TRIU
THE ETER

"The Ice will advance, not far, young smith, not far; but far enough to reflect some small portion more of the sun's heat, and so cool the clime of the world just a fraction further. And that will be enough! As a morsel of snow set tumbling down a mountain may grow, unstoppably, to a mighty avalanche, so the margins of the Ice shall grow of their own moving force to encompass and cleanse this carrion world. And the peace that is cold will settle about it, and our day shall come again! Then we shall live free indeed, free from the strife that devours us, free from all the ills, demands, indignities, free from the burning tomb that you call flesh!"

Other Avon Books in
THE WINTER OF THE WORLD *Trilogy*
by Michael Scott Rohan

VOLUME 1:
THE ANVIL OF ICE

VOLUME 2:
THE FORGE IN THE FOREST

THE WINTER OF THE WORLD

VOLUME 3

THE HAMMER OF THE SUN

MICHAEL SCOTT ROHAN

AVON BOOKS ◆ NEW YORK

AVON BOOKS
A division of
The Hearst Corporation
105 Madison Avenue
New York, New York 10016

First Avon Books Printing: August 1990

Contents

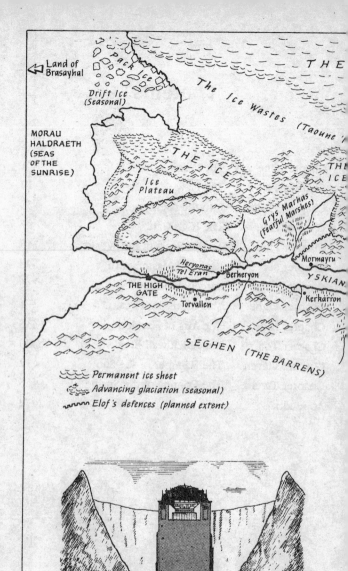

← Land of Brasayhal

Pack Ice

Drift Ice (Seasonal)

THE Ice Wastes (Taoune '...

MORAU HALDRAETH (SEAS OF THE SUNRISE)

THE ICE

Ice Plateau

THE ICE

Grys Marhas (Fearful Marshes)

Mormayru

Y·SKIAN

Heryonas
Tel Eran   Berheryon

THE HIGH GATE   Kerkarron

Torvallen

SEGHEN   (THE BARRENS)

〜〜 Permanent ice sheet
〜〜 Advancing glaciation (seasonal)
〜〜 Elof's defences (planned extent)

THE HIGH GATE OF KERYS
Viewed from the seaward

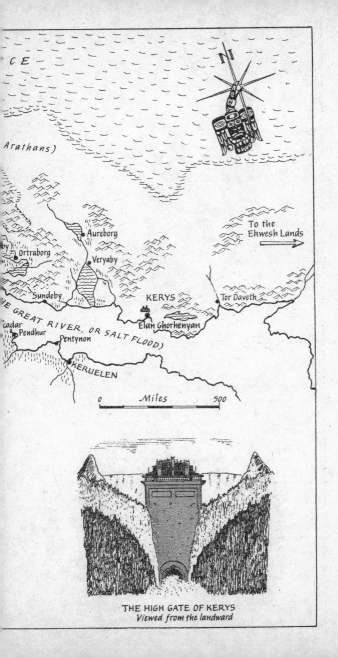

...CE

(Arathans)

...by
Ortraborg

Aureborg

Veryaby

Sundeby

KERYS

Tor Daveth

To the
Ekwesh
Lands →

...cadar
Pendhur

Pentynon

Elan Ghorhenyan

...E GREAT RIVER, OR SALT FLOOD)

KERUELEN

0   Miles   500

THE HIGH GATE OF KERYS
Viewed from the landward

Seven years have passed since Elof the Mastersmith, Kermorvan of Kerbryhaine, Ils of the duergar and their fellows came to the legendary lost city of Morvannec and vanquished the Power that had overcome it. In those seven years, the city has been reborn; but in the West the onslaught of the Ekwesh raiders, driven by the relentless malice of the Ice, has continued unabated. And so each summer Kermorvan has mounted an expedition, by sea and by land, from shore to shore of the great continent to stave off the fall of the Westlands and to bring their folk eastward.

For Elof, these years have brought great happiness with Kara, whom he wrenched at the bitter end from the Power that ruled her. But that very happiness makes him afraid: that Kara, herself no mortal, and drawn by unseen forces, will one day leave him. And in his fear, Elof calls on his own uncanny skills to weld Kara to him with unbreakable bonds. Of all mistakes, this is the greatest: Kara flees, and Elof can only follow. With his old friend Roc, he must set out upon a journey no man in living memory has undertaken, far across the Seas of Sunrise to the east where lies, if the ancient legends are true, the mighty city of Kerys, the origin of Kermorvan and all his people.

And it is there that the chronicles of the Winter of the World reach their climax. For it is in the legend-haunted lands of the east that the malevolent Powers of the Ice see the key to the final extinction of life that they so desperately crave; it is there that the final confrontation will come; and it is there that Elof must finally confront the truth of his past and his destiny.

Prelude

The happiness of men is fragile; for so are we made that all our gains carry within them the seeds of loss, and too often we ourselves may sow them. After the events chronicled in the Book of the Helm, many long years of such happiness awaited Elof and Kara whom he loved, and the friends they had won; and for all he knew, in the pride and prime of his years, they might have lasted forever. But it was he himself who was to end them, in such folly as only wise men may create, and endure terrible trials in consequence. Yet from that ill sowing much else was to grow; and of that the Book of the Armring tells.

CHAPTER ONE

The Forging

IT WAS HER RESTLESSNESS that roused him, the slender body beside him twisting and turning beneath the covers of heavy tapestry, admitting the keen morning air to play over his naked skin. For a moment he lay half-drugged with sleep, dimly aware of a deeper chill growing within him. He knew it well, that chill, all too well of late; in part it was excitement, oddly tinged with guilt. But even more of it was fear. In sleepy anxiety he rolled over, put out an arm to enfold her; it brushed her flank as she rose, and dropped on the warmth of the empty sheet. His eyes blinked open; she was stepping onto the balcony, her skin pale as the dawn sky beyond, lifting something to her shoulders. A swirl of white hid her back, fell back to her sides, its lining black as her hair. Then her outstretched arms raised the cloak in a great spreading sweep, hiding the sky; fear stabbed him awake. He sat up, cried out. Her arms dropped, but in falling the cloak billowed out, the lining flashed, and the air whistled with the downstroke of wide black wings. A great swan surged up from the balcony and wheeled dark against the pallid airs, lifting and swooping with a lazy grace out over the sleeping rooftops and down towards the sea.

He cursed and sprang from the bed, his feet tangling in the spread skins beneath, and flung aside the curtain of the aumbry behind; from its highest shelf he seized a light metal cap and clapped it onto his head. A spray of mail fell icy about his cheeks, chilled his neck as he closed it with clumsy fingers. Fear flamed in him, fear and a fire still hotter. So it was, as the tale is told, that there awoke in his heart that wish, wholly loving and yet tainted by darker and more ruthless desires, that was to turn the course and flow not of his brief existence alone, but of the whole Winter of the World. He drew breath an instant, forced himself to think, while the black speck dwindled in the swelling light.

An image formed in his mind; he gave it substance, shape, and as it burgeoned a wave washed over him, a prickling surge of pain, cold and metallic, that trailed behind it a sense of vast pressures. He let fall his hands, and felt the air grow thick beneath them, a sudden urge of overwhelming power at his breast that lifted him high, higher, across the tangled bed and out over the balcony in a single thrusting embrace of the air. His legs trailed, he angled his feet in the rush to steady him as he rose; his eyes, grown newly keen, sought out the distant wing-beats. Already they were out beyond the harbour; with a fierce, voiceless hiss he angled his wings and plunged down the the sky in pursuit. Below him the ships of the great fleet rocked gently at their moorings, no-one stirring on their decks, and at the sight of them a cool thread of doubt grew among Elof's anger. He threw all his strength into his wings, arced high above the sea wall and out over the swell that heaved like the breathing of some vast monster, low but deep. Over it, now low, now high, sped Kara, but for all her speed he was gaining, he was upon her, the shadow of his wings flickered on her back as he stooped to her. She wheeled effortlessly, and rose to meet him. Level with him she flew, and passed so close that her back brushed his breast and their flight muscles rippled together under the sleek black down. Her neck snaked against his, writhing teasingly, then, suddenly, down ruffled against bare skin, her skin. Up and past him she surged, in woman's shape once more; but from her shoulders vast black wings still beat, and among their feathers was a single flash of gold. Startled, he threshed clumsily after her, and her laughter rang bright in his ears. He struggled to concentrate, to clothe himself in a new shape as she had, but he could not imagine himself so, could not accept the strangeness of it. He faltered, fluttered on the freshening wind, panicked, and felt the shape that masked him fall away, the rushing air chill upon his naked skin. He flailed at emptiness and dropped like a stone.

The uprush took him, flung him about, showed him the steely sea sweeping up to meet him. Then it whipped him around again and Kara filled the sky, swooping down upon him, a vision of eerie loveliness. He reached his arms out to her, and her great wings closed about him, enveloped him. He touched her, clung, and felt her legs twine around him. Her lips pressed down on his with bruising force, her tongue flickered against his and her breasts thrust against him with every wing-beat; he hooked an arm about her heaving shoulders, caressed her with his free hand, felt the taut peak of her fierce excitement, the heart that leaped beneath. He stroked his fingers down her ribs to her flank, across her taut belly, and she threw back her head and cried out. They were rising now, the sea swaying away beneath them with every beat of the black pinions, faster and faster; he felt a surge of strength to match her own, and crushed her to him. Her back arched, her legs quivered against his, then she folded fiercely forward and crossed them about his waist. Joined, they scaled the heights of the sky while beneath them the horizon rolled away to reveal the sun, and they lifted into its first clear flare of gold. It blazed on Kara's pale skin as she swayed back in a tremor of delight, and to Elof's eyes she seemed to flow with a flood of molten light; it spilled over into him, rushed searing through his body, a torrent that burst into his mind and blotted out thought. He felt Kara stiffen convulsively against him, her wide wings outthrust, quivering. With the high scream of a great bird she toppled backward in the air; they went spiralling down into emptiness, uncaring.

Only in the last instant, as the sea seemed to reach up and grab at them, did Elof recover his wits. Kara gave a wild yell, then he felt a great stinging slap of cold across his back, that all but drove out what little breath was left him. Water rushed into his open mouth, stung his eyes, roared in his ears; it sucked the heat from him, though his skin burned with the impact. Instinctively he kicked out against the icy embrace, felt himself rising, and in a sudden qualm of panic snatched for the precious helm. His fingers touched metal, and he knew it hung still fastened about his neck; it was no greater relief when an instant later he burst through the surface and could draw breath. Gasping, he clawed his streaming hair out of his eyes; a wave lifted him, and he looked anxiously about. He was floating naked in a strong swell, the shore no more than a sun-reddened streak of grey in the distance, and he could see no other shape among the wavecrests. Then came a splash, and Kara's light laughter rippled like harp strings among the soft rush and thunder of the ocean. Two warm and wholly human arms slithered around his neck, and her slender body was a startling warmth in the dawn-chilled waters.

"*Kara!* You …" Then he had to hold her close and kiss her, taste the salt on her soft neck. Her dark eyes sparkled into his, and he sought to see past the gentle mockery he read there, and heard in her voice.

"But you were not worried, surely? For *me*? Who in all the world has less to fear from any element than I?"

He held her to him, tight, as if at any moment she might slip away into the depths beneath. "I was afraid you might have … changed again. Gone where I could not follow."

She stroked his forehead. "Why would I do that, my heart, even if I could? Have you not bested me before, you and your cunning helm?"

"Aye, but it strains me, Kara; I was not born to this constant shifting and change. And I love you as you are; I would have you so – "

She lowered her eyes and smiled a small smile. "And did you not, just? In what counts, at any rate …"

Elof laughed, though it rang hollow in the emptiness within, and bent his head to hers. "That I'll grant you! Though the rest was strange enough, in all conscience it was good. But I'm wearied now, and the ocean's ice-chill yet at this hour; let's be swimming back for breakfast, eh?"

She threw up her arms above her head, as if about to dive; her serpentine gold armring flashed warmly in the sunlight. "Gladly! In what – "

"As ourselves, Kara. Please!"

She pulled free of his arms, rolled idly on her back in the water and let a wavecrest bear her along. "If we must!" Then suddenly her long legs thrashed, sprayed water in his face, and she was torpedoing off through the waves, almost as fast, it seemed, as in any unhuman form. Elof groaned and launched himself after her. He was a powerful swimmer but a graceless one, and in another moment she was rolling and plunging about him like the dolphin she could be, tickling him, nipping him, tangling his thrashing legs or simply brushing herself against him and darting out of reach, and that he found most disturbing of all. She was seldom so skittish, and unease swelled in him.

"All right!" he protested, coming to a halt and treading water. "Have it as you will! Match me now – " He reached up and pulled the helm over his head once more and ducked down. Side by side, twisting in the first shaft of sunlight, two seals arrowed towards the coast.

But it was in human form that the two clambered onto the warm stones of the sea wall and stood dripping a moment. "Well?" laughed Kara, leaning on Elof's shoulder and clutching her swancloak about her. "May I shift shape once more? Or would you have us stride through the streets as we are?"

"We've scandalized the night watch enough already, I doubt not. Shift, and I'll follow."

Kara, already in swan's shape once more, chose to hear that as a challenge; rather than flying straight home, she led him a lively dance around and about the forests of masts, diving and weaving among the tangles of rigging with a leisurely grace that was wholly deceptive. Plunging after her between trailing clumps of blocks and tackle that every moment threatened to snare a wing and send him spinning down to the deck or sea, Elof felt the terrible sinking of doubt grow ever greater in him. Soon, very soon now, this great fleet must take to the sea, sailing southward as they had every spring these seven years past, on a great voyage south and east, making landfall upon the barren coasts of the inland seas. From there the King and his crews would

retrace the way overland through the borderlands of the
hostile Wastes to the fair coasts of the West, the road by
which, a thousand years past, Vayde had led the Last-
comers from Morvan to the land of Bryhaine in the
West. There they would help to hold off the advancing
Ekwesh marauders for another summer, and at its end,
as the raiders retreated for the winter, bear back with
them still more of Kerbryhaine's unhappy people. And,
with the fleet, as in every one of those seven springs,
Elof and Kara would go. Long and arduous that way
would be, yet it was none of the many perils of the Wild
that awoke such unease in Elof's heart; to the menaces
of the Forest realm, Tapiau'la-an-Aithen, they were as
nothing, and through that he had already passed, and
bested the will of its shadowy lord. *It is the perils we
may bear with us that I fear ...*

By the time he landed upon the high balcony of the
palace Kara was already shaking the seawater from her
swancloak, whirling it this way and that in a rain of
droplets. "There! And what, pray you, was so terrible
about that?"

"Nothing," said Elof sombrely, "as well you know.
And yet ..."

Kara's dark eyes seemed to narrow further. "And
yet?" she echoed, and her arms fell to her sides.

"It happens ever more of late. You grow restless,
the fit falls on you of a sudden, and ... you are gone. By
strange ways, in strange forms. You are often hard to
follow."

"Not by design! Are you not as apt as I am at the
sport? You proved that long ago!"

Perhaps. Though it is natural to you; other shapes
are but masks to me, and they soon gall. But is it any
longer a sport, Kara?"

She stared at him, bewildered. "Why – "

"Why indeed, Kara? What is it stirs in you, calls you
so?"

"The spring, perhaps ..."

"Nothing more? No other behest, no other voice,
nothing that would summon you away from me?"

"*No!* From you?" Her arms went out to him, and

hearing the hurt in her voice he could only take them, hold her to him. "What could ever be strong enough to do that?"

He shook his head. "Then what is it, Kara my love? For there is something, I would swear it ..."

In the palace towers above bells chimed, sounding the first hour of the day, and she pulled away from him, laughing again. "What a mood for so fine a morning! Come, dress if you're so set on your breakfast!" Other bells were echoing the hour from the city below, an instant apart, so that the peals rang together, but not as one. Elof, struggling into tunic and hose, watched Kara flow into her gown with liquid grace. *Even so it is with us*, he thought.

But as he followed her out onto one of the open galleries that circled the palace like a coronet, he said no more, only listened intently to the music of the bells. Many he knew intimately, could distinguish their individual tones clear among the clangour; good chimes, well pitched, ringing brightly without crack or flaw. Those bells he had cast himself, making good the destructions of the Ekwesh occupation; he knew every stage of their making, from the alloying to the final raising. He could trust them. Then he grew wroth with himself for what that thought implied, whether about Kara or others; his trust was not so narrow as that. He had friends enough who had risked their lives with him, for him, and for whom he had done the same, or would gladly; those bonds were of nothing so fragile as metal, nor so easily forged. Then why think worse of Kara? A gleam of gold caught his eye, and for all the warmth of the sunlight he went cold. He had shaped her the armring, that was why, the ring and all that went with it. Without those virtues, those patterned forces in the gold ...

Once, a lonely, desperate youth, he had pressed it on her; she had taken it, in sympathy perhaps, and – Suppose she had not? What would he be to her then? He bit his lip savagely. But then she turned and laughed, warmer than gold or sunlight, and tucked her strong slim arm in his, pressing closer to his side, and he could resist her no more; he hugged her close, and they made their way thus down the long stairs to the lower galleries. The cold core of doubt and fear within him seemed to melt and dwindle; yet, tempered and hardened by fear, fear of loss, some tiny sliver still remained.

Under the new kingship and the restored peace the great halls of the Palace of Morvanhal through which they walked were flourishing as they never had before the Ekwesh came. There was not one of that fierce folk now left alive east of the mountains, so far as any could tell. In a swift and bloody week the land had been scoured of them and of those others, shadowy followers of the Ice-worshipper Bryhon, who had guided and prepared their invasion. Freed from the Ekwesh, the Eastlands had begun to grow and flourish once again. From the day he took possession of his halls the new king had made his first priority the feeding of his folk, organising the fair sharing of what supplies there were, and the urgent clearing and planting of land that had been left fallow and overgrown for many years. But even as the first planting was ending he was setting out with what ships and men the land could afford for the Westlands and for Kerbryhaine, the City that two years since had all but driven him out. He found it in a very different mood, harried by famine and disease, the power of the Syndicacy in tatters. It might have been in total anarchy, save that the threat of the Ekwesh had grown so great there that internal differences had come to seem light by comparison; and perhaps also the death of Bryhon had led to a lessening of the strife. Ironically enough, it was the Nordeney fugitives the syndics had once sought to bar who had become the staunchest supporters of order, and the fiercest fighters against the invading reivers. But they were not enough. Slowly but surely the lands of the great landowners were being overrun, and their peasants were fleeing within the walls of the city, reducing the flow of its food supply even as they increased the demands on it. The prospect of an eastern realm which neither Ekwesh nor Ice could easily reach, with a diminished population and land to spare, became suddenly appealing even to those landowners, and to those partisans of the Bryheren faction, who had long opposed the line of Morvan. When under Kermorvan's generalship a mingled force of men of Nordeney, Kerbryhaine and Morvanhal decimated or drove out all the larger bands of marauders, all opposition fell strangely silent, and many who had most fiercely opposed the kingship became most vocal in seeking its shelter. More sought to go with Kermorvan than he could possibly take; he promised to return for them, and this promise he had kept. That first fleet sailed back in time to help with a harvest of unlooked-for abundance, and from that day forth it became only a matter of time until the west was abandoned. That time drew nearer with every passing year.

During those years the palace saw many rich and splendid feasts, commanded by the king as token of its reborn prosperity, or to welcome unhappy refugees from the Westlands. But at the first meal of the day there was no pomp or luxury; lord and servant ate together if they chose, the fare was simple, the mood quiet and relaxed in preparation for the labours of the day ahead. In this it reflected the nature of the king himself; as often at this hour, he had forsaken his high table and ate at his ease out on the gallery, contemplating the harbour and the muster of his fleet. His lean frame was wrapped in a light robe, his bronzen hair was unkempt, he wore plain rope-soled seaman's sandals and seemed wholly at peace with himself and the world. When he saw Elof and Kara approaching he rose at once, smiling, and greeted them with his usual slightly stiff good nature.

"My master, my lady, come and grace my table! I'm glad to see you so early, Elof; much must be settled today ere the shipyards can begin their labours, and with Ils away our wisest smith should advise me – "

Kara laughed. "Then you will excuse me, will you not, my lord Keryn, and you, Elof? You know such matters have little hold upon my mind. I'll breakfast with our friends within." She kissed Elof lightly and glided down the steps into the cool depths of the halls; the men watched her go. Elof a little ruefully. Kermorvan smiled.

"She adorns our halls. It is good to see that you and she have still your share of the happiness we have found –"

Elof slumped down into a chair so hard that its light frame protested. "Do we?"

Kermorvan sat down more slowly, and his misty blue gaze grew suddenly piercing. "A tale reached me but moments since," he remarked with dry disapproval. "A wild tale, such as the watch are wont to dream up at a dull night's ending … " Elof groaned faintly. Then the king's stern features were suddenly illumined by a mischevious twinkle. "I can only say that you both look remarkably fresh! And while I'm no authority, I think it is hardly so that love lessens … "

Elof felt his scowl harden. "Our love, no! But … " He hesitated, but his need to speak, to mould words out of his inner blackness, was too great. "It is our trust I fear for! And Kara's safety! Kermorvan, she was seeking to escape me, I am sure of it!"

Kermorvan sat up, startled. "*Escape* you? Talk sense, man – "

"I mean it! She changed, flew, I woke and followed. But if I had not woken, what then, what then? How far would she have flown? And where? To whom? Kermorvan, there is another voice calls her, of that I am sure!"

"Another voice … " Kermorvan's face darkened once again, and his voice took on an edge that belied its quietness. "She who mastered her of old, you mean? Yes, that would not surprise me. Inevitable that Louhi would try to summon her back. The Lady of the Ice is hardly one to forgive or forget, were the thing snatched from her less precious, or less … "

"Less loved!" Elof heard himself blurt out, and the bitterness lay like metal on his tongue.

Kermorvan inclined his head sympathetically, yet a little distantly, as if to set himself apart from Elof's jealousy. "What of that? It is past. Whom Kara loves, that is what matters, that is what must counter the call. That, strengthened by your love. Your trust … "

Elof flushed. "That alone was never enough to win her free of Louhi! Not even though she had my arm-ring, with all the virtues I set upon it … "

"Not while you were apart. But from the moment she saw you once more, she began to struggle. You called upon that ring. And she triumphed."

"Aye, for a moment. Then I had to hunt her down …"

"It was the moment that mattered!" said Kermorvan sharply. "That set you free, to free her! Do you remember, I was there! I saw!" He stroked his chin thoughtfully. "And that was when you hardly knew one another, when she could scarcely believe your love was possible. Now you have had years together, happy years, the links will be stronger – "

"But strong enough?" blazed Elof. "Dare I trust her, for her own sake?"

"If they are not strong enough, then seeking to tighten her bonds may only weaken them further." Kermorvan smiled thinly. "Even I can see that, little versed as I am in matters of the heart. If you doubt her strength, lend her your own; do not force it upon her. Have patience, wait! There lies the best counsel I can give you. That, and don't forget your food." He gestured to the table at his side, which held dishes of smoked meat, cornbread, curds and fruit. "Now, about the *Alaven*'s refit. The shipwrights report that the old tackle will not bear the new rig. We cannot rely on Ils returning in time, and other than she, only you truly understand shipwork – "

For the next hour Kermorvan kept Elof so busy discussing shipyard problems that he should have had no time to think of anything else, and perhaps that was in part his purpose. But instead Elof found himself answering and eating in a kind of abstracted daze, while the core of his mind wandered along other paths. He heard his own voice as if it was another's, though it spoke sense enough, while through his inner self fears and worries stalked. He found himself longing for Kara to return, constantly fighting down the urge to run and find her, to be sure she had not somehow vanished away once more. When he heard her laughter, soft and bright as fine gold, echo unmistakeably out of the shadows of the hall he felt his whole being relax in re-assurance. Yet only minutes later he was anxious again. *Wait!* he told himself sarcastically, *Have patience!* That was not the turn of a smith's mind; they could be patient only in action, not inaction. No more was it their way to leave weak links lying; they would sooner forge the whole chain anew.

All throughout that day it was that vision that haunted his thoughts, of a chain stretched to breaking. How he got through the many tasks that devolved upon the Court Smith and chiefest counsellor of so active a king, he never knew, for Kara was ever in his mind, Kara whom he loved too well to risk losing once again. Yet somehow it was evening, and he came to the door of their chambers in the palace, those high rooms where Kara's chains had been broken, and they had first become lovers. A great weariness was upon him, and a need for comfort, and the sight of Kara, reclining upon a daybed on the balcony, was balm to his tormented heart. She sat there in silent silhouette, contemplating a sunset of eggshell greens and blues beneath a canopy of clouds streaked fiercely red and gold, and when he approached her she did not turn, but waved him to the couch beside her. He stooped to kiss her, then stopped as he saw tracks of fire upon her cheeks, as though the angry clouds wept, and not she. She looked up sharply into his face, and began to speak, then hesitated. "You .. you asked me earlier ... if there was any other voice that called me ... that sought to part me from you ... And I denied it. But, heart, you were right."

For a moment he felt a vast sinking away beneath him, and then a sudden recovery; at least she was admitting it. He would help her now. "Yes. It's that she-wolf Louhi, isn't it?"

Kara gave a short bitter laugh, and gestured dismissively. "Her! Oh yes, she is always there, far off, whispering, tugging. But I had almost ceased to think of her. This is something more, a thing hard to understand. Something I cannot know for certain ... yet with every fibre of my being I sense it. A great change coming, a balance swaying this way and that, and whichever way it tips it must alter the world." She turned and leaned on the low railing of the balcony, gazing out at the sea; the wind had turned westerly now, by the gilded vanes on the high roofs below, and it was driving grey breakers in against sea wall and shore, booming upon block and gravel. Above them flocked gulls, bright in the last of the light, and their harsh cries awoke new fear in his heart, that at any moment she might fly up from him and be lost in their numberless throngs. "A wave rises over all things, and soon it will break ... Much that is new must flow in, much that is old must be swept away. And I am old, heart, very old."

Elof caressed her crisp dark curls, stroked her smooth cheek. "You are no older than when first I set eyes upon you. And you have little memory of the years, you have said."

"Little, till first I came into bondage. Till first I set eyes upon you."

Elof frowned. "Are the two then so close?"

"Only in time. You do not bind me; I am not your property, your instrument and plaything, as I was ... hers. Once I roamed the world uncaring, unremembering, save when I served the Steerers in war, and that too was in my nature from the first. So, to be held again, save by my own will, by myself ... even to think of that sickens me. But with you I am happy ... "

"As before? As when you were free?"

She gazed around at him, her green eyes wide with astonishment. "But surely! Why else should I stay?"

Elaf nodded. "Why indeed? But ... this change you sense ... it comes soon, you feel?" The sun rolled beneath the horizon, and all things beyond the balcony, tree, rooftop, cliff, darkened to shapes of shadow against the sky, golden now as peach-skin, shot with grey clouds.

She smiled. "Soon need not be as men conceive it!" Then she looked away again. "And ... a day may come when I would welcome it, embrace it. Having known you, I cannot ever be the same."

Elof knew what she meant. In all the years he had loved her she had not aged, nor would she, perhaps, within the circles of the world. Whereas he ... He would share the common lot of men. But he had accepted that, for himself, with an ease that surprised him; was it selfishness that he so seldom thought what it would mean to her?

"But suppose it did come soon," he persisted, "soon as I would see it, I mean. Would you resist it, then, and stay with me? Could you?"

"I don't know!" she breathed. "How can I know? Were the choice mine, yes, my heart, I would try, I would strive, with all my being I would! But ... "

Elof leaned over, gripped her bare arms, gazed deep into her eyes that had the shade of a forest pool, the alert gaze of deer that drank there. "Do you fear you cannot resist, heart? That you lack the fortitude, the strength? Let me help you! Join my strength to yours!"

"How may I do that? How can you help?"

"I will study! I will seek! It would not be the first time I managed what a Power could not. But I need time, Kara, time; you must trust me, give me that time. Hold yourself as safe meanwhile as you know how."

She flashed him a sudden, uncertain glance. "What do you mean?"

"I mean, rein in your urge to change; it is that betrays you. Hold your human form, cease to shift and wander through the world, save at great need. For now; only for now ... " She turned her head away indignantly, and he heard his voice go very cold. "I trust you, when you say you love me, and do not want to part; I need no proof. But in trusting me this ... for now, only for now ... you will be showing me how strong that love, that wish, can be – "

Her teeth gleamed white, biting hard against her lower lip. "I would promise, gladly I would!" she cried out, desperate. "But dare I? Can I? Have I the strength? You cannot imagine how strong is the urge ... "

"I can," he said softly. "If only by the pain it causes you. But you have the power to see that you never break your promise, by one simple act. Give me your swan-cloak, that you need to take on new forms; give it me, and I shall lock it in my strongest chest, returning it to you only at need. Believe me," he added, to forestall her cry of protest, "I guess how great a trust that would be. But for now, at least, we have no better answer, and no way to find one. Take time to think, if you wish."

But at once she rose, and from the seat beside her she plucked the cloak, swirling it around her shoulders, but instead she folded it carefully, neatly and held it tight to her breast a moment, burying her face in the down. Then impetuously she thrust it into Elof's hands; it hung there lightly, like a sliver of cloud. He lowered his eyes, and turned away into the inner chambers, where stood several chests, some metal-bound, some wholly of metal. It was to a large one he turned, and with a small key and some murmured words he unlocked the lid and laid the cloak reverently upon the piles of cloth-wrapped volumes within, shifting some of the bright jewels aside so that there was no chance of any snagging. He closed the lid again with more words upon it, and went back to the balcony; there stood Kara still, gazing out into emptiness, her shoulders bowed and her crossed arms hugging her breast, as against a chill. He laid his hands upon her shoulders, very gently, meaning to slide his arms down to embrace her. But she whirled around, gazing into his face with eyes large and liquid.

"Hold me!" she whispered. "Hold me, for the world grows dark! Let us live, let us seize love and joy while we can!" He felt her arms suddenly cold under his fingers, and he held her tight, let his mantle fall around her, cover her from the onrushing night.

"I will hold you!" he whispered. "But even now I can do more, Kara, if you will let me. I can shield you –"

"*No!* You would forge your love into a cage – " He knew well what was in her thoughts, how she had wept with rage at her first sight of caged songbirds in the city markets. Before the day's end Kermorvan, not easily swayed on any matter, had found himself forbidding the practice altogether. She shook her head insistently. "You would temper bars for me to flutter against, till at last I grew weary, ceased to care, and shattered them altogether. We must find some other way. I would not be

pinioned ever again, love, by any force save one, and
that is myself."

He looked into her intent eyes, on a level with his
own, and ran his hand through her dark hair. And even
as he did so, a cold thought came into his mind, and
there took root. "So be it!" he said quietly, and bent to
kiss her on the brow.

CHAPTER TWO

The Flaw

THERE REMAINED ONLY a few weeks till the fleet must sail, and in that time Elof had more than enough in hand to occupy every waking hour. Though the Eastlands had not, as Bryhaine, lost the true smithcraft, the art had fallen into decline. Few smiths of any great ability had escaped there from Morvan, and though many books of lore survived, fewer still were born able to make proper use of them. Certainly there were none in these lands now to compare with the Mastersmiths of Nordeney. Of these many had perished in the sack of that land, or in the hardships of the flight south, and with them great reserves of skill and learning had been lost. Only a handful had survived to come east, and some of those too old to do more than teach and oversee. It fell upon Elof to apportion the labours of the rest, and of such likely journeymen as he could find; what remained, he most often had to do with his own hand, and always when the utmost craft was called for. For whatever their degree of mastery the magesmiths of either land were loth now to measure themselves against Elof Valantor, still young though he might be, and the craft they saw ablaze behind his strange-hued eyes.

Yet the idea he had had would not quit him, but grew and took shape even when he seemed to have forgotten it, like a serpent uncoiling in darkness. He lived in peace with Kara, and she never asked her cloak of him, but busied herself as much as he with preparations for the voyage. But the thought would come to his mind at odd moments, as he proved chain and tackle on the launching slips, or fashioned strong fastenings for sheet and hawser; and each time it would be that fraction clearer, that step more advanced. When he dwelt upon it too long, and upon its implications, it began subtly to disturb him; then he at once forgot it again, because he had to. Right or wrong, it hardly mattered

17

when he could not spare a tenth of the time he would need to make that thought real. Indeed it might never have come to fruition, if help had not arrived from an unexpected quarter.

One chilly dawn the clear note of a horn drifted up to the watch on the City's main gate; Elof, already making his way down the steep main street to the shipyards, saw them hasten to the windlasses and stayed to watch. The huge doors ground back in their sockets to reveal an extraordinary caravan, a cluster of hooded figures, short and square, who were leading a train of baggage-beasts that looked like vast shaggy hill-goats. But Elof knew them for musk-oxen from the mountains, and that only one folk could be leading them thus. He went racing down the slippery cobbles with his tool-pack bouncing and jingling at his side; the caravan's leader looked up, hailed cheerfully and came running to meet him also. Man and duergh collided with a solid smack in the centre of the road, and clung to each other as they threatened to fall over; a hood spilled off thick dark curls, bright eyes, a flashing, breathless grin. With irresistible strength two firm arms drew Elof's face down for a kiss as solid and smacking as their first encounter, and he hugged the girl tight, intensely aware of how different she felt from Kara, the hard buxom breadth of her. Ils, still breathless, pulled back a little too sharply, but then laughed as if to lighten her reaction. "Well then, young human? Do I find you well?" She prodded him amiably in the midriff, and frowned. "On the thin side, even for a man!"

He smiled. "I've been busy this last week or two. More smith's work than we bargained for –"

"And is she seeing to it that you don't forget to eat? Well, I thought you might be running into a little trouble, so I've brought back some help." She gestured at her companions, busily goading the half-tamed and rebellious musk-oxen into these unfamiliar surroundings. "Smiths, all of them. Not the finest we have in the east by a long chalk, just middling, but I wanted them day-hardy, so they must needs be young. And with them a fair stock of finer ores such as we've so far found in the old delvings."

"Ils," said Elof reverently, "you're a marvel! Even middling duergar smiths can strike sparks off our best men!

And we've been too harried to go and hunt down new metals …" He paused a moment, feeling the cold thought blossom in him once more. "You wouldn't have any silver ore among your panniers, would you?"

"Silver?" snorted Ils. "Silver overflowing, take it and welcome! We dwell among silver, we tangle nuggets in our river nets, we strike new seams with every old air-shaft we open; comes in handy for making new light-mirrors. And we need 'em! Huge they are, those old workings, and twisty as a greased worm; even our eyes need all the sun we can carry down."

"Even when you can capture sun and fire in your crystal lamps?"

She grimaced. "Could we but craft them like that one in your gauntlet, we'd have less swink, aye! But we've not matched it − not yet!" she added hastily. Elof kept his face rigid; for all her friendship with men Ils ran true to her race. "Maybe when some more of our folk come east …"

He was careful to avoid offering his own help. "You think they will? There've been few enough till now −"

"We're a slower folk to change, Elof, not like you mayfly men; they'll be watching and waiting to see how the first few have fared ere they up roots that go back many a thousand years. Even Ansker's of that mind; we've never before lived so openly around men. But now we've reopened the ancient mountain-halls and have some rich workings of our own to tempt them, away from human gaze, aye, more'll come. And if they can't manage …" She regarded him levelly, and took a deep breath. "Why then, Elof Valantor, you might teach us much."

He blinked in astonishment, and with a wicked glitter in her eyes she added "Never thought to hear that, did you? But I only said *might*, mind! Well, the sun's all but up; I'll have the silver sent over to the Hall of Guild in the noontide, and my lads when they've rested. Right now I want some breakfast! So we'll go pay our respects at the palace, though it's plain enough eating there, in all conscience." A note of amused affection crept into her voice. "How fares the long lad, by the bye?"

Elof smiled. "Still king, driving himself harder than any servant, and looking well on it. But all the better for seeing you, I've no doubt. Roc's down south in Pendyra port on business for him, but he's due back within the week."

"And your lady?"

"She's well as ever, thank you." Elof was sure he had spoken naturally, he had taken pains to, but he was suddenly uncomfortably aware of Ils' piercing dark gaze.

But all she said, equally naturally, was "So? I am glad to hear it. That we've travelled those hard hills before won't make them the less perilous; we'll be happier, having her with us." She hesitated a moment, then, before adding "Take good care of her, Elof. She is a rare creature."

He nodded, knowing that her concern was not for Kara. "I intend to, Ils. Believe me, I do."

Thus it was the coming of the duergar smiths that left him free to put his purpose into effect; and how matters might have gone otherwise, none can say. That afternoon, when he had sent them about the many tasks he had in hand, he found himself suddenly with a little time to spare. Quitting the great forge that was his in the vaults of the ancient Halls of the Smith's Guild, he strolled along wide corridors that rang and chimed with the strokes of heavy hammers, roared with the breath of bellows and furnace; the weighty hangings that were mounted over the walls of smooth stone to deaden these echoes had long since darkened to a sooty black. He mounted the wide stairs into cleaner air and quieter, past the newly refurbished libraries and scholar's rooms to the upper floors in whose smaller chambers the master jewellers and fine artificers kept their workshops. Here the din echoing along the walls was shriller, swifter, a tingling and chiming of light hammers and fine instruments against rare metals and gems; here it was the acrid stench of solders, corrosives and cleansing pickles that tainted the air, the hangings stained and faded and in places charred or withered through. At a high window a bent old mastersmith, surrounded by a gaggle of black-garbed apprentices, was demonstrating a delicate instrument, explaining the virtues of orientation and steadiness worked into its metals. Elof nodded to them as he passed, thinking back to his own apprentice days. He knew the device, an aid to navigation made to determine very precisely the elevation of sun, moon and stars; he wished devoutly that some instrument might measure as minutely the courses of their Steerers.

He paused before a tall door of hardened oak marked with a name in fine-laced silver, knocked lightly and entered at the muffled summons. A lean woman of about his years looked up from the gilded chalice she was burnishing, and her large eyes widened further. "Good day, Master!" She rose awkwardly from her bench, but he motioned her back with a smile.

"And to you also, Master; don't let me disturb it!" She smiled hesitantly, brushing brown locks back from her forehead; a nervous gesture it seemed. He knew from Roc that Marja was always nervous in his presence, yet she looked at him with the eyes of a fellow smith. "My errand should devour little of your precious time, a minor matter upon which I would know the mind of a master jeweller, one whose craft is turned so closely to adorning the body. Which, think you, of all the noble metals, has the greatest affinity with the body, with human flesh and blood?"

Marja subsided slowly onto her bench, her face already slackening with the distraction of thought. "Why ... gold, I suppose many would say. That is the tradition, anyhow. For the softness of it, they say ... and the seeming warmth ..."

Elof sat down in front of her. "And you?" he prompted.

"I ... I am not of that mind, not wholly. Less so, since I read some scholars of the old Eastlands here. For the greatest affinity might you not need to look beyond metals altogether? To some of those odd stuffs the ancient mastersmiths made, akin to metal in their properties but more malleable?" She knitted her fingers with enthusiasm. "There was a tale old Hjoran told me once, of a stuff that was spun ... *spun* ... from the very stuff of life itself, living matter reduced to its ultimate pure ash, and it was stronger than any metal, lighter too. It was one of the heroic magesmiths of Morvan made it, I remember ... or of Kerys, even. Thyrve, or Aluki Three-finger, or Vayde ... somebody like that!"

Elof grinned. "I know; Mylio told me of that, too. They make good tales to fire apprentices with, don't they? Sets them dreaming of discovering such wonders for themselves. But the secret of that strong stuff is lost, if it ever existed, and none of the others we know of will serve. No, it has to be metal."

She had grown nervous again. "Well then ... It is a subtle point, on which few can be certain; but whatever tradition says, I ... I would choose silver."

Elof nodded with slow satisfaction. "I thought you might, in your hard-won wisdom. Tradition once had it that women did not make good smiths, also."

She flushed at the compliment. "It's that the warmth of gold is an illusion ... It can be a barrier to heat, in many instances ... and as for being soft, well, flesh is soft, but it holds its shape, and there's bone beneath. And the bonesetters, they come to us smiths, do they not, for alloys of silver – plates and pins of it to join and patch shattered or splintered bones; the bone may well grow out around them with little hurt, the flesh and skin heal over them. A hardened silver will endure the fluids of the body better than any metal save some special steels, and those hard to make and harder to fashion ... save perhaps for the Duergar," she added ruefully, "or yourself."

Elof grinned and shook his head. "For armoury, perhaps. Not for fine tasks. Silver is subtler, as you say, readier to take fine shape upon itself, and deep craft. But of course, to maintain the affinity it need not be set within the body ..."

Marja smiled. "Hardly! Though I have found service-able a setting in some way symbolic of the union ... a zoning, say, an encirclement. A girdle, a necklace, an ... an arm-ring ..." She hesitated; evidently she had heard something of that, from Roc or from Kara herself. But Elof only chuckled, putting her at ease again.

"That indeed! Though I was but a prentice when I crafted Kara's, and used gold at my master's behest. There was one who lacked the woman's insight! But for yours I thank you, and leave you to your tasks; I was half of your mind on a difficult point, and now you've settled it well. No word of Roc? Well, he should not be long now. Again a good day to you, Master!"

She looked at him a little curiously as he took his leave, but made no move to ask him why he had asked what he had. It was common enough for mastersmiths to be secretive about their work, especially in its earliest stages, and to pry would be a grave breach of manners as the Guild understood them. That would not stop her thinking, but she, only recently made master, would hardly be likely to guess at his true purpose; he himself had been slow enough to conceive it. Even now he balked at it, half yearned to let that thought remain a thought; but then consuming fear came upon him all the more strongly, and a great horror at the thought of abandoning Kara to the cold mind, dark heart that had first ensnared her. Should he let that happen, when he might so easily prevent it? How could he live with himself if he did? The prentices, still taking sights with their instruments, turned to greet him as he passed, but fell silent. He saw his look mirrored in their dismay, and turned it to a rueful smile.

Back once more in his forge, he sat gazing at the panniers of ore left him by Ils' fellows, picking out chunks and turning them over in his fingers. Silver was among those metals that could be seen clearly even in its natural state; his knowing fingers traced the threads and streaks with which the living rock was shot, as if they were its veins and nerves. And was not that another affinity with the living? It remained for him now to render it, concentrate it, distill the essence of this stony flesh and set within it … Once more his mind shied at the thought, and once more that iron purpose, forged by fear, tempered by desperation, goaded it to its crucial leap. He roused himself, went to the door to call in apprentices from the training forge nearby, then stopped. The fewer hands that mingled in this work, the better, for many reasons. With all his strength he heaved the first pannier from the ground and began to tip the ore into the crushing trough. When all was done he spun a heavy bar pivoted in the stone wall, and water came gushing from a metal chute above, swirling the loose dirt from the chunks and herding them slowly down the trough towards the iron block at the end. As the flow quickened he lowered into it a tall flanged wheel set in a framework among levers, and two heavy shafts tipped at their end with iron blocks as big as his head, shaped to bite against the iron below; the levers worked as the wheel spun, lifting and letting fall the shafts, catching and crushing the ore between iron and iron, the shattered pieces ground to finer fragments as they passed beneath the centre of the wheel, a hub of hard stone.

Retreating from the noise, Elof smiled in satisfaction. He had adapted this engine from those in the forge of the Mastersmith Mylio, and if it was smaller, driven by Morvanhal's ducted water supply and not a mountain torrent, it was also subtler and less cumbersome. One day, perhaps, if he needed more power he might harness the pounding of the waves below, or, as some smiths had of old, the contained and perilous force of heated steam. But not even that could match the blast of the earthfires by which the Mastersmith's furnaces were fed, and which, at times, he missed most sorely in his work. The duergar might have helped him harness them, but there were simply no such fires near enough the surface in this rolling seacoast region. Smithlore had taught him that nature held many other sources of great heat, from the sun's gathered light to the inner turbulence of certain metals subtly purified, but also how hard they were to tap, and how perilous. For one brief minute of wonder and terror he had trapped the lightning in his fist, and seen how small man stood against the compass of such forces. To draw upon the least of them would require long study, and though he had bent some time to his researches, always some matter of greater urgency had intervened; and always there was Kara. He had ideas; but as yet he was far from any answer. He rose, and busied himself about his furnace.

Water drove the bellows; behind the panel of sooty mica in the door their glow changed from red to glaring yellow in the blast, and thence to a core of dazzling white about the foot of the crucible he had thrust in.

The coals sizzled and sang, and as he watched the little pyramid of crushed ore slump and trickle inward he caught the note of the singing, rising and falling, and found within it, as visions are seen in hearthfires, the music of songs. One, ringing and compulsive, he knew well, though from where he could not say. The other was something new, quite new, a slower, lilting, flowing phrase that seemed to lead him on to others. That was good, that the songs sung over this work should arise out of it, one upon another, phrases that grew and burgeoned like twining flowers. Should flowers also be the starting point of the pattern he must set upon his work? But there might be something better; something closer ... He ran his fingers idly over the blocks of fine beeswax he had set out, humming vague snatches of tunes, seeking for the shape they suggested within the amber depths of the wax; after a moment, forgetting the array of knives and carving tools beside it, he plucked up a long thin block, and, warming it at the furnace wall, began to work it between his fingers. It flowed and responded under his powerful grasp. "Even so," he muttered. "Even this ... you learn well what you must do. Your proper pattern you shall have!"

And that night, as the stars wheeled beyond their balcony and Kara tensed and flowed beneath him amid the tangle of their sheets, he ran his hands through her crisp hair, forcing her head back to kiss her fluttering throat; he had meant to grip lightly, but in the force of his passion his hands clenched tight, and when they fell away, trembling, they grasped a whole wisp of her hairs, not the single one he had need of. But this they could smile at, for he in turn bore the impress of her nails upon his back, sharp as talons. Later, when she slept, he padded over to the chest where her cloak was bestowed, unlocked it and very softly raised the lid. There lay the cloak, gleaming so white in the faint light that when he lifted one corner the blackness of the lining seemed absolute, and he had to riffle the little feathers with his fingers to find their roots. At last he chose one, inconspicuous yet near the garment's edge, caught it between finger and thumb and plucked it loose. There was a sudden slight gasp, and to his horror he heard Kara whimper in her sleep, looked up and saw her, curled up on her side, straighten out suddenly and reach up to rub at one shoulder. He felt moisture on his fingers, a slight warm stickiness he could not mistake, and froze unmoving where he knelt. But her eyes did not open, her arm fell away onto her breast and she slipped back once more into sleep. When he dared move again he reached down, caught the cloak between his fingers; beneath the feathers he felt some fine silken fabric against the outer cloak, no more. He folded it back carefully into the chest, smoothing it with what was almost a caress, and quietly locked the lid once more. He rose shakily to his feet, sick with self-disgust half minded to hurl away the feather and the hairs he clutched, sticky with a spot of drying blood. But instead he forced himself to tuck them into the fold of cotton he had laid ready, and returned it to the aumbry. Then, clambering back into bed, he reached out almost desperately to Kara; sleepily she came to him and clung, and he buried his face in the warmth of her shoulder. Had she woken then, he might still have blurted out what was on his mind; but sleep held her as fast as any human. So it overtook Elof also, and so the first light woke them, to love again half sleeping and in loving, forget. By the coming of the day Elof's doubts had receded like a troubled dream, and it was easy to blame the blood on one of his own smarting scratches.

The next day, in between his official duties, he set about further extracting the pure silver from the reduced ore by amalgamating it with quicksilver, a subtle but hazardous process. Only after there was no further chance of fumes could he bolt the doors of his forge and lay out his prizes upon a scrubbed clean workbench, guarding against the least draught that might snatch them away. For a while he toyed with them, setting the lock of hair and the feather together in various ways till he had an arrangement that pleased him; he chalked a quick sketch of it upon a slate, multiplied it to form a frieze, then drew the frieze in various perspectives, in circles, rings, spirals. And it was as he completed the spiral design that he found himself humming again, those first faint serpentine phrases of the new song, ever more clearly. A spiral ... He took up the shape he had already made. A flowing spiral of feathers interwoven with locks of hair, winding forever onward ... but winding about a torus, and so coming forever back upon itself. Free, yet unchanging, forever fleeing yet forever returning ... He nodded to himself. It would take great care, but it could be done. He scrubbed his crude sketch from the slate, took up ink and parchment pieces, and set to work constructing a large and intricate version of the design. It took him many hours, and several false starts, and all the while singing softly to himself. The floor around him was littered with discarded sheets, and when he had at last finished he was careful to gather these and thrust them into the forge. The parchments curled and whined and sizzled like living things upon the hot coals, but he scarcely noticed; his hands were already upon the wax, probing its smooth contours with a burin finer than the finest of the hairs it would portray.

By now it was late at night, but for all his distrust of wearied mind and hands, he laboured on, driven as he had not been since his youth, singing still under his breath, hardly aware of it. It was not easy work, for the glabrous wax was not parchment to be inscribed, nor wood to be chiselled clean. Any mark caused its surface to swell and change; it might flake away where it was too brittle, or ooze where it was soft. Every stroke had to be incised with care and foresight, its shavings minutely cleaned away before the next. Flat lines had to be translated into incised channels or raised ridges, and the tapering of the hairs, the fine fluff at the feather's bases, represented; even the dark stain on the quill he sought to match by subtle texture. It was master's work, and in the mere precision of its detail it was fair. "As if already there is something of her in it," he thought, and was pleased; yet that pleasure only sharpened the spurs of fear. On and on he laboured, till he found the delicate tools slipping between fingers sweating or numbed; many times he managed to avoid damaging the work only at the cost of cuts and punctures, and it was his own blood made them slippery then. When at last some shred of sane caution told him to lay down the thing he held, to get it free of his trembling fingers before he ruined it, he felt almost sick with frustration. Only little by little did reason reassert itself as he hobbled back up towards the palace under skies whose stars were already beginning to pale; he told himself angrily that it was too easy to become obsessed with lonely work like this, easier still to ruin it with impatience. Yet he still could not be sure he would find Kara there awaiting him, that he would not find the chest broken, the cloak gone, and nothing save perhaps a black quill left him as a token. Along high stair and vaulted passage his thoughts haunted him; and though his relief at finding her curled beneath the covers, her hair a dark corona amid the white pillows, was great enough, it barely lasted him into sleep, and fled with waking.

On the next day he hurried through his duties in the shipyards like a man possessed; that carving haunted him like a persistent irritation, an itch in the mind. Even when he found himself dangling head down from a masthead to free a salt-encrusted block, rather than reeve a whole new set of tackle, he could not stop running over and over the patterns in his mind until they made him dizzy. He swung himself upright on the little platform, and to avoid looking straight down to the deck he glanced out across the harbour, enjoying the cool breeze and the look of the town in late afternoon. Down here, walls were mostly half-timbered and limewashed, or timbers laid clinker-fashion and painted very much like those of his childhood village. Many had been repainted after the ravages of winter, and garlanded with flowers in hanging baskets and window shelves; they looked bright as toys clustered around the feet of the more august buildings of the upper town, in their rich shades of red and yellow stone. But inevitably, somehow, his glance was drawn across the lower rooftops again, towards the dark bulk, itself a little like a louring anvil, that was the hall of his guild; his sight seemed to pierce through those walls and down, down towards those

half-formed secrets they held. He cursed; the joy had gone
out of the scene for him, the irritation had infected it
too. He hated what he was doing, yet it would not let
him be. Moodily he lobbed the useless block into a cluster of seagulls bobbing on the harbour waters, and
watched them explode upwards, cursing and squalling
just as he wanted to. Then he shrugged guiltily. It would
not have amused Kara, that; one of them might even
have *been* Kara, if he had not ... Very slowly he inched
out along the shrouds and slid down with gloved hands.
His duty was done for the moment; he could get back to
his carving once more.

By late evening it was complete, carved surfaces
more detailed and more delicate than any he had ever
made till now. The living lock and feather he took and
set among the patterns, and save for the hues of life they
were matched to perfection. He laid them apart, then
swiftly turned to preparing the moulds, lest in the
warmth of the forge the wax should soften further and
lose some tiny point of definition. By that much might
its power be lessened; by so much might he lose what
he fought to preserve.

It was with the gentleness of love that his practised
fingers worked a soft slip of burnt and powdered chalk
about the delicate shapes he had made, to take the finest possible impress of the pattern. Over that he
smoothed layer upon layer of clay, gradually firmer, till
at last the prepared shapes could be manoeuvered
gently into position in his moulding flasks, sprues carefully aligned with the openings, then encased and set to
dry well away from forge-hearth and furnace, lest the
sudden heat should crack them. Now he brought the
water thundering down, washed the clay from his stinging cuts and set the bellows-wheel spinning till the
breath of the bellows roared through the coals like
buried dragons. Then with long tongs he set the crucible of purified silver among them, and several of other
rare metals for his chosen alloy. He sat by the maw of
the furnace, humming idly under his breath and watching its dulled surface gradually shiver with remembered
heat and change into a flowing mirror. He remembered

his tumbledown smithy among the saltmarshes, these ten years behind him and the breadth of a land away, and the silver wires he had worked there for a sword-hilt. Believing his craft lost to him, he had not sought to set within them any virtues; and yet they had absorbed something of his essential self and shown it him as an image of the Marshland skies, a rushing of grey clouds, a sweep of rain and storm. Now he must make this silver do likewise; save that now he would determine the image, and the essence would not be his own.

He began to sing to himself quietly, vague snatches of that new song, wordless still or with only a single word, yet heavy with a meaning that was growing continually clearer. Firing the moulds, he felt a chain of words take shape in his mind as the wax rushed molten from the sprueholes, spitting and flaming onto the coals, and after it the boiling water to clean them. He set them at the edge of the fire, and took a deep breath; then he lifted the glowing crucible to the furnace door, and one by one, in careful order, tipped in the lesser metals. Some were to make the silver harder and more durable, some to add slight spring to it; but others, added in merest traces, were to bear special virtues of their own. The heavy liquid hissed and seethed sluggishly as he stirred it with a long rod of steel, and all the while, listening carefully to the thin high note of the coals, he sang the chant that had come to him. That swirling rythm went well with the stirring, and the coils it awoke in the crucible's heart.

In silver the shaping, enclosing, embracing,
In silver a shield-ring of signs interlacing
Set firm within silver the circle shall close.

In silver the melting, in silver the blending,
As ramparts of steel shot with moonlight defending,
No call from without them may pass what they hold.

Tiny droplets of metal spattered his hand, the rod grew hot through the rag he held it by, the furnace heat drew the skin taut over his cheekbones, cracked his lips,

stung his eyes, yet still he sang, dry-tongued, till the last
part of the alloy was added and the blend complete.

As freely you flow now a form shall enfold you,
In cooling, coalescing, a pattern shall hold you,
In shaping, in firming, grow strong yet grow fair.

What now I trust to you, embrace it, enfold it,
Against yearning for change, against wandering
hold it,
Encase as in armour the heart that is torn.

    With frantic speed he threw his weight upon the
great forge bellows, pumping them faster than could the
waterwheel, till the hill of coals glowed searing white at
its summit, as if earthfires fed it indeed. Urgently he
heaved out the crucible in the long tongs, whitehot
metal slopping and sizzling against its flanks, and
whirled it across from furnace to forge; it seemed to
leave a trail like a falling starstone in the heavy air, and
hissed onto the angry coals. The lock of hair and the
feather he caught up, raised them to his lips a moment,
then reached out over the fire to the crucible and
dropped them in. A light plume of flame danced up,
ghostlike, and they were gone.
    Gathering his strength, he took up the crucible
once more, swung it around to the moulds waiting on
the forge-rim ... then cursed himself luridly. Fool that
he was to try such a task without one forgehand at least,
to steady the mould, to correct his aim, to vibrate out
airlocks and bubbles, to warn him when it was almost
full ... Hideous difficulties loomed over him; one
mistake, one only ... But there was no help for it now;
delay would only cool the silver further, make it harder
to pour. He would have to reheat it, risk dissipating
what he had set within it ... and would he ever dare to
replace it? Better at all events to have no forgehand hear
what he must sing now. Gritting tooth on tooth he
tilted the heavy thing, saw a swelling of red at its rim, a
fine thread falling ... Straight into the mouth of the
mould. Steam whistled from the other spruehole; he

breathed again, and on that note he sang, clear and
fierce, that older song his memory had taught him. Yet
the words were new; and as he sang his hand never
trembled, the thread of falling silver never wavered.

Sheltered in silver
By craft and by flame
Be no more now drawn from me
And captive again – As once you chose,
Choose to remain!
Your own self shall enclose you,
More firmly than fetter or chain!

Silver sprang and spat, and he swung the crucible
away. But was the mould full, or was it only an airlock
which would leave a damaging flaw? Too late to tell;
already the mirrored meniscus was dimming, he must
pour the other quickly before the silver cooled. This
was worse, his arms aching with cramp, his fingers
trembling with weakness. His head swam, but he sang
the words clearly through the smoky air. A long age it
seemed before the silver leaped and spattered down the
flanks of the second mould, and so great was his relief
that he all but dropped the crucible, and had to set it
down at an awkward angle on the rim before coaxing
the moulds gently out of the coals; even unshaped, that
silver could be potent stuff. He would be safest making
some other work of it as soon as possible, set with
different virtues. Meanwhile ... He left the moulds on
top of the coals, to cool slowly as they did; that helped
lessen stresses within the metal. Exhaustion burned in
his back and arms, and suddenly the air choked him; he
flung the air-vents wide and collapsed by the forge,
listening to the wind sigh in the passages of the stone.
His head drooped on his breast, he jerked upright once,
and then it no longer seemed worth the effort; his eyes
were hot and sore, his head ...
    Thunder crashed around him; suddenly he was in
many places, on a storm-wreathed tower-top, a grim
and night-bound forest, by a forge in a marshland
hovel – or was it in the mountains of the north ... Then

he knew where he was, shivering by a stone-cold hearth, with pounding, pounding upon his doors. Speechless he stumbled up, his throat ashen as the forge. Something in his dreaming, a memory of other such summons, filled that sound with dread, made his hands clumsy on the heavy bolt. For a moment the figure that stood there in the shadowy corridor, cloaked and hooded, seemed ominous; but he was shorter than Elof, short and rotund, and from beneath the travel-stained hood blazed a mane of red hair. Elof forgot all his alarm and seized the proffered hand. "Roc my lad! So you're back, then!"

"Sort of looks that way, don't it?" grunted Roc gracelessly. Elof looked at him narrowly; though Roc was nominally a Guildsman, he was seldom seen in the Halls. There was no mystery about that. In the Southlands he had been a respected master of his art; but what status had a smith here, skilled as he might be in the mechanics of his trade, who lacked the least trace of true smithcraft? The short man grimaced. "You're the only waking soul in the place! And here's me just in the gate, all the hostelries still shut up snug for the dawn, and me too dry with the dust of twenty roads to make the climb up to the palace –"

Elof took the hint, and poured them both wine from a jug on a side-table; Roc downed his in one gulp, and held the beaker out for more. "Not bad," he wheezed. "Distinctly passable, in fact, though the soot's got into it again. Don't your forgeboy keep it covered up?"

Elof peered suspiciously into his own goblet. "I don't keep a forgeboy anymore; I get the prentices in to help as I need them."

Roc snorted. "No wonder place is a mess, then. I've half a mind to take up my old post again; you're not fit to look after yourself. What's this that's got you out of your bed so early?" He glanced at Elof from beneath his bristling brows. "Or kept you out of it all night, eh? My, my, must be something good and juicy!" He squinted at the small moulds, into the cold crucible. "Silver? Not stuff for the fleet, surely?"

"Hardly!" smiled Elof. "That's day-labour. This is to

be a gift, a surprise, so not a word of it. Even to
Marja . . ."

"Scant danger of that!" grunted Roc. "Smithcraft's
not a thing we talk about; jewellery least of all. Well,
these moulds look about ripe for cracking. Want a
hand?"

"If you're not too weary," grinned Elof, striving not
to let his misgivings show. But it would be a worse risk
being seen to hide anything from Roc; he was no fool.
And since he could see nothing of the craft within the
metal, what harm was there? His stubby hands were
every bit as deft as Elof's as they prised apart the metal
shells and chipped at the crumbling clay within. Below
lay the chalk, sintered now to the hardness of the rock
it came from; but under Elof's impatient grip its edges
flaked away, and he shelled it like some strange fruit,
catching his breath at the gleams of bright metal that
showed through. He brought down a jar of corrosive
from the high shelf and mixed a weak solution in water.

"So!" said Roc, as they watched the chalk fizz and
bubble away, revealing the clear outlines of the pieces.
"Not bad. Not bad at all. Neat as Marja could manage, or
any other master jeweller I know. But that's no surprise.
They the way you wanted them, then?"

With great care Elof hooked the gleaming pieces
out of the cleansing bath, ran them a moment beneath
the waterchute and held them up, first to the red-tinged
duergar lantern, then to the thin light that was filtering
down the air-shafts. "Yes," he breathed, seeing the
intricate pattern of lock and feather wind its way around
them without the tiniest flaw or bubble to break its
inexorable course. "Yes! They are. Indeed they are."
They set a catch in his voice, for he had the true smith's
love of all things harmonious and fair. Yet not only their
perfection moved him, but the sight of the shimmers
and flickers that to his eyes darted this way and that in
the metal, like fish below clear ice.

With a friend's privilege, Roc reached up and
plucked down one of the gleaming things, like rare fruit.
"Bracelets, eh? But why open like that?"

Elof smiled. "Anklets, rather."

"Mmmh. I see; so they'll fit over the foot. But won't they need hinges?"

"No; the natural spring of the metal ..."

Roc nodded, and his powerful fingers closed around the thick ring of silver, narrowing the split. "No!" barked Elof, and wrenched the fair thing from his hand. Roc raised his eyebrows mildly, and Elof smiled in apology. "After it's annealed, I was going to say. A long slow heating and cooling, to heal any inward stresses."

"All right," grunted Roc. "I wasn't going to risk closing it all the way, anyway; guessed you'd be wanting to work on the catch. Can't see how it'd undo, as it is."

Elof shrugged. "It's important they stay on securely."

Roc grinned in wry agreement. "Fair enough. She's an active girl, your Kara, more active than most. You'd be wanting anything you gave her to fit close and stay close, all right."

Elof relaxed, trying not to show how shaken he had been, how vital it was that those clasps should close only at the right time and place, and in no other. It was a fell thing he had shaped here, in its way, but there was no help for it. He had only to think of her drawn back to Louhi's clutches to make it all worthwhile again. He balanced the anklets in his palm, and was startled to see blood on the metal. It was his; he had reopened some of the worse cuts when he snatched the thing back. Well, on the outside of the piece it could do no harm; he turned to wipe it away on a clean rag. Then he froze. On the outside... But he had paid little heed to his injuries earlier in the work; he could have bled at any point, onto the wax, into the silver... The tokens; he could have added his own blood to that feather. And there was no way now he would ever be able to tell.

"What's amiss with you now?" grunted Roc. "You've a face on you the colour of milk, and sour at that."

"I ... It's nothing. Just ... an effect, one that might turn out good or bad, I've no idea." He choked down his sudden flood of anxiety. There was always slight contamination when you touched something, a flake of skin, its natural oils; that mattered little, so why should this? And after all, could he really be bound up any more closely with Kara than he was? It might even strengthen the thing. He smiled wearily. "I was really wondering ... I've a fair amount of silver left that I'd like to find a use for. Do you have any notions?"

Roc fingered his stubbled chin. "Not just now, but then my mind's that muzzy, I've not slept; something to help us on our jaunt south, that's a good an idea as I can hatch right now. Me for the palace, and some breakfast. And a bath; they should have the bathhouse warming nicely by the time I get there. You could use one, after your labours; set you up. Coming?"

Elof considered a moment. "Why not? But hear me; if Kara is there also, not a word of the gift, remember!" He shut away the anklets in a secure cabinet of iron, and closed up the forge with as much care. Then they went together out of the Guildhalls and into the winding streets of the northerners quarter, at whose heart the great building stood. A light spring rain was falling, making the scale-tiled house-roofs shine, gurgling out of the open-mouthed dragonheads at their gable-ends or running in sheets down their wall timbers, caulked tight as ships with the figures brightly limned in red and black upon them; little rivulets chattered down between the cobbles into the central gutter. Roc looked at the ships rolling at anchor, and up to the ornate weather-vanes on the house-roofs, and groaned.

"Wind's swinging around the compass again; clear dawn when I came in. Ah well, that's spring for you; that'll give us an interesting time at sea, that will, just like always."

Elof grinned sympathetically; Roc was unhappily weak of stomach in a lively sea. "You know," he remarked, watching the vanes creak back and forth over the tiles, "that was no bad thought of yours. Something to help on the voyage, indeed. I'll think on that!"

And so he did; even as they took their ease in the royal baths, stretching out weary limbs on the steam-room slabs and drifting in the heated pools, his mind dwelt on it still. Then friends and fellow-courtiers came to join them, and later Marja and Kara, and the demands of the day took over his thoughts. His other, deeper concern he forgot entirely for that time, the matter of the blood. Yet in the years to come he had cause to remember it, and wonder if this petty accident might indeed have played a strange part in his fortunes. For to the effects of true smithcraft, say the annals of that day, it was ever hard to put any bounds, and never more so than in the hands of Elof, called Valantor.

From that day forth he had in any case little leisure for thought; the day of departure was near, and his was the ultimate responsibility for all the work his helpers, men and duergar, had made ready. What spare time he had he devoted to reforging the extra silver; he would leave nothing so perilous behind to suffer the whim of chance. This work was less subtle, for the forces of nature might be stronger than the turning tides of heart and mind; but it cost him much hard labour incising its pattern with maul and chisels, and beating down an inlay of gold wire into the troughs thus made. He had chosen the complex pattern, coiling and intertwining in the Southland style, that represented Amicac, the Sea Devourer, embodiment of the terrors of the oceans. But it represented also their regality and strength and as such it was the favourite emblem of the boldest corsairs, and fitted his purpose well. From time to time he would sing snatches of old fisherman's shanties he remembered from his youth in Asenby village, songs chiefly concerned with summoning fine weather and catches, simple but strong. More often, though, he whistled hard between his teeth as he worked, recalling the pipe-whistles the seawise smiths of Nordeney used to forge for mariners to summon up the breeze. And as often happened to him, a work he had started casually took hold of him, and ere it was finished he had set within it a surpassing craft and strength.

Such was the turmoil of those last days that he could not finish it till the very eve of the fleet's departure, checking its balance carefully on its steel mounting and giving it a last buff and polish. It only remained for him then to gather up the tools he always travelled with, and close up his forge for the summer. Last of all he took the anklets from their cabinet and thrust them into an inner pocket; then he locked the doors behind him and hurried out and into the ways leading up to the palace, seeing that the sun was almost down. That night Kermorvan was feasting all the mariners of the fleet, some two thousand in all, at a great banquet of state that would fill all the wide halls of the palace, and he should attend. Not that it mattered much if he was late; but Kara might be anxious. As it was, they managed to make their entrance a few minutes before the King himself took his seat. Till then the centre of attention had been Ils, queenly in white among her guard of thickset duergar, but Elof was uncomfortably aware of all eyes turning to Kara, for the beauty of her and the mystery, garbed in a gown of forest green and set about with the jewels he had made her.

"Do you hear them stir, down there at the crews' tables?" she whispered, as they took their seats at the high table. "Do you know why? Folk from the west or the remote townlets, who have not seen me ere now, they turn to their neighbours and whisper, *"Is that not she, the strange one, the shapeshifter that he took from the Icewitch? What is she, in truth? And what is he, that he loves such a one?"*"

Elof chuckled. "And their wiser neighbours will answer that if they cannot see good reason, they must be blind! Or fish-blooded! And for your inner self, they'll cite the courage you showed in freeing their king, the ways you've helped us on our journeys ... scouted for us, healed for us, fought for us –"

"For you!" she said quietly, clutching his hand beneath the table. And then to a flourish of music Kermorvan entered, and as one the crews rose to cheer and stamp. He acknowledged the rowdy tribute with a quiet nod and a lifted hand, and moved smiling to take his place between Ils on his right hand and Kara on his left. The feast began then, and it was a merry one, though neither long nor drunken; Kermorvan wanted his crews fit on the morrow, and would have a severe way with any who were not. It was well before the

middle hours when Elof and Kara made their way back
to their apartments. As Kara laid aside her jewels Elof
opened the chest, took out the cloak and made as if to
drape it about her shoulders. But her own strong hands
held his wrists, and she shook her head, smiling. "Do
you keep it for me still; pack it among your own gear,
and give it me only at need, take it back when that is
past. I would not add to your worries on such a voyage
as this!"

Elof's mouth quirked; he understood only too well
that she was paying him back, very gently, for having
asked it of her. He put aside the cloak and drew her to
him, and the anklets he left in his pockets, without a
further thought.

But on the next day's dawning, when they went
aboard the longship *Prince Korentyn*, flagship of the
fleet, at its anchorage in mid-harbour, Elof had his other
work ready to hand. Kara, bare-legged, swung through
the boarding port with a lithe grace; he clambered
unsteadily after her, while the wherrymen swayed up
their heavy packs to the deck. Together they made
their way aft to the sterncastle, where stood Kermorvan,
directing the disposition of his fleet. His clear voice was
ragged and cracking with the effort of shouting orders;
messengers scurried this way and that about the gently
heaving deck, and the signal flags fluttered like bright
butterflies in the crowded harbour. He had no more
than a glance to spare for the newcomers, and that of
relief; they were the last aboard, for Elof had been carrying out some final refitting aboard other vessels. Already
aboard with the king was Roc, and also Ils, as she often
was in these days; that was natural enough, in that she
also was a ruler, seeking to establish and extend her
realm in the Meneth Ledannen, and was hoping to bring
many more of her folk eastward on this expedition. Only
Elof, who had once by chance overheard a strange
conversation, was inclined to wonder what more might
lie behind this, and he kept his own counsel. She was
leaning on the rail now, squinting in the morning sun,
regarding the confusion with her wide sardonic grin; it
broadened, if anything, when she saw Elof and Kara, and

she waved them lazily over.

"Scurry, scurry, scurry! Everyone rushing about at the behest of their feelings, too busy to stop and think! That's men for you. Or humans ... eh, lady Kara?"

Elof stiffened slightly. He was very fond of Ils; but what she thought of Kara he had never been sure, and this stress on humanity made him uncomfortable. In many ways Kara was more human than the duergar, and knew it. But Kara only smiled, and took Elof's arm. "I find they have some uses, both of them. What's amiss, here?"

Ils jerked a stubby thumb at the sternpost, where a gilded wind-vane in the shape of a gull creaked to and fro, swinging with each slight shift of the ship. "The wind, it would seem ... a few points short of favourable, by the look of it, so we are windrode, with scant space to manoeuvre. The small craft think they will clear the harbour mouth close-hauled, the larger longships and dromunds fear they cannot; it is hard to be sure."

"And getting them out under oars could take all day," said Roc uneasily. "We could miss the wind and sit wallowing for hours ..." He looked somewhat green already.

Elof nodded, stepped forward and tapped Kermorvan unceremoniously on the shoulder. "Would it help you to have a true gauge of the wind?" he called out against the breeze.

"Would it not!" snapped the tall man over his shoulder, brushing his bronzen hair out of his eyes. "Why, can you shape us such a thing in time? It would help us to know whether to risk sail –"

Elof reached into his pack. "I was going to give you this today anyway, as a luck-gift for the journey." He handed the glittering quarter-moon of metal to Kermorvan; his brows lifted as he looked at it, then he grinned to Elof.

"Amicac, eh? Well we've sailed under his sign before, you and I; it shouldn't hurt us to play the corsair again!" He reached up to the carved stern-post and lifted the golden gull from its socket; into its place he slid Elof's vane, the raised finial that was the head of the pattern gleamed gape-jawed to the wind.

"Once it takes the wind properly," called Elof hopefully, "it should hold it tight with every twist and turn –" He watched it saw from side to side a little, just like its predecessor, then … "There!"

The vane had stopped sharply, quivering slightly, gripped as if by vast hands in the dead centre of the wind. "Remarkable!" said Kermorvan, "Even though its tidings are not hopeful … What if it were pushed out of line?"

Elof shrugged. "It should centre itself once more. But it should not be so easily shifted."

Curiously, Kermorvan reached up and pushed at the blade of the vane; it did not move. He pressed again, and then harder, with a real effort. "Like … trying to close a door in a fierce gale," he gasped, "though the … breeze is no more … than middling …" He pushed with both hands, and all his weight, and now, very slowly, the blade began to shift. And as it did so Elof caught his breath, felt Kara's hand tighten suddenly upon his arm; a sudden chill grew in the pit of his stomach. Something else had shifted also, he knew not what. But it felt like the balance of the world …

Ils cried out suddenly, and pointed, not to the vane but to the streamers on the mainstays, the signal flags above; it was hard to see at first, but … had they also shifted? Kermorvan had released the vane, staggered back; it stayed where he had placed it, as firmly as before. He threw his weight upon it again, and once again the streamers shifted, the flags flapped to a different angle. Elof swallowed.

"That's all!" panted the king, releasing the vane and doubling over, hands on knees. "You, Elof, your thews might shift it a fraction further, but no more …"

"That's scant surprise!" said Ils, a little shakily. "To alter the wind at all … Winds are not single things, says our lore of weather, but a net of flows and currents, vaster than the oceans. To shift one, even a few points … I cannot conceive of it!"

"Nor I!" muttered Roc. "What've you gone and done this time, my lad?" Elof could only shake his head, feeling like an idiot.

Kermorvan leaned back against the gunwales, waving off the messengers clamouring for his attention, abruptly very much the ruler. "Elof, did you plan this?" he asked with a grim quiet in his voice.

Elof drew a deep breath. Kara's hand lay tight upon his shoulder, and somehow that gave him the wit to speak. "I planned no more than I said. Now I see it, though, I can see … something of how it came about. It is logic, of a sort. I sang over it, I whistled .. old songs of the North, to encourage sea-luck, fair winds … They are part of me, those songs, they run deep in my memory; they must have drawn more out of me than I guessed … I never dreamed of giving it the power to compel!"

Kermorvan nodded. "I can believe that. This … it is a startling power, but perhaps also a dangerous one –"

"My lord!" cried one of the messengers suddenly, desperate to be heard. "The dromunds are all signalling! The wind has changed, it will serve them now!"

"And the longships!" called another. "My lord, we may lose the hour, the tide –"

Kermorvan snapped to his feet. "Well," he muttered, "What that power has already given us, let us not waste!" And cupping his hands to his mouth he shouted out to his crew "To your places, all men! Winch and cable crews, ready! Mainmast men, ready! Slip the stern moorings! Hoist the mainsail, ready the headsails! Bow moorings, haul in!" Tumult broke out on the maindeck, and the shipmaster and his mates came running aft to the sterncastle. Kermorvan rounded on the messengers with a blast of orders that sent them scurrying to the signal halyards, then back to his own crew. "Do you take command, Master! Warp her around into the wind, mainsail first, out into the main channel and through! We'll lead them all out!"

The shipmaster saluted him, and turned to bellow across the decks. In the bows a capstan winch began to clank, and they felt the stern swing suddenly free of its moorings, the long hull begin to sway and sidle in the choppy harbour waters. The huge mainyard creaked and rumbled up the mast, the hemp-stiffened mainsail fluttered and boomed as the breeze caught and shook it. "Keep hauling, the bows!" bellowed the master. Into the wind swung the great ship, and for the space of a breath the mainsail hung limp; then it was across, and almost at once the wind caught the sail, bellied it out with an explosive crack. "Slip moorings, the bows!" roared the master. "Helm, steer for the harbour mouth!" The great ship surged forward, the deck leaped under them and then began to dip and raise more smoothly as it gathered way. Behind them the wheel spun, hauling on the tiller lines that rose up taut through the deck; Kermorvan cast a glance at the helmsman, who nodded calmly. This manner of rudder was a new thing, learned from the duergar, and still unpredictable; but it seemed to be working smoothly enough now. The *Prince Korentyn* nosed her sleek bows out into the main channel, while all around her sails blossomed out upon the other ships of the fleet, and their standards dipped in salute.

Kermorvan gathered up his armour of black and gold from the bench where he had laid it, and moved forward to stand at the rail of the sterncastle, proud and resplendent; he wore no helm, and his long locks shone like bronze indeed in the morning sun. From the walls of the palace came a fanfare of trumpets, the call of the garrison who would remain to defend the town, from tower-tops a loud pealing of bells, and from the shore a great cheer went up; as ever, all the town had turned out to watch their king and his great fleet depart. He waved, and from the bows his own heralds answered the town's salute; then at his command the rest of his music, gathered by the companionway, struck up a strong and buoyant tune. Like sudden wings the headsails spread out above, white water swirled at the bows. Kara, still clutching Elof's arm, positively danced with excitement as the great ship swept towards the harbour mouth, its fellows sliding out one by one into its wake in the order the king had laid down. As it glided between the tall towers that flanked the mouth, the music of the other ships took up the tune, and the notes of thudding tabors, shrilling flutes, silver cymbal and brazen horns and trumpets rose and rang around the whole shore of the bay, as their white sails spread out, dazzling against its sparkling waters. Thus in pride and splendour that great fleet set forth; and though from shore it must have been no less splendid a sight, no account describes it so. Those who chronicled it were among its numbers.

Hard on the flagship's heels the greatest of the dromunds came, still spreading its great fields of sail; the creak of ropes, bellowed orders, the dull boom of sailcloth shook the air. Flanking it raced two smaller craft, chase cutters rigged in the strange new patterns derived from duergar ideas, their sails slanting fore and aft instead of square to the hull. Kara went running to the sternrail to watch them, bouncing and skipping impudently up through the wake like puppies snapping at the ankles of a bull. "They're so beautiful!" she breathed. "If we could only sail one of those!"

Elof laid his arm around her. "There'll be time enough, on this voyage; no doubt their crews'll be glad of the rest, for a day or two. We should ask Kermorvan."

"Oh yes!" she said, her eyes sparkling like the waters beneath. He felt her quiver from head to toe with excitement. "So light, so fast, it would be almost like ..." But there she stopped herself, and said no more.

As in previous years, the first few days of the great fleet's voyage were leisurely, more like a ceremonial royal progress than a venture of moment. By day the ships would race each other, or contest in manoeuvering and skill, which Kermorvan encouraged for the practice it gave crews and commanders alike; Elof and Kara had their chance then to sail the new-rigged cutters. Each night they would anchor in sheltered waters, or the harbours of lesser ports where the king would receive deputations and petitions, settle disputes, and renew acquaintance with those of his people who seldom or never came north to Morvanhal the City itself. In the remoter areas the fleet was greeted with almost delirious relief, as a living token of the strength and solidarity of the land; the wounds of the Ekwesh occupation, short as it had been, were slow in healing there.

Those were pleasant days for most; yet for Elof they were marred. For Kara grew more restive, spoke less and seldom settled; she would pace the decks, or sit for long hours in the bows, gazing at the empty expanse of the ocean off the port bow. She did not object to his company in such times; she would smile at him as he came to sit by her, perhaps rest her head upon his shoulder, yet ever her gaze was turned away into the void of earth and sky. Once he found her still there in the midst of a storm, clinging to the forestay and squealing with delight as the bows clove the wavecrests and showered her with chill spray; he grew angry then, and upbraided her for courting foolish perils. She made no complaint, but took to climbing, in clement weather, to the lookout's place at the summit of the mainmast. Elof followed her up, admiring the grace of her tanned legs on the rigging above, the animal ease with which she swung herself up onto the narrow platform. Elof bent and struggled through more cautiously, and once up he hastily looped his belt through the ring provided. Kara took no such precaution, but leaned out over the rail, rejoicing in the feeling of height and pointing down delightedly to the flocks of dolphins come to race around the fleet's bows. Elof smiled, only a little thinly, and sought to share her joy without looking down too often at the deck; he found himself too ready to notice how distant it seemed, and how narrow, and how unsteady, heaving wildly back and forth beneath him on a surface of churning green and white ... But if he studiously ignored that, the view was worth it, and so was the sense of space after many days cramped and confined aboard ship. He felt a sudden pang of sorrow for Kara; she had come of her own will, she would say nothing, yet if her life on land was confining, how much worse must this be?

"Would you like your cloak back?" he asked impulsively, forgetting his other concerns for now. "Without ... obligations. So you can ..." He shrugged. "Take the air whenever you wish. As you wish."

She leaned on the rail, her crisp dark hair ruffled by the wind and tinged with a corona in the clear light, and looked at him speculatively a while. Then she smiled, shook her head again, and put her hand affectionately on his arm. "No need. This is enough for me, to feel the rushing airs and see afar, far. I'll wait till you need me."

Elof shrugged again, and took her arm. But within himself he felt slightly resentful; she was still paying him back, it seemed. He glanced at her, watching those fierce bird-like eyes, green as the water beneath, flicker this way and that across the vast horizon, and was suddenly glad she had not accepted. What could he have been thinking of? Dislike it though he might, his chosen way would be the safest, after all.

It was not long after that that they passed beyond the southern borders of the realm of Morvanhal, and into the Wild, beyond the habitations of men. Yet still it was a rich and wholesome country along the shores, well watered by many rivers, and they were able to land for water and provisions at many anchorages they had charted and explored upon previous voyages. The worst perils here were wild beasts, and an occasional nest of human outlaws many times more savage, ready to sally out and assail any small vessel in difficulties or separated from the body of the fleet. Kermorvan had taken strong measures to guard against this, however, and such attacks were swiftly dealt with. On one occasion such a straggler was attacked by two pirate longboats in fog; Kermorvan brought the *Korentyn* alongside with sweeps and himself led the clearing of its decks. Out of some thirty raiders no more than three escaped him, and that by leaping overboard, swimming for a boat and rowing frantically off into the shadows. "Were it clear, I would have pursued them in the cutters," he remarked, wiping clean his grey-gold sword. "As it is, let them save their hides, if only for the sake of times past ..."

At last, after some three weeks of generally easy sailing, they came to the last of these anchorages and the greatest, a wide river estuary that was of old named Ancarvadoen, the Deep Roads. Beyond it the coasts became rougher, stonier, dangerous in the approach; no voyage had passed without the loss of one vessel at least along this stretch, and many lives. Nor were the lands they guarded any safer; somewhere at their heart stretched the long arm of the Great Forest, turning to tangled jungle with its manyfold traps and terrors.

Ancarvadoen was remembered in this uninhabited country chiefly because it was known that the last great band of fugitives from doomed Morvan, led by Vayde and the princess Ase, had encamped here through one long winter. On the last voyage men of the fleet had stumbled upon the traces of that brief settlement, a few overgrown hummocks of drystone walls and upon the hill overlooking the estuary, three or four graves, well marked but nameless. It was a melancholy place, but Kermorvan wished to land there once more; he had brought with him memorial stones fairly carven for the graves and the ruins. "And may they lay the unquiet spirits of this land!" he remarked quietly to Elof, as the two of them clambered back down the steep grassy slopes to their shore camp. "For I feel they walk here still, or some memory of their sorrows. Let them learn from this that their suffering was not wholly without result, that the line and heritage of their land lives still, and does not forget them."

Elof nodded. "I sense something of what you say, strongly. It is wholesome enough, this land, but over-hung with feeling; anguish, sadness, loss. And beneath it anger, rage at the injustice of fate. I have felt it somewhere before; in the hollow bones of Morvan the City, perhaps. And not only there ... I do not think those stones will assuage it, worthy notion though they were. It does not bode well."

"I agree. And in any event, we are on the edge of difficult and dangerous country, and a treacherous coast." He looked at Kara, tripping lightly through the tangled grass where others slipped and stumbled. "I think it is time we called upon your unique gifts, my lady. If you are willing, you could scout out our way on the morrow for many leagues ahead ..."

She looked demurely at her feet. "If Elof is willing, my lord, then of course."

"He does not normally raise any objection," said

Kermorvan quizzically, glancing at Elof. "No? Then whenever it pleases you, my lady..."

"I'll fetch your cloak from the ship, then, Kara," said Elof, a little self-consciously. "You can be getting something to eat, meanwhile..." He hurried off, feeling the king's gaze like a cool gust at his back.

When his boat came back to the beach he could see her waiting there for him, a slender silhouette against the glow of the campfires, half hidden against the shadows of the bushes around them. "I have it," he said quietly, stepping up to her, holding out the precious garment. She received it in her outstretched hands, held it, did not put it on.

"Kara..." he began. "Heart ... why the reluctance? Why do you hesitate, why have you twice refused this already? Is it because ... were you only delaying the moment? Do you yourself think you'll fly away, never come back?"

"*No!*" she hissed, and then, more softly, "No, heart, I will come back. Never fear but I will come back..."

He nodded, took the cloak from her hands and himself draped it around her shoulders. Then he reached into his pocket. "I believe that is what you truly want. But I have brought you a small token, keepsakes; wear them for me, and you will not forget."

Swiftly he stooped to her ankle, one open band of silver in each powerful hand; he felt the first slide over her cool skin – Then his wrists were seized. Elof was stronger than most men, but he could not move a finger's breadth against the strong slim fingers that gripped him thus, that drew his hands up and into the light. He saw the glint of the silver mirrored in the chill green pools that were Kara's eyes, and, to his horror, the shimmering that ran within the silver also, as bright as ever he saw it himself. "Fool!" said a voice of steel he hardly recognised. "Oh, you unutterable fool! Did you think a Power had sunk so low in loving a man, that it should be blind to the forces within his works? Did you dream I donned your arm-ring that day in ignorance of what it would do? That I would not see through this silver of yours as into clear water, and read there what you have set in play? Did you think so little of my life, my existence, to trifle with it thus?" He saw the streaks of silver that coursed her cheeks, and his heart withered within him.

"I sought … I sought only to reinforce our own truest wish … steady you by your own will …"

The steel broke, and burst into flame. "Aye, by ensnaring that will! By goading it along the paths you choose!"

"I sought only to embody what I knew you wanted! I set no compulsion of mine in the work!"

"No more than you would compel the winds! And yet you did! And shackled them with fearful force! Can you not see that you cannot harness any desire of mine? Only as your own eyes see it can *you* give it form!"

"But …" Elof swallowed. "If it is so close to yours … If it is what you want … then how can it harm you? If you truly love me, how should it mar that?"

"How?" She laughed, but not as humans laugh. "By taking away what is most truly mine! How would it harm you to be whipped to breathe, beaten to eat, goaded to love? How would it harm you if Kermorvan drew smithcraft from you by prison and torment, not friendship and honour? Then my cunning child, my deceitful heart, then you would understand!" She lifted his wrists, shook then fiercely before her face, and the rage of the Morghannen shone there behind the tears. "And how would it mar love? By forcing it to tread one single path … one circling, spiralling, endless path! Never free to change, to grow, to find new ways and new reasons to love. Love of all things, that must change from moment to moment to live! That you would keep for yourself, aye, but never trust me with it! Must I be the same to you in age, when you will not be the same? Be to you then just what I am now, no more, no less? How fine a lover will you find me then, fool, how fitting company for your cooling blood? Yet to that you would bind me, shackle me in my own imprisoned spirit, encircle me about in the mazes of my own mind! You would deceive me, drive me by my very feelings, just as your damned mindsword drove men by their deepest fears –"

A sudden shock drove deep into Elof's breast, as cold and breath-devouring as that blade's bite. He clutched at the scar, remembering. That older song, that tune that had arisen unbidden from his memory, as it seemed – he knew it now, knew the first words he had ridden upon its rising fervor ...

As sundered I found you,
In flickering flame,
As once then I bound you
I bind you again ...

Over the mindsword, embodiment of command, compulsion, driving by terror – over the last completion of that unhallowed weapon, upon the fixing of its cutting edge, he had sung that song. And he had sung it again over the instrument of his love ..

A new flood of fury filled her, overflowed in tears. "And the risk! How could you? What if those anklets had closed, other than on me? What then? And if they were ever opened again ... You who broke Louhi's fetters on me, how I loved you for that! And then you, *you* sought to fetter me within myself!"

Now Elof wept also, as he had not even in childhood, tears of shame and rage and scalding self-disgust. His own vast folly billowed up before him like a banner of blackness, and blindly he reached out to her through its enveloping folds. "Kara ... I see now ... I ..." If he could reach her, hold her, tell her how much he had been at fault, then she might still forgive him.

His hand clutched at her arm, closed around metal over warm skin. "*Don't touch me!*" she screamed, and with that astonishing strength she jerked away her arm. The metal caught in his desperate fingers, he felt it bend and break. Then the darkness seemed blasted from his eyes, and he was staring at her and she at him, wide-eyed with shock, unsteady on her feet. She was holding her arm as if injured. On the dark grass between them a shard of gold gleamed, a curved, distorted shape; and from between her fingers a broken end gleamed. The serpentine arm-ring of gold, Elof's first great work, his first gift to her and sign of hope between them, had broken in two.

She stumbled back a pace, and even as he reached out to her once again she threw back her head and screamed aloud, a terrible shriek of grief and despair that echoed out around hill and water like the feelings that haunted them given fearful voice. All in that camp or aboard the ships, awake or sleeping, it brought instantly to their feet, hearts pounding, ridden by fear beyond thought and reason. Before those who had seen them the empty wastes of Taoune'la opened out once more, the Withered Lands; so the winds might cry there, with the voice of the imprisoned dead. So they might have stirred the cloak about her, so billowed it forth to reveal its inner blackness. Shadow enveloped her, she sprang and vanished. Wings of shadow beat upward into the night.

With a cry of horror Elof snatched the Tarnhelm from his belt and clapped it on his head. The cry changed in mid-breath to the scream of an eagle, and into the heights he soared in her pursuit. There was starlight enough over the ocean for his keen eyes to pick out the black swan flying seaward, high and straight, never wheeling, never turning. After her he sped, feeling his wings bite into the wind, his keen head crest it like a speeding swimmer. Yet she flew fast, that strange creature, and even in seconds she had a lead of him he would find hard to break. And time was on her side ...

Far into the night they flew, till the land was no more than a streak of shadow far behind. Elof had looked back once, and dare do so no more, for the distance it had cost him; he was no nearer now than at the first. And already he could feel himself tiring, his masked form yearning for the lineaments of a man once more. Never once did he see her neck turn; did she even know she was being followed? So fast, so straight she flew, it made little difference. He had no voice to call her, and the call of his heart was emptiness. He had betrayed her, and brought about what he had most dreaded. What more could he do for her now but fly in her path till he reached its limits, or those of his failing strength? One way or another, he would find an end.

How far he flew he never remembered, or for how long; but at some point some shred of sanity must have asserted itself. For his friends of the fleet found him at last, in the small hours of the morning, sprawled face down and soaking upon the tidal sands of Ancarvadoen. They feared him dead at first, but he breathed; and in one hand the Tarnhelm was clutched, with a grip they could not break.

CHAPTER THREE

Into the Night

KERMORVAN HEARD ELOF'S TALE out in silence. As king he had the right, if he cared to use it, to judge any aspect of his follower's lives; as commander of the fleet he had an equal right. Elof expected harsh words of condemnation when he had done. But Kermorvan only looked at him with troubled grey eyes and asked "What will you do now?"

"What I sought to do first; follow her, find her. Make what amends I can. Aid her, if she is in need."

Kermorvan rose with a sigh, went to the railing and looked out across the sea. Ils shifted uneasily in her chair, her wide face lined with unhappiness; then she rose, put a beaker of wine in Elof's hand and her arm about his shoulder. Her cheek rested on his head a moment. "Yes, you were a fool!" she muttered. "But who is not, when torn apart by love and worry?" She turned abruptly away. Roc, the only other hearer, was looking out to sea also, avoiding his gaze.

Elof gulped the wine, grateful on a throat made raw by salt water and long speaking. He had slept the day out in his exhaustion, and now the sun was setting behind the hills in furious flares of red and gold. Kermorvan turned, and watched its glorious decline. "The world is wide," he said darkly. "Which way think you to start your search?"

"The way she told me to, when first we parted," said Elof. "It was the way she flew last night." He gazed out across the open oceans into the darkening East. "Thither. The path of the dawn."

Roc turned his head; Ils drew breath sharply, Kermorvan nodded, as if he had expected that reply. "Across the trackless ocean, that none has crossed these last thousand years. Once the ancient realm of Kerys lay

on its farther shore, home of our fathers; who knows
what lies there now?"

Elof waited to be told he was mad. But Kermorvan
only remarked "You will need ships. You may choose
them from the fleet, and pick their crews."

Elof stared, and spluttered with surprise. "My lord
… I, I … it would be … I have no right …"

"You have bought them many times over with your
labour for me, even were there no stronger claims of
friendship; without yours I would have no throne. Now
it is my turn to help you. I shall come with you."

Elof stared up at the tall man, scarcely able to
believe what he heard, and much humbled. To have this
man's aid in his search … The years and experience of
rule had deepened Kermorvan's wisdom, without
making him any the less fearsome a warrior. It was his
firm hand, in peace and war, that had built up this
whole kingdom from the ruins of two lands, raised it to
peace and prosperity in less than a decade. It was his
iron hand that held back the incoming raiders in the
Westlands, that struck even up into the ruins of Nordeney to free those imprisoned and enslaved. Against his
command, year after year, the Ekwesh battered as at an
immovable wall, till it seemed that many grew weary of
war for war's sake, and preferred to settle in what land
they already had in peace. In that, as in many other
ways, he thwarted the will of the Ice, that fed and prospered
upon the strife of men, and had made the Ekwesh its
chiefest instrument. With a man at his side who could
thus uphold a land there were few roads he would not
willingly tread. And that man was willing to leave all
that he had built up, for no profit of his own …

But behind all these thoughts Elof had felt a growing unease; he glanced now at Roc and Ils, and the
alarm he saw on their faces brought it to a head. He
rose, a little unsteadily still, and shook his head. "My
friend, I am more grateful than I can say. But I cannot
allow it. You are the cornerstone of this land, of the
lives of all men in it; how am I to draw that out on my
own poor quest, and leave the rest without support?
You have no deputy of stature, no heirs, no successors;

your place is here, and your duty. And I have selfish folly enough to live with."

Kermorvan nodded. "So be it. It is an honourable answer, and I confess the one I hoped for; yet for my honour, and my debt to you, the offer had to be made. You speak the truth, though I wish to the depths of my heart it were not so. I burn to help you, for your sake and Kara's; and I yearn still for the free adventure I once knew, and to see more of the world." He sighed again, and his voice took fire a moment, ere it sank to embers. "To cross the Seas of the Sunrise, to gaze upon the fabled lands beyond, I could envy you that in a happier cause! But I am bound to stay, to go on with my labours and my worries, and I add to them the fate of a friend adrift in the unknown without my aid."

"Well," said Ils lightly, "not quite; he'll at least have mine ..."

"Which just leaves me," rumbled Roc, irascible and offhand as ever; and yet his words were hollowed out by deep disquiet. "Can't be sitting around here getting bored while you two go gallivanting –"

But Elof could not let them finish. "The same for you as for the King, my lady! If not more! For his folk follow him all, and willingly. You still must win the trust of yours, for the east and for men; and if you cannot, who can? No, princess of the Elder Folk; you also are bound. And you," rounding on Roc, "what of your bonds? I'll not ruin your life for the faint chance of mending mine! Marja bade you farewell for a summer only; what of her, if you do not return?"

Roc shrugged, seeming very uneasy, and turned away once more. "I can't say!" he said between his teeth. "But I should still come, damn you!"

Elof shook his head. "No more, any of you. We have seen too much together to say more, I think. I should wind no other in the webs of my own folly, no friends, no crews; I should not weaken the fleet. I'll make my own way back to Morvanhal, find a boat there –"

Kermorvan dismissed the idea with a curt wave. "None fit to cross the wide oceans in! All such we have with us; if there were others, I would have brought them. Take one, at least; do not burden me with so great a debt!" There was genuine pleading in his cold eyes, though he added crisply "And do not martyr yourself in foolish penitence! If you have a purpose, carry it through with sense; if you would help her, do it properly!"

Elof drew a deep breath. "I will take a boat. But only one I can handle by myself –"

"One of the cutters, then; though they are barely large enough for your need, and hard for one to handle. But we have nothing better. Unless … here!" He rose, and striding to the stern-post he unlatched the heavy wind-vane and tossed it to Elof. "I return you this, with thanks; we have fared well enough in the past without it, and it may make all the difference to you. When do you wish to leave?"

Elof looked at the dimming sky. "At once, I fear. As soon as there is a wind; the land breeze after dark, perhaps. But first I must go back and find those damnable anklets; I let them fall in my panic. They could still be perilous; I will destroy them, as soon as I have the chance. But it must be done with care, to release what is within; unless –" He paused a moment, reflecting, "Unless they might be of some help. But first I must secure them. By your leave –"

"Go, then," said Kermorvan sadly. "I will give the orders for the best cutter to be provisioned and made ready; it should not take long."

It was now early dusk, the sky grey-clouded save where the sun glowed still through great streaks and slashes, like rich garb showing through a beggar's cloak. That made Elof's search all the harder; the campfires were not yet lit, and he had not thought to take a lantern ashore. Over root and through thicket he stumbled, cursing the dimness, unsure even quite where they had stood those few hours since, she and he. But the last thin gleam of the sun awoke an answer among a tuft of long grass well down the beach, and there he found first one anklet, then the other, already half buried in the dry sand. He must have hurled them from him in those blind moments; he could not remember. He loathed the sight of them now, scooped them up as if they were poisonous snakes, but forced himself to blow the sand from them and stow them carefully away. He straightened up, dusting his hands, and glanced out across the waters; the lanterns were being lit aboard the *Prince Korentyn*, and the other ships were following suit. By their light he made out a lesser, light-hulled shape in the lee of the flagship's bulk, with many figures busy about its deck. That was in hand, then. No more now remained to be done, save to bid farewell to his friends, his home, all he had worked for these last nine years and before; all he had grown to love. But the shaping was his own; he had no right to complain. He turned ... stumbled back in sheer alarm, lost his footing and sprawled amid the dewy grass, so close behind him the figure stood.

Tall it seemed and more than tall, a column of darkness against the dark; the immense figure of a man, all muffled up in a black cloak. Only at the edges of him did the shiplights find a gleam; upon the curve of the great shield at his back, the shadowy visor of the helm beneath his hood, the long black spear balanced in his black-gauntleted hand. Beneath the visor a pale-skinned face caught the light, a great eagle nose and bushy grey-black beard around lips hard and unsmiling. His breath smoked in the evening chill.

"Oh no ..." breathed Elof, raising himself on one elbow. "Oh no, no ..."

The hood moved; the tall man was looking him up and down. "Where to, at such an hour? And in such haste?"

Elof swallowed; he knew the voice, deep and stern. "To seek out a thing I have lost," he said, scrambling up. "How should it concern you?"

The man appeared to be considering. "If you have lost it," he remarked, "how do you know which way to search?"

"By my own eyes!" barked Elof impatiently, and then, plaintively, "Why would you hinder me? What harm can ..." He stopped; the figure had held up its empty hand.

"Suppose another now has it? What then? How will you take it back?"

Sudden anger swelled in Elof, and putting hand to belt he swept the sword Gorthawer snarling from the scabbard, and it gleamed as black as any of the other's armour. "With this, if need there be!"

The hood bent down over the levelled blade. "A mighty weapon; yet there are mightier, and the finest sword is no stronger than the arm behind it. Who made it, I wonder?"

Elof reined in his patience as best he could; great aid and great danger hovered over him here, and he could not guess which. "How would I know? It came to me from the hand of one long dead –"

The hood turned slowly from side to side. "You do not speak the truth. No hand save yours has ever held this blade."

Elof's control snapped. "Do you name me liar? Or mock me with riddles? One truth I'll tell you! That if you think to delay me here bandying idle words, then Power though you may be, you're sorely mistaken! If you can aid me, do so without tormenting me! And if not, leave me to go my own way for once!"

The hood rose to its full height. "That you have done, and to what end? If you address a Power, should you not show some respect, instead of tempting its wrath?"

"Respect?" blazed Elof, with a bitter laugh. "Now truly you mock! What have I seen of the Powers, what have they been to me save trial and torture?"

"Help," said the deep voice quietly. "And love."

Elof felt the veins throb at his temples. "Help, from you? Did I not hear you yourself say it, that it was only to balance another Power's meddling? Better far to have had neither! And love? That was the worst torture of all! And though mine was the fault, yet I was sorely driven to it! Leave me to work out my own destiny! Why have you come to plague me now? If you'll not aid me, then let me pass!"

The hood was thrown back; the helm shone clear against the clouds, its eyes dark shadows, unfathomed. "I came to tell you this. What you did, is done; leave it, lest worst befall! More rests on it than you can ever know!"

Elof shook like a wind-blown aspen. "Leave it; leave Kara? Never see her more?"

"Leave her; wait and be content! A great change is coming, upon a vast brink the whole world trembles; even to the Powers its end is not revealed. Be not too eager to leap into the balance, till you know which way it must tilt!"

"I know this; that Kara may need me! That I must find

her, free her if need be, were I never to see her more! And
that I will seek her thither, in the sunrise, whatever you
place in my path!"

The voice grew cold, harsh, daunting in its power.
"The way you would seek her, you must not go!" The huge
spear swung in his hand, barring Elof's path to the shore.

In a single movement Elof drew his armoured gauntlet
from his belt and thrust his left hand within. "And who are
you, to forbid me? I have broken the will of Powers ere now
.. beware lest I sweep you also from my path!" He raised his
hands; in his left palm the crystal glittered, ready to drink in
whatever was hurled at him, and in his right Gorthawer,
poised to strike in its turn. "Wield your spear! But weigh
well the craft in my hands!" He took a swift pace forward
and brought Gorthawer against the dark haft of the spear,
between the massive hands that held it. The tall figure did
not move. With gritted teeth, feeling a sudden sweat break
out on his brow, Elof drew the black blade's edge lightly
across the shining surface of the haft, and saw a faint score
appear there, finer than a hair. Then he sprang back, almost
dropping the blade. The figure had not moved; but across
the sky behind it there leaped great fronds of searing white,
that seemed to join and meet behind the crest of the helm
like a crown of blasting force. In its light the right eyehole of
the visor shone ghastly white; the socket beneath was
eyeless, empty, blind as bone. A moment later the sound
reached him, a sombre crackle and crash as if high above
the cloudroof a vast door slammed closed. A cold breeze
blew in his face, and great raindrops began to fall, like
tears.

The tall man stepped forward, lifted a hand, and Elof
scuttled back, weapons at the ready. But there was no move
to attack; he was simply pulling up his hood. Again he
looked at Elof, and when he spoke the voice was heavy with
many things; weariness, contempt, sorrow, and perhaps
also pity. "Go on, then. I cannot prevent you." He strode past
Elof into the shadow of the bushes and was gone.

Elof stood gazing after him, his jaw sagging, his head in
a fearful whirl. The flare of his anger had passed, and a great
uncertainty was upon him. What had he done? What should
he have done? What could he ... Not abandon Kara, of that

alone he was sure; his lips pressed tight at the thought. And yet till now the Raven had always aided him, however harrowing that aid might be ... And he too had spoken of a great change impending. The Powers seemed to sense it, yet they could not foresee what it might be. He thought then of the tremors of the earth that at times shook Kerbryhaine, and of how it was said that animals both wild and tame sensed them hours before they came, heard perhaps the stirring of the earthfires upon which the hard rock floated; then, it was said, they grew uneasy, chafed at restraints, and fled. But a thing of this magnitude, whence could any flee? Save beyond the circles of the world, perhaps; which for men meant only the River. "I have no choice," he said aloud to the surrounding darkness, and liked little the tone of helpless complaint in his voice. "I must go! I must follow!" Slowly he turned and walked towards the shore. At his back the fires sprang to life, but from their warmth and light he turned away.

When he clambered back up to the flagship's deck he found his friends awaiting him. "A storm brews," began Kermorvan. "Would you not be better to put off – "

Elof shook his head. "It only comes on a land wind," he answered. "And it cannot be bad; I heard only the one thunderclap. It will serve to speed me on my way." Of its true cause he said nothing, and strove to conceal that he knew; Kermorvan revered the Powers, and Raven most of all. Such a warning he might heed, and feel it a king's duty to enforce it. "Is my boat made ready?"

"It is," said Kermorvan, and sorrow weighted his words. "The cutter *Mordan* awaits you overside, that is *Seafire* in the Northern tongue. Your gear is aboard, and supplies in plenty; though how long your voyage must be, we cannot tell. We have no charts that can help you, and no records; none have sailed east these last thousand years or more. The last to sail westward was your great forebear Vayde, and he left no account. Sun and stars must keep you on your course ... and may they be favourable to you!" His face was as Elof had seen it in their worst adversity, set like flint. "We would stay you longer if we could; but our debt to you will not allow that. You leave our land bereft of your skill and power; you leave me bereft of my chiefest friend. Do you return one day if you can, whatever your case or condition; then we shall rejoice indeed! May your quest's ending be a happy one!"

"Speeches!" spat out Ils, and seizing Elof she embraced him so hard he feared his ribs would crack, and buried her face a moment in his shoulder. "Now get on with you!"

Elof did his best to nod and smile, but he could say nothing; the crew were flocking around him, extending hands to him, slapping him on the back, calling out their good wishes. It was goodwill he felt he did not deserve, and it came near to breaking his heart. By the ladder Roc awaited him, with no more than a nod and a slap on the shoulder; Elof was grateful for that. "Down you go, and when you give the word I'll cast you off at the bows," he said.

Elof nodded, and hurried down the rope ladder. His feet thumped onto the cutter's polished deck; it was less resonant than usual, and closer to the water, so great was the weight of supplies below. He hurried to hoist the headsail; it would pull his bows free of the flagship. He kept his head lowered, so those on deck would not see how close he was to weeping. The headsail caught the breeze and billowed out; he ran astern to set it with the winches, and slip the stern mooring, "All right, Roc!" he cried then. "Cast off forward!" The headsail filled, the cutter began to move, and to a chorus of farewells he leaned on the tiller and turned her nose out from under the curve of the *Korentyn*'s timbered flank. Around her bows he swung, heading out into the wide estuary of Ancarvadoen; but as the cutter's bows crossed the pool of light from the flagship's lanterns he had to turn and look back. Ils stood by the rail, gripping it in her plump fingers, and he cursed himself that he had said no word to her; he raised a hand to touch his heart, and she nodded quickly, and turned away. But high upon the carven bows Kermorvan stood, tall and pale and grim as winter, his arm raised in solemn salute. Elof rose quickly, and lifted his hand in return. It is said that they seemed for a moment like the statues that stood upon Morvanhal's sea wall, of an earlier Keryn and the grim old lord Vayde who was his friend; for in that time many years seemed to fall upon Elof, and score his face deeply. But all too soon the vision passed; out into the night the small craft glided, became a ghostly glimmer upon blackness, and faded then altogether from *Korentyn*'s sight.

Though they could not see him, Elof could still see them, the great ship in its glowing circle, and the fleet beyond; he stood a long while watching. He had made many farewells in his life, but surely none more bitter than this; his thoughts moved like the craft beneath him, upon blackness. Only the thrash and creak of the boom called him to himself; it was high time and past to hoist the mainsail. He turned the *Seafire* into the wind, set the tiller and clambered up to free the lashings; one was stiff, he tugged at it and swore. Then he started so violently he all but went over the rail: out of the darkness another hand had reached, and twitched the other strand of the knot free. "Thought you were supposed to be the sailor!" jibed Roc.

"What in the jaws of Hel ..." Elof shouted, and then he gathered his wits. "You sprang on board once you'd cast off, I suppose? Right, you can help me with the mainsail, but the moment it's done, keep your head down; we'll be going about. Back to the *Korentyn*."

"Think so, do you?" inquired Roc with an ominous calm as they struggled to free the heavy gaff from the boom and begin unfurling the sail. "And why might that be, may I ask?"

"Why?" snorted Elof. "Didn't I tell you to your face, once already? You can't just cast off all your obligations like that, public or personal; you're needed back home, man, needed ..."

"Oh aye? Am I?"

Elof, checking the hanks around the mast, paused and looked up. "Marja needs you. And you've a place in the state —".

"Oh aye? As what? Not a bloody smith, I'll tell you that. Hammering bits of iron, aye, without this messing about with virtues, chants, I'm fine at that. I did all right in Bryhaine; they'd lost the true craft there. But here? There's a smith's guild here, with flaming mastersmiths and all. And there's you. Whenever folk look at me, they see *you*, behind me like a shadow; only the shadow's the brighter. Just think! Here's one with no true craft; how'd he ever get to be a smith? And here's t'other, and *he*'s got craft enough for two. Hella, but it's been hard! And now my woman's a mastersmith; what's she need me for? Contrast? Can't even talk about her work with me; haven't a bloody clue what she's on about. And her work's her life. So we don't talk; haven't for a while now. And precious little else, either. Different in the Southlands; I was the rich one there, the one they looked up to; who looks up to me here?" He turned, spat into the wind and swore at the result.

"I'm sorry, Roc," said Elof quietly. "I had wondered … I should have realised … But I can't tear you away from our other friends. There's much good you could do in the King's service …"

"Why d'you think he's been making this much use of me? He knows; not much he doesn't notice, our long friend. So he's been sending me on all these weighty errands – "

"Well then …" Elof freed the main halyard, and passed him the end. "Wind it around the winch there, *carefully* … People will come to respect you for that, soon enough; King's trusted emissary, there's many a role of less honour to play. Now wind when I say … yes, that way …"

Roc chuckled. "Indeed, that's so. It's the role I play now."

Elof, who had been about to give the command, stopped and stared. "You mean … He knows you're here? He sent you?"

"By royal warrant, aye; read it if you like, got it in my hip pocket somewhere. Charged to return to him, intact if at all possible, the person of his right worthy and well-trusted Court Smith … well, you know the form. Said he wouldn't sleep easy with you milling round the whale-roads on your own. And, well, I jumped at the commission, didn't I?"

Elof shook his head feebly. "But his … You can't! This is folly, this voyage … for any other, I mean – "

"Aye, well, don't go smothering me with gratitude, will you?" A sudden gust buffeted the cutter, plucked at the unfurled edge of sails; the gaff swung violently, caught Elof in the chest and stretched him flat on the deck.

"Hel's black belly, man!" roared Roc, trying to restrain the threshing spar, "Will you lay off flapping your lip and sail this thing? D'you want us wrecked not ten minutes out at sea?"

"We're not at sea yet!" wheezed Elof. "Still in the estuary ... you hate the sea, Roc ..."

"I'll not like it the better for being dumped in it!"

"The winch, then! Not too fast ... that's right!" Smoothly the heavy gaff rose to its proper inclination and creaked its way up the mast, the stiff sail creaking and flapping like a vast dry wing in the quickening wind. Elof kept a careful hand on the mainsheet winch till the gaff hung tight at the top of the mast, then showed Roc how to fasten the halyard securely and turned to the tiller. "Now back here with me, out of the way of the boom! Take the mainsheet here, pay it out little by little as I tell you –"

Roc looked askance at him. "Fine old time you'll have, doing all this on your own –"

Elof, too preoccupied to understand, set hand to the tiller and swung the *Seafire* about. In a thunder of sailcloth the boom scythed across the deck, thudded up short as the mainsheet restrained it. At Elof's word Roc unwound the winch, the mainsail caught the wind and grew full with it; the *Seafire*, spurred like a spirited horse, sprang forward over the whitecapped windrows. The headsail sang and strained at the sheets, dangerously tight; Elof thrust the tiller at Roc and sprang for the winch. Swiftly he slackened the headsail, let out the mainsheet a little, then very carefully he eased the tension on the winches with the heel of his hand. He saw there was little or no flutter at the luff edges of the sails, against mast and forestay, and glanced at the trailing hempen strands sewn in rows across the sailcloth; the rows fluttered at a slight angle to each other. Sails not quite set, then; but if he ...

Then another consideration slashed across the rest. "Well?" came Roc's sardonic inquiry. "If you're wanting rid of me hadn't we best be turning tail now? Or won't you have a long tack back?"

Elof bit his lip. "You're right."

"What do I do? Swing the tiller ... "

"*No!* I didn't mean that, anyway; I meant what you said earlier. I can sail the cutter on my own – just. And in easy conditions; how I'd fare in a storm ..."

"Um," said Roc dubiously. "In a storm you might *be* on your own ..."

"You'll get used to it, soon enough –"

"Whatever you say ..." sighed Roc; but he did not sound convinced.

Unhappy as he was, Elof summoned up a grin. "You could still change your mind ... No?" He chuckled. "Roc, I'm glad, I've got to admit it. But it's a mad venture, all the same. Scarce a hope of returning, let alone succeeding –"

Roc snorted. "Think I need you to tell me that? But then, when the whole world's daft, maybe it's as well to be dafter yet ..."

Elof nodded wryly, and from that time he argued no more, but took in the mainsail a little further and pulled the tiller gently towards him. The cutter heeled slightly as it bore away, and the slap of the wavelets beneath the hull quickened like a pulse. Before the land wind and the oncoming storm that rode it the *Seafire* ran upon a broad reach, away through the dark roads of Ancarvadoen and out, out until the horns of the bay dwindled to strips of shadow upon either flank, and their bows reared and plunged upon the higher swell of the open ocean beyond, unsheltered and unforgiving. Thus it was, as the chronicles record, that the two friends set forth on a quest that was to prove darker, more perilous and more painful than any in their lives before, and of greater moment. For in the end it was to cast them, as the Raven had foretold, into the very balance of the changing world.

How long their voyage endured no account is certain; it may be that no exact record survived. Upon the open sea, with nothing above but clouds constant only in their inconstancy, it might indeed have been easy to lose track of the hours, the days that passed by, forever alone at the focus of a vast arena of empty water. Yet it is unlikely that they did so, for they were not aimless wanderers, but steering a course by sun and stars. Elof at least had studied the simple principles of navigation, as were then understood, with the Master-smith, that he might learn to make the necessary instruments. In later years, as friend to such a mariner as Kermorvan, he had learned more, and much sea-lore besides. Yet it is said only that for many weeks they sailed swiftly and well, and that the *Seafire* bore them safely through many a time of peril. In that first storm, that hunted them from the land there was hard going, for as it came upon them the rudder fought like a living thing, Roc and Elof struggling desperately to lash it down while the wind yelled in their ears, fresh rain drummed upon their heads, and heavy seas broke every minute over the stern. Long hours the weather lasted, and they were left sodden, exhausted, bruised and sore from the tossing-about they had received; their hair was rimed with salt, salt that stiffened their garments and flayed the skin from them as cruelly as the ropes that hissed and ran through their fingers. But the cutter was a finely made craft, and though it rode low in the water under its weight of supplies the sea washed harmlessly across its well-caulked decking and slopped out through the scuppers. It scudded on before the storm, bounding impudently across the wavecrests, and when at the end of the night the clouds broke and the risen sun beamed down on them once more, they saw mast and rig as firm as ever, and the bilges scarce wetter than before. No line had parted, nor any seam loosened. And Elof smiled at that, for in the shipyards he himself had laid such virtues of strength upon the metal fastenings. Even Roc, though he groaned and grumbled as loudly as the waves that ran still high beneath the hull, was impressed, and more confident that they might somehow come through the voyage alive.

Elof had always wondered at the daring of the hero Vayde in braving this same passage in what was, by all accounts, no larger a craft, a feat that many ascribed to necromancy; he found reason to doubt that, in the weeks that followed. The sudden squalls he had come to fear around the coasts he could ride out easily here, and worse weather also. For though the storms of the ocean were terrible, when the chill airs came blasting down off the Ice to whip the waves into white-capped peaks that loomed high above the *Seafire*'s masthead, and between them sudden sickening troughs that swallowed it up, yet at least there were no lee shores at hand to worry about, no rocks or shoals lurking, hungry to rake the belly from the boat like a dagger-tooth its prey. And down into trough and up over peak the little cutter rode, where sleek longship or massive dromund might have been caught across the crests and twisted apart, or plunged in bow or stern and been overturned in the troughs. It could climb the rising slopes of waves that would have burst like falling mountains upon the decks of larger craft, sweeping off rig and crew alike and tumbling toylike the mastless hulk that remained. Like a gull it floated upon the heaving hills of ocean, lurching madly this way and that; often no sail could be carried, the rudder had to be lashed and a sea-anchor thrown out to keep the drifting bows into the wind. Yet though sorely soaked and battered it came through whole, its crew with it, and Elof came to conclude that in refusing Kermorvan's ships he had all unconsciously made the wiser choice.

Those weeks at sea were by no means all storms; it was spring, and though that brought gales and rain in plenty, they carried warm weather in their wake. There were cool, crisp nights, when the stars shone among ragged clouds like gems beneath grey velvet, and their wake came alight with the phosphorescence the ship was named for, a shimmering stream of cool fire like the reflection of some invisible moon. There were fair days, when the foamcrests were dazzling in the clear light, when the expanse of seas shone like a vast disc of sapphire under a cloudless sky.

At times the sunbeams slanted down into the deeps, picking out shoals of fish, ranging from tiny things glittering like glass shards that swept this way and that in clouds of light, to bulky, barb-finned things as long as a man, their flattened flanks gleaming irides-cent as they glided effortlessly past the speeding ship.

Mostly the men marvelled, but from time to time Roc would lower a line among the speeding mass, and the formation would dissolve into a threshing tangle of jaws as ready to snap at hooks unbaited as baited; it often took the two of them a long struggle to hoist up the catch, and many of the huge fish flipped themselves free against the ship's flanks. Often a school of porpoises would come to leap and sport like merry children around the bow, mocking its man-made sleekness with their speed and grace; for Elof and for Roc they could never come often enough nor stay too long, but they soon grew bored with the unresponsive ship and sped off. More than once their greater cousins came to alarm; immense whales rising singly or in vast schools that appeared in a line of white water mist-crowned along the horizon, like breakers upon some vast and impass-able shoals. Remembering the Hounds of Niarad, Elof steered well clear of them, feeling like a mouse among the tall cattle he had once herded, and for the most part they left the *Seafire* equally alone.

Not all such encounters were as harmless. Very early on they grew used to sharks circling the cutter, and after an alarming experience of Roc's they were careful never to trail hands in the water; the beasts came in all sizes, but even a small one was well able to remove a finger. Some were vast and solitary monsters far longer than the cutter, but apparently harmless, idling by the *Seafire* with enormous mouths hanging witlessly agape. "Though I have heard of others as large that live in deep waters and hunt like their lesser cousins," Elof remarked. "The headman in Asenby kept a tooth of one ..."

"And?" prompted Roc nervously.

"Bigger than my two hands," Elof said tersely. "You could drive a cart through such jaws as held it."

"Do you try it if you like! How'd you tell'em from these peaceable brutes?"

Elof shrugged. "Go for a swim around one ..." Roc shuddered. Needless to say he never took Elof up on his suggestion; and Elof himself came to regret making it. For it brought home to him very uncomfortably, when he had already had time to grow used to the sea and considered himself a hardened hand, just how vast a deep there lay beneath these fragile boards, where light and warmth gave swift way to blackness unending and chill; what secrets might not such depths contain?

Yet it was not from any depths that their next hazard was to come. In all their voyage till that day they had seen no other craft, and that was no surprise to Elof. So when one clear morning in the sixth week of their voyage he heard Roc's hail, he came running up from the little cabin at once. "A sail? It can't be! Where?"

Roc simply shrugged and pointed northward into the wind. Then Elof saw it at once, a high triangle of whiteness just rising above the horizon that might indeed have been some great sails gleaming fair and clean in the sunlight, spread wide to run before the stiff breeze. But when they had watched it in silence for some minutes, Elof shook his head doubtfully; he strode forward to the mast, scrambled up it as far as he dared with the ship thus heeling on a beam reach, and, shading his eyes, strained to make out what lay below the horizon. Roc, seeing him start, called up "What manner of hull has it, then?"

"No hull!" was Elof's curt reply, and he came sliding down to the deck and ran to the helm. "No hull, because it isn't a ship, and that whiteness is no sail; it rises sheer from the water."

"Hel's blue teeth! What is it, then, man?"

"Something I should have known sooner; I saw enough of them in my childhood home, come the fall. When the ice-islands came drifting southward, then it was time to beach all the larger fisher-craft of the village, and only the little skin-boats would go out, buoyed with blown-up skins."

"Ice-islands ..." echoed Roc uneasily.

"Aye. Great drifting chunks of it, fallen from the greater mass to the north, no doubt; some are very hills and towers afloat. I thought them evil things even before I learned what lay behind the Ice. But they were harbingers of winter, then, and melted away with the spring; I would never have looked to see one this far south, and in this season."

"Might be a stray," suggested Roc, "a leftover from this winter past, slow to melt ..."

Elof nodded "It might; though if that is melting, what size was it at first? And where one strays, so might a flock; we would do well to watch for more. At least we will be able to outrun them, if the wind holds from the north."

And hold it did; for so long, so steadily and so chill, that Elof came to conclude it must be blowing straight down across the Ice from its northernmost heart in the frozen oceans at the summit of the world, where no man might pass. That, too, seemed strange in late spring; what little weatherlore there was of the open ocean predicted cool easterlies off the Ice at this season, and some milder westerlies further south. But the cold blast southward reigned, and though it might falter at times it seldom gave way to any other wind for long, a day at most; they began to think of it as the only thing constant upon the changing ocean. And on its back, as they were soon to find, it bore many ice-islands more. On that first day they only appeared to northward, but on the following afternoon a great jagged band of white lifted against the leaden sky almost in their path. It was no danger to them, being easy enough to avoid in the wide ocean, though to do so meant a series of long and annoying tacks. They glared at it as it glided by them, its flanks glistening against the dull clouds, scoured into strange bluish ridges by sea and sun, slick now with meltwater like the slime of some unclean beast.

In the few days of peace that followed Elof steered to the southeast as far as he dared, to avoid more ice. The sailing was all too easy, bearing away effortlessly before that southward wind when it blew, or running comfortably on the weaker westerlies; in these latitudes the air was milder, and while there was some heavy weather even the water that came roaring over the bows seemed warmer, or at least less chill. Roc revelled in the change, but Elof distrusted it, fearful of straying into the sudden calms for which southern waters were notorious. He kept careful watch on their position and progress; and thus it was that they were not taken by surprise. For it was as he attempted to trace the sun one overcast noontide, by a subtle instrument with thin sheets of spar crystal, that he noticed the dark speck cresting the southward horizon; against that sullen sky, shaded in charcoal and lead, they might otherwise have quite missed their peril till it was too late. But now it was his turn to hail, and Roc's to come running in disbelief. When he saw, though, he whistled, long and low. "Well! A sail it surely is this time, and a big 'un! Now what ..." He stopped then, and swallowed audibly.

Elof nodded; his own mouth had gone suddenly dry. "It's black, yes."

"But ... Not *here*!" burst out Roc, in violent disbelief. "They've no way onto this ocean!"

"I know!" muttered Elof. Memories arose at the sight, old and bloody. "And yet ..." He stared suddenly. The black speck was distorting, shivering, settling into a new shape. "They're going onto a new tack! And I'll give you one guess why ..."

Roc nodded grimly. "They've spotted us! Want to hang around and see who they are?"

"No, indeed!" grated Elof. "Ready on the winches! If I bring her closer to the wind we should be able to keep our distance long enough to lose them ... whoever they may be!" He unlatched the tiller and bore down on it; the nose swung around from southeast to due east once more and the *Seafire* heeled as Roc wound in the headsail, riding the strong northerly like a spirited steed. It was the first time he had been wholly thankful for that wind, as they began to pick up speed and skip and slice along the wavecrests, and he saw the black sail seem to slip away beneath the horizon once again; he smiled with cold satisfaction. But then Roc seized him by the sleeve and pointed, and what he saw dashed that smile from his lips. Over the brink of the waters ahead two more dark peaks arose and grew with startling speed, their squaresails angled to sail close to the wind; they were hurtling down on him as fast as he toward them. Another minute, while he hesitated, looked wildly about, and their bows lifted into view, high-arched, knife-edged and cruel, black as the sails save for the white beast-patterns they bore.

"Ekwesh they are!" cried Roc. "Turn back! Go about! Or within the hour they'll have us –"

Elof felt a sear of bitter cold in head and stomach. "They're too close! They'll have us anyway if we turn! There's only one way now – ready on those winches, I'll take her on as close a reach as I dare!"

"Close to the wind?" yelled Roc. "You mean northward again? Among the ice-islands?"

"Northward indeed!" barked Elof. "And right up to the Ice itself, if need be!"

"*Are you gone stark mad?*"

"Think, man! They're four times our size, and what rig have they, but one squaresail? On the open sea they can run us down – but among the narrow ice-roads? Now stand to that winch, and haul, man, *haul!*"

Roc shook his head, but he flung himself on the winches and wound with all his strength, while Elof leaned hard on the heavy tiller, and felt the *Seafire* begin to shift beneath him, take the waves from a different angle. Her bows dipped, and great wings of spray burst over the bows before he had her properly trimmed, flying shards of water that stung his face as if already hardened into ice. They were on a northeasterly heading now, sailing toward the wind on a close reach, good and fast. The chill of the northerly played across him like a hoary breath, and he clutched his jacket close about him. An inner chill was on him that no warmth could cure, save one; and from her now he felt as far as ever he had been.

Perhaps Roc sensed this, for he began to bustle about below, and soon reappeared bearing mugs of their precious ale, cakes of hard bread and deep bowls of stewed smokemeat. "There, get this down you while you can! Times like this you never know when your next meal's likely to be, and the longer the stove's quenched, the better, till our little friends are well out of the way!" He snorted. "Speaking of which, how in the iciest parts of Hel did they ever get into it? They were stuck the whole breadth of the land away!"

"Yet they took Morvannec that was," Elof reminded him.

"Aye, by marching a few thousand fanatics half to death across the Ice! You telling me they hauled a warship on their shoulders? Anyway, we cleaned out every last man-eater of that pack!"

"That we knew of! They had a year, they might have built one, and a few survivors fled in it ... But where have they been since?" Elof clawed a hand through his dark hair in frustration. "Ach you're right, it makes no sense! But look south, and there they are ..."

"True," muttered Roc. "And so's the Ice, look you north! And here we are, rushing like loons between them! And what sense d'you find in *that*?"

Thus they ran, through many long days and nights, and thus they were pursued. It was a time of terrible strain for them both, for the ice-islands arose in their path once more, monstrous jagged things that gleamed in daylight like the fangs of harsh mountains, and under moon and stars glimmered like fragments of a sickly dream. Elof feared a night of overcast and storm, when they could only heave to and await what the waves would send them, ice or Ekwesh; but the skies grew clearer the further north they went, and the hours of darkness shorter. Nonetheless they slept little and poorly, for neither could linger away from the deck; Roc could not handle the cutter on his own for long in the best of conditions, and in any difficulty Elof needed him – all this, while the enemies at their heels were well-crewed and tireless. Whenever Elof could, he studied them at their manoeuvering, saw how they twisted and turned their loose heavy sails to tack around the ice-islands he had passed; clumsy he found them, but skilled and swift, and in their pursuit inexorable. It was small wonder that at each dawning the black sails loomed that trace larger, that fraction nearer.

They were growing bitterly chill, those dawnings, and the rime upon the rigging was slower to disperse in the sun. The ice-islands were more frequent now, appearing on every quarter, and the sea between them was no longer clear but filling gradually with smaller floes and drifting chunks still large enough to stave in a small craft's planking or to spring its seams. Elof steered with minute care, and gritted his teeth at every scrape or rumble upon the hull. At nights he had to take care lest the sail grew too heavily coated with ice, whose weight might easily capsize them; in such seas that would be death too swift for even their pursuers to pick them up. And one clear night, when the ocean seemed like a shattered dish of white under the full moon, he saw a dread sight rise up above its crazed rim, a mist of white like the starry River overhead, but lying all across the northern horizon. As a boy he had seen it first, as a man on the verge of a new life he had watched it fade behind him; what was he, now that he faced the Iceglow once again? Almost like a ghost he felt, a troubled spirit wandering uneasily in a body that galled it, yet dared not be cast off. He huddled deeper into his fur-lined cloak, and yearned for sunrise. But when it came they found themselves plunging on a freshening wind toward a sea that seemed almost solid with drifting islands and floes of white, and ended in a high wall of white that arose in the farthest distance, a strength and rampart that stretched all across the northern horizon, and on either hand vanished with it into the blur of distance, beneath the curve of the world. And as they looked they felt that cold, constant blast strike full in their faces, pouring down those frozen heights like an invisible foss, washing their ancient malice out across the oceans of the world.

"The Walls of Winter!" said Elof darkly. "Cliffs and fortresses of the Ice! But at least it grows thick enough in those waters; there we may manage to evade our hunters."

"Or cheat them of their prey!" grunted Roc, hopping from one foot to another and flexing numbered fingers to keep the blood flowing. "Can't eat meat that's fifty fathoms down and frozen solid, can they?"

Elof laughed. "That's true enough!" He glanced back once with weary eyes at the sails that flocked like stormclouds behind them, then rubbed his hands and took firm grip on the tiller. "Well, to your place and stand ready; the most perilous course we can steer, that's where our hopes lie now!" And with iron care he edged the tiller around, swinging closer and closer to the northward, trying to watch both the streamers and the vane and the channels that opened between the wallowing ice-pack; one whit too close and ...

It happened. Elof saw the dark speck from the corner of his eye just as Roc shouted in sudden alarm; he could not help being distracted, looking round. Kermorvan might have carried it off, but Elof was not half the seaman he was; his hand jerked on the tiller, and edged the *Seafire* too far into the wind. In the smaller boats he was used to sailing it might have mattered less, but the cutter was four times their size, and undermanned; he lost control. Roc yelled and ducked as the sails emptied overhead and the boom flailed loose across the deck, the gaff threshing this way and that against sheet and stay, raining flakes of ice down upon the deck. The tiller kicked, Elof lost his hold and fell sprawling. Their speed slackened, faltered, and the *Seafire* wallowed uncontrolled, left for vital moments to the mercy of the waves, and the keen-edged floes around.

Dodging the wild swing of the tiller, Elof scrambled up. He knew only too well that the two of them could not regain control quickly enough to swing her away from the wind again; if they lost so much of their start it would only be a matter of time before they were overhauled, or driven against the Ice and sunk. Without the wind ... It was almost before thought that he had sprung to the stern-post, seized the rimed metal that hung there, gripped it, pushed it ...

It quivered, but it did not move. Like holding a door against a gale, Kermorvan had described it; but he had striven only with a brisk breeze in a sheltered harbour. Now it felt as if Elof strove with the naked force of the gale itself, all flowing through the very metal, or sought to dam a torrent with his fingers. And worse; he seemed to sense some other guiding force behind it, as if other hands pressed or pulled at the vane's far side, constantly opposing his own. He was losing his grip; his chest ached, his breath whistled between his clenched teeth. His fingers slipped over the incised pattern, the spray-encrusted salt crackling beneath them in its serpentine; but he felt something else there also. Darkness swirled before his mind's eye, depths green and gloomy through which he sank, drifting down, down ... and something was rising to meet him. A sudden smothering fear gripped him, and it unleashed new strength; crying out aloud, he thrust violently against the vane, and felt it give a little, swing, then stick, immovable.

It was enough. Hanging there exhausted, he saw the streamers leap up straight and shivering, heard the stays thrum and quiver. The lashing boom suddenly jerked out straight as the sail filled with a crack like a whip of the Powers, and the cutter surged forward once again, heeling wildly. Elof grabbed the tiller; Roc, crawling to a winch, gave a whoop of delight and pointed astern. The same slight shift in the wind that had filled their sails had spilled it from the black squaresails astern, leaving them wallowing as helpless as the cutter had been.

"And see how soon you get out of that, my fine man-eaters!" yelled Roc, shaking his fist at them. But Elof caught him by the shoulder and gestured. The wind had shifted a little to the east, and they were sailing on a close reach northeastward now; and ahead of them was the black speck that had startled them, clearly now another Ekwesh sail. It had been tacking well wide of the ice, but already they could see the sail begin to shift, the momentary collapse and sudden billowing tautness that meant it was sweeping down the wind to intercept them.

"How many of the bastards are there?" howled Roc, brushing his red fringe out of his eyes. "Is it a whole fleet they've got on our tail?"

"They must have been searching," reasoned Elof absently, measuring his distances from the newcomer. "Or on guard. Quartering the seas, beating about, each ship to a sector, or they would have come on us

together. Now they flock ... And perhaps this one was
astern of the rest, and they signalled it to sail north to
cut us off; their shamans have such arts." He bit his lip,
and felt it numb as wood, "He is nearest now, that one,
and fast upon us. It will be a close run, Roc, within
bowshot even; you might want to don your armour ..."

"No thanks! Sooner not face a swim in that, if it's all
the same to you. And metal's bloody cold. But bowshot,
now, that can work both ways can't it?" He turned and
ducked quickly through the companionway, and reappeared with two bundles of arrows and two large bows;
the arrows he thrust into racks by the tiller, and set
about stringing the bows. "Not the best shots, you and I,
are we? Wish we'd Kermorvan here, or old Gise even –
what's he about now, d'you think? But we'll maybe pink
their arses for them, if only these thrice-damned strings
– ah, there! Now yours – how long have we, think
you?"

Elof had been asking himself the same question.
"Less than an hour; the horizon's a bare league distant,
and they're coming in fast. Shoot if you wish, but stand
ready on the winches; we cannot fight a whole war
craft. What hope we have lies in flight."

It was not long indeed before they saw the Ekwesh
ship more clearly. Long and narrow in the hull, but high
of side and decked, it was much the same as that one
Elof had helped to capture, one wild foggy night many
years since. Now, though, the long sweeps were stowed
away, and the bare sides bristled with men. "They have
not even hung out their shields," said Elof tautly. "They
think us such easy meat. Well, so much the better;
they have been mistaken ere ..." He heard something
then, and Roc also; a distant drumming boom, borne to
them down the wind. And as they drew closer still they
could make out the platform upon the wide bows of the
warship, and the strange figure stepping up onto it, clad
in spreading robes that swept this way and that, and
some form of masked head-dress. They looked at each
other.

"What in Hel's black breasts is that?" growled Roc.

"A shaman," said Elof. "To dance up their battle

craft, and counter ours. Maybe they do fear us, after all."

Roc made no reply; they sat in breathless silence as the Ekwesh craft knifed through the swell towards them, white foam spurting and spraying past the black prow, disdaining the ice-floes with ruthless grace. The drum rolled and thudded down the bitter airs, but the sinister shape in the bows stood motionless, the mask drooping as if the head beneath was sunk in thought. Suddenly it lifted, and the drumbeat changed, stuttered like an excited heartbeat; from side to side the mask swayed, and the robes spread and billowed beneath. Faster and faster the shaman danced, leaping from one leg to another so the robes wove and wagged behind him like a tail, throwing back the long mask till the jaws dangled, shaking them in a sidelong snarl. They could see now that the robes were streaked in grey and white, the mask crested with low grey curls and ending in a large black muzzle rimmed with gaping fangs and black gums.

"Wolf!" muttered Elof. *"Ouashkas,* the Wolf clan! I know the mask from Mylio's records; but we have faced few of that line in the Westlands."

"Then make ready for a new treat!" growled Roc. *"Here they come!"*

Caught in the inexorable play of waters and winds, the two craft charged down upon each other like great deer sparring in the forests of the Northlands. Elof gripped the tiller tight in his fist, counting the time against a quickening heartbeat, fighting off the urge to flinch, to swerve away; that would not save them now. The black bows lifted over them like axe over twig, ready to ram; Roc shouted and ducked down, the *Seafire* bounced and heeled violently on the war craft's bow wave, and Elof thrust hard on the tiller. A handspan only he moved it, sharp as a measure, but the cutter answered instantly as any living mount; its bows swung, the sails pressed closer to the wind and the little craft heeled sharply. Roc whooped in triumph as the black prow slid harmlessly alongside and passed them, the painted beast-face leering in baffled fury. From the awesome figure of the shaman came an ululating howl

of rage, and longbows lifted over the rail above. But
Roc, still on his knees, had already drawn bow, and the
range was a few strides only; he loosed, there was a
yell and a black-garbed figure toppled between the
two hulls, so close he almost struck the *Seafire*'s deck.
That held back the storm a heartbeat, when every
instant was a gain; time enough for the hulls to draw a
small way apart, and Elof to shift the rudder a fraction
further. The little craft heeled further away from the
Ekwesh ship, even as the first ragged volley of arrows
was launched. Meant to sweep its deck, they thudded
instead into its upraised flank, or spat through the sails
with little harm. Before the last had passed Roc bobbed up
from behind the rail and fired again; he hit nothing, but
Elof fired across the stern transom and struck one of the
yelling faces above the steering oar. More arrows hissed
and rattled into the *Seafire*'s timber, then they were
past and away.

"Kerys, you timed that close!" gasped Roc. "But
what now? They'll be about in a moment and snapping
at our heels ..."

"Will they indeed?" asked Elof quietly. But even as
he spoke the black ship was sweeping around in a wide
circle, its hands frantically paying out the sheets till the
great yard swung almost parallel to the hull and the
black sail ballooned outward from it like a child's kite.
With majestic ease the war craft leaned over and
came gliding after the skipping cutter.

"At least we're almost past bowshot –" began Roc,
then ducked hastily as a flock of arrows sang close over
the deck. "That's not natural!" he protested. "Shooting
against the wind, at that!" His eyes lit on the shaman,
still hopping and leaping at his post. "It's that bastard!"
he cried. "Guiding the arrows by his craft –" Something
heavier crashed into the planking; wide fletches of black
and white stood quivering in the stern transom. "And
they've brought a catapult to bear!"

He was about to spring up recklessly and shoot, but
Elof pulled him down. "Wait!" he commanded, flinching
slightly as another catapult arrow riffled his hair with a
ghostly breath. "Ready to trim sail! Now we may test

them, in their turn —"

With calculated suddenness he bore down hard upon the tiller, and the cutter swung still closer to the wind, heeling so sharply now that, arrows or not, they both sprang out to the rail and leaned back to balance it. Behind them the war craft seemed to hesitate a moment, then slowly and ponderously eased itself onto the new heading.

What happened then was startling in its suddenness. The taut black sail appeared to tremble, then all in a moment it spilled, collapsed and snapped taut again; the huge craft listed alarmingly, then with an explosive crack that carried even upwind the strained sheets parted and the sail whipped free, streaming out like a bedsheet on a line. The black hull plunged and bucked, and the shaman, springing for the safety of the foredeck, was hurled out and away like a stone from a sling. His robes billowed out as he struck the water; they saw him struggle a moment, win free of the wolfmask but become tangled in his soaked furs and borne down. Even amid the chaos of the warship's deck a line was thrown to him, but in that chill water it was already too late; he vanished in a swirl and rose no more. Only the gaping mask bobbed empty among the drift-ice.

Elof's laugh was a snarl. "You see, Roc? You see? Just as when I lost the wind, but worse with that clumsy rig; they can't shave the wind so close, and never dreamed we could — so they were all aback in an instant, their sail loose and flailing this way and that ..."

Roc nodded grimly. "And one shaman the less; they'll waste their arrows now. But they'll follow all the harder for that, and there's the others in their wake, still —"

Elof pressed his lips tight. He eased the rudder now, and the *Seafire* settled a little further from the wind, on the reaching course that was its fastest point of sailing. "Then we'll see how they fare among the ice! *The race begins!*"

So began the maddest of mad dashes, a fearful plunge between floe and floating island, fleeing the servants of the Ice upon the very winds it spawned. It

took the ship of the Wolf-clan no more than ten minutes
to rein in its sail and start after the *Seafire* once more,
and that was all the lead they had; nor were the other
ships so very far behind. For narrow channels and
passages between and around the thronging slabs of ice
Elof drove, ever seeking a place where the cutter could
pass unscathed and a larger craft might not; but he soon
found this was less easy than it seemed. For the Wolf-
ship was like all Ekwesh ships of war, narrow and lean
for its length, and its bows were well reinforced for
ramming other ships; also, it had many hands to fend off
dangerous ice with the long sweeps. More than once
Elof and Roc saw these bend and splinter against some
immovable floe, or snag in a crevice and topple their
wielder into that murderous ocean which sucked out a
man's life in seconds; but they were not discouraged, so
hot now burned their thirst for vengeance. Through the
fringes of the pack-ice raced the *Seafire*, the cold sea
hissing and slapping at its flanks, but the Wolf-ship still
closed till once again they hung only just beyond
bowshot, and the wildest chances Elof took could not
dismay them.

But all the while he was sending the little craft
weaving and twisting between the floes, his thoughts
were elsewhere. Even as he noted the huge ice-island
ahead, weather-sculpted to the shape of some fantastic
crooked claw, he was ranging though his wide memories for any scrap of knowledge that might serve them in
their desperate need. It was almost summer now, for
what that meant in these regions; it would not melt the
ice-islands, but at least the drift-ice would stay free, and
probably not close in around them. That was some
comfort. What had he heard of ice-islands, so long ago
in Asenby? That the greater part of them lay hidden
beneath the water; but that was an old saw. There was
something more; that even the seal-fishers would steer
clear of them, though mere collision could not harm
their resilient skin-boats ... Why? He gritted his teeth
and sent the *Seafire* gliding in towards the shining mass.

Roc was dozing where he sat, exhausted, but the
changed note of the water awoke him to see the mass of

ice seemingly rush towards them. His bloodshot eyes bulged, but after one look at Elof he sat tight and let him steer. Closer Elof took them, and closer still, till the crooked peak of the ice-mass loomed over them like a gigantic image of the Ekwesh prow; he risked a swift glance astern, and gestured to Roc. "Come, take the tiller!"

"Me? Here?"

"Yes! Just hold it as it is, put it down a little when I give you the word! Hurry!"

Roc scrambled aft and seized the tiller, while Elof moved stiffly over to the rail, and drew his sword. He weighed Gorthawer in his hand a moment, and then as they swept under the crooked overhang he seized a stay and swung himself up to balance on the rail, reaching up with one arm. Then he struck with all the strength he could muster, once, twice, again and again, and the ice clanged like metal. "Now!" he yelled, and Roc swung the bows away from the island; he turned back, and gestured defiantly at the Ekwesh. A catapult arrow buzzed past his shoulder and shivered into the ice-wall behind; a flight of darts followed it. Hastily Elof ducked back, sheathing Gorthawer and seizing the helm once more.

"What was all that about?" inquired Roc with sinister calm. "Aside from scaring me awake, that is?"

"A guess..." said Elof absently, looking quickly ahead and astern by turns, as if loth to lose sight of the Ekwesh whatever the hazards ahead. "A throw of the dice ... weighting them a little, perhaps ... we'll see, any moment ..."

The Wolf-ship was nearing the ice-island now, and the sweeps were going out as before to fend it off. Riding higher in the water, it could not pass under the clawed peak as had the cutter, but swung as close as possible; and it was at the claw that the sweeps thrust. Fragments of ice broke away and fell, some into the water, some on the decks, but the black-clad warriors paid them little heed. Then there was a warning shout and scattering from the rail, as the whole tip of the peak cracked and dropped away where Gorthawer had hewn it; but it fell well clear of the black hull.

Roc swore. "It was a worthy try, though, that!"

Elof shook his head sharply. "Wait! Wait and see ..
there!" He pointed, not at the ship, but at the island,
and Roc gaped in horrified awe. The broken claw was
swinging back, away from the war craft, tipping back
into the sea. And rising from below ..

For a moment the war craft seemed to float on
green glass. Then the great mass burst through the
surface into blazing whiteness, straight under the stern
of the black ship. Those aboard it had no time to move,
scarce enough to scream, ere the whole sleek craft was
flung upward, tipped over with a crash and sent sliding
down the new summit of the island to nose downward
in the foaming waters. It twisted there a moment, its
shattered stern upthrust, while dark flecks flailed and
struggled in the turmoil around it. Then, as the *Seafire*
swept away down the channel, it fell slowly forward,
and was gone.

"Glad I'm no enemy of yours!" said Roc darkly.
"You planned that!"

"I hoped for it." Elof fought the tiller as the swirling water overtook the cutter and set it bobbing like an
angler's float in the narrow way, struggling to keep the
bows away from the floes on either hand. "Gambled that
their commander had never sailed around such islands.
I'd heard fishermen say they kept away from them
because they were unstable; they melt, they weather, the
balance changes and the least breath turns them turtle.
When I saw that odd outcrop, I thought we might speed
matters along and as well I did! See what comes!"

But Roc had no need of the warning; he also had
seen the black sails of their other pursuers billowing out
like some vast bat above the floes, far closer than they
had a right to be.

"They've found some other channel!" spat Roc.
"Aye, and leading this way. Might even cross this one!"

Elof nodded, but glanced up at the sails. "That's a
chance we'll have to take; we could go no faster among
the drift, even if we dared."

But it soon became plain that Roc was right; the

southerly channel was drawing ever nearer their own, and ere long the first of the reiver ships had caught up enough to see clearly. Once or twice an arrow arced up from the throng along its side, and twice they saw a catapult aimed and fired; but dart and bolt fell far short, into the sea or scuffing harmlessly along the ice. Roc shaded his eyes. "Don't see any shaman in those bows, do you?" They both grinned, as wolves may grin.

"But the two channels must meet right enough, somewhere ahead there," remarked Elof. "Not far. Then shaman or no, we'll have them closer on our tail than the others, and forewarned; this channel's too easy for them."

"So what can we do?"

"Turn away, down the channel if it goes on, or another. One that's harder; one that'll take us closer to the Ice."

"Fine choice!" muttered Roc. "But so be it!"

It was little more than a thousand paces ahead that the two rough channels came together, in mockery of a crossroads; and the new one did indeed weave gradually away to the northeast. Elof glanced at the dark ship, now running almost parallel with them, and with scarcely a touch on the helm sent the *Seafire* gliding down the new channel, angling towards the high walls of the Ice. To their pursuers it must have looked like the last act of desperation; and Elof kept having to remind himself that it was not. There would, there must, come a point when the unwieldy sailing of the black ships would tell against them, and the cutter could slip away. That was a reasonable enough hope; but it was also the only hope they had.

All the remainder of that day the cutter sped northward, racing and weaving like a seabird over the white-strewn waters; the only seabird, for the skies were bare of life. Not so the sea; once or twice upon flat-topped floes the voyagers saw dark smudges, as of ink on paper, that lifted round alert heads as they drew closer And if they came too near, close enough to see the patterns on the sleek fur, the seals would cry out in gulping alarm and go humping and slithering off to plunge into the dark waters. Once, a bulky, bloated-looking monster half the length of the cutter only raised a majestic snout crowned with a crest that bobbed like an inflated bladder and bellowed a hoarse challenge to the intruders.

"Not today, brother," muttered Roc. "Save it for the Ekwesh ..." But upon another floe they passed a heap of sprawling reddish shapes that were each of them larger and bulkier than that huge beast, and when they raised their heads Roc cried out, for some were armed with immense protruding teeth. "Like dagger-teeth!" cried Roc, and snatched up his bow.

"Leave them be!" said Elof quickly. "I've heard of them, called *valros* in the northern speech; they are harmless shell-diggers, save when provoked. Anyway, you might make little impression on such beasts; their hide is thick. It was valued for cables in Nordeney."

Within the shadow of the blue-white cliffs, though, even these signs of life vanished. Cruel and stern they gleamed, mountain-high they reared, or so it seemed, and as majestic in their power. Yet barer than the starkest stone were they, with no substance on them or around them that was not their own, no tree or plant, no soil, not even the rocky debris borne by glaciers of the land, nothing save the snow which was their first and primal stage and by whose accumulation alone they could grow. Here the Ice contemplated only ice, and the water it hoped soon to freeze into itself; all else was intrusion, And by that they seemed somehow diminished in Elof's eyes, and he looked upon them with contempt and defiance in his heart, where there might else have been awe.

Once only, when the cutter came to a clear patch where the sun struck down into the blue waters, they saw huge pale shapes like Ice-ghosts glide beneath them in the depths. Ere long they surfaced, not far off, with snorting spouts that clearly made them some white-skinned breed of porpoise or small whale, and suddenly they seemed heartening company in this cold waste. But they did not play like porpoises, and all at once they dived and were gone; they had seen the black shape that came sweeping up channel, heard perhaps the squeal of the catapult windlasses echoing through the hull. Elof ducked at the snapping ring and hiss of a shot, even though it splashed harmlessly astern, then turned to Roc in real alarm. "How could we hear that at this distance?" He glanced up at the streamers, the vane, and could see them begin to sag and falter.

"The wind's dropping!" howled Roc. "Now of all times, after it's come pouring down on us day in, day ..." He looked suddenly at the cliffs, and at Elof, and freckles blazed on his paling cheeks. "You don't reckon *they* ..."

"Now, of all times," echoed Elof. "and our pursuers may use sweeps, and we not. Yes they know someone is here, the masters of that wind. But they cannot stop it all in a minute, so let us get the best from what is left!" He swung the tiller over, and the cutter went racing in even closer beneath the lowering cliffs. "Into the very embrace of the Ice ..." he said grimly, as they passed within the arms of a wide bay. Roc made no answer; he was staring up at the cliffs. From afar they had seemed a solid wall of whiteness; this close they looked ancient, crumbling, their faces lit a ghastly blue, riven and shadowed with cracks and chasms through which white avalanches came tumbling and smoking to drop into the sea beneath. Such an aspect, noble yet blasted, might a lord of old have worn who had fallen from youth into a cruel and dissolute old age, and bore the marks of all he had wasted and corrupted. Against such a background even the black ships in their wake seemed almost innocent, vessels of a merely human viciousness.

"And they're falling behind at last, by Kerys's Gate!" Roc slapped his fist into his palm.

"Aye, and are they!" said Elof, between his teeth. "With their rig and their weight they need far more wind for steerage way. And within the shelter of the bay there isn't enough! Whereas for us ..."

Roc grinned back, tapped his nose in understanding, and glanced up at the wind-vane. Then the grin was struck from his face, and he yelled hoarsely; shadow fell across the cutter like a cloak, and all the sea about. Elof turned swiftly, and for a moment he could only cower, so vast and looming was the threat. It dashed thought from his mind, and for a moment he was an animal, or less. It seemed that the whole immense cliff was moving, tilting above the stern of the cutter, leaning forward to rush down upon these tiny creatures and scour them from sight.

His wits returned to him, and he saw that it was only a part of the cliff, splitting along fissures that were already there, down which those avalanches had fallen. Yet that part was the size of a goodly hill, and though it leaned with the slowness of nightmare it seemed already to fill the sky. Under that lowering shadow he saw only one faint hope of escape. Feeling as if his limbs were weighed with lead, he slammed the tiller hard over and sprang up, as if through thick oil, to seize the cold wind-vane in both hands.

Again he sensed vast weight, and beyond it the presence of another will, opposing hands, but momentarily relaxed, distracted; he thrust with all the force of his fear, and the vane swung round a good two points. Then abruptly it stuck. Elof's hands slithered over the pattern, and for a moment he thought he had fallen overboard. Green light billowed around him, clouded and chill; he could not breathe, he was sinking, twisting among silvery threads of dwindling air-bubbles. And from the forest-green depths below something else was rising to meet him ...

Roc shouted and pulled him down, or he might have fallen indeed, as the sails snapped suddenly full and the *Seafire* heeled and bobbed around. Forward it surged on its new heading towards the far arm of the bay, racing the shadow of that toppling death across the ice-strewn water. Elof, gasping with the reaction, glanced back once at the foremost war craft, saw the sweeps arise along its sides and beat frantically at the water. But whether they sought to pursue or back off, he never saw, for at that moment the cliff face fell.

From the glacier it broke with a crack like thunder and a great cloud of powder snow, one vast single slab. It did not slither like a landslide, but tilted forward like some petrified giant, to crash down face-first and rigid across the black waters of the bay, With a booming explosion the waters leaped skyward amid a spray of shattered ice, then fell back in a great arched wave that welled out with a devouring roar to fill the bay and rise in wrath against the very cliffs themselves, hammering upon the uncaring face of the glacier with the floes it had spawned.

Had the dying wind not shifted, the *Seafire* could not have escaped annihilation beneath that titanic fall. As it was, it had hardly reached the arm of the bay when the mass struck, and barely escaped being tossed into the air on that first gigantic upsurge. But the failing breath of the breeze bore the little craft clear of the wall a moment before the vast wave struck it, and out into the ocean once more. After it the wave came racing, a tide of thundering blackness crested with teeth like white glass, but with its first energy spent, else the cutter might not have survived. As it was, Elof and Roc had time only to fix tiller and hatch and lash themselves in before the breaking waters crashed against their stern. For a time that seemed centuries all was racing, rushing confusion, an endless torrent of ice-laden sea sweeping over them like the flow of every mountain foss in the world together. It was drowning and worse than drowning behind the curtain of rushing waters, for they were battered and bitten by the fragmented ice it bore, and the black chill of it made them gasp in agony for air they could not get. Ice boomed and crashed against the hull. The jagged rim of a floe swept by above their heads and plucked at the starboard mast-stays like a finger at harp strings. Then it was past, and the cutter wallowing and twisting upon the lesser waves that followed, riding outwards like ripples in an infant's pond.

Elof and Roc tore free their bonds and scrambled around as one, to see what had happened behind them. The sheer force of it dazed them. The vast slab had split upon impact, and two huge ice-islands slowly bobbed and spun in the bay, with a million lesser shards and fragments of ice around them. But beyond the mouth of the bay a great fan of sea lay black and bare, scoured almost clear of ice by the passing of the wave.

"The Ekwesh..." croaked Roc, as the turmoil subsided.

Elof spat out a mouthful of seawater and coughed violently before he could speak. "Under the slab. Dashed to nothing, as we would have been, but for the vane. Little their masters cared, if only they could strike at us!" He looked around suddenly. "But the other two? Were they..."

"'Fraid not!" said Roc unhappily, and pointed. Beyond the dark gap in the drift-ice dark masts lifted like leafless trees against the greying sky. "And they're not running, neither."

"They'd time to see it coming," said Elof grimly. "Lowered sails and rode it out with sweeps ... and now they'll row for us, fast ..." He looked despairingly up at the sails, but they hung soaked and limp in the sluggish air, gaff and boom swaying idly. "Not so much as a breath ..." He stumbled wearily up, rubbing where the ropes had bruised him, and clambered unsteadily to the stern-post. The vane still hung in its socket, but it too was swaying idly, and swung to the touch of his finger, one side to the other without the least resistance. Calm settled like smoked glass upon the windless sea.

Roc's voice came to him distant, distorted, as if through deep waters. "Can't it do something? See the speed of the bastards! They'll be upon us in minutes now!"

Elof shook his head. "Nothing ... nothing ... no wind to work upon. The virtue I set on it was to summon, to direct ... But it can't summon what's not there anymore!" In dazed despair he hung on the vane, feeling the swirl of the pattern, the sense of drifting down into green depths and the vast black shadow-shape below, nearer, even nearer, the two faint gleams, dim points of light ...

He stiffened suddenly, gasping, clutching the vane in shaking hands as if he feared to release it. "Is it a wind?" cried Roc, and then "No, man, what're you about?" Elof heard him, but it was too late; he had wrenched the vane from its socket, held it a moment to his brow, then brandished it high over his head.

"Since the wind fails you," he breathed, "show us what else your craft may command!" And with a great effort he hurled the precious thing from him, straight into the path of the oncoming ships. Far out over the waters it spun; Roc flinched, as if he half expected that calm surface to shatter like some vast dark mirror. But the black waters swallowed it with scarcely a ripple, and he cursed. Elof hardly noticed; his work was fixed still in his mind's eye, falling, sinking, drifting down into the green cold depths, down to a rising shadow . . .

The ripples faded, the mirror lay calm once more, open to the cutting onslaught of the black bows. For the pace of two slow breaths it seemed that nothing would happen; then, around the spot where the vane had vanished, a little spurt of bubbles pattered up. Elof swallowed, painfully, for his throat and mouth were suddenly very dry. Another breath, and Roc leaned forward suddenly, eyes narrowing in alarm. In the same spot, but with scarcely a ripple, something else broke the surface, something small, rounded and glistening that gleamed dark as the sea around it, and yet was no bubble. Slowly, steadily, it arose and grew to a tapering pointed shape, and Elof was momentarily filled with disappointment; that sleek black head, as large, perhaps, as a horse's, must surely belong to one of the very large seals they had seen, curious at all the disturbance above. Then the head lifted, clouds of steam jetting from narrow nostrils; the eyes blinked open, and with a shudder of fascinated horror Elof saw they were like no ordinary seal's, set small on each side of the head. These were immense, with a green and catlike glint in them, and they were set as forward as his own. This way and that they turned as the huge head swung, water streaming from a crest of coarse fur that ran like the main of a horse down the narrow column of neck beneath. Still it rose out of that eerie calm like some vision of nightmare emerging from a mirror, higher and higher on a neck of impossible length; it seemed it would never stop, as if the legends were true that made it an endless serpent engirdling the earth. Yet it was no serpent; beneath the water a wide whale-like body was becoming visible, and around it in shadowy outline four limbs like the flippers of a seal, and a long and tapering tail. When the rolling curve of the back at last broke surface, that head stood taller than the *Seafire*'s mast; higher even than the mastheads of the Ekwesh warships it rose, swan-like and graceful, immensely majestic, infinitely terrible. Their rowing slowed, the long sweeps clashing in disorder as the rowers turned to stare at what they saw mirrored in the calm water; then the sweeps dug hard into the water, their fierce onrush faltered. They glided to a halt and hung there, rocking gently.

"What *is* it?" gasped Roc. "Not ..."

Elof clamped a hand over his mouth. "Not a sound!" he hissed into his ear. Don't attract his attention! Aye, the Sea Devourer it must be – Amicac himself!"

He sensed Roc stiffen, and felt little better himself, overshadowed by that long head, those enigmatic eyes. It was a sight to make the heart shrink, to bring home to him how different was the order of the ocean, a monster harbouring monsters. A good seventy strides in length were those great war craft, but the creature before them was at least as long and many times outweighed them. It floated now between them and the cutter, motionless save for the briefest flick of limbs beneath the surface, and the watchful swing of the great head. Elof held his breath. He could not guess what it would do next, which way it would turn, but his foes, who had seen this creature summoned, could not know that. Yet they were not craven, the Ekwesh; their codes demanded they avenge defeats and deaths. After that first breathless pause a sudden defiant howl rang out; upon the leading ship a wolf-clad shaman sprang forward to prance and posture at this new apparition, while behind him came the bark of harsh commands, the creak of catapult winches, the rumble of feet upon the decks as the archers ran up to form battle ranks. The drums rolled, the oars swept down in a single surging thrust that sent the black ships lancing forward; the icy air seemed to crack like a whip, and volleys of arrows came sailing up from their decks like leaves in a sudden gust. Against ships or men that hail of shafts might have told terribly, but the Devourer was greater than the greatest whale, and that massive back bore thick hide or even bony armour; what few arrows struck served only to sting and annoy him. His head tossed back, he gave a single barking snarl, and the long neck snaked down so swiftly that the arrows seemed slow in their flight. Against the length of him his head seemed small, but it was three times longer than any great cat's, four times that of a wolf; along the decks it raked with jaws agape, and strewed the helpless archers like chaff. One, too slow or too bold to leap for his life, was seized and borne bodily into the air. Robes streamed and fluttered about those jaws; it was a chieftain or shaman who threshed in their grip. Catapult bolts sang up from the decks; they were harder to aim, but by skill or chance one struck high on that narrow throat and sank deep into its iron muscles.

The reeking jaws parted, their prey dropped to crash unheeded upon the deck, and a whistling cry of pain split the air. Then it was as if the whole sea around the Devourer boiled up, lashed into foam by limbs and tail as the vast beast gathered itself up and hurled itself forward, to strike like a true serpent at its tormentors. The vast flippers slammed down upon the decking before it, their blunt claws tearing at the planking, and then amid a tumult of howls and screams, like a seal mounting an ice-flow, the Devourer hauled its great bulk bodily out of the sea and onto the deck. The mast was brushed aside like a twig, the timbers creaked and shivered, and beneath that vast weight the whole great ship was flattened down into the water, Elof saw the terrified oarsmen springing from their benches, but the sea was already flooding across the high gunwales, and they were swept away in foaming turmoil, or plucked from handholds by the water that fountained up through the shattered deck as the hull timbers gave. The broken ship lurched, twisted and canted over, and together with its destroyer it sank from sight; the sea swirled in where it had been, setting the drift-ice bobbing and spinning, and only a few scraps of wreckage spun above its grave.

For long moments nothing more happened, and Elof guessed that the Destroyer had dived deep, as might a whale, seeking refuge in the depths from tormenting humans. The last warship, it seemed, had as urgent an aim, its oars beat the water with frenzied strength, and the sleek craft came scything on across its fellow's tomb. Elof and Roc watched helplessly as the Ekwesh bore down on their cutter; bent the man-eaters might be on escape, but they would not miss the chance to sink their prey first. Then a shadow passed once more over Elof's mind; staring down into the black ocean he saw what must happen, and could barely restrain himself from crying a warning to his enemy, so near and certain was their doom. Up from below surged that vast body, and the Ekwesh warship seemed to explode as if a volcano had erupted under its keel. They saw the hull shoot up under the impact and crash down upon its side in a wall of spray, and then all was hidden from them in roaring havoc. This way and that flew sweeps and timbers and the helpless shapes of men amid a seething cauldron of sea, stirred up by limbs and flippers that lashed and pounded the black hull to fragments. Into the black ocean plummeted its crew like ants spilled from a nest, and like ants the shrieking swimmers died beneath the crashing impact of those broad limbs, or were plucked up by the jaws that plunged and darted this way and that; though perhaps the few who were left to kick and struggle a few seconds longer were the worse off, for the cold took them more slowly, and the waters swallowed them living and aware.

"We've got to get out of here!" screamed Roc above the uproar, as the cutter lurched and heeled on the boiling sea. "That brute'll have us next –"

"There's still no wind!" shouted Elof, fighting helplessly with the tiller and empty sails. "We're drifting – just drifting! There's not a thing more I can do –" Abruptly the cutter lurched and lifted beneath him, and a hummock of black water swept by, almost gunwale-high, a crestless wave that was the first outrush from that explosive emergence. It caught up the little craft like a hand and swept it forward, heeling and wallowing wildly; Elof had to wrestle with the tiller to keep it from capsizing. Other waves overtook them from that maelstrom of carnage astern, sweeping the floes before them and adding to their speed.

"We're heading towards the Ice again!" Roc growled.

"Can't be helped!" Elof answered, though he felt a sudden cold breath upon his neck. At least they were not headed back into that terrible bay, but around the arm of it, where the cliffs were less sheer and looming. "Just so long as we get out of sight –" The drift-ice clustered more thickly here, but the waves they rode cleared it from their path, and spent their energy in doing so. The cutter's speed dropped to a quiet glide, and they relaxed a little. Suddenly the boom creaked and swung, the sail fluttered and crackled with falling ice. That breath played about Elof's head again; it was real, a movement in the still air. It even seemed to stir his hair a little, soaked and salt stiffened as it was. He read the same pang of hope on Roc's face, and together they looked up at the streamers. They too were stirring slightly – even fluttering a little ...

"A westerly!" groaned Roc. "Oh no – not here ..."

"Afraid so," sighed Elof, sagging wearily over the tiller rack. "We'll have to tack out of here, it'll take hours and the sun's falling fast –"

Roc's cry alerted him; he whirled, and forgot the wind, so appalled was he at the sight of that fierce silhouette, held high against the darkening clouds, surveying with regal calm the waste of waters around. Beneath it no trace of turmoil remained and on all that wide surface no trace of the last of their pursuers. From that lofty vantage there was nothing here that could hide them, and a strange urge gripped him; he staggered to his feet in the stern, met that calm gaze with his own, striving to read what lay behind it, life or death, and felt the cool touch of awe and great wonder in his mind.

"That ..." breathed Roc, equally unnerved. "What

manner of ... beast is it? No seasnake, that's for sure! ͵ ."

"I cannot say," Elof whispered, without turning. "Some ... cousin to the seals, I think; a giant among their kind ..."

"Where's he come from? It was you, wasn't it? What'd you *do*?"

"That vane ... in my lightness of heart I set its image upon that vane, not knowing what virtues of command it would bear. So, when I turned the wind to my will, I summoned ... him, also. All this while he must have been close to us, far below; a happy chance we did not use the vane more, or idly! Each time I – sensed something, though I did not understand it till the last; then I called upon him in desperation, not knowing what he would do. And still I do not!"

"He made no move to attack anyone till those maniacs quilled him," Roc pointed out. "That's something. He just sat there like he's doing now, as if he was waiting ..."

Then Elof gave a deep sigh, as of sudden understanding; he lowered his gaze, and made as deep and courtly an obeisance as he knew how. And even as he looked up once more the long neck drove forward among the drift-ice, and as it swept forward it sank, slowly and smoothly, that proud head held level. The ice-floes scattered before it like panicked sheep, and it trailed a wake of whiteness over the shadowed seas like a royal mantle. At last only the head rose over the waters, and with startling suddenness it ducked down and was gone.

Elof turned away at last, upon unsteady legs, to find Roc looking up at him, his broad face unreadable and pensive. "Well?" demanded Elof. "I suppose you'll think me mad to go bowing and scraping thus?"

Roc considered a moment, gnawing idly at his lip. "Had it in mind to do much the same thing myself, as it happens. If, that is, I didn't just kneel down and bang my head upon the decking. I'm not one to stand on my dignity, me ..."

Elof sighed and sat down heavily. "So you felt the same? I'm glad. That head ... that *face* ... as if, as if – "

He never finished. A booming crash rocked the *Seafire* and he was flung flat on the deck amidst a shower of ice from the sail. The timbers quivered as something jagged rasped along the keel like a giant saw, then came another crashing impact that set the rigging thrumming; the mast-stays sang like harp strings, then where the floe had plucked at them they frayed, snapped and flew free. The gaff reeled and dropped down in a flurry of sail-cloth, the mast tottered, sagged in its footing and toppled. Elof could only clap his hands over his head and hope; he felt and heard the thudding fall, and the broken rail that pinioned his ankles and the tangle of cordage and blocks that struck him painfully in the back felt like the end of everything. But in the next breath he looked up, to find himself face to face with Roc, only a few inches away, peering out from under great swathes of grey sailcloth. In Roc's face he read the same realisation, the same overwhelming horror and momentary panic; they spoke no word, but their thoughts ran in dark communion. Held in the thrall of the Devourer, they had forgotten the other perils all around them; for that moment of forgetfulness they might well be about to pay the price. At any instant black water might come welling over those gunwales to stop their hearts in its chill embrace, as it had so many others this day.

They scrambled to their feet, forgetting their pains, and stared anxiously about them. The deck felt strangely still and heavy underfoot, and across it lay the mast like a severed tree, the sails strewn beneath it, trailing half in the water. But that water was not black; even in this failing light it was the palest of blues, like a mockery of warmer climes. They stumbled to the side, stared down for a moment, and then they turned as one, still without speaking, to look across at the other side, and beyond, and up. They knew now why the deck was still; wind and water and their own folly had conspired to drive them aground, but where there was no ground. They had come to rest upon the margins of the seaborne glaciers, upon the utmost shores of the Ice.

CHAPTER FOUR

The High Gate

ROC TORE HIS EYES AWAY from the heights above, and tugged his fur jacket closer about him. "Well. How long before they come for us, d'you reckon?"

At first Elof could not understand the question, so numbed was his mind by the mere presence of the Ice. Even standing on the deck he seemed to feel something of that sickening, burning pain that contact with it had always brought him; the very air ran like fire in his nostrils, already raw with the cold, and pulling up his scarf made little difference. "Come for us ...?" Then he realised who Roc meant, but was carefully not naming, and as he considered he felt a sudden flicker of warmth awaken. "You know ... they may not be able to find us so easily –"

Roc raised a sceptical eyebrow. "They're not daft; they've only to look, haven't they?"

Elof rounded on him. "That's just what they can't do! They've senses we haven't; they're aware of us, yes – but they can't see us; not as we would see, anyhow!"

"They managed just fine when they dropped that cliff, didn't they?"

"Only with their thralls' sight to guide them! And even then they weren't close enough, were they?" He scanned the cold cliffs in the greying light. "We're too small for their minds to grasp. Even to Tapiau we were only shadows, and ... these will be far less attuned to live things than he. They can only gain living senses by taking on living shape, and that'll be their last resort!"

Roc grabbed him by the shoulders. "You mean we've still time? Then what're we standing here for? Let's get this hulk afloat again!"

But it was scarcely that easy. First, most urgently, they had to haul in the sail, leaden-heavy with water and

97

already half-frozen, and disentangle it from the jumble of twisted cordage around the fallen mast. Then they had to clamber down into the bilges, which, poor seamen that they were, they had failed to clean out often enough, there to struggle through slime and stink by the light of a sputtering lamp to check the hull for damage They found less than they feared, but several seams had been sprung, and Roc at once set to work melting their small store of pitch on the stove, while Elof went back on deck to begin what Roc could not do, dismantling the ruined rigging and reeving new lines where needed. From time to time as he worked he would glance up at the sun, now resting like a redhot brazen shield upon the rim of the Ice cliffs. He wondered, almost idly, how much of the day remained, and how they would fare after dark; the powers of this place hated and feared the sun, however weak, and were doubly formidable in its absence. Beneath him the hull boomed and quivered to the thump of Roc's caulking mallet; it was the only sound not born of wind and wave, and to Elof's ears it seemed to echo around the cliffs above. Surely the Powers must sense that as tremors in the Ice, if nothing else. It was a great relief to him when it stopped, and a minute later Roc emerged, streaked with pitch and slime, gasping with exhaustion. Elof helped him up and found him a flask of wine.

"Enough ..." Roc wheezed. "Must've been just about shouting *Come and get us!* to 'em, with all that row."

"Probably!" agreed Elof. "Couldn't be helped, though. But you've finished? Good! That was hard on you ..."

"Not so light on yourself!" grimaced Roc, looking at Elof's raw and bleeding hands. "And at least I was out of the cold. What now? The mast?"

"If you're strong enough ..."

"I'll manage."

Manage they did, though raising that mast can have been no easy task even with block and tackle. Neither of them had the advantage of height, and had they not both possessed the sinews of smiths, and an exceptional endurance, they might well never have achieved it. The sun was setting by the time the mast stood stepped, and the headsail at least was made ready to raise; but by then Roc, who had had the heavier labour of caulking, was near to collapse.

"Come on!" encouraged Elof, as they warmed themselves over the cooling stove. "We've only to launch her now, that's all –"

"Go to rest," mumbled Roc. "Jus' minute ... arms won't move ..." He slumped down against the stove, and curled into himself.

"All right!" said Elof, and sighed. "I'll keep watch – but remember, a few minutes may be all we have ..." Pulling his furs tight, he scrambled back up on deck, and peered anxiously overside at the fearsome water that washed and gurgled under the scarred hull, lurching it a little on the ice-shoal. It was hard to make out the tide on this mockery of a coast, but it seemed to be more or less at its height; they could hope for no more help from it. He could rig some kind of spring cable, such as the corsairs had used to launch their ship, but that required a fixed point somewhere, a very strong one ...

Elof swallowed. There was no getting around it; one of them, at least, would have to get down hip-deep into that fearsome water and wade ashore. And it could not be Roc; in his exhausted state the sea might kill him. Elof was hardly more sure of himself, but he knew he had little choice. There were things abroad to which death might well be preferable. Swiftly he set about gathering gear, made fast a long line about his waist, and lowered himself gingerly over the curve of the hull. Only as his feet touched the water did he realise he had not told Roc what he was doing, but left him sleeping. He hesitated, but decided not to turn back; the longer Roc could rest, the better, he reassured himself. But in truth, he feared that if he once turned back now, he would lack the courage to try again.

The bite of the water about his legs was fearful at first, smiting the breath out of him, yet after that it seemed possible to endure; down he clambered, shivering uncontrollably, fearing the touch of the ice below. He had reason; it felt as if his boots touched molten glass, and he almost put his teeth through his lower lip with the effort not to scream. For long seconds he could only cling to the hull timbers, cursing his own folly; he should have let Roc go, Roc would not have felt this nerve-searing, nobody did but he. Why? Was it the smithcraft afire within him? Yet the Mastersmith had trodden the Ice freely; perhaps, like other votaries of the Ice, that dark creature had welcomed the pain, treated it almost as a mark of honour, a special summons, or a call . What the Mastersmith Mylio had endured, then, so could the Mastersmith Elof Valantor. Hammering away at his will as he might at toughened steel, he set his back to the hull, took up the slack on the line, and took a stiff, staggering step forward. He had moved not a moment too soon; already his legs were deadened, tingling masses, hard to control. He would have fallen on that glassy slickness, if he had not been able to dig in the heavy metal spikes he carried for support. But after only a few strides he was already rising into the shallows, and scouting about him for a suitably flat spot. Choosing one with no rough edges to chew and fray rope, he plucked the great hammer from his belt, tapped a spike to seat it and then drove it down deep with a few tremendous blows; the other he drove in a few paces further on, wound the line around the two stanchions and straightened up with a sigh. The wind was rising once again, rolling down over the cliffs above, and he peered up at them uneasily. Who could tell what he might have awakened now? But with so sound a leverage point he could almost launch the *Seafire* by himself, in minutes ...

He squinted suddenly, pulled off a glove to rub his tired eyes; was he starting at shadows in this dismal half-light? He was sure he was not; something had moved atop the slope there, at the notch which led between the lowest cliffs. He cursed, turned to get back to the ship, then stopped, hesitated; he was afraid, afraid of what might rush down upon him while he was off his guard in that water, and the pain in his limbs was

almost an exquisite thing now, fair and clean as a flame.
His head whirled with it; he must see, he must know ...
With a savage growl he drew the dark sword Gorthawer,
and with his hammer in his other hand he stumbled up
the short slope. Once or twice he glanced around to see
that the cutter was all right; but not often. The slope
demanded all his attention, and once or twice he had to
fall on all fours and crawl; the agony in his hands almost
made him laugh aloud. At last, as he reached the crest of
the pass, some shred of his wits he won back, and with
a flash of fear and anger he understood; he had been
drawn here, he had been summoned. Cautiously, fighting down the piercing ache, he shuffled over into the
shadow of a riven pillar of ice, stood up and looked out
to the openness beyond.

He had seen the Ice before; but at its landward
margins only. He had marvelled at its bitter beauty,
bright as a hoard of jewels and as perilous; but this was
a new aspect. He saw a flat plain that seemed to reach
out to an infinite horizon, broken by nothing save a few
low hills, grey against the twilit sky as if they had been
painted on it with shadows. Nothing moved on that
plain but low wind – rows of powder snow, too cold
even to lie and compact with the rest, rustling in the
wind as if to mock the soft sigh of growing things. Here
nothing grew, not the humblest mould or lichen; no
feature was different from another. Hill, plain, snow
were all one single, uniform thing, forms without meaning, movement without life. The flakes that danced
before his eyes were swelling, thickening, but the one
that melted to nothing upon his palm had as much
meaning, as much identity, as the whole vast expanse
before him, for they were made of the self-same thing,
no more, no less. As free water it had been forever in
motion, flowing, evaporating and condensing; it had
been a vital link in the great chain that was life and it
had had a beauty of its own. Yet what was it as ice? Frozen
into a single shape, a fair shape indeed, but incapable of
adding to or enriching that beauty. A snowflake was the
opposite of a seed, of a thought; it could spawn nothing,
it *was* merely an end in itself. It might endure till the

end of all years, and then still be no greater, no less, than it now was. Standing in the failing light upon that lonely ridge, he knew that he had looked into the deepest heart of the Ice, void of the glamour it might lay upon itself; and that he had found there only the ultimate sterility. It was not reverence that lowered his eyes before it. He thought back to the Halls of Summer, and the undying ones that Tapiau sheltered. Exactly as they were, the Ice was immortal – and useless. What could it be that bred in so many Powers this need to hinder the passing years? A dread, perhaps, of themselves, of their own inability to cope with any new order?

Then he looked up swiftly, for it was as if a curtain was flung over his eyes. A rush of snowflakes blotted the last light from the sky, and he was lost in featureless greyness. He ducked down a moment in breathless panic, and it was as well he did; across the slope of the ridge he saw a shape move, and it was like the shadow of a man in a dark robe, with a high hood drawn low across the face. But this shadow was immense, and it drifted, as on some wind milder than the blast which blew. Past him it glided, higher than the mast of his ship, the peaked cowl nodding with a slow regularity that seemed anything but benign; he had seen gelatinous things drift thus in clear waters, pulsing things that could sting and envelop. He shrank away, quaking, lest it chance upon him as it swept by.

Across the ridge it advanced, nodding slowly, and near his side it appeared to stop and turn, as if casting about in the growing blizzard. He grew deadly afraid that it might start down the slope, and clutched at his swordhilt, though unsure what effect it could have. He had seen something like this once before upon the Great Ice, and in evil company; but whether it was material enough for any blade to bite on …

The wind howled impatiently; the shadow floated on behind the swirling snow, and vanished behind the arm of the pass. Elof waited only long enough to be sure it had really gone before hurling himself down that steep ice-slope, not stopping to climb but skidding so fast he had visions of overshooting the ship and sliding into the sea. But his furs snagged and tore and slowed him, and he arrived at the shore on unsteady feet, caught up the line he had wound around the stanchions and plunged unhesitating into the water, drawing Gorthawer to support himself. Up the hull he clambered, and so great was the release when his feet left the Ice that he almost fell back in. Roc, roused by the booming of his climb, came staggering up on deck to help him in.

"'Mazing what a little rest'll do for a weary man ..." he began, but Elof cut him short.

"Take this a turn around the stern capstan, Roc, and back here quick! We've got to get off – they're coming!"

"Are they, by Hella!" exploded Roc, and rolled off along the deck. Elof hung gasping for the minute it took him to return, and together they looped the line around the winch.

"Now!" snarled Elof, and began to crank the winch. It wound freely a moment, taking up the slack, and then it stopped dead as it encountered the weight of the hull; Roc threw his weight upon it, the winch creaked, and they felt the hull quiver and shift a little under them.

"Shall I ... get overside ... and shove?" wheezed Roc, the veins starting out under his thick fringe. The hull lurched upright, the line slackened a moment and hummed taut.

"No ... not much use ... a good-sized boat!" gasped Elof, feeling as Roc had that his arms would not obey. "Just keep ..."

There was a sudden grating rasp beneath them, too like the sound they had made grounding in the first place; the boat heaved and they hauled harder before they realised it was sliding of its own accord. Next moment they were hurled to the deck as it bucked and bounced under them. "Sail –" gurgled Elof, clutching at his side where his sword-hilt had bruised a rib, and together they crawled forward to raise the headsail they had rigged ready. The blast of the blizzard shook it and filled it, and swung them violently around; jubilantly Elof seized the tiller and let the sail out further and further till it goose-winged out. The *Seafire* sprang forward, frisky as a tired horse let loose among fresh green meadows, and went skipping across the troubled waters as if it had never been aground, running brisk and easy before the wind off the Ice. The water slapped resoundingly at the hull, but there was no ominous sound of filling, and the little craft rode level and true.

"We're away!" said Roc, as if he hardly believed it, and then, exulting, "Kerys' Gate, we *are* away!"

"Not yet," said Elof absently, for he had to concentrate on controlling the cutter. "We've yet to see if we can raise the mainsail. Then we've got a good three leagues of pack-ice to get through – and in the dark ..." Roc caught his arm, and pointed so vehemently astern he had to risk a look. The high cliffs were walls of shadow now, as darkly cold beneath the rising moon as they were pale and chill by day. But above their summits the Iceglow burned, and shooting through it in bands of furious colour blazed the North-Lights, a banner and a challenge. Fiercest they burned above the promontory the cutter had escaped from, and by their eerie glow Elof and Roc saw something move. Yet this was nothing above the Ice, such as Elof had encountered, nor even on it; something was within it, as bruise beneath raw skin; a patch of shadow, a pool of dark liquid that flowed beneath the glinting surface of the Ice, freely and swiftly. Down the slope that Elof had climbed it poured, and out across the promontory, one long portion stretched out in front of it like an arm. Suddenly the shore lit up with an appalling flash of green light, and they saw green flames leap like lightning between the steel stanchions Elof had left, saw the strong metal sag and melt like candles of tallow, and metal run in spitting rivulets across the ice. It cracked explosively, and again, filling the air with bright shards, and suddenly the crack was racing across the whole promontory, wider and wider, till with a rumbling roar the whole mass of it split free and dropped like an avalanche into the sea.

"No more, if you please!" said Roc hastily. "We're leaving, believe you me, we're leaving!"

And indeed, though perils enough yet lay in their path, from those blazing crags no further assault came. In the first clear stretch of channel they uncovered their lantern and hoisted the mainsail, mending its battered tackle as best they could and holding their breath while the remounted mast took the strain of the snow-laden wind. But it held firm as ever, save for some stretching of the stays which they foresaw and dealt with. Thus, as the long night wore to its close, they were scudding back along the channels as easily as they had come. Elof steered with nervous precision, but he could not avoid every encounter, and they winced at each judder in the bows, each rasp and scrape along the cutter's flank. Every hour or so one or the other would check the hull, but, though it creaked and groaned more loudly than before, the *Seafire* was shipping only a little more water than was usual through the working seams. To right and left of them the tall ice-islands glided, but, being blown southward by the same wind, they were more easily avoided or out-paced. As the stars faded and pale light crept up along the ocean's rim they cast about anxiously for any trace of black sails; but there were none.

"You took us a good way further east, as well as north," said Roc thoughtfully. "I guess we've passed a cordon, and left any other searchers behind."

"As I hoped," said Elof quietly, keeping a wary eye on the thinning ice round about. "But what was that cordon guarding, I wonder? And how far have we yet to sail – if we can?"

Roc made no reply to that; for though the little cutter bestrode the waves as lightly as ever, they were both aware they could no longer rely on it as they had. Sound it might seem, yet it had been most terribly stressed, and probably damaged in a dozen ways they could not hope to detect – not, at any rate, until the contant warring of wind and water around every sailing boat had worked upon the weaknesses, and made them serious. And then there would be little or nothing that could be done afloat; only on a boatyard slip, or at worst a favourable beach, was there a chance of repair. The two travellers sailed forth from the clutches of the

Ice, yet they were not free. It had laid a sentence upon them more implacable than any edict of a human king; find land within a certain span, or find their last long rest beneath the Seas of the Sunrise. And what that span was they were not told.

That day and night the snow pursued them, and, fearing it would grow to a storm, they set their course southeastward in all haste. Those were hard hours, for the seas waxed high and rough, the wind gusty and fierce, and the little cutter juddered alarmingly in that double embrace. Wild flurries of snow came lashing across the deck, coating the rigging, caking in every cranny, rushing across their faces till they could scarcely breathe, let alone see. They could feel and hear the working of the hull timbers, and it was no cause for comfort; yet for all her wounds the *Seafire* rode out the weather gallantly. As the sun arose the snow faded, as if in disgust, and they fell to baling and caulking anew.

Yet there were distractions enough from their concerns, in the days following. As they quitted the marches of the Great Ice life seemed to return to the sea, and they no lnger felt quite so isolated from the world of warm blood. Seabirds were still rare, yet from time to time fine-winged shapes could be seen against the clouds, gliding high beyond the reach of any. Seals of all kinds were common, bobbing up in the seas or sunning themselves on wide floes; by night their cries could be heard for many long sea miles, eerie and yet strangely melodious, and with a yearning quality that spoke deeply to Elof. Once or twice, too, they saw the huge white bears that hunted them, padding across the floes with their low heads swinging, or actually swimming between them; they seemed too much creatures of the land to be able to survive in that appalling cold. Strangest sight of all, though, was a group of creatures that Elof at first took for some kind of large porpoise, from their grey backs and speed of swimming. But as they cut across the *Seafire*'s bow he saw that those backs were dappled, that the tall flukes were rounded to the shape of a fan, and, more strange than any, that they had a single long spear of a horn set slightly to one side of their heads which rose and fell at a vicious angle as they swam. Elof and Roc found it only too easy to imagine one crashing through the *Seafire*'s distressed timbers, with many tons weight of whale behind it; curious as they were, they kept a respectful distance, and never saw the beasts again.

High winds still blew, constantly, but they scoured the skies clear; Elof and Roc looked eagerly astern as each night fell, for they hoped to see the Ice-glow fading from the sky. So it did, astern; yet it seemed to linger curiously in the eastward sky off their port flank, glinting on the grey clouds that rolled imperiously by, till Elof, alone and gloomy on night-watch, wondered despairingly if it were not somehow reaching out to bar their path. He knew the idea was idiotic; it could not move so far, so fast, and would have crushed them directly if it could. Yet there it was, reaching out like the pallid tentacle of some seabeast ... Something flickered by him, a thought almost too swift to grasp ...

He had it. Always, always the Ice strove furiously to reach as far south as it could, so those cliffs he had trodden must have been the limit of the glaciers' reach, out here at sea. In which case, what were they seeing to port? There were still ice-islands about; could a great mass of them make such a glow? Surely not; so if the Ice there reached further than it could at sea. ...

"Then by Hel, it's not at sea!" said Roc forcefully, when he came on deck near dawn. "There's land over there!"

"Land under the Ice," Elof reminded him dryly. "It may still be far away; the Ice might curve in towards it, as it does north of Morvanhal, only further. The tales say that east of the oceans it *did* reach further south; that was why Kerys the Great was founded, when the Ice drove out the ancient kingdoms of men in the old North, forgotten now in the deeps of time. And then its advance on Kerys drove folk from there to settle in Brasayhal, to found Morvan there, and our own homelands.' He frowned, feeling suddenly slight before that creeping, inexorable advance. "Roc, that was some four or five thousand years past. Who knows how far it's come now? There may be no land there at all ... "

"There's something!" shouted Roc, springing up and squinting into the growing light eastward. "See there! Breakers! A shoal! It's land, right enough!"

"It couldn't be so close!" objected Elof, puzzled, and he clambered up onto the unsteady rail beside Roc. But he could not deny what he saw. All over the wide seas eastward spread a great turbulence, white water and spray spurting like breakers over some rough coast of black rocks, and behind it a low line of shadow that might indeed be distant hills. Then they both saw at the same time that the shoal was moving, that the apparent rocks were shining serpentine backs, glossy and wrinkled, rearing and plunging with the strength of living waves; the spray was the jetting vapours of their breath, blasted from cavernous lungs. They had seen whales before, but never so many and so large all together. Like breakers indeed churned the bow waves around their blunt-walled heads, and the foam about their flukes. Elof eyed them suspiciously, but when he saw that they would pass well south of the cutter he grew thoughtful. "One piece of good tidings they may bring us, Roc; I've heard that the great whales never herd so in cold waters. We may be coming to warmer climes at last."

"Not before time, then!" Roc grunted, and waved a hand at the hatchway. He had no need to say more; they could both hear the heavy slopping of water below, and yet they had baled it out with great labour only the evening before. "And all their news may not be so good; if those aren't hills behind them, they're clouds. And filthy black ones, too ..." Elof glanced at him, and read in his lined brow the same fear; it was early summer now. A time when, along the coasts of their own country, where the cold air off the Ice met the warm winds from southern lands, fierce storms were common.

Elof stood silent awhile, but at last he shrugged. "Well, what can we do but endure it? We'll have to turn in towards the land, storm or no storm – Ice or no Ice." As if to punctuate his words the sea beneath the clouds glittered grey a moment, and a full minute later a rumbling rolled across the waves, like a cascade of stones. Elof breathed deeply; he could almost smell the lightning on the racing breeze. "Come, we'd better go batten down all, reef the sails. And gather some gear together." Such things as they might need on shore, such things as they might risk drowning to save; but that he left unsaid. The slow complaint of the timbers was eloquent enough.

The storm advanced like a dark mantle drawn up the sky. "You see?" Roc pointed out. "Smith's clouds, right enough ..." Elof smiled wryly at the old Nordeney folk-name, only too apt; the high crests of the thunderclouds were flattened and peaked like vast anvils, their bases hidden by the rainclouds that rolled and boiled like sooty forgesmoke. Flashes leaped among the peaks, and he thought of the image of Ilmarinen in the duergar halls, Master of Masters, Smith of the Powers who smote out the very mountains; on such anvils might he work, with such storms for a fire. His hand crept to the precious gauntlet of mail at his belt, the sword slung opposite. Once he had dared to intrude upon that forge, to use some fragment of its strength; sheer presumption, like so much else he had done. Now he must hope to dash through its midst. "Ready about!" he called, and saw Roc wind the winches furiously. They had sailed as far south as they could; to sail across the storm would only lengthen their time within it, increase their chance of being sunk. As well head straight into it, and hope that somewhere beneath it lay the land. Slowly, smoothly he swung the tiller across.

It was as fierce a storm as they had faced in all their time at sea; all around them, closer and closer, the lightning stabbed and flickered through the driving rain. The wind's sharp gusts raised ever greater waves that plucked up the cutter's bows, bursting athwart them in vast wings of spray that were lit molten silver by the levin-bolts. Down their steep slopes it plunged as if to dash its bows into the trough, while the thunder drummed like harsh laughter overhead. But due rather, as Elof suspected, to her fair shaping than his own seamanship, the little ship rode out each trough and climbed each crest anew. Even over the bellow of the storm they could hear her timbers creak and moan, as from the pain of old wounds reopened, now and then cracks like snapping bone. Yet for all those wounds she held firm, even when they were forced at last to strike the sails altogether from the tortured mast, and struggling and slipping with ropes along the storm-lashed deck, toss out an improvised sea anchor to hold the bows into the wind. Then they could do no more than lash themselves at their posts by tiller and rail, and bow their heads to the wind and their destiny.

But that was the worst, after which the storm soon slackened; and as it passed, and the heaving waters turned from black to grey, they found themselves blinking in the light of a cloudy afternoon. "Two or three hours, that was!" gasped Roc indignantly. "That's all!"

Elof sagged down over the tiller. "Seemed like an eternity, didn't it?" Then he pulled himself weakly up. "Roc, we've got to check the hull –"

Roc pushed him back with a grimace. "Sit tight; you had the worst of it at the helm there. I'll check; you gather your strength. Maybe you'll be needing it," he added as he undogged the hatch and disappeared below.

He emerged a short while later, fouled and grim. "You'd better come. I've never seen the seams work so, there's no getting the caulking to hold and we're shipping water faster by the minute ..."

Elof glanced up at the sails, racked the tiller and staggered past Roc and down. All the seams were indeed working loose, the more so the lower down he checked. "It shouldn't be so ... Unless ..." He stooped into the blackened slime at the bow and ran his hands slowly and carefully along the huge timber that was the keel. Some third of the way along he stopped, pressed his fingers down and felt back along. His hands were half numbed by the filthy water; but his blood ran colder yet. "Roc!" he said, when he could "I know why she's working so much; the keel's cracked."

"What?" roared Roc. "Can't be! She'd have broken up at once –"

"Not right through; but with every wave ... The Ice

did it; it did get us, after all ..."

"We can't brace it? Patch it?"

"It's past that! She's filling, faster by the minute. Within the hour, a few minutes maybe –"

"Back on deck!" growled Roc. "This stench softens my brain!"

Elof sighed as he climbed up after him. "As you will, though there's little enough to think on now –"

"That so, hey?" Roc's red thatch was thrust back down the companionway. "Up here with you a minute – now, tell me truly, what d'you think that is?"

Elof scrambled up into the grey light, and peered the way Roc was pointing. Upon the eastern horizon there lay a smoky-hued smudge no different from a hundred other cloudbanks, save that its high crests ... He had to swallow hard ere he could speak.

"It's land," he said softly. "A league and a half, at least, two if those are mountaintops ..."

"Can we make it?" demanded Roc bluntly.

Elof shook his head mutely, choking down the bitterness rising in his throat. "She'd pull apart the moment we hoisted sail. We might make it on a raft or swimming with floats, a spar or a hatchcover –"

"Scant chance of that, with it so freezing and us weary! We'd never last long enough! Hel, but it galls me! To have got this far, and ... There's no other way?" They could feel the little cutter settling under them now with every passing second.

"There is, by the High Gate!" blazed Elof. "Roc, take up your gear, and swiftly!"

For answer, Roc dragged a bundle out from under the thwart, and slung his bow across his back, with a closed quiver of arrows. "And yours?"

"All about me," said Elof, eyes sparkling. The cutter lurched sideways suddenly, and they staggered to the rail. "It's that will serve us – if you think you can hold tight for a half-hour or so?"

"For my life? Like the grip of the Ice its own self! But what to?"

"To me!" cried Elof. "Follow!" And springing up on the port rail he sprang for the sea. Roc shook his head only once before he scrambled after.

They rose together, gasping with the water's chill. "Should've slung my furs – " gurgled Roc.

"No need!" cried Elof, and dashed the salt sea from his eyes. "See, our *Seafire* lists, true friend that she was! We'll need to be out from under, fast, or follow her down!" He was delving in his jacket as he spoke, and drew out with a cry of triumph a thing that glittered in the murky air.

"Hella's claw ..." Roc yelled, but was cut off by the rush of water against the cutter's deck.

"Hold you tight now!" shouted Elof, and drew the metal about his brows.

The cold sting of it seemed to surge through him. He shuddered, and felt the water boil around his massive limbs; dimly a protesting shout reached him, and he remembered to stay still a moment, felt a weight at his side, arms close around the roots of the high fin at his back. Then he kicked out once, and was away. The sea surged behind him, and he was aware of the long mass that slid slowly down into the green depths; but he forgot his brief flicker of grief in the rushing joy of the waters. He had taken this shape for its strength, and because he had worn it briefly once before, hoping that might help him endure it longer. He had not bargained for the gradual change it brought to his perceptions. Sight and scent dimmed, but a strange new awareness filled his mind that had some aspect of hearing about it and some of sight; a world of floating shapes it drew him, swaying and darting, suspended among shimmering swirls and currents, a world of beauties and mysteries he could only guess at. It allured him to dive down, to explore all the marvels half-guessed at in this alien setting, this otherworldly sea; so strong was its call he came dangerously close to forgetting his burden, and in panic he forced the new sense from his mind. Lifting his head above water, he could dimly make out the shore, and that way he drove, acutely aware of how little time he had. Already his thoughts were beginning to blur, to waver with the strain of maintaining the mask; sooner or later it would slip, and be hard to regain. On he swam, the world an unregarded wonder about him save for the weight that dragged at his back, and the explosive outburst of his own breath.

The current came as a shock, a sudden upsurge, warmer than the rest, that lifted him suddenly and dashed him forward the way he was headed. His eyes lifted above the surface, and suddenly they saw only too clearly the high and jagged barrier out-thrust before them. In a sudden flash of panic he thrust out his hands to stave it off – and they were human hands. The mask had dropped, and his heavy clothes were dragging him own. He heard one sharp cry from Roc, felt a hand clutch at the soaked furs on his shoulder and tear free in the swirling water; he reached out blindly, but there was only water – and scouring, scraping stone. The surf threw him against it, dragged him back, threw him again – but this time he caught it, gripped and clung though it scraped the skin from his finger, clung as his legs were dashed against the stone. He let the flow carry him to a foothold, then with one desperate heave he kicked and hauled himself up ere the undertow could pluck him away again, clasped tight to the stone as the next wave roared over him like green glass, and painfully pulled himself to a secure hold.

Only then, gasping with effort and the chill of the water, could he spare a moment to look up. He found that he was crouching on a long spit of jagged black rock, one of many out-thrust into the sea by a coastline that was all rough cliffs, sculptured strangely by the sea that besieged their walls. He scrambled hastily higher, beyond the reach of the waves, and stood up, scanning the sea and the rocks around, ready to dive back in at the slightest glimpse of any form. He could see nothing living save himself and the few gulls that swooped and screeched about the wild air. "Roc!" he yelled, over the drumming of the surf, and again, many times, till his salt-raw throat protested. A gust of cold panic closed over him, and he scrambled back up the rocks, higher and higher, yet from every new point of vantage he saw no more, nor were his calls answered. He looked up desperately at the promontory above; it would be no hard climb, and it would give him a commanding view. As swiftly as the thought he set his weary limbs to the rockface.

There was some snow on the ledges, and he wondered briefly if he would find the Ice beyond the cliff top; but when he thrust over a hand for some hold to draw himself up, his fingers closed upon coarse plants and earth that was relatively soft. He scrambled more confidently over the rim and stood a moment, staring around. It was a bleak landscape that met his eyes, cold and hard, a rounded expanse of rocky, stone-littered slopes and vales clad in sombre shades of brown and purple; but it lived. Its colours were those of tough grasses and flowering scrub, moorland hues not unlike the Starkenfells of his Nordeney home; in the valleys there were clumps of green, and here and there a stand of stunted birches, but all over the slopes there were thick patches of spiky gloss-green, dotted with yellow flowers. A great clump of these bushes rose near him, and he knew they were a kind he had never seen before. It was only then that he fully realised what he had done, that he had crossed the sundering oceans, come to the lands of the ancient east, first among men to do so in well-nigh a thousand years. And he had taken a great step on his quest; yet desperately he wished it undone, so bitterly it stuck in his throat.

This way and that he gazed from the crest of the promontory, out to sea, along the cliffs and the little beaches that nestled below them. He could see clearly and far yet he saw nothing that he wished to, no trace of any human shape. Again and again he called, but his voice alone challenged the gull-cries over the bleak land, the empty sea. At last he slumped down at the cliff-edge and sank his head in his hands. He was beyond the release of mourning, of tears; the void that opened at his feet seemed less than that within him, and his loneliness infinite. Love lost, homeland renounced, friends forsaken; and now he had doomed his oldest friend, failed to save at this one crisis the man to whom he owed his life many times over. His life; what use was it to him? All that he had won with such effort he had tossed away. He sat here on a barren coast, in no better case than if he had never quit his hovel upon the Great Marshes, half a world away and many long years. Worse; for there he had its shelter, at least, the means to live, and a guilt that he could hope to expiate. Here he had – what did he have? Sword, hammer, pack with its precious burdens, all hung at his side – yet something was missing. He lifted his fingers cautiously, and clutched his salt-stiffened hair in tearing handfuls. There was no helm on his head. There had not been, he knew now, since he had climbed from the rocks; nor was it about his neck, for he had fastened it only loosely in his haste. The loss shook him rigid; yet he would have laughed it off to find his friend alive once more. The sky above descended on his shoulders, and it was made of granite harsher than any beneath.

But it was not so very long before he raised his head again. If there were the least thing he could do, he should do it; one folly did not excuse others. He must search for what he had lost. The Tarnhelm had almost come ashore with him; it would be folly to abandon it so easily. It could not have borne him across the oceans because he had never seen this shore and could not hold its image in his thoughts; but now he had. If he could find it, it might serve to bear him back, though the distance involved unnerved him; Bryhon Bryheren had travelled across the Ice with it, but only in short stages, with rest. He could not rest in mid-ocean. Meanwhile, there was a little food in his pack; while that lasted he would search for Roc. The clouds parted a little; the sun, still hidden, shed long beams over the land, touching the hilltops with a sudden glow of warmth, but shining cold upon the green waves and the steely peaks of distant ice-islands. He watched the sea awhile, noting the run and flow of the surf that had borne him ashore, and how it varied and shifted with this wind. Alive, Roc should have come ashore some-where near; dead, he still might. The place most likely was a beach some way down the cliff from the spit he had climbed, wider and less steep than the others he could see, and leading up to a shallow valley, a depression in the cliffs filled with bushes and birch that had grown straighter than was usual here in its shelter. And yet the wind seemed to be stirring them now ...

There was movement in those bushes. Too much to be just one man – and yet among the dark foliage there was a brief but definite flash of red that could easily be the hue of Roc's hair. He leaned forward, eager to shout or wave, yet hesitant. Whatever moved, it would be out in the beach in a moment; then he could see. If it was Roc ...

It was! He sprang up as the square, burly figure emerged from the bushes, cautiously, as if expecting trouble. Elof waved, hailed, and saw him start, look up, and wave back – no ordinary joyful wave, but a scything, flattening gesture, urgent, sinister. *Danger! Come down!* Or did he mean *stay out of sight?* Elof half turned, hesitated –

Caught a glimpse of armour, copper skin, as a great weight ground down on him and forced his face into the earth. With sickening suddenness, as if not a moment had passed, he was back in the last day of his childhood, some twenty-five years ago, taken unawares by the raiders who had ravaged his village. But now though he was weary there was strength in his arms, smith's strength, and as they were wrenched behind him he struggled and snarled and fought. He jerked one arm the way it was being pushed, felt his attacker lose his balance, and thrust out once again. The hard hands tore free, the man was flung back, but there was no sound of him striking the ground, only a rattle of loose earth and stone, a terrified shriek, and a moment later a thudding splash from below. The other attacker hesitated, Elof swung around, seized the fingers that held him and twisted them back; the man let go with a scream and Elof was on top of him with fist swinging. He sprang up as another came running with spear levelled, seized the shaft and snapped it with bruising strength across his knee, then fell on the spearman with the bladed truncheon. But as he raised it for the killing stroke another blade passed across his throat, one more

pricked his neck below the ear, and a narrower blade
jabbed him painfully over the kidneys. He let fall the
truncheon, and rose very slowly to his feet. The faces of
the men running up, hard and brown and scarred not
only by wounds but by ritual cicatrices, were all too
familiar in their cast; with bow, spear and sword a ring
of Ekwesh warriors hemmed him in.

Ekwesh! Till then, confused in time, it had seemed
only natural that he was fighting his lifelong foes – but
now the implications pierced him like a catapult bolt.
For a crazed moment he wondered if he might not have
somehow sailed on around the world to the Ekwesh
homeland; it was said to be a bleak place like this. But
he knew better than that. What then were they doing
here? His blood still boiled; he had half a mind to try
and break through their ranks and run for it. He might
make it. But then they would comb the area, and might
capture Roc. Better to wait, bide his time ...

A broad man in a fur-trimmed cloak strode forward,
cheeks hatched between cheekbone and jaw with a chieftain's scars in the shape of wings, and gestured at his
pack and sword-belt; Elof did nothing. Two warriors
dropped their weapons, seized him and tore the pack
from his shoulder. Elof thought of the hammer at his
side; if he could keep it from their sight ... One warrior
tugged at the buckle of his sword-belt, and Elof made a
furious lunge for the hilt, struggling with the men who
held him; it availed him little, but it was not meant to.
The scuffle lasted only a minute, and ended with Elof on
the ground being kicked with ironshod boots, but the
hammer was tucked safe among his furs. The chieftain
gestured him up, and Elof lurched to his feet more
unsteadily than he needed to; let them be off their
guard only a moment ... The chieftain caught his arms
and spread them wide, then ran long fingers through his
jacket and gave a grunt of satisfaction; he plucked out
the hammer and hefted it before Elof's face. "You are
soldier?" he demanded, in some barely comprehensible
form of the sothran tongue.

"No!" spat Elof, then reined in his temper, remembering the exaggerated prestige this reiver people

attached to warriors, and their contemptuous treatment of any who were not as fair game. "That is – I am, when I have to be. But by choice I am a smith." The chieftain's face was blank. "A – a shaper, a *shaman* of metals ..." It was the Ekwesh word he used, and the chieftain drew back as if he had trodden near a copperhead. He spat on the ground and gestured to the others, and they searched Elof from top to toe; he ground his teeth as the chieftain fingered through his precious pack, knowing what danger lay in the jewels he bore. The chieftain plucked out the anklets and the half arm-ring, admired them a moment and to Elof's astonishment replaced them, handing him the pack.

"You carry this, for now," he said. "Answer with your head!" He spoke with an atrocious, guttural accent, but better than other Ekwesh Elof had heard; also, he used terms that had a strangely literary or archaic ring to Elof, and others he could only guess at. "So! You speak for self now, then before *Iltasya.*"

Elof knew some words of the Ekwesh common tongue, but that one he had never heard. "My ship sank out there," he said, pointing out among the floating ice. "I barely made it to shore."

"We see the sail sinking," said the chieftain. "Guards search the shore. You come from West-over-sea, from Br–Bras'eal?" He mangled the name. "Alone?"

Elof was thinking rapidly; of the two Ekwesh who had first crept out upon him, one was dead, one still unconcious. The others could not have seen Roc; two were looking down the cliff, but that was evidently for signs of the man who had fallen. "My crew was drowned, I think. I called in case they had come ashore, but ..." He shook his head resignedly. "It was a long swim ..."

It would have been, for a man. The chieftain eyed him a moment. "Other guards will find them, if living; we go!" He turned to his men and clapped his hands. "*Ouakia'ma!*" With no more than the one command the patrol formed ranks around Elof, two of them carrying their unconscious comrade, and strode off down the promontory, winding in and out of the thorny bushes that had concealed them. They glanced about them as they went, stabbed a spear at likely-looking concealment, but made no serious attempt to search. Elof wondered about the "other guards"; at least they were not here yet. Roc would have time to take cover. But who were those others with him, that he had not seen? It seemed that even if the Ekwesh were masters of this dour land, they might not be unchallenged. And Roc was free; there might not be much he could do unaided against eleven armed men, but with aid ... That was something; definitely something.

All the rest of that afternoon they marched, more or less southward, along an unchanging coastline within sight of the ice-strewn sea, and into the long summer evening that followed until no slightest trace of light remained to show their way. They halted then, and Elof, muscles weakened and gait unsteady after long weeks in the little cutter, fell groaning to the ground, clutching cramping muscles in calf and foot, but glad he had held out till the end; though it would have been little use his asking these grim folk for any rest. And yet he had already noticed many things unusual about them. For one, their armour of stiffened black leather was much thicker and heavier than the usual Ekwesh pattern, and the chieftain wore a short shirt of scale-mail beneath his cloak; the clan emblem on their gear was reduced to a stylized image sketched in with a few flowing lines, and they wore fewer jangling ornaments of metal, precious or otherwise. Only the chief had gold rings in his long ears, and bronze and gold tips to the braids of his coarse black hair. He himself was unusual, like none of their chieftains Elof had met before now, neither a malevolent old man nor a steely young fanatic. This was a heavy man of late middle years, stone-calm, granite-hard and grim of aspect; yet neither he nor his men indulged themselves in the casual brutality of most Ekwesh towards their captives. They neither beat nor bound Elof as they marched, and that itself was unusual; yet in some ways it made them more alarming. Their eyes were never far from him, and he guessed that if he had shown any tendency to slacken or sought to escape, he would have suffered both; but not necessarily as retribution, more as a cooly considered means to an end.

They built a great fire of brushwood that night, too great for anyone with anything much to hide or fear, and cooked over griddles among the ashes. Elof, seated in the smoky lee between two brawny spearmen, was wondering how long the food in his pack would last, when one of them passed him a deep wooden bowl of some boiled grain, a slice of bread and a chunk of smoked meat. Elof took the bowl and bread hungrily, but when he refused the meat it was thrust at him. "Eat!" barked the soldier, in an accent worse than the chieftain's. "Is long road, at first sun!"

"Be damned if I will!" exploded Elof, forgetting all restraint in his loathing. "What carrion is it, flesh of some helpless thrall –"

The blow spun him round and stretched him flat on his back, blood trickling from his mouth across his burning cheek. "That word you swallow, or I strike it in your teeth, shaman of filth!" It was the chieftain who stood over him, almost slavering with rage; he had evidently sprung straight across the fire. "We are the Proud Ones! We eat no man's-meat, us!"

Elof heaved himself up on one elbow and glared at him. He should not have been so rash; but having spoken, to show any weakening now might be dangerous. "So?" he said, as sarcastically as his swelling lips would allow. "What do your shamans have to say about that, proud one? And the Hidden Clan?"

As he expected, that rocked the chieftain back on his heels; the spearmen sprang up and back, weapons ready. "What might you know of *Tlasuka*, shaman of West-over-sea?" He spoke very softly, fingers flexing near the short sword at his belt. "You are of their pale masters, maybe?"

Elof fought to keep up his arrogant front. "I am not; I have met them, though, men and non-men. And though they claim the Ice runs in their veins and their guts, I know that for a lie. I have spilled enough of both!"

He was appalled at the howl his words raised, till

he realised it was laughter. Even the chief was staggering around clutching his sides. Evidently, he reflected a
little queasily, he had achieved some degree of Ekwesh
wit. "How many?" gasped the chief, when he could
speak properly. "Five score?" More laughter, and Elof
understood; wit for them lay in outrageous boasting, the
more outrageous the better.

"Five score and one!" he snapped, straightfaced, to
new howls. "But that One I only pinked in the shoulder,
and she fled me!"

Silence chopped down like a blade. He had said
something too much. But his blood was up, and he
would not now back down. "If it's proof you're after,
then do you only give me back my sword!"

Abruptly the chief straightened up, wiping his eyes
irritably. "Oh no, word-shaman," he said. "You are
captive, you stay. Not free to chase *hala'yu*!" That word
Elof understood only too well; it meant 'deathbringer',
and also 'fame' or 'honour'. "But know this of us; no Ice
runs in our veins! Ancestor-laws, ancestor-duties we
hold still, from days when clan first made compact with
clan, to conquer …"

"And those duties, do they include playing thrall to
the Ice?" blazed Elof.

The chief would not be baited into losing his
temper and his face a second time. He met Elof's gaze
with contemptuous stolidity. "No bonds bind us, save
sworn word and honour. Our chiefs are no thralls to
shamans! And we take no flesh of men, that is forbidden! We are the Proud Ones, the Kok'uen, the Raven
Clan —"

"*Raven?*" Elof stared at the chieftain, unable to
credit what he heard, or its import. Surely it meant
nothing; all the Ekwesh clans were named for the totem
animals familiar to the peaceful hunter-gatherers they
had once been. Yet long ago, when Kermorvan had first
told him who Raven truly was, he had added that many
among the Ekwesh also revered him. In which case … "I
too have heeded a raven's cry," he said softly. "He is the
banner and sign of my land. Can it be the same?"

Heads turned in surprise, but the chieftain only

grunted. "That Raven is totem to some among you, I had heard. Let us see who he favours!"

Elof smiled quietly. "He has favoured me."

As he expected, those words from a prisoner provoked a great wave of savage scornful laughter; he let it subside, and when he spoke again even he was startled by the ringing pride in his words. "He has favoured me, I say, my land and my king! To my poor door in such a wasteland as this he came, ere I knew who he was, a tall rider in black mail upon a mighty warhorse – " One or two warriors interrupted with crows of disbelief, but their voices faltered when they found themselves alone, and faded to silence when Elof's gaze fell on them. The chieftain and the others listened in silence, unstirring save for the firelight that leaped in their eyes. "He gave me aid I did not know I needed, aid that … that helped me to undo a great evil, that in the end raised me from the least of smiths to among the great of my land. More than once he has come, sometimes in other guise, always with aid and counsel …"

"What guise?" The chieftain's voice was soft, but his demand cracked like a whip.

"An old man, bearded and mantled, leaning on a staff … an old wanderer …" Elof sighed, and a black gloom overwhelmed him, reaction to his moment of pride. "But last in his warrior guise. Wiser I had heeded him then, and never come here …"

"Wiser!" agreed the chieftain sombrely, and gazed at him a while before he said more. "Shaman, you burn from within, and the flame is clear. I do not think you lie. We too know Raven in these shapes, warrior and wise shaman, though no man living sees him so. We follow his path, straight path of the warrior, no matter the price – though lies whispered, though trust denied. Though they set us to rot on land, to guard outlands bare of blood or fame or booty, though they trust us with no honourable station at sea, yet we Proud Ones serve as sworn to by our ancestors." The chieftain's face was an implacable copper mask, his voice pitiless as winter wind. "From word and duty we do not turn. *To Iltasya take all strangers* is said, to *Iltasya* you must go.

Does Raven come to you now? I think not." He rose and returned to his chieftain's place on the more comfortable side of the fire. "Eat and sleep; you tread a long road, come dawn."

It proved so indeed. The Ekwesh treated their captive with greater regard, and even something like awe, but they drove him as hard as ever through all the daylight hours. It was a lonely road, too, for few had language or inclination to talk to him, and what he understood of their speech told chiefly of strife and bloodshed. Only the chieftain came to quiz him now and again, on why he had come, and what he sought; most often Elof also said nothing, or adamantly changed the subject, because he knew the Ekwesh took a direct rebuttal or denial as an insult, and to insult rather than challenge these fierce folk could be a deadly error. A straight path they might walk, but they were a warrior race nonetheless; their orders to bring in soldiers alive would not stop them shedding his blood in some less than fatal fashion. He took his cue from the chieftain, matching his studied calm and his frank speech, and found it well received. It could not be said that any liking arose between them, so alien were they to each other, but a degree of understanding came, the more so as they sought to practise each other's tongue. Each spoke more freely to the other than they might to any who shared their concerns. The chieftain was a bitter man in his way, on behalf of his folk as well as himself; for generations now they had striven to serve both the expanding realms of the Ekwesh, and their own notions of what was upright and fitting, and inevitably they had suffered for it. Their code was fierce and pitiless, but it had within it some concept of order greater than continual and bloody conquest, of duty to weaker peoples greater than mere enslavement and exploitation, of holding and building on gains. Such an attitude had made them influential in the uniting of the scattered, quarrelsome tribes and the rise of something like a coherent realm. But beyond that realm it also made them poor agents of the Ice, whose interest lay in bringing havoc and disorder, in scorning the very name of

Raven and teaching its initiates likewise. As its influence had grown among the Ekwesh, so the prestige of the Raven Clan had fallen, their more purposeful ferocity branding them cowards, their careful consolidation of conquests earning them the name of fainthearts and laggards. Elof understood now that his bid to overawe this little group, though it had won him better treatment, had had no real chance of success. The Ravens were determined to reinstate themselves with a show of zeal and loyalty, and he was a prime opportunity. Even had they wanted to let him go, they would not have dared.

When that gruelling day's march came to an end, Elof again fell down in agony. He guessed, as he lay curled on the ground, that they had covered some ten leagues of rough going, over hill and heathland roadless save for the occasional beast-track. Only once, in a marshy place, had he thought he detected a fragment of an ancient roadbed buried far beneath the mud. But on the next day's march, begun as early and as swiftly, he began to see the small heaps and circles of rough-hewn stone that he knew were the remains of simple buildings, cot and sheepfold perhaps; beneath the grass and heather underfoot he heard the rasp of laid stones. Once this had been inhabited land. And ere long he came upon clearer remains, many of those ruins with the weathered walls and gable-ends bare of any roof that Nordeney folk had come to call 'Ekwesh footprints,' the marks they left upon a countryside. Yet these looked ancient, far older than the Ekwesh incursions into Nordeney. How long had they held this land? Or who had held it before them? And how, how could they have reached it?

Elof restrained his impatience. The chieftain might be persuaded to tell him something, but he was some distance away, striding ahead of the others as if he too were impatient; it would have to wait till they halted at nightfall. But there was no halt; for as the sun sank down towards the clouds in the distant west, setting the ice-islands aglitter on the sea, the chief, reaching the top of a low slope, cried out triumphantly to his men. Elof

understood, and he felt a host of new fears; they had
reached their destination, with all that it held for him.
What new menace must he face? Yet such was the
majesty of the sight awaiting him that it drove all lesser
concerns from his mind.

At first he hardly took it in. He saw only a wide bay
of the sea, awash with floating ice, and behind it an
encircling arm of three smallish mountains, low and
craggy, joined by a thin-topped ridge; its stark flanks
sloped precipitously down to a strip of flat brown land
at the water's edge. Then a long ray of the low sun
escaped the clouds and rested a moment upon the
lower central peak, tinging it with warm fire, and Elof
saw that it was no work of nature. A high castle
crowned the ridge, and he thought it the mightiest
work that he had ever seen.

In that he was right; for no mightier then existed in
the world, save only the citadels of the Ice itself. This
was its fashion, as it became gradually clear to Elof
while he and his captors traversed the remaining half-
league from the hills. From the base of the ridge two
vast square towers of the same sand-hued stone arose;
their flat-roofed capitals reached three-fourths of the
way to its crest. Between them was a wide wall, bridged
at its top by a great gallery between the towers, lined
with many columns, graceful and fluted; below this
opened many lesser galleries, but the lower half of the
wall was featureless save for a single arch at its centre.
Vast this must have been, taller at its keystone than the
masts of great ships, but against that height of wall it
seemed small, no more than a gate. And seen above the
height of that first immense wall reared another, after
the same pattern, a gallery between two towers; but this
was lower and narrower, and the overhanging pedi-
ments of the towers were level with the ridge. At each
corner stood a statue, and between the statues a tracer-
ied rail of carven stone. But above these vastnesses
loomed a third level still, round like the base of an
unseen column that upheld the sky, like a crown fit for
the brows of Powers in their majesty. A high palace it
was, in itself greater than the citadel of Kerbryhaine or

the palace of Morvanhal that was his home. Windows
and galleries latticed its walls, statues encircled its roof;
its every line spoke nobility and power – chiefly power.
This was a place made to daunt, and daunt it did. With
the sun's fire upon its walls it seemed rich and noble, fit
for the court of the living Powers; but the sun was slipping behind the clouds, and as Elof was shepherded ever
nearer the air turned murky and cold, and the fire fled.
A low mountain it seemed once more as the shadow
wrapped itself around, and few lights showed upon
those towering walls. It was at the foot of the ridge that
lights shone out, the bleak land flickering under the
flares of a myriad torches, warmed with the kindling of
numberless fires, as if beneath the castle a sprawling
town had sprung up, almost a city by its extent, huddled
at its feet like hound to master. It was towards this lake
of lights that Elof's captors led him.

   The sound of harsh voices reached him from afar,
of flutes and drumming, and he guessed that this must
be some huge encampment of the Ekwesh. It proved to
be that and more, however, for instead of tent and shelter there were many boat-shaped longhouses of rough
tarry planking set within sturdy compound fences, above
whose gates hung sign and symbol of the clans. Curiosity overcame fear in him, for he had never before seen a
full Ekwesh community; also a sense of regret and anger,
for the houses with their flanks of pattern-painted clap-
board were very like those of his own village, that the
Ekwesh themselves had devastated. It was their own
cousins, their own flesh they had been induced to scorn
and betray. And the gap between even modest civilization and savagery was all too apparent. Livestock
wandered free and untended between the houses, and
there seemed to be little or no attempt at drainage; they
walked on boards among filth, and the stench of the
place was terrible. Life in all its aspects seemed to be
carried on in the open air, amid howl, hubbub, and the
beat of drums from the open spaces between the
compounds; as they passed one of these Elof saw a
shaman dancing some rite with warriors. He was an
eerie figure, clad only in a long skirt of leather strips,

his scrawny body painted in many colours with the emblem of the Mosquito clan, and his white hair flying as he whirled about among the warriors, hurling a much shorter figure from one to another. It was a girl, wearing only some rags about her thighs; ochre plastered her cropped hair flat, but her skin gleamed a much lighter brown than the rest. That would make her half-bred, and therefore by definition a thrall here; he wondered what her fate would be, and then remembered with a sudden jolt that in even more immediate question was his own.

They wound a way through the outskirts of the encampment, down ways of mire and slime, often having to leap aside to avoid horsemen who came cantering through, and once a column of thralls being driven like ponies, at the run. The compound they finally entered was broad, but few fires burned there; the door before which the chieftain paused and called was wide, but the light within dim and smoky. Swift words were exchanged, and Elof was thrust forward into the gloom. His smarting eyes could barely pick out a double row of figures seated around a trench of fire, many white-haired and bent. Words flew again, and a burst of harsh laughter. Then he was seized by the arms and bundled outside once again, with the chieftain by his side, his face a grimace of satisfaction. "So!" he said, savouring the words. "A great prize you are, and one awaited! You bring us fortune, West-shaman! Come, we go to *Ilta-sya!*" He pointed up into the darkness where the heights of the castle were hidden.

They passed out of the Ekwesh town then, and up the slopes of the ridge to the side of the nearer tower. It was an easy enough climb, for there were steps sunk in the stone, ancient and dished with weather and wear, but well-formed and serviceable. The air blew strangely chill from below. Looking down, Elof saw beyond the town a harbour of many ships, large and small, behind a strong sea wall; and that was needed, for the whole bay was speckled with ice-islands in various stages of decay, as if some freak of the currents drew them in here in their last melting. He shivered, and was glad when they passed through a narrow wicket into the blackness of the tower. Torches blossomed, flickering in the air flow, and their light fell upon a narrow flight of stone steps, steep and cramped between high walls. Elof swallowed, remembering how tall that tower had seemed from without, but hard hands at his back thrust him forward. In single file they climbed into an echoing vault of shadow, lit blue-gray only by faint spills of moonlight through the narrow windowslits; the right-hand wall dropped away into emptiness. They were mounting the inner wall of the tower, by stairs that ringed its hollow heart.

As his eyes grew accustomed to the dimness he saw that it was not wholly empty, that heart; a curious engine of cables and pulleys hung there, extending both above and below in the tall well. It seemed to him like some enormous lifting hoist, able to raise great weight of goods or men; that this place should have such a thing made sense, and it looked in reasonable repair. But in that case why did the Ekwesh not use it? However hardy they were, in time alone it offered advantages over this endless climb, this overpowering darkness. Because they couldn't? It was more than likely; this place was nothing of theirs. Here all voices were hushed in awe; the least word spoken went fluttering away into the cavernous dark above, and after a while no man spoke, but concentrated on the exhausting climb. The only sounds were those of rasping breath echoing around the enclosing walls, and the monotonous thud of heavy sandalled feet upon the steps. It seemed to merge, that constant rhythm, with the leaden passing of the hours, until he forgot that he was walking, that the distant ache was his weary limbs. Space and time were one, and he was floating upwards, ascending out of the past that lay below into the future above, and all was as shadows, dim and indistinct in that strange undersea light. Somewhere above many deep bells were tolling.

Suddenly it was as if the world had turned on its side, the great space above opening out instead before him. Dreamily he looked up, and saw revealed through the blue dimness vaulting so high and wide-swept it might have been the very roof of the sky. Gradually, as his exhausted trance faded, he realised he was climbing no longer, that he was stumbling along the smooth and level floor of a majestic hallway towards a high-arched door where points of fire burned, gleaming red on the metal of armed sentinels. Weapons were levelled, a harsh challenge raised the echoes, was answered as harshly; he caught no more than the name *Iltasya* once again. Other sentinels appeared from within the gate, and herded in the Raven clansmen much as they herded him, into an even darker corridor behind; the roof was hidden, but from the echoes it sounded less high. A screech and a crash made him start; an upheld torch shone fire upon a heavy door, thrown back to reveal a small chamber, its walls of dusty stone, windowless. The sentinels seized his arms and flung him down on the flagstones; darkness slammed shut about him.

He almost welcomed it, in his exhaustion, so restful it seemed. It felt impossibly good simply to lie still and silent, no matter how hard his bed. He was half aware that he no longer had his pack, but he was too weary to feel any concern. His eyelids fluttered, his head sank down; he struggled to stave off sleep, to guess where he might be and what might happen next. But what was the point? He could do nothing about it; as well be rested when it came ...

Thunder and light jerked him awake, his eyes sticky, his limbs stiff and aching as he was hauled bodily to his feet and shoved stumbling into the corridor; it was still gloomy, and he guessed he had slept at most for an hour. Ekwesh guards with swords and spears surrounded him, and it disturbed him that none of them bore Raven crests; and many only a meaningless pattern of white bars; he had seen too many like them in Morvanhal, acknowledged members of the Hidden Clan. Yet though they prodded him along roughly enough, hustling him round corner after corner and up long echoing flights of stairs, they were never brutal; in fact they seemed to be taking elaborate if cold-blooded care of him, as might one charged with carriage of some precious thing. Yet the brutality lurked there in their blank dark eyes; acknowledged or not, they were all of the Hidden Clan, if any were. In the shadows above the stairs a tall double door was seamed in yellow light; it opened, and the flood was dazzling. Into the midst of it he was thrust, blinded and squinting foolishly; he reached out to steady himself, and closed his hand on what was unmistakeably worked velvet, heavy and costly. A heavy, aromatic scent filled the air, and a welcome warmth crept up through his boots. One of the Ekwesh pushed past him and spoke, his harsh tones sunk almost to a breathless, awed whisper; Elof heard no reply, but he was pushed forward at once and his jacket was pulled from his back, his tattered clothes and boots stiffened with filth and salt, ripped off him. He started to struggle, but as his sight cleared of its swirling colours he was astonished to find himself tottering on the glossed stone steps of a wide bath, filled almost to floor level with steaming water. He stared at it unbelieving; a bath was what his whole frame ached for, and he could almost believe this some tantalizing torture. Before he could hesitate any longer, however, the grim-faced guards seized him and hurled him bodily into the water. The heat and the impact of it struck his breath away, and he rose gasping and spluttering, eyes smarting with pungent oils. But water-filled ears heard only the receding ring and slap of sandals on the stone; he turned, and saw the doors close smoothly on their heels. All his guards had gone.

That alone made a great difference, and though he was still confused and apprehensive he felt himself succumbing to the water's grateful warmth. Whatever was to come, he reflected, he could face it better rested and relaxed; it could hardly put him in any worse case than he was already. With a deep groan he sagged back into the water, wincing as it bit at his scrapes and bruises, and blinked his eyes clear. He could hardly believe them. Only once before had he seen rooms so richly furnished, the old royal chambers of Morvan; but they had been dusty and ill-lit, and Kermorvan had had them cleared to suit his own more austere tastes. Here the floor was of polished stone, black as onyx, the walls smooth white but overhung with velvet in rich blue hues of night, worked about with gold and silver; if there were any windows they were hidden. At each corner the bath was lit by lamps on ornate stands, blazing with scented oil, and though he saw no fire the stone at the bath-rim was warm to the touch. Many ewers of lye-oil and balms stood there, mingling their fragrance with the heavy air; in an idle humour he reached out to one, but as he touched it it rattled and rocked on its base, so sharp and sudden was the tremor in his hands. The tall fair woman who sat in the shadows of the hangings rose from her chair, stooped swiftly and caught the ewer before it could overset.

"Have a care, young smith. This is a rare and precious stuff you trifle with here. Lean forward – bow your head."

Elof, slack-jawed, could not bring himself to move, let alone obey; for he could conceive of nothing save his own immediate and helpless death. Had he been clad and afoot he would have been casting about for some weapon, some way of escape; but now an absurd and paralysing vulnerability held him in thrall. The tall woman snorted with impatience, pushed his head down on his chest and poured a measured flow of the stuff in the ewer over his head and shoulders, and into the water beyond. It gave off a strange scent, dark and slightly bitter, and tingled on his skin; but where it flowed the worst of his pains seemed to dissolve away, and he subsided into the water once again, utterly at a loss.

"*Louhi* ..." he said, or meant to say; it emerged as a ghastly croak.

The woman smiled in wry acknowledgement. "Even so. The Ice lies all about the earth, south and north, west and east; why should you not expect to find me here?" She set the ewer down and stepped hastily back to her former place. "Enjoy your bath, young smith; make yourself as clean as you would wish to be. Doubtless you will be more at ease so, and I also. No offence! But you have come through great hardships of late, that cannot but have left their marks upon you; and I suffer from too keen an awareness of such things. Of senses other than smell also," she added with rueful grace, "not being born to them. I lack a lifetime's practice in ignoring their importunate messages, such as you mortals enjoy. To me they come new-minted, undulled, each time I take on form, and they are a continual torment."

"A wonder you can endure the Ekwesh, then," Elof grunted, his head still awhirl.

Louhi shrugged her shapely shoulders in answer. "I cannot, save with difficulty. I deal with them through more civilized minions, or from a distance; you may have heard what they call me – *Iltasya*, the Old One Unseen. But they are apt to the hand, and they are brave. As are you, young smith! All across the Seas of the Sunrise you have sailed, to their eastern shore – and all in vain."

Elof tensed, but remained lying where he was. "Who says so, lady? Yourself? But you cannot be sure of my purpose, can you?"

Louhi, her face grave and impassive, almost sad, turned to a low table beside her, of black marble white-veined, and took up from it something that caught and enhanced the gold of the lamplight, mellow and fair. Elof's heart gave a terrible leap. It was his half of the broken armring. They had given her his pack ... She came forward again, gathering up her white robe to kneel by the bathside; to his astonishment she held out the half ring, and put it into his hand. But then she reached up to her throat and drew up a thin golden chain that hung there, and from her breast lifted another such twist of gold upon its end. And that, too, she put into his limp fingers ere he could speak. He looked from it to her, feeling its warmth contrast with the coolness of his half, then seized the pieces and thrust them together, telling himself frantically that it was a trick, a copy, that such a thing might easily be confected in a few hours, were the jeweller skilled enough ...

But it was not. They fitted, and not only in physical form. Elof knew the unity of his own work, none better, and his fingers could sense the sudden reviving flow of forces within the metal as it touched, his eyes saw the tremulous gleams that shot this way and that like small fish in a pond, independent of the lamplight. This was in truth his first gift to his love and his last, the making of it and the breaking. He glared up at the pale-haired woman, silently daring her to gloat, or even smile, so that he could dash it from her face. "You ... took this from her?" he grated. "Where have you caged her, you wolf's bitch? Where is she?"

But Louhi's face remained calm. "She gave me it," was her quiet reply. "Without benefit of cage, or any such barbarity." Gently she slipped the pieces from Elof's nerveless grasp and, ignoring his belated grab, replaced them on the table. "You see," she said, without a trace of a gloat, "I have what I have long sought. And I fear you need not think to take it from me ever again."

It came to Elof's mind then, what part of it could still think, that Louhi had ordered her ground for this encounter with great subtlety. None among his folk save the upper orders were especially squeamish about nakedness; no others could afford to be. And he was no highborn, yet he found himself fettered by his situation, fettered and depressed. Before those cool blue eyes he was as uncertain as a child, unwilling to leave the sheltering water, yet within it vulnerable and at a loss, too easily dominated. He saw it clearly; yet he was powerless to change it. For those quiet, unforgiveable words he might have sought to attack Louhi with his own two hands, to stifle the life of her body or even try to hold her hostage before her followers. But thus naked and enmeshed he could hardly summon up the spirit. He could not possibly hoist himself from this deep bath swiftly enough. He would look ridiculous. He would probably slip on that glassy floor and split his skull, anyway. And what good would it do? What did it truly matter? It, or anything. He had no trouble believing Louhi's words; in her very mildness he could read their truth. Kara, in her fury and her sorrow, had obeyed that nagging call, and fled back from the company of men to the security of her bonds, the shelter of her own kind.

He could hardly blame her. A deep misery, deep as the roots of the world, came pressing in upon his mind, and depression like a rolling wall of mist, distancing and darkening the very hues of life. It clung to him too closely for the release of fury or of sorrow; he had done with caring. He laid his head back wearily against the lowest step, and closed his eyes.

He jumped when Louhi spoke again, for it had seemed there was no more she need say; also, she was again close by, kneeling and looking down at him with that same grave mien. "I find it in me to pity you, young smith ..." Elof flinched in angry disgust, but she held up a restraining hand. "No. I speak no hypocrisies, truly. What need have I to? What I said, I meant. Have I not felt as you feel now, and at your hands? Believe me, I would not mock it; I know. But do not despair too soon. I said that you need not hope to take her from me, and that I meant also. But it is possible that I might relinquish her."

"Re-*relinquish* her?" Elof felt more adrift than ever.

"So. Oh, not wholly, not forever. Would you, had you the choice? For a time, a span – the span of a mortal life." Her full lips pressed tight till the colour drained from them. "That is not easily offered, or lightly. Even to think of it is ... oh, pain, revulsion; look into yourself and understand. Yet I have had to see her pass from me once already and to me one life would be a short enough time to bear ... though that life might be made very long indeed, young smith. If you were willing to join Kara, in my service."

"Consider!" she said, almost pleading, before Elof could even gather his startled thoughts, let alone utter a word. "Why not? Consider what you have seen here. Has the dominion you call the Ice not won far further southward than in your own land? Most of the world is thus, Elof. A great change is coming, and it totters in the balance. Only a little further, a small advance, and the balance will tip, beyond recall." She rose on her knees, staring out into infinite distance, and shook back her smooth cascade of pale blonde hair. "I had hoped to make that advance in your land, young smith, thinking it easier than here. You taught me my mistake, you and yours! But here it shall still come about. The Ice will advance, not far, young smith, not far; but far enough to reflect some small portion more of the sun's heat, and so cool the clime of the world just a fraction further. And that will be enough! That, cast into the scales, will turn them. From that moment on we need no longer strain to advance the Ice. It will become a process of growth, clean growth without the taint of life. Its advance will chill the world further, and that chill will advance the Ice; as a morsel of snow set tumbling own a mountain may grow, unstoppably, to a mighty avalanche, so the margins of the Ice shall grow of their own moving force to encompass and cleanse this carrion world. And the peace that is cold will settle about it, and our day shall come again! Then we shall live free indeed, free from the strife that devours us, free from all the ills, demands, indignities, free from the burning tomb that you call flesh!"

Slowly she subsided, leaned sideways to rest on one hand, her hair hiding her face. Elof sank down in horror, the warmth of the bath lost to him in his shock, recalling all the duergar lore he had learned of the Ice. It was all too plausible, what she had said; it could come about ... But when? How soon? How long remained?

She looked down at him suddenly, high breasts heaving, but serene of face as ever. "But it would not all happen at once, young smith. Not in one lifetime of men, or even two, though it could not be stopped. You could live on happily enough. Even your friends would be left alone to live out their lives, if they wage no war against me; for I would no longer need to assail them."

"And those you assail here?" demanded Elof sternly, though his words rang hollow within.

She shook her head sadly. "Them? You need think nothing of them. In their unceasing folly they deserve disaster; almost they court it. They will bring down the Ice upon their own heads. I cool the water about these lands, mass the drift-ice at its gates, freeze the rivers that feed the land. The Ekwesh serve only as the living spearhead of the Ice; and the haft is half a world wide, and hurled by many hands. Fair young smith, I and mine are on the verge of victory; and yet that victory will only win back what was so unjustly wrested from us, long ago. We have yearned for that, yes; but is it so terrible to yearn thus, exiled and dispossessed? Can you find no scrap of sympathy for us, no understanding? Have not you done the same, in all your wanderings? And along the way, from haste or need or plain folly, we have done some terrible things; and have not you, also? But we will have what we yearn for; and perhaps you shall, also."

"If you would gave me what I yearn for," said Elof dully, "you would slay me here and now. It would be kindness, perhaps."

She gazed back at him, and shook her head. "Once I might have. But smith, I have warmed to you. You are brave, and you harbour a force of your own, mortal though you be, that is rare among the herd of common men in any age. And I have learned much about you, aye, from Kara. You have awoken a Power to love, young man, and that is no small thing. Our kind knows love indeed, but of a different nature. It is not the same as this mortal huddling, this passion that spurs on the lowest, laughable urges, the mingling of flesh in filth. It is no desperate snatching at happiness made more precious by its own mortality, by its own inevitable end; it is no fire, doomed both to blaze and burn out, no flake of snow to melt even as it is grasped. For the force of the lower love to touch the higher, that is rare, and not to be lightly thrown aside. I say again, Elof, I would have you at my side." She rose, tall and beautiful as a crest of sun-bright cloud, and turned back to the table, began sifting through the things that lay there. "You are a smith of surpassing craft, like none other I have encountered in this age. That helm ... I have marvelled at its power. But I do not see it here; lost in your wrack? A terrible loss; but you may live to shape another. And this gauntlet ... from among the duergar, perhaps, but no other men; and the same for this hammer. And these, these are surely the fatal anklets ... I find it hard to blame you, young smith, truly I do; you have my sympathy, even if I have none of yours. And this sword, that you call Gorthawer ..." She drew it with a hiss and a flourish, but in her hands the black blade was silent. She gave a bitter laugh. "This at least I have felt from you!"

She balanced it in her hand a moment, then suddenly she sprang forward in a fierce lunge, and sent it stabbing and cutting through the air in graceful exercises of formal sword-play that bent her lissom body like a bow, drawing her robe tight about her and loosening it at breast and flank. Elof watched her in fascination as she danced back and forth about the bath, cleaving the columns of steam into swirling panic, till at last she paused with a peal of silvery laughter and stood panting, her straight hair clinging in dishevelled wisps about her damp face, her cheeks and breast flushed bright with unaccustomed colour. "This at least ..." she repeated, her blue gaze bright and intense. "And small wonder; it is a magnificent blade, a noble weapon." She stooped beside him like a plunging bird. "Here you wounded me, in the shoulder. Do you think I would hate you for that? But I, I at least, can forget wounds when they have healed." She reached out suddenly, and her long strong fingers closed on his; their warmth was startling. She lifted his hand unresisting to her shoulder, and with it drew down the loosened shoulder of her robe. "See; not a scar remains."

It was true; where Gorthawer had struck, the skin was milky white, unmarked, unmarred, glossed with a faint sheen of perspiration. She drew his fingers over the spot, and down over the curve of her breast, the robe falling away before them. Colour surged beneath the skin, and she breathed quickly through parted lips; her blue eyes were half hooded by their fluttering lids. Her breast jutted firm and damp into his cupped hand, and he traced the nipple with coursing fingers; her other hand reached out, touched his neck and quivered there an instant, then moved on to caress his neck and ear, his throat and chest. She gasped slightly, throwing back her head, and caught his hand to her. Only then did he try to snatch it away; but she was as strong as he was. Then she relaxed, slid it down across her ribs, the taut plane of muscle at her waist and down, pulling her sash away and parting her robe, down till it slid over soft curls and pressed in between her thighs. Abruptly she pulled away and rose, and stood a moment with parted robe clinging to her damp body, fixed in his gaze, gazing at him with an intensity that blazed like the North-Lights. Suddenly the air was heavy with a scent, whether it rose from the water or from her, that stirred his thoughts into a blurred confusion. "Hate if you will, Elof!" she said softly, almost chanting her words. "Only hate fiercely! They are the great twins, Mastersmith, the great unities – Hate and Love, Ice and Fire. And when the force of the stars themselves is spent, when rights and wrongs alike are forgotten and darkness claims all things, they shall lie down together, and become one ..."

Loss and misery, drowning in the beauty of her, foundered in her gaze. Then she shrugged the robe from her shoulders and peeled it away, and stood naked and fair as the vision of her true self amid rivers of falling stars. Yet fairer still than that vision she seemed, for she was present and real, though her skin shone translucent as milky ice. When she padded to the steps and down, thigh-deep into the lapping water, Elof caught his breath, as if the heat might melt her away. But the hand that touched him, that coursed along his body and encircled him in its caress, was warmer even than the water, and the lips that pressed on his flared like fire, traced burning trails of it along him as he floated, catching flame in his turn. The arms he closed about her encircled glowing heat, his fierce caress unleashed its flows. And as she pressed closer to him, flung thigh across him and drew him close, he remembered what he had once been told; that deep within the Ice the fires of the earth might still burn, a furnace contained that could burst out with searing force. They closed, and within the furnace she drew him, and as one they burned.

After a time, when the seething water grew still, she led him by the hand from the bath and across the room to the alcove where she had sat, and drew back the heavy hangings there to reveal a carven door. It

opened onto suffocating luxury, a wide galleried
bedchamber hung all around in gold and saffron yellow,
save where a tall narrow window gleamed upon blackness. Against the far wall was set a great bed of silken
cushions and counterpanes. Upon a side table stood a
pitcher and goblets; she poured him a glass of thick
yellow wine, honey-scented and strong, and slipped back
into the bathchamber a moment ere she came to join
him. Together, sipping their wine, they walked hand in
hand to the bed, and there as she lay down he poured a
trickle of wine across her breasts, and kissed it away.
Among the cushions, as time passed, they twined and
thrashed and sweated to their shuddering conclusions,
each contesting the other's limits, till they fell at last to
the dalliance of exhaustion, and from that sighed down
entwined into sleep.

   After some time Elof shifted, as the heaviest sleepers may; but his hand fell idly free. Some time later, as
he stretched comfortably, his leg slid gently from under
the other's, but he made no move, and his breathing
soon grew still. It might have been half an hour before
he moved again, and that slowly, flexing the hand she
had trapped between her thighs, gently, insistently, till
she herself shifted and flexed. Then, though he might
have slipped away, he lay still beside her, listening
intently to her breathing. Another quarter-hour or so he
lay still before beginning to inch his way over the cushions and onto the thick carpeting below; once there, he
did not get up, but moved on all fours, reflecting wryly
that he would have distrusted his legs anyway, so tremulous they felt.

   The door opened as silently as he had hoped, but
only when it was shut behind him did he pull himself to
his unsteady feet by the frame and draw a deep, shuddering breath. Relief and revulsion surged through him
with such force he almost vomited; and they were made
all the worse by the inescapable memory of how he had
responded to her. His clothes lay where they had been
torn from him. He gathered them up and forced himself
into them, binding them about him as best he could
shuddering; they were half-soaked with slops from the

agitated bath, and none the better for it. Then, gathering his wits, he padded swiftly over to the small table. She had extinguished all but one light, and it lay in deep shadow; he reached out gingerly, and touched only bare marble. Panic shook him, but he forced it down; she had been gone only a moment, so unless some servant had removed them ... He began to twitch the hangings aside, and behind the one directly opposite he encountered a plain blank door with the look of an aumbry about it. But it was locked, and he could find neither the key nor the means to make a pick. In desperation he plucked loose the heavy belt that had borne Gorthawer, forced the strong buckle between door and frame and began to pry them apart, leaning on the hangings to muffle the creaking and snapping of the wood, and forcing his fingers in between. In seconds he had a gap through which he could thrust his hand, and he managed to grasp the crumpled hide of his pack. Drawing it out through the narrow gap was less easy, but fear drove him; he did it, and when he had rummaged through his possessions he clutched it to his heart in deep relief. As he had hoped, Louhi in her haste had simply scooped all the smaller items into it. Gauntlet, anklets, they were there – and even the two halves of the arm-ring, one still on its chain. That left Gorthawer, and his hammer; by dint of much straining he had the sword, and with it he could just touch the haft. If he could only hook it towards him; if the gap were that fraction wider ...

He forced his broad arm into the gap, feeling the wood quiver, thrust further – and fell sprawling among the hangings as, with a crack like a blow in the face, the whole door snapped across and swayed from its hinges. He struggled free and, still on his knees, tore the sagging door aside; the hammer spilled from a dislodged shelf onto the floor, but even as he snatched at it the inner door crashed back, and Louhi stood there before him.

"*So!*" she said, and the very sound of her voice, controlled and calm as it was, chilled him rigid. Still unclad, still fair, she was no less a sight of terror, her blue eyes glinting like the sunken Ice, her lips drawn dead-white and snarling. "A beast returning to his vomit. A sacred trust is shattered for this, for this deathless Taounehtar abases herself! She opens the treasures of this body her temple to an animal, accepts the degradation, undergoes the pollution, the foulness ..." Loathing contorted her like a serpent; her voice sank into hissing incoherence, and a ribbon of saliva ran unregarded from one corner of her working lips. Elof shrank back, afraid as he had seldom been of anything; for a moment she seemed wholly inhuman, a moving window onto a landscape bleaker even than the material Ice, yet alive with a blazing wrath. She looked ready to spring at his throat. Before his eyes, his own hair bristling, he saw hers, palest silken blonde, rise straight up into the white mane of a fiend.

Against that tide of inhuman fury the blade in his hand seemed an irrelevance; flight filled his mind to the exclusion of all else, a frantic, feral panic. But he could not forget the hammer, and made one wild grab. Louhi, though she was out of reach, stooped even more swiftly, and touched her fingers to the wet floor. It was as if a window were thrown open onto a winter storm. With a shock that hurt Elof's panting lungs all the warmth was blasted from the air, and in the blink of an eye a white film raced like ground glass over hanging and tapestry around the alcove. Over the marble the water from their bath and their bodies crackled to solid ice. The hammer did not move; it was frozen solid to the floor. Elof cried out at the agony in his knees as the ice enmeshed them, and barely in time tore free and fell aside, against the wall. The floor was drier there, and the ice did not follow; but Louhi clenched the steam-sodden hangings, and they stiffened to stinging glass above him. On all fours he scrambled back, feeling the sodden clamminess of his clothes, knowing she had only to touch him and he would suddenly be encased in a cast of burning ice; enough, perhaps, to freeze his blood, or stop his heart by the shock alone. Now he saw that she had chosen her ground even more carefully than he had guessed, and how subtly she had put him at her mercy; that bath had made him vulnerable in body as well as mind. She paced forward now with the measured pad of a snow-tiger, and he could not even rise properly, his feet slipping on black ice beneath him as he scrabbled towards the door.

Suddenly she cried out, a piercing summons, and from outside came the rattle of feet and harsh cries in answer. The door quivered under a blow and flew open, and the gap filled with Ekwesh guards. Against them Elof could lift his sword, but knew it was no use; there were too many, and some had bows. He moved slowly back, scanning the room for some faint advantage, and they made no move, content to bar his way for their mistress. Now the wall was at his back, and all avenues of escape blocked ... all? Something jutted against his hunched shoulder, that must be, had to be, the edge of a window arch; but a window to where, opening upon what? It hardly mattered, when swift death was the alternative. He seized the chill hangings, bunching his fists in them, and with reckless strength he hurled himself against what lay behind.

He had a brief glimpse of narrow leaded panes that gleamed with a hundred jewelled hues, before his shoulders, shielded by the rime-stiff velvet, crashed against them and through. Over the frame he rolled and out, clinging to the hangings as he kicked about, feeling them begin to give under his weight. Edged stone scraped against his leg, and he looked down to find a foothold.

Emptiness roared beneath him, the very shock of it like thunder in his ears; like a blow it dashed his breath out of his breast, strangled a cry in his throat. A fly enwebbed, he dangled and kicked upon the outermost walls of that fortress mountain, and beneath him the abyss gaped and growled, its depths a dizzying, smoky blur as he spun. The sudden sweat on his palms stung against the ice-caked cloth, and he slipped down a span, caught himself with a jerk and felt the rending in the material. Swallowing hard, he kicked out to reach the ledge he had felt, and found it, barely wider than his boot; be braced his leg against it to stop him swinging and reached up desperately with his swordhand for some hold above. All he found was a narrow lip of masonry, barely wide enough for his fingers to clutch, no more. With the care of desperation he caught at it and pulled himself up, gasping, against the cold stone. The hangings billowed suddenly and collapsed, falling past him into nothingness; he clung to the stone lest they pull him loose. Some hand above had severed them, only just too late; he could only have been dangling there the space of a heartbeat, though it had seemed like hours. He looked up, and found himself below a lip of masonry; he could neither see the window nor be seen from it. It must be deep in a recess, as proof against weather perhaps. But he could hear guttural shouts and guessed that they knew he had not fallen; at any rate, they would hardly take it on trust. They had only to throw something down on him; water, even …

He struggled to repress the sweat that made his fingers slippery, and began to inch his way along the ledge and out from directly underneath the window, sliding foot and fingers along a careful turn. Gorthawer seemed to weigh tons in his fingers, yet he dared not try to thrust it through his belt, lest it trip or dislodge him; after a few minutes he rested it by its hilt on the ledge and pulled it along in stages, little by little, as he moved. After a few minutes his breathing steadied, and he felt able to risk a look along the ledge to see where it might lead him. To his astonishment he found himself looking at the shadowy outlines of trees, leaden in the first grey light, upon a steep hillside no great distance away. With great care he turned his head, rolling it back so it would not force him from the wall, and saw the same. Then he understood; this was the far side of the fortress, rising not in imperious stages but in a single sweeping wall, and much narrower. He yearned to turn and see what lay behind, but did not dare; time enough when he was off this terrible perch. Then movement caught his eye, and he saw what must be a rope come snaking down from the window recess, and a moment later a lean figure scrambling down it, apparently barefoot, but with a sword slung across his shoulders. The Ekwesh reached the ledge and clung tight with fingers and toes. The sight of it almost unnerved Elof, so precarious did it look; it brought home to him his own plight. The moment the first man was free of the rope, another came slithering down, and after him a third. But the third, perhaps overconfident, or weaker in the fingers, lost his handhold, clawed frantically for balance, and then with a scream that sickened Elof's stomach he toppled out into emptiness. His shriek seemed to go on for ever, and Elof had to steel himself not to look down after him. Another warrior came sliding down the rope, as if quite unconcerned by his fellow's fate, and joined the others; above his head one more appeared. Setting his teeth in his lower lip, Elof began to shuffle along, as fast as he dared; there was more effort in this controlled, cramped movement than in a mad dash, and he felt his much abused leg-muscles beginning to tremble. But the sentinels were gaining, and the leader was already freeing a hand to draw the long sword from his back, the others readying their stabbing spears; Elof realised there was no way he could turn to bring his right hand to bear on them. Gorthawer felt strange in his left hand, that usually bore the gauntlet, but he had no choice. He inched along with only his right hand for support; the leader came within reach, and as Elof had hoped he swung out and cut at Elof with a great sweeping stroke. He brought Gorthawer crashing down in parry, a blow that moved outward from the wall, so that as the blades clashed he was pressed closer against it; but the Ekwesh was driven outward by the impact, his grip slid and faltered, and he too dropped shrieking into the deep. Even as he toppled a spear stabbed past Elof's shoulder, close against the wall; but the black sword was closer, swung up from beneath and slashed open its wielder's arm. The spear flew wide, and its wielder after it. Now Elof took the offensive, two shuffling steps back and a straight thrust that ducked under the next blade and took its wielder between the ribs; he cried out and dropped his spear, but clung there gasping, blocking the way for his fellows. Elof was appalled to see the next one lift his spar and callously dash the wounded man loose; but in falling he caught the other's leg and drew them both from the wall. The warrior behind stared after them, then made the cleverest move, hurling his spear along the wall; but Gorthawer struck it aside. Then, though he bore an axe at his belt, the thrower made no move to advance, nor did those behind press him. Elof, with a sudden surge of confidence, went shuffling along at what seemed like a great speed, and soon left them behind.

As he had expected, other windows were flung open above, and all manner of things flung down the walls, water, rubbish, offal and other filth, even rich furnishings; but the throwers could only guess at their target, and their aim was poor. Nets and chains swung and swept from the crenellations above came closest to unbalancing him, but once, when a carved waterspout gave him a firm handhold, he was able to reach up and seize such a net, and by wrenching it suddenly pull his unwary assailant right over the parapet. There were no more nets, then; but also no more such spouts within reach, and he began to grow very weary. He dreaded arrows from among the trees, but none came; he guessed they grew too thickly for any clear shot. But up ahead, blocking his path, was a squat tower, evidently the guard-tower for this end of the wall; he could see that the ledge he stood on ran out around it, past waterspouts at each corner, but equally clearly the lip that was his handhold did not. And when he came out along that ledge he would be briefly in clear sight from the parapet above, and in clear shot. The far side was not so bad, for so steeply sloped the hill that the tree-tops almost reached it; if worst came to worst he could cast himself down among them. But that bare wall, without a handhold ... He fought down his shivering, lest it lose him the hold he had. He twisted his head back, and saw light in the hazy air behind him, the serrated tree-tops along the hillside growing clear against it. Sunrise was upon the heights, and it would be his friend.

All too soon he had reached the tower, dodging only a few half-hearted missiles; but before he essayed it he waited a few precious moments, resting as best he could. Let them wait, and be less aware! He held up Gorthawer to his weary eyes, saw mirrored in its black sheen a tiny seam of pure fire open between hill and sky. A shaft of gold struck suddenly through the haze, and another, lighting on the tower, the treetops, the wall with dazzling warmth … It was then, when night-eyed watchers must be suddenly blinded, that he made his move, reaching out to straddle the gulf beneath and pull himself across onto the tower. It was worse than before, far worse. The weight of the sword clamped between his fingers, face and chest and knees pressed flat to the rough stonework, he shuffled as fast as he dared, but knew he was far too slow. Upon the very thought a shaft sang over his head and struck dust from the stone. He glared up and saw two archers scrambling up onto the parapet, leaning out to draw, and others running to join them; and useless as it was, he lifted Gorthawer in a dark flash of defiance …

Suddenly it was dulled. A shadow blotted out the sunrise, wings widespread sweeping down its rays towards him, skimming the heads of the startled bowmen; one loosed wildly and fell back behind the parapet, the other leaned out to take new aim and fell shrieking from his perch to crash against the ledge and tumble down upon the treetops below. Elof, heart leap-ing in his breast, lifted his hand, then ducked as wings thrashed deafeningly above him and half-webbed claws raked the air. He flung up a hand, and suddenly, as swift and sudden as its coming, the great swan was gone. Only then did he realise his hand still held the sword. It was Kara, beyond any shred of doubt; but what had she meant? To help him or to slay him? She had come close to dislodging him also; might easily have done. And yet and yet …

Cursing, half-weeping, confused, he scrambled and staggered to the corner of the tower, only to find that the waterspout here was large enough to block his path. To free his hands he had first to reach Gorthawer over, and scramble gingerly after it. He managed it safely, finding it a great relief to see the tree-tops so much closer; but when he reached down for his sword it was not there. He looked up, straight into a pair of blazing blue eyes. A window opened above that narrow ledge, and upon it, one foot outstretched, stood Louhi as steadily as she might upon any floor of stone, though the wind plucked wildly at her robe and hair. Her mouth was twisted, her lip bitten to bleeding; he was astonished to see the tracks of tears upon those cheeks like milky ice. And she held the black sword in her outstretched hand.

"So it ends, young smith!" was all she said, ere she thrust.

To few men can it have been given to feel that agony twice; but it was to him. It tore a gasping shriek from him, and he curled around it as if to hold in what was spilled, clasping the sword to him, tearing it from her grasp. Ice was everywhere, and pouring into his entrails; his legs lagged beneath the weight of it, and he toppled from the ledge into open air. A sickening, suspended moment, and the world was full of whipping, crashing, the reek of pines and sickening, numbing impacts. Then something huge hammered into his back, and there was a new agony as the sword was jolted free. Dimly he heard Louhi shouting from above "*Gather me all he bore! And then burn the carrion! But first – set his head atop the Gate!*"

CHAPTER FIVE
To the Heart of the World

HE LAY AMONG COLD shadows untouched by the sun, unmoving. He was shrouded in a deeper night, aware of nothing save the hot life pouring out of him from the roaring furnace below his heart. It flooded his throat; he had to cough, and stiffened in agony as its white fires racked him, blasting thought. But as they ebbed his mind cleared a little; his body felt cold, numb, immovably heavy, as if it had turned to metal. Dimly he remembered the long sickness he had endured through lack of blood, though mysteriously healed of the wound that caused it; he knew, in a strangely detached fashion, that he must seek to staunch the flow somehow. But floating in darkness, lit and limned only by pain, he could not imagine how; divorced from limbs, from senses, he forgot the use of them. Instinct instead led him inward, into the furnace-glow and past it, to a flame that burned and glittered brighter still at his core, at the meeting of mind and heart. As into the works of his hands that secret fire was channelled, so now it spilled along his veins like solder of silver along some riven seam, to seal, to join, to set secure and weld. The white fire it overtook and quenched, damming its progress, ebbing the outflow of his life. Gradually he grew aware that his throat was clearing, felt his breath grow deeper and steadier, stinging needles of sensation return to his heavy limbs. His eyes fluttered open, saw the familiar floor of a pinewood, and sagged weakly closed again. He was too weary even to be amazed at what he had felt himself do. There was still pain, but better far than the deathly numbness that had passed. If he had turned to metal, he had tempered himself anew.

But as his body healed itself his thoughts grew more agitated. They fluttered like dry pine-needles in

the wind, shivering, scattering withering; only two
visions stayed fixed and clear, the dark wings shining in
the rising light, and the tears that gleamed upon a milk-
pale cheek. Kara! He was sure of her now in any shape.
She had come, but to save him or assail him, which?
Either was possible, but he feared the worst – the more
so if she knew what he had been about with Louhi.
Though surely she must realise he had succumbed only
to seek a chance of escape ... Except that he had not.
He had told himself that to justify it, and he had lied in
his teeth; he wanted Louhi, he had ached for her even as
he hated her, and the memory of it was a writhing
torment. What had he done, lusting after an unhuman
shadow? No, that at least was rubbish! That body was no
false seeming, it was the expression in human terms of
what she truly was, perilous and fair; and the peril had
only added a sensual sting. Had that alone been enough?
Surely not. Perhaps she had drugged him with those
unguents; equally possibly she had not needed to. He
had gone too long without love, thinking only of Kara,
hardly noticing other women; no wonder Louhi had
made such an impression when she thrust herself at
him. Yet still ... Still, there had been something else. It
could not have been, surely not, the thought of Kara and
she ... if they ... He clamped down hard on the half
formed thought, and damned himself for it; but if he
was honest, there had been something ... Her vulnerability. Of all things, that was it! He had been drawn to
her for all those reasons, even the worst; but it had been
sympathy for her, sudden and instinctive, buried till
now in the depths of his heart. He felt, as he had
never once felt in all the fervour of their coupling, a
sudden pang of compassion for that lost creature, half
formed shadow of a greater self, tormented by the urges
of a body she both loathed and scorned to understand.
She too was driven to love; yet for all her boasting she
could not possess that love, save by force. Kara belonged
to neither of them, whatever bonds they might impose,
but was at heart only herself. Now, when it was too late,
he had come to understand; but he doubted if Louhi
ever would. Till then he had thought of her only as

trying to ensnare him; but he wondered suddenly if Louhi might not have been drawn to him in just the same way ...

Weak and feverish, wrapped in his imaginings, he failed to hear the footsteps till it was too late; those who made them were practised hunters, and accustomed to moving quietly. Only the sudden crash of bushes upslope alerted him, and the guttural bark of triumph. He wanted to spring up, but hesitated; better they thought him unconscious still, and stayed off their guard, especially if they sought to carry him off. Instead he was left lying. Puzzled, he let his eyelids fall open a hair's-breadth and saw them, tall Ekwesh warriors standing casually by, some four or five at least. One pointed with his spear to a long dark stain upon the steeply sloping forest floor, and they both laughed, a short cruel laugh. Then he understood; that strange stain was his own blood, and they thought him dead already. As well he had lain still; if they left him, if they did not seek to plunder his body ... Then one grounded his spear in the soft earth and plucked a short axe from his belt, and Louhi's words came back with sickening impact; they were about to execute her command, and he did not even know whether he could move.

But the footsteps crunched among the needles a span from his head; he had no choice but to try. With an agonized groan of effort he thrust himself up on his arms and lashed out desperately to ward off the blow he feared. None came. He managed to lift his head, and was astonished to see the axeman frozen in the act of raising the weapon, his eyes glaring wide, the clan-scars standing out livid on his graying cheeks; from his fellows came only yells of sheer terror. A blood-boltered corpse, as it appeared, had come to life, and there were few things the Ekwesh feared more than the dead; for if their victims could arise, they had much to fear indeed. Spears clattered as they fell among the bushes, and the axe dropped from its wielder's hand. Had Elof been whole, he might then have ventured escape, but the effort even of rising was so great he could only stumble back against a tree, retching with the sickening reek of clotted blood that choked his mouth. Dimly he saw the moment pass, the flicker from fright to fierce resentment in those cold eyes, resentment at being fooled into showing fear. As one they snatched up their weapons to blot it out, and with faces twisted into sneering masks of anger, slowly, contemptuously, they closed in around him.

The sound then might have been a bird cry, a whistling soft yet shrill, and they paid it no heed. But Elof had heard it before, and it woke wild memories in his muddled mind, told him the best thing he could do; he threw himself flat amid his own blood. A sudden soft sussuration filled the air, and his enemies turned uncertainly. Then they yelled in earnest, and threw up their arms to ward their heads; but the hail of stones that came whistling down upon them through the pines brooked no such slender shields, and shattered both together where they struck. Elof saw one warrior's brains dashed completely from his skull, another dance grotesquely under a dozen impacts, a dead pulp before he fell; the axeman whirled about with three arrows through his leather cuirass, wrenched one out, sank down and died with it in his hands. Elof, braving the stones to grab his axe, saw that it looked familiar somehow, graceful yet roughly worked. Ekwesh raced about the clearing, one with an arm drooping limp from the shoulder, but they found no way out; arrows and slingstones felled one, the other made a mad dash at the bushes, stopped short with a horrible yell and sagged down upon the spear that transfixed his stomach.

The sight was too much for Elof in his weakened state; he was violently sick, and almost fainted with the pain it caused him. He lay helpless as feet rustled across the clearing, and he was seized and lifted in strong hands. A strong odour flooded his nostrils, familiar yet unpleasantly altered, a scent he knew grown rank and harsh; that spurred him enough to force open his eyes. But he thought he was wandering in fever then, for the first face he looked upon was Roc's.

"Easy there!" said Roc breathlessly as Elof sagged with the shock in the arms that held him. "Gone to

Hel's own trouble to get you out of here, don't go turning your toes up on me now! You see, dammit?" he added swiftly to the shadowy shapes behind him. "He can't even talk, let alone walk! We'll have to carry him ... "

"Not yet!" said a harsh deep voice from behind him, and he was shouldered aside. A burly shadow took his place, slightly shorter than he but as broad or broader. A hard hand clutched Elof's hair and forced back his head so that a face could stare into his, a dark-bearded face that seemed twisted out of a mass of browned cordage, set with eyes of black opal that burned beneath heavy brows. A fine fillet of twisted gold crowned them, and the unkempt beard bristled over a thick golden collar. Those eyes glared deep into his own, and the sunken cheeks seemed to grow hollower still, as if eaten away by those fires within. There was no trace of mildness or mercy in that look; it was hard, proud, suspicious, and above all it was voracious. "Well?" said a voice whose accents had the same half familiar ring to them; but by the face, even by the odour, Elof had already recognised the race of the speaker. The words were heavily sarcastic. "What token can you show us, smith among men? What marvels to amaze us?"

Elof spoke with difficulty. "None ... none but this." And reaching inside his torn tunic, he pulled out the little oval of onyx that the great duergh Ansker had hung around his neck. Gnarled fingers plucked at it, rubbed it, the opalescent eyes peered closer and looked up in startled disbelief.

"Whence stole you this? By what right bear you it?"

Elof forced himself to stand upright, though the trees seem to be swaying too violently around him. He looked the dark one in the face, and demanded "I am the Mastersmith Elof Valantor. Will you not give me your name? *Ti shkazye khto?*"

Duergor voices rumbled their astonishment that a human should speak any tongue of theirs, and he relaxed a little; he had been afraid they would not understand him. The gold-crowned one glared at him a moment, then nodded curtly. "*Ieh tyak, uznye. Ildrya-nye korolye! Iye!*"

"Then hear my answer, Lord Ildryan. That stamp I was awarded by right as a journeyman, after two long years of service; and by the achievement of mastery was confirmed in that right!" Again he heard astonished words, mingled with disbelieving sniggers; but he concentrated his gaze on Ildryan. "For myself and my helper I claim the shelter of that right! Is it granted? Or do we tarry here till the man-eaters return? *Khazhto myetdylas!*"

Out of the shadows around they crowded in around him, and there were fewer sniggers. Elof saw for the first time that the gold-crowned one seemed surprisingly ill-clad for any of the Elder Folk, let alone one of authority; he wore a shirt of the fine-meshed duergar mail, ornamented in gold, but it looked to have been altered from one shaped to fit another's form, and the leather breeches beneath were worn and stained. But then the garments of the others were as rough, and even less clean; bags of game, bunches of roots, even a brace of hares hung from their belts, and many of their mail shirts were ill-fitting. Only their weapons were well made and richly ornamented, even when they hung from rawhide baldrics. He felt his mind whirling with the puzzle of it, and suddenly that dark face was all he could see; it seemed to hang unsupported in space, and he forced himself to hold those unreadable eyes with his own, until at last they lowered in a quick, unwilling nod. "We waste time indeed!" growled the voice. "The price is accepted! *Talyazkha na zyevar! Nazh skary-enje!*"

Elof let himself collapse with relief; Roc supported him, and demanded what had been said. "He said we should go with them," croaked Elof, and added, as quietly as he could, "Or ordered it, rather ... and told us to hurry up!" The idea of that seemed suddenly hilarious to him; he could hardly put one foot in front of the other, and that stupid ringing in his ears was drowning whatever Roc was saying. Unease swelled in him. "But what did he mean, the price ..." Suddenly the trees were whirling around him, and the ground surged up beneath his feet.

For much of the time that followed he hovered uneasily in the shadowland between consciousness and unconsciousness, dimly aware of being borne on some kind of litter, swaying on broad shoulders, of lines of tall trees looming over him, with moon and stars between them. At other times he was swirling once more in that awful tide-rush, or seeing Louhi's face contort with wrath, or feeling that sickening agony of the sword thrust, or walking paths that were darker and more confused still. Then, very suddenly, his eyes were staring up at a circle of blue sky, and he was wholly awake.

Roc was bending over him, waterbottle in hand; as Elof stirred he nodded as curtly as Ildryan and sat back against a tree, but gave no greater sign of relief. "Well," he said, "Had a good sleep, have we?"

Elof stirred and looked around him. All he could see were bushes, and above them, picked out between black outlines of limb and leaf, patches of deep blue sky strewn with the rose-hued clouds of sunset, and the high summit of some cliff or crag of greyish stone. It gave him a welcome sense of peace; uneasy and short-lived perhaps, but still peace. The air was full of a strong resinous scent, and as he moved he saw he was lying on a long heap of soft spruce tips, a comfortable woodland bed. There were trees in the background, but Roc sat at the base of the only one near, a substantial pine, with Gorthawer and their packs by his side. "Yes," Elof said, and though his dry voice rang already stronger in his ears. "Yes, I have. I feel … strengthened."

"And so you should," said Roc severely, "the rate you've healed. We guessed Louhi had muffed it; but she didn't did she?" He saw the look that crossed Elof's face, and sat back. "Calm down, my lad; take your ease. We're safe enough here for now. Ildryan and his lads say Louhi doesn't control this land. They're holed up in a nice shady place nearby, waiting for night; but I thought the sun might do you more good, and they seemed glad enough to be shot of us."

Elof sat up gingerly, feeling his head clear. "Roc,

how did you fall in with that crew? What happened to you after –"

"After you lost hold of your shape? The Powers know how you held it that long, but I'm bloody glad you did. Well, I was swept off, whirled down; then I saw the Tarnhelm go by me ..."

"You saw it? Did you get it? Roc, is it safe ..."

"Easy does it, there! Aye, I found it; I saw it dashed away among the rocks, and dived for it as it sank. Got myself swept off in a current for my pains, but I brought it ashore all right. Much use I thought it, without you! And I didn't know whether you were alive or dead. Then our friends found me." He snorted. "Friends I call them; that's giving naked truth clothes. They're not fond of men, those ones. They'd have settled me on the spot if they hadn't come upon the helm, and seen there was something about it; that made 'em more ready to listen. Afraid I sounded off a bit about it and you, to bait them into helping me look for you; they wouldn't have cared a toss otherwise. But the Ekwesh got to you before we could ... Tried to warn you, but well, too late. And there you were, prisoner; and there we were.'

Elof smiled. "My own fault! At least you tried."

Roc grimaced. "We saw you taken, but they wouldn't attack the patrol, not in that open land; can't blame 'em, there were too many others about. But they tracked you neatly, every step, and when the man-eaters took you to the castle we were near enough to see you then – and me close to tearing my hair out, or rushing into that tower after you. But they said we'd get closer round by the rear walls, and that I might scale them by the mountain's flank and slip in, that place being built to keep folk out to the front ..."

"Slip in?" laughed Elof weakly. "Roc my lad, what'd you ever hope to do in there? You must've seen it's a crawling hive of the man-eaters ..."

"Well ..." Roc grinned, a little self-consciously. "I thought I might just nose around a bit; make myself out to be a thrall, like ..."

"Ass!" growled Elof, to cover his real feelings. "Even after weeks on short commons you'd still look like the best fed thrall I've seen!"

Roc chuckled quietly. "Ach, maybe they fatten them up now and again. But I'm glad you saved me the swink, with that acrobatic act of yours ..."

"You saw that?"

"From a ways downslope. Couldn't miss it, when it started raining Ekwesh! Then you. Hella's teeth, I thought you'd had it that time! Born to be hanged, you are. But it seemed as well to look a bit closer, just in case; and you saw the rest." He shrugged. "Mind you now, it's as well these tykes aren't friendly enough to be interested or they might start thinking, from a scar front of your breastbone and another back of your spine. Quite a wound; and we all saw it made. Might even say a mortal wound; yet here you are. It's happened again, hasn't it?"

Elof swallowed and nodded, remembering the unhappy gulf that strange incident had opened between him and his friends. "Yes. It has. And I still don't know why ..."

Roc reflected. "See, now. You can be hurt, just like the rest of us, that's certain. Right from your first days prentice at the anvil, when you'd smite your thumb or burn your fingers, I've seen it. And you wouldn't so much as swear, not aloud, so bent you were on acting like our Master." He chuckled at the memory, though it made Elof shrivel. "But you bled right enough, and took as long as any to heal. And as a grown man, too. Except these two times. Now what was so special ..." Then his eyes widened with wonder, and Elof began to see the drift of his thought. "Both wounds made with swords; and both swords from under your hand ... You who so often make your work more powerful than you mean. As if you'd poured so much of your craft into them that they'll not wound you properly, but heal the breach they've made, seal it with the fire that forged them ..." He whistled softly. "It sounds damned unlikely, but of you ... aye, of you I could believe it."

Elof shook his head. "Ach, Roc! I set no such virtue upon either blade!"

"There's spells in your very blood."

"Then I've left the forest floor well enchanted! Listen, Roc, it may be as you suggest; who am I to say? But this I know, it did not stop me shedding that blood, I'm kitten-weak and starved; is there any food to be had?"

Roc chuckled. "Very well then, you're on the mend." He pulled over the packs, rummaged within them and handed over leaf-wrapped lumps. "Let's see, we've meat, bread, some kinds of root, strange but wholesome enough. At least they haven't stinted with food, our short friends; and no more they should, the damned price they – "

Elof, tearing ravenously at the tough grey bread, looked up sharply. "Price? And now I remember, Ildryan said something about a price being accepted. What price, Roc? And for what exactly?"

Roc twined a dangling lock of red hair around his broad fingers. "Well … That's the rough side to it. Hadn't meant to mention that till … well, till you were better."

"Roc, I'm better now. What price?"

"Better? Grey as that bloody bread you were, and weak you still are. Ach, what's the use? The price – well, it's that helm of yours – no, do you lie back there and let me explain!"

"You've got it? *And yet you're bartering it away…*"

"Elof, hear me out! It was the price of our lives…"

Elof exploded. "Roc, you stupid bitch's get, that helm's the most powerful thing left me! It's mine, and to Hel with your damn-fool bargaining! I've got to have it, d'you hear me? *Got to*! I can't hope to catch Kara without it – "

Roc's eyes screwed up till they almost vanished, and his cheeks flamed. "Catch her, is it? Where's all your repentance fled to, then, eh, sir cock-a-hoop? Haven't you thought a sight too much of catching already? *And would we be here in this stinking midden if you hadn't?*" Abruptly Elof bowed his head, and Roc blew out his breath impatiently. "Ach Mastersmith, I'm sorry. But what was I to do? I couldn't rescue you on my own; I can't work that thing! What profit in hanging onto it and losing you, then? They had it already, anyway; there was nothing to stop them just hanging onto it, taking it without another thought and leaving me high and dry. Or slitting my throat. And so far at least they've been honourable; they've taken nothing else, nothing we had in our packs or anything."

Elof nodded, though he was sick at heart still. He ate again, but without gusto, as the last sunlight faded above the bushes, and the first stars began to appear. The crag seemed to loom larger in the dark, a steep shadow against the luminescent twilight. He reflected that with the duergar also appearances could be deceptive. Their character had many facets, not all to be judged by the standards of men; they could be a dark and suspicious folk, selfish even towards their own, though he had never known them half as sheerly brutal as the worst among men. Perhaps in cases like this they were only being less hypocritical. Ansker and Ils exerted themselves to respond to men on their own terms, and most younger duergar copied them. But even Ils, generous in heart as she was herself, might consider such a bargain only somewhat rigid, and in no wise dishonourable. "And as you say, Roc, they might have taken the helm away, with no risk ... But much good may it do them! For though they have smithcraft enough to use it, they do not know the ways. Let them only try!" he added grimly.

"Dark comes!" said a harsh voice. He looked up sharply. There stood Ildryan and his gaggle of followers, and in the deepening shadow the lined faces seemed even less human, the black eyes stony and opaque. From Ildryan's fingers the precious helm dangled, and Elof's heart leaped and laboured; he could see some damage, dents, and links offset here and there. To his fury, another had caught up Gorthawer in its scabbard. The duergar lord motioned to one of his men, who pushed through the thorny bushes to the root of the crag, parting them gently: the thorns seemed to make no impression upon the leathery hands. What more he did was hidden, or else it was another of the duergar beyond their sight, but his intent became apparent. For as they watched, the shadows upon the rough face of the crag deepened and darkened, and seemed to flow into one another; a whole section of the stone, apparently unbroken a heartbeat since, was inching silently back, swinging aside upon some hidden hinge. Even as it opened one of the duergar stepped into the blackness, tinderbox in hand; light kindled, a mote of red he touched to the wall, and suddenly it grew to a flower of mellow gold that sparked off another and another, a racing line of trembling flames shining a dim, warm light upon a wide chamber of stone, long and deep also, its bare walls ornamented with dark-hued scenes of beasts and the chase. Old and faded they seemed, but at the rear a great grille-work of metal shone untarnished by time, and the lamps themselves glittered in their own light.

"Silver, gold and crystal!" whispered Roc. "And yet they're clad like peasants ..."

Elof felt the hair prickle on his neck; he was suddenly very near the answer to his puzzle, and he did not like the picture that was taking shape in his mind.

"Come!" said Ildryan gruffly. "Enter our ancient halls, be our guests as you were of our kin oversea! And feel honoured, for no man has been permitted sight of these gates for many a lifetime!"

Two duergar bent to Elof's spruce-lined litter, but he half rose suddenly, forestalling them. Ildryan's brow knitted. "Why linger?" he barked. "Where else can you go? Here there are no *zhaliki* near, but in the lands around the eaters of men will be combing the woods in wrath for you! Fools, shall we leave you to them?"

Elof hesitated. Warmth and light allured him, and a thirst for the security of old memories; he strained his eyes, and it seemed to him that beyond the inner gate he saw a tunnel sloping down to a dark mirror of still water, a sunless lake on which the dancing flames gleamed like gems in coronet. By that tranquil shore he yearned to lie and rest, rest from need, from thought, from love; he had endured too much of all, they were bound up in his agony and he pined only for surcease now, and recovery. But that other picture was becoming all too clear. He remembered another king under stone, and how loath he had been to let strangers depart, once they had passed such mountain-gates as these. If anything he trusted this one less, with his hungry face and burning, devouring eyes. Behind such defences, in apparent shelter from the turmoils of the outside world, it would be all too easy to forget that not only one's own folk might be entitled to justice, or that there might be some good, some right greater than their immediate gain.

"What is it you want of us, lord Ildryan?" he asked quietly. "That we shall show you how to wield that helm? But that was never in our bond – was it, Roc? Well then; since you forced us to it, we shall hold you to the letter of it. I will not teach you the use of that helm, here or below. I will bind myself to shape you as worthy a price in its stead, if you so wish; but I will make you nothing till I hold the helm in my own hands. Nor will I enter your gates till I have it. Hold the helm if you will, and much good may it do you. But if you are sensible, you will let me ransom it from you with other works – "

"The helm you shall not have!" spat Ildryan. "You who dwell above, creatures of fierce light and wayward airs, think you we are blind? Or fools? Will you seek to wrest our price from us, and fob us off with some trash of your tinkering? The Elders of your own land you may cozen, but we, we shall guard what is ours. No helm! Nor anything more from us, save blade and blow! Get you within, or die!"

Dull iron gleamed as arrow sprang to bow, stones into sling, and the duergar sprang forward, their eyes chiefly on Roc, not the sick creature they had been carrying. But he sprang up with ease, straight at the one who held Gorthawer, felled him with a single blow and snatched scabbard and belt even as they dropped; the black blade sang into his hand, and he stood there defiantly, swaying slightly. Roc stepped quickly to his side, and he rested a hand on his shoulder.

"So the duergar race forgets its honour indeed," rasped Elof, in so fell a voice that Roc jumped. "Along with all else ..."

Ildryan's glare smouldered, but he raised a curt hand, and no shot was loosed. "We do not forget," he said contemptuously, "even to human filth. Get you from here, now, whither you will, to the cliffs or the Ice for all I care. Linger here but a moment and we may justly slay you as intruder and spy!"

"And the helm?" demanded Elof.

"*Adyitze!*" At Ildryan's curt command the duergar turned and strode by him within the gate. Teeth gleamed behind the tangled beard in what was no smile, and he hawked and spat on the grass beyond the door. Against the flickering light his hunched figure seemed to swell with the very intensity of his malevolence. "Bargain is bargain. What we have, we hold. *Dal'budye!*"

Even as the duergh spat his last dismissive contempt at them the huge slab of stone was swinging out across the soft light, and severed it with the smoothness of a sigh. For an instant the crag-face was seamed with glowing gold, then it faded and vanished. Sheer fury overcame Elof's weakness, he staggered forward and hammered the stone with his sword's pommel. But it rang as firm in one part as another, nor could his skilled eye and finger detect even the faintest breach.

"Come away!" growled Roc, dragging him back. "You heard what they said, another minute's about the extent of their honour. Then they'll shoot ..." He jerked his thumb expressively at the heights above, that might conceal a hundred arrow-slots or a thousand, and draping Elof's arm about his shoulders he bore him almost bodily down the slope.

At the foot he paused, gasping, and they sank down amid some clumps of yellow-flowered broom. The first thing Elof said was "I could break that door ..." His eyes wandered upslope. "Oh, more than mere skill shields it so, true. There is some great persisting virtue, something deepset, very ancient and strong. But ... Yes, give me the time and I could break it."

"Aye," said Roc drily, "And to what end? To give their archers a clearer shot? You couldn't storm that place with an army, my lad. Anyway, they'd only repair the door soon enough ..."

Elof coughed, and pressed his hands to his breast-bone, wincing "Would they? I wonder."

Roc looked at him. "Anyhow, if you were so eager to get within why'd you balk so at entering? I was suspicious, aye — but it looked as if you'd seen some good reason not to trust 'em, the blades behind their backs or whatever."

"I did see something, yes. Not blades. It was the contradictions, Roc, the gold and the crude clothes ... Ils has told us often enough that the first coming of men to these lands, many thousand of years ago, drove almost all her folk to flee oversea. So, these duergar must be the descendents of those who remained. And of so close-knit a race, who would remain? Chiefly the outsiders, outlivers, solitaries, eccentrics, the cloven-minded ... no great number among the duergar. Those least likely to come together in any kind of community. And the duergar need to live together to support their great arts and skills, more even than we do ourselves. What then? Separated, weakened, without the solid core of their folk, those remnants must have grown weaker still, their skills and knowledge dwindling. Some united at last, or more likely their descendents, but by then it was too late; too much was lost and they were too few to recreate it. Poor sorry remnants! All their ancestors' realm to wander in, all the riches they had had to leave behind them, yet aware that they could not shape anything half as fine. So, though they walk among lamps and gates of gold, Ildryan and his folk, their descendents, must live as hunters and gatherers, being too few and too unskilled to farm their mountain slopes properly. And so also they grow greedy and avaricious, even more than the worst of their kin in our land; they are hoarders more than makers, fiercely inward-looking and jealous. I did not dare put our lives in such hands."

"Should've thought they'd jump at your offer of another price, then ..."

"Admit me to their forges, and betray the decay of their own craft? I, a human, and a pupil of a true master of their kind?"

"They could have learned from you ..."

"They are too proud, and too afraid of being betrayed. If once we had entered those gates they would have found reason to keep us there, honour or no honour."

Roc frowned. "I'll give you that. I doubt they'd suffer it even from Ils or any other of their race, the black pride of them." He sighed, and his red hair flopped listlessly over his face as he bowed his head dejectedly. "Well then. Here we are, leagues from nowhere, adrift and helpless as ever we were, and without the helm. So ends my bargain, and a piss-poor one it was, it seems."

Elof laughed, though it stabbed his ill-used stomach muscles, and clapped him on the shoulder. "Never say that! From under that axe it looked fair and good to me. And I've my pack, entire, and Gorthawer! So if we've lost the helm, yet we have the gaunlet and all else; if my poor hammer's left to Louhi, I've the other half of the arm-ring in exchange, and count it cheap at the price. Most of all, we've our lives! That, and a few bites of food; and we've seen times enough when we'd have sold the one for the other, eh?"

Roc chuckled with reviving humour. "Truth enough. And no haggling! But it's the poor trade that galls me still; those chiselling bastards hadn't even the grace to set us on a good road."

"Perhaps there is none. Or none as they see it. But they did tell us something, without meaning to; they told us that Louhi does not control this land, and later said that no man had been permitted sight of their gates for many lifetimes."

"So?"

Elof grinned. "So, that implies that once men had such sights. Which tells us that men and duergar once had dealings, however slight; that once there were men in these lands. And since these ragged duergar alone would not keep the Ekwesh out of this land, almost certainly there still are. Strong men, at that."

Roc whistled softly, and looked around him. The sun was all but gone now, save for a few pale streaks upon the dark overcast, and a last slash of fiery orange at the horizon, barbed with the silhouettes of the trees. "Maybe. May well be. And enemies to the Ekwesh could be good friends to us. But where? Which way do we turn, in this wild country?"

Elof gathered his strength, and hauled himself shakily to his feet. "We are still high up among the hills, here. We should be able to find some vantage point without much effort ..."

"Aye, but can you ..."

"I told you; I'm better. Come!"

Roc's doubts were evident; but he did as Elof bade, and sought only to support him when he tripped over tangled roots or loose stones in the soft earth slopes. They forded a small stony stream that chuckled as its cold fingers tugged at their ankles; Elof drank deep of its waters, and seemed much refreshed. Slowly but steadily they climbed again, and very soon espied a pale notch of sky between the shadows of the crags; towards this they climbed for their vantage. The slope was very steep, but it was carpeted with tough grasses whose tussocks gave hands and feet good purchase, and they soon neared the top. On the ridge they paused to catch their breath and await the moonrise, for there was little light to see by through the overcast cloud. But Elof, looking down, could make out that the grass on the northward face of the slopes was far less lush, low stuff unfit for grazing; bare rock showed through the soil in places. It made him uneasy, and he strained his eyes northward. So it was that when the moon arose he saw its first glimmer alight upon a rough terrain of dark hill and mountain, the same as that through which the Ekwesh had borne him, broken only by the winding silver threads of broad rivers and the sparkle of the mountain snow-caps. But above them another light leaped up, like a mist of silver spray from a breaking wave, and it hung there pale and clear, gleaming upon the clouds till they too seemed turned to rivers of ice, walls of winter looming above the world. And Elof, in his wounded heart, cursed the day that first he saw it.

"The bloody Iceglow!" said Roc. "This close?"

Silently Elof pointed. Between two of the most distant snow-caps shone a speck of something whose light put them to shame, a glittering frost-jewel in the brittle air. "Its herald," he said softly. "Or its child. It is there, and it advances. It is causing the snow-caps to spawn new glaciers of their own."

"So much for the North," said Roc, after a moment. "Westward lies the castle and the seas and the man-eaters; our best hope there'd be to pass their cordons somehow and steal a smallish boat. Don't much reckon on that, d'you? Thought not. Which leaves east and south." They turned, and looked out over a dimmer, softer landscape, where crag gave way to high hill, and the dark tangle of lush forest softened the contours of the land; there was no trace of snow. A light mist, or perhaps a passing rain shower, made the distance hazy, yet they could just make out there the mellow gleam that might be some wide river or lake. From south to east as far as they could see the view was the same, a generally lower and well-grown range of hills, and beyond it haze and uncertainty.

"Looks all right," said Roc. "Got to be better than the north, anyhow."

"And if there's anywhere better yet, inhabited lands even, southward's where they will be," agreed Elof. "There lies our road. To the South!"

Yet even as he said it he cast a last glance up at the crags. He could not quell his heart's ache to recover that miraculous work which had given him a brief glimpse, at least, of the keen heights and dizzying freedom of a Power. He doubted that he could ever shape such another, without the unparalleled library of the Master-smith Mylio to hand, or the ancient lore of the duergar. Worse without its aid he could hardly believe he would find Kara again, or keep her if he did. To memories of bright light and rushing air and fair laughter he bade farewell, and to the free sharing of strange shapes and sensations, a world untrammelled by mere human limitation. Sorely as that life had taxed him, he yearned for it, as for a fair dream too suddenly shattered. But hard upon that yearning came a gust of bitter self-mockery and disgust, and it drove him so fast down the slope that Roc was hard put to keep up.

So it is that the Tarnhelm fades from the Chronicles. Yet though it has left this tale, it has not left all tales, nor the legends that grow out of them. In the end, after many years, perhaps many lifetimes, it seems that the duergar learned to unleash at least some of its powers, and though many claimed it as the wisest of their work, its true maker was never wholly forgotten. For it was to become a great treasure among the fading Elder Folk of the north, and at last pass on to those fated few who inherited their hoard and the shadowy name they earned, and were to bring its tragic history at last to an end.

Of the three great works of Elof's corrupted youth, a second had now vanished from the world. Fit prentice-pieces as they were to herald the mightiest of mage-smiths, yet each in its own way could not escape the taint that was then upon him, and each in that way worked great evils. Even as the greatest of them, the sword of the mind, drove whole hosts of men to needless suffering and death untimely, so the helm, worker of secret change, became an instrument of treason and deceit, and the arm-ring, binder of love and tainted the least, came nonetheless to bind love in coils that stifled and tangles that cut. Broken as it was, the tale of its ill-doings is not yet done.

No account remains of the passage of Elof and Roc southward through the hills and the forests. It must have taken some few days at least, since so many heights and valleys lay in their way, but it seems to have been uneventful; the land was empty, is all that is said, and game was scarce. What this meant to them can be guessed, for they had only the little food the duergar gave them, and no easy means of hunting save Roc's bow and few remaining arrows; and the effort of healing was draining Elof's body. On the other hand, they walked free and alive when all too often they had stood in deadly peril, and they had both strong spirits to sustain their flagging frames. It must have been warm summer in those forests, the air tangy with resin, and

flowers glowing among the pine-needles on their floor.
They were still afoot and in no bad heart when they
reached the wood's edge, and came out among a few
scattered trees onto a bare and stony upland slope, leading to what seemed a hill-crest. It was a warm midday,
and beyond the crest only clouds glided by; there were
no more treetops, and as they looked to either side it
seemed that there also the wood was thinning and
diminishing. With growing excitement to steady their
shaky limbs, they clambered up the slope. "Let's ... hope
the downslope's ... easier," wheezed Roc, face purple
and glistening as a berry. But as they drew nearer the
top, they realised that there was no downslope; they
were at the top of a cliff. And it was no mere hillside
crag, such as they had come upon out of the Meneth
Aithen, but part of a long irregular wall of golden stone;
as far as they could see from east to west the forest
grew down almost to its edge. Then they came
cautiously to the cliff-edge, keeping low lest some
unfriendly eye catch them against the skyline. But when
they reached it and looked out, they forgot all that in
wonder at what they saw. For to their right, westward,
they first made out another such line of cliffs, and
thought themselves overlooking some deep valley. But as
they rose higher, and looked out east, they saw that line
of cliffs turn away from them and plunge deep into
cloud-shadowed distance, till they became no more
than a dark streak upon the horizon and merged with it.
And below them all the broad lands between lay spread
out clear, as on some vast map, some boundless living
tapestry. For if this was indeed a vale, then it was the
greatest in the world.

About the feet of the distant cliffs were green
woods, glowing with the lighter hues of seasonal trees,
but these soon gave way to low hills, plains and grasslands wider than any Elof had seen since he crossed the
desolate country off ancient Morvan. Through them a river
flowed out of what seemed to be a chain of small lakes,
widening swiftly as tributaries, like branching veins, led
into it from the cliffs; as the cliffs turned away into the
distance, so it snaked after them, growing ever wider

and wider till it seemed to become a great lake again. And if distance did not deceive him it broadened still further, became like a sea lapping at the horizon's lip as if eager to spill out across the sky itself; many long islands were set in it. Yet it was not this sight alone that set Elof's pulses racing, but what he saw thus far off on the edge of sight, extending between grassland and river, a rolling country mottled with a regular mosaic of many shades, chiefly green and brown. Upon this side of the river the same pattern repeated itself in the lands eastward, woodland, grassland, mosaic, till they blurred together; so fine was that mosaic and so great the area it covered, he still found it hard to accept it could all be fields. Around great cities he had seen such chequered patterns of fields; but from here they seemed like flecks as fine and as numerous as the lichen upon the rocks beneath his clutching hand. So small they looked that he might almost reach out and scrape them away as easily; yet he looked upon the works of men.

"It's a rich land," said Roc, his voice unwontedly soft. "Rich and spacious. Makes home look pretty damned small, doesn't it?"

"So it should!" Elof retorted, equally softly. "And so it should, Roc. Or have you not guessed where we are? To what place we have come and by what paths? I know it, Roc – I *know* this place! I know the stone of those cliffs, layered and tortuous like that; I know the colours of those fields, the span of the river beyond them, the contours of that hilly island there; even how the winds play about the cliffs as they converge ... see, you can see it in the swirling of the clouds there!"

Roc stared at him, astonished. "When you've lived all your life half a world away? Or," very darkly, "is it that you can look back along the River to some life you have lived before? How in Hel's name else could you have set eyes on anything here?"

"Through page and paper, scroll and book, words enscribed! They showed me this whole scene, little by little, a word here, two words there; but I never realised it, I saw only the parts, never the whole picture. But now, here, I see it! It springs out at me from every corner of my reading, so strongly it shaped the minds of those who wrote. I pieced it together from a hundred casual examples, a thousand chance comparisons. The cliffs, the coloured fields, they came from manuals of mining I pored over as prentice. That island there from some old treatise on mapping; the river and its currents from clauses in some leaden-heavy charter of commerce. The winds blew about the pages of ancient almanacs. Roc, from a fraudster's scrawls on divination I could tell you the very stars that will rise!" He gazed out solemnly over the expanse before him. "This is a cradle, Roc; a mighty cradle, for it bore within it high beginnings. It is our cradle, Roc; the birth and nursing of all that makes us what we are, our folk, our histories, our wisdoms, our follies. All that has driven us since our first youth began here; all that we achieve now is measured against the best of this place. This below us is the Vale of Kerys, greatest of all vales; and greatest of all rivers is this which flows through it, the Saltflood, Yskianas, the River at the World's Heart. In this vale, by this vast stream, for centuries beyond count was encompassed the high and ancient realm of Kerys, the City of the Lowlands, the very heart of the world itself."

Roc paled as he contemplated that awesome prospect, and his voice grew choked. "Is that so? Then I'm given a gift I've longed for since I first heard those names, in old tales my poor mother told me. To see them as you name 'em, that shakes me to my core. How my lord Kermorvan'd envy us! Worn and wan as we are, he'd change his chair of state to be with us! But then ... what lies there now?"

Elof shook his head, and his voice sank to a whisper. "Ah, there the words have no answer. Five thousand years have passed since the fleets left this land to found our own! Yet longer than that it had endured already; more than twice as long, some say, more than ten thousand years. Therefore it may endure still; yet if so ..."

"What is it?" demanded Roc. "Your face just went like a wet midsummer, clouded over ..."

"If so ..." Elof swallowed. "If so, then the Ice comes

hard upon it, to be so close. And its strength must have waned terribly. Do you not know now that fortress to which they took me? Yet you've sworn by it often enough! That was, that must have been the High Gate of Kerys, legendary strength of strengths, built to deny any enemy access to the valley mouth. *And who holds it now?*"

Roc's hands clenched on the stone as if to clasp it to him, to deny it furiously to others. Elof saw the horrified anger seething in him, and understood it well. To the sothrans, far more than to the northerners among whom he had grown up, the ancestral land and all things about it were sacred, imbued with reverence, enshrined in memory. They had made it the measure of all their aspirations and the warranty of their oaths, the more so as they thought it lost to them among the impenetrable shadows of time. And no part of Kerys was more sacred to them than the High Gate. "That's the bloody worst of all! In her damned cold clutches! And if that's fallen, what else stands? Will we just find a nest of her thralls here too?" He stopped, and blew out his cheeks with sudden relief. "No, surely not! Or else this land'd be lousy with them, too. No, it's got to be as you reasoned it; there's men in the Old Country still, true man and enemies of the Ice. Might be glad to know they've kin fighting the same fight, eh?"

"It's possible," agreed Elof, straining his eyes for any trace of life across all that wide vista. "We should seek a way down these cliffs, I think, in any event Where else is there to go?"

Roc shrugged. "Where indeed? Short of trying conclusions at the High Gate." He peered over the brink, and shuddered. "Damned if I'm beetling down that! But it's lower to the east here, more of a slope than a cliff. And the sooner we get you some food and rest, the better. Feel up to another stroll?"

They grew weary indeed as the day wore on, and they clambered and scrambled along the overgrown margins of the cliffs; hunger shook their limbs, and though root and berry grew more plentifully than above, still there was little to lessen it. It remained a wild land, with no sign of man's hand upon it. But Roc in particular refused to be downcast, and kept searching the landscape all around with squinting intensity that earned him many a stumble over obstacles nearer to hand, and once or twice great danger at the cliff-edge. His persistence, though, was rewarded while the sun was still well up the sky, for as they came down a steep bushy slope towards a deep gully in the golden cliffs he let out an abrupt whoop of triumph, and pointed to tiny flickers of light in the distance.

"That's mail, or I'm an ape of Hella!" he swore. "Yes, see there; soldiers, and clad in no Ekwesh fashion either!"

Elof shaded his eyes, and let them focus. "Yes … they are pale-skinned …"

"I'll take your word for it!" said Roc good-humouredly. He stepped forward, waved his hand and let out a hail that went echoing away down the gully's water-eaten walls. Elof's keen eyes saw pale specks of faces look up, hands point, and a great scurry break out; one went running back down the steep slope – a messenger, perhaps.

"Ah, Roc," he said, shaking his head, "I wonder, was that wise? You're not normally so trusting. I would sooner have watched them a while from hiding first, weighed them up …"

Roc shrugged, a little shame-facedly. "Well … maybe you're right; though I'm sure they'll be no friends to the Ekwesh, at least. Do you go hide, then, and watch over me …"

"Too late, I fear; they've seen two, and finding only one would breed suspicion in the mildest breast. I'll come down with you. No don't bother yourself, the slope looks easy enough and I'm feeling much better …" He knew well that it was as much concern for him as eagerness to gaze upon Kerys that had made Roc impetuous. But he had spoken only the truth; the sun was shining, the air was mild and filled with strange fragrances from the sun-warmed bushes, bay and thyme and myrtle, and whatever his doubts, whatever the weakness of his limbs, it was no effort to relax. As they reached the gully's head Elof heard a distant jingle of metal rise on the light breeze, the crazy carillon of mail and harness, and the rolling clatter of hooves among the loose stones. A cloud of dust rolled up over the edge of the slope, and out of it, with a roar like a breaking flood, a squadron of horsemen in light mail came charging up the gully, long rows of pennons fluttering from the lances upright in saddle racks behind each rider. Behind them on foot ran a file of mailed soldiers with halberds levelled. Across the gully the horse spread out, lances poised to sweep its length, while their leader, with the foremost of the footmen at his stirrup, came trotting forward to loom over Roc and Elof.

'Well, what marvels have we here?" He did not deign to lift his visor, but it was a young man's voice, clipped and scornful. He eyed their tattered and blood-stained garb. "Whose men are these, that he lets them stray about the borderland? Or could it be that they're masterless men, good-for-naught outlaw vermin? Out for pickings?" That was evidently what he believed. "Those men there! Let them declare themselves, person and purpose! *In the name of the King*!"

Curt and ominous as the words were, the travellers exchanged wild glances, hearts pounding. For though the speaker's accents fell strangely on their ears, they had understood his words, and all that they implied. Peculiar though it had become, it was recognisably some form of the sothran tongue he spoke.

"With no hesitation, friend!" exclaimed Elof, and saw the men start, listen and then understand. "We sought you with that in mind, for we are charged with an errand to him. But we are fleeing the Ekwesh –"

"Oho!" exclaimed the leading footsoldier less harshly, for all that his voice was rough, and with a glance up at the rider he advanced upon them. The other footmen looked scarlet-faced and panting, but he seemed to breathe easily enough. The face below the helmet was lantern-jawed, of late middle years and weathered the hue of brick; his nose and cheekbones were a mess of scarlet veins, and wispy colourless eyebrows shadowed very cold blue eyes. His expression was still suspicious, though he was evidently taking in the marks of their exhaustion and Elof's bloodstained clothes. "Been mixin' it with the man-eaters, have yer? Well, but what'd you expect if you go strayin' off into the Highlands, then? As soon clamber up Hella's quim; what sort of a way is that to be gettin' to my lord king?" He stiffened suddenly. "Or don't tell me the bastards bore you off from the Lowlands ..."

"They took us some way northward," said Elof. "A week's march, maybe. For that is where we came ashore, when our ship foundered. We are not of your land, soldier, but from its sundered kin across the oceans; we come as emissaries and as friends."

The mounted man straightened up in the saddle so sharply his armour rattled, and the other soldiers exclaimed in a blend of excitement and disbelief, cut off at once by a peremptory wave of his glove. "A marvel indeed, it seems!" he remarked to the footman. "An emissary from all the way over the seas, he claims?"

"I do," answered Elof calmly, but with weight. He seldom minded how he was addressed, but he was not going to defer to this young puppy who would not address him directly.

"Well now!" remarked the footman, with an elaborate show of courtesy. "That's fine, very fine. Because, by Verya, an emissary's got no cause to conceal his name and quality from lawful authority, has he now? From a captain of the First Line like his lordship 'ere?"

"No indeed!" said Elof, increasingly nettled, though he knew well he could not reasonably expect to be believed at once. "I make you free of them. I am Elof, called Valantor, Mastersmith of my land's guild, and this is Master Roc, my friend and helper." He raised a hand to his neck, striving to stop its trembling, while the captain swung himself dubiously out of his saddle. "As earnest, my stamp of rank."

Captain and sergeant took one look at the carved jewel Elof held out to them then looked hard at each other. "Ah ..." began the captain uncertainly; but the sergeant seemed in no doubt. He rapped out an order,

and behind him the ranks rippled like mown grass; the
horsemen bowing low to their saddlebows, the footmen
hastily kneeling. So did the sergeant, but upon one knee
only; the captain, after dithering a moment, bowed low
from the waist. Roc cocked a sardonic eye at Elof.
"Know any more tricks like that?"

"I'm not quite sure what I've done!" admitted Elof.
He had murmured, and in northern dialect at that, but
the soldiers were on their feet so fast he feared they had
overheard. Then he understood; the salutation had been
impressive but perfunctory, a purely formal honour to
someone they were giving the benefit of a considerable
doubt. These folk evidently valued appearances.

"Still, shows they've a sound respect for smithcraft
anyhow," remarked Roc. "You ought to like that."

"And something about the land itself, perhaps,"
answered Elof quietly. "If so, I like that less."

Captain and sergeant were conferring, while the
horses began to stamp and chafe in the lines. Now the
captain turned back to them and doffed his helm, revealing a square, slightly boyish face below blond curls, with
a nervous flutter at the corner of one eye. "Well, noble
sirs," he began, a fraction more politely. "I regret,
though it is hardly surprising, that I have no orders
concerning such unexpected guests. This is too deep for
me, or any, I think save my lord the King himself. And
his Court Smith." His eyes, lighter blue than the
sergeant's were studying Elof's face for any sign of
dismay at that, and themselves grew uneasy at what they
read there. "I am taking steps to send you to him at
once, and speedily; the transport that landed us awaits
still at the riverhead. Aurghes here will command your
escort. For your own safety, please be guided by him in
all things, however restrictive this may seem. As you
have had occasion to find out, these are troubled times.
We will provide horses for you – or if the mastersmith
cannot ride," he added, considering Elof's blood-stained
clothing and forestalling an angry outburst from Roc,
"we will happily draw him down in a litter ..."

However polite, it was a command; Elof shrugged,
unwilling to be hoisted about like a sack of potatoes.

"Of course. If it is not too far, I will try to ride. But ere we depart, we have endured days with little food, and stand in some need ..." The captain nodded curtly, gestured to the sergeant, who snapped his fingers at his men; they fumbled around belt and harness, and produced the usual scraps and morsels that patrolling soldiers will carry with them. They were mostly young men, some very young, their faces much like any of their contemporaries in Morvanhal, but without the open quality he might have expected there. When he thanked them they neither grinned nor saluted, and some bowed their heads in an instinctive way that irritated him. Then at a word from the captain two dismounted and held their stirrups for Elof and Roc; evidently they were meant to do their eating on the move. Elof wavered as they helped him up; the saddle was not the kind he was used to, high-bowed and stiff. The captain rode past and the troop wheeled into formation around them, Roc urging his mount clumsily up to Elof's side. "All right?" he growled. "I know you rode a bull bareback and all that as a lad but ..."

"I'm fine," said Elof impatiently. "Just let me get some food in me ..." But the captain barked an impatient order, and the troop wheeled about as one, fell into file and went thundering away downhill. The travellers' mounts responded with the rest, so swiftly they almost toppled their riders from the saddle; there would be no sudden escapes on these well-trained beasts. Over the slope they clattered, stones scattering and rattling away in little avalanches beneath their hooves, and a cloud of yellow-white dust boiled up around them, sparkling with mica. Not even that, though, could keep Elof from the food he had been given. It was rough, some kind of tough dark bread and even tougher morsels of dry meat and cheese, but it heartened him so much he had to take care not to overeat, and be sure Roc had his share.

He needed it, for the ride that began thus soon gave him cause to regret his pride, and ere it ended left him slumping in his saddle, borne up by Roc at his side. At first he could still take notice of the view from the path, looking down upon low and tangled scrubland and then the tops of dense pinewoods, cool in the evening haze; but by the time the troop went thundering among them the light was failing, and his sight blurred. They looked strange, stunted, so much lower and thinner they were than the pines of his own land. And though their familiar scent drifted around him, it was oddly mingled with others he did not know. Even the soft bird-calls among the branches sounded strange. To his exhausted mind he rode through the distortions of a feverish dream, subtle and sinister; he doubted even the flecks of light that flickered in the distance, flitting this way and that about a great bulk of shadow beyond the trees. He half feared that even the solid shadow of Roc at his elbow might suddenly distort and melt into some nightmarish shape. Only when he heard the sharp challenge of a sentry, in much the same words as in his own land, did he realise the shadow was a wall, and that they had come to some kind of strong place; he heard sounds he knew well from campaigns with Kermorvan, the familiar firelit bustle of a busy military post.

"*Stand! Who goes? Under which King?*"

"Under Lord Nithaid," answered the captain coldly. "And about his business. Anehan captain of horse, with ..." The hesitation was slight, but it rang in Elof's hearing. "*Arrivals* to take ship for the City at dawn. So pass us to the landing-stage, and look lively about it!" They clattered on through a narrow arch; the wall was high, and had a strange look about it, but in the torchlight Elof could not be sure why. They passed between a cluster of buildings, low and austere, and into the looming shadow of a tower. It was of no great height, not more than four or five stories, but very strong in the building, and fortified all around its peaked roof. It reminded him unpleasantly of the Mastersmith's lair, and that added the final touches to the nightmare. The riders passed through another gate, and beyond the lights; darkness fell deep again. He could not think why the hooves sounded so hollow all of a sudden, and when they helped him from his saddle, heavy-limbed and shaking, he stepped down into that darkness as if it were deep water.

He awoke, shivering, beneath a pile of coarse blankets that reeked of horse. Looking up, he saw only the canopy of a leathern tent, silvered with dew; beyond its open end the air was grey with heavy streamers of mist. A chill droplet struck his bare neck, and he reached about in sleepy haste for his clothes. They lay beside him, foul enough to make him shudder as he pulled them on, but he was heartened to find his pack and sword with them, all intact; whatever the captain had meant, they were not prisoners to be disarmed yet. There were voices not far off, indistinct yet tantalisingly familiar. He swung onto his feet, then staggered and fought wildly for balance. A moment he thought himself still sick, then realised that he stood upon caulked planking, that truly was heaving gently underfoot to the tune of a hundred muted creaks and groans. Gingerly, still striving for his balance, he peered through the opening and stepped out.

He found himself on the deck of a beamy barrel of a boat, of the old-fashioned kind called a cog, with high bows and stern which might have looked comical had they not been topped with catapult platforms. Beyond the stern, and the sail that hung limp and slick with damp, the top of that ominous tower glimmered through the mist; they must still be at mooring. From the bows, where the smoke of a brazier entwined with the mist, Roc's voice hailed him to break his fast. Aurghes the sergeant was there also, seated crag-like by himself, and some eight troopers lounged around the decks, wrapped in cloak and blanket; three or four dark-haired sailors, busy with line and tackle, were cursing them roundly in a rolling speech. The soldiers seemed not to know it, or they might not have lain so docile under its lash, but Elof understood; it might have been the Nordeney speech of his boyhood, for all the strange turns and twists it sometimes took. Roc made him known to the shipmaster, Trygkar by name, a smooth-faced old man so expressionless and bland that Elof guessed he was enjoying his crew's barbed humour.

"It is only the wee breeze of dawn we are after," he

remarked, "to shift this mirk, and then away downriver to the capital. What river? Why, Heryonas, to be sure, that we northerners call Eran; you have come down into the Vale of Heryonas, Tel Eran. Down Heryonas to Yskianas lies our road, and down Yskianas to great Kerys the City herself." A cool breath touched Elof's neck as he named that august name, as if it had some summoning craft of its own; suddenly the mist-serpents were writhing weirdly in a freshening wind. "By your leave, gentles!" said the shipmaster hastily, and strode past them to bellow orders at his crew. Elof turned to watch, and found the sergeant at his back; he must have moved noiselessly as a cat, to listen in on their conversation. Pointedly he turned his back on the man.

"So, not a foot further to ride," grunted Roc, as the squaresail flapped and fluttered above them. "Which will at least give you a chance to recover a little ..."

"Thanks, Roc. But I'm well enough now."

"To gather your strength, then. You may have need of that; we both may."

Elof made no answer to that. They leaned on the rail and watched the cog pull away from the fort at the riverhead, that seemed to materialise now out of the thinning mist. Suddenly Elof leaned over and peered, and swore under his breath. "You see that?"

"What?"

Elof glanced at the sergeant out of the corner of his eye. "I don't want to point. Just look at that wall ..."

"Kerys, yes! You can see it against the tower, the buildings; they're ancient, of weathered stone, but that wall's spit-new!" He watched the emerging sunlight play on the raw face of the stone for a moment, sucking his teeth as if at some ill taste. "So even well within its bounds Kerys needs strong walls now. Those reivers have a long reach." The cog glided out peacefully into the centre of the stream riding easily on the freshening wind, and the mooring soon vanished behind a slight bend in the river, hidden by the vale's steep flank. But for some time the tower could still be seen above the pines, and it loomed longer in their thoughts.

Before that first day's end the pines themselves had

fallen away behind. Tired of having his every word marked, Elof was wearily content to sit quietly and watch the changing banks of the vale; by day and at ease he no longer found its blend of familiarity and strangeness so unsettling. He soon began to notice other trees among the pines, of the broad-leaved, seasonal kind, and as the hours passed he saw their dominance established; straight birches, some of kinds he did not know, were joined by ash and elm and what he learned were chestnuts, but few of them approaching the heights he was used to. The same was true of the beeches, and Elof was beginning to think that this was a poor land for trees when the cog had to steer hard to avoid the corse of a great willow uprooted and toppled of its own weight into the river, almost blocking it. Its pale hair still lay outspread and waving upon the water like the locks of Saithana daughter of Vellamo, and branch and twig raked the cog's hull as it passed. There were more willows then, massive brooding trees trailing their grey crowns in the water like aged and brooding powers of the forest, casting their shadows cool and dank along the banks. And as the land grew less hilly they passed the first of the great oaks, gnarled and ancient and regal as kings of old, their broad branches overspreading the stream and diminishing it in their shadow. Not even in Tapiau'la the Forest had he seen any greater or more aged, and his awe grew when he saw that an immense avenue of them stretched out before him, flanking the river as if it were a road. When Roc pointed out the weathered remains of a high marker stone, with a carved figure of distance half hidden by thorny undergrowth, his suspicions were confirmed. The oaks had not simply grown thus; they had been planted beside that stream, surely at a time when it was a much used thoroughfare. They asked Trygkar; though taciturn by nature, he had taken some fancy to them when he found they both spoke the Northern tongue, and were experienced mariners. He agreed. "But how many hundred years since, who can say? Not me, gentles, not me, and there's few know the old Eran any better. These were wild lands in my grandsire's day."

So they passed downriver, sped along by the swift wind behind them and the current beneath, and saw the wide lands of a great realm open out upon either hand; yet the works of man in it were few. By the next morning the only trees in sight were the tall willows, set at clear intervals along the bank; beyond them the steep forested vale had opened out into the green hills they had seen from the cliffs, low and rolling. In the course of that day these in turn flattened out into a wide grassland country, so dismally flat and featureless and so thickly carpeted with green that even the Eran was almost invisible beyond the next bend. Yet though the grasses bent and nodded in waves under passing windrows, so that the cog seemed to ride not the river but an ocean of green, still they lacked the ocean's boisterous thunder, yielding only a soft rattling hiss, the dry play of stem against stem, husk upon husk. It soon grew monotonous, even with the birdsong. Never before had he heard the trilling songs of larks arising but they were poor substitutes for the wild gull-cries of his homeland. Nor could he warm to the harsh merriment of raven and carrion daw, and the scream of raptors stooping for the kill. Of other creatures, or of men, they saw none; the land, though rich, seemed unpeopled, and though once or twice towers had lifted from hill top or river promontory their windows gaped empty as skulls. They did not look that old, but to most of those on board they might have been made with the stones of the cliffs, things too impossibly ancient for any man to know their history. Only when they passed one such tower, and saw that still visible among the grass at its foot were the blackened remains of a village, did the travellers begin to understand.

"Don't tell me that Ekwesh have struck this deep into the land!" exclaimed Elof grimly. "And so long ago? That's been ruined many a year ..."

"Never believe it!" said Trygkar behind them, in the northern tongue. "That's not reiver's work, more's the shame of it. That, now, gentles, that was put down in the times of the last Ysmerien kings, maybe even when my grandsire was young. A bloody business they say it was; but then the Line of the Bull would never spare chick nor child in such a matter. Called it breeding rebels if somebody did. Never recovered properly from those times, did this region ..."

"The last Ysmerien?" Elof pricked up his ears. "Then what line rules here now?"

Trygkar blinked casually around before replying, but the sergeant was, for once, not on deck. "Did you not hear? Lonuen, the Line of the Bull. And well named!"

"We've none of that name in our land," said Roc. "Still, at least it's not the Bryherens – or Herens, as they were."

Trygkar whistled. "Have a care, my lads! There's a connection. The Lonuen are a bastard offshoot of the Ysmerien, but they've Heren blood; why, the king's own mother was almost the last of them. Their line's gone now, too."

"And good riddance, I don't doubt!" muttered Roc.

"They had some bad lots, aye; on your side of the ocean also? Though they stood up to the Bulls as they had to the Ysmerien, and that was something; but the Bulls broke them –" He stopped. Aurghes had surfaced again, and though he was to far off to hear, the old shipmaster fell silent and would say no more.

All through that long summer day they glided across the grassy plain under a sky in which sunlight and cloud contended, and saw never another work of man. As night came the clouds thickened, and the air became cooler; after the evening meat Elof and Roc sat by the brazier only a short while before returning to their deck-tent, which was considered better quarters than the noisome lower troop-decks of the cog. So the next morning they were already awake and shivering before dawn, eagerly gathering by the brazier again to claim fried hunks of some kind of peppery blood-sausage and bowls of small ale mulled and spiced. In the gloom the clouds hung in grey overcast, shot with streaks of darker grey, as if to mirror the grassland beneath. The sunrise took them unawares; a rift had opened in the clouds, and the sun came pouring through it in radiant glory, turning the air to hazy gold. And looking out across the yellow-green waves of the grassland, it seemed as if they now mirrored the clouds. For among them also a golden seam opened, threading away in rippling fire along the eastern horizon.

"Yskianas!" said Trygkar quietly. "But 'twill be even ere we reach it, gentles. Harder sailing from thence, not like on this mild wee stream."

Elof smiled. "I think we may endure that, shipmaster, having survived the open seas." Trygkar shrugged, and said no more for that time; only long after did Elof wonder what deeper meaning might have lain behind his words.

Near the mouth of the Heryonas they at last began to see the distant wisps of smoke that marked human habitation, and here and there the grassland flecked with herds of horses or cattle. At length they passed by their first village, a straggle of houses in a shallow dell that was evidently home to drovers or herdsmen, by the great spread of animal pens that surrounded it. Beyond that a plume of smoke arose; but as they came closer it became evidently too big to be a town, or anything of human origin. "Why, it's a fire-mountain!" exclaimed Elof. "Just like in the Nordenbergen of my old home! But not so fierce, I hope!"

For once the sergeant joined in the conversation he was listening to. "Wouldn't be so sure of that, gentles!" he said grimly. "My home village was in the shadow of another such, for there's many in the land; we'll be passin' a good few. Well, that village is under a man's height of ash now, and it seems there's vines being planted on top already. Fierce enough for yer, sirs?"

"It'll serve," said Roc dryly. "Why'd your people build so close to it, in this wide land?"

The sergeant scratched his head. "Now that's a thing I used to ask as a lad. Seems that an awful time back, three hundred years even, that mountain wasn't near 'alf that size. And I can believe it, by Verya, for I've seen others spread too. But that's the way of 'em, isn't it?"

Not long after that they sighted the first town, or

rather the grim castle that dominated it; the scatter of streets was hardly visible behind its walls, until they drew much closer and could make out the roofpeaks. And these walls were manifestly not new; they looked as old as anything over the oceans. The whole community was first a fortress and a place of strength, clearly placed to dominate the rivermouth, around which white sails flocked like so many wings. As they drew nearer two longboats with five oars a side, flying a flag of purple and white and heavy-laden with men, detached themselves from the flock and steered towards them; but at Trygkar's order a dark bundle was sent soaring to the masthead and there broke out into a long pennant striped in black and gold. At once the longboats went about and vanished among the other ships. "No tolls to levy on a king's ship," grinned Elof. "Do you note our colours, the same as Kermorvan's?"

"I noted more the numbers of men under theirs," said Roc sourly.

"That's the Holder of Berheryon," said Trygkar, tilting his white head at the castle. "A hard hand he lays on such trade from the uplands as goes not through his town and his tolls."

"And the king permits that?" asked Elof in surprise, knowing how Kermorvan would react if any noble of his sought such advantage.

Trygkar glared around, but the sergeant was watching them with a benign bloodshot eye. "The king needs peace and loyalty from the lords of outlying burgs," he said, and turned pointedly to his helm once again. Elof and Roc exchanged glances, but they too chose to guard their tongues. For that time, though, hard thoughts were forgotten; they were beyond Berheryon town now, and Yskianas the Great opened up before them.

It was more like the approaches to the sea itself, thought Elof; gulls flocked screaming about the banks, and the freshening wind carried an unmistakable tang of salt coasts in the clear air. More like wide estuary or sea-lake than river the waters looked, already some two thousand paces between banks and still widening, save that the current ran so clear, even near the banks where it was slowest. It seized the cog as it cleared the inflow and swept it onward, swaying and wallowing till Tryg-kar's crewmen trimmed the sails; the spray that reached Elof's lips tasted salt. With the wind at their beam now even the unwieldy cog could race the clouds above, and the banks swept by them at a great rate. Ere the light left them the lie of the land was changing, and when they rose at dawn it might have been another country altogether they sailed through. The grasslands had gone, and in their place the river shone between steep hill-sides, riven by deep valleys through many of which other tributaries flowed. It was often at such conflu-ences that they came upon more towns. "Or more castles!" muttered Elof, as the channel carried them close beneath age-blackened fortifications. "It seems they're the same thing here. Never one without the other!" They had been two days now upon the great river, and he was growing sick of the sight of them, from the smallest tower perched high on a promontory above the water, the nest of a marauding osprey, to the vast and sprawling fastness that filled whole hilltops, or hunched upon the lower lands like some beast snarling over its kill.

"Well, so is it with us," Roc pointed out. "Every-where larger than a village has its own walls, its own strong place or citadel."

"Yes, but as a refuge, a defence chiefly, never to dominate the place as do these. Every one built as both palace and garrison, as was Morvannec at the first; a home for a lord, and the stony kernel of his power. Even the larger towns herd like sheep around the feet of the fortresses. And they cast a long shadow over the coun-tryside; nobody, villager, cottager or outdweller, could hope to live free of it." He nodded his head at the blan-keting of fields beyond the walls, and the rows of minute figures who toiled in them. "Do you look there! Never an orderly chequer of single fields and farm-hold-ings, such as you'll see around any town of ours. Just a great sprawl of huge fields, and a few small strips at their edges; the same with the vineyards on the hillsides, always the same. A lord's holding, a master's portion!"

"Aye, and who works it for him, I wonder?" Roc gazed at the toilers under the hot sun. "I wonder. But I'll be damned careful how I ask."

They passed by many more towns in the days that followed, and large or small, all wore the same aspect. Strong fortresses of yellow stone or a curious patchwork of yellow and brown, their peaked roofs usually red-tiled or of black slate, gathered their flock of lime-washed houses tight within high yellow walls; beyond those walls the larger towns might have a quarter of ramshackle huts, but never more, save where here and there some ancient and august ruin arose. In those towns many of the houses rose several stories high, as if they were plants constrained to shoot upward; they had few windows on their outside walls, and looked somewhat fortress-like themselves. The Great River was widening swiftly now, and the towns of the southward shore had long been no more than blurs even to Eloof's keen sight. However, the cog kept close to the northward bank, and so brought him closer sight of those there, the more so as by many of them Trygkar would slacken sail, or even heave-to altogether, till flag or trumpet gave him the signal to proceed. But by some, notably those on the offshore islands, he would clap on all sail and steer swiftly out into the choppier open waters; evidently there were places the king's pennon was no passport. At one point, where a pair of squat square forts sat flanking the channel between a town on a promontory and an offshore island, he called the soldiers on deck and raised strong mantlets along the side. The travellers were ignored, but Elof loosened Gorthawer in its sheath, Roc fetched his heavy bow from the deck-tent, and together they joined the watchful sergeant on the sterncastle. His coarse face seamed with surprise when he saw them, and he unbent slightly. "You do well to 'elp us, sirs," he said, his pale bloodshot eyes weighing them up. "For this one, I doubt not, would slit the throats of emissaries as freely as common soldiers."

"Fitting we share in the defence, then," answered Elof crisply, as the towers glided by above the slatted

screens, staring down with blank slit eyes. "For I doubt
not we'd bleed the same colour."

The sergeant eyed them with even sharper surprise.
"True enough, sirs. But there's many that might not 'ave
said that," he added, and strode stiffly off to order some
mantlets shifted astern. The old shipmaster nodded
approvingly.

"Bleed the same colour! Aye, that's the right line to
take with that one; or myself, for that matter. Told him
you were worth twice the popinjays we're used to deal
with. The same colour!" He laughed quietly. "Well, let's
hope it won't come to that. Shouldn't, if we seem hard
enough; he's no fool, this lordling here. Pays his dues,
sends his levies to the king, not a word out of place; but
still from time to time boats vanish along this stretch,
and he fares better than that starveling townlet of his
can afford him. Most often such boats as are too weak
or too unwary to defend themselves; easy enough to
make such a one vanish utterly, if you've a swift shipyard
to strip the timbers and no scruples about the souls on
board. He's not the only one doing it, by all accounts.
No wreckwood to float ashore, and no corpses
neither..." The shipmaster leaned out beyond the mant-
let to check the progress of the channel. "Ah, but he'll
not try anything now, we're well by him already and the
next town's not so far ahead. Still, no harm in keeping
the mantlets up for now."

Elof looked back at the suspect town; it seemed
quite large. "An evil thing, if it's true. Unlikely it could
happen in our land; there we tend to gather in one
great city, and the outlying towns and holdings are small
and weak by comparison."

"Why, so we do here also!" chuckled Trygkar. "Do
you think those towns you've seen are of any size? Then
it's clear you've never looked upon Kerys! Kerys itself,
Kerys the City, Kerys the Golden; not the largest of the
towns we've passed, not Keruelan of the Five Castles in
the South can stand compare with Kerys itself. What
d'you call cities over sea, then? Ten cottages and a byre?"

Though the raillery was kindly enough, Elof could
not help bridling. "There's no denying the breadth and

richness of this land, shipmaster; it's a legend among us. But so is Morvan the Great, that the Ice laid waste; and Roc here and I have walked among its ruins. It took us a day to cross its southern quarter alone."

Trygkar raised his brows. "A right noble place then; a fit match for Keruelan, or better, perhaps. But Kerys, now, just its port quarter – but why do I waste my spittle, eh? Only another se'ennight and you shall see for yourselves."

"A week!" exclaimed Roc, when he had digested the unfamiliar expression. "But ... we've been six days in this damned boat already!"

Trygkar shrugged. "Such is Kerys, my lad, and I can nor widen nor shrink it to suit you, nor speed my ship; she makes some nine knots already, by the mean, and that's as fast as you'll find of her build."

"No offence to her or you, shipmaster," said Roc, abashed. "I was startled, that's all, the more so because I knew we were sailing swift. Nine knots! But that makes the distance ..."

"Some four hundred leagues and fifty," confirmed Trygkar soberly.

Roc whistled. "As long as the old Southlands and Northlands together!"

"And that is only to Kerys the City; the lands extend beyond that perhaps half as much again, perhaps more. Boundaries are uncertain, out in the furthest east where prowl the eaters of men."

"The east?" Elof caught the old shipmaster by the arm. "The Ekwesh, you mean?"

"Aye, who else? That's where the devils first appeared, and then all along the Northlands that were my kinsfolk's once, skulking along the margins of the Ice. A few at first, then small raids and sharp assaults, larger raids that were harder to beat back, a hundred years of harrassing us and dividing us – till a great force worked their way westward and fell upon the Gate, that we never dreamed they'd dare. But east's where they came from; some say their homeland's out that way, far upon far. I wouldn't know; I've no desire to go visiting there, I'll tell you ..."

"*But in our land they came from the west!*" blazed Elof, not caring how he overrode the old shipmaster; he was boiling like a lidded cauldron. "Over the sea, across the Ice ... but always from the west! Where their homeland was said to be ..." he swallowed. "You do see, don't you? How they came to be on the Seas of the Sunrise, without first passing through our land. East one way, west the other ..."

"Oh no!" exclaimed Roc hollowly. "In Hel's name, do they hold so much of the world already, those savages, that they can spread two ways around it?"

"They do not," said Elof quietly. "But the Ice ... yes, it does. And whither it can send them, they will go. *A great change is coming*, she said, *and it totters in the balance* ... Powers!"

"Powers indeed!" said Roc darkly. "This is their fight, not ours; what's there for such as we to do against the likes of ... that force? Might as well fight one of these fire-mountains! Halfway around the world ... The more I learn of it, the lesser I feel."

Elof shook his head. "In yourself, perhaps; who wouldn't? But as a folk, as a kindred, no, Roc, we're not small. Remember this; where there's been unity and order, free men with free minds, there the Ice has made little headway. It fears the strengths that makes us human! And if Morvanhal can resist it, if this vast realm of Kerys can only stay both ordered and free –"

"Aye," said Trygkar quietly. "If. If, indeed." They looked around at him, but his taciturn mask had dropped like a gate of blank iron. The only answer he would give to their question was "You'll see, lads; it's not for the likes of me to say. You'll see it, soon enough."

The week that followed was all days of hot sun and cool wind, brisk but easy sailing that sent the cog skipping ponderously along the riverine coast, like an old horse released into green fields and acting the colt once again. Green fields indeed carpeted the banks, pastureland whose well-tended richness contrasted with the empty lands westward; towns, however, were few. It seemed rather to be divided up as were the lands around Kersbryhaine, into a few great farming estates whose manor-houses dominated the landscape. One such they approached quite closely, an ancient-looking and nobly proportioned building of age-darkened stone perched atop a hill-spur overlooking the river; below it at the bank a fortified tower, squat and brutally ugly, huddled over a well-sheltered landing stage. But as the cog drew nearer the house took on a very strange aspect, and they soon saw why; it was no more than a facade, a ruin gutted and stripped from the back, hardly higher than the ground.

"Aye, it's a crying shame," agreed Roc. "A grand-looking place, yet it's that toad of a tower they've chosen to rebuild first!" Even as he spoke the cog had drawn close enough to the tower to make out the high scaffolding lashed together out of stripped wooden poles, writhing with the shapes of men like ants in a tree. But Elof peered at the construction for a moment, and shook his head grimly.

"Rebuild be damned!" He pointed at the wall as they glided past. "Build! Look at that wall; see now where the chequerboard pattern comes from? Those stones, they've been well weathered, but not where they lie now!'

"You mean ..." Roc brushed back his red hair with both hands. "Hella's tits, d'you mean they're tearing down a good sound hall to build that overgrown jakes? They must be running daft!"

"Or fearful."

"Daft, I still say. If they're so afraid why don't they get together with a neighbour or two and build a proper-sized castle? One they might just be able to defend properly?"

Elof grimaced. "Well, even in our lands not every-one cares overmuch for neighbours. And here it seems they don't trust them –"

"Wait you, though!" said Roc sharply. "We've seen that pattern on half the walls along the river – can't all ..."

"Not all," mused Elof, "but many, I think; casualties of a time when men need strength more than comfort or fair craft. And too long a time to blame on the Ekwesh, I fear."

"Aye. There's trouble in this land, right enough. Look where the despoilers come now!" A long dray, drawn by a team of many horses, was labouring down a road that wound from hill to shore; it flexed strangely as it rode, for it was made of many sections, each with its own wheels. Even at this distance there was no mistaking the stone it bore. As it arrived at the foot of the tower a gaggle of men slouched out and scrambled up to begin unloading. Elof could not see what happened next, but there was a sudden confused swirl at the side of the dray, and a rumbling crash drifted out over the water. Its load was indeed stone; but a good half of it lay in a heap to one side, amid a rising fountain of dust. Evidently its unloaders had been careless. Men were sprawled among the mess, or groggily picking themselves up; others strove to calm the startled horses. More men came running; but not to help. Roc leaned over the rail and cursed aloud at the sight; Elof was too shocked. The fallen were being kicked and pummeled to their feet, cowering under a rain of blows to head or body from what might have been cudgels or short whips; even some of the horse-holders were being dragged away and thrashed till they sprawled upon the ground. Then the cog passed beyond the curve of the tower, and the scene was hidden from them.

Roc glared at Elof, his face turned so white with anger that the freckles blazed beneath his tan. "Well," he said with dangerous evenness, "What d'you make of that, then?"

Elof felt the muscles of his own face tighten. "Much as you, I guess. Do you say it."

Roc growled. "Those farm-workers, and now these. Maybe they're free folk swinking for pence, ready to swallow a blow; but I wonder. Hel's gape, but I wonder! You never had a chance to know Kerbryhaine, ere the Ekwesh changed all, and then Kermorvan. But there were many reckoned it was heading down a bad road, with no strong lord to rein in all the little lordlings on their own land. Hiremen and tenant being bound to the land, to their masters, ever more closely till they were free men no more."

Elof whistled softly between his teeth. "And of all our lands Kerbryhaine was ever said to be the most like Kerys …"

"Aye. So perhaps what was happening there had already happened here, grown from the same roots maybe." He snorted. "Villeinage, serfdom, whatever they chose to call it; common thralldom's my name for it, and this place stinks of it!"

Elof glanced around, and nudged Roc; he had almost felt the eyes on the back of his neck. There in the sterncastle stood the sergeant, apparently exchanging a few words with Trygkar; but his gaze was unwavering in their direction. "Maybe. Maybe. But best we say no more of this for the moment. Mouth shut –"

"And eyes open!" grunted Roc. "As you say, Mastersmith! I'm not sure I can find fit words, anyway!"

But thenceforth there were no more alarms, few excitements of any kind; the mantlets were never again raised, and no more towns avoided. The sailing was calm, and save for the fire-mountains the sergeant had promised, they saw no more such disturbing sights upon the shore. In fact there were few excitements of any kind; they saw little that was new, and what there was, such as a lava-stream that flowed right down into the waters and turned them to steam, they could not stop to explore. Roc sought to make the best of his enforced idleness, but Elof paced like a wild beast caged; however much rest the delay gave his body, he could find none in his heart. The appearance of any town, however small, was a welcome distraction; they would lean over the rail and strain their eyes to make out more of this enigmatic land. But they learned little, till the first time they passed a town by night; it struck Elof then how few lights showed, given its extent. "Just like Morvannec when the Ekwesh held it!" he remarked to Roc.

"You're not ruddy well suggesting –"

"No, no, not this deep within the land. But Morvannec had already been struck by plague, and lost two third parts of its folk. Here also it seems there are fewer folk than there should be – than there were, for they would hardly build whole streets of houses they do not need. Empty land at the borders, empty towns in the heartland ..."

Roc grew thoughtful. "Not nice. But there's other things than plague could cut down a folk thus. War, for example. Not necessarily with outsiders. Remember that burned-out village?"

Elof nodded. "Though we've seen no more. It could simply be that Kerys the City has drawn too many folk, leaving the rest bereft and dwindling, as Morvan did to Morvannec."

"Mmnh. Which'd go some way to explaining border banditry; nobody who counts cares much about it, 'cause they all live weeks away. Could be, could be. But we'll just have to wait and see, won't we? Not long now!"

"No!" said Elof explosively. "Not long! And then ..."

"What then? You've something in mind?"

Elof tapped the rail with his clenched fist, gently; but it was the gentleness of iron restraint. "I don't know ... I can't be sure. So much depends on what they're prepared to do – and why they haven't already done it ... If I only knew more about this land!" He gazed in anguish into the night, as if seeking upon the horizon some distant glimmer of the lights of Kerys itself.

But he was given no such forewarning. Six nights later they took to their tent, expecting they might see the city in the distance the next day. But around dawn they were both sharply awakened by a clamour of voices and the creak and rumble of tackle, unusually loud; when they scrambled out into the cool air they found the cog hove-to in the midst of a flock of other sails. These were of many types and colours, but they spared them scarcely a glance, for above them towered a vast squaresail, golden in the grey dimness, bellied out by the wind. Yet no such wind blew, then or ever, for the sail was of stone, and rode not upon a mast, but two slanted pillars of like stone that flanked a vast portcullis gate of dark metal, meshed very close; the waves of the Yskianas slapped about its bars and boomed hollowly in the arch behind. A great seagate it was, in a wall of the same golden stone higher than the highest of the masts now gathered before it.

The breeze drew cold fingers across their skin, but they stayed; for even as they watched a light golden as the stone climbed up the cloudy sky, and golden also came the cry of distant trumpets, and a call in answer from the wall. Trygkar bellowed to his crew, and other shouts echoed him from neighbouring ships as the ponderous clank of a ratchet winch echoed out of the arch, and the gate began to lift. Water poured from clumps of weed draped over the bars, but the full sheen of the metal beneath was untarnished. Elof nodded quietly to himself; there was fine smithcraft in that gate, such as all the tales said flourished in this land. A sudden excitement arose in him beneath all his other concerns, taking fire at the thought of all the rich smith-lore he might find here, and some of the discoveries he might himself unfold. He felt a sudden surge in the deck underfoot, heard the rigging creak overhead as the sails were angled to catch the wind once again, and forgot even that in his eagerness to see beyond the gate. All the other ships were making ready, beamy merchantmen of all shapes and sizes laden with merchandise, other cogs crowded with armed men and what seemed to be military stores, and a host of barges and lighters of all sizes. In between them slid long lean war galleys, some ornate and blazing with colour, even with ornate canopies on their decks. But the cog, flying the royal pennon, was suffering no dispute over first entrance to the gate; the prow dipped and rose gently as it got under way. Elof and Roc grinned at each other like excited boys, and as one they made a run for the mast shrouds and went swarming up the laddered rigging to the masthead. Most ships had only a spar there to sit on, and possibly a loop for a rope or one's belt; but being a ship of war the cog had shielded platforms for archers, and the travellers could stand in relative ease to take their first sight of the City at the Heart of the World.

But for that first moment Elof felt a keen pang of disappointment. It was a vast expanse he saw stretch

out before him through the narrow aperture of the gate;
large enough, he guessed, to swallow the two greatest
living cities of his land. But it seemed to have not a half
of their grandeur. The sun was not yet over the curve of
the world, and the distance was no more than a shadowy frieze against the luminous sky, broken only by the
looming silhouette of a jagged hill; over the nearer part
of the city the morning mists rolled like slow waves
down towards the Great River, for the land was well-
nigh flat. He could see that it had a network of ancient
walls, many times greater than those of which Kerbryhaine was so proud, but the level ground made them so
much less impressive than Kerbryhaine, rising on a steep
and ancient volcanic rock, or Morvanhal on its high
promontory above the sea. The stolid bulk of the distant
hill served only to diminish them further. Nor could he
see any likeness of the noble masonry which made
Morvanhal so fair, towering on its rust-red terraces
above steep streets; if there was any, it was lost among
the welter of lesser roofs. Worse, he could make out no
axis, no heart to the city, no equal to the citadel of
Kerbryhaine, ivory-hued under towers roofed in bronze
and gold, nor the darkly graceful palace of Morvanhal,
its carved columns and galleries weathered to the shade
of long-shed blood, with its lesser palaces on the
terraces below. "This has overgrown itself," he thought
contemptuously, "become bloated with its own vigour,
and now simply shapeless, a mere tangle of walls and
streets."

   But then the sun arose, and laid its first honours of
scarlet and gold across the true regality of Kerys. What
till now had been lost in black silhouette blazed into
life, and left Elof staring, unable to believe what he was
seeing; he turned to Roc and found him wild-eyed,
agape, one hand clutching at his fiery tangle of hair.
The sheer expanse of Kerys the City was greater than
they had guessed, but that alone could not have daunted
them so. It was the sun's slow progress across the
jagged slopes above that held their gaze as by rivets; for
hill there was none.

   Over wall upon wall of sand-hued stone that rich

light played, through high arch and carven buttress, over terrace, court and gallery and colonnade, behind turrets of every size and shape, and across the two high towers joined by a wall that were its crown, towers curved and shaped into a stylised shape that suggested the horns of some vast bull. The height alone of that vast edifice was astonishing; it reared above the mists like some lonely island in the ocean, and looked as ancient, as immovable. And all of this the sunlight turned to gold.

That first sight of it sent a cool shiver of awe through mind and body. Higher rose the red rim, hanging behind those crags of masonry like a mantle of fires, and higher yet, till to the astonished eyes of the watchers it seemed to settle between those graceful twin towers, rest upon that wall like a brilliant gem set in the crown of the world itself. For so it had been contrived with vast care by those who built the castle and the shore walls long ago, that around dawn each day the sun should be seen so from the first gate to open, appearing to hang there for a time, and from the last gate to close at evening; as the sun's road shifted with the seasons, so also the choice of gates, for there were many. Not the sight alone held Elof rapt, but the concept behind it and the cunning. It was contrived, that effect, with an equal insight into the paths of the heavens and the ways of the minds of men. Those who lacked wisdom would be astounded; and those who had it would still be daunted, by appreciation of the skill involved.

Yet about that majestic citadel itself there was nothing monstrous, as there might have been; some stark tower or castle of that scale might have spoken more of folly than of grandeur, of brutal domination rather than airy strength. It might have loomed like a threat above that great sprawl of humanity beneath; instead it seemed to grow out of it. This was no single heap of stone, no one palace or fortress. This was a palace manyfold, a city in itself of a hundred levels, as if an astonishing host of halls and towers, tall and fair, had somehow been caught up in a web of woven stone, or in the tangles of some petrified tree. It was as if the city itself reached upward towards the sun and offered it a throne, as if its moving spirit sought to embrace the radiant source of life itself.

That noble vision held the travellers hard in thrall as the cog glided smoothly towards the gate. Then, all too abruptly and with no more than a shout of warning, the spell was shattered; the cog heeled violently as the helm was thrust hard down, lurching dangerously for such a top-heavy craft. Roc and Elof clung frantically to the mast as it swung, their feet scrabbling uselessly againt the sudden steepness of the floor planks; a soldier on the deck below was less lucky, and slid down it to crash painfully against the starboard rail. The cog swung upright with a force that threatened to hurl the watchers from the masthead, and he lay groaning in the scuppers.

Across the river from the southward, on a huge squaresail even less wieldly than the cog's, came the largest ship Elof had ever seen, a monstrous broad-beamed barge half as large again as the longest dromund of his homeland; low in the water with a heavy load, it wallowed sullenly even in the calm waters of Yskianas, and the two galleys escorting it seemed torn between keeping close to lend support and darting away lest it might roll over on them. Lesser traffic scattered before it, and Trygkar and his sailors let out a fearful volley of oaths as the vast thing cut unheeding across the cog's bow.

"Grain from the south!" he spat, as if it were a foulness in itself. "Takes precedence over all else afloat, by my lord king's edict, does that bloated bastard breeder, and acts as if there's naught else on the bloody River!" The great craft glided on regardless, and he swung the helm around again, scarcely more gently, to fall in behind it.

"And yet," said Elof breathlessly, still clinging to the masthead, "I can see why, after a fashion. That monster was so overloaded that any sudden check in its course would risk swamping it completely!"

"Then why in Hel's name must they load it so?" Roc snarled, as the cog glided into the archway, and the boom of the water echoed deeply about them.

"Because they need so much, I guess. Look at the size of this place! And with craft as crude as that they must need to wait for the fairest winds ... Roc, I don't think these folk are very good sailors. Their ships are of kinds we've long since laid by."

"Hardly surprisingly, with naught but an overgrown river to play on. By this lass Verya they all swear by, our ancestors were braver than we thought, if they made that crossing in tubs like these! Or just plain daft!"

"Well then! We may have some things of value to teach them." The cog cleared the archway, and came out into a wide basin lined with stone quays; all were worn with age, and one or two were crumbling, collapsing into the waters of the dock. But whatever their view of repairs, evidently those in charge here believed in wasting no time on vital cargoes. The huge grain barge was already moored, and a chain of hunched figures were filing down onto its deck; the first were scrambling back up to the quay, bowed double under huge sacks. Nothing visible drove them, perhaps they were only eager for some extra payment for speed, yet he had seldom sensed so tangible an air of frantic haste and unhappiness; he could not hear one of them shout or laugh, let alone sing as did the dock workers of his own land. Free men or serfs, they were driven indeed. That sight, and the image of the fallen stone, brought back what that glorious vista had driven from their minds.

They were silent for a moment, for it seemed almost impossible to reconcile the two visions. But Roc echoed Elof's own though when he added "Maybe! If we can trust them! *If!*"

CHAPTER SIX
King and Mastersmith

THE COG SHOWED NO SIGN of heading towards any of the berths, but rather moved out into the centre of the channel where the wind was clearest. Looking ahead, Elof was surprised to see that the channel led on into the bounds of the city, between hard walls of grey stone, faceless and windowless, much like the dockside storehouses of their own cities. He was even more surprised that it was only one of many such that wound about between the buildings, till distance dwindled them to threads glistening in the shadow of the citadel. Here and there he could even make out a mast against the rooftops. "Yet the ground does rise, however slightly ... can it be they've some kind of lock system here, as the duergar do?"

This proved to be so, for when the cog rounded a bend in the channel it slackened sail, and two heavy water-gates closed behind it. Roc, who had never seen the duergar's dark rivers under stone, was fascinated as the waters came churning through the sluices; he had a great love for all cunning devices that needed no smith-craft in their operation. The cog rose swiftly, and as the further gates swung open it went gliding off down the new channel. This brought a further surprise. After the blank dockside buildings they were now passing between unmistakeable rows of houses, though there was little life about them as yet; only a chimney smoked here and there, and a baby cried in the distance. The streets were empty and the water of the channel glass-calm, mirroring buildings and blue skies; the cog glided cloud-like over the reflected rooftops, and strewed flecks of golden light in its wake. The houses themselves, built against one another in blocks large and small, were pleasing in proportion, many-storied and high-gabled;

some had lime-washed walls, others were even plastered
smooth and painted in pastel colours, pink and apple-
green and soft blue. But most looked old and faded, and
in some the plaster had faded to a flecked brown and
begun to crack and peel away. A few had bands of
decoration across the frontage between floors, so
tangled and florid that even Elof, used to archaic scripts,
was slow to recognise them as old saws and mottoes,
fragments of simple verse and the like. The town was
beginning to come to life; a pump creaked noisily in a
courtyard, chimneys smoked, one or two figures could
be seen going about the narrow lanes. A breeze wafted
them the odour of baking, and though different from the
cornbread they knew it was no les irresistible; when the
odour of frying meat drifted up to them from the deck
braziers not even the excitements of the view could
match it, and they went sliding like madmen down the
shrouds.

At first Roc bolted his breakfast, afraid they might
arrive at the citadel soon, till Elof pointed out that its
towers, still visible over the rooftops even from the
deck, looked only a little nearer; at this gentle pace they
had a good half day's sailing ahead, at the least. This
turned out to be too slight a guess; for to the scale of
that great sprawling burg their minds were not yet
attuned. Now and then, too, the cog must slow its pace,
as the wind grew less or some other ship slid by it,
fresh sails glistening in the bright sun, barring the
breeze from the cog's stained square of strengthened
linen; then Elof almost had to restrain Roc from springing ashore, so eager was he to tread these ancestral
streets. By this one and that the channels led them, from
lock to lock, ever rising. Quarter after quarter rolled
smoothly by them, like illuminations on some vast
unending scroll, divided by the channels and the grim
encircling walls, now breached in many places and even
plundered for house stone. As they went deeper the fine
dwellings grew gradually more dilapidated, and gave
away to older streets of sullen tenements, upper stories
overhanging their muddy alleys till at the top they all
but met; often crude gangways, rattling like dry bones in

the breeze, ran between them in rough parody of the
flying buttresses in the citadel above. But this poor
quarter, large as it was, ended sharply at a broad channel; on the far side were blank walls of brick, more faceless storehouses. Here and there among them narrow
sluices spilled fast streams into the channels and when
Elof climbed to the masthead again he saw huge waterwheels turning under artificial falls; behind them a few
tall chimneys smoked, spewing smuts and cinders at him
along the breeze. Here evidently was a gathering of
manufactories, with kilns for pottery or baked brick.
Huddled in their smoky lee was a patch of decent
houses and a bustling little market, and beyond them
more of the faceless storehouses, ending in another
canal. Past these were more canals, and
then a long and august rooftree of some five stories that
was unmistakably a guildhall, built much as they were
in Morvanhal. Other guildhalls followed, and beyond
them the tall narrow counting-houses of a merchant's
quarter, very like that of Kerbryhaine; it set them thinking of their old friend Kathel the merchant, and how he
was faring far off in the embattled west. But it was
another quarter that brought home most sharply the
kinship of this land with theirs.

They came first upon a wall of dense woodland, a
slice of hunting park isolated like a veritable island
between two curving channels that might once have
been natural streams. Into the furthest of these the cog
turned, and they saw that beyond it reared a row of
walls so blind and windowless, so weatherstained and
streaked to such a dismal shade of grey, that they might
have been more storehouses, save only that they were
too tall and too noble in proportion. And as the cog
sailed gracefully by, with two white swans as heralds,
Elof could make out that their wide roofs were not
solid, but hollow at the centre, and also that the few
outer windows they displayed, all in the uppermost
stories, were many of them glazed with jewelled
colours, and flanked by richly carven shutters.

"Remind you of anywhere?" Roc inquired.

Elof gestured at one doorway, surmounted by a

carven shield whose blazon was blurred and unreadable with weathering, a mere mass of hollows and pits upon the stone. "Need you ask? Kermorvan's ancestral house, any other noble house in Kerbryhaine. Courts, four walls of rooms, almost all the windows facing inwards; well hidden from the world outside, from their noble rivals and the assessors of levies."

"And from the commons," growled Roc. "That's what it really means, I guess; wall out even the sight of the poor, that you can wallow in your wealth in peace. Look at the way the woodland screens off the whole fine quarter!"

"It may not be wholly their fault," said Elof. "Under some kings, even quite good kings, it might be bad for your purse or your standing to appear too openly rich ..."

"And under the not so good, for your health also? Well, maybe," grunted Roc, unconvinced. "But hear this. I asked Kermorvan about the fashion once, seeing it wasn't the way in Morvannec, with all our palaces clear and open; rich or poor, folk have always trusted each other there. He told me it dated only from the declining years of Morvan, taken thence like much else rotten by the rebels who became the first syndics; that it was never the way in Morvannec – *nor in Kerys*! And you'll allow my lord Kermorvan's a bright lad; when he says the lore is so-and-so, thus it is."

"Then it must have come about at some time since the lands were sundered. Powers, there's been time enough!"

"Aye ... but in both countries? Following the same path, the same ill path? *Again*?"

Elof frowned. "Well, they spring from the same root; they might well grow the same way – but no, you're right; I cannot believe it either, not when Nordeney and Morvannec have managed to be so different. It is more as if ... as if the others display the symptoms of the same disease."

"Ahh," breathed Roc. "Like it might be a cold, you mean?"

Elof smiled grimly. "Caught in a chill wind off the

Ice – yes, it might well be. Its hand can be subtle at times, and no less cruel; and it has many generations to study the flows and currents within the hearts of a people, and seek to channel them. Remember that as well as yours and Kermorvan's, this is also the ancestral homeland of Bryhon Bryheren."

Roc shuddered. "But if even Kerys is infected, what's the chances for the rest of us?"

"Every chance! Remember Tapiau, who despised men too much to be able to understand us. The Ice is ten times worse off, Roc; it hates us, it makes the worst assumptions about us. If we do not live up to them, we stand a better chance of escaping its snares!"

"Ah!" said Roc moodily, eyeing those walls, whose forbidding drabness seemed almost a reversed mould of the richness within. "But what's the likelihood of that here, d'you think? Eh? After all we've seen?"

"Still a good chance," Elof answered him calmly, "so long as the infection has not yet reached the heart. And that, I guess, we are about to find out."

The cog was gliding out from between the tall and insular houses of nobility and between another belt of woodland, growing against and over the most ancient walls they had yet seen, long since abandoned to the ravages of weather and wood. The channel lost its straightness and began to wind mazily about the buildings ahead; clearly it had once been a river here, before stone built up its banks and its channel was dredged. The buildings themselves took on a less even and upright look. There was no prevailing shape or size or fashion as in the outer quarters, save that they were all many stories high and built against one another, with few wide ways between; but here and there archways opened onto stairs and alleys that ran through the buildings themselves like worm-holes, as if space had been too precious to leave them open to the sky. Some buildings seemed more ancient even than the walls, others were brash and brightly new; some – and not always the old ones – gaped empty like skulls, while their neighbours stood in fine repair. And in many of their windows lights shone, although it was still only the middle of the afternoon. For in the shadow of the citadel they huddled, and behind its towers; for them, the sun had already set.

Some half-hour later, around a shallow bend in the river, appeared a row of wharves, with tall buildings behind them; walkways and galleries ran across their faces, overhanging the river, and between them many a complex hoist and crane for unloading. Elof and Roc stood beside Trygkar at the helm as with a heady blend of cursing and great dexterity he swung the cog along-side the furthest of the wharves, a vast grim affair of tapered stone blocks. Under the eyes of two bored-looking sentries men in dark liveries ran to take up the lines thrown ashore, hauled in the cog bow and stern till the long fenders of straw-stuffed canvas grated and squeaked against the stone, and made it fast. The crewmen were already beginning to strike the sail, and as it slid rustling and flapping from the mast it unveiled, like a curtain before a picture, the most startling prospect Elof had ever seen.

"The Strength of Kerys, masters," said Trygkar. "Within the Old Town, by the Royal Wharves. Great artery of the city, Heart of the Heart's Heart, the pivot about which the wide world spins. And for your worthy selves, voyage's end. May it be a fair omen to you. Pray don't forget the poor skipper!" But he chuckled quietly as he spoke, as if he knew he would get no answer; evidently he was well aware of how this sight struck a newcomer. As a distant hill or a bulk looming like a low cloudmass behind rooftops it had been an easier thing to accept, or if need be to ignore. But it could not be ignored here, for they stood at its very foot, and behind it the sky was fading to layers of blue-gray cloud inter-leaved with hues of peach and gold, a royal mantle draped about a crown.

Like a crown indeed rose the Strength of Kerys, a crown of many tiers and ornaments, and faced about with jewels and these jewels were edifices tall and fair in their own right. Of every kind and form they were, low and long and robust, square and strong, squat and forti-fied, tall and graceful and spire-crowned; palace and

castle, hall and hallow, all were here, set high about
those slopes like fruit in a tree, with a hundred smaller
shapes scattered in their shadow. Seeing them from afar,
Elof had not guessed how great they were in their own
right, nor how fair in their several ways; not one but
would have graced the heart of any city among men.
The High Gate might be greater than any of them, but it
was far less fair. His eyes followed a long stair, picked
out in the long sunlight like the many-branched limb of
a vast tree, from one of the tall, tapering gatehouses set
in the walls encircling the slope's foot up to the level of
a bulwarked fortification, out-thrust in the arc of a half-
moon to dominate the slope with dignity and strength.
Around this and above the staircase wound, between
smaller halls and up to a great frontage, bearing two
sweeping spires that echoed the towers above. The stair-
way parted before it, swept up around and behind its
steep-pitched rooftree to the two ends of a wide terrace.
Upon this stood a palace built like embracing arms, a
wide-windowed residence with nothing of the fortress
about it. Up the slope it rose in curving steps, the stairways
weaving about it, till it ended in a single high conical
turret. From there, over a bridge that curved like the
rainbow, the stair crossed to the first of a stepped
pyramid of terraces; from the highest of these the
towers arose.

So much he saw along one stair, from one gate; but
in that side of the wall alone there were a dozen such
gates, and as many stairs, and around many of those the
buildings clustered more thickly. Elof could not take in
a half of what he saw there; time was not given him. He
jumped at the crash of the gangway upon the quay, and
the roar of the sergeant's voice, mustering the guard.

The soldiers came clattering along to form up on
the deck, and suddenly, after two weeks of lazy informal-
ity, they had the look of guards once again. The sergeant
clumped up the gangplank to exchange words with the
sentries on the quay. Elof, without turning, spoke to
Trygkar. "Shipmaster?"

"Aye, Mastersmith?"

"You're of northern stock, and the seas are the

northerner's birthright. Are you happy, sailing all your life upon river and channel?"

"Happy enough, lad," said Trygkar guardedly. "We never reckoned much on the sea, not knowing who or what lay beyond it. Anyhow, birthright or no, the man-eaters stand in the way of it now, as of so much else. And not only them."

The sentries, looking agitated, were summoning somebody from the building at the rear. Elof bit his lip; over the last few days they had told the old shipman much of their voyages, and he had seemed enthralled and envious. But there had never till now been a free moment when they might safely sound him out; and there was little time for persuasions. "Search your heart, shipmaster. Is there not, deep down, the least longing to make one great voyage, unbarred by bank or boundary, to sail like the sky-wanderers, free upon the winds of the world? To find a fair land and a free kindred, and help against our common foe?"

"Not in this here cog, master ..." Trygkar grinned as he might at an over-enthusiastic boy, but Elof had seen his light green eyes shift suddenly, seem to gaze at a far grey horizon.

"And if I found you a fit craft?" hissed Elof.

"A seaworthy craft? Couldn't get one past the Gate, and there's no seacoast free to build on; where'd you ever get such a craft?"

"From the Ekwesh, of course!" said Elof impatiently. "If you could find a crew?"

"From the ..." repeated Trygkar, and began to laugh, softly. "By Saithana's belly!" He shook his head in happy disbelief.

"Then you'll come?"

The sergeant was saluting two plump men who came striding up from the rear, evidently officials of some kind; they were quizzing him rapidly, and darting surprised glances at the travellers.

Trygkar fell silent suddenly, pressing his lips till his small moustaches bristled. "By the Horns of the Bull, with such lads as you twain I just might! There'd be no problem about a crew, not among us old northerners! I might! But when?"

"Who can tell? so much depends on what we may do here ... upon your lord's word, among other things. A day, a year ..."

"So that it take not ten years ... Past that I might be too old. Get you word to me when you know – whatever my lord may say! Then we'll see!" There was sudden fire in his soft tones. "Lads, if it's at all possible I'm your man! Daft I may be, but I'd not miss this last endeavour if I did have to wait ten years!"

"Maybe it will not take so long," said Elof quietly. "But however long, I shall still call upon you, shipmaster!"

"Do you so! Fare you well – Mastersmith! And my thanks!" The officials were nodding vigorously now, and abruptly one turned on his heel and stalked away; the sergeant turned back down the gangway as swiftly, and tossed Elof and Roc a crisp salute that was as good as a command.

"By your leave, gentles ..."

One of the sailors sought to take up the bag that was all their gear, but Elof forestalled him, graciously enough, and let the sergeant usher them over the gangway, with the escort clumping behind. He heard a sharp intake of breath from Roc as he set foot upon the deep-worn stone of the wharf; at long last his feet rested upon his ancestral land.

But they were not to remain there long. The sergeant led them towards a great gibbet crane at the rear of the wharf, and ushered them up short steps onto the dais beneath, a broad square of stone wall supporting a raised floor of wood with a low railing around it. It looked so like a hanging gibbet that Elof found himself uneasily scanning the boards for signs of a trap; he told himself angrily that he was growing foolish, and turned to the doors at the back. Then he recoiled in alarm, suspecting he knew not what snare, as he felt something snap taut underfoot, and the dais judder. "Do yer take hold, sirs!" warned the sergeant, himself seizing one of the rails. Roc swore in horror as with an alarming squeal the whole contraption, themselves, their escort and all, was plucked bodily from the ground.

The doors swung open before it, and Roc swore again. A long ramp of smooth stone stretched out before them, rising straight and high among the buildings above, and running the length of it two deep parallel slots. Through them ran two heavy cables, singing with tension; looking back, he saw the same two running down into the empty space beneath the dais and into a mass of pulleys and wheels. They were standing upon some kind of winched platform, set on an angled carriage to keep it level as it was hauled up the ramp; he peered over the edge to see the small iron wheels running in the slots, and was all but tipped over the side by a sudden jerk. "Have a care, sirs!" the sergeant warned. "Faster and easier than the thousand stairs, is this, but no smooth ride. Stretchin' in the cable, they always say – though like as not it's their own idle hands shirkin' the task!"

"Hands? You mean it's men hauling this weight up?"

"By a capstan, to be sure," shrugged the sergeant. "Expensive by paid labour, but there's never a shortage of sturdy rogues from the jails, even if they need their backs tickled now and again!" Elof hoped he had not noticed Roc's tactless grimace; evidently they were thinking the same thing. Water power would manage the job better and cheaper, even if the cost of building was higher; either Kerys had lost its once, famed skills in that art, or it no longer cared. He did not like to think which. At any rate they had not learned the art of drawing and plaiting wires of steel into strong – and unstretching – cables, that was clear. They were rising high now, cresting the rooftops; the platform was catching the breeze and beginning to sway. After the first shock Elof and Roc, not long from the mastheads, hardly minded the sensation, but the soldiers clung grimly to the stanchions, and even the sergeant was a shade paler beneath his bricky colour.

Already they were over the outer walls of the Strength, and passing among its host of roofs. It startled Elof to see so great a mass of stone reaching such a height; it seemed to war with all he knew of the mason's art, this tower thrust at the heavens. But as they passed the terrace and gallery, square and street shelved out from the slopes, he began to appreciate the vast skill of its shaping. Grand and imposing as was the Strength from a distance, at closer sight it seemed far less substantial, a thing of lightness and air and outlines rather than of bulk, of arches that soared like an arrow's flight made stone, heavy buttresses that surged like carven waves, lighter flying buttresses that fountained up in sprays or rose in fluttering excitement like a flock of birds startled from a cornfield. They tapered into a surprising thinness, those buttresses, both for lightness and exaggerated perspective, till with the carven foliage that adorned them they stood out against the sky like bent saplings. Roofs of vast height were narrowed, built in against the slope on their hidden side; many of the spires and towers that seemed so solid proved to be chiefly openworks of pillars and carving, intricate and delicate.

But as the platform neared the top of its run and he came among the buildings, he saw that all this too was a work of skill, and not just a vainglorious facade. Had the Strength actually been as it was made to seem from afar, it would have been ugly and intolerable close to; the streets through which their escort hurried them would have been overshadowed valleys, deep and dank, the noble arches and doorways around dark cavern-mouths – a gloom-ridden place, horribly airless and oppressive. Instead their impressions were of brightness and space captured within the lightest possible cage of stone. Enormous windows in walls reduced their weight, and left pillars within to uphold the roof; but fair works of coloured glass filled them, and the rays of the sinking sun shining through them and playing over street and wall turned the Strength into a shimmering hoard of jewels. From any reasonable angle or distance the whole vast edifice had been contrived to seem fair and consistent in itself, both its several buildings and the greater whole they made up. Some strength, perhaps, had been sacrificed; it might not have withstood the rigours of endless northern winters, so much closer to the winds and the snows off the Ice. But then it was built for the south; and it was yet a place that great armies would break against, and lesser ones flee at the very sight of, and nonetheless a dwelling fit for all the arts of peace.

Winding their way along the walls they came at last to yet another such platform and ramp. As it lifted under them Roc shaded his eyes against the dust glare, and, looking out over the hazy magnificence of the view, he sighed in deep content. "Well, whatever else there may be, this is all the legends tell of this realm, and more. Can't you see here all the roots of Kerbryhaine, of Morvan and Morvanhal that now is, aye, even of your own little towns in Nordeney with their painted slats – see, in yonder patterned window, the same style? It's well named; the strength of our folk it is, sure enough."

Elof nodded slowly. "It is; for it embodies so much wisdom and skill and sheer cunning of mind and hand. This must have been a fair size of hill once, but what can you see of that? Nothing. As if they'd melted it down and moulded it anew from the hot blood of the earth. But there is something strange about some of these buildings – sergeant!"

"By yer leave, gentles?"

"Those buildings down below there – yes, that one … and that. Look down through those huge windows and what d' you see? Exactly. Nothing. They're spic-and-span, they've some of them painted walls or hangings, but scarce a stick of furnishing in them all."

"Small wonder there, sir; them as dwells there are well content with little. They're tombs, those are."

"*What*? Every one?"

"More'n a few, sir, aye. For in what better hallow should the kings who built the Strength wish to lie, in halls befitting their glory and power? All their lives they'd be working on them, as splendid as they could make 'em. 'Twas always intended thus, as I've heard, sirs, hallow and palace and place of strength together, a living show of their power. As the old saying goes, *The Strength of Kerys is its mighty tombs.*"

"So long as it lies not buried with them!" said Roc quietly, as the sergeant turned away once more. "What a pile of wealth to heap upon your own dry bones!"

Elof nodded. "What needs the greatest of men more than two strides of ground, if only he leaves a worthy name? And all the show in the world cannot enhance that. Remember Dorghael Arhlannen, how simple it was, and yet the feeling there?"

"Aye, that I do! These gilded boneyards fare ill by comparison – whup, here's the end of our ride!"

There came more streets, more looming buildings, and another ramp; this one was shorter, and ended before tall gates in an encircling wall; upon their dark wood the image of the bull's head with gilt sun between its horns stood out in weathered relief. The platform creaked and juddered to a halt, and Elof thought he heard, echoing up from the slots below the winding gear, the distant groans and gasps of exhausted men. Then the sergeant bellowed at his shaken men, and they formed up around Elof and Roc more closely than before. As the gates ground open the travellers saw they had at last reached the brow of that carven hill, for against the sky of evening, taller even than Elof had guessed, arose its mighty crown, the Horns of the Bull that held the sun.

Cobbles rang beneath their feet as they were marched briskly off the platform and across a wide square. Elof slipped and stumbled, for he was gazing at the towers. They looked subtly newer than the others at their feet, and their resemblance to horns was no accident; their outermost faces were flat and hard-edged, but the inner faces were shaped carefully into a graceful continuous curve, as across the brows of a gigantic bull. Below them, at the level where eyes would be, stood two round drum turrets, many stories high and faced with graceful colonnades that flanked the front wall of a palace, a greater than any on the hill below, and a fairer. Midway in that wall a tall arched doorway opened, and above it a wide balcony whose canopy was in the form of a high helm crowned with a circlet. The helm shone silver, the circlet with the lustre of fine gold and the sunlit fire of encrusted gems. To Elof that crown, like the overwhelming towers, seemed more vulgar than splendid; it hardly seemed to belong against the calm strength of the palace, almost as if it had been added later – recently, even. Then he frowned with sudden understanding. That balcony fell midway between the towers. When they captured the sun, it must seem to stand above that balcony, that helm like a crest; and how would a man seem who chose to appear beneath it then?

There were sentries waiting within that arch; a great many sentries, their mail brightly gilded, the shafts of their long spears a gaudy scarlet, as were the bobbing horsetail crests on their helms. One among them bore a surcoat of black worked with the crest of the sun between horns in heavy gold thread. He stepped forward unhurriedly, without surprise, a slender man with greying blond hair, and the sergeant saluted with great deference. Somehow, swift as the ascent had been, some message had passed more swiftly, and they were awaited. The man in the surcoat inclined his head politely to Elof. "I am Irouac, officer of the King. He will hear you at once, gentle sir, if you will come this way; but your sword, I fear ... Not in his presence; no-one may, save his guard alone. I myself will bear it beside you; and I must search your burden also."

Elof's teeth clenched and his fist closed unbidden on Gorthawer's silvered hilt, but he knew he would achieve nothing by resisting; with the best grace he could summon, he unslung the bag from his shoulder and passed it to Irouac, then slowly drew the sword from his belt. The officer's eyes widened as he touched its edge, and he held it gingerly by its quillions. "A noble weapon, this! I understand you are a smith; of your own forging?"

"Of my re-forging. It was forged in the deeps of time, by a hand unknown to me. It came to me ... as an inheritance."

"A rich one, then! It is fit to be a legendary blade of old, such as Belan that was Glaiscav's, or Talathar; that would fit its colour."

Elof smiled; his lore was being gently tested. "It would indeed, *talath* being a word in the Old Northern for the Dark; the Coming Dark. But whose blade might that have been?"

Irouac waved them in before him; the red-crested sentries closed in behind him, leaving their escort unceremoniously out on the steps. "This way, good sirs! The king will receive you in the main hall, only within these doors ahead – *Open, there*! Whose sword, sir? Why, I hoped rather that you might know that, for the last that is told of that hero was of his setting out over-sea to seek the land you come from; Talathar was lord Vayde's sword, Vayde the Great. Was he simply lost at sea, then? Did he never come among you, and find the hero's death foredoomed to him, after all? Well, well. And has this blade a name?"

Elof swallowed in a dry throat; he was aware of Roc beside him, staring, speechless. "Vayde did come among us, sir," he answered with an effort. "I am thought by many, though by what ways I know not, to be distantly of his kind. And the blade has a name, sir, of my bestowing; it is Gorthawer. Know you what that means?"

"Why yes," said Irouac. "It means ..." Then he hesitated, licked his lips, almost let fall the blade he held. "It means Nightfall."

The officer hurried on. Elof followed after him, but he hardly noticed the tall arches of the outer hallway, windowless and gloomy, nor its rich murals, dimmed now in shadow save where the declining sun shone down through the windows of the gallery above and shed a splash of sudden colour on the walls. He was elsewhere, wandering lonely over infinite grey marshes. Under cool heavy skies, with the smell of salt in his nostrils and the sharp black rushes rattling like an enemy's spears, the grass-flowers sprinkled like a spray of fresh blood; he was seeing the mass of bodies the bog had brought up in the spring thaw, cloven corpses from a thousand years past, some thirty or more, and one huge frame whole, still grasping a black-bladed sword. A sudden pang, and he was back at Morvannec as it then was, on that terrible, glorious night when a free people had bought their freedom anew in blood, when the light had first shone on that great statue of the Watcher, and shown him a face so like and so unlike his own. Vayde's face, Vayde's blade – and Korentyn who had known Vayde had seemed to recognise his very voice ... Yet he was not Vayde; whatever twists and turns the River had taken, whatever the unknown parentage he cared for so little, he had never been more sure of that. Vayde was reputed a giant in stature, and so the Watcher's image showed him, Vayde, by such chronicles as Elof had bothered to consult, was a warlord, a schemer, a man of unpredictable and frightening temperament as his wrath-stamped countenance suggested, wielder of a cold and deadly justice; worse, he was certainly a necromancer who trafficked with strange forces in his strange tower, who had prolonged his life to twice that of ordinary men, and only incidentally a skilled smith. He had served good kings and good causes with ruthless loyalty, and sometimes by fell deeds they would never have countenanced themselves. What could Elof find of himself in all that? Little or nothing. If he was honest with himself, a certain ruthlessness; but not half so much. No word of love, and what had driven Elof most of his life save the quest for love? If Vayde had ever loved, no chronicler had thought to mention it. Uncertain tales were told of his eventual end, but all agreed it had come about in the turmoil when Kerbryhaine drove out the refugees from Morvan, whom he favoured. It could well have been in the Marshlands, then ...

He came back to himself with a start. Roc had jogged his elbow. Glancing quickly around, he saw that they stood now on the threshold of a long hall, stone-flagged and shadowy, save for a window at the far end, through which the sky of evening showed ruddy and fierce. The buzz of voices hung heavy on the darkening air. Torches and lanterns were being lit along the walls, and by their flicker they revealed a considerable company there, seated around long tables, strolling about or simply lounging, kicking their heels against the rush matting that covered most of the flags. "Not here yet!" breathed Irouac thankfully. "Come along! Come!

Not to be kept waiting!" He led them swiftly down the middle of the hall, where lines of pillars marked out a central aisle, lit very brightly by lamps before curved mirrors of metal cunningly worked into the pillars; they revealed the flagstones worn almost into grooves beneath the mats. Irouac halted them some twenty paces from a wide dais of white, not very high but surmounted with an immense carven chair of oak and some kind of yellowed ivory, clearly ancient work. Its back reached twice the height of a man, with a heavy canopy of ivory above it shaped to seem like cloth blowing in a wind, cloth intricately inlaid with gold, and each arm was a small table of ivory, their carven edges worn almost smooth by the rubbing of robed sleeves. There were images in the carvings that looked like scenes from a tale, and he was just striving to make them out, when th crowds at the side rustled into sudden life, there was a single clear note upon a trumpet, and a voice called out "Clear the way! Stand aside, all men! He comes, the Lord Nithaid of the Lonuen and of the Ysmerien comes, High King of the Land of Kerys and all its folk! *The King comes*!"

There was a frantic stir and rustle in the background, chairs scraping against the floor and feet shuffling, and a growing hubbub. Forgetting his other concerns, Elof waited eagerly to see this king of an ancient line, this remote kinsman of his friend Kermorvan. "Think he'll be like him? Like as was Prince Korentyn?" Roc whispered.

"In body, who can tell?" Elof whispered back. "In mind and spirit, let us hope so; there is a bond of blood."

"Aye, but that's no guarantee; some of Kermorvan's kin were right sons ..."

He said no more, for the crowd to their right scurried apart. Many threw themselves upon their faces and beat their brows upon the matting; everyone else fell to their knees, and all but a few, Irouac among them, bowed to the floor. He tugged furiously at Roc's sleeve; Roc glanced anxiously to Elof, who rebelled at the thought of grovelling as no man did before his own revered king. But not wishing to offend, he compromised by sinking slowly to one knee, Roc copying him, and with head erect sought his first sight of the monarch of this enormous land.

But strangely enough, it was not he who appeared first. A little girl in a bright red gown, a child of no more than ten summers with a gold fillet around her chestnut hair, came skipping unconcernedly along the cleared way, stopping to look back and giggle. Behind her stalked older boys, tall and sturdy in cloth of gaudy green and gold, with gold bands twined about their brows; at fifteen or sixteen they were almost men, but their faces, though well enough, were set as arrogantly as only rawest youth can be. Elof could see that they were chafing under the weight of the huge hands laid on their shoulders, at least in public; well, so might he have. Perhaps he himself, at the height of his own blind self-regard, had managed to look that unpleasant; and such a father as this might lay a formidable burden on his sons.

Nithaid, High King of Kerys, looked at first sight not the slightest bit like his kinsmen oversea, past or present. Elof stared in surprise as a man of middle height, no taller than himself and even broader, a thick-set wall of a man with a round tun of a belly, bustled his children aside, then came stumping and wheezing at a great pace up onto the dais and settled into that noble old seat with an alarming crash. The robes that streamed and billowed about him were of dark velvet, gaudily worked with a wealth of gold and silver, but neither new nor especially clean nor closely tailored, hanging comfortably loose about his immense shoulders. He was bareheaded, revealing a mane as thick and waving as Kermorvan's, but black instead of bronze and shot with streaks of grey; his beard was the same but even thicker, spreading down to his heaving chest. Kermorvan, by contrast, preferred to go clean-shaven like most folk of consequence in his land, Elof and Roc included; in fact he carried it to extremes, shaving with his sword's edge if he had nothing better. But then,

Kermorvan's face was lean and handsome in a hawk-like fashion, whereas Nithaid without the hair would have been coarse as a puddock, as Roc was later to put it. His skin was white, his jowls heavy and fat and his mouth a wide thin-lipped gash; his nose was narrow and straight, but slightly bulbous at the tip, and his brow, though high, was furrowed into a permanent frown. His eyes were oddly slanted, under heavy brows; but in them some likeness to Kermorvan did lurk, the same shade of mist-grey blue and a fierce raptor's alertness that spoke of great energy of mind. Sweeping the prostrate throng before him, they fastened upon Elof and Roc, and widened as if in surprise; but any other feelings they held back like a stone wall. He grinned suddenly, his teeth gleaming very white against his beard; it was a merry grin, with the impish innocence of a child delighting in his own vast cunning, but above it the eyes were intent, considering, more like Kermorvan's than ever. The children also were looking at them, the little girl with wide-eyed fascination, the boys with a mixture of alarm and disdain. Elof guessed suddenly that word must have been sent well ahead, that this whole court must have been buzzing with news of their arrival, so that even the children had heard. Suddenly Nithaid vented a wordless bark, like a laugh cut suddenly short, and his huge ham of a hand slapped the throne-arm; Elof felt the whole court twitch in fright, then warily they looked up and began to rise.

"Well?" His voice, though tinged with an accent that sounded rustic, at least compared to Irouac's, was neither as deep nor as coarse as his looks suggested; in fact it was clear and mellow, with the suave music of the trained orator. He spoke words as if he relished the taste of them, his tones slightly drawling and sibilant, constantly on the brink of a chuckle. "So these are our emissaries, are they? The Mastersmith Elof Valant', and his companion Roc, hmmm?" The slight accent cut the ending from Elof's second name. "Welcome at last to your homeland, sir emissaries – though from all I hear the savages gave you a harsher greeting first. That's one more insult we'll be repaying in due course!" He eyed

Elof's bloodstained clothes uneasily. "Before anything else, d'you need a surgeon?"

Elof bowed courteously. "No, my Lord Nithaid, though I thank you. I'm well enough now."

Nithaid gestured at the roughly mended tear in his tunic. "That the wound? Horns of the Bull, it's a marvel you're still alive!"

Elof smiled ruefully. "Sometimes it happens that way with me, my lord; I heal fast. I'm not sure how or why."

"Ah, well, you're a smith, of course," grunted Nithaid, "and smiths is strange cattle, as our country folk say. Now, do you tell me, how come you to be here? And to what purpose?"

Elof gathered his wits; this fierce character would not be easily impressed. He had not missed the awe in which his court held him. "My lord, I will. We also, in the several lands west oversea, have been beset by the Ice and its minions. My lord Kermorvan sent me on this quest, to reach our ancestral lands and there find, and if possible recover ... a thing of value which was lost to the Ice, and we guessed was brought here."

"A thing you'll not name, then? Not in open court, anyway. Very well. But do you tell me, are mastersmiths so common in your land, that they are sent on missions of great danger?"

"No, my lord. But what was taken I regarded as mine."

"Some powerful work, then? Ah well, let it pass for now. A heavy trust, and a perilous one; you must have had adventures. Tell us some!"

Elof had not expected that, and flushed like a child; he looked hastily at Roc, who shook his head. But under Nithaid's goading Elof told a few of their experiences, and was surprised to see how the courtiers hung on his words, how the King's beard bristled and his cheeks flared. When the Ekwesh ship was lured under the ice-island he literally roared with laughter, throwing his head back and guffawing; even the princes lost their arrogance and listened all agog, while the little girl simply gazed at Elof with immense eyes. "And I not there!" sobbed Nithaid, thumping on his throne-arm. "Do you go on, man, go on!"

"... and so we made our way south," Elof eventually concluded, 'until your patrols found us. That is all, my lord. We are now as you see us, and that is a poor state in which to continue our mission. We sought the lord of this land in the hope that either he would assist us against the forces of the Ice, or at least aid us in returning to our own land, where we may seek help of our own." He paused slightly, but Nithaid only sat back in his chair and stroked the corners of his moustache with his thick fingers; his keen eyes fixed them both, but he said nothing. "In any event, my lord." Elof resumed, assuming his most ceremonial manner to underline the formality of his request, "we are, apart from our main quest, also ambassadors from our own lord, bearing assurances of good will to any realm afflicted by the Ice, and of particular friendship to our ancient kin of Kerys, whose name is still revered among us. To them he offers the renewing of ancient ties, no matter the span of leagues or centuries that has hitherto parted us, and where alliance or aid is wished for, any he can supply. He requests also, in the name of good will between rulers, and lords of the Ysmerien line, free passage without hindrance for his ambassadors, and any help you may be able to give them. This, through Elof Valantor his counsellor and Court Smith, and Roc, his trusted and confidential courier, from Keryn Kermorvan, Lord of the Ysmerien, last king of the line of Morvan, first king of Morvan Arisen, and the folk of Nordeney, Kerbryhaine and Morvanhal together."

He stopped. He had said something, some word too many, there was no doubt of that. Nothing had changed, nobody had stirred, Nithaid still sat stroking his beard, but the atmosphere had changed dramatically. The very stillness was electric, like the first hush before the storm. Suddenly he found the air of the hall stinking, stifling with the smutch of torch and lamp, the smell of human sweat, and beneath that the almost tangible reek of fear.

"What did I hear you say?" inquired Nithaid softly,

his voice so suave it was almost creamy. "King, was that it? Last *king* of somewhere, first *king* of somewhere else, and of some people nobody has ever heard of. *King*..." He leaned forward suddenly, grinning still with an immense satisfaction. "Well, my learned Mastersmith, do you learn one thing more, and that is that there is only one rightful king of all the people of Kerys, wherever they may have spread to and in whatever land they have settled, whatever barrier lies between, be it ocean or Ice or the very fires of Hella herself! And that is *me*! *ME*!"

His voice had risen to a roar of startling volume, from that almost to a scream of wrath, a stormcry that bent and uprooted his courtiers, quailing like saplings before a blast. "Nithaid, of the ancient line of the Ysmerien! By birth, by acclaim of the nobles and by main strength! Not some upstart! Not some spawn of a rebel and runaway! Not some tag-end of the blood, reared and raised ruler of a scrape or two of soil! Learn you that! And learn it well ere the mood takes me to have it branded onto your hide!" He subsided, panting, still grinning with ferocious enjoyment of his own temper. "And by Hel's black belly, when I've whipped the Icewitch and her man-eaters from the Gate I'll sail a fleet of Kerys across this ocean and show your princeling what it means to be a king!"

Elof, standing shocked and silent, saw Roc's face turned red as his hair with fury; but this was a dangerous animal, and anger was no safe way to deal with it. He caught Roc's arm, felt it tense and subside; Nithaid noted the gesture. After a moment he muttered, more thoughtfully. "Needn't sack the place, of course. Knock it into order, that's all, take proper account of your landholdings, lick your peasants into line and set them swinking as they should, tax and toll a bit, h'mmm. Need a few nobles to take it in hand. Or even a good viceroy, it being so far away; if this Kermorvan's done a good job till now, might even leave him to look after it, so long's he makes me the proper submission and tribute. Could use a new source of thralls — and timber — is there good timber in your land, lad?"

"More than Kerys and Morvanhal together could use," said Elof evenly. "And great store of all else that your folk may need, if it is sought in friendship. But you will find us very short of thralls, I fear."

The intent eyes fixed on Elof, unblinking, but nothing was said. Instead he turned and beckoned peremptorily to Irouac, who had been careful to stand well clear of the others. The officer scurried forward, and laid sword and pack upon the throne-arm. Nithaid reached for the pack, and rummaged inside it, then tipped the contents out into his lap. Elof took a step forward, opened his mouth to protest, and found scarlet spearshafts hard across his throat. Behind him Roc cursed. Nithaid looked him in the face a moment, then called out "*Amylhes!*"

A figure detached itself from the shadowed mass of courtiers and stepped forward. He wore a livery in the black of the smith's guild, much like Elof's own as court smith, only far gaudier, broidered over breast and sleeve with gold and silver and gems in garish signs and symbols. To Elof they looked remarkably meaningless, and he guessed they were meant to impress the credulous. Otherwise the newcomer cut an unimpressive figure, middle-sized, scrawny and none too clean, his thinning white hair brushed sleekly back from a narrow face whose stained teeth seemed too large for it, giving him a fixed and mirthless smirk. He bobbed his head to Nithaid with cool deference. "At your command, my lord!"

Nithaid's great hand spread out the jumble of jewels and tools in his lap. Elof could not suppress an agonized breath as he saw the few things he truly treasured so roughly treated; Amylhes evidently heard him. "What d'you make of this, then?" the king demanded. "Is he any kind of a smith?"

The Court Smith plucked each piece up one by one and held it close to his eyes, squinting and peering as he turned it round and round in his fingers, grimacing with concentration and sucking his teeth. He clucked with surprise when he came upon Gorthawer, and as he looked up from it his watery blue eyes fastened on Elof with a malice so immediate and obvious it startled him. He shrugged, and his horse's teeth bared in a smile. "Oh aye, it's pretty stuff enough, but bare and barbarian, not enough ornament, no style. Old-fashioned. Rough. What's this supposed to be?" He bent down and rummaged in the tool-bag, and to Elof's alarm he drew out the gauntlet with its crystal in the palm.

"It protects my hand when I must handle ... hot things," said Elof, perfectly truthfully. The smith tossed it back, and straightened up with a high braying laugh.

"We don't coddle ourselves thus in this land, sonny! I was taught to take my burns and like it when I was an apprentice, half your age. And you claim you're a mastermith!"

"I bear the stamp," said Elof evenly, though the spears still crossed at his throat. "Come paw at that, if you will. But I am not *the* mastersmith, only one of many. And I serve as Court Smith, I allow."

Amylhes shrugged. "Not here you wouldn't, my lad. Not at *your* age. Got to sweat for your mastery here ..." Nithaid, whose brows had drawn together at mention of a court, cut him short.

"One of many, eh? Well, well. Can you make anything of him, Amylhes, that's what I want to know?"

Amylhes wrinkled his nose as if some bad odour lay beneath. "Well, since I never have enough help – aye, I might, given time. He's got good thews on him. And at least I'd not have to teach him to tell gold from brass ..."

Nithaid waved his hand. "He's yours, then. And the other; he looks strong enough, too."

Elof stood speechless, aghast. Amylhes' heavy-lidded eyes drooped, and he thrust out his head like a turtle's. "Many thanks, my lord. But since he's shown himself so forward and unruly, he might prove recalcitrant, eager perhaps to seek his native land ..."

"I'd thought of that for myself," said the burly man shortly. "Well, I'm not having him tattling tales back to his dunghill cock of a princeling, I've troubles enough for now without one more fly to squash. Make sure you keep him well fettered, that one."

"My lord, fetters of iron and steel will hardly hold even a half educated smith ... Might it not be better to ..."

Nithaid grimaced. "Oh, very well, then. If you must!"

The smith gestured, and suddenly Elof found himself seized and flung forward on the ground; he gathered his strength and flung off one of his captors, but many more piled in upon him, and when he still threshed something solid rapped the back of his skull, not hard but enough to jar and confuse him. Moments passed as his mind whirled, a wooden gag was thrust between his teeth and his worn britches ripped up from calf to knee. Still he did not understand, not till his sight cleared and he saw Amylhes bending over him, with the black blade in his hand –

He heard Roc swear hoarsely, and a sound of furious struggle. Then into his leg, just behind the knee, a dart of searing agony drove. All his muscles knotted with the pain of it. Fire roared in his head, his heart hammered against his ribs till he though he must die, wished he would, then knew, in a flood of dull panting agony, that he would not. The hands that held him did not relax, he caught his breath, and in that instant it happened again. Somewhere in the roaring furnace he was aware of the gag splintering between his teeth, and then the bellowing redness surged up and overwhelmed him.

He blinked, aware of a sudden blessed chill, of flooding wetness; he still lay face down upon the same flags, but they were soaking. Somebody had thrown water over him. He raised his head a little, saw a guard tipping more water from a leathern bucket onto Roc, stretched senseless on the matting with a trickle of blood running from his nose; he stirred and groaned. Somewhere a young girl was sobbing; Elof, confused, looked around and saw it was the child, kneeling beside the throne and gaping at him wide-eyed with horror, hardly hearing Nithaid's bluff attempts to comfort her.

"... happen all the time! See, see, go to, he's not sore hurt, he's looking at you now! No need to take on so, he'll be right as rain in a few minutes. It was just to stop him running away, that's all, when he might be valuable. You'll have to learn to look after your own thralls one day, if it's a proper princess you want to be. Come now, here's a pretty present for you ..." And with no more ado he picked up the two halves of the arm-ring and slipped them over the little girl's shivering forearms.

It seemed to Elof that something actually snapped inside his head. He struggled furiously to spring up, to cry out, to howl in horror and outrage; but the splin-tered gag filled his mouth, and such a bolt of agony lanced through him when he tried to move his legs that he almost vomited against the gag. He forced himself to be still; his legs had refused to obey him, had scrabbled and scraped limply against the stone, as he had seen in dying things, beasts and men. The pain faded, and he lay there gasping, breaking out in a cold sweat. But as the agony faded there was a sudden sickening sense of release in his lower legs that was almost worse. Fear caught at his throat. As through a fog he heard Nithaid crooning "There, that's better, isn't it? And you can wear them as two for now, and then when you're older ... no, don't go bothering Master Amylhes, he'll be too busy. Run along now and show them to your nurse!"

Elof was fighting a frantic battle with the jagged panic in his mind; he could not face what had been done to him. Slowly, choking down his rising gorge, he forced himself to rise a little on one elbow, and look at one outflung leg. One glimpse was enough; he slumped down so limply that his head rang dizzyingly on the flag-stones. It had not been hewn off, as something in him had whispered. But behind his knee there were deep wounds, still bleeding, and he knew they meant some-thing almost as terrible. Amylhes had simply severed the great tendon behind each knee, and so destroyed the leverage of the limbs. They had hamstrung him beyond healing, and made a lifelong cripple of him.

He would never be able to walk again.

Nithaid and the Court Smith were looking at him. There was open gloating in the older man's eye, but not in Nithaid's; he bore the satisfied look of one who has seen a disagreeable matter of business done with. Fury went shuddering through Elof like the winds through a forest and sent his fears whirling away on the blast. To the forest he thought back, to the pine floor. What had he achieved there? What had he unleashed, to heal himself? With that fury for a spur he delved deep into his mind, searched for the same source he had tapped, the same inner strength he poured into his work. He imagined it like some precious pure metal spilling white-hot from the furnace, flooding through his veins till they shone hotly bright, spreading, searching, seeking the flaw in his flesh that it might flow into, heal and restore.

Almost at once, though he had scarcely managed to believe it, the pain grew less, that sickening limpness began to fade. If he could keep this up ... Then from behind him came a gruffly alarmed shout. "My lords! He has stopped bleeding!"

"What?" he heard Amylhes exclaim. "Impossible! let me see! Unless he's dying –"

"No, noble lord! Even as I watched the bleeding slowed suddenly and stopped – just stopped, formed no clot, nothing! And the wound, the sides of it, see!"

"What is this creature?" he heard Nithaid mutter, and his wrist was seized. "He said he healed fast, and by the Powers it was no lie; would it had been! Is it safe to hold him, Amylhes? Had we better not simply slay him out of hand, and scatter his ashes?"

Amylhes snorted furiously. "I've a better remedy than that. And he himself has supplied the means!"

Quick footsteps sounded, and from across the floor he heard Roc's warning shout. Looking up, he saw the Mastersmith Amylhes bearing down on him; but it was what he held in his hands that chilled Elof's heart. "*No!*" screamed Elof through the gag, and forgetting the agony he struggled somehow to rise, fought like a madman to find something he could spring himself up on, to roll away. But at the smith's curt order more hands seized him; he snarled like a wolf and bit, but a spear-shaft pinned him to the floor. Then, for the second time, two brands of pain unimaginable thrust into his legs.

Terrible as the first pains were, he had not yet screamed. But now he did, and shattered the gag with the force of it. The pains were no worse; but the torment of heart and spirit was a horror he could not endure. He clutched at death even as he had clutched at life, willing his heart to shatter, his mind to blow out like a candle in a cold wind, and the shadows around him to rush in. Horrifying as what they had done to him already was, this was worse. He howled his sorrow like a beast, for indeed it defied words. Yet somewhere, some part of him in a strange mad isolation, he could think with frightening clarity. Had Kara felt that last agony even as he had, wherever she was, far or near? Had she too felt bars of metal shut about her soaring spirit, the measure of her days caught in? Did she curse him then, knowing it was his doing? For Amylhes had spoken truer than he guessed. He himself had forged the fetters that henceforth must bind him to the end of his days, that he would never dare force open. He had sought to bind Kara; far more terribly, he had bound himself. For he had shaped those silver anklets which Amylhes had thrust through the wounds in his legs, between the very bones, and snapped firmly shut.

The clasps were cunning; who knew that better than he? Since they were meant to bind Kara, he had shaped them never to be opened again, once shut. As Amylhes must have seen, he had also made the anklets strong, almost impossible to break. Kara might have done it, in her power; but caught up in them, she would not wish to. Elof might manage it; but he would not, for with them he would break Kara. As they closed, a circle closed that should never have taken shape anywhere save where it was intended, around Kara's own flesh; for into the anklets, with a hair, a feather, no more, he had woven a part of the fate of that flesh. Closed around her, that would not have mattered; if they were somehow broken there, what was taken could return to her. Only the virtue would be dispelled. But if they broke now, that vital shred of her existence would dissipate; the effect upon her could only be guessed. She might

not die, as a mortal might, but that change she had foreseen would surely come, in ways he could not imagine;
and surely she would be lost to him. That was the risk
he had chosen to run; that was what Kara had hurled in
his face. And never more clearly than now was his own
confident and ruthless folly brought home to him.
Unless those bonds were broken, he could never ever be
healed.

He screamed, or he wept like a child; he did not
know. He hardly noticed that hands were smearing
numbing salves upon him, tying rough bandages about
the wounds. Not until the face of Amylhes swam into
the emptiness of the world before him did he take
notice. Then all in an instant the fit passed, and he
raised himself upon one elbow; he saw the King's sons,
staring at him with amused, gloating looks on their
faces; evidently they had enjoyed what they saw. He saw
Roc sitting up beside him, clutching his head and staring in wordless horror at what had been done to Elof.
To neither did he pay any heed, any more than to the
fire between his bones. For a moment another face
seemed to swim before his eyes, seamed and grim. A
clear cool wind of hatred and wrath blew through him,
and brought him sudden strength. On one arm he raised
himself and looked clear-eyed at the Court Smith. Then
he spoke, and the man took an involuntary step back.

"*Amylhes!*" The name grated from his throat. "Liar
and fool I name you, and false to your lord. You knew
me for what I am from the first moment you saw me; a
smith of craft and skill far greater then you could ever
command. You feared me, lest I show the world how
feeble you truly are; and you hated me, because I could
not help showing it to you. So you lied to your lord, and
you sought me as a thrall, to pass off my work as your
own, or at least keep me from others, and in time be
quietly rid of me. All this, to stop me supplanting you!"
He felt light-headed; he seemed to have no body, as if
the fire had burnt it to ashes and the wind dispersed
them. He existed only as feelings, and the words they
spawned. "Yet you had nothing to fear from me,
Amylhes. Not then. But you do now. For your mean

ends you crippled me; yet that is not a tenth part of the greater wrong you have done. You are a flawed casting, Amylhes; and I shall shatter you."

The voice he spoke in had stilled the babble of the court; his words echoed with sombre certainty between the stone walls. The Court Smith flushed red, then white, so choked with his wrath that he could not get out his answer. But it was the king that Elof looked to, Nithaid to whom his words had truly been addressed, slumped reflectively in the great chair; and it was Nithaid who answered him, with not a trace of the anger that had gripped him a shorter time since. "It fits a thrall to guard his tongue better, Master Valant'," he said soberly. He gestured out into the shadows of the hall, towards a pillar upon which something hung, gleaming red in the deceptive flicker of the light. It looked horribly like a dismembered body for a moment, till Elof realised it was a suit of armour, with a bronze-hued breastplate. "Amylhes is no mean smith. He's made for me some fine things, the latest that armour, better than any king of Kerys has had since the old days and the lost arts of our ancestors."

"Are they lost?" asked Elof softly, though a sudden shiver of weakness gripped him. "That sword of mine that this nithing turned against me, take it from him and look! Be wary – aye, it cuts, does it not? And is it not fair? A thousand years could not blunt that edge; I know, because it is older than that. But when it was ruined and bent I was able to reforge it; could he? Craft and skills I have that have never been lost, king; and others that I have found anew for myself. But do not think me an idle boaster, king; put us to the proof. Set my sword against his armour!"

The court erupted. Nithaid looked at him wide-eyed a moment, then let out his barking laugh. "By Verya's sweet apples, at least you promise good sport! What say you to that, Court Smith?"

Amylhes elaborately did not look at Elof. "My lord, even a broken-backed serpent may be dangerous. By my counsel you will not risk yourself even slightly –"

"Risk?" inquired Nithaid quietly, but with a flash of

his frightening eyes. "What's this of a sudden about risk? After all you've told me of that armour –"

"My lord," said Amylhes, treading confidently but delicately as does a man used to avoiding traps. "You yourself called my armour the best and strongest since the elder days. Yet kings were slain even then, clad in their mightiest armour – not least by the sly hands of traitors. I would not have you expose yourself to such perils lightly. Test it at need, my lord, in battle, but not for so petty a matter!"

"In battle!" repeated Nithaid, and suddenly his blue eyes were very like Kermorvan's. "In battle. Aye, that would be more appropriate, would it not? In battle, where if it fails, I fail, and am in no case to take the matter further. Interesting!" His voice had a mildness in it that made Elof squirm. "However, as usual you are right, I cannot risk it. Not out of fear, lest it should have crossed anyone's mind; but because I will not put my land in jeopardy lightly, not with my sons still young, the Icewitch sniffing about our doors and now this outlander princeling." He shook his head over the many iniquities of life, then looked up. "Therefore, Master-smith Amylhes, I think that you shall don the armour, and meet the challenge in my stead."

Someone at the back of the court gave a snort that sounded like sudden laughter, instantly stifled. Amylhes' hooded eyes were unreadable, but he bowed. "A worthy idea, lord; but I crafted it most painstakingly to fit only your frame –"

"Oh, come, Amylhes!" Nithaid rumbled. "No need for such tact! We're much of a height, and you can pad yourself out all you like to match my belly and the rest; you'll have a few days to prepare, till this one's fit to face you. So that's settled, eh? Good. Very good. Guards! Take 'em off, these two; see they have healing and all else they require, but keep 'em secure. Your heads answer for theirs! And while you're about it, see their food is tasted. A shame if they met some ill fortune before the appointed day, eh? Off with you, then!"

The appointed day dawned earlier than any of them had expected. "Nithaid seems to be impatient for his sport!" remarked Elof.

"Sport?" growled Roc, as he helped Elof step by painful dragging step to a bench. "This is plain murder! Tell him you're not healed yet, refuse! You can hardly stay upright on your crutches, let alone put any weight on those legs of yours, splints or no – "

"Roc, I'm aware of that! And so is he! Do you think he'd care? Was I strong enough to strike a blow, that was all he wanted to know!" They turned to look at Nithaid, sprawled across his chair; he waved a jovial hand at them, and turned to bandy some remarks with his sons who stood beside him. Elof was glad that the little girl, at least, had been spared this. Courtiers came out as they neared the bench, and helped them in. They seemed cruelly amused, some of them, but not unkindly; Elof guessed that the Court Smith had made himself no great favourite, and they would be glad to see him fail. But from the wagers he could hear bandied about, few favoured Elof's chances.

A murmur parted the crowd, and from out of the shadows strode a figure it was hard to recognise as Amylhes. From head to toe he was carapaced in metal of a shimmering bronze hue, shaped to Nithaid's bulky frame; upon the breastplate, from midriff to throat, it bore in traceries of gold the sign of the bull's horns holding the sun, in a coiling, cluttered, florid style. The same gaudy decoration wound across every surface, spreading out along the limbs, for instead of mail they were encased in metal shells, with discs bearing the sun design to shield the joints and hinges, and at the brow and sides of the visored helm. In one hand he bore a heavy mace of matching hue, with many narrow ribs, and a sun-disc at its head. "Plate armour!" hissed Roc. "A whole suit of plate! And solid, by the ring of it!"

Elof glared and said nothing, but there was a sickness in him greater than any pain. He had bargained on some plate armour; but this was a whole suit of it. It was far easier to fashion, but crude compared to the subtle shapings of mail that the best smiths could accomplish. Few active men sought to encase themselves in so heavy and cumbersome a guard, preferring ring mail with added body plates. Knights of the warrior order of ancient Morvan, with their fast, fluid craft of fighting, preferred less plate; Kermorvan used only light plates at shoulder, elbow and knee, and sometimes the breastplate that bore the crest of his line. Plate might shield the wearer from some blows, but hindered him in avoiding others. Here, avoidance was not at issue; if Elof could not make good his boast at one stroke, he could not move to avoid its counter. That mace would dash out his smithcraft forever, and all the hopes and fears and follies that went with it.

"Let me do it!" hissed Roc fiercely. "I've the strength, I'll have the bastard's head off before a man can move – "

"And yours would follow! No Roc, you've got yourself a bad rap on the head already by trying to help me; look to yourself, rather, don't worsen my fall by sharing it!"

"'Twasn't much. I gambled a dunt on the head against the chance of wringing that scrawny neck. Had the same idea as you now, I guess; only I might have saved your legs, and ... and worse. Those anklets ..." He groaned under his breath. "Oh Powers, what's the point? What can we ever hope to do now?"

Elof's heart sank like an ember; if even Roc was despairing ... But Nithaid was speaking. "You there, give the man his sword! And you, his friend, get him to his feet! be you his prop for now!" He left unsaid what was obvious; that if Elof failed Anylhes would soon see he needed no support ever again.

"Listen, Roc!" said Elof suddenly as they shuffled into a circle lit by many lamps, summer eve though it was outside. "When I give the word, let me go! Yes, let go! Only for a moment! You'll see why ..." But then Nithaid raised a peremptory hand, and Amylhes clanked forward to face him, only two strides away. Irouac put the cool hilt of Gorthawer into his hands, and with it the memories of that last shattering stroke against another and greater evil, of the lightning that had bathed it and driven it deep into solid iron. Elof drew a deep shuddering breath, and Nithaid let fall his hand.

Amylhes stepped forward with a clatter of metal, and raised the mace high. "*Now!*" cried Elof, and swinging up Gorthawer he flung his arm free from Roc; both hands met on the hilt, and with that singing snarl the black blade flew high above his head. Amylhes looked up, he could not help it, and for all his own wiry strength the weight of mace and armour told on his arm. He lost the moment of his swing; and in that instant, swaying on legs that were already collapsing under him, Elof brought Gorthawer hissing down.

Weakened as he was, his arms still held a strength few even among smiths could equal. The black blade struck like the lightning that had forged it anew. It met the mace, reaped the head from it like a cornstalk and fell upon the helm beneath, smashing away the visor; the breatplate rang like a bell as it passed and leaped up in baffled fury against the flagstones. The rebound tore it from Elof's fingers, and he toppled; Roc caught at him, but he crashed down onto the stones, and agony convulsed his half-healed legs. The black sword skittered away across the floor to Nithaid's feet. Amylhes' face, revealed in the broken visor, wore a look of startled relief.

But only for a moment. A flicker of vast surprise crossed it, he opened his mouth to speak or cry out, choked, coughed and staggered in a jangle of metal, fighting with the collar of the suit. Blood gushed out of his mouth, and bloodstained tow erupted from the riven breatplate, slashed like soft tin from breast to waist. He hit the flagstones with a jingling crash; plate squealed and scraped as his legs kicked along the flagstones a moment, and fell gradually still.

In the hushed silence that followed Nithaid rose ponderously from his throne, bent down with a breathy grunt to pick up Gorthawer, and gingerly thumbed the edge that had struck. "Not in the least blunted," he announced, as if not in the least surprised. Elof, fighting to breathe against the shock of pain, could not answer. Nithaid prodded the corpse with the toe of his boot. "So there you lie, Amylhes," he said dryly, "for all your craft and cunning. Fool! Did you think me so blind I could not tell for myself the better man? But you were ever a schemer, and wont to force matters. Guards! Take this trash away. Armour and all."

Elof found his voice, though his head was swimming. "You knew? You *knew*? Then why did you force me to this?"

Nithaid shrugged. "As I said: good sport. Though as it turns out I am rid of a mediocre smith and accomplished intriguer, in a way that his powerful kindred cannot lay at my door. I could not be absolutely *sure*, after all, could I?" He hefted Gorthawer and clucked at it delightedly. "And I have a new Court Smith who is related to nobody and ill-placed to interfere, or even go where I do not want him. Your first task, by the way, will be to make me a new armour. And I have a most remarkable sword."

"*That sword is mine*!" grated Elof.

"And you are mine, Valant'," replied Nithaid levelly. "And so also all that belongs to you."

"I am nothing of yours! You may have tricked me into becoming your murderer, Nithaid; but you cannot compel me to work for you!"

Nithaid motioned to the guards, and they dragged Elof swiftly to the dais foot; the jolting pain sickened him to silence. He could feel blood oozing from an opened scar. "Let us understand one another, you and I," said the king. "You are mine, either as an outlander thrall, or as a subject of the rightful king of Kerys and all its domains. It makes no difference; but it could. Do well by me, and you both will prosper. But if not – well, I would not coerce a mastersmith such as you with common threats. I would only apply to you the law which governs any man, left to himself, that if you do not work, you do not eat." He shifted his glance to Roc. "But this sturdy fellow here –"

Roc growled deep in his throat. "Do your worst!"

"This sturdy fellow, as I was about to say, I would not waste so. You also would have to work – but in some heavy labour, fettered among felons, or if need be blinded, as I guess you are also some kind of a smith. I think we would have years of work from you, after hunger and thirst first began to bite; but I would rather leave you to look after your friend. He may need you – and he cannot flee. You alone would not get far if you tried, for from his account of your voyage I learned you are scarcely a sailor. The one cannot escape; the other cannot use any freedom he might gain. What do your own efforts tell you?" He leaned forward earnestly, fixing them with a gaze grown suddenly keen. "But do not mistake me! The Ice is your enemy; so also it is mine. And does it not threaten us more closely here than in your homeland? Well then! Do we not need you more urgently here? I would far rather count you as free servants, helping me with the same skill and valour you have displayed. You came asking me for aid; and I never gainsaid you. I mean to drive back these reivers, storm the Gate and make it ours again, hang the Icewitch from it by her own ensnaring hair! But to do that I need to unite this land, build up my power! Help me in that, and you'll flourish! When I trust you I might even have those fetters struck off –"

Elof shook his head violently, too violently; the palace chamber shook around him. "*No, king! Never!* That, never! These are deep waters of smithcraft you cannot understand. Let the fetters be! I am resigned to them. But that broken arm-ring ... I can forge another as fair for the little princess. Let me at least have that back, king for it is a dear and bitter memory to me."

Nithaid tapped his teeth with a ridged thumbnail. "As Beathaill is to me – all that is left me of her mother ... I will not take from her what I have bestowed, and I know she will not give it up for any reward. Not now, anyway; in a few years, when she is suitably wedded, perhaps, she may put it aside. I can only counsel you to wait. But what's that, man, however dear, to what you could gain? A man like you could earn a title, even, and estates; you'd hold them a hundred times better than many born to them –"

Weakness and bleak despair welled up around Elof; his breath came fast, and fearing he would faint he threw up his hand to stop Nithaid in his flow. "No, King! The Ice is our enemy, but we have little common cause. I have seen your land, and how you rule it; and beside the king I serve you are a brigand chieftain, Nithaid – no more!" A horrified buzz of voices arose in the court, and many shrank back; but though Nithaid's eyes narrowed, he did not interrupt. "To suit yourself you have maimed me, made me your tame murderer, and taken from me things greater than you can guess. I will serve you because I must, under duress, as a thrall only. Never freely, never loyally; you lack the coin that could buy that of me! I will set great craft in your hand; but only as long as it is turned against the Ice. Cease that struggle, turn aside from the fight, and I will serve you as you deserve. I will crush you, Nithaid!"

The silence when he finished could not have been more shattering than while he spoke. Nithaid's hands had closed hard on the leading edges of the throne-arms, white-knuckled, quivering, as if to tear the ivory asunder; his face was bloodless, his eyes staring, his lips working with words half formed. A great lock of hair had fallen across his eyes unheeded, and they were screwed up to inhuman slits. Then suddenly he threw his head back and bayed like a wolf, a great whooping crow of laughter. "You'll crush me, will you? How, lad, how? Under your crutches? By hopping on me? Ho, it'd be worth it just to see you try!" He doubled up with the force of his mirth, hugging himself till tears shone on his cheeks and his nose ran into his beard, and his courtiers, as soon as they were sure of his mood, joined in, whooping with laughter and even mimicking a cripple's gait. "*Enough!*" barked Nithaid suddenly, slapping his hand down on the arm of the throne. "Learn this one's courage, some of you! Then you may mock him! But you, Valant', hear me! Serve me as anything you like, so long as you serve me well! And as for slaying me, why, when you feel ready I give you leave to try!"

Elof had raised himself on his arms at that, though they trembled under him and the blood roared in his ears. He thrust out a hand, and he could not see it tremble. "I hear you, king! So be it! *So be it!*"

The walls spun about him, faster and faster, the torches flared up and danced like marsh-lights. And like the marshes, weighing down his limbs, pressing suffocatingly upon his chest, the darkness behind them reached up to enfold him, envelop him and suck him down.

CHAPTER SEVEN
Sorcerers' Isle

SO BEGAN, IN SHED BLOOD and desperate pain, the time of Elof's thralldom; and in blood and pain also it was to end. But that end was to be long in coming, and destined to be the ending of many other things besides. Neither Elof nor Roc could foresee it, and for them those first days were black days, as black as any since their youth. They knew they could count on no aid from Kermorvan and Ils; to their friends they would simply have vanished into the ocean's trackless wastes, and grieve as they might, with the weight of kingdoms upon their shoulders they would be unlikely to risk themselves or others on the same voyage. "And here's hoping they don't!" said Roc glumly. "For they'd simply sail all unwitting into the arms of the Ekwesh, and without your ways of winning help!" He swore, and sank his head in his hands. "How about his weirdness Master Raven? Now I'd even be glad of his brand of aid, though the thought of it puts years on me; can you not get word to him?"

Elof, curled up on a pallet with his maimed legs tucked under him, stared into the darkness and sighed. "Since I began this voyage all has gone amiss as never before; so he warned me, and I defied him. He will not aid me now; perhaps he cannot." He listened a moment to the sound of the river waters lapping against the shore far below, and leaned his weary head back against the timbered wall. "No, my old friend, this is something I must accept –"

"Well, you may, but I bloody well don't have to!"

Elof shook his head at Roc's sharp outburst. "I spoke only of myself, Roc; this is no affairs of yours, any more than it was in the marshes. You are not crippled; you have nothing to hinder you escaping."

Roc snorted like an ox. "Oh yes I do! That get of a mongrel bitch Nithaid landed his darts right in the gold, neat as pie. For one, I haven't got you this far to leave you now; or why the hell'd I spill all that sweat in the first place? For another, where can I escape to? The duergar? The Ekwesh? Or the depths of the bonny blue sea? I can't sail a ship worth a damn, still less can I plot a course! No, my lad, I'm taken in the same snare; here I am, and here I stay, till we've some way of prying you loose."

"But do you not see?" Elof groaned. "You're his chiefest hold over me! If you weren't in his hands too, I could refuse to labour for him, even if he had me tortured half to death –"

"Which he would! And then the whole way, if you still resisted! He'll baulk at nothing, that one – as we've cause to know. Think I could suffer escaping, knowing it meant that? Could you, in my place?"

Elof grimaced. "I like to think not. Very well, Roc, you have the advantage of me there."

"Not I. Circumstances. And it's surely not worth having your gullet slit just to keep your smithcraft from his paws; it's a king of our kinsfolk, he is, after all, and foe of our foe."

Elof laughed bitterly. "So I told myself, and so sought his aid; should I have not been warned by the manner of land he ruled? A chieftain of brigands I named him, and brigand he is, ruling by main strength and by fear, by no law save the absolute whim of his will. He hates the Ice, I guess, as he would hate anything which threatened aught that was his. For the evil behind it, for its threat to all men, he cares nothing; let it do its worst, so long as it leaves him alone! And it might, Roc, one day it might! If he gives Louhi a hard enough fight – as he is strong enough to do, can he but hold his realm together – she may decide our land is the easier target, after all."

Roc's alarm was evident in his voice. "You'll never get him to go after her then! And a sudden assault, after years of peace ... Powers, Elof, what do we do?"

"What we can!" Elof felt a change within himself,

deeper than any mere mood: his voice grew suddenly harsh in Roc's ears, as grim and dark as time-eaten iron. "He is a fool, who incurs without need the wrath of a mastersmith! For had Nithaid used us with any honour, we would have worked strong smithcraft enough for him; it fitted our purpose. Even so fell a hand as his I might have strengthened, seeing no other way to unite the land. But now we will bide our time, you and I; and use that time to seek the means of freedom for us both. And shall we not find it, who in our youth defied the will of Powers? On that day all pacts shall fail, all reckoning fall due; then let him beware! His reckoning is heavy enough now; if he lets fall the struggle against the Ice, the weight may crush him!"

"Great words!" said Roc, the more acidly because he himself was daunted by the voice in the darkness, so unlike the friend he knew. "But breath alone won't bring 'em to pass!"

The voice grew softer, slower and yet more sure. "Yet for all that, we shall make them be, you and I.

We shall quarry our misfortune, we shall smelt it, you and I;
Out of suffering render vengeance, molten in the forge of pain;
We shall strike it on our anvils, ere the fires within shall die.
And from vengeance temper freedom that shall shatter every chain!
The more firmly I am fettered, all the freer I shall stride!
The more cruelly I am pinioned, all the further I shall fly!
The more harshly I am crippled, all the more I shall be free ..."

It was sinking now, like the last embers of a dying fire, almost to a whisper on the edge of sleep, mingling with the circling wind in the trees.

"And he shall see it!
The more clearly he shall see it! And in seeing ... shall
he ..."

King Nithaid had been generous, after his lights, to
his valuable thrall. Also, perhaps, he had not been
unmindful of his own safety. When Elof collapsed he had
had him taken and cared for in rooms of the palace,
rather than any of his dungeons; but every door and
window had been well guarded. In a day or so, when
Elof was recovering his strength, their old acquaintance
Aurghes the sergeant had come with a detachment of
the royal guards, to which he had been promoted, and
conveyed them unobtrusively down to a light longboat
and out to one of the islands that lay in the Yskienas
around a half-league offshore from the city. Its southern
face was unwelcoming, yellow cliffs rising to a roughly
fertile country of scrubland and small woodlands, with
many oaks, chestnuts and pines on the upper slopes. Its
northern side, though, rose more gently, and over a
wide part of it a single sweeping slope, smooth and
grassy, led to a hill-top crowned with a great stand of
oaks, ancient and gnarled, contorted like grotesque
dancers as they swayed in the river breezes.

There he had settled them in the shell of an old
building, built half of wood, half stone, in a pleasant
nook high on the island's upper slopes, by the side of a
swift stair of waterfalls and well sheltered by the oaks.
Once, he told them, it had been a comfortable hunting
lodge, used by those who came to hunt the island's
game, which was rich and diverse; it included small
herds of rare creatures, perfect cousins of the enormous
mammuts found in both Elof's land and this, yet no
larger than a dog. In later times the lodge had sometimes housed noblemen sentenced to mild terms of
exile. That, he said, might account for the slightly
unhappy reputation the island had among the more
ignorant peasants; and certainly nobody cared to come
there now. So, since neither Nithaid nor his father and
grandfather before him indulged in such lenient punish-
ments, it had fallen into neglect and near decay, leaving

barely one room sound, abutting the rockface behind. But that very decay had stripped away enough of the wood to reveal, unmistakable to Elof and Roc, the unshaken foundations of a magnificent smithy in the stone. Here beneath the lodge's fireplace was a hearth, wide but well shaped, with the remnants of what must have been a tall chimney, cunningly flued; other lesser hearths were ranged around. Here were solid bases for huge anvils, such as they had not seen outside the tower of the Mastersmith Mylio; and, as in that eerie place, there were recognisable mounts for tall waterwheels, and channels from the many falls above. "He was a master indeed who built this!" said Elof admiringly. "How came it into disuse?"

"Can't say anythin' of that," said the sergeant, rather uneasily. His manner, though not unkindly, had become noticeably more curt and domineering, as if to underline that he had to do with thralls now and not emissaries. "Must've been three hundred years past, or more even. The Lord Nithaid commands you build it anew for yourself."

"All by myself?" inquired Elof sardonically, tapping the stones with the crutches of green birch the guards had cut for him. With his legs splinted straight he could already move surprisingly well for short distances, aided by the great strength in his arms.

The sergeant sniffed humourlessly, and handed him a sheaf of waxen tablets. "Tomorrow we return with a first load of stone and all else necessary. If there's anythin' special you'll need in the buildin', do you write it here. Lord Nithaid grants you such tools as you bore, and all else in Amylhes' smithy; it will be packed and sent when the smithy is ready."

"Before!" snapped Elof, scribbling furiously. "I'll need to forge ironwork for the building. And it must be packed by a smith. If he had a library, I'll want that also, and safe housing for it here. And any other books Nithaid can spare, of smithcraft or otherwise."

The sergeant sniffed again. "I doubt there'll be many; what'd a king be wanting with books, now?" He glanced down the long list Elof had scrawled, and his wispy eyebrows shot up. "By the Gate, I'd as soon not be the one gives him this! Him in a rage, he'd do nigh anythin' to anybody!"

"So I have observed," said Elof flatly. "But this is the smithy I must have, to work of my best. If he wishes less, he has only to choose. Tell Nithaid!"

Shaking his head, the sergeant shambled away down the slope to the boat, and left Roc and Elof to spread their bedding in the last remaining room. It was there, alone and free at last to speak openly as the long summer twilight faded into night, that they held that desperate conclave. It proved the first of many they were to have during the weeks, the months that followed after, which at last grew into long years.

At the next day's dawning the guards returned. To the sergeant's astonishment, when shown the list the king had simply grunted and told him to see to it all, adding that there was no measure more wasteful than a half-measure. All that Elof had asked for had been sent; including, to his delight, his precious pack of tools. He tore it open, and sighed with relief at finding it untouched; the guantlet was there also, his explanation evidently believed. But to the dismay of the smiths 'all else necessary' turned out to include not only building stuffs but also a pack of thralls to do the actual labour, peasants passive and stolid, stooped by continual labour and poor feeding, burned to a brick red by the strong sun of these southern lands. Though the guards were not especially brutal, they drove and harried these hapless ragged creatures to their labours like mere livestock, till Roc felt his blood boil, and Elof no less. But at the same time he would seize upon some detail and goad all within reach to amend it, guards and thralls alike, till it was to his satisfaction; impatient at his own weakness, he drove them so furiously that even the cowed thralls called down curses upon his head. At last, maddened with frustration, he plunged in among them and, crutches and all, began trying to heave about blocks of stone with his own strong arms. Roc had practically to haul him away lest he injured himself any further, and he sat aside with his hood drawn over his face.

They might have thought him angry; but in truth he wept, and despised himself for weeping. What had been done to his body any man might have found hard to accept; but for Elof, who from his youth had always been impatient of the weaknesses of flesh, it was a terrible torment, and it almost broke him. It was a torment that he could not forget, even for a second, even in sleep. Each night he dreamed of running, free and strong and tireless; then his maimed legs would jerk and thrash, and the pain of his scars would awaken him. Already despising himself for the follies that had led to all this, he could hardly have felt less of a man now had they truly unmanned him. He had learned to walk on crutches quickly, not because he had adjusted to his present fortunes, but because he could not. It was this same impatience that made him drive himself, and led him to bully the thralls. But when it came time to eat he fed them well from the store of decent provisions Nithaid had sent him, though the guards protested it was better than their own. "Why not?" he inquired coldly. "If I am to share their fetters, they are my brethren, and shall share what I have. You who deem yourselves free servants, be content with what your master provides – or try a thrall's life for yourself! I am sure he will oblige you."

The soldiers grumbled still, but made few attempts to hinder him thereafter. They feared him for his influence with Nithaid, but still more as a mastersmith of proven power, which to them was a unique and fearsome thing; had he not been a thrall, they would still have had to salute him as they had Amylhes, falling to their knees before him. From talking to them he had come to expect this, and from his reading in Amylhes' library, when it arrived, he understood why.

Smithcraft in this land had long been caught up in the struggle for power, the secrets of its mastership ever more jealously guarded; they had become something to be handed on only to a chosen few, and in great secret. The fewer mastersmiths there were, and the less widespread their knowledge, the greater became the power of the remaining few. Over many generations that process had taken its logical course, their number being constantly whittled down until in the end there was only one true mastersmith in the land at a time, a powerful servant of the king. But with the dwindling of the mastersmiths the breadth of their experience also fell away, and hence their knowledge; much was lost and little added. Thus the craft of jour-neyman and apprentice was impoverished, as was that of the masters who rose from among them. It was a slow process; but it had been going on, he guessed, since before his own land of Nordeney was founded, a thousand years past. He found now he could understand Amylhes better, pity him almost; any man who had risen to where he had would inevitably have had to be more the scheming courtier than the smith. And for such a man to be confronted with another he could see at a glance was infinitely more powerful, more capable, and half his age – how could he help viewing him as a rival?

"But Nithaid saw through him!" objected Roc. "Seems he always did; and yet he didn't stop the old bastard crippling you ..."

"Why should he?" inquired Elof bitterly. "Did it not suit him well to lose a bad smith for a better, a free man for a thrall, a whole man for a dependent cripple? All without having to lift a finger?"

Roc grimaced. "So that was what you meant! He expected it. He was letting you do his dirty work for him all the time."

"He was," Elof replied coolly, running his fingertips over the wallstones of the forge with an absent-minded caress. "He is clever, Nithaid; too clever for Amylhes, too clever for me, who saw through him only when the deed was done. In every way he has ruined me, that wise brigand; he has stolen from me all the things I still treasured most, he has made me both his victim and his tame murderer. For that I told him I would crush him; and so I shall, Roc. So I shall."

"But not today," said Roc quickly, his eyes darting to the approaching boats.

Elof smiled thinly. "No my friend, not today. My wits may be crazed across, but they are not wholly shattered. Today he comes to see what is costing him so dear. See he shall! And may his cleverness teach him due respect for true smithcraft!"

"It might, at that," said Roc, relieved. "It's impressive enough, that forge; almost as fine as old Mylio's lair, or your own in the Guildhall – and may I live to set foot in there again one day! Who'd have thought this old ruin would shape up so neat?"

"Well, I did!" smiled Elof. "Right from the first moment I set eyes on it, there it seemed to be, just as you see it now, exactly the way it was – "

"Oh aye?" cut in Roc sharply, but Elof had already stopped short. "How're you so sure of that, then?"

They looked at each other a moment, questioningly. "I don't really know." Elof admitted. "I just ... saw it, that's all. That's all!" he insisted, as Roc opened his mouth to ask something more. "Come, the boats are beaching. Come!" He snatched up his crutches and with ungainly energy slammed the shutters closed and swung himself out of the door. Roc lifted his eyes to the naked rafters in mute appeal for patience, and stumped out after him.

With no less vigour Nithaid swung his heavy frame over the gunwales, thumped down onto the chalky sand and squinted up at them. Behind him, splashing into the shallows, sprang his guards. The king waved an imperious hand upslope, and set off at a great pace, the guards doubling to keep up with him, their plumes tossing in the breeze. He reached the forge red-faced and asweat, and stood with hands on hips, glaring at them and saying nothing; the guard, a dozen or so, closed in around him, their scarlet spears held trailing but ready for immediate use. Elof gave no sign of noticing them, and inclined his head politely to Nithaid. "Your thrall regrets his inability to come down to meet you," he said with elaborate politeness. "Or make the usual obeisances. The crutches, you see ..." For a moment their glances clashed; but Nithaid's smile was all bluff and genial condescension.

"Well, I'd hardly insist, would I now? Take it that you're relieved of all such obligations to me. Valant'. As to the least of free men, eh?" He gestured impatiently at the smithy. "What do we tarry for, then?"

But he glanced uneasily at the freshly painted door as he entered, and many of the guard baulked visibly. For Elof had set patterns and symbols upon it in strangely worked brass, and they guessed unhappily at their potency. At its heart was the mighty character of the sun, worked in the Nordeney style, and the look in its central eye was bleak and baleful indeed. What they saw, as their sight grew used to the shadows beneath the temporary roof of sailcloth and boards, was no more reassuring. Two huge waterwheels dominated the forge, and as the king entered Roc spun open the sluices; water diverted from the falls leaped and thundered under the roof and crashed down upon their blades of iron unrusting, and with many a protesting creak strange devices came to life. Sighing like a giant, bellows taller than a man drew breath and blew in the same pass, and all around the room the hearthfires roared into sudden dazzling flame. The red-white light danced about the strange-shaped ironwork that supported the roof, browning the beams and bringing eerie life to the grimacing masks of the crouching beasts that formed the brackets. Grinding wheels and shaping lathes, crushers and sifters, driven by pulleys of many sizes, hissed swiftly to life, and with ponderous smoothness a tall column of blackened steel surged straight up towards the rafters, slipped free suddenly and dropped down upon a high anvil with a crash that seemed to shiver the air. Lesser hammers beat a rippling rhythm on blocks of chiming iron, sharp sounds that lanced through the ears and severed thought from thought. Against this torrent of sound Nithaid stood stolid and unmoving on his squat legs, his guards clustering close about him as if he might protect them. Elof waved to Roc, and the sluices were shut again; the abrupt silence seemed as terrible as the noise. But Nithaid was yet undaunted.

"That's a pretty show!" he remarked sceptically. "But I've seen better in the arena, Valant'. Fine to look upon – but what may you do with it all, there's the rub! Crows you may scare off with such a din, but never the

Icewitch! So much expense upon the thrall, and now he's demanding still more! Time we saw some results from you, my lad!"

Elof smiled calmly. "Do you look over upon that anvil, then!" Nithaid stared, blinked, then with a muffled curse he stalked forward and lifted from the anvil some pieces of plate armour with patches of mail about their edge. They had something of the same bronze hue as Amylhes' but no other resemblance. Each link of the mesh was most cunningly and intricately worked against its neighbour, so that when Nithaid laid a piece across his hand the mail became almost a solid surface, merging imperceptibly with the plate. "You commanded an armour of me," said Elof quietly. "These are its trial pieces, made of such materials as Amylhes kept to hand; I will need more, and better. It will be a suit of plate and mail combined, in the style of Morvanhal; and the mail will also close thus under the weight of a blow. The harder that falls, the more firmly it will be driven together. The mesh as a whole has virtues of strength and unity within it, but upon each ring is set a virtue of moving freely and unhindered; I have learned to value that of late. Well, as I have begun, shall I go on? When you send me the makings – "

"You'll have 'em, you'll have 'em!" crooned Nithaid absently, greedily caressing the mail as if it were costly silk, "Aye, finish it, soon as you may!" Then, recollecting himself, he added gruffly "I've need of haste. Summer ends, and with the mists of autumn the reivers grow bolder; the king must start a new campaign, or lose even more support from the outlying lords who bear the brunt. I hate to fight in armour that was dead men's, and what's borrowed never fits my belly. So! List all you need – but no waste, mind you!" He peered around suspiciously. "Like these heavy roof-timbers you've the nerve to demand! Each one the month's keep of a cavalry squadron! If any can be found of that size, that is! We're forever short of large timber in this land. Why not just cut down that oakwood stand atop the hill and use them, as my lads'd have you do?"

Elof snorted impatiently. "Aye, and lose the roof

itself to the next winter gale, without their shelter! Anyway, you feel the heat of the fires, even under this high roof; it takes well seasoned timber to bear the heat of a forge for long!" He forbore to add that he was simply too fond of the trees, anyway; fortunately it was highly unlikely that any such idea would occur to the king, though Nithaid had a mind both acute and acutely suspicious. It cost Elof most of the day's work, not to mention all the shreds of patience he could summon up, to convince him that the timbers and materials he had demanded were necessary. "Well, then," grumbled Nithaid at last, as he cast a last severe look around the forge, "at least you'll not be able to claim I denied you aught, Mastersmith. If I'd a court as perfect as this forge I'd hammer out a sound enough realm, let me tell you!"

"Would you?" inquired Elof coldly. "A master does not despise his metals, king. And though the forge is well enough as it once was, it is hardly perfect; I need more heat! Fierce heat, fiercer than a common fire can yield! Heat to soften stubborn metals, to consume others and bear new substance from their blending. At the very least I need a furnace of some kind, for my studies and trials! Amylhes cannot have understood a tenth part of that library of his, there's much new to me within those books that I must wrestle with."

"Is there now? And to what end?"

"To what end is a babe new-born? I have known the strangest oddments prove vital. But where knowledge is dangled before me I must have it, king, as you must your dominion. No other passion rules me save one, and that is deep in eclipse."

"Well, do you burn your heart to feed your forge, then! No, you'll have no costly construction of me; if fiercer fires you want, you yourself must find them. And meanwhile, have a care of that armour!"

As Nithaid's boat pulled away and his guards scrambled hastily back into the other, Elof flung the shutters wide and drank deep of the cool air. Roc grinned as the sunlight flooded the smithy, and made it an airier, fairer place altogether. "You were right; far better show it made, all in shadow like that! Fairly shook the brute, for all his calm! And look at those guards hop! They'll not be too eager to come back to Elan Ghorenhyan again!"

"Sorcerers' Isle, is that what they're calling it? Well and good! Let them keep a clear berth, there'll be fewer prying eyes and ears for Nithaid then. And with those timbers we'll have the forge complete within a week." He pondered. "Save for the furnace. But any ordinary furnace would barely meet our need, anyway. He was right, Roc; we must find some means for ourselves ..."

The makings of the armour arrived the next day, heaped on the shore by a nervous boatman, who all but fled when the smiths approached him. Elof set to work then in earnest, forming stiff wires of bronze and many other metals, shaping and entwining them with soft sung words into intricate forms; most he left free and flexible, but some, for the vulnerable surfaces of the joints, he shaped into the close-knit chains that flowed like thick cloth through the fingers, yet braced and locked against one another when struck. Forming the plates was an easier matter, but he did not skimp it, and set their surfaces with ornament carefully shaped to deflect any impact; then little by little he linked them with the mail, fitting them carefully around the same form Amylhes had used. It was a hard task and tedious, hardly taxing to a mastersmith like Elof, but he threw himself into it with such fierce energy that by the time the thralls returned with the new roof-timbers, some three weeks later, the armour was nearing completion. It stood on the form in a corner of the forge, squatly grotesque, to his tormented mind a disturbing likeness of Nithaid; all the worse, in that he had not yet shaped the helm, and it was headless. It haunted him, and he longed to be rid of it; yet for his pride's sake he would not hurry the work. But a strange quirk grew in him, and when Roc, who had been supervising the work on the roof, saw the completed helm he was appalled. "You're never sending him *that*!"

Elof shrugged. "Why should I not? He will know it for better work than any he can have seen!"

"Aye, but ..." Words failed Roc. And indeed, the

effect of the helm was not easily described. It was of the same dark bronze hue as the armour, beautifully ornamented in gold; but there was little fair in its aspect. It sat upon the armour's broad shoulders in the shape of a huge bull's head, shaped as from the life, as closely as one could who had herded such beasts in his childhood; its horns were short and turned down against the brow to ward off blows, lowered as if for the charge. But there was also a strongly human cast to that countenance, though it was hard to find it in any single feature; and the look upon it was appalling, lowering, threatening, basely brutal yet fiercely aware, most bestial in its likeness to men. Or rather, to a man; for the whole cast of those features, and most of all the look in those pouched golden eyes, cold and menacing, was beyond mistake. That helm, work of craft and strength though it was, was a mockery closer and more deadly than any dart it might deflect, a distorted likeness of Nithaid.

All Roc's objections Elof brushed aside; the armour was packed up and dispatched to Nithaid that evening with the returning work party. Roc groaned as he watched their boat pull away from the shore, but Elof only chuckled. "Even he would not slay us for that, not when it is such a proof in itself of our worth to him! But I would I were there to see the conflict in him, between his greed and his pride! You saw how he drooled over it; but what will he do now, I wonder?"

"Ah well!" sighed Roc. "He might well burst a vein in his rage, that's always something. We can only hope. But it wasn't so much that that was worrying me; it's *you*. Dependable soul you've been all the years I've known you, from the moment you got out of the Mastersmith's clutches onward; serious like, never your braying merry-andrew, but a good lad nonetheless. And now? All of a sudden you show up this quirky jesting side; and a jest with savage teeth, at that! What's got into you? You're changing!"

Elof's brows knitted, and for a moment his own face wore the look of the bull-mask. "Say rather, I am changed. In lasting pain, my sword and my freedom torn from me, even the power to walk, what may I do but put a keen edge on my wits? But I am still myself, Roc; have no fear."

"You're still the man I know, aye," grunted Roc. "But there's a hint of one I'm not so familiar with, also. and I do fear; for you most of all."

But when the guard returned, early next morning, they bore with them tidings from the king that neither man expected, and more besides. Nithaid, it appeared from the sergeant's account, had gazed upon the armour a long while in silence, as if astonished, while the court held its breath. Then he had crowed like an enraptured child, insisted upon being fastened into the armour at once, and had jingled around the palace in it for the rest of the evening. "And for all I know 'e slept in it!" grunted the sergeant. "For sure I saw 'im set off for a ride in it at first light!" He scowled at them. "As sharp a piece of kiss-my-arse as ever I saw, that likeness! A fly pair you are, for all your fine words! Brown-noses with the best of the courtiers!"

"You mean," asked Elof faintly, "you think that image is a flattery?"

"Well, surely!" trumpeted the sergeant. "Fairly brings out the king in 'im, that does! And doesn't 'e know it! Wait till the lords clap eyes on 'im in it, he keeps saying, that'll scare 'em into line! And the army! And the savages, by Verya's curlies, they'll brown their britches and run a league! Don't believe me? Well, believe this; 'e's sent you by me a mort of delicate meats, enough for a two days' feast, and a hogshead of strong wine all to yourselves! Though by my lights the bearer of such glad tidings might rate a swig, it being such thirsty work telling 'em ..."

"Help yourself, and gladly!" said Elof, sagging on his crutches.

"You don't think Nithaid was just bluffing it out?" Roc inquired, as the sergeant stalked purposefully back to the boat.

"He might have been," said Elof. "He has the wits ... but no, you heard the sergeant; he liked it no less. What a folk to fall among! What a land ... "

That evening Elof climbed by himself to the hill

top, and with him, though he was little given to deep drinking, he took a large jug of the wine. There he sat a long time on a rocky outcrop, watching the sun sink through a sky that flared in shades of scarlet and smoke, looking to the west that held so much he had lost. Roc, sensing his mood, let him alone until well after dark; when he did go to search, bearing a brand from the fire, he found his friend sprawled insensible among the roots of the oaks. He was stirring and moaning, as if ridden by nightmares, but the next day, though little affected by the drink, he remembered nothing; only the flesh of his legs about the silver fetters, which had been healing well, was bruised and bleeding again, as if someone had been tugging at them.

But from that day on Elof grew calmer, and outwardly at least more content with his lot. He readily agreed with Roc that their life on the island called Elan Ghorenhyan was no great hardship in itself; they had both endured far worse in their time. The smithy was comfortable, and seemed well sheltered from inclement weathers. It was lonely, perhaps, but no worse than the Mastersmith's tower in their youth; and it was infinitely better than being cooped up in Nithaid's palace. It held even some slight consolations for his worst sorrows. The loss of Kara still burned in his breast, but here at least he dwelt far closer to her than if he had remained at home; and that could only increase his chances of seeing her once again, even helping her somehow. Beyond that he did not dare think. And he was also closer to Louhi, well placed to work for her downfall; and that task was next most dear to his heart.

As the autumn drew on, and cold winds from the north whipped up the waters of the Great River and scoured the island, he buried himself even deeper in his studies; these were copious, for Nithaid had sent him not only Amylhes' library, but great numbers of scrolls and fan-folded tomes from the palace. For the most part they were dirty and neglected, spotted brown with sharp-smelling fungus and even chewed by vermin; evidently the sergeant was right in thinking the court had little use for books, least of all such difficult and crowded texts as these. But Elof had, for among them were not only works of smithcraft, but recondite histories and minute chronicles, profound studies of the earth and the skies and the waters that freed his restless mind from the confines of his hobbled body and sent it questing back and forth across the world. He laboured long on good arms and armour for Nithaid's courtiers and lords, but these were to him casual and trifling works that occupied only half his thoughts. While he twisted the cooling breastplates this way and that beneath the fall of his hammers, or set keen edges on sword or halberd against the grinding wheels, his mind turned over strange and arcane fragments of his reading, purified and refined them, welded them together into larger, stronger structures of knowledge.

So time passed – a year, autumn to autumn, and another year after that. Scant detail is given those years of captivity in the chronicles; they are recorded in the terse and cursory fashion common in matters which the chroniclers must have thought unimportant, or of which Elof was not proud. Often they are like pages read beneath the gloom of gathering stormclouds; yet from time to time a bright light illumines some event, and it stands out in stark relief against the rest. So, perhaps, these must have seemed to Elof and Roc in their thralldom, rare blazes of levin-light against the oppressing skies.

If the chronicles recount them in such detail, while ignoring or merely glancing over so much else, that is only to be expected. All through the years of his thralldom a fierce strife was raging throughout the land of Kerys. In small bands at first, and sometimes, unpredictably, in substantial armies, the Ekwesh were striking more and more often into the lands of Kerys itself. They never sought to hold territory, or even linger any longer than they had to in one place; they came to destroy and pillage, and when they had done they moved on. Fighting them was like chasing quicksilver; yet fought they had to be. The border lords who bore the brunt of their incursions grew more and more restive under Nithaid's hand; what were they paying his levies for, they demanded, if not protection? But that protection he simply could not give to each and every one. He had to guess as best he could where the next strike would come, and gather his forces there, or risk losing them piecemeal. Often, too often, he was wrong: because, he suspected, hostile eyes were watching him and his movements. So did Elof, though whose he never said; and only because of this is it mentioned.

Those great events the chroniclers choose to treat remotely and from afar, as Elof himself saw them, and not without reason; for in the end it was he who mattered. To those of Kerys who lived through that time, who saw their fields laid waste, their homes burnt, their kinsfolk slain and at last, perhaps, their own blood freezing even as it spilled across the uncaring snow, it was the breaking of a world; yet in small things, the fall of a feather, the opening of a long-closed door, lay the roots of other events against which that strife was to seem almost insignificant. Not even the Powers who from their strange heights watched the wintry slaughters, or the no less bloody counters that followed, when Nithaid the Bull with the black blade would hunt the reivers back to the very snow lines and set heads upon every burned tree in gruesome mockery of spring – not even they could weigh events with the certainty of the chronicles. For theirs in all its stark irony is the judgement of time, and time ruled those many lives and deaths to be ultimately of small account. Perhaps there was a purpose in each; but if so, even from the Powers it is hidden. For they also dwell within time, and it is mightier than they.

Elof and Roc, for their part, eagerly followed Nithaid's campaigns, when they could come by any news of them, and were grateful even for such scraps and rumours as the guards who brought provisions could tell. The sergeant, when he came, was most forthcoming of all. The first news he brought set the pattern; that Nithaid had won his most telling victory against the reivers for many a year, decimating and driving off a powerful war band in a series of pitched battles over the northern grasslands, himself leading the charges of horse as was his custom, clad in a fearsome new armour that no weapon could mark and doing great slaughter with a black sword, whispered among the common soldiers to be the gifts of a dark sorcerer. By the next spring it was being said the armour transformed its wearer into a raging beast-man with the strength of ten, and the Ekwesh had come to fear their enemy as a warrior of the Powers, many fleeing at mere sight of the bronzed bull's crest advancing. Elof knew that word of this, and of the many like victories in the years that followed, must inevitably come to the ears of Louhi, and even as the thought of Gorthawer in Nithaid's ham hand galled him, it filled him with a grim satisfaction, and a desire to thwart her still further.

So it was that he and Roc were anything but idle. There are clues both in the words of the chronicles, and from marginalia and drawings copied in the earliest texts, as to their many works and achievements in these first years of their captivity; and if these were not spectacular in themselves, they were undoubtedly of vast value to Nithaid in the defence of his realm. In addition to the fine weaponry they crafted for the noblemen, the two smiths shaped many templates and pattern pieces that lesser smiths could copy in large numbers and at low cost, setting upon them simple virtues by fixed formulae, so that the common soldier also could be better armed and shielded. And it is said that many lives were saved so, and Nithaid grew greatly in the regard of his men.

When, in that second winter, a town fell bloodily to the Ekwesh through poor fortification, its walls shattered by frosts and the weight of snow, Elof grew interested in the art, and applied to it some of the techniques of smithcraft, among them principles of flow and of fracture. He produced many designs, and under Nithaid's command and the spur of fear, thrall and soldier were pressed into feverish labour to give them form. Walls were strengthened with subtly formed buttressing, and gates reached by ramps cunningly shaped so that the press of an attack would spend itself against its own numbers, catching them in tight curves or forcing them off sides that narrowed suddenly and imperceptibly, or across bridges that seemed rock-firm, yet could be collapsed in a second; the gates themselves often led into lanes or corridors that were worse traps, bringing the attackers under the defenders' fire from unexpected angles and penning them against another and stronger gate. And the following summer an ambitious barrier began to be built across the northwest of the land, linking the various fortresses and walled towns into a defence to replace the Gate fortress. It was not to be a plain wall but an intricate, meandering tangle of corner and curve, sometimes linked by bridge or tunnel and filled with hidden traps and barriers as before. This, like the rest, was born of Elof's restless mind, but he took no part in its building, did not so much as set eyes upon the site; for Nithaid forbade him still to leave the island. It became ever more clear, though, that at the least the builders had to keep in direct touch with him, and so, grudgingly, the king allowed Roc to go to the sites and report the problems. At first he was heavily guarded and restrained, but by their third autumn of captivity this was proving too cumbersome, and he was free to travel with only a pair of guards, and to go more or less where he willed. He enjoyed these excursions for many reasons, and often returned looking smug and well cared for, but Elof grudged him none of the diversions he found. Had he missed the company of women, Nithaid would have lavished them on him as he did all other good things, but he shrivelled at the idea, as the maimed wreck he saw himself. He had little stomach, too, for bedding thrall-girls who would not dare refuse him; and always Kara was a flutter of wings across his heart.

He had, in any event, always more work than he could manage, and when that palled he had a strong interest of his own, almost an obsession, to eat up any spare time he could find. This was the search for some greater source of heat than his forge. So many of the texts he had surrounded himself with half hinted at great secrets of his craft that high heat might unveil – or unleash. And nested within one such, like a pearl within a pearl, might lie the secret of his release. When the fourth winter of his captivity came it added urgency to his quest, for it grew bitterly cold even before the year's ending; blasting snowstorms swept land and river, and though they settled only lightly upon the island, they cut it off from the city for days on end, and though the smithy seemed to remain warm the supply of fuel for his forge was often very near its end. The trees of the island tempted him, but still he could not bring himself to cut them down.

So he set himself to study all that he could set down upon the nature of heat, and went in his reading from the minuteness of nature to the heights of the sky, yet remained, it seemed, little the wiser. Into the strange affinity of the sun with glass he delved; he gazed at it through smoked glass, shattered thick glass into slivers so sharp they split its very light into streaks of gorgeous colour, he concentrated its rays through fine-ground globes and sections of globes until it grew to a firing heat. But even gathering that within his gauntlet could not bring him the fierce radiance he needed; and the sun was anything but constant. He considered the gauntlet itself, and sought to shape new crystals that would drink in all forms of heat and direct them as that one within the gauntlet did, but with greater duration and intensity. He failed, achieving only such weaker crystals as the duergar used in their undying lamps; and from then on the steady glow of the forge became a new mark for mariners on the river, but one at which they shook their heads and spat. And searching through the other skills taught him by old Ansker and Ils, he began to inquire into the strange properties manifested by certain of the metals ordinarily less useful to smiths, being too heavy and soft even for jewellery. But some of the old texts confirmed what the duergar had hinted at, the uncanny dangers encountered in the refining and storage of such stuff. He grew excited at that, for it seemed to hold the promise of great power, but at the same time he furthered his researches very slowly and carefully.

He grew more interested in the stuff called stonesblood, which was a pitchy seepage that issued from the ground in some southern regions of the land, as it did more rarely in his own. It was little thought of; since it burned poorly in lamps and smelt terrible, only the poorest used it, but an early smith whose accounts he read, in seeking to purify it had arrived at some strange substances, some very combustible. Even though he improved greatly upon the processes of purification, however, they remained cumbersome, and the results were disappointing. The essences of the stonesblood proved incredibly dangerous and volatile to store, and more than once the smithy was almost burnt to the ground. But that impelled him to turn them to other uses, and through blending them with a variety of other substances he was able, in the fifth summer of his thralldom, to place into Nithaid's hands a weapon of devastating effect.

At first he used a thick form of the tar, mixed to a sticky paste with sulphur, wax, and powders of rare metals, that was formed into a bolus and shot flaming from a catapult. Where it struck, it clung and burned, and could not easily be dislodged or put out; against wooden walls or roofs it had fearsome effects, and landing among close-packed troops or horsemen the bolus could cause panic. By its aid the siege of an outland tower was raised, and the town of a lordling who had in desperation sought to ally himself with the reivers was bloodily taken. But the Ekwesh had by now reached the main rivers, and were seizing enough boats to make them a serious threat to traffic; Elof distilled a thinner essence that floated when it was poured upon water, and could be fired there to form a barrier of flame before pursuing ships. This, though effective at first, had many disadvantages, chiefly that the flames were liable to blow back in the wind before it could bear the boat free of them; also, once the Ekwesh came to recognise the tactic, they could steer clear in time. When poured from a battlement its flames often exploded about the wall, enveloping defender as well as attacker. When word of this was brought to Elof he laboured long and hard, drawing again upon his memories of his time among the duergar and the mysterious weapons they could wield, and produced yet another essence of the stonesblood, this time a thin jelly that could be passed through a pump. Even the crude syringe used to clear the bilges of little fishing boats could jet it through the air to spatter an opponent's sail, where an arrow with the merest spark of tinder would fire it. From larger ships special pumps could spray it in a dense cloud that would soak into sail, clothes and deck alike, or, with great daring, could be enflamed by a heated wire at the pump's mouth, engulfing whatever it touched in a searing cloud that rivalled dragon-breath. After a while the mere sight of pump and fire-arrows caused all but the hardiest of the reivers to hang back and delay their attack, if not turn aside altogether. On land also it was effective, able to spit its venom beyond a besieged wall or into the rearward ranks of an assault, and so split its force. This magesmith's fire, as it came to be called, was not a conclusive weapon; it was perilous to produce, perilous to store, most perilous of all to wield in the panic of a battle, where more than once it claimed those who used it uncautiously. In the chill of that fifth winter, when the malice of the Ice was strongest and the hardened Ekwesh had the vantage, its flame burned feebler and less certain. But still, Elof had armed his captor with the most terrible weapon of war that ancient land had seen, and one of enduring effect.

Such were the concerns in which Elof lost himself during the first five years of his captivity. He did not, however, cut himself off from the world; on the contrary, he still took an almost fanatical interest in the progress of Nithaid's campaigns, when he could get any news of them. But as his sorcerous repute grew, so this was becoming harder. Even the guards were loath now to stay and talk, save a few who remembered him from the first; the sergeant alone would linger for a stoup of wine and a few words, and let slip once over some strong wine that his men held him in great awe for his daring. Few others ever appeared. The king had commanded that none should set foot upon the island without his express permission, and most were glad enough to leave it so. When a fisherman was wrecked there during a winter storm Elof and Roc would have sheltered him gladly enough, but the wretched man would not come near the 'sorcerers' tower', stayed out all night in the howling rain and seemed vastly relieved to be summarily arrested by a guard-boat he contrived to signal next morning.

The nearest they had to an intruder was one morning, when they were awakened near dawn by a sudden crashing from the forge. Rising in haste with weapons, they found that one of the little mammuts had strayed in, lured by some leftover fruit; it led them on a wild and shattering chase between the benches, trunk and tail held aloft, squealing and trumpeting wildly, before they at last ejected it. Beyond that, they were hardly disturbed from one month's end to the next.

So it was that Elof had another reason to be glad of Roc's frequent excursions. So, also, he even came to welcome Nithaid's occasional visits to demand some new labour, when he would bombard the king with barbed questions about the state of the wars, and the advance of the Ice. Nithaid was curt in his answers at first, but as the years passed he would appear more and more frequently at the forge, sometimes for no very important purpose. Once or twice, in the earliest days, he would bring one or other of his sons to be outfitted with some gift he had commanded, armour or weaponry fit for a young prince; but he would often linger to talk long after the work was done, though the boys, their greed assuaged, grew bored and clamorous to return. Eventually it dawned on Elof that the king also had come to enjoy these visits to men with whom he could speak straightly, and be answered as straightly, without thought of fear or favour. He would spend long evenings sitting by the forge, drinking mulled wine with the man who had sworn to kill him, and bandying hard words about the state of his realm. They were strange evenings, for between king and captive there was no slightest mellowing of feeling; at times the air seemed sulphurous with their rancour. Yet equally there was a kind of fellowship between them, a sense of bearing swords in a common struggle, and of satisfying a common need; Elof was desperate to know all that was passing, and sometimes it seemed almost as if Nithaid were seeking counsel. "Without having to ask for it, either!" Roc pointed out cynically. "Saves him lowering himself! He knows you're all too ready to bend his ear." This was the truth; for though he might approve Nithaid's valour on the battlefield, Elof never masked his contempt for his way of rule. This was not only to suit his whim; by provoking Nithaid he often learned more.

"The poor folk of this land?" Nithaid jeered at some such sally of Elof's, one dark night in the middle of the sixth winter. "Where's your own fine concern for them, then, be you so eager to see me dead? Where'd they be without me? Rags rent between the teeth of the battling barons, that's all! And easy prey for the Ice, after that! Who d'you think'd take my place? You, eh? Is it that you had in mind? Think they'd follow a limping tinker, do you?" He buried his blunt nose noisily in his wine-mug, and blew a deep rumbling sigh. The lines in his face seemed to deepen, and Elof noticed with a quirk of surprise how much greyer his hair had grown since their first encounter. "No, Valant, if you truly wish to help the drudges you'll swink as you're doing, and forget all your foolish fancies. They're born to burdens and blows, it's in their blood; they've not the mind to feel the pain of them like higher-born folk. Or even mastersmiths! A strong lord over a quiet kingdom, that's when they fare best; they know it, too, all save a few malcontents, and it's what I'll give 'em. The throne's no chair of ease, but I've no mind to quit it yet, for you or anyone. At least, till my lads are of age ..."

When he had gone, Roc grimaced at Elof. "I didn't like the sound of *that!*"

"Nor I," mused Elof, remembering the flushed faces of the youths who had watched his torture, and the bright greedy eyes. "You've heard something of them, these lads of his, I remember. Are they like their father?"

"I have, and more," Roc rumbled disdainfully. "There's chatter enough about them round the court. Aye, it's said that they're like him, but I think not.

There's two of them, Geraidh and Kenarech, and all too close, in years not the least."

"Jealous, then?"

"Aye, so I've heard, for all they're so alike. Of each other, but more of him, for all he dotes on them and spoils them rotten. Not that they show it, though; they're careful to play the devoted sons and brothers before him, and the merry swaggerers before the common folk – but less so of letting their tongues wag before servants, or bragging to the thrall lasses they bed. So I get all the gossip, for the girls don't like 'em a bit; cocky young bastards and nasty-minded with it, that's the word. A lot of the troops favour them, though, and so also a lot of the folk; Nithaid's too hard a taskmaster for some, and they blame him, would you credit, for not seeing off the Ekwesh sooner. Seems to me the lads are taking pains to foster that ..." He paused significantly.

"You mean, they've already got their eye on the succession? Before they're even of age?"

"Wouldn't surprise me a bit. No less did Nithaid, at their age; but he worked hard to inherit the kingdom, and fought hard and brutal for his father, putting down rebel lords and Ekwesh reivers. These two don't seem of the same mettle; they want everything the easy way, and now. There's been talk of compounding with some of the more troublesome lords, giving them local independence for the sake of quiet –"

"Or support," mused Elof. "But don't the young fools see there's no end to that, save with the Ekwesh? All Nithaid's vicious ambition, but without his vision, or his driving will. Ready to sell the morrow to buy the moment ... I'm glad I made that armour as well as I did, Roc. I'd as soon nothing happened to Nithaid; not yet."

That thought brought him some greater consolation for the loss of Gorthawer; for it was borne into battle as he no longer could, and he heard of Nithaid doing greater deeds than ever with the black blade in his hand. That sixth long winter of his captivity was the first time in Nithaid's reign that not even one Ekwesh raid penetrated the heartland successfully; most were met and driven back among the wild lands to the north, and the few who slipped through broke harmlessly against the new fortifications. But neither blade nor walls could turn the weather, and where the Ekwesh failed to go the stormwinds came. Sieges they laid with floods and drifting snow, and after them, quieter and deadlier, the frosts, to crack stone in the still night and lay deadly fingers upon the hearts of those who lacked shelter and fire enough. Nor was that the only terror of the night; the weather drove wolves down in hungry packs from the wild lands, and the huge forest bears, with many other beasts, some among them of an unheard-of strength and ferocity. From byre or pen a terrible screaming would be heard as of beasts fear-maddened, so terrible that many feared to go out to them even though all their wealth and livelihood were threatened; the more so, as many who did never returned, and were found in the first light butchered among their flocks. The beast responsible was never caught, or even seen clearly, and so wildly did accounts vary that it seemed there must be many; yet the manner of attack was always the same, the skull crushed and the brain devoured. Often wayfarers were attacked thus on overgrown paths, by some thing that lay along a stout branch above and struck downwards with a vast paw; yet this also was never clearly seen. And through storm and blizzard still stranger shapes stalked, and men abroad were missed till the thaw uncovered their gnawed bones; on the clear nights shadows thin and spider-limbed lurked in thickets for the unwary traveller, or beneath the haloed moon climbed through unbarred windows to suck the lifeblood from sleepers within.

"This is how it must have been at the fall of Morvan, Roc," said Elof on one such clear night towards the winter's end, as they opened their door before sleep to gaze upon the Yskianas sparkling in starlight. The distant shore shone white with snow, but upon the island it lay lightly among the grass. "Do you remember how Korentyn spoke of it?"

"Aye, do I. But Kerys is far from falling yet. The glaciers are a long way from even its outermost walls."

"Yet they can travel fast, at need. And Louhi spoke

of only having to tip the balance a little, make the world a trace colder ... but how? To overrun this great land is scarcely a small work, even for the Ice."

Roc grew thoughtful. "If it froze the Yskianas as it did the Great Waters of Morvan ... no, that couldn't work ..."

"No; sea-lakes are one thing, a river well-nigh the width of a sea another. The most Louhi and her kind might do is freeze the Gate falls and dam the main inflow, and I guess they would be hard put to it to do that till the Sea-Ice itself came south –"

His words faltered; he choked, caught his breath, and suddenly, with a great thrust of his crutches, he hurled himself out of the door into the darkness. Roc, plunging after him in astonishment, saw him raise a hand to the sky as if to claw down the very moon or stars. But then he also saw the shadow sweeping over the snow, the shape that cast it, blacker still against the shimmering sky as it glided down towards them. Low it came, and lower, long-necked and graceful, shivering the moonbeams with its speed and the still air with the slow pulse of its wingbeats; nigh over Elof's head it swept, so close that the wind of its outstretched wings uplifted his tangled hair, yet not quite close enough to touch. Despairingly he lunged upward, arms out-thrust in a wild embrace, and shouted out in his great voice a name like a cry of agony. "*Kara! Stay, Kara! Only stay awhile!*" A wild embrace, but futile; for even as he gave voice the dark wings lifted over the rooftree and vanished over the snow-hung crowns of the oaks. He fell headlong among the frosty grass, and screamed aloud in frustrated fury. "*Damn these corpse-legs ... Kara! Ach, Kara!*"

He called after her again and again, but the great swan did not reappear. Out into the icy silence of the night his strong voice rang, across the River at the Heart of the World, and it seemed that the waters trembled in answer, and the mirrored stars shook. But it was no more than a breath of wind, coming to stir the leafless trees above, and rustle the grass about their feet. Elof, scrabbling for his crutches, looked dimly down at it.

"Roc," he inquired in a wholly different tone, vague and distracted. "I've hardly looked at this grass of late. There's scarcely any snow here ..."

Roc shrugged, and helped him back to his feet. That sudden vision had left him almost as shaken as Elof; he was glad of anything else to talk about. "There never is, not much. Same every winter ..."

"Yes ... Hella's fires! Idiot that I've been, never to think of it! And the smithy, so warm and comfortable ... Roc, whoever built it as it first was, he was a great smith, building a forge to suit him, a worthy forge. I should have seen that at once!"

Roc looked hard at him. He seemed almost to have forgotten what he had seen. "You did. We both did. So?"

"So would not he also have needed great heat?"

"He might; aye, he might, at that. But whatever he got it from, it's gone now."

"Is it? Come inside – come!" He hobbled towards the bench laden with his present studies, bent beneath the weight of books and notes. "So many forms of heat I've studied!" He picked up sheaves of parchment scraps, tablets, wooden slips, tossing them aside one after another. "The sun! Crystals! Stonesblood! Strange metals! All this time and I forgot what was most obvious to me!" He seized a map from among the clutter, brushed a table clear of tools with a single sweep of a crutch and in a crackle of crisp linen unrolled the map across it.

"Roc, you've travelled widely enough in the land by now, you can tell me – those *loskveneth*, those fire-mountains like the ones we saw, whereabouts exactly do they lie? No, don't show me – mark them in with the charcoal here ..."

"Well ..." began Roc slowly, and then with growing irritation, "Does it have to be now? I need my bed, I'm too sleep-ridden to remember! I don't know where every single one is – there's too many, large and small, it seems they've been spreading lately, and in some places there's a whole lot close together –"

"Just the major ones – and mark regions where they're grouped – yes, so ..."

Yawning, Roc cudgelled his weary brain, and made his charcoal circles, here and there as they came to mind, in no particular order. But after a moment he stopped, blinked down at the map a moment and swore.

"Yes?" demanded Elof keenly.

"This ... did you foresee this? You did, didn't you? I can see it in those cat's eyes of yours. Or ... has somebody whispered something in your ear?"

"Foresee what?" grinned Elof.

Roc's mouth twisted impatiently, and he drew a single savage slashing streak across the map, and plucked it up under Elof's nose. "*That!*"

Elof whistled softly. "That they'd form a pattern, yes. I learned something about the flow of earthfires from the Mastersmith, and more among the duergar – that within the shell of the world there are vast and shifting stresses, that the shell is broken along many lines ..."

"Like fractures in fatigued metal, you mean?"

"Aye, very like. And it is along these that the earthfires break out at their fiercest. One such ran up through the Meneth Scahas in our old homeland, and among the Nordenbergen; but in our Eastland, almost none, and no fire-mountains. Whereas here ... But I never foresaw that the line would run *thus*!" His finger traced the streak of dark ash that linked the marked firemountains in a single straight line, dead straight across the land of Kerys. And some two-thirds of the way along that line the finger slowed and rested, and a tremor of excitement crept into his voice. "Nor that Elan Gorhenyan would sit so squarely upon it!"

"You can't be that precise!"

"Close enough! Somewhere here, somewhere by here ..."

"Such as?" objected Roc, seeing Elof cast about like a hunting dog on the scent. "Do we not know every corner of this island by now – who better? Have we not trodden over every damned finger's breadth of it, aye, even you, in all the years we've been here?"

"The warmth, the half melted snow!" Elof flung back at him.

"Aye, but how would we get to it? Have we not even seen the forge stripped down to its foundations and rebuilt? So where could anything lie hidden?"

Elof stared at him a moment, then snapped his fingers and swung about on his crutches. He turned towards that last room left of the old lodge, that was still Roc's bedchamber. But Roc seized his arm.

"No, damn you! You're not going to start ripping up walls or floor before I've had my this night's sleep, at least! If there's anything there it won't be gone by morning!"

Elof glared at him, then half smiled and threw up his hands in defeat. "Very well! Till morning, then!" And he appeared to compose himself for sleep no less willingly than Roc; to all appearances he had indeed forgotten the coming of the swan altogether. But more than once in the night Roc was awakened by the restless tapping of crutches about the forge, and a muttering voice that seemed to be repeating questions to itself, over and over in a tone of growing desperation. "The fires ... *what was she doing here?* .. what did she mean? ... what could she hope to gain ... would it not work against her ... was it mockery? ... was it? *Was it?*"

It was as much in pity as in irritation that Roc turned over and stopped his ears with the blankets. But he swore loudly when he was awakened at the very first light by Elof, hunched on his crutches, ripping a length of timber from the rear wall. He had seized a boot to hurl when he stopped, sat back among his blankets and stared at the surface that was being revealed.

It had been covered, once, with some kind of sandy concretion, plastered tight against the surrounding rock; then the new surface must have been hard to tell from old. But now the concretion was decayed, and it was crumbling back to damp sand as if the immense weight of years had suddenly descended upon it. Beyond it was a jumble of heavy rocks, some that looked naturally fallen, others piled clumsily as if by hands hasty or nervous; these Elof was already pulling away, and finding beneath them a blackness that was not emptiness. He plucked away another stone from the pile, and half of it slid into the gap he had opened. But it landed with a dull clangour that no stone ever made. Roc, amazed, put down his boot and grabbed for his clothes.

It was midmorning before the two smiths had the door cleared, for door it was, though all of metal and bound with steel, and set at a slant backward beneath a low arch in the rock; clearly there was a descent beneath. "Stairs, I'll wager!" said Elof breathlessly, running his fingers over the surface, stained but only mildly corroded for all the damp. "Now those locks must've been full of muck already when this thing was walled up, they're set solid; but I'd guess we could cut the stone around the bolts, or if not, chisel through to the hinges ..."

"Hold hard!" grunted Roc. "First, I want my breakfast, I do; second, if you're right, who knows what that door may hold back? Could get more earthfires than you want!" For answer Elof banged his crutch hard down upon the centre of the door, and Roc nodded as he heard the hollow boom die away. "All right. But there's still breakfast!"

Elof's first idea proved the best; the stone was hard of its kind, but their chisels were harder. They cut clean through to the recess that received the bolts, and all around the sleeve of steel that lined it. Elof levered it free, peered at it and scratched the bared bolt-ends with a sharp probe. "Strong work, scarcely touched by corrosion. There are virtues on it for that, but it owes as much to skilful alloying, I would guess. What of the hinges, I wonder?" Before Roc could stop him he dug in his fingers beneath the lip of the ancient door and heaved. Roc sprang up with a cry; he heard clearly the cracking of Elof's muscles, and a minute later the sharper crack of wood as the prop of Elof's crutch bent beneath the weight. But he was too late to prevent, he could only hurl his weight against the door as it lifted with a metallic screech that tore his ears. Half way it rose in a shower of grime and rubble, and there it jammed, even as the tortured prop snapped beneath Elof's left armpit and stabbed like a blunt knife into his arm.

"Might've been your heart, and serve you right!" raged Roc, tugging out splinters of wood no more gently than he needed to, "Into your fifth year thus and still you won't learn what you may and mayn't manage!"

Elof winced and mumbled rebelliously as the wound was bound up, though till his outburst of the night before he had hardly even grumbled about his infirmity these last two years. He kept staring down into the opening his haste had made. It looked like a well of darkness, gathering from the skies above; for their labours had lasted all the short day. The moment Roc was done Elof seized another pair of crutches, with no sign of pain, lit a plain oil lanthorn and leaned over the sloping lip of metal and into the dark. "A stair it is!" he exclaimed, with grim satisfaction.

"If you're feeling generous," added Roc, looking askance at the roughly stepped stone slabs, covered in dirt and fallen rock, and the dim earth floor they led to. "Do you use your wits for once and let me take the lead!" Elof grinned, and made no protest; Roc helped himself to a stout spear from the litter of arms about the forge walls, and gingerly lowered himself down the metal ramp that led from the rim onto the first step. Then Elof's hard hand landed on his shoulder.

"Stand a moment! Do you not smell anything?"

Roc shrugged. "Stale air; are you surprised?"

"Stale, but not damp; no mould, no nitre, as we found in Morvan, dry though it was."

Roc nodded. "It's warm, right enough; I can feel it in the air. And there's something more..." He hooked the lanthorn over the spearhead and dangled it down into the dark. Its light swung tantalisingly over shadowy shapes along the walls, then dimmed as the wick guttered and flickered. "Bad air."

"But breathable. The lamp still burns. And there's no mine-fume to flame in the air about us, at least." With gasps of painful effort Elof heaved himself down onto the stairs; Roc tactfully ignored him, but swept a path clear as he went. Elof worked his way down after him, clutching at every shelf and outcropping in the rock to steady himself; but before either had reached the floor he stopped. "Feel it!" he hissed, and Roc, reaching out to the stone, started at the distant thrill and quiver that was almost like touching the flanks of a living beast. He knew it well, just as it had shivered through the stone foundations of the Mastersmith's tower where he had grown up.

"Earthfires it is," he nodded, grimacing at the altogether too generous layer of grime that had come off on his fingers. "You were right. And look here!" He stepped down onto the floor and swung the lanthorn around the wall ahead. Rows of murky shapes stood ranged upon stone shelves cut out of the very wall, pot and crucible and mould-case, draped deep in ancient spider-webs that the fine grime had turned to black lace. An encrusted block, like a petrified table, stood in midfloor. "An underground workshop, it must've been! See there, all those shelves, the walls go right back … and those vents in the wall there, full of rubble, they'd be fireplaces, but with the chimneys stopped up or fallen in … Have a care, the floor slopes down!"

"So it does!" grinned Elof. "And where to, think you?"

"Another door, of course!" Roc announced. "I can see it, too, good and solid, set deep in the stone − sliding back into it, I'd say. Looks like there's your furnace, right enough!"

Elof nodded absently, running his fingers along the litter on the shelves. But for the deep layers of grime they might have been his own store, or any true mastersmith's, a jumble of uncompleted pieces, old moulds, leftover metal and offcuts, coils and coils of wire … or was it wire? It felt fine as hair − disturbingly like hair, in fact. He made a mental note to rummage through the mess at the first chance he had; who could say what fascinating relics his predecessor might have left? But then he heard Roc swear explosively, and turned to hobble down the steep floor after him.

The reason became obvious as Roc held up the light. The air here was worse, if anything, and it shed only a faint glow upon the wall around the furnace door. But it was enough to show the wheel which must work the door's running gear, and the broken lengths of chain which dangled from it. He pointed up to the ceiling. "Must've run up through those holes there; to some kind of counterweight system, probably, up above. That must have gone with the original forge, decayed or torn down, or both. Be damned to it! We'll have to rig the whole thing again before we can get at the furnace!"

Elof chuckled, and turned away up the slope. "Now who's turned impatient? If we must, we must. I've hauled open doors enough for one day. Let's go and see whether there's any sign of the holes above, or those chimneys; I could use a breath or two of clean air ..."

He looked back when he reached the stairs, but Roc was still engrossed, and not listening. "If the wheel still moves," he muttered, "It might just be ..." He thrust the spear-shaft through the spokes of the wheel, and leaned upon it hard. Nothing happened; the wheel showed no sign of stirring. But Roc, brushing his hair from his eyes, was not to be thwarted; now he was throwing his whole weight upon the spear, dangling from it almost as his feet left the ground.

"Leave it, Roc!" called Elof. "Later's soon enough."

"No, by Hella! A moment more!" gasped Roc through clenched teeth. Elof wondered if the bad air had gone more swiftly to the shorter man's head. "I'm getting there ..." And indeed there was a faint sound, a hum, a groaning of ancient wheels at the edge of hearing; and beyond that the deeper rumble that he had felt in the walls. "It's moving ... shifting ..."

Elof sighed and turned back to help; but then his glance fell upon those fireplaces in the walls. They did not really look like ... Something, a flash of understanding, seemed to whirl around in his head. He shouted aloud, and sped for the wall in great swinging leaps. As was bound to happen, his crutches skidded from under him on the grimy slope, but he flung himself forward and, even as the dark door moaned and squealed into movement, he crashed against the wheel, clutched at a spoke and sagged down so that his weight blocked Roc's leverage. "No!" he yelled. "Don't you see? Those aren't fireplaces! They're air-vents, and this muck, it's *soot* –"

"*What?*" bellowed Roc, but he dropped from the spear and let it clatter to the floor.

"That's not the furnace; we're *in* the furnace!"

There was a sudden sharp hiss, and Roc stumbled hastily back as a jet of white fumes burst around the rim of the door. Then Elof's weight told, the wheel sank back that vital fraction and the rumbling died away. Roc staggered over, coughing and contrite. "Belly of Hel, what was I going to do? What was I going to *do*? They'd have seen us on the mainland and never known it, one flash, a wisp of smoke and farewell smiths –"

"And a brace of hot cinders down Nithaid's fat neck!" coughed Elof, and fought to keep from laughing hysterically. "Powers, these vapours, they've got me too! They must pool here like water –"

Roc hauled him loose and got his crutches under him, and they more or less dragged each other up the slope. When they got out into the open, they sprawled gratefully on the cold grass under a sky grown murky and showing few stars, Roc still muttering reproachfully to himself "Why didn't I bleeding well *see*?"

"Those vapours are cause enough!" coughed Elof, hugging his ruined legs.

"Maybe; but *you* saw ..."

"I was further up the slope, they took longer to get to me. And even on crutches I'm taller than you. Ach, we should both have realised at once, from the soot; but it's so ancient it's congealed, halfway to earth. Or the door mechanism – meant to be opened from above, and for good reason. We weren't expecting it, that was half the trouble; who'd have thought of so vast a furnace? What'd he ever use it for, that's what puzzles me!"

"Aye, me too! I've seen forges no bigger than that, he could've worked in there –" He stopped short, and they looked at each other. "Don't suppose he *did*, do you?"

Elof shook his head in awed disbelief at the image of some huge figure standing silhouetted against the fearsome glare from that open door, hammer rising and falling as the vapours swirled around him, labouring away at ... "That block! In the floor! It could be an anvil!"

"Those things on the shelves – stuff he wanted

kept warm, ready to hand! Powers! What sort of a creature can he have been?"

Elof shook his head again. "Not human! No creature of flesh and blood could live long in such a furnace at its full heat, among those vapours. No, the idea's impossible! Unless ... yes ..."

"What?"

"A dedicated smith. Very dedicated. Ready to go down and work there – before the furnace had cooled ... Yes, he might have achieved a great deal. A very great deal ..."

Roc smote his brow. "Aye, he might, if he'd no mother-wits! And two good legs to get him out whenever his clothes took fire!" He seemed to see Elof's wince in the darkness, for he added, more gently. "No point in sparing you that truth. For it's as true as that you saved my life there once again, legs or no."

"Ach, chalk it up to luck; we'll settle the slate at the end. I've done well out of it, Roc; I've got my furnace now. We'll rig that opening wheel again, and clear the air-shafts, and set the whole thing to work again! There's things I've been thirsting to try ..."

"Speaking of thirsting," interrupted Roc, "I've laboured enough for one day. Me for a drink and a bite and bed – down by the hearth as you've torn my fine bedchamber asunder! And the same for you, if you're wise ..."

"No. I've still got the stink of those fumes in my chest. I'll sit out a while longer."

"As you will! But don't go to sleep in the frost, or it'll take more than that forge to unstiffen you come morning! Sleep you well!"

The door clattered shut, and left Elof alone with himself beneath the clouds. He bowed his head almost to his knees, and sought to rein in his racing thoughts; of smithcraft, of pain and humiliation at his crippled state, of half formed, half dreamed ways of escape that the furnace might now make possible ...

Then he looked up.

Roc came running when he heard the cry, and found him halfway to his feet, one leg kicking uselessly against the slippery ground, as he stared frantically into the night. Roc caught the faintest glimmer of something that came fluttering slowly down, like a dark snowflake. Then he jumped as Elof hurled away his crutches and plunged to his knees so hard that one splint broke, scrabbling furiously among the whitened grass.

"What, man? What is it?" demanded Roc, horrified, as he stooped to help him; he snorted with surprise at what Elof held up with a gasp of triumph. "Is that all? A crow's cast-off?"

The long feather shook in Elof's grasp, and he swept the skies with his gaze. "This is too great for any crow. Should I not know the pinion of a swan, none better? And what other swan have you seen in all the world that is black?"

Roc sucked in his lower lip with shock. "Can you see anything?"

"No ... nothing. Not even a star ... *Kara!*"

The shout was so sudden, so anguished, that Roc jumped. But to Elof's own ears it sounded like a wail of weakness, and he bit it off; what woman would come to a call as miserable as that? "Help me up!" he muttered, devouring the feather with his eyes.

"What can it mean?" Roc demanded, handing him back his crutches. "Is it a token, or ..."

"A token? Yes. But of what ... Hope? Scorn? Roc, I ... I know not what to think! But that she's here in these regions at all, this deep within the land, it may bode ill; does Louhi ready some sudden assault?" Swaying on his crutches, he clenched his fists at the skies and howled with sudden anguish. "Was it scorn she meant? *Was it?* A curse eternal light upon my helplessness, and upon him who brought it about! You stern powers of life and death, be my judges! Are the sorrows of men worth no more than laughter? Are we in our miseries mere playthings of your scorn? Then shatter, world, as in the end you must, and shorten all agonies! *And the fires of Hella at your heart consume us all!*"

CHAPTER EIGHT
The Cleansing Fires

THE ASSAULT THAT ELOF feared did not come. He sent a guarded warning to Nithaid, without saying why; it is some tribute to his standing with the king that he was taken seriously. Nithaid alerted his marchwardens, but they reported no signs of any great mustering of their foes. On the contrary, the Ekwesh armies were if anything dividing their numbers, avoiding battle and returning to their raiding habits. More often now they would strike in small bands at weaker targets, as they had at Elof's village in Nordeney; they seemed less eager than before to lay siege to strong places and larger towns. Nithaid was once more kept busy chivvying his forces from one town to the next to reinforce the house-troops of his lords; but he had fewer pitched battles to face. To Elan Gorhenyon he returned an impatient answer.

Elof was left furrowing his brow with worry. What then had been Kara's mission, if not to spy out some assault? For mission there must have been, and a grave one; Louhi would hardly have loosed her for less, knowing she might turn such freedom to her own ends. "Why did she come, then?" he muttered, staring up at the sky as it lost its deep sapphire lustre, and took on the misty sheen of a pearl. For three nights now he had waited, sitting cold and forlorn on a bench against the stone wall of the forge, sleepless even after long days of toil restoring the furnace; but he had seen nothing, not so much as the sweep of wings across the paling stars. "What was she seeking?"

"Has it occurred to you," said Roc's voice behind him, "that it might've been you?"

Elof looked around in surprise; his friend was as fond of his sleep as all other comforts, and rarely rose this early save at great need. "Of course; she turned aside to seek me out. Though whether out of scorn or spite or ... something more, I still can't guess –"

"No," said Roc, treading carefully. "I mean, that she didn't turn aside from her mission – that she fulfilled it. That a certain lady gave her the order to seek out *you* ..."

"I?" Elof laughed. "Surely not, Roc! Once, perhaps; but what would the warlord of the Great Ice want with me now? Why should she come hunting one crippled smith after six long years? How could she even know I still lived, let alone here of all places? And surely Kara would not ..."

"You won't face it, will you?" demanded Roc, less carefully. "The turn in the war, all your fine new walls and weapons, you can wager Louhi's taken good mind of those! Wouldn't be that hard for her to guess where they've sprung from all of a sudden, whose hand lay behind them! What more likely than yours? All but branded your name on 'em, you have, for those with eyes to read!" Elof was silent, and Roc pressed home his attack. "Then she'd have prisoners to torture, maybe even spies of Bryhon's ilk to call on; what'll they tell her? Rumours, aye, but think of them; some outland sorcerer, a cripple – she might think she'd done that ... And Gorthawer, by the High Gate! Nithaid new-armoured and wielding a black sword! Then she'd know, all right! Do you ask yourself what she'd do then?"

"Why have I been so blind?" demanded Elof of himself. "Why did I not see this for myself?"

"Because you wouldn't credit that Kara could hunt you," said Roc sombrely.

Elof shook his head. "Still I cannot! Not for Louhi! Not even after ..." He bit his lip savagely. "Why would she show herself to us, if she was hunting us? I cannot credit it!"

"And yet once she came close to slaying us all at Louhi's behest," said Roc quietly, "though bravely she broke that bond ..." He grimaced, disliking what he had had to say. "But only with your help. That lost, why should she now have any greater strength?"

"Because of what has passed!" said Elof, clutching his hand convulsively to his breast. "Long years, longer even than this unending thralldom, this imprisonment in a maimed shell! Can they all count for nothing at all?"

Roc regarded him gravely. "In another man's mouth, and of any other woman than her, that might sound more foolish. Happen you're right, I hope you are. But dare you trust in that? And does it matter? Whether she hunted us by design or found us by chance, think you she could keep it from Louhi?" Silence fell, save for the small noises of the night. It was a long time before Elof finally shook his head.

"No. You have the right of it. Louhi would crumble her will like a dry rind." He slammed a fist against the doorpost. "That was why she left the token! She couldn't help herself; but she wanted at least to warn us! To warn us we had been found, that something might follow ... what, I wonder?"

Roc rasped a thumb across his chin. "A strike like lightning, I'd guess; a sudden swift raid, to bear you off or slay you. Here! This raising they're about, maybe they're just limbering up ..."

Elof frowned. "Surely not! That would be folly for them; let the first strike fail, and they alert us all. Nithaid would spirit me away at once, perhaps to Kerys the City, and how would they find me again among all that great hive of humanity? Louhi will have something else in mind, something surer; slower, maybe – she thinks like the Ice – but more sure. I cannot guess what."

"But we've got to!" Roc protested. "So we can do something; we can't just squat here and wait!"

Elof rose up on his crutches. "Any move could be the wrong one, when we know so little. Save one; and that is to escape Louhi and Nithaid together! As we planned to. All Kara has done is make our need more urgent." He frowned suddenly, and thrust a hand within the breast of his jerkin. "Unless ..."

"Unless what?"

"I ... cannot be sure. But one thing I know; we have that furnace now, and no excuse for not using it!"

He stretched his back, swaying alarmingly, and clapped Roc on the shoulder.

Roc groaned. "Will you not even snatch an hour or two of sleep, lest you lose the habit?"

Elof laughed. "Was it not you who was so eager to do something? Well then! Bestir yourself; the Ice itself is on our track!"

The forge roared as he hauled a last time on the bellows lever, and light swelled among the heaped coals. He seized a bar of steel in his tongs and drew it out, sparking and sputtering white, just on the edge of burning itself; then he swung about on his crutches, laid it against the anvil's edge and snatched up a heavy hammer. Down on the steel he brought it in swift bouncing blows, never letting the metal settle as he twisted it this way and that, humming to himself all the while a tune, light and rippling and yet with an eerie undertone, that took on words in his mind.

Hark to the words of the one that shapes you!
Know you the sound that is struck into you!
Look that you hold what is laid upon you,
Fail you shall not nor the flames consume you,
All the fires of earth restraining,
All the heat of Hel enchaining,
So at the last to my words you hearken,
Hear that the moment I choose is come!

The steel wormed and twisted beneath his ceaseless blows as if he tormented something living, till at last he laid it over the anvil's beak and stilled it with two smart raps before plunging it swiftly into the trough; and even then it seemed to shriek among the steam. After a few minutes he drew it forth, and leaning on his crutches he turned to the open door of the furnace. Very slowly and laboriously he clambered over the lip, swinging himself over by his hands and barking his weakened shins painfully; but he was all too used to that by now. He longed for a rail to help him down the steps, but any metal he could think of able to withstand the furnace would hold its heat too long, and be deadly dangerous. He had to make do with the rough handholds they had cut in the wall, and sockets for his crutches in the steps and the sloping floor beyond.

"You all right?" echoed Roc's voice from below, as it had a hundred times in the last few weeks.

"I manage!" was Elof's gruff reply, as it had been just as often. They both knew it was not true, but it suited Elof to act as if it was; before they found the forge he had grown at least partly reconciled to his condition, but the difficulties of working on it had revived all his raw resentment. "Here!" he said, when at last he reached the floor, and tossed the bar to Roc, who caught it deftly and began to clean and file it to a close fit with the mechanism he was working on. Elof hobbled slowly across the sloping floor to join him, then leaned against the wall, mopping his brow.

"You're a fine artificer," he said more cheerfully, leaning over Roc's shoulder. "That's as good a job as I could have done ..."

"Save that you'd have had it sit up and beg!" puffed Roc, reaching for a finer file. A few strokes more, and he wormed his way on hands and knees into the re-opened cavity till only his substantial rear protruded. "And how you made it so close a fit ..."

"I measured the bar closely to start with," said Elof. "I knew how the heat would expand it; and while it was hot I looked among the crystals in the duergar fashion, and saw where to lay each blow ..."

"... is quite beyond me, I was about to say." A chain clanked suddenly. "That's it! Snug and in place! Well, there's the air-shaft mechanism, counterweight and all! Your furnace is yours for the testing anytime." He reappeared, brushing grime out of his thick thatch of hair. "Whew! How'd you like your soot? Congealed, caked or just plain loose and powdery; do you take your fancy!"

"There's a great deal of it ..." remarked Elof thoughtfully.

"Only just noticed that? Times were when we were working down here I thought we'd kill every fish in the Great River, bathing at the day's end."

"Yes ... but why? There's more here than there should have been if he was only burning coal or wood with the earthfires; and it's too pure, some of it. As if ... as if the soot itself was part of what he was creating ... almost as if he were seeking to reduce it somehow ..."

Roc raised his eyebrows. "Soot? What use might that be to a smith? More like a curse to this one!"

"You did not study among the duergar, or in Morvanhal. The pure stuff of such a burning has many uses. For one, it may change steel, smelted deep among its very crystals; so was Kermorvan's sword made, that can hew plain iron unscathed. And when very pure it can be formed into many strange substances; it was Marja who reminded me of that, long since. Wood or coal will yield it, but more easily still stonesblood that is their cousin. The duergar know of many. Some of the true mastersmiths in Kerys of old made trial with the stuff, and I have many of their accounts among Amylhes' library; I may be able to improve upon their methods. In fact it was some of those I meant to try here first, for this furnace is so well suited ... so that now, by all the Powers, I begin to wonder if that smith of old was not upon the same trail ..." Suddenly he snapped his fingers, and reached up to one of the wall ledges so sharply that he all but overbalanced; clouds of soot flew up as he swept his hand impatiently along it. "Not that one ..." he muttered, brushing another. "Nor this –"

"Are you out to choke the pair of us?" coughed Roc, but Elof paid him no heed, scraping along the shelves of stone till at last his hand closed upon that same smooth hank that he had first felt.

"This!" he hissed. "By all the Powers, it can't be! And yet what else? Spun ... *spun!*"

"It's not hair, that's for sure!" muttered Roc, tugging at a loose strand and managing only to cut his finger. "Is this one of your strange substances, then? You never know, it might well be. I've never seen or heard of anything like it before, and I'll wager you haven't either."

Elof riffled the glossy stuff between his fingers. "Then you might lose," he murmured. "I think – I am not sure, mind you, but I think – that I have. Heard, and seen."

"Among the duergar, I suppose," grunted Roc, but Elof shook his head.

"No. They knew of something like it, but they did not make it. Can you not tell by the very look of the stuff? And by the very feel of it … Powers, it burns in my hand!"

"Seems cool enough to me!" muttered Roc in surprise, stroking it gingerly. "Just black, shiny, fine, and sharp as …" His voice tailed away, and when he looked up into Elof's face his ruddy cheeks had paled beneath their sooty crust. "*Gorthawer?*" he whispered, and Elof inclined his head.

"Remember what I told you once, of those moments when I poured the lightning down upon it – and of what I saw?"

Roc's voice fell very quiet. "That it was no single substance at all, but made of a tangle of fine filaments, compressed somehow …"

"Into a sword. My sword. Someone's sword before me. Whose, I hardly dare think …"

Roc whistled, and hefted the hank in his fingers. "So that's the secret of that blade, eh?" He twisted it in his muscular hands. "Stronger than steel, it could well be. So likely it was some smith of Kerys made it, then, by binding filaments like these …"

"No," said Elof dully, staring beyond him into nothingness. "Not like these …"

"But you said –"

"Not *like* these. These."

Roc dropped the filaments as if they had turned to snakes. "*What?* Don't be daft, man; how can you be so sure?"

"The gauge of them is the same. I have held that sword too long not to know the stuff of it again. I feel it, Roc; I can feel the blade in my grasp even as we stand here."

"I think you've shed your wits!" barked Roc, backing away. "There must still be some bad air here –"

"No, Roc. *You never know*, you said. But for once I

do know; it is not only a feeling. Do you look on those
shelves behind you, and see again what we saw when
first we came down here."

... "Old vessels, pitchers, moulds – sword-moulds,
by Hella's tresses!" He snatched one off the shelf and
held it up, then turned to Elof with a look of dawning
understanding. "It's much like the shape of Gorthawer
... much! But it's not the same, not wholly ..."

"No," said Elof quietly. The crystal lamp was
beginning to dim, the light of day it had gathered to
fade; from the corners of that ancient furnace the long
shadows were beginning to close in. "That one was
flawed. You are not quite tall enough ..." And he
reached high over Roc's broad shoulder, to where the
shorter man saw a sudden gleam among the disturbed
soot. "He who laboured here was a taller man than
either of us; and I would guess, a better smith. But even
he had his failures ..." And from the long-neglected
shelf, amid a cloud of soot, he drew forth a twin to the
black blade, bare-tanged and gleaming as he had first
drawn it from the marsh, from the hand of one centuries dead; save that midway down it was warped and
cracked as if some impatient hand had wrung it and
flung it disgustedly aside.

"*Vayde?*" Roc's growl had thinned to a dry whisper, and it trembled. Elof had seen him stand indomit-
able against so much; but he feared the dead.

"*No!*" cried Elof, himself desperately afraid as the
only friend left him backed from him, to the stairs. "I
tell you, *no!* I am only who I am, whom you have
known ... Alv, Elof! That's all! Not some long-dead
necromancer – of that at least I was never more sure!"

"But you are linked with him," breathed Roc heavily, and suddenly he began to shout. "Can you deny it
now? Dare you? What then? Did he come and visit you
in that marsh? Has his power reached down the years to
you and shaped your destiny? Do you dance to a dead
man's strings, that his blade you wielded, his furnace
you have found, *his very face you wear?*"

Elof stood dumbfounded in the sooty air, swaying
before this assault, helpless and confused. "I don't

know," he cried, "I ... don't ... know! Roc, I'm as unnerved as you are ... more! Help me, Roc! Or I'll be truly lost —"

Roc stopped in his tracks, and ran his hands down his forge-apron; soot crusted on the sweat in his palms. He breathed like one who has run a long course. "I tell you straight," he said, "I'd half a mind to be up those stairs and slam down that door."

"And what then?" said Elof bitterly. "Open the other doors?"

Roc hung his head. "I don't know ... Half a mind, maybe. I'd have thought better of it once I'd got my wind back ..." He picked up the lamp, now scarcely brighter than a glow in that gloom. "Hel, man, let's get out of here, into the clean air; this murk's got into our minds. I wish to Hella I'd never come down here! I never will again! And no more should you!"

"I agree, my friend," sighed Elof, as Roc gingerly helped him up the steps. "But I must. What was made here must be made again; or our doom may yet be more certain. Have you forgotten our need?"

"No. But what makes you so sure the answer's in this pit of sorcery? The makings of another sword? It'll take more than that to set us free!" Elof shook his head, too spent to speak. "What then? The Tarnhelm again, do you think you can shape another such out of that stuff better than you can from metal? For I can think of naught else you were sure of!" Again Elof shook his head. But as they came to the door he reached within his tunic, where he kept Kara's token, and drew out something that slipped from his grasp and fluttered to the ground like a golden leaf. Roc stooped to it; and gazed up at Elof in greater awe than before.

"You can't mean ... You do! Well, I've said once or more than once I'd believe anything of you; but *this*... " A shadow crossed his face. "You're not meaning *I* should — " He could not continue.

But Elof shook his head and smiled. "No indeed! Have we not said often enough that you could get free with ease? Nithaid hardly cares about you. I am the halter about your throat, and to me it falls to take the risk, or perish in trying. But whatever befall, you will still have a part to play, a hard and a dangerous one ..."

Roc grinned and rubbed his hands; his fright had drained out of him. "So long as we're getting somewhere at last!"

"We may be. But who knows how much time is left us? Kara showed us that, whatever she intended, and perhaps also pointed us our way. But it is not yet ours to take!" He slammed the sloping door of the furnace, and twisted the screws that held it tight; then he turned to the remade mechanism and began to wind the wheel.

The soft dragging squeal of the doors in their runners echoed up, setting Elof's teeth on edge. Then beneath their feet a dragon coughed, and the stone quivered to a vast remote roaring. Roc watched tensely as he wound the wheel still wider and set in motion the waterwheel that drove the air-vents. They both kept a tense eye upon a row of tall stems rising from the ground along the length of the furnace, stalks of dark metal set about with leaves of gold; in seconds, no more, the first leaves quivered and began to curl in upon themselves, and the second soon followed. But only when the leaves of the third were curled tight did Elof spin the wheel backward, to close the doors below. The whine of the air-shafts died, and a last puff of vapour came spurting up through the vents, mephitic and biting, before Roc was able to close them, and choke off the growl of the unquiet earth beneath. "Well, they work, by all the Powers!" exclaimed Elof, peering through streaming eyes at the writhing leaves. He had shaped them from webs of many metals laid together in layers, often gossamer thin, and with many virtues worked into them, of consistency not the least. Each layer was chosen carefully to expand at a different speed under the heat that rose up the stem from its roots in the furnace roof, and so pull and twist each leaf this way or that, gauging for those above the intensity of the fires below. He frowned slightly. "Fiercer even than I had expected, for so brief a firing! We must take great care, Roc; Vayde or whoever, it was a brave man who worked this forge before!"

"Or a cracked one! Unless the fires are burning hotter since his day? It's a long time since, remember."

"Maybe ... but wouldn't they rather have cooled, being so close to the air?"

"Why should they, when nothing else has?"

"How do you mean?"

"Don't you remember? How Trygkar said the fire-mountains have grown fiercer since his grandfather's day; and I've heard others say the same. As if the land itself was warring with the Ice ... Ach, leave it, man, it's safe for now! Do you come outside for some air and a drop to celebrate; my face'll fall off if I don't get a stoup of wine into it!"

But they had to walk some way from the forge, for that last exhalation from the vents still hung in a dark cloud in the still air, and the oak trees drooped with darkness on their leaves. Elof watched it, preoccupied, till the reviving river breeze whisked it away like the remnants of a dark vision; only then did he feel at all like celebrating. "To our labours!" he said crisply, clinking his goblet against Roc's. "For though now I know the thing I need can be made and I have the furnace to make it, yet it may be a while before we have cause for toasts again!"

In that he was a true prophet; for all through spring into summer ran his trials, and more and more frustrating they grew. Many and subtle were the stratagems he was driven to devise, the compoundings, blendings, reducings he had to essay in the search to shape anew that hair-like filament with the dark sheen. A dark miasma hung often over the forge and the small beasts of the island fled its environs. Once the very spring was poisoned below the forge; the fish died in its outflow, the swans came no longer to the quiet pools, nor the little mammuts to wallow and spout. Elof, for all his desperation, was grieved at this, and more careful in future, even devising measures to shield the trees from the airs of the furnace. But he did little else; and had his master been more demanding he could hardly have escaped detection. Nithaid, though, had other and more pressing concerns, for the Ekwesh went on as they had begun, harrying the lands in small bands that did less actual harm than before, yet wrought havoc and spread panic by their very elusiveness. Nor had they any need to slacken their campaign in the summer months, as when they were mustered in a full army, for a part of each clan could direct the thrall-gathered harvests in turn, while the rest were raiding.

Only where Elof's new fortifications stood were the raids blunted, for they rarely dared afford the time to lay siege to a town so defended, and the labyrinthine barrier as it spread blocked the quick influx and escape upon which their strategies depended. When Nithaid could fall upon such a band of raiders heavily engaged against a town, or trap them between the slender garrison of the barriers and his own army, he wiped them out to a man; but otherwise he was left floundering with his heavy forces from place to place after reivers who darted in and out like fish nibbling a bait. Only by surprise and good fortune could he intercept them; and he seemed to be having less of both. In many places he left garrisons, but one might fall into undisturbed idleness, another be overwhelmed by unusually large numbers, another worn away by repeated harassment; all were equally destructive. Often he had to face minor mutinies among his levies when they heard of their homelands being pillaged while they were kept chasing some elusive threat halfway down the border. All this grew worse, and his standing, which by Elof's creations and his own fierce energy had been greatly enhanced of late, began once again to suffer. Even his own warriors grew louder in their grumbles, and more ready to remember that for all his claims to Ysmerien blood he held the throne by the right of a usurper only, and that through an Ysmerien great-grandfather his children had a better right than he. Even at his court, since he was so often absent, this came to be said openly, and less than eagerly discouraged by his sons. So Roc reported, for as often as ever he went abroad to aid in the fortifications, and Elof was left to his lone and gloomy labours.

It was from one such excursion that he returned, early in the next winter that was the seventh of Elof's thralldom, and found his friend seated at their table with a great mass of filament before him, and a strange smile on his face. He was clad as if to celebrate in some of the fine garments that Nithaid had sent them; but Roc did not fail to notice how stiffly and gingerly he rose, nor that his crutches were new and of steel, nor that the end wall of the forge had a stained and blackened cast to it, as from the passage of great heat. As Elof offered him his hand in greeting he took the arm instead, and saw Elof wince as he gripped the bandages beneath; looking closely, he saw that his friend's cheeks had a sheen to them as of new scarring, tight and papery.

"You've been doing it, haven't you, you daft bastard?" Roc hissed, gripping harder in his anger. "Going down there to work, and all by yourself – fired your bloody clothes, didn't you – *eh*?"

"It was the only way ..." said Elof faintly, and sat down, clutching his arm. "The only way untried ... The lesser the wound, the slower it is to heal, so it is with me, I think. No grave burns, but many scorches, that is all ... And it is done, Roc! Done! I have burned the rock-oil with minerals to its finest form, and spun it into thin chains of matter, crystals finer than thread. Was that not worth a flaying from the fires? The filament is made anew! And with it our hopes!"

Roc shook his head resignedly. "The filaments, maybe; but all the rest? How'll you come by the materials you need? Crystals take time to grow; and where can you find enough gold for ..."

"That taxed me also!" said Elof, smiling darkly once more, "But no longer. Nithaid is returned, have you heard?"

"Aye; he had me to the palace, to quiz about the state of the fortifications. He is hard-pressed, that one; he leaves the field only to tighten his grip on the heartlands, and raise more money for the campaigns. It's rumoured he plans a new minting of coinage ..."

"He does," said Elof, still smiling. "But he has need of my aid with it. Last week that slime-ridden lord his treasurer came calling on me with great chests of gold, his knees knocking at the very sight of me; but still he demanded that I use my arts to so debase the stuff as to increase it by a quarter, and leave even the minters unable to tell. Wonderful, is it not, to what heights I am elevated in the hands of this king? He makes me his thrall, his murderer, and now his counterfeiter; a noble advancement, is it not?"

"Tell him you can't do it!" urged Roc, outraged. "It's no more than the truth –"

"I sent word back that I could, and would," rejoined Elof.

Roc shook his head in surprised disgust. "But man ... can you do it?"

"I believe so – though that reflects less on the skills in me than the lack of them in the coiners. They would scarce notice if the gold were debased by half, so long as it took their die-stamps prettily enough."

"By half –" exploded Roc, and then he began to chuckle. "You'd better be right, my lad!"

"About the coiners?"

"About your plan! Make the best of that gold, for I fear you're going to need it! But whence comes the other stuff?"

"I sent word I needed that for the coining. The first boatload arrived this morning." Roc stared at him wide-eyed, and exploded into laughter.

"He's fostered your felon's instincts only too well, I see!"

But Elof's smile did not change, and Roc understood suddenly that it was rigid with self-disgust. "He has. And if one day it should lead me to forget that I am a mastersmith, and no common assassin, be it upon his head."

The winter that came was harder even than those before, and it was among banks of snow and bitter winds that Elof entered the eighth year of his thralldom. He scarcely noticed; he was too busy, labouring with Roc upon the king's gold, or by himself in the depths of the furnace chamber. Roc was glad to see that his burns were healing, and that he took no further such risks; he seemed to feel now that he had greater cause to keep himself as whole and ready as he could. Only at times, when he could not sleep of a night, he would go stand hip-deep in the snow that not even the rising earthfires could dispel now, and gaze long into the skies, whether clouded or frost-clear; and for that Roc hardly had the heart to rebuke him. But he saw no more wings. It seemed that Kara had vanished as mysteriously as she had appeared. Chests of gold went ashore and were received at the mint without complaint, the more so as Elof had set within the tainted gold a potency which might cloud a prying mind; the new-made blanks rang as clear and heavy as any pure gold between the dies. Upon one face, as was customary, the sign of the Sun between the Horns was set; but upon the other was shown Nithaid in his armour bestriding a dying Ekwesh warrior, for he wished the coins to embody the confidence of his realm and rule.

"And so it does!" said Elof bitterly. "For it is as false at heart! More false even that he himself suspects!" He let the coin slip through his fingers onto the table, and from there roll unregarded to the floor, and wiped one hand against the other as if to shed the taint. Then, gathering his crutches, he heaved himself upright, swung towards the door and slammed it behind him in an icy blast of air. Roc looked after him and shook his head sadly; but he did not neglect to pick up the coin and stow it carefully in an inner pocket.

Elof floundered out through the snow, climbing laboriously to the summit of the hill, drinking in deep draughts of the clean air as if to wash out the clinging taint of dishonesty. A cold north wind had scoured the sky to a dome of onyx traced with diamond, glittering and hard. The oaks looked suddenly aged, for the snow clung to their bare branches in place of missing foliage, and they drooped beneath its weight. In summer this little grove was a place of peace for him, a green shade where he could lie and be lulled by the drone of insects and the thousand shifting shadings of the broad leaves. Stark and cold now, it held little promise of peace for him; and yet it helped strangely to lean his aching head against the coolness of the gnarled bark, and know that somewhere beneath life and growth went on in hope, readying for the spring that was not far off. He had done well to spare these ancient trees.

You did well indeed.

Elof jerked back from the trunk as if it burned him, and barely kept his balance on his crutches. The voice was impossibly faint and distant, vast as a wind over infinite forests, the susurrus of unnumbered tossing treetops, and blowing like them in gusts that came and went; yet he heard each word clear in his mind, and knew who it was who spoke. "You again!"

I indeed. I am glad you remember me. Moss and creeper invade that cunning forge you built in my realm. Dead leaves blow over the floor, gather and rot to fertile earth. Seeds swell and split among the crannies of the walls; roots slither under flagstones, small beasts tunnel beneath the cold hearth. In the spring gales the roof shall fall at last. You may wall out the forest, but you cannot keep it at bay for long.

"What do you here, so far from that realm?" demanded Elof, seeing his breath smoke against the trunk. "If you've come only to mock me –"

I have not come anywhere. I am here, as I am where stands even the smallest sapling of a tree. And I do not seek to mock you, or enchain your heart as before. As the world is now we have common cause; and I speak only to bring warning.

Elof snorted. "Warning? What have you to warn me of, who set me such a snare?"

Heed me nonetheless! Too gravely stands the cause of life to let any enmity divide its defenders now!

"If you could bring some kind of help, I might believe you!"

You must believe me! I can give you no help; I must put forth the utmost of my strength even to speak, in this land of men that has slain its trees! I can only bear warning!

"Then ... a message; could you not bear one to my own land, to Keryn Kermorvan its king? There are trees enough!"

But none to hear their voices. Few hear me, save at the edge of thought, who have not dwelt long in my realm, or trafficked otherwise with the Powers. You have tasted the blood of the worm, that is a minor Power embodied; and you have your smithcraft, that is the gift of a power to men. Few have as much; in your Eastlands, none.

Elof caught his breath. "But you can see that land? Then do you tell me at least how my friends there fare! How stands their realm? I beg of you ..." For a moment no answer came, only silence. Then in a sudden gust the great voice called again.

I look, and it is well! Though trees are felled others are sown; the land is tended, and not laid waste. A land at peace, a land that looks to the coming years, a wise land; were all such, I would have less quarrel with your kind. I see men and duergar meet in harmony beneath the trees, and praise their lords who drew them from the west. Of the city I see little, among stone; but on the shore are stood two Watchers more. You would know their likeness. I can see no more.

The sudden heat of tears over his cold cheeks startled him. "I thank you, Lord of Forests! It is more than enough! Of what then would you warn me?"

Of one thing more I cannot clearly see. For in the realms of the Ice less grows even than among the stones men raise. Yet something is stirring; moss and lichen feel it, and the seeds that sleep beneath the frozen ground, against the day of its withdrawing. They are my spies, and they bring me word. The Ice prepares to tip the balance at last, and this is the place appointed. Against Taounehtar I cannot stand, where trees are so few; but you who break the wills of powers upon your anvil, it may be that you can. It is laid upon you to try!

"But how? What will the Ice do? It is too far off to strike a spearhead against Kerys as against Morvan ..."

It is nearer than you may think. Already Taoune's ground-ice gnaws the roots of my highland forests, and they falter. This winter will be long; but the next one will seem to have no end! Then, some time in the summerless months that must follow, the glaciers themselves will throw their weight upon the scales ...

Abruptly the voice broke off, grew harsh and shrill as a stormwind.

One is here who listens! I speak no more, you know enough ... reflect in care and fear!

The silence was as sudden and absolute as the slamming of some distant door.

"Wait! Who listens?" Elof whirled around wildly, searching the tree-shadows; he fought for balance and toppled into the crisp snow, his crutches clattering apart. The icy chill on his neck was so sudden it was terrifying; he felt his heart race, his breath grow shallow, so strong was the sense of presence, of being watched – closely, intently. His mind flooded with thoughts of those terrors, thin and shadowy, that stalked the outlands on just such nights as these; he had to get up, to jump up and run, and to know he could not was to live a nightmare. He fought to call for Roc, but his voice was dry in his throat; frantically he twisted about, grabbed his crutches and struggled to find a footing on the hill. But even as he somehow managed to rise he stopped, swayed as if struck, and reached out a hand not to strike, but unbelieving, to touch ...

She stood there at the margin of the grove, a pale face atop a mantle of shadows, her eyes wide and gleaming. But what he read in them he could not be sure, whether it was love or hate, pity, disgust, scorn, all of these or none. She saw him in all his weakness and shame, broken, halting upon his crutches, and what she thought he could not guess. Another moment, another fraction of a heartbeat and he might have read the mystery of her gaze, fathomed the pools darker than the darkness that were her eyes so long lost to him, so dearly, so painfully remembered. But even as he reached out, her mantle became a flurry of motion; even as he cried out her name a great wind beat upon his face, a shadow passed over the moon. And when Roc, horrified, came running from the hut, he found Elof staring lost and empty-eyed at the distant skies.

In a few curt words he told his friend what had passed; Roc could do nothing but shake his head. "It's beyond me, either of them – if you didn't but dream them both up –"

"*No!* It was more like awakening. This could be the dream … and I would to all the powers it were!"

Roc scratched his head, and chuckled. "Sorry; I'm all too real. Tell you what, though, I'll stand here awhile with you, if you will, and scan the skies; though your eyes are sharper than mine, and I don't think she'll come back. Not tonight, I mean," he added hastily. "But another night, for certain. And each time she's come closer; that's something, isn't it?"

Elof scraped a crutch in the snow. "Thanks for that comfort; I should accept it, I might – if she had not come so hard on Tapiau's warning! What did she mean? What was her purpose – and whose, her own or Louhi's?"

"Who am I to say? But it's a question better pondered within doors over warm wine. Or better yet, slept on. Will you not to your bed?"

Elof resisted, but soon let Roc draw him away. But ever and anon he looked about him as they made their way down into the hollow where the forge stood, spilling golden warmth across the snow from its open door. As they turned the corner towards it Elof cast one lingering look back; and stopped dead, though his crutches sank deep into the snow.

"What is it?" Roc whispered. "Do you see her again?"

"No!" whispered Elof. "Do you look there!"

"What then? The slope, the water, the further shore. Snow upon snow, and the first clear night we've had for an age and an age –"

"Clear it is, clear as glass … and as brittle. Look up, man, up! To the shore, the hills, the far horizon – there the night is not clear. A fell word is written on it, have you the eyes to see." Roc saw; and caught his breath in anguish. For that sight he also knew too well, and too many memories came flooding back. More than the light of moon or star picked out the peaks of the most distant hills; faint and tenuous though it was, there was no mistaking it. Like the light of some distant lake, impossibly still, the radiance of the Ice flew across the night;

and in it, through it, the lights of the aurora danced and flickered.

"But it's hardly closer than it was!" exclaimed Roc. "Still far too far for any direct assault, whatever Tapiau told you ..."

"There are other ways of being close! Perhaps he sensed Kara's presence, for something of the Ice must cling to her. Or did he mean ... Roc, what wind has chased the clouds so swiftly?"

"Why, a bloody north wind, can't you feel it? Straight off the Ice, brrr ..."

"Yes! All along the horizon, so the Ice can shine out clear. Like a signal ... or a banner ..."

Roc shrugged dismissively. "As far off as this? It'll not daunt us!"

"Aye, but is it for us? How will it look close to? Remember what Kermorvan and I told you of, on the glacier?"

Roc whistled. "As if the sky'd frozen and the stars come down to dance! A fine rallying for the forces of the Ice!"

Elof nodded. "That assault I foresaw – I'll wager it's that! It would make sense! To have it two years in the brewing, building up their forces – and these raids a mere sham of Louhi's devising, to keep them well blooded but preserve their strength!"

"And wear down Nithaid's!" muttered Roc. "We'll have to warn him!"

"How far will he credit me, after I warned him last? Hel, they won't even be able to see that display from the mainland, they're too low! A few lights in the sky and words in my head, you know what he'll make of that!"

"Whatever he does, we've got to try!"

Elof frowned. "Yes. But there's little we can to till daylight; none save Nithaid himself, or one or two of the guards, would come near Elan Ghorenhyon by night!"

"Not even if we fired the whole forge!" growled Roc. "And they're all up at the palace. So be it, since it must! At first light, and may it be in time!"

But there was no need. If it should seem strange that the chroniclers count that one night's happenings as crucial, then let it be remembered that the weightiest of balances turn on the finest of points. It is known that, even as Elof and Roc spoke, lights danced in the sky over Kerys as over the Wild Lands, angry sparks of red and gold; the beaconfires sprang from hill to hill like the first sparks of a racing forest fire, and after them the golden flashes of the signal mirrors. Even as Elof flashed a mirror towards the guard-post on the harbour wall, royal messengers were spurring their lathered mounts across the slippery cobbles around the harbour, and ere he had sent his warning he saw beyond the walls the masts of the tall cogs stirring as they were warped from dock to loading quays, ready to re-embark the troops they had but lately released to homes and families. The assault had already begun.

More word soon followed. The first assault had spent itself among the maze of Elof's defences, with terrible slaughter done by the light garrison; but they themselves had taken great losses, and feared another such attack would leave them unable to man the wall. There were signs that one was mustering, greater than the first; but strange beasts prowled the lands around, and terrors stranger still, and trackers and spies who sought to discover more did not return. Nithaid was needed, and that very afternoon he set sail with such force as he could gather from the city, leaving his commanders to raise levies from the other lands and follow.

Elof and Roc were watching from the vantage of the forge as the flotilla departed; but they were surprised to see the king's cog drop anchor in the lee of Elan Ghorhenyan, and Nithaid himself be rowed ashore. His greeting was unceremonious. "What's this about a warning of yours?" he was bellowing before his boat scraped onto the shore. "How'd you come to know something was afoot?"

Elof told him only of the lights over the Ice, making no mention of Tapiau or Kara, and he tugged angrily at his beard. "It looks bad!" he muttered. "And you can't tell me more? No more cunning tricks to hand?"

Elof studied the king a moment. His heavy face

seemed to have loosened, coarsened; he had grown fatter, and there were dark pouches under his eyes, stale wine on his breath. "I have nothing ready to show you, King."

Disappointment and desperation chased like clouds across Nithaid's face, and the veins at his temples bulged. "*Nothing?*" he barked, then, with a glance at the men in the boat, he lowered his voice. "Nothing at all? What've you been about these past weeks, then? What d'you think I treat you this well for? You're still a thrall, by Verya, and you'll serve as one! Are you needing the lash to remind you?"

"I do have a work in hand," Elof answered truthfully, "which may be of great service against the Ice. But it is not yet finished –"

"Then finish it, man! Finish it today, while I watch!"

"King, if I could, I would, believe you me. But you should know by now that smithcraft cannot be hurried. It will take some weeks still. But when it is done, I promise, the first to see and wonder will be you!"

"If I'm still here," muttered Nithaid, and then added "If I'm not, you are answerable to my sons, remember! The throne will be theirs soon in any event. I grow old; I can stand little more of this ..." He drew a deep breath, then straightened up, turned on his heel and stalked back to the boat. Over his shoulder he shouted back "I'll have it the moment I return, mind you!"

"There goes a man afraid!" observed Roc thoughtfully as they watched the king rowed back to his ship. "Looking for some straw to clutch. Now he'll be telling the rowers he's had counsel from the sorcerer, so they can spread the rumour to hearten his troops ..."

"And so he can blame anything that goes amiss upon me!" said Elof, with a grim smile. "Well, to work; I have a promise to keep now. At least it will be many weeks more till we are disturbed again."

In that, as it turned out, he was wrong. It was only some three weeks later that Roc's cry brought Elof hurrying and stumbling up from the depths of the forge, the light hammers and shapers he had been using spill-

ing from the pockets of his forge-leather. He leaned on
the window-ledge and squinted into the bright morning
sun. "You're right!" he said in some surprise. "A royal
barge, painted like a jaybird and flying the Sun emblem!
But Nithaid never uses such a thing to come see us ..."
He and Roc looked at each other.

"Someone more fond of pomp and luxury ... I'll
wager it's *them*!"

"No stake!" said Elof dryly. "I can see them; and it's
here they're headed."

"Then do you go clean up and don a robe, something ceremonial! The more magesmith these two see and
the less thrall, the better!"

Elof nodded thoughtfully.

When a horn sounded a flourish from the hill
outside, it was Roc who swung open the heavy door of
the forge; Elof smiled to himself as he heard the flourish
falter. Someone was evidently nervous at finding himself
here. The two tall figures who stepped over the threshold, however, could hardly have radiated a more arrogant confidence in their manner and their rich dress,
scarlets and greens; it might only have been interest that
had caused them to hesitate before the great sun symbol
upon the door, or the dimness within. Elof had closed
the shutters and plied the bellows to the forgefire by
whose hearth he now sat. He had donned a robe Nithaid
had given him, and which normally he hated; it was of
smith's black, full about the sleeves and hood, worked
about breast and cuffs with symbols of smithcraft in
gold, and he suspected it had belonged to Amylhes. But
now it served his purpose admirably; he had pulled the
hood over his face, and as he rose from the hearthside
he felt he looked every inch the sorcerer. The crutches
he could not help, but to offset them he held, as if cere-
monially, a huge long-shafted hammer. The sight of him,
shadowed against the head-high forgeflames, stopped the
princes in their tracks.

"Hail, my lords!" he said, and his voice rang
beneath the high rafters of the forge. "You honour the
Isle of the Sorcerers with your presence. How fares the
king your father in his wars? Does he send word by you?"

Behind the princes he saw Roc striving not to laugh; he evidently thought Elof was simply out to keep these young popinjays off balance. But Elof's purpose was more serious, and he pressed it home. Were these the new lords of Kerys he spoke to? The thought that Nithaid might be dead flamed agony in his heart. "Do you set foot here today by his command?"

The older one – Geraidh, was that his name? – looked Elof up and down with elaborate unconcern, and then turned to a workbench and idly picked up an elaborate piece of gold-work, a gem setting in fine wire. "Quite cunning!" he remarked. "I see now why he trusts you with so much gold. But then you have shown yourself worthy of trust, have you not? Many and oft a time; and yet you have reason to hate him – is that not so, Master Valant?"

"I have never pretended otherwise, prince."

Geraidh rounded on him sharply, taken aback by this casual mode of address. But he held back his words, and stood stroking his curling black beard, though something burned still in his eyes. "You hate a man, yet serve him faithfully ..." He looked around. "And for a poor reward, it seems to me – eh, Kenarech?"

The younger prince chuckled. "I wouldn't kennel my hounds in such a hovel as this. You're a puzzle, sorcerer; gold flows through your hands, yet it seems that little sticks. I think our respected father has been rather unfair."

"Quite so," mused Geraidh. "I think that such service deserves its proper reward. You know that he has left the kingdom to us jointly, Master Valant? Well, if my brother is agreeable, I think we can certainly do better for you than this."

Kenarech chuckled. "Of course! We'll set you free, sorcerer – how about that, eh?"

"At the very least!" said Geraidh emphatically, gazing a little reproachfully at his brother. "Freedom alone is small repayment. In the old days a king would have ennobled a smith for that armour alone. I think a barony might be in order – a titular one, of course, with a stipend instead of land, to free you from respon-

sibilities. To allow you to remain with us at court and
practice your art there."

Kenarech chuckled. "Say then, would you not
rather serve a better master? One who rewarded you
more to your liking?"

Geraidh stiffened, and his dark eyes flashed a
sudden anger at his brother; Elof read in it a warning. If
it were possible to have them talk more freely ... They
would have to believe they were on safe ground for that.
He bowed his head slowly, and laid down the hammer.
"I have done so, in the past. Gladly would I do so once
more."

The two young men visibly relaxed, and Kenarech
smiled mockingly at his brother. "You will serve us,
then, sorcerer."

"That may be," said Elof cautiously, "when your
father wills it."

"Yes!" chuckled Kenarech, "And willed it he has!
For his last testament is made. Made – and witnessed."

Elof bit his lip. "Do you tell me he is dead, then?"

"Cannot your dark arts reveal the truth of that?"
inquired Geraidh sarcastically. "What if he is?"

"What indeed?" said Elof calmly, and shrugged.
"That, if I mistake not, you will tell me."

Kenarech glanced nervously about him. "Send your
man away! This is not for the ears of thralls ..." Elof,
smiling inwardly, glanced at Geraidh, but saw only
fierce and wary attention. Well and good; for all their
scorn they had soon forgotten that he also was a thrall.
Imperiously he waved Roc outside; Roc tugged his fore-
lock and altogether overdid his show of deference,
mopping and mowing. Fortunately neither prince paid
him the least attention. Their eyes were fixed on
Elof. On Kenarech's smooth brows beads of sweat
had sprung out; he sought to speak, but his voice had
dried up to a hoarse croak. Geraidh's eyes narrowed,
and he tossed the gold-work into the air and caught it
deftly. He was a burly man like his father, but taller and
leaner, and at some twenty-four years a far more impressive figure. Save in the eyes; his were narrowed, and
without Nithaid's glittering vitality. "Under his will we

inherit you with all else. We may do with you as we will, sorcerer. You would not wish to displease us, I am sure; but I need say no more than that." He smiled suddenly, a handsome, engaging smile. "You see, it is not my way to govern with threats. Or my noble brother's. We are not ... shall we say, so single-minded as our father. We would not spill blood needlessly, nor dice with the lives of men. We believe in justice and peace."

"I would be glad to see such a one king of this land," said Elof smoothly.

"You will work your wizardry for us, then, Master Valant?" broke in Kenarech impatiently. His brother hissed wordlessly between clenched teeth, and he added "I mean, since it is willed so. Aid us and you'll find us generous ..."

Geraidh gestured him angrily to silence. "This sorcerer is a wise man. I'll avow that he and I understand one another; he'll serve us far more willingly than ever he has Nithaid." He paused a minute, tugging at his beard with an air of deep reflection, and met his brother's eyes a moment before adding "When the time comes, of course. No, sorcerer, it is not yet here; our father lives still. Word has reached us that he has beaten back the worst the Icewitch could do, at a great cost in lives, and there is talk of peace. He stays only to be sure her forces have all drawn back. Soon he will return, and take up his throne again."

"For years and years, maybe!" spat out Kenarech, a frustration in his voice that sounded close to tears. He was shorter than his brother, and though little more than a year younger the plumpness he kept gave him a boyish look, which his trim moustache only served to accentuate. "You couldn't ask for better, could you, smith? Years more swinking under his thumb, in this place! Years before you can come into our service!" He gazed moodily into the fire. "No more could we! Years of guzzling mouths, of endless levies, of eating, sleeping, breathing nothing but war ..."

"Of shedding a Great River's worth of blood!" put in Geraidh. "Terrible, of course; but absolutely necessary, you understand."

"Oh, of course!" complained Kenarech, sprawling back on a bench. "To win back all those wild wastelands on our northern borders – absolutely! Why should it matter, after all, that they've not been ours for two generations past, and that we've never missed them? Or the Gate, that had become a punishment posting for mutinous soldiers, so far was it from anywhere civilized! Let the savages have them, that's what some people might say; give up chasing about after every flea-bite of a raid! After all, those border folk are half savage, anyway; leave them to fight one another, and the rest of the country in peace! That's what some people might say, but never us!" He snorted. "We're with our father, every step of the way. We can't wait to go blundering about the backwoods with a huge force every time the savages lift a few cows from the peasants! So we stir them up and have to spend another fortune quelling them! Eh, Geraidh? Can we? We're afraid the Icewitch is going to come and get us!"

Geraidh smiled thinly, like a kindly adult entering into the spirit of an infant's game. "I lie awake worrying about it," he remarked. "Never mind that I've never seen the Ice moving any nearer in my lifetime; our father is quite right to encourage all that cloud of superstition about it, and this Witchwoman the savages worship. How else would he drum up so much support?"

"How else indeed?" laughed Kenarech. His brother seemed content to let him run on, as if confident what opinion of him Elof would form. "After all, if it isn't the Ice he has to deal with, it's these border lordlings. Now there are those might be content to let them run free and be hanged if they like, with their endless provincial bickerings; not as if they brought in their worth in taxes, after all! But no; let's butcher every savage and whip every lordling into line, say I, and beggar the kingdom for a century to come, if we need to ..." He bit off what he had been about to add, and spat viciously into the fire.

Geraidh, who had been looking wary, relaxed and nodded calmly. "Our esteemed father is certainly a man of great and war-like ambitions. If he makes peace with the savages, he will turn next to uniting his borders; that will be a bloody business! Yet already he talks of it. And then? Why, he dreams of the lands across the sea, whence I believe you came! Naturally you would wish to see him rule there also. There is no limit to his ambition – and of course," the prince shrugged, "he is fully entitled to it. He is, after all, the king. But there is no treason, after all, in favouring, as we have on occasions counselled ..."

"A less dedicated approach?" suggested Elof, resting heavily on his crutches. The rumour of peace had shaken him, and he could think of little else at that moment.

"I see you understand. But, as he is entitled to do, he has ignored that. These things cannot be helped, of course. Our father is the rightful king, and we his loyal sons. There are those, of course, even many great lords and men of wealth and influence, who feel that our father's rule grows daily too costly, and not only in money, that he throws away lives like so much wine-lees. They complain, if you will credit it, that they are weary of glutting this strife with their taxes and their sons. But this is dangerous talk, talk of rebellion even, and there has been far too much of it around the court of late. We have done our best to suppress it, of course; but these things are particularly hard to contain. Especially while the king is away. You take my meaning?"

"Of course," said Elof, with a slight bow. Having endured Nithaid's doting upon these his own flesh, he felt an almost physical surge of sickness. He had seen without difficulty the way they were leading, and without surprise; but to hear this monstrous ingratitude from their own lips was almost beyond bearing.

"We are particularly afraid that some such foolish rebellion might be prepared to strike before he could return. In such a time we must move with circumspection. A personage such as yourself could be of material importance in assuring the success or failure of such a revolt – if, for example, you are preparing some powerful engine of war for Nithaid on his return, as it is rumoured. You might be approached, or even abducted by such rebels …"

"Tortured, even!" Kenarech chimed in. "They'll baulk at nothing, men like that!"

Geraidh nodded, tugging his beard. "It is possible. I do not like the idea, but it is possible. When the stakes are so great … We came to warn you, therefore, and to assure ourselves of exactly where your loyalties might stand in this matter, were you approached, pressured even, by any such misguided faction." He paused, expectantly.

"You may be sure," said Elof slowly, "that my loyalties are engaged as you would wish them to be; and that if the worst should come to the worst, I would hope to serve you and your brother in exactly the same manner as your father. As it happens …" He leaned on his crutches and steepled his hands, watching the sudden flaring of interest in their faces. "As it happens, I am indeed working on such a device, which could be of signal advantage to either side in any rising, if they were clever enough and enjoyed sufficient support. I would feel a great deal better if you knew about it …"

"And perhaps took charge of it?" suggested Kenarech. His brother glared at him.

"Some details, at least, might be of assistance; a demonstration, even – if you are not saving that for Nithaid."

Elof smiled. "For him, yes; but in the circumstances I consider this more important. Provided all this is kept in the utmost confidence –" He looked at Kenarech and then, meaningly, at Geraidh.

"That goes without saying," said the older prince sharply, with a sour look at his brother.

"Then I will be pleased to show you what I am working on. When it is ready."

The two keen faces clouded with impatience and disappointment. "Why not now?" demanded Kenarech. "At least give us some idea …"

"If we are to forestall any such treacherous action," put in Geraidh quietly, "we must – *must!* – have some sight of it before he returns!"

"Till it is ready there is nothing to demonstrate,"

said Elof firmly, thinking of the shimmering beauty that hung concealed in the cooling furnace below. "How long will that be, think you?"

"No more than three weeks away, I'd guess. Well, can you achieve it in that time, sorcerer?" The tone was a threat in itself, but Elof smiled as if he had not heard it.

"I believe I can," he said. "I must consider, and study. If I may send word to you, no later than fourteen days hence ... By my thrall; he is to be trusted entirely," he added, as their faces darkened. He watched greed war with caution in them both, as clearly as metals that cannot alloy.

At length Geraidh nodded. "Very well. But take care! The conspirators may be all around you. Why, we have not even dared warn our father yet, so certainly would any such message be intercepted, and the rebels alerted. There is no need to bother him, for now."

Elof smiled broadly, and bowed. "You need have no fear I will turn aside in this matter. What more could I wish, after all, than to enjoy the gratitude of the heirs-apparent, and the just reward of my toil? I would wish you no less, my princes."

Kenarech chuckled. "When our father returns, we will see to it that you have your reward! Whatever a cunning sorcerer takes delight in, eh?" He chuckled, and clucked his tongue lightly. "Whatever your desires – whatever your tastes – set yourself no bounds, you may indulge them all!" His moustache worked as his mouth pursed at the thought.

Geraidh shook his head reprovingly. "This learned and cunning man would scarcely bother with such things!" he said with calm certainty. "Come, brother, let us take our leave ere you offend him further. We await your word, sir; and leave our lives, and the good of this poor bleeding realm, in your hands. Come, Kenarech!"

Elof bowed deeply as the tall young man turned his brother towards the door; Kenarech acknowledged him with a jaunty and patronising wave, but Geraidh studied him a moment out of his narrowed eyes, and then inclined his own head slightly. Elof watched them step through the door and out onto the hill, and was about to sink down in his seat when Geraidh plunged back inside and strode over to him. "My gloves!" he remarked, somewhat loudly. "I must have laid them down somewhere … Ah, there!" They lay on the bench beside Elof. As Geraidh bent over to pick them up he paused, and murmured, "Hearken to me, wise man! You heard my brother prattle, you will have formed your own view of his discretion. He is scarcely to be trusted. I counsel you, when you send that word, do you send it to me alone!"

Kenarech poked his head around the door. "What keeps you, brother?"

"I had left my gloves. And I was remarking that I will wish to command an armour also, when times are more settled!"

"No, sir sorcerer!" laughed the younger brother. "Do you shape me one first, for he hardly cares to bestride a horse, this one, let alone fight with his own two hands! He'd sooner crouch over the coals and plot –"

Geraidh ushered him firmly out, and Elof slumped down and rested his head in his hands. When Roc reappeared, having seen their boat safely away, he looked up at him. "Pour me a stoup of wine, will you? I've a foul flavour needs rinsing from my mouth …" He tossed back the cup at a gulp. Roc refilled it, and Elof nodded his thanks.

"When I think how the king has doted on these two young vipers …! How that old brute has driven himself half into his grave these past years, killing himself with the effort to leave them a kingdom secure, united and at peace …" Elof shook his head furiously. "I could almost find it in me to pity the man!"

"As he raised his seed, so he must reap it!" said Roc censoriously. "It might be a hard and scarring thing to be raised by such a man; I'll wager his devotion could make twice the tyrant of him, and crush those it fell on!"

Elof nodded. "Crushed they are, out of their natural shape!"

"You don't know the half of it!" grunted Roc. "That little swine Kenarech, as we're turning down to the boat he makes as to toss me a coin, and stands fumbling in his purse. Well, I'm playing the daft mechanical, so I stand and wait, and damned if he don't whisper to me that I'm to warn you his brother will betray and cheat you as he's cheating *him*, and you're to send the word to him alone. Or, failing that, that I'm to bring it to him anyhow; and he gives me a gold piece, no less, as an earnest." Roc tossed it on the table. "Another of yours, damn it!"

They laughed, but Elof swiftly grew serious. "I wonder if Kenarech is quite the fool his brother thinks him; Geraidh did not think to bribe you, which might have been the surer way of getting the message, had you been the usual thrall. Though he did contrive to assure me he would still have a use for me afterwards, with that mention of armour ..."

Roc poured more wine. "There's not a handsbreadth between them; Hella have the pair of them, for me!" He looked anxiously at Elof. "Not really going to aid them, are you? Not even for revenge on Nithaid?"

"And give Kerys to the Ice? Hardly! I could simply betray them to Nithaid; for what revenge could be keener than showing him the treachery of what he loves the most? His own flesh and blood ..." Elof considered. "But I do not seek so base a vengeance. And as they warned me, I might not manage it. Yet ..." He sipped absently at his wine. "There is too much that does not satisfy me, Roc. Too much I fail to understand. This talk of peace with the Ice – what in the world could induce Louhi to offer that?"

"Maybe the hiding Kerys has given her; you suggested that once. Made her think she'd be better off turning her powers elsewhere – against Morvanhal, maybe as we feared."

"It might be – and yet I cannot believe it. Nithaid has only just held back the Ekwesh, and they are no more than the advance guard of the Ice. There is none of that unity of heart and mind here that the Ice seems to fear. As witness those two! They endanger the land.

And something more worried me – "

"So it bloody well should! Bugger the land! What about you and me? Can't you see? They fear what you've shown you can do! If you don't help them they've as good as threatened to slay you, just to deny their father your help."

"I know!" said Elof calmly. "I meant something else, something lurking under their whole approach to us. They spoke as they did so that no word could be reported; in another's voice the true meaning would be lost. Yet would you have babbled out so perilous a plot so lightly to one you hardly knew? However badly you needed his help, however sure you were he hated your victim? They seemed in such haste, too hasty to make caution worthwhile for them." He paused. "Or for me. As if they knew something might happen to me –"

"Or they planned it to!" muttered Roc, "the treacherous little swinesheads!" Then he brightened again. "But you must still be all right for those two weeks, or they wouldn't have swallowed the wait. And after that …"

"After that we'll see. I will deal with them another way. But we must hasten our plans, Roc. At least I've won time to work without interruption, still." But in that, as before, he was mistaken.

The days that followed were a time of unrelenting toil. They had known many such in their lives, but seldom if ever had they had so clear and steep a brink marked out before them, or so dark an abyss beyond. They knew their span; in fourteen days they must be ready, for after that might lie ruin for themselves, and so, perhaps, all that they cared for in the world. Their work began before the sun, and finished after it, though it was high summer and the evenings growing long. Through light and dark they laboured, and sought rest only when they were close to falling, when the arm would no longer support the weights it must, when the fingers trembled perilously over delicate work and the details of it became dull blurs under aching smoke-ridden eyes. Once in a while rest was forced upon them, chiefly when the furnace must be left to cool, but Elof grudged the rest even as he welcomed it. For him sleep became a monster that drew him down unwilling into shadowy deeps, into nightmare and turmoil that left him feeling almost worse when he awakened. Roc slept better; but all his food smacked of little save smoke and soot.

Late one evening, that of the twelfth day since the coming of the princes, such an enforced rest found Elof slumped upon the hearthside seat where his aching limbs and shoulders could draw in the milder warmth gratefully, taking bread and drink he could scarcely taste. His eyes burned from the endless intricacies of his task; the urge to haste burned in his veins, and with it the fear that all might come to a crux too soon. He felt a fierce restlessness, and the need to distract his racing mind. It was a jeweller's craft he exercised here, yet the power in it was vast, and must be tightly secured, firmly controlled, lest the work shatter under its own stress. So also it was with him. Roc was throwing open doors and windows to clear the manyfold smells and smokes of the labours, and let the scent of the myrtle bushes nearby drift in on the warm airs, alive with the creaking of cicadas. But at the window that looked down to the River he stopped, gaped out and swore horribly. "What is it?" Elof shouted.

"There's a bloody boat down there! Beached and all, sail furled and a couple of sailors dozing in her lee! Someone's sneaked ashore!"

"But who? Is it that Royal barge?"

"No; half the size! But it looks rich enough!"

Elof swung around on his crutches, but even as he did so he saw the shadow that crossed the doorway. He raised his voice in an impressive challenge. "Who comes unheralded to the Socerers' Isle?"

The voice that answered him was a woman's, hard and clear and proud. "No herald needs the Princess Beathaill to any servant of the King her father! Bow down to receive her!" Through the doorway stepped two tall and haughty women, angular in rich-hued gowns of court, and stood flanking the entrance, their eyes flickering nervously about the strangeness of the forge. After a moment, seeing no lurking peril, they turned and bowed, and between them stepped a shape shorter and more shapely of a girl of at most twenty years, probably a shade less, startlingly pretty, clad in a divided hunting gown of green as bright as her eyes, with breeches of the same beneath. She hesitated only a moment before she saw Elof, standing stunned behind a great anvil, and advanced to meet him. Her body, slender and lissom, moved with a skipping grace that set her mane of long chestnut hair asway; that and the hair alone allowed Elof to recognise in her the little girl of eleven who had witnessed his downfall and disgrace. And now, of all things, she was holding her hand out to be kissed.

"I seek the mastersmith," she said in a soft voice, slightly tremulous, as, speechless with astonishment, he took it to his lips. "The crippled one, the ... Valant, the sorcerer ..."

Elof placed his hand at the open neck of his shirt, upon the small stamp that hung there. "I am the Mastersmith, my lady, Elof Valantor. You will find no sorcerers here." And he bowed as best he could on his crutches.

She made no reply at first, but stared at him wide-eyed, her feelings coursing undisguised across her face. There was fright at first, and surprise; she stepped back a little, and her hand flew to her throat. Then came awe, and sudden interest, and she looked him up and down with a heedless arrogance that made him acutely aware of his maimed legs. "But ... you are so much younger than I thought to find!" she said. Then her eyes grew apprehensive again. "Or ... is that only the way you choose to look?"

"I am as you see me, my lady," he answered, a little stiffly. She had looked on him last with the eyes of a child, eight years since, and though even now he was not yet in his middle years, she had evidently been expecting some snaggle-toothed spellmonger out of romances. Perhaps her brothers had been telling tales, and exaggerating the mysterious figure he cut.

"Of course!" she laughed, a little too blithely. "Why, you might almost be handsome, if you kept yourself cleaner. And if you could manage to smile now and again; or are you so set in grime and grimness that your cheeks would crack?"

"You come upon me in the practice of my craft and mystery, my lady. At the day's end you would find me scrubbed as clean as you could wish to look upon. And should I in my plight smile as lightly as any careless mayfly of your father's court? I saw you weep once at a certain sight."

She laughed again, and wrinkled her dainty nose. "Oh, I was only a child when last you saw me; father would not let me come here, in all these years."

"Then should you have come now, my lady? Will your father not be wroth with you? If you go swiftly he need never find out ..."

She arched her brows at him. "So eager to be rid of me? Do you have so many high-born ladies visit you that you must drive one forth ere the next arrive?"

Elof smiled wryly, and bowed again. "Doubtless they would all pale away before your fair presence, my lady Beathaill. I spoke only out of concern for your gracious self."

She laughed, and clapped her hands. "Ah, so you can smile when you wish, I see. And play the courtier, also. But my father is far off, deep in endless wrangles with the barbarians or some traitorous lord, I know not which, and besides he grows old. He will hardly care about such a petty thing, not now ..." She checked at a thought, and began to rummage in the long and heavy sleeves of her outer robe. "Not now my brothers have set foot here, I meant. But still, I have no time to waste, there is dancing tonight in the hall. I came not out of vulgar curiosity, I wish you to mend something for me ... a gaud, an ornament ... ah, here it is." And before Elof's appalled eyes she cast the two halves of the golden arm-ring chiming upon the anvil beside him. He stood staring at it, and felt the blood drain from his face.

"Is aught amiss?" he heard her ask, sudden concern in her tone; but her voice reached him as from some infinite distance. "Are you unwell? Or can it not be mended? Has it been re-soldered too often? Speak freely, you need not fear my displeasure; it is the least of my things, but I have had it since I was a child and am grown fond of it, only it is forever breaking and my ladies insist that I cannot wear a broken thing now I am no longer a child, and that I must give it up or have it made whole. Only," she added, a little wistfully, "there is no goldsmith in the city who has ever been able to heal it neatly or lastingly, not without melting it down altogether. And I fear they would spoil it, then!"

Elof drew breath, and recovered his calm. He guessed there was more, that word had indeed got round of the princes' exploit; probably Kenarech had been boasting of it – though hardly of his true reasons, save to a select few. Almost certainly she was not among those; but she had been delighted at having such an excuse for a slightly daring exploit of her own, of being able to boast that she too had bearded the mysterious sorcerer in his den – all the more because her father would not approve.

"It can be re-made well enough here," he told her, caressing the pieces with his fingertips, feeling the ridges of solder built up about the broken surfaces. He would gain little from lying about that; she would only take the pieces away to cherish. "And so it should be. But my lady, do you know what you have brought me?" He chose his words carefully. "This ... gaud was made by me, and taken from me against my will, and the loss of it all but broke my heart. It was the first gift from me to my wife, who is lost to me."

"Ohh," breathed the young woman, and laid a light finger on one of the serpentine pieces, so that it rocked back and forth. "How sad that she is lost, sorcerer! But my father would have found you another if you had asked him, a very fair one, even though you are not a whole man."

"I have never wished another," answered Elof as calmly as he could, still holding back from open appeal. Beathaill looked at him more closely, and her green cat-eyes grew softer.

"That is sweet; you must have loved her very much!

Make me the ring again, Valant, and maybe you will find another to love ..."

Elof grew desperate, and clenched his hand on the anvil's rim. "Princess, I ask it of you; I beg you, do not keep it from me! If I could, I would throw myself at your feet for it. Give it me, and I will shape you such jewels as never blazed about the body of any princess of this earth! I will draw down the light of moon and stars and girdle you with them, I will crown you with the rays of the sun! I will make you a vision among the Powers! But do not keep it from me!"

She was all astonished attention now, biting at her neat forefinger with unconscious childishness. "Could you do that, indeed?" she whispered. "How soon? Would it take long?"

"It could not be hurried, my lady!" admitted Elof. "A year, perhaps, if my labours are as light as now; a brief time, for such an end ... my lady, give it me!"

Sadly, regretfully she shook her head. "Alas!" she said softly, "it may not be. I would have you work your wonders, but soon ..." She checked herself once more. "But Valant, *I* did not take the ring from you, and it was given to me and I love it; I cannot let it go for a promise. You may keep it a few days, at least, to remake it. Do that, and make me these jewels you promise, and then, maybe, I will let you ask it of me again; and I shall take good care of it in the meantime, never fear."

"My lady!" cried Elof in anguish, "Do not sport with love, as you hope for love yourself ..."

Her neat mouth pursed, and she stamped hard on the earthen floor. "You presume upon my good heart, smith! What are you but a thrall, my father's broken bondsman, unfitted even to address me, let alone beg? All you have is mine by right, all the jewels you can make me mine if I but wish them! It is not for you to bandy bargains with a princess of the Lonuen! Five days from now my father is due back; I shall return on the third. If the ring is not made whole, then do you look to that wise head of yours! And seek not to gull me with substitutes; I have worn that ring these many years, and even re-made I shall know it! Meanwhile you may reflect on what respect is due a princess!" She spun on her heel, waving her women away before her; the wide skirts of her gown flared about her, her riding boots clattered on the threshold, and the door slammed. Elof bowed his head down over the anvil till his forehead almost touched the cold iron, and his fingers gripped the rim of it as if to dig deep into the metal.

"Whew!" Roc breathed eventually, breaking the tense silence. "Old Nithaid's losing his grip for sure, if even that chit and child rushes to defy him!"

"No, Roc!" said Elof; his voice was stern, though the grime on his face was streaked and moist. "There is more to it than that, I am sure now! She also was strangely in haste; and twice she all but let slip that time, my time, grows somehow short ... That *is* why her dear brothers were in such haste, then! And it all has some connection with Nithaid's return ..." He hobbled laboriously to the window, and watched the little boat pulling away from shore, the sail hoisting and swelling, shining suddenly scarlet as if the rays of sunset filled it. He could not see whether she was looking back at him. "It grows shorter than you dream of, lady, that time ..."

"But can you?" demanded Roc. "In five days, if it's true what you fear ... Can we finish our work in that time?"

"We must — must we not? And one thing more, even. For this, *this* —" He caught up the halves of the ring, clutched them to him, held them to his lips, his eyes, his breast. "Whatever may befall, this shall be made anew!"

What means Elof used are not recorded. Most probably he encased the two pieces together in the finest clay or sand, as the ring was first moulded, and fired it with long and delicate care as it first was, in the upsurge of earthfires. He would have sung the same soft songs over that chrysalis within which the sundered gold sweated, shivered and at last grew liquid, as it seethed and flowed in currents of convected heat, pent within the shell of its own shape. But within that shell there would be nowhere it might flow, save into itself, uniting, mingling. Within that shell the process of change was brought to its absolute, only to be turned back upon itself; a dissolution so total it restored form, a turmoil so fierce it imposed unity, a storm that served only to create a greater calm.

However this may be, there is no doubt that Elof succeeded; for as he gazed upon the ring re-made, it is set down that he wished aloud he could do as much for himself. "Melt myself down in my own furnace, mold myself anew, mended and whole! And in doing it I might even skim away the clinging dross of all my past, all my follies and my cruelties; all the wrongs I have done, all the wrongs done to me, I might forget them all together! I could just escape then, and have done with it, this damnable hunger for revenge! I grow to hate it, Roc; hate what I must do to glut it. It is a master almost crueller than Nithaid! I hate to deal in this way, even with such as they!"

"What's this, then, from you of all folk? Mercy? Compassion?" Roc looked around from the bag he was packing, and his voice grew edged and bitter. "It's never yet held you back from what you thought needed doing. Didn't stay you with poor old Ingar, did it? Or Korentyn. Or Kara. Why then now, with these creatures that are a hundred times the worse?" Elof writhed beneath the sting of the words, but he made neither protest nor denial; for they both knew too well there was none. "You've never scrupled to mess with your friends; why baulk at your foes? Regret's cheap when it comes too late, my lad. What you've planned now, you must do, or all's to wrack and ruin ... more, maybe, than you know. You'll not make yourself a better man by turning stupid!"

"No!" muttered Elof, still burnishing at the gold, though it shone bright as it ever had in the midday sunlight. "But I may yet make myself worse. Enough! High time you were on your way; the guard-boat is waiting! And take care!"

Roc nodded curtly, and turned to the door. "I'll do my part, never fear. Only do you yours!"

The door closed behind him. Regretfully Elof wrapped the bright fair thing in a square of dark velvet and laid it aside on one of the benches beneath the window. He leaned there for a moment, resting his weary shoulders, and watched the guard-boat with Roc on board pull away across the great smooth flood of the sunlit Yskianas. It was the last piece he could move, in a play that stood either to lure his foes into the check he had laid with such care, or to rebound upon him so utterly as to sweep him from the board. And Roc with him, perhaps, and many more. Had he been over bold? Too late if he had; he should be thinking of his work. They had loaded the furnace earlier; high time he shut it down.

He limped over to it and began to spin the wheel back. Beneath him he felt the door grind across, though it seemed to be growing harder than usual to move; when it was three-quarters closed, it began to stick. He cursed, tugged at the wheel, wound it back and then sharp forward; it turned a little further, then stuck. Alarmed, he had to jerk it again and again, throwing all his weight upon the wheel till it seemed to clear the obstruction. At last it slid a little way smoothly, then a sharp clang told him the door was shut. He cranked the air-vents open wider, knocked free the bolts on the outer door and heaved it up, ducking back to let the gush of searing air disperse. Then it was only a matter of more waiting, until the stalks had spread their leaves wide enough to show him it was safe to enter. Waiting; and he could not even pace up and down. With rags wrapped around hands and feet he swung himself down onto the stairs and shone his lamp into the mephitic gloom, coughing as the fumes caught his throat. The floor seemed different somehow, its slope changed and less regular; he limped down the steps, though the rags were charring, and saw that at the rear by the door's foot the floor was no longer a smooth incline, but had across its centre an irregular tongue of smoking slag. Small wonder he had had to fight that door shut! Whatever the reason, the earthfires were certainly growing fiercer; now, from out of whatever vein lay open behind that door, they had come boiling up into the furnace itself.

The sight filled him with horror. His labour, his creation, his last gate to freedom all depended on the furnace, his very life even if his play went as he planned. And it was no longer safe to use; yet, safe or not, he must open it again – if he still could – and risk unleashing what dire consequences he might. Suddenly he became aware of the smoke arising round him; his rags were smouldering, and one trailing strip burst into a little yellow flame, easily stamped out. Only he couldn't! He cursed and swung himself up the stairs; but that took time, and the rags were well alight as he emerged. He had the sense to smother them in sand first rather than pour water over them, which would have carried the heat through too swiftly. Angrily he peeled off the scorched cloths and slumped down with his back to an open window; he must think, and fast.

On reflection, he decided, it could have been worse. It must have taken time to rise, that flood. It could only have happened moments before he shut the door. So it would again, most probably; he should be able to work in short bursts, ever watchful for what might be rising beneath. It would slow him, perhaps too much; yet there was no help for that. He would have to work all the faster now. Thoughts of what that would mean, problems present and foreseen, whirled and tangled in his mind; and though the forge and its engines stood quiet now, the creak and tick of contracting metal, the wind in the air-vents and the flow of water in the troughs were so loud that he did not hear the hull that ground onto the beach, the footsteps on the grassy slope, till they touched the very sill of the open door. He sat up in sharp surprise.

Upon his threshold stood Beathaill, alone. She was clad now in a light silken gown of a leafy pattern, girdled with silver; the low sun behind it made a willowy silhouette of her body. She seemed tentative, almost shy in her manner, but she stiffened as she saw him. He bowed to her from where he sat. "Good even to you, lady. I expected you tomorrow; you return earlier than you said."

A haughty smile quirked her lips. "Why should I

not? It is up to me. You have had ample time, in any case. Well? Is it done?" Elof bent to gather up his crutches, and did not reply. "Well?" she shrilled, and stamped her foot. "Have you mended it as I bade ..." Then the arm-ring caught her eye, gleaming on the velvet like the sun over stormcloud. "Oh," she said flatly. "You have ..." She sniffed contemptuously. "I see you know how to obey your betters after all, like a good thrall." To Elof's acute ear the tinge in her voice was almost clear enough to be called disappointment. She stalked over to the ring, and was about to take it when Elof's hard hand closed over the shining gold.

"Lady," he said quietly. "I have made that fair thing whole again; but I never said it was for you."

"How *dare* you!" she squealed, and stamped again.

"Lady, that arm-ring is not for you. There is a potency in it, a strong one, its virtue a binding bond. It cannot create one where none exists; but where one is, it may act upon it, lend it strength, in what ways who can tell?" She snatched at the gold unheeding, but he did not release his grip. "Lady, I warn you only for your own sake!"

"Give it me!" she said, her front teeth white against her carmined lips. "And have done with your conjurer's cant; have I not worn that ring all these years? Do you think I am still a child, to be frightened with tricks and shadows?"

She shook the ring in Elof's grasp; and though she had none of Kara's strength, the memory defeated him, and he let it slip through his fingers. He caught earnestly at her arm, preventing her donning it. "Lady, upon your head be what follows if you take that ring to yourself ..."

"Get away from me!" she cried, springing free and forcing the ring onto her arm. "Thralls have died in torture for less gross offences! Ach, you soil me, you stink of sweat and soot —"

Elof sighed; he would achieve little by offending her, in her nostrils least of all. "Lady, I apologise. I was about to wash when you arrived." Doffing his sweat-stained tunic, he turned to the trough that flowed through the forge, reached for the bag of fatted lye hung beside it, and quickly splashed the cold spring waters about himself. He was half afraid she would simply march out on him, but knew she was still standing there; he could almost sense the intentness of her. Upon the ring? Then he heard her say sardonically "That is a fine crop of scars you bear, thrall. One might almost take you for a warrior or an adventurer, rather than a sorcerer and an artisan."

He laughed, and tasted the bitterness on his lips. "I have been both, at need," he said, without turning. "Once. I have crossed a whole wide land, and sought out the duergar in their mountain fastnesses, and lived with them two long years; I have lived with the *alvar* of the forests, Tapiau's Children, and escaped the forest's power. I have sailed the Seas of the Sunrise, I have fought beside an exiled lord against the Ekwesh by land and sea, and when he won himself his kingdom. I have battled a dragon beneath the earth, and the Icewitch herself on a palace stair – aye, and bested her! And yet I would far sooner be a man whole and at peace, in the land I made my own, with my true love by my side."

He heard her laugh. "A braggart, as well as a boor!"

Elof turned about in annoyance and heard her gasp. She reached out suddenly, and he felt her soft fingertip trace out the faint mark on his breast. "That is a scar also! That is ... the same scar! As at the back ..."

"Your father remarked on that wound once; shortly before he had me crippled! Before he made me a pinioned swan, a tethered hawk! Less than a man!" He turned away impatiently, and again she caught her breath.

"I see another pair, even more faint! But ... one such wound should have been mortal! How did you come by them? And how survive them?"

"Ask rather why!" he said, and went on washing.

Behind him there was silence; until a small voice said "Would you tell me some of your adventures?"

Slowly he rose, and turned, reaching for a cloth to dry himself. "To a wellwisher or a friend, I might. But what joy or profit can there be for a listener who does not care?"

To his astonishment a hand was laid lightly on his arm. "Did I say I do not wish you well? I will listen gladly – if it please you?" He looked down at her, and suddenly her hand seemed to sear him worse than the forgeflame. It was long, long since a woman had touched him. His breath faltered and grew fast, and forgetting all he hoped to gain by patience he crushed her hand beneath his own, hard against him. She stiffened, but made no attempt to pull away. He swallowed, and heard his breath whistle through flaring nostrils. Hesitantly she lifted her free hand, and laid it upon his breast.

"Your heart pounds like your hammer!" she said, and giggled softly, her eyes lowered.

He felt a taut smile settle on his lips. "Does yours?" Her grip tightened on his arm, and slowly tentatively, she bore it to her side. Equally slowly, with deliberate malice, he stroked his fingers down her ribs to her waist, and then up again, to slide one by one across the curve of her breast, gently passing over the peak taut beneath the gown's silken lightness. He bent to whisper in her ear "It does …", and stayed to kiss the lobe of it, the neck beneath, the satin cheek and so, at last, her parted lips.

She met the kiss fervently at first, a little clumsily; then suddenly she squirmed, wrenched free, gasping. "How dare you?" she squealed. "What are you – what have you done? What have you done to me? What spell have you …"

Elof shook his head. "I have cast no spell upon you, my lady. But you took one upon yourself. Will you be able to shed it so easily? It has power. Yet remember, there is none in it to create what is not already there …"

"*No!*" she shrieked, and plucked the ring violently from her arm. It tangled in her gown a moment, fell and rolled against some sacking. But then she let out a despairing wail, hugged herself tight and burst into hysterical sobbing.

Elof reached out to her, cupped her face in his strong hands, and she did not resist. His thumbs wiped the tears from her cheeks and tilted her head back to meet his gaze. Her eyes looked into his, and now his hands ploughed among her crisp hair, stroking her neck from behind her ears to the neck of her gown, tracing its edge around to the front. Her eyelids fluttered and her head relaxed, lolled back, as the topmost fastening parted under his deft fingers and they met and caressed in the hollow of her throat. She clutched at his shoulder to steady herself as they swept back, parting another fastening, and so on down till they curved around her neat small breasts and laid them bare. He clutched her close then and kissed her breast to breast, and she did not pull away, but drank at him as if he were a spring.

He felt her heart flutter, and a flutter of a different pace below her ribs, down the whole front of her body, as though it were a bird imprisoned behind those bars and beating to be free. Slowly, carefully, as her gown fell open and apart, his fingers tracked it about her and down to its source, tracing it tangled amid damp curls. Gown and girdle slid unheeded to the silver sand. Her forehead lay on his shoulder, her shifting thighs imprisoned his fingers as they explored, and she clutched at him in her turn, tugging at his belt, pulling at his breeches. A wave of hesitancy welled up in him suddenly; all these long years he had half believed himself become less than a man, maimed in more than limb, and he feared to find it true. But as her long fingers discovered him, probed and plucked at him, spiderlight, his fears were fiercely overborne. He managed to croak a word in her ear, and together they swayed and stumbled towards his bed, her fingers playing about him still, her lips smearing his chest with their colour like so many fresh wounds. He flung aside his crutches, and they toppled together among the coarse blankets. She raised her head to kiss his lips, his throat, his shoulders and armpits where the crutches galled them; he lifted himself on his arms, his lips touched her breasts and lingered, then swept down, drinking her in, a feaster after famine, till her back arched like a bow and her fingers wrung in his thick hair. Then, with a single shuddering gasp that two throats shared, they writhed together like serpents and joined.

There was no love in that unity save its very intensity, only a community of need drinking from a common source, clambering, one upon the other, to reach a common peak. So savage was that need that it knew no barrier, no obstacle; even braced, Elof's legs were almost useless, but by strength of arm alone he bore up the girl like a leaf in a whirlwind. The single fire that burned between their thighs breathed and quickened in that wind, grew hotter, brighter, and at last swelled out in a searing globe to envelop them, the room, the world in a scalding burst of light, in which nothing existed save their shared flesh. Timeless, rigid they hung there; and then it passed, and the world rushed in on them again. They fell sweating among the blankets, their thighs still thrusting convulsively one against another, the spasms of fighters dying upon each other's blades. They gasped for breath, through lips that trembled and would not form words.

But as the fires in Elof's heart were slaked, so it fell to embers and ash. A black mood settled upon him, in which all that had passed seemed to him little better than rape, and an ugly parody of what he had felt with Kara; missing her was an acute ache in his heart. Beathaill sensed something amiss, and sought to distract him with mumbled endearments and caresses. She was inexperienced but not unknowing, and gradually, despite himself, the brush of her breasts against him, the play of her lips, brought a reviving warmth. He stifled his sense of loss beneath cold cynicism, telling himself it scarcely mattered and he should enjoy himself while he had the chance; he had held back long enough. She giggled again as he caressed her and she felt him revive, and with a mischievous flicker in her eye she laid her head in his lap, tongue darting; he gasped, laughed, rolled his head ...

And saw the long shadow that stretched out across the forge, seething, shapeless, demonic. Saw beyond the open door the slender woman's shape that cast it, the cloak that billowed from her arms, the short mailshirt that was her only garb, the helm above like the head of some great bird of prey. Beneath its eyeslots, slanting, narrowed, bitter rage burned in the dark gleam of her gaze, a rage he saw echoed in the very stance of her, tensed as against a high wind, spear outstretched. Then Beathaill saw her too, screamed and sprang back among the blankets; but Elof had all but forgotten her, save as a fragment of his shame. He sprang up, forgetful still, in hope of running to the door, but only managed to sprawl headlong upon the sanded floor. Half stumbling, half crawling towards the light, he reached out an arm to her; but it seemed to him he read words in those wide dark eyes, heard her voice clear in his mind.

Now you have lost me! Lost me forever!

His arm fell; he could not face her, and bowed his head. The long shadow changed, as if the cloak swirled now from arms upraised, and suddenly a great wind scoured through the forge, lashing his face with blown sand; the light pulsed, then was clear, empty. Elof turned away, blinking gritty eyes, and sank down by the bedside.

Beathaill sprang up from the bedclothes and clutched his arm. "Sweetheart, who was that? Will she tell ..."

In a fury of loathing Elof rounded on her, swinging his arm to lash out viciously. "Away, you riggish little viper! Get out, out and leave me be! Get you to Hella, you empty she-whelp! And beg a heart of her, that some better soul has lost!" She shrank back with a squeal and began to wail, open-mouthed like an infant. Elof sank his head in his hands. "No! No. I am sorry; the fault is mine alone." He looked at her. "Mine alone. Only the folly is yours. You came here for no good purpose, came to taunt and tease the tethered bear —"

"*I came because ... I was sorry for you!*"

Elof shook his head sadly. "No, princess! Not so, whatever you told yourself. True, you pitied this man you thought fair, for being alone and womanless. And since you do not understand love, you thought to dangle your charms like a toy before him. Why not? It would be an extraordinary condescension from one of your rank;

he should feel honoured. You came alone, and when you had made sure he was alone; you thought to sport with him a little, assuage your own feelings but escape unscathed, unstained and laugh at his frustration. But such feelings are dangerous to play with, my lady, most of all one's own; you were tethered by them in your turn, they were the chains. Well, do I speak false?"

She had stopped crying almost at once; a look of blazing outrage crossed her face, but Elof held up his hand. "Shall I tell you why I am so sure? Because if you had been truly sorry for me you would not have sought to deceive me. You would not have kept from me what your father plans for me as soon as he returns. What it is that made me one of the few men you could safely indulge yourself with – because you thought that soon my mouth would be far away, or stopped forever. But of course, you had to have me repair your precious arm-ring first!"

Her mouth opened in a shriek of anger, the tantrum of a child humiliated; but then she saw his bleak eyes, and slowly she subsided, cowering among the bedclothes. "Do not look at me so!" she whimpered. "Do not hurt me!"

Elof gazed down at her, unrelenting. "What does Nithaid intend?"

"He means ... the Icewitch, she offered him peace, complete peace! On one condition only ..."

"*That he hand me over to her?*"

She nodded frantically, clutching the blankets to her bare body. "He ... he didn't agree at first; he's been haggling ... Now they say she has offered the Gate back, and all the Wild Lands, to leave Kerys be and take her savages to another land ... They say he is coming back to announce his decision ..."

"Aye, before I get to hear of it!"

"Yes!" she breathed. "So ... so ..." She began to weep again, slowly, looking up at him in terror. He sighed deeply, and when he reached out a hand she cowered; but it was only to stroke her shivering shoulder.

"I spoke too harshly," he said. "There was some

pity in you, though much else. I alone am to blame. I wish you no ill, Beathaill, and none shall hear of this from me. Get you dressed and go. Leave me here with my own company; I deserve no other."

So afraid was she that she sprang up and ran to the door, almost forgetting to gather up her gown as she passed. Once she looked back, at Elof, still sitting by the bed, and at the arm-ring, gleaming against the dusty sacking; but she made no move to take it. For a moment it was her shadow that filled the doorway, then, still naked, she ducked out into the light and was gone.

Early next morning Roc returned, staggering up the hill apparently much the worse for a night's wine. But once within the door, beyond sight of the departing guard-boat, he became alert, even elated, and thumped his fists exultantly on the great table. "That's it! All your errands discharged, every message delivered; say, have I not done you proud ..." He stopped then, and peered at Elof, saw him seated at the other end of the table, toying absently with the ring. "What's the matter, then? Not want to hear? What've you been up to, then?" He circled the forge, peered into the furnace and turned on Elof savagely. "Not your bloody labours, that's for sure! You've not done half of what was left you! And when every flaming *minute* counts ... Man, what's amiss in your head? A fine damned trial you can be to a patient man, and at what a time! Want to toss away your own life and mine too? All because you've suddenly sprouted a tender shoot of conscience – and for a crew of bastards and betrayers who merit it less than most I can set mind to! You and your bloody maunderings! Stop mucking with that thing, pay some heed –" And in his anger he might have sought to strike the ring out of Elof's hand, save that his wrist was seized in a grip that, for all his own solid strength, held him clamped like his best vise.

Elof glanced up, and he sounded as grim as he looked. "You mistake me, my friend!" He released his grip. 'It is not that which concerns me; I have managed some work, and I had a new task to complete. What remains we can finish in time – just. Beathaill was here ..."

Roc looked at him sharply, and at the arm-ring, then his eyes widened as they took in the blankets rumpled and stained upon a bed that had manifestly not been slept in. "Oho, was she now?" he breathed.

"And so was Kara ..." He held up a hand to cut off Roc's exclamations. "Wait! I know now what Nithaid plans; and it is ugly. Whatever else befell, it was a mercy Beathaill came when she did. Roc, there is no time left you, none at all; you are sure all is done?"

"So you do want to hear, then? So be it!" It had seemed simply one of his usual errands that took Roc ashore, this time to the palace; he had delivered a minor order for necessaries, and contrived in doing so to exchange words elsewhere. It was with a full purse, and little extra effort, that he had managed to entice his guards to come in search of some old friends to drink with, around the harbour quarter. So, all was indeed done, and the hook swallowed. "Just as you said. A summons to come to you, alone and utterly in secret, all conditions as you laid them down and at the hours you said, tonight. It wasn't too well received, that – not with the name this place has got for itself! But then I gave the rest of the message. *Then I will show you a secret that shall give you mastery over your brother at a single stroke* – your very words. And didn't that summon up a grin!"

He was grinning himself as he described it, but Elof seemed grim and preoccupied, and drew little cheer from the tidings. He nodded wearily, and with an awful tenderness he wrapped up the arm-ring and put it gently aside. "Thank you; you've done well, Roc, as always. Would there were no more, that I could know you at least were safe! But as you say, we must work, and not forget to make ready to receive our visitors as befits them. And you must hear of the new cloud that hangs over us; for you are proven right. Louhi has guessed where I am; and if Kara has not told her already, I fear she may now ..."

That day's labour was the worst they had endured, all the worse for the sense of apprehension that swelled in them both. Like the heavy air before a storm it hung about them, setting their nerves on edge, distracting their thoughts; a hundred times that day they might have exploded into foolish quarrels, save that they could not waste the time. They would look up to dash sweat from weary eyes or free a cramping muscle, and their gaze would meet in a sudden mutual awareness of dread. Only once did Elof break off for what seemed to Roc no good reason, and that was to search out two wide silver cups, plain things he had made long since as trial pieces for a gift Nithaid wished to bestow. Only at the day's end, though, did Roc find time to ask about them. Elof turned over the wide cups in his hand. "They are not important in themselves; scant art and no virtue. Just a little of Nithaid's silver. I mean to show him one small mercy, Roc."

Roc stared. "Even after what the girl ..."

"All the more so – though little he may appreciate it! As I said, I'll not betray those treacherous limbs of his to him. Let him go on thinking them loyal."

Roc shrugged. "Why bother yourself? He's no fool; he's bound to guess the truth, when he starts to think about it."

"Yes. Unless he cannot; unless the shock to him is too great ... So, I must see that it is ..." His voice faded. Roc waited, but when he spoke again his words were brisk and lively. "What's the hour?"

"The last before the middle hour," Roc answered calmly. "And there's a small boat tacking in towards the west beach. They gather, Elof; do you cool your head, and your heart'll harden once more!"

Two weeks had passed since the coming of the princes to Elan Ghorenhyon, and for Elof they had been two weeks of remorseless labour, both arduous and minute, work that might have killed a common thrall outright. To that he had been hardened since his youth; he made no complaint. But he was heart-weary, and that which he strove to make was not finished. Yet he must now lay all aside; for this was the night he had laid down in Roc's message, the beginning of the hour.

"It's Kenarech right enough!" hissed Roc. "A showy sailor he is, but skilled to my eyes. And he's taking care to hide the boat, as you asked. Aye, here he comes now!"

It was not long before the younger prince stood on the threshold, his face so reddened by excitement and the climb that in the forgelight he seemed to glow. A dark mantle covered his rich garments, and Elof was sure he detected the line of a mail shirt underneath them. He bowed. "Enter, my lord! Surely you do not fear to come to Sorcerers' Isle, when you have met the sorcerer?"

Kenarech scowled. "I do not *fear* any man. But this place was so called, and bore a bad name, long before my father set you here; why think you it was kept for exiles?" Roc and Elof exchanged swift, significant glances, but Kenarech did not seem to notice. Nettled by any suggestion of fear, he stepped briskly into the forge and glanced about. "Well, Master Valant? What's this secret you have for me?"

Elof bowed again, and pushed back the hood from his face. "It has been long and hard in the preparation, my lord; it wants only a short time more."

"Oh?" Kenarech scowled around the forge. A wheel was turning slowly, silently, and the forgefire was glowing; but there was little else intelligible for him to see. "How long?"

"Before the middle hour, my lord, it should take shape."

The prince's face cleared. "Oh well, *that's* well enough. D'you have any wine?"

The wine was the best Nithaid had sent them, and though he made Elof taste it first, it mellowed Kenarech's mood even further. He seemed content to wander round the forge and cluck with admiration at the bits and pieces of work lying around, not least many crystals set in webs of gilded wire. He remarked how weary Elof looked, and hoped the effort would be worthwhile. At last, very close to the middle hour, Roc, whom he had disregarded completely, appeared from the shadows and bowed. "It nears completion, my lord."

"Then bring it to us!" said Elof quietly. "My lord, we will need darkness –"

"As you will!" said the prince uneasily. Elof saw his hand settle near his sword, and smiled.

"Take whatever precautions you will, prince. But I shall keep my word." Kenarech nodded curtly, striving to appear unafraid. Elof lifted a long left sleeve, and darkness seemed to fall in upon the forge like a net. He heard Kenarech's sharp breath in the darkness. "Silence, my lord, only for a minute longer! Have patience! *It is here –*"

The door creaked back, a faint outline of silver in the darkness; a shadow filled it, and a heavy tread rang upon the floor. Elof drew a deep breath and let his sleeve fall back; upon his arm was the gauntlet, his fist clenched tight upon the crystal at its heart, that only a short time since had drunk the blinding glare of a rare metal in flame. He heard Roc slam the door shut once more, and his hand flew open; the forge blazed into sight, stark and demonaic in its glare, impossibly sharp and shadowless. And in that terrible clarity stood revealed, frozen and grey as a mantled statue, the shape of Geraidh the prince. For Elof's message had been delivered to them both, differing only in the time of their coming, and the place where they must land; and in that fearful light he had revealed them each to the other, beyond the reach of bluff or hypocrisy, in the very moment of their treason.

"So then!" he cried, as the glare died, and the lights of the forge burgeoned once again. "So you would think to enlist me in your treacheries, and betray me in my turn? But do you bear witness that I have kept my word! For each of you has only to draw and strike down his brother before him, and mastery shall be his indeed!"

They stood there, those baffled princes, for longer than Elof would have thought possible, blinded both in body and mind by the bright light of their exposure. He could measure that time by his own heartbeats, that roared so loud in his ears it seemed the walls must be shaken. Then, with perhaps a greater unison than ever in their lives before, they turned their bloodless faces upon him; and their gaze was fell.

They snatched their swords from their scabbards,

though Elof stood unarmed. Kenarech, who was nearest, advanced on him, breathing heavily, with the menacing pad of a cat to its kill. Elof made no move, but held him with his eyes. Geraidh circled the benches to get to him, but slowly, content, it seemed, to let his brother strike the first. Closer came Kenarech, till Elof could see the quiver of his lower lip and the tears of rage hot in his eyes. Then he swung up his sword and brought it down upon Elof's unguarded head.

Like a snake striking, the gauntlet sprang into the way; the blade passed between fingers and thumb and struck the pale jewel in the palm. And there it lodged without even a sound as the fingers clamped tight, for the jewel had drunk the force of the blow. Elof clutched the blade, twisting it, pressing it back with a strength so great that his left arm prevailed over both of Kenarech's. The prince saw what promised, his mouth fell open to shriek; but then Elof unclamped his grip. The blow had not been so hard, for though both princes were polished swordsmen they had seldom if ever had to fight in earnest, but it would have served to split a skull. Now, though, the blade was turned back against its wielder while it was still in his hand, and its force unleashed. Straight through Kenarech's throat it struck, and in a great spray of blood his head flew from his shoulders and went bouncing away across a bench. His body dropped convulsing to the sanded floor.

Geraidh sprang back, remembering all too late that he had to deal not with a helpless cripple but a sorcerer of craft and might. He sought to break for the door, but found himself facing Roc, grim-faced, his heavy longbow drawn to shoulder. He wailed like a beast and raised his sword as if to throw it, then whirled about and hurled himself with desperate frenzy on Elof. Elof seized his sword wrist as he struck, but the impact knocked him off his precarious balance, back against the great anvil. Kenarech's dark-smeared sword lay almost at his feet but as he sought to stoop for it Geraidh's other hand clamped tight on his. Fighting to stay on his feet, Elof could not bring his greater strength to bear, and so they swayed there, locked together for what seemed an eternity, though Roc had barely time to down his bow and seize a forgespike. Geraidh was screaming like a lunatic into Elof's face, spraying him with foam and spittle, snapping at his throat like a wolf, while Elof's back creaked agonizingly under both their weights against the sharp edge of the anvil. It might have gone hard with Elof, unable to use his legs; but Geraidh, desperate to escape, suddenly let go Elof's wrist and twisted to snatch a poniard from his belt. Even that slight relaxation was enough. As he raised the dagger Elof's powerful fingers clenched in the gaudy slashes of his jerkin and thrust him back, staggering; then they jerked him forward and to one side. The anvil's edge caught the taller man in the midriff and he folded over it with an impact that drove the wind from his lungs. Elof stooped with an equally painful gasp, and even as Geraidh rolled over, wheezing, to bring his blade across in a slashing cut, Kenarech's sword glittered high against the shadowy roof.

So near came Geraidh's sword that it slashed Elof's robe across and left a deep scratch over his ribs. Kenarech's smashed down upon the anvil with a dreadful clang. It was not a blade of Elof's making; it shivered like glass into flying fragments against the time-tempered iron. But it had done its work. Geraidh's blade clattered to the ground; slowly, leaving a great smear of blood like the trail of some unclean creature; his body slid down off the anvil, nerveless fingers scrabbling weakly at the iron. Roc exclaimed in disgust at the head that rolled past his feet.

But Elof paid him no heed. The bare hilt dropped from his hand, he tore off the ruined robe and cast it across the severed heads as they lay. With a strength that appalled Roc he seized a limp arm and began to drag the corpses to the back of the forge. Roc bent to help, but Elof waved him away. "This is for me to endure! Do you keep your hands clean of it!" Roc shuddered as he heard the furnace door creak back on its hinges, and sounds first of one heavy fall, then another, and at last the deep dull clang of the closing door, final and dreadful as a passing bell. A wheel spun; chains clanked and rattled, the floor trembled, and the leaves of silver writhed and curled like their live selves caught in an autumn fire. Then, letting fall his props, Elof half sat, half fell upon the seat of bricks at the hearth. For long minutes he huddled there, head bowed, the back of his hand to his lips, as if listening to that devouring roar beneath.

"Well?" demanded Roc. "Not having second thoughts, are you?"

Elof shook his head. "No!" he said, and his voice was steady though very bleak. "All other gates are closed to us now. Some blood splashed upon my lips, that is all; and it has a bitter tang."

Roc nodded. "They say it does," he said, "I'd better look to my packing now."

It did not take him long. When his pack was full he gathered up his steel-shod bow from the floor, unstrung it and brushed it clean, and slung it carefully on its quiver at his back. Only then did he turn back to Elof, and found he also had been busy. Of the robe there was no sign; but by Elof's side was a good-sized casket of plain wood, with a richly worked clasp. Roc hefted the pack. "Time I was away ..."

"Aye," said Elof quietly. "High time!" He lifted the box. "You know what you must do with this?"

Roc took it gingerly, made as if to open the catch. Elof's hand restrained him. Roc tapped his foot a moment, considering. "I'll take Kenarech's little boat, it looks the handier for a no-sailor like me; Geraidh's I'll leave for you, just in case –"

"No. Do you scuttle it or set it adrift in the channel. I am weary, Roc, bitterly weary. Of suffering, and of making others suffer ..." From the breast of his tunic Elof took the feather Kara had let fall, and beside it another almost as black, but with a faint sheen of gold. "If I succeed, well and good. If I fail – I fail."

"But our warning –"

"That burden falls on you then. Steer as truly westward as you can; err to the North, if anything. At worst, follow the margins of the Ice ..."

"If we make it in time!" said Roc quietly. "All right.

West and north – I'll try."

Elof heaved himself up suddenly and caught the shorter man by his broad shoulders. "Roc, fare you well! Truly well! A hundred times you've been my good fortune; the Powers know, you've earned some of your own!"

Roc cocked his head to one side, and grinned. "It's not every forgehand gets to serve such a master, that they know also! Whatever else, it's never been dull!" He clapped Elof on the arm with his own heavy hand, and turned away. At the door he paused, then flung it wide and filled his lungs with the clean night air. "Aah! I'd all but forgotten how fresh a tang it has, freedom! Fare you well also – Mastersmith!"

He closed the door softly behind him, and left Elof alone among the muted thunder of the forge.

Elof sat awhile, feeling more profoundly alone than ever in his life before, and then wearily he rose and began to sweep the bloody muck from the floor; in its place he sprinkled clean silver sand. The hardened earth beneath had drunk its fill, and the stains did not reappear.

That luxury he allowed himself, meaningless though it was; then he threw himself into his labours once more. He had lingered long ere he opened the furnace, almost too long. He felt the earthtides fight him at the door, and when at last he went down the steps he heard their grinding thunders behind it; but they hardly stirred the pile of cooling slag at its foot. All through the night he laboured, pausing only to gulp down a cup of wine, a morsel of meat, whenever the work allowed him. The work grew in his mind, under his hands, till it seemed to fill the whole universe; he almost forgot there was anywhere beyond the stifling forge, any future beyond its completion. He hummed at first as he laboured, and soon he was singing, singing with little heed of the smoky airs that arose from the furnace to claw his throat and burn in his breast. Into that song he poured his heart, a lilting ecstatic music of joy that knew nothing of treasons and bloodshed, that soared high above that sombre vault of fire and the toil that

scorched his flesh and drew blood even from his hardened fingers.

I am a leaf, a leaf on the stormwind
Sailing, sailing
I am a flame, a flame on a feather,
On the wide air
Dancing, dancing
I am a cloud, a cloud on an eastwind
Bearing me homeward,
Singing, singing . . .

And into the work that song was woven.

Yet for all his absorbtion, in some remote corner of
his thoughts he could not help imagining the train of
events he had set in motion, so minutely that he seemed
actually to be seeing them all, building up like strange
simultaneous layers of motion. He saw Roc's little boat
glide across the dark Yskianas to shore, beaching clumsily, no doubt, but safe; Roc leaving that casket with
some of the gate guards he knew, repeating the instruc-
tions on its lid that it was for Nithaid's eyes alone, and
then melting away into the end of the dark. Taking to
the boat again, though not for long; Roc would sooner
make his way ashore. Roc on his way, the casket borne
by mounted courier through the sleeping streets of that
immense city to the walls of the Strength of Kerys, and
within, to await the coming of the king. He saw the sun
arise over the Horns of the Bull more clearly than
through his own shutters, his own eyes blind to all
except the piecing together of things delicate into a
binding whole. But then it grew less certain; Nithaid
might return by water, sailing leisurely up the channels,
or by land, to ride in triumph through the streets and
enjoy the acclamation of his people. That was more
likely, now that he brought peace to offer them, and the
appearance, at least, of victory. He would come by the
westward gates, then, and reach the palace sooner;
about midday, perhaps. He would find troubled faces
awaiting him; the princes would have been missed by
then. Perhaps Beathaill would tell then, something at

least. They would bring Nithaid the casket ...

Elof swallowed, and bent himself to his labours; that scene he had no wish to see. Ironic, that mercy should be cloaked thus in the appearance of fiendish cruelty; or was it mercy? A strange kind, if so, twisted and deformed; but so Nithaid had made him, and must take his mercy as it came. He could not banish it from his mind; Nithaid, grim-faced, being handed the box, the courtiers who gave it melting away into the crowd, beyond the reach of his wrath. Nithaid, pale and apprehensive, balancing the box on his knees against his bloated belly, hesitating, then angrily snapping back the catch and swinging up the lid ...

Elof started, and almost burned himself on the furnace's outer door. There, in the two wide cups, with clasps of gems and gold to weight down their eyes, to uphold the sagging jaws, the severed heads of his two beloved sons ... Even in memory that vision almost unmanned Elof; yet without it the King must begin to wonder how Elof had enticed his sons – and inevitably somebody would talk. Now, though, there would be room only for horror and grief, agonies of grief; and then wrath such as even Nithaid had rarely displayed, wrath against Valant the dark sorcerer, Valant the murderer. He would draw the black blade, and then ... soon? How soon? Elof threw back the shutters, and was appalled; the sun was already past its zenith. Little time remained. Hastily he flung back the furnace door, and smelt the hair scorching on his hands in the air that blasted by; the inner door must be scarcely closed. Most of the delicate work was finished, woven already into the web of the whole; what remained was chiefly smith's work, making joint and frame strong and true against the forces they must endure. But that he must manage soon, soon ... He glanced at the stalks, at the leaves that clung curled, and bit his lip; he could not wait for it to cool. He gathered up his tool-pack; the arm-ring, after a slight hesitation, he looped around the chain at his neck, for it was too small for either arm. He had not expected to feel anything; yet he was aware of a sudden strengthening, a reinforcement of his will, as if the power he had poured into that gold long ago had returned to him now. Over his left hand he drew the gauntlet, and slowly, carefully, he heaved himself over the hot metal rim and down into the depths of the forge.

The walls were shaking around him now with the thunder of the earthfires, but he set his hammers as counterpoint against them. After a while, though, it came to him that the little chamber was growing hotter, not cooler. He paused in his hammering to risk a glance over his shoulder, saw the inner door too hot to touch, the layers of dross beneath it still aglow. He could guess what had happened. He had left the door open too long, and the earthfires had broken through whatever restraints the original builder had placed there. Now they must be welling up directly against the far side of the door; even as he looked on it began to change colour slightly, developing the dull bloom of heat. No matter; it would hold long enough. Longer than he, perhaps; every breath seemed to sear his lungs. He set his teeth, still humming his tune, varying it, broadening it and finding words for its sweeping coda.

Far from here bear me now,
Off to the smiling land of the spring,
Where what is lost I regain
And more than I was I become!

He hammered with redoubled urgency, shaping and forming metal uncannily obdurate for all its lightness into the last fine welds of a framework for a light corselet of mail. The crashing chime of his blows rang dizzyingly around the stone walls; would they hear it, out there upon the Great River, and look up to see the plumes of smoke, the red glow, atop the shadowed crest of Elan Gorhenyon? Would they pull their oars to that frantic hammering time as their king urged them on, threatening, promising, half crazy with his wrath? He could see them as the thought came, the galley leaping through the water, the wavelets hissing and booming beneath its bouncing hull, its bows stirring the shallows, growling hollowly as they clove through the gravelly sand of the beach. Nithaid now, leaping the gunwale into the shallows, his warriors at his heels, charging without pause up the slopes of the Sorcerers' Isle. And in that moment it came to Elof that he was seeing a truth, a vision that was happening, and even as the metal leaped and twisted beneath his hand he listened for the roar of voices, the thunder of feet on the floor above.

It came swiftly; Nithaid, for all his years and the bull's armour he bore, must have made an almost unhuman pace up that slope, borne along by the wrath that boiled in his brain. "*Valant!*" he screamed, while he was yet some distance away. "*Come hither and be paid for the jewels you sent me! Valant! Valant!*" His voice had a shriek in it like that of a man racked to the tearing point; it froze Elof's heart. "*Come hither, you skulking slayer! Coward, come forth!*" Already he was nearer; he must be running like a man possessed –

Running. Running as once Elof could have, eight years past, on two strong legs. His teeth ground with fury. Eight long years of misery, loss and torment! He beat them out beneath his hand, with his last few strokes he hammered them away –

"*Valant, come forth!*" It was Nithaid's weight alone that crashed against the sun symbol on the door and tore the whole thing from its hinges. His onrush carried him stumbling into the forge, crashing over table and bench before he could stop, staring at the red-lit smokecloud that came boiling up into the empty room and swirled beneath the roof, as a rumble like unending thunder shook the walls. But against this sorcery he swung up his shield and shrieked "*Stay, fiend and fight! My hounds have a claim on your carcass!*"

Then out of the cloud, as it seemed, a voice answered him. His guards heard it, as they came running up behind him. And though it had seemed to them till then that no voice could be more terrible than Nithaid's in his torment, yet this one stopped them in their very stride as they came spilling into the forge. Where his was crazed, it echoed bleakly calm; where his screamed, it spoke in tones elegiac, dark and measured. But they quailed all alike at the pain it bore, and the judgement it pronounced remorseless, final as a passing bell.

Unworthy borrower of your name!
Oppressor of the land you rule!
King without honour, truth or shame!
The measure of your crimes is full!

Nithaid beheld, in that last instant, a dark shape rise amid the glowing centre of the cloud, shadowy, formless, unlike a man's. Then with a last deafening roar the floor before it split with a line of fire and collapsed, caved inward beneath him in a roar of incandescent smoke. Into the gap slid benches and tables, sweeping men with them. The wheels and engines, baked dry by long heat, burst into flames and toppled; the troughs split and the water blasted out into scalding steam. Tongues of flame roared against the roof and fired it. Great cracks raced up the walls, and they too sagged and split; before any in the forge could move those immense timbers of the roof shook free and dropped like the very props of the sky itself. Then toppled the upper walls, and with a crash and a roar the whole forge crumbled like a hollow coal and fell inward in a thunderous fountain of smoke and flame. All the soldiers outside sprang back, dragging with them comrades who had leaped free at the last moment, escaping with bruise and burn. But they knew their lord was within, and they did not flee. Not at once, not until one cried and pointed, and they saw the figure that rose out of that incandescent ruin.

In man's shape it was, yet more than man; for on immense wings, pinions of shining black shot with gleams of gold, anchored in harness set with glittering crystals, it arose radiant into the rich evening light. Most fled at the very sight of it; but some stayed to cast their spears or shoot, for they were brave men. But from one outstretched arm, sheathed in metal, a spear of fire sprang that blasted the grass before them. Then all who could turned and ran for their ship.

But Elof, rejoicing in the surge and power of wings once more, paid them no heed; for he was searching the wreckage, and called aloud the name "*Gorthawer!*" A gleam like a night of stars shone out in answer, and a faint, broken hail. Men, looking back, saw him glide down like a gigantic eagle, and they shuddered and ran on. But Elof came low, and hovered, and made out amid a great mass of rubble that shimmer of darkness, and not far from it Nithaid's tortured face. One side of it was crushed and eyeless, the heavy locks matted dark with ashes; yet he lived, and saw, and as the wind of the vast wings blew back the dust around him his lips moved.

"*Your ... armour ... was made well! Yet ... your revenge ... better! Leave ... my people ... lordless before the Ice!*"

Elof reached down among the rubble and plucked out the black sword, unmarked, unmarred; and the silver of the hilt poured a healing marshland coolness into his hands so sorely burned. "No, king!" he cried. "For better or for worse, I go now to bring them a worthier lord. Die in peace!

In the ashes there lie with your kin!
For them you fought
And schemed so long –
Now together you all may find rest!"

Slowly now he arose, higher and higher into the sky. And as he gained full mastery of the great work he had laboured on so long he turned as a bird turns, and flew off westwards, towards the setting of the sun.

CHAPTER NINE
The Airs of Freedom

ON AND UP THE wings drove him, soaring towards the white clouds while the land plummeted away beneath and the airs of the heights streamed by, cool and exhilarating as new wine. The very power of their beat was intoxicating, awesome, for they felt almost like limbs of his own, and in those moments the maiming of his legs diminished in his mind, the shadow it had cast over him dispersed. In the face of such overwhelming strength and freedom it scarcely seemed to matter any more; what he had lost was made good a thousandfold. He shouted aloud and sang for the sheer joy of it; he had passed through the fires, and was made whole again. A soft air surged beneath him, rising from the sun-warmed land, and he spread his wings and rode it easily as any bird.

It came to him as an instinct; had he not worn bird's shape many a time? Few who had not could have mimicked their flight so closely, none controlled it, for the wings were made in every detail as he remembered them, able to move in the same complex patterns, to sweep and angle and shift their shape. He had modelled them on the feather Kara left him, even to the tiny barbs that link each frond of the quill into a single surface; his material the dark substance of the filament light yet strong, with traces of gold to line it that could bear the virtues he needed. Yet though he flew thus as he had flown before, it was different, better. Now he was not cramped by the helm's powers into the mask of another shape, nor did it tell upon his strength, save to guide the flight with slight shifts of shoulder and thigh; for not even his steely arms could have freed him so from the clutch of earth. It was the gems of the corselet, drinking in the radiance of the sun as they had the furnace glare, that through the subtle virtues of the gold caused the woven web to shift and stiffen, expanding and contracting as the thews of a living frame.

He was stronger and greater now than anything else that took the air, save a dragon or some other unnatural fosterling of the Ice. Even the eagles of the Nordenbergen, shadows across the moon in his childhood, even the condors of the Meneth Scahas that came drifting down like dark clouds upon the slain of many battles, had scarcely half that awesome span. The shadow he cast was huge, and looking down and back he saw it pass at an incredible speed over the darkening blue waters of the Great River, over golden shores and green fields and forests and brown walls of town and tower, as free as himself. He did not then notice, not consciously, the dark specks against the distant clouds that kept pace with him nonetheless.

That first night took him far from Elan Gorhenyon; how far, he had no idea. As the sun sank, so the power in his wings began to dwindle and the high airs grew colder; he had expected this, and looked for a place to settle. He chose at last to land on the outskirts of a lonely wood, far beyond the towns, on a narrow spot of riverbank protected by thorn thickets. Drink he had from the river, but he had not had time to bring any food; save for a few coins in his belt, he had carried off only his precious tool-pack, the arm-ring and seal at his breast and Gorthawer at his side once more, and that seemed to him more than enough. Above all, he had his freedom. As darkness fell he folded his wings about him, and was surprised at how sheltering and warm they were. A great weariness took him then, and he slept.

Lulled by the soft ripple of the stream, the whisperings of the trees, he did not dream. Birdsong awoke him, and he laughed to find himself spreading wings of his own in the dim light; he washed swiftly and drank, finding his burns healing cleanly, and kindled a great fire with his flints to feed his wings. The gems drank it to dark ashes in minutes, and he sprang up with the sun, high into its first light. He felt hollow with hunger, light as a foam-bubble, and still did not notice the distant followers; what concerned him was food. When he saw two peasants breakfasting outside a cottage he swooped down to them, but they bolted like maddened horses in opposite directions. Fortunately they left their food; it was rough country fare, coarse bread, goat cheese and summer fruits, but to his heightened senses no less than a feast. He ate swiftly between gulps of rough wine, impatient to be aloft once more, and ere he rose again he threw down one of his gold coins in payment. It occurred to him, though the coin might have bought the cottage twice over, that for all their fright it might mean even more to them to have such a tale to tell.

It was then, beating up through the sky once more in a great spiral, that he first truly noticed the wings far off; but he thought no more of them all that day, so full was his mind of the joys of freedom, and of the heights. He tested his wings to the full, riding ever higher on the warm air-streams till he was among the clouds, sporting in and out of their chill contours as he might in water, and at last rising higher still, to where the sunlight grew sharper and the air thinner, till a tight band began to close about chest and temples, and his wings seemed to be losing their force. Then he plunged down, down in a long sweeping glide towards a swirling fountain of clouds, awaiting the moment when they would part like curtains before him and the great Vale of Kerys burst out like a bright banner beneath.

Suddenly he was in trouble. The sun was blotted out, and for a moment of horror he thought he had somehow fallen back into his crumbling forge. Sulphur boiled in his mouth and nose, hot ashes stung his eyes, cindery particles lit agonizingly upon flesh too recently raw; a vast exhalation seemed to fill the universe, louder than a stormwind but all too like the last breaths of a man half buried. He could have believed himself in the clutch of ghosts then, save that far beneath him there sounded a deafening explosion; the floating dust was blasted upward, branding his skin with new pain, and behind it the air filled with enormous masses whose passage he felt as much as saw, huge flowing gobbets the size of a house cutting the air with an eerie whistle, trailing a wake of red-hot turbulence that tumbled him madly down the sky. Another blast, and this time a shower of such gobbets almost smashed into his left wingtip. He knew now where he was, and that he must flee or die; he folded his wings and dived like a swimmer through the mirk. Another concussion, and a spraying bolt passed where he had been a tenth-second before, sent him spinning like the merest leaf away and out, out of the cloud and into clean sky. The air seemed to sing around him as he spread his wings and fought to brake his descent, the huge pinions lashing the air. Low over the waters of the Yskianas he swooped till it seemed he must be sent skipping across their crests as a boy will skim a stone, but at the last he managed to pull up, and take the sun on his shoulders once again. He looked back as he circled for height beneath the spreading ashcloud, riding on the very airs that had threatened his doom, and saw the fire-mountain blast again, spewing its glowing lava skyward. A volley of small stones passed beneath him, and he banked hurriedly across a glowing torrent of earthfire to ride the heat that rose from it. It was an eruption greater than any he had heard of before in those lands, as great as any he knew of in the Nordenbergen where he grew up. The ashcloud towered over the mountain, hanging as if motionless in the air, high enough to mask the sun from the lands beyond; its shadow lay far across them in the likeness of an arm, upraised and threatening. Around a widening spiral he flew, and was high enough now to catch a glimpse of startling contrast in the distance, the ramparts of the Ice glittering beneath the sun in all their deathly stillness.

A contrast indeed, each with an awesome ability to destroy and lay waste; abilities totally opposed, but with the same results, a land blasted and sterile. Strange that so often they should lair together, and at their fiercest – Ice and earthfires in the Nordenbergen, and now here ... Could there be some link? Could Louhi be out to make use of them somehow? If there were Powers of the fires – or whether there were or not, could there be some more material link? The fires had grown worse here as the Ice advanced, as it ground down the land, crushing it beneath its overwhelming weight ... His spiral swept him through the shadow of the cloud; he shivered violently, and his wings seemed to falter, though they had plenty of power left them. These windy airs, the sun's warmth banished, were suddenly bitterly cold ...

He passed out of the shadow, into sunshine so warm and bright it felt almost like a caress. The chill remained with him, nonetheless, sinking deep into his bones. He shifted his weight a little, and without seeking greater heights he struck out to the westward again. He had begun to understand.

The land sped by beneath him, the clean air whistled past and soothed his burns once more, and his mood of exaltation returned. Less concerned now with the sheer marvel of his flight, he began to enjoy the view, to seek the sight of places he recognised or had been told of. Only now did the full extent of the land of Kerys come home to him, only now did he begin to understand the might upon which that great city was founded. A vast land opened beneath him, an expanse even that first sight from the cliffs had not prepared him for; there, where the Vale was narrowest, he had seen only a miniature, a model of the true extent of the land. From the height he now enjoyed he could look across great sweeps of field and forest to the northern wall of Kerys Vale, and the Wild Lands beyond; or he could turn his gaze southward, and see for the first time the Yskianas' farther shores, and the different hues of the warmer southlands, the grassy meadows yellowed by midsummer, the light green of orchard and wood, the grain fields fast ripened to gold, and above them, on the slopes of the Vale, the long stretches of dark green olive grove and fig orchard, the brown of vineyard and scrubby goat pastures. So clear was the air that he could make out among them the larger coastal towns, with their walls lime-washed in dazzling white and their roof-tiles green rather than red; Kerbryhaine had adopted that style. In the south man's dominion did not stop at the margins of the Vale, but went on further than the eye could reach, into the shimmering haze of distance where the southern deserts began. Once it had been so in the north also, beyond the cliff tops a tamed country, rustic but civilized, much like Nordeney that had been his home and settled by the ancestors of its folk. Now it was the haunted half-barrens he and Roc had escaped through, helpless before the inexorable advance of the Ice; and the scars of war that had made it so had spread down into the very Vale itself.

He slept that night beneath the trees of an outlying orchard, overgrown and neglected this season; it yielded him some food, and its fallen boughs a sweet-scented fuel for his ascent next morning. By noon that day, less than two days after the fall of the forge, he reckoned he had come the distance it had taken Trygkar's cog well-nigh seven days to sail. Prompted by that thought, he looked up and down the Great River, but there were few ships of any size abroad. He saw the distant wings then, a pair of flyers as fast as himself, and curiously he swung towards them; but they scattered in panic, as what birds might not before something as huge as he? Ever westward as he flew he saw more signs of war, at first those that the greater towns were inflicting upon themselves in their frantic haste to build new fortifications on his pattern; many an ancient building was torn down for the materials, and the lands about gouged up with trench and dyke. But soon he came upon sharper devastations, wide slashes brown and black across the green earth below where holt and hamlet had been overrun and fired, walls tumbled or whitened with flame, fields trampled to muck, pastures empty of beast and herdsman. A wide ring of such ruin marked out many of the greater towns from afar.

That next evening he slept well in a proper bed with blankets, high in an abandoned tower; but he slept hungry. Every morsel of food seemed to have been stripped from the lands around; hardly a bird sang, and no small creatures disturbed the undergrowth in darkness. At dawn, as he was kindling a fire upon the tower-top, he heard the approach of horses, and looking out saw a patrol of horse-soldiers, come to investigate the smoke. He had no wish for trouble with them; but he had little cause to worry. When he spread his wings across the tower-top the horses neighed madly and bolted, their riders making no great effort to restrain them. Elof was surprised at how fearsome he seemed to be; perhaps word of the sorcerer who had slain the king and flown away had reached them – yet why should he scare the horses? Puzzled, he kicked the ashes apart, and rising upon the parapet, he launched himself out in a great glide. His quest for rising airs took him far out over the Yskianas, and when he passed high over two large cogs beating southward he decided to try diving down towards them; one might be Trygkar's, and if not he could at least see how the sailors reacted. It was almost the end of him, for even as he came gliding down the sky, confident in his invulnerability aloft, he saw a flurry of activity at the lee gunwales, but was slow to realise what it must be. He lurched aside just in time as the spurt of flame roared up at him. His swooping escape took him across the other ship's sails, and so only arrows were launched at him; but he left them far behind, and soared high to safety once again, very thoughtful. They had fired before they could possibly have made out what he was, the moment they had seen something with wings. What had they learned to fear, out here in what had become the forward lines of the war?

That night he huddled, hungrier than ever, in the lee of four broken walls, and burned the fallen timbers for his morning fire in the damp dawn; the scoured land offered little else. Yet this was still within the lines; no enemies had passed here save a few reivers. Even the defending forces had left desolation in their wake. And not only they; for as he took to the air again he saw snaking across the land ahead what seemed the worst and ugliest scar of all. But it was not long before he could recognise it for the great line of defences he himself had planned, yet never seen. It held still, for the banners of Kerys flew bravely above its battlements; but it was severely marked as by repeated assaults, and in places its outer lines looked from above as if someone had beaten on them with a vast cudgel. Bodies unburied were strewn like chaff about all the ground before, partly burned but still all too recognisable. He did not dare dive closer, lest the fire be turned on him also.

Westward still he flew, and followed over many a forest and field the bruising tracks of wholesale war, the devastation that attends the passage of great armies, and their meeting. Long swathes of grey-black ash streaked the hills, and he knew that his fire-weapons had been at work here; at times the devastation was so wide-swept it seemed as though duellists had slashed at each other with vast swords of flame. Nothing moved in the land below him, and save for distant dots now and again the airs were no less empty. Here and there, all too often, his wings shadowed low mounds set about with rusting spears, to mark where men who would defend their soil had at last become part of it. As in a vision a sound of lamentation rose to him, faint but clear, the weeping of countless voices, the groans of overburdened hearts, and he never knew whence it came, whether by some trick of the airs he heard what passed far beneath, or whether, as one blended out of many, the voice of Kerys itself cried out to him. The earth had swallowed blood here, and sickened of it. It was a land laid waste, marred as a swordcut mars a fair face; and healing was a long way off. The winds that hissed through the shattered forests called after him, bidding him make haste; the rolling music of the wide waters below urged him on. *Fly, Elof! Fly! You are destiny now!* He had no reply; he could only speed on his way, chasing the sun down the sky till evening. There lay his only hope; he could do no more for the land.

That last night of his journey he spent huddled in the lee of a stand of resinous thorn-bushes, sleeping little, watchful for intruders, and in the morning he had to fire it to charge his wings. He rose swiftly and banked away towards the Great River. As the day passed he saw it narrow beneath him, and the cliffs beyond begin to converge. He had come a good part of the length of Kerys, and ahead of him, when he rose high enough, he could see the Gate as a minute blur of grey where the cliffs converged, far ahead. Two week's journey by ship he had matched in the space of less than five days. Though he had left earlier, Roc could not possibly have kept up; he must find one of the places they had chosen as safe tryst. The shores were bleak and eerie places now, and his heart rebelled at risking a night on them, here where the Ice's terrors walked abroad; he settled at last upon one of the islands he and Roc had first seen from the cliff-tops, many years since.

It seemed at first as if war had not touched this lightly wooded little crescent of land, till, in searching the island before the sun sank, he came upon a small beach scarred by a ship's keel, and above the waterline, still recognisable, the ashes of fires. He landed, kneeling, and found they were cold; but his raking fingers uncovered bones that were unmistakable. Ekwesh reivers must have held some rite here to the Ice they served; for even they did not eat the flesh of men as casually as any other. He rose in fury, and buried the ashes with the thunderous downdraft of his wings; then he settled in shelter high up on the island. Gorthawer, unused since he recovered it, seemed to nuzzle his hand like an eager hound, and he found himself wishing those reivers would come back; but he was weak with hunger, and knew the idea was folly. Berries grew on the island, and he managed to catch some small crabs and roast them; poor fare for a man who had eaten little for days, but it would keep his strength for tonight. Tomorrow he would try hunting, and find some way to fish; that should keep him alive until Roc came. He should not be long; for all their sakes he had better not be ...

"Well, you haven't withered away, anyhow!" was that worthy's only comment, some five days later.

"Not quite!" Elof admitted, between gulped mouthfuls of the hot stew they had brought him. He set it down a moment to cool, and took a long pull at a pitcher of ale. "Though it felt like it at times. Poor hunting, I expected that; but the fishing as well? Surely even armies couldn't deplete that, not when they were mostly ashore ..."

"Maybe Trygkar'll know something –" But the old shipmaster was busy getting the cog under way; already the anchor was clanking up the side, and the sail booming out overhead. He spared Elof no more than a curt but friendly wave. "He won't linger in these open waters, lest we attract a stolen lugger full of hungry reivers! Ach well, you got through, that's what matters." He patted the massive wings outstretched on the deck. "Must've been quite a show; sorry I missed it! And these – I'm disappointed; I was looking to see you swooping down on our mastheads, not hailing for a boat from shore ..."

"So you might have, if another cog hadn't set flame on me at sight!"

Roc blew out his cheeks. "Aye, that's reason enough for care! Can't altogether blame them, though; you must have been a pretty fearsome sight! And if they'd heard about Nithaid ..."

"No!" objected Elof, swallowing a mouthful of stew too quickly. "The news couldn't have travelled that fast, not to a ship far from the nearest town! Anyway, they were racing to fire while I was still well aloft, before they could have seen anything but wings. And some cavalry ashore bolted at just the sight of wings ..."

Roc tapped his broad foot on the deck. "You're saying they've reason to fear wide wings –" Then he stood up straight. "Ach, no ... you're not thinking ..."

"Kara," said Elof flatly. "Yes, I am." For a minute their glances locked; but then Trygkar, seeing the cog well under way, felt able to leave the helm for a word, and hastily they changed the subject.

"Poor fishing here?" he repeated incredulously. "Why, man, it's the better part of the river, saltier for the seafish!"

"Then do you try your luck!" said Elof sourly. "Trawl a few lines and try! Line and spear, I've tried both from land and from above; and I've lived by fishing before. Not so much as a sprat! The waters are empty, that's it and all about it!"

Trygkar shook his shaggy white head in puzzlement but found no answer. Eight years had changed him little, save to bow his shoulders a trace; he

bellowed as vigorously as ever at a young seaman amb-
ling by. "My youngest," he said, jerking his thumb at the
lad with evident pride as he scurried off.

Elof stared. "You're bringing a son on this voyage?
Shipmaster, it's a deadly dangerous venture – would you
risk him?"

Trygkar chuckled dryly. "They're half of this crew
my lads, Mastersmith; and the rest close kin, or good
northerners – comes to much the same. I'd have
brought my old wife along, if she were living yet, sooner
than leave her here; the perils of the sea can't be worse.
Stand or fall, I fear Kerys'll never be what it was; she's
too far gone."

"There's wisdom in that. We cannot hope to
restore it to what it once was; at best we may salvage
some hope for its people. I do not regret what I have
done; but for the land's sake I wish it could have been
otherwise. Without a strong king ..."

"Without Nithaid, mean you?" Trygkar hawked and
spat overside. "He wasn't strong, no more than his
father and grandfather before him. Save as brutes are
strong, and that's the wrong way. The land's well rid of
that line. I served 'em all; I know. And I want something
better for my lads."

"Judge of our land and our king, then!" said Elof.
"Your kin have a new home for the asking, shipmaster!"

"I'd that in mind!" said the old man judiciously.
"Given he knows the worth of a good sailor, mind ..."

"None better," grinned Roc, "him having been a
seafarer himself in his wild youth. But if we're to save
anything in that realm or this, we must make haste,
shipmaster!"

Trygkar jerked his thumb at the taut sail. "I don't
call that dawdling! We're running for the southern shore
now. But we'll have to beach her in another day or so,
anyhow; daren't get too close to the Gate!"

"Daren't?" blazed Elof. "We'll have to! We can't
carry stores so far overland!"

"Well, Mastersmith, let me give you the same
answer: we'll have to! By day the Gate guards would
spot us afar off, and by night – well, it's a madman's

risk! That's a rocky shore, beset with shallows and rough
water; the flow from the falls through the lakes is fierce,
and the nearer the Gate the worse it gets."

Elof considered. "There you know best, shipmaster;
but to trudge overland for days, laden with supplies,
that too could well get us spotted. At the very least it
will put the Ekwesh on guard if they find our tracks.
But suppose ..." He bent and stroked the plumes at his
feet. "Suppose you had a watcher who could pass over
the waters ahead, spy out such obstacles even in the
dark?"

Trygkar looked at him in great wonder. "You can
do that? Then by Verya's sweet apples, we might just
risk it!"

So it was that in the dimming end of twilight, two
evenings hence, a shape was flitting about the river that,
from afar, might have been a great black bat in search of
fat moths. It settled itself at last upon the foredeck of
the cog, and the light of an uncovered brazier flared
briefly behind the widespread wings; then it was as
quickly quenched as they folded and enveloped it. It was
an eerie sight, and Elof was acutely aware of the white-
rimmed eyes of the watching sailors. "It's nearly clear
now!" he whispered urgently to Trygkar. "Round the
point, skirt the sandbar there, and some jagged rocks
well under the surface, and there's a sheltered little bay,
fine for a beaching!"

Trygkar gave a curt nod, hissed a command, and
the eyes vanished in a flurry of motion. Elof spread his
wings, wider even than the cog, and let himself fall
forward on the air. It was cloudy, moist and still,
strangely tense and breathless as if it had caught their
excitement, and flying was cooling relief. Over the bows
he glided, and circled over the channel the cog must
follow. As had happened once or twice already, the tip
of a rock gouged into the protesting timbers; depths
were hard to judge, even skimming the very surface of
the water. It sounded deafening in the stillness, and Elof
winced; but no great damage was done, and the cog
rode free into haven.

There was still force in his wings, and finding a

light updraft from the land he swooped high over the tangled forest, spying out signs of movement, yet took care not to rise above the slope and be silhouetted against the stars. The forest was silent and still, save for the scufflings of the tiniest beasts, and, greatly encouraged, he sank to the treetops and ventured a closer look at the grim bulk that bridged the narrow vale no great distance ahead.

His teeth clenched with a snap as he saw the lights that burned yellow in the upper windows; but he forgot the dreadful memories that aroused when he noticed that there were no outside lights at all. Normally sentries needed a few, at least, to save them slipping down long stairwells or over low balustrades; here there were none, and not a single guard to be seen. He did not know what to make of that. But then his wing-beat began to falter, and banking swiftly in the air he glided back down to the cog.

Its barrel hull looked absurd, canted over to one side in the shallows; from the side a frenetic unloading had already begun, with figures scuttling ant-like up and down the gangplanks. A few, Roc among them, made no move to help, but stood with bows to hand, watching the forest. With little force in his wings Elof landed awkwardly, and they ran to help him up. "Safe, I think!" he gasped. "Even up by the Gate; no guards, nothing stirs there ... And yet –"

"And yet!" echoed Roc, with a shiver. "We'll take no chances passing *that* place by! How goes it, Trygkar?"

"Well on, Master Roc! First of the portage sleds loaded to the limit, the others almost. Five men to a sled, and we'll manage what's left on our backs! And swiftly, for I smell a storm in the air!" The old man paused, embarrassed. "But what of you, Mastersmith? These paths will be too steep for you. Will you ride on one of the sleds, or shall we carry you also?"

Elof felt his blood race; he could not go back to being a cripple, a mere burden, not now. "Neither! Kindle me a good fire, and I'll fly!"

Roc growled. "What'd we agree? What if you're seen?"

"In this haze? A bird, that's all! There's no telling distance or detail! Besides, what if I'm needed aloft on the far side? We can't just stop and build a fire there!"

"True!" said Trygkar decisively. "I'll have it laid, but not lit. You must wait till we're hard by the crown of the hill! Then if it is seen they'll at least start looking in the wrong place; and you can catch us up in minutes."

So it was agreed; and as the little party began its long haul up the slope Elof was left, doubly helpless under his powerless wings, to watch the cog steered out by its three remaining crewmen. Since they were moving with the current now, they had less trouble in regaining the main stream and heading west again. It would be a long time before they were in safe waters once more – but how much longer for him?

An hour passed, and another, more wearisome. He looked at the fire, and at the heavy clouds overhead; a breath of cold air stirred the heavy leaves around him, ruffled the plumage of his wings. Was that a distant rumble? At the first drop of rain he would have to light the fire, or risk being stuck here; but some of these summer storms came on very quickly and heavily. He twisted around, and his keen eyes pierced the murky air, following the slight disturbance high among the trees that marked the progress of the sleds, marked where a brace of birds flew up, squawking in alarm at the intruders. They were making good time, better than he had feared; but they must be tiring, plodding along on legs that felt like molten lead, hot, heavy and agonizing. He found himself pitying them; flight seemed so natural to him already, his braced legs a minor hindrance. If there was a clear patch he might even be able to help them with their burdens ...

He sat up straight. A chill droplet had touched the back of his neck. He looked up, and after a moment another touched his cheek. That was more than enough; he fumbled desperately with the tinderbox they had left him, blew a glow into the shavings and struggled to transfer it to the kindling of the fire – *Powers, was it damp already?* Down the vale from the southeast echoed a crackle, a rumble. The kindling steamed and sputtered and sizzled, then quite abruptly it flared, a single yellow flame that spread into a wavering line. The wood above it blackened and caught, a sudden swirl of air only swelled it, and in minutes the pile was a roaring cone of flame. Above it hung the great wings, hiding its light, shielding it from the rain; then they swept down, and in a moment the droplets hissed upon spent embers from which the last glow had been drunk. The crystals in corselet and gauntlet had turned the fire back upon itself, redoubling its ferocity till the wood was consumed in an instant. Now the wings thrashed with its heat, and their wind scattered the ashes among the damp sand, dispersed even the smoke. Nobody would see it now. A flicker raced through the sky above the cliff tops, even as Elof rose from the beach and soared up the slope.

The storm was following fast; he went leaping out of its gusty vanguard like a dolphin from a bow wave, and swooped down over the heads of his fellows as they reached the crest. But there was nowhere clear enough for him to land, he swept past and saw with alarm that he was circling past the upper levels of the High Gate. They looked strange, somehow, as if their louring profile had been changed. And still he could see no guards –

Then a blade of awful light smote across the sky. Somewhere far behind him the lightning struck, blazed through the heavy air, and the High Gate stood out stark in its glare. Elof recoiled at what he saw there; for it was not that the profile of the tower had been changed. Above the colonnades, curled protectively around the circumference of the tower, he looked upon a vast length of back all set with scales like smooth irridescent shields, the curving flank of a body narrow only in proportion to the thing's sheer size. Above it lay folded wings that dwarfed even his; one leg jutted out like a crazily angled buttress. The vision came and went in an eyeblink; darkness returned, and hot red images behind his eyes. then the thunderclap came, a tearing, unending crash, and the air took hold and shook him. At the far end of the tower scales rattled, and a huge head lifted and swung like a ship's spar; yellow eyes larger than Elof's head cast about, this way and that, malevolent glitters in the renewed blackness. Rigid with fright, he let himself fall, drift down on stiffened wings, cursing himself for not having been warned by the sights he had seen – great flame scars on the earth, a land devoid of food, sailors and soldiers scared of the very sight of wings. And a sight this must be, aloft; for it was twice the size of the dragons that had assailed the duergar capital. In developing his fire-weapons he had forgotten that the Ice could command a living flame of its own; small wonder no sentinels need be posted. He was almost among the treetops before that huge head sank down again; it had missed him in the gloom. He turned wildly and went plunging after the others.

He reached them just as they were about to cross the bare crown of the ridge, and was able to land among the thickets. "Makes little odds!" said Roc, though he spoke from a dry throat. "We were going to beware of Ekwesh sentries anyway –"

"This thing is sentry and army both! And it must move more swiftly than any, aloft. If sentries spotted us we might still get away; but not if it does!"

So they crept slowly across the clear land, lifting the laden sleds bodily rather than run them over even the slightest obstruction; here Elof could help, for there was still power in his wings, and without the added strength in them and his own arms they might not have managed, for they were weary after their climb. No man spared a thought for the view ahead till the sleds were under the trees lower down; but then Roc and Trygkar slunk back up, with Elof above them casting many awed glances at the indistinct bulk on the terraces and cursing the gloom that made every shadow seem to move. They fell flat among low and tangled bushes, with Elof's wings to cover them, and took stock of what they saw.

Against the ocean's faint glimmer it seemed for a moment to them all as if the shore directly below the Gate was lined with thickets of dead trees, stark and skeletal. Then lightning pulsed among the clouds, and by its glow Elof recognised them for the bare masts and spars of ships beached, or riding at anchor in inlets and streams. "Quite a bloody fleet!" whispered Roc. "And no wagering whose – look at the shape! Ekwesh longships, every one!"

"So much the better for us! Trygkar, a few of the lads can get the supplies down the gentler slope to that point there, while we head down this steeper way; then we can take them aboard as we head out!"

"But won't we need all the crew to ..."

"I think not! Better to do this quietly, if we can; and with the rain to aid us, we might! By the way those fires are scattered about, they can't imagine an enemy coming within leagues of them; and there are no lights on the ships. I'd guess they'll have set no more than a token guard, and that mostly to watch the weather, or one clan thieving from another. And if that's so ..."

The rain came as they were scrambling down the precipitous slopes that flanked the Gate, making an already perilous climb far worse; Elof flew, and more than once he had to rescue some unfortunate who slipped in the rivulets of mud that came gurgling down through the undergrowth. Every time the lightning flashed overhead they froze, pressing themselves flat to the slope, while Elof swooped away to avoid drawing attention to them, fearful that at any moment he would see that vast yellow gaze staring down at him with the malign intelligence of a minor Power; its fire he might resist, but those jaws could pluck him from the air with a single bite. The storm lingered on the ocean's edge, as if waiting for a change of wind, and it took them a good three hours to reach the gentler slopes below the Gate. They had come a way no army could hope to, and they were exhausted and chilled; but here of all places, on the margins of the Ekwesh encampments, they did not dare rest.

Nor were they grateful when a lull came in the storm, for they had hoped it would cover their escape. Here and there sentinels began to emerge from shelter and relight campfires; and one of these stood squarely in the way to the ships. So it was that a terrifying winged shadow descended suddenly upon that fire, and with a single sweep of its pinions snuffed it out; in the instant of darkness other shapes swarmed over the stunned guards. The act was swift and merciless, and because of that it was silent. "Now light that fire again," ordered Trygkar, "lest any of the other swine notice! We'll have to wait for the rain now ..."

Elof held out a restraining hand. "Not necessarily! We will need the rain later; but meanwhile there may be another way ..."

Now he was high over the longship they had picked out, the guard no more than an outline leaning over the rail, gazing out into the bay as if listening to the soft boom of the surf under the rain. Perhaps at the last second he saw in the dark water astern some glimpse of what was coming, for he whirled swiftly about, his spear lifting, his mouth opening to shout. But they were his last thoughts, his last acts, and he did not live to complete them. The next moment he was high in the air, breathless as a fish plucked from the ocean in the talons of the swooping raptor; he was a strong warrior, but those talons broke him, and let go. The other watchers heard no more than a faint splash from out in the bay.

Lightning lanced down over the hills behind the Gate, thunder shook the air. Elof swooped low, hoping he looked no more than a large seabird, and skimmed the waves back to the ship, Gorthawer in hand, ready to fall once again upon any who resisted there. But a familiar shape waved to him as agreed and he settled swiftly to the deck. "Any others?"

"Three, all asleep in shelter. They never woke. And one in the next ship who chose that ill-starred moment to come on deck for a leak. I dropped him overside with an arrow before he even saw. Like sheep in a stall; just slaughter!"

"But hardly up to their own standards. Where's Trygkar?"

"Here!" came a gruff whisper. "As I thought, this one's newly ready for sea; the rig looked fresh-trimmed, and it is. But better we take her down to the point on oars, they're slower but quieter –"

"No!" grinned Elof. "Just get her afloat the moment the rain comes back; I'll see to the rest!"

With poles and sweepshafts as levers they began to inch the longship down the beach, lifting anxious eyes to the skies. In this dimness it was unlikely any guard would see much at first, until the longship began to move in earnest; then the one mast moving would stand out among the rest, and they could not lower it without hindering their escape. It had better be raining again then. Lightning sizzled across the sky, thunder hard on its heels, and the masts stood out in stark relief; every man froze in the glare as if it had struck him, but the ship's stern was already rocking slightly in the waves, the mast swaying visibly. Trygkar let loose a stream of appalling oaths under his breath, but there was no disturbance; probably this area was the responsibility of the sentries they had slain, and nobody else was paying it any attention. With that monster above their heads, thought Elof, they had some excuse for being complacent. Trygkar passed him a heavy cable; he looped it over his shoulders, and they waited. Now and again a cold droplet would splash on arm or neck, but it was only the wind blowing them off spar or stay. It was a warm wind, but in his soaked jerkin it made him shiver; an angry tattoo of drops spattered on his neck, and he winced. Then came another, then a few slow drops more struck him with mounting intensity and speed. He turned in sudden hope to look up at the clouds behind the heights of the Gate, and felt a stab of sheer terror. Lightning clashed like twin lances against the tower, and he saw the immense body churn and stir like the sea, its scales dazzling with reflected glare, saw the spear-shaped head rear up, yellow eyes alight, jaws flung wide, the vast wings stir and spread above the Gate like some demoniac crown. A cavernous roar mingled with the thunder, and their contention shook the air.

Then, like a steel gate falling, the rains came once more. And into the midst of them as they crashed down upon him Elof launched himself, catching a last glimpse of the others springing to the levers below. Then he

could see no more than shadows; he hoped the rain
would dim those yellow eyes as thoroughly. The cable
snapped taut, a tremendous weight bore down on his
back and then suddenly eased as the longship slid down
the sand and into the surf. Dimly he heard Trygkar calling that all were now aboard; he could not answer, but
took the strain once more, and felt the whole weight of
the longship seek to haul him down. But it was afloat
now, and the strains slackened as it began to move, sliding smoothly through the water behind him; he towed it
as a small boat might, his wings mocking the rain with
their powerful beat. It gathered speed more easily than
he had feared, riding smoothly through the swell, and as
the others settled at the sweeps it fairly leaped forward.
They had chosen it well, a craft of no great size, built
more for speed and sea-handling, for long journeys
ending in swift assaults rather than carrying huge
cargoes or many men. In fact, it could have been any of
the ships that had come gliding in towards Asenby so
many years since. He laughed aloud at the irony of that,
and the thunder seemed to laugh with him, mocking the
ways of fate.

No voice was raised from the shore, no shot was
fired after them; the rain was still shielding them, scattering the lightning's glare. They turned in towards the
point where the others awaited. There was a moment's
alarm when an impact threw the rowers from their
benches and caused the mast to waver like a grass stem
in a gale; but they had only touched upon a hidden
sandbar, and Elof still had enough power in his wings to
haul them off and set them on course for the beach.
They grounded alongside, and one party went to a
nearby stream to fill the Ekwesh water-breakers while
the others set about loading. They could not spare the
time to unpack the sleds, so they laid down planks and
hauled them bodily on board, though the half-decking
seemed too light; as it turned out, only the last sled
cracked it. The water-bearers came scurrying back and
stowed the heavy barrels beside their own lighter flasks
of metal and thick glass. "That's it!" barked Trygkar.
"Draw us off, Mastersmith! To the oars, all, and back

water! Fast, ere the rain slackens again!"

Elof rose up and seized the bow line, but felt his wing-beat falter as he took the strain. The oars were already thrashing against the surf; urgently he heaved, felt the lean prow swing around to face the waves, lift and plunge. A gust of wind caught him then, his wings faltered and fluttered against it; he spread them wide and dived desperately for the deck. With no power in wing or leg to stop himself he landed with bruising force; the wind got under his wings, dragged and skidded him across the tarred, greasy timbers and almost over the far gunwales. "No more power –" he gasped, as crewmen ran to hold down his wings and help him free of the metal harness. "Can't help any more now –"

"It doesn't matter!" bellowed Roc in his ear, as the thunder drummed overhead. "Doesn't matter, d'you hear? We're out! Headed out into the bay, out to sea! We're away!"

Elof gave a great sigh. "Then their work is done!" he said, and even over the storm there was no mistaking the regret in his voice. "And so they are clipped; on a ship this size we can hardly build a fire big enough to fuel them! See them well stowed, Roc." He let the wings be slipped from his shoulders. "Lie there, my new life!"

He brooded a moment, while the deck plunged and the wind whined around him, but soon roused himself. "Ah well, at least I'm still good for some labour! Help me to an oarbench, will you?"

"Ach, I don't doubt you could row the ship by yourself if you pleased, but why bother? Trygkar'll be setting sail any minute ..."

"*No!* He mustn't! Help me to him!" Roc shook his head, but helped him up, and they staggered aft together. Trygkar stood on the after deck, clasping the steering oar in his corded old arms with no apparent effort; the moment Elof sighted him, he cried out "No sail, shipmaster! Oars only! Till dawn at the earliest, as I said!"

The old shipmaster frowned. "But Mastersmith, in this rain ..."

"And if it clears for a moment? They might miss a bare mast by night, but never the expanse of a sail! That's one reason!" He slumped down against the gunwale, and pointed. "And by all the Powers, there's another!"

Out to sea the rain was thinner, and through it they could just make out the high pale outlines that seemed to muster around the mouth of the little bay. "Sails!" barked Trygkar, clapping hand to the axe at his belt. "And they're a size, by the powers – three, four, no, more, a bloody fleet of the savages ..."

Elof shook his head. "Not Ekwesh! Those woven sails of their never look white!"

"Then who ..." began Trygkar; then the lightning came again, and the truth glittered clear and bleak. "*Ice!* Are those the ice-islands you warned me of, Master Roc?"

"Aye," said Roc grimly. "But twice the size of any we saw, this far south! Why, with so much above the water, they must be just about touching –"

"They are," said Elof bleakly. "I saw; the waves lashed them, but they never moved. They are aground – a reef of ice!"

Trygkar shook his head. "You were right, then, Mastersmith – as well we didn't go sailing smack into those, in the dark and rain! Navigating them's a job for sweeps alone! Why, they're all around the Gate –" He snapped his fingers. "*That's* why you didn't find any fish! All around the Gate – all around the inflow, the High Falls! Think what they must be doing to the waters of the Yskianas!"

"Of course!" breathed Roc. "This must be Louhi's doing! She's chilling it! So that's the plan you guessed, is it, Elof?"

But Elof shook his head. "A part of it, perhaps; a preparation ..." Then something boomed against the bows, and the ship lurched. "Floating ice! Even this far in!"

"You've met this before, Mastersmith!" said Trygkar shortly. "You give the orders!"

"Three men in the bows, with heavy poles or

sweeps!" barked Elof. "Shift what you can, sing out to the steersman if you can't! Roc, you'd better be one of them! But help me to an oar first!"

It was hard to sit down at the bench, to grasp the rough wood of the sweep and turn his back on what must be happening at the bows, to fix his mind on the pace and rhythm of the shoulders that bent and strained before him, broken only when they must hurriedly back water, or push poles and sweeps against some cruel fragment of glacier. It was a fearful toil, for there were not enough rowers, but that he hardly noticed. As the time passed he could look up, at least, and see through the veil of rain the white crags slip slowly by, their twisted summits aglitter with the lightning. It was more distant now; the storm seemed not to be following them out over the sea. So much the better; it would cover their escape all the longer, and give them a more peaceful ride. For all that it had played them some uncomfortable tricks earlier, in fact, it could hardly have served them better –

The thought came to him so suddenly he almost missed his stroke, earning the curses of the others on his side; but he hardly heard them. He was too busy thinking of the other fliers he had seen, remembering how even in the most deserted lands or skies there had always been birds within sight, near or far two birds, great birds, black birds, so great, so black they could be seen easily from afar. More than once he had seen such a pair, and always on their traces rode a storm; a storm that was no common storm, that cloaked a cunning and a quirky mind, a Power and a jester both ...

Then a hand on his shoulder startled him from his thoughts. Trygkar was kneeling on the half-deck by his bench, and there was a young man's urgency in his voice. "Mastersmith! Master Elof! I think we're through the worst of the ice-islands! They're all afloat now, wider apart save to the northward, and we can dodge those! But it must be drawing nigh to dawn!"

Elof looked up sharply, realizing that he had heard no thunder for some time. The rain was lessening, and the blackness beyond it was developing a definite greyish tinge. "Then by all means hoist sail, shipmaster, and get us away from here! On the wings of the wind!"

Trygkar rose and bellowed orders, and the sweeps lifted from the water like rippling wings; Elof copied the othes, shipping his in a shower of seawater. The chill of it stung him, and he shuddered; there was something there of the agony the Ice caused him. Then Trygkar bellowed again, and the other rowers shipped their oars and sprang for the halyards, leaving Elof helpless on his bench, wild with resentment at being unable to rise and see, though he could guess at what was going on easily enough. He heard the rough spar go rattling and creaking up the mast, and twisting round he saw the black sail billow and catch the wind. It filled with a dull thump, wholly unlike the crisp crack of the sailcloth he was used to; this black stuff was a much heavier and cruder weave, strengthened with a crosswise net of tarred cords. But it took the wind well enough. The yards sang taut, and beneath him the hull answered with a single deep drumming note; water slopped and gurgled in the bilges, and the sleek ship sliced through the water like a flung knife. A wild cheer rippled the length of the ship. "*Quiet!*" barked Elof, and it was instantly quelled; he held up a hand, listening, but the sound he thought he had heard did not come again. He scrabbled and struggled to haul himself out of the benches, and Roc came running to help.

"Why be quiet?" he demanded as he hauled Elof bodily out of his seat. "We're away, aren't we? And you can't blame 'em for a shout or two; crude these reiver craft may be, but they've a keen edge of speed on 'em!"

"And we may need all we can get! Help me aft, Roc, and fast! They'll have discovered it's gone by now; there'll be pursuers combing the Seas of the Sunrise for us! Sound may reach them where sight cannot!"

Roc, helping Elof up into the sterncastle, cast a worried glance at the sea, all shades of dull metal now, and at the land that had held them so long, dwindling now to a grey streak across the horizon, its hills no more substantial than the remotest band of cloud. "But surely we've a good start ..."

He stopped. Elof was listening, gesturing urgently for quiet. The rumble that was borne down the wind might have been the last of the night's thunders, had there been any lightning with it. "Over their ships, yes! *But look!*"

All eyes followed Elof's hand, high into the growing light. The dark stormclouds were breaking up now over the land, riven with gulfs of lighter grey. Through one of these a strange shape glided, serpentine, yet borne aloft on a wide spread of wings, more like bat than bird; so uncanny it seemed that it took them a moment to gauge the distance, and realise how huge a thing it truly was.

"The dragon!" hissed Trygkar, pale with horror. "The dragon hunts us!"

"As he would have sooner, had the sail been espied last night!" said Elof absently, peering into the growing light. Again that ominous shadow crossed the cloud. "Keep on your course, do nothing else! He hasn't seen us, not yet – and if he does ..."

If only this wind doesn't drop –

Somebody shouted. Out of the clouds, far nearer to them, far larger, the winged shape dropped like a spent arrow. Frightened gasps arose, and men looked to the side as if weighing the chill of the deeps against the venomous flame. But the dragon only hung there for a moment below the cloud canopy, vast wings sweeping between sea and sky, then abruptly it turned and sped away eastward. Elof let go his breath, and swayed a little. "He fears to go further, lest he grows weary, or is wounded! Dragons hate the sea, that waits to swallow them and their fires together, quenching them without effort. Not even at Louhi's behest will he go further! And if he cannot catch us, their ships will also find it hard! So –" He sighed, and turned to gaze out past the great bow platform, across a vast expanse of sea and sky to the farthest horizon, where air and water met and shadows of the night still lingered.

Roc swallowed. "Then – that's it? No more than that?" A look of mild astonishment spread over his face, and he shook his head slightly, as if to clear an ear. "We've escaped. We're away –" He sat down upon the helmsman's bench, very hard.

Elof nodded slightly. "West by west-north-west . . there lies your course, shipmaster!"

Trygkar looked dubiously from the clear grey waters southward to the flow-strewn north, and back again, and scratched his head dubiously. "As you command, Mastersmith. But it's a chill road, bitter chill!"

"No more chill than the heart of Louhi! No more bitter than the lot of men! *Sail on!*"

They gave that black ship no name, though it proved steadfast and strong, sliding through stormwaves as lean and supple as an eel; for it was none of theirs, and they found it better not to think what might have passed upon those greasy planks. The altar-pyramid of cemented stones on the sterncastle was bare of all dark ashes, but Elof cast it into the sea, and after it all the banners and shaman's gear he found, all bearing emblems of the Otter clan. The design on them was not unpleasing, showing well the sleek and sinuous movement of the beast he knew; he had watched them sport and dive in the seas of his childhood, menacing none save the shellfish they broke between flat stones. Once the ancestors of the Ekwesh, simple hunters themselves, had sought to identify with such creatures, seeing mirrored in them the qualities they valued, and their own place in nature; how had such a folk been twisted into predators, builders of a cruel empire, eaters of their own kind's flesh, feared servants of all nature's deadliest foe?

All too easily, he reflected; for on that long voyage he had ample time for such lonely musings. He had only to consider how the onslaught of the Ice had begun to twist the folk of Kerys, once noble and high of spirit, into the sorry images of the folk they fought. Between Nithaid and the best of the Ekwesh chieftains, such as those of the Raven clan, there was little enough to choose. And yet however malformed, there still must be a great grain of humanity in the Ekwesh somewhere; in their spirit of battle-fellowship that gave them some discipline, perhaps, their courage, or their sense of order and hierarchy. Yet it was with qualities such as those, lacking the mindsword of his own evil making, that Louhi bound the Ekwesh to her service – those, and the lure of simple riches, and where all else failed, sheer terror. An unwholesome fellowship links those who have committed acts atrocious beyond the common course of men; those who in great peril have saved themselves at the cost of others, those who, starving at sea or in the wilds, have been driven to eat the flesh of their fellows, who have joined in some dark crime, or witnessed horrors beyond the bounds of nature. All these things the Ice demanded of Ekwesh warriors, through the medium of the shamans and the secret society of the Hidden Clan, with its masked ritual and mastery of magecraft; and it reinforced them with terrifying penalties. The best it left them was the sombre pride and warrior's honour he had met in the Raven clan. But still, somewhere, there lurked the spirit of the men who had watched the otters in the bright waters, and delighted in them. If he could somehow reach that ...

Such musings were a useful distraction from the monotonies and hardships of the voyage, and those were many; but there was nothing idle about them, and they were only one strand among his tangled thoughts. Their passage was swifter than it had been outward, for they met no greater perils than wind and rough weather and made no detours, but sliced a smooth arc over the curve of the world, tacking across the chilly airs that flowed off the Ice. With a crew able to stand two watches the sailing was far easier, and though many of the young men had never before seen the ocean, they were Northerners bred to it over thousands of years, and took to it at once. The black ship, though crude and simple in its building, proved steadfast and strong, sliding through stormwaves like a serpent, shipping surprisingly little water over its low gunwales and between its planking. Their living space was uncomfortable, for the Ekwesh made a fetish of hardihood, and scorned the least of civilised comforts. To the surprise of many it was also scrupulously clean, for they had learned the need of this in conditions so cramped that disease could race like a forest fire. If there were pursuing ships, they never saw them, nor did they encounter any patrols; it seemed that Louhi had withdrawn them, perhaps to provide more manpower for her campaigns, perhaps also because of the ice-islands that were gathering in such numbers now.

"They'll freeze together come winter," remarked Roc.

Elof nodded, and leant a little on the steering oar, swinging the black ship that much wider of the clustered floes. "And maybe next spring, or ten springs hence, they won't thaw apart again, and though they're blocked on the land the glaciers will creep a bit further down across the sea."

Roc eyed him dryly. "By any chance would that be this plan of Louhi's you suspect?"

Elof frowned. "A part, probably," he admitted unwillingly. "But still not the core of it. I – I *think* I see it; but not clearly enough. Not yet." He tipped the helm back as the floes slipped by, watching a shadow creep back along a curiously carven disk of wood and bronze till it fell straight along the course he had marked. Roc looked at him a moment, then shrugged.

As the weeks wore on the ocean grew colder about them, so that even in high summer rime formed upon rigging and spar by night, and by day was slow to disperse. In the northern skies the Iceglow burned baleful above the horizon like an unending banner of spiderweb, dimming the stars as they arose, a silent presence that preyed upon men's minds. Many of the crew grew anxious at their northward drift, and began to eye their fast dwindling supplies with great concern. They could not understand, though Elof sought often to explain to them, the necessities of navigating across the curve of the world; their minds, bounded all their lives by the walls of Kerys Vale, could scarcely comprehend distances so vast, and in confusion they grew distrustful. Even Trygkar, who had looked upon the ocean as a child, remembered only that there was some special art, and not what it involved; no man of his time had known it. He trusted Elof, however, and that kept his crew in check.

At last, one chill morning, Elof took careful sight on the sun as it shone red through the swirls of freezing mist, and shouted to Trygkar to bring the ship about onto a new heading, west by west-south-west. "For this is the mid-point of our voyage; we need go north no longer! Now for the South, and home!"

From that day on the climes grew warmer again, and though there was still rough weather enough to occupy them, their main concern was whether the food would last. "We always knew it would be hard!" Elof told the crew, when they must needs reduce their daily portions still further. "We could not have carried more and still seized the ship so swiftly! But be steadfast, and I will make you all amends yet!"

Trygkar chuckled. "We'll hold you to that, Mastersmith! We've water still, though it's piss-poor drinking, and water's the main thing; for the rest, a feast was never made the worse by a few day's fasting first!"

But the water was down to the scummy dregs of the casks, and the fast had endured many days, before the sunset came that brought their lookout's hail. The sinking sun flooded the skies with still flame, reddening the grey clouds till they turned to glowing embers crusted with black; fire ran among the steely waves till the black ship seemed to ride a path of metal half-molten. But at the apex of that path, hard to look at as the sun descended upon it, a dark streak showed at the waves' ending that seemed more solid than any cloud. The sun was almost down before those on deck glimpsed it, and then only for a moment ere the dark came. They were not sure; hope stuck painfully in a parched throat. But the lookout was sure, as he came sliding merrily down the mast, and bade them hold their course and await the dawn. That night no man slept.

So it was that when the first feeble light dimmed the sinking stars the whole crew crowded the deck. They had seen little by night, moonless and cloudy, and now they quivered like hounds at the slip, thirsting and hungering for more than mere sustenance. When the clearing greyness showed them that shadow grown more solid still, the whole ship went wild; they laughed, they danced, they pounded Elof and Roc upon the back with bruising force. Both men scarcely noticed, for a deeper hunger yet burned within them; for hours it held them at the gunwale, their eyes fixed on the changing silhouette ahead. They were approaching the coast at a shallow angle, passing further southward the closer they drew, and they were torn between the urge to turn straight towards land, and the more sensible course of waiting till they were nearer. "We've got to be close to home!" asserted Roc for the twentieth time, twisting his fists about the gunwale till the layers of encrusted salt crackled and crumbled. "We can't be far north or we'd still have seen the Iceglow –"

Elof writhed uneasily on the crutches he had whittled from ship's timber. "It was hard to set our southward course exactly. Too far south, and we come upon empty country – wild land, forest. Desert even, or the salt flats of Daveth Holan ..."

Roc squinted up into the afternoon sky, shading his eyes against the declining light. "You couldn't be that far out in your reckoning! Mad you may be, but not daft ..." He tensed at a sudden hail from the masthead.

"What d'you see?" shouted Elof. "Whither away, man?"

"*Dead ahead – beyond the bows! Look ... oh look!*"

On a ship of their own land they would have been able to scramble up the stern-post, but the reiver ship lacked one. They could only wait long minutes, while the ship sailed on and the world seemed to hold its breath – all save the lookout, for he had become totally incoherent with excitement. But as what he had seen appeared above the horizon, a great shout went up of wonder and joy, from all save Elof and Roc; for astonishment held them mute.

This was not the land they had left, not far short of nine years past. And yet beyond doubt it was the city once named Morvannec, renamed Morvanhal; but now it seemed in truth that the ancestral seed of Morvan, a thousand years crushed beneath the Ice, had risen and flowered into triumphant strength once again.

Roc gulped. "Is it real?"

"Could all this have been shaped in a mere nine years?" breathed Elof in wonder. "Or have we been wanderers in time, as we have upon the oceans?"

"Lesser than Kerys!" growled Trygkar softly. "That you told me – but not that it was like this! And you have brought us straight here!"

So entangled in wonders were they that this further one seemed scarcely to matter, then; it was only later that it came home to them all. For dead ahead of them lay the promontory of Morvanhal, and across all the trackless wastes of the seas Elof had set their bows straight towards it.

But as they drew ever closer they had few thoughts save for the majesty of the sight; they forgot empty bellies and parched throats, for their minds and their hearts were filled. All that Elof and Roc had looked to see was there, the smooth solidity of the outer walls with their rotund towers, cone-capped in grey, the streets and terraces rising up the flanks of the ness, and at its crown the lordly tower of the palace. They were still too distant to make out much detail, even in this clear afternoon light; but memories touched in what their eyes did not see. Yet those memories they began to doubt, for so much was overlaid upon them; they saw familiar pictures in new and splendid settings, but so contrived that their splendour only enhanced and dignified the older work. From behind the old walls new walls arose, their stone vividly red-gold in the clear light, and they spread out to embrace the land around and beyond the promontory, and the hills that overlooked it. On the slopes behind the ness, where tangled forest had encroached upon overgrown field, new streets wound their way up from the old; but they were tall, spacious and widely separated. Between them both forest and field were maintained, each within their proper limits, save where they gave way to the familiar patterns of vineyard and orchard. It was an image of harmony, a contained balance of man and nature such as Elof had never looked to see within a city wall. And as the palace crowned the promontory, so on each hill a tall tower rose out of the trees; yet though they far over-topped it, they did not overwhelm it, but were set about it like standing sentinels to an enthroned lord, like flourishing youth about venerable age. Of ivory stone were their walls, their roofs of bronze capped with gold, and many a brave banner flew above them against the white clouds.

"Those are the towers of Kerbryhaine!" Roc burst out. "What magecraft translates them here, right across the land? Copies, maybe – but where'd they get the stone? There's none like that here!"

Elof shook his head in sheer wonder. "Surely the duergar have had a hand in this! Only they could achieve so much in so short a time."

"The duergar?" whispered a young crewman nearby. "Is this a magical place, then?" Nobody laughed.

"It's a peaceful one, anyhow!" said Trygkar contentedly. "That shows! We'd never get even this near to any city of Kerys in a ship like this ..."

Elof and Roc exchanged shocked glances; they had both forgotten what manner of ship they were coming home in. Then they turned as one to look up at the black sail. "One wins you ten," said Roc carefully, "that they're warming up our welcome this very minute!"

Elof swallowed, remembering the lethal rams he had fitted to Kermorvan's great warships. "And they would use them at full speed! By the time they got within hailing range it would be too late!"

"Even if they heeded any hails!" grunted Roc. "Or they'd use catapults – one volley from the *Prince Korentyn* would turn this hull into pickteeth! If we lowered the sail –"

"The reivers do that before the attack, often enough!"

"One ship against a city?" demanded Trygkar.

"A city the Ekwesh have held within living memory!" said Elof quietly. "Not an experience you forget! They might think us daft, but they'd still strike first and hard ..."

"*In the harbour!*" cried the lookout. "*A ship, a huge ship, warping about, readying sail!*"

"That's it!" said Elof decisively. "Head for the harbour-mouth and they'll smash us to flinders. We can't anchor outside; it's too deep. Sweeps or sail, we'll have to risk coming alongside the sea-wall, where they can't use the ram; can we do it, shipmaster?"

Trygkar grinned. "We can have a stab, Mastersmith! But we'll be taking a slow pounding between waves and wall –"

"Better that than the ram!" said Roc fervently. "And I've few soft feelings about *this* ship – have you?"

"Well … she bore us no small way; and a skipper hates to lose any ship. But better that, as you say – *to your places, the pack of you! We're going about!*"

The city was confident of peace, that was evident, for it had no war-craft in readiness; but by the time the black ship reached the sea-wall the longship *Saldenborg*, next in size to the *Korentyn*, was sweeping out of the mouth. "She'll have to tack ere she can come back at us!" shouted Elof, helping Trygkar with the unwieldy steering oar. "If you can get us alongside at once –"

"Any moment now, Mastersmith!" said Trygkar intently. "Down helm a little – a wee bit more – *let her go, there! Stand by to fend off, you others!*" The old shipman took a deep breath, and bellowed "*Now!*"

The two of them leaned hard on the oar. The black ship swung sharply around, spilling wind from its sail, the waves caught it broadside and lifted it with a sickening lurch; a dark bulk loomed suddenly over the gunwale, there was a jarring impact, another and still another that rattled their teeth in their heads. Then, as the ship lost way, the beating slowed down to a juddering scrape. "*Get that sail down!*" Trygkar ordered, and then, as the spar slithered down the mast, he breathed deeply again. "That's it, Mastersmith!" he said. "You're home." Elof bent over the oar, and closed his eyes.

There were stone steps set at intervals in the outer face of the wall, and to one of these they made fast, bow and stern. But even before the knots were tied Elof was at the gunwales, and Roc helping him over. He hung on the steps a moment and looked back; out to sea the *Saldenborg* was coming about. By main force he hauled

himself up the steps, and collapsed over the top onto
the flinty top of the wall. He felt it drum beneath him,
and looked up; the low sun dazzled him, but he saw a
column of men come thundering down the narrow crest
of the wall, a knot of horsemen at their head. He hauled
himself up on his knees, waved and shouted, and to his
infinite relief the horsemen reined in, the foremost so
swiftly that his huge white mount reared in the narrow
way, its hooves thrashing the air over Elof's head. He
looked up, shading his eyes; and the world seemed to
stand still in a moment of infinite silence.

"*By the High Gate!*" He still knew that clear voice
at once. "*It's Elof!*" The tone of utter amazement was
unmistakable. "*And Roc!*"

Elof felt a sudden inane, breathless laughter
bubble up within him. "All hail – m-my lord!" he
managed to say, and lifted his hand in a limp parody of a
formal salute. Then Roc was beside him, helping him up
onto his crutches, and he was able to grin up into
Kermorvan's face, slack with astonishment as he had
seldom seen it. But as he took in Elof's condition it set
instantly in shock, and his grey eyes grew bleak and
hard. "Who has done this to you?" he demanded, and
swung down from his saddle to seize Elof's hand in his
own iron grip. "*Who has done this?*" he repeated, and
glared at the black prow beneath.

Elof shook his, and forced himself to find words.
"No! These are friends, none better, and I ask you to
welcome them; they are men of Kerys – aye, Kerys," he
repeated, seeing shock flicker across Kermorvan's face.
"As to who did this, don't concern yourself; that score is
settled forever."

Kermorvan raised an eyebrow, then nodded. "And
Kara?" he asked softly.

Elof shook his head. Kermorvan looked down.
"Truly I am sorry . . ."

"And Ils?" Elof asked hastily, but he had hardly got
the words out when the gaggle of men around them
burst apart as a short figure bounded through, and
slammed into Elof with a force that would have knocked
him over into the harbour had the arms embracing him

been less strong. He swayed, breathless, all too aware of the body pressed against him, sturdy and square and thoroughly female, of the pert face laughing up at him though it was streaming with tears.

"The lady," said Kermorvan carefully, "appears to be very well."

"Elof!" she gasped. "They were yelling about reivers ... so I thought I'd not leave all the fun to *him* — but you ... what ... where —"

Elof rumpled her curls affectionately, unable to find the right words. "As fair as ever!" he said lightly, though his own eyes prickled. "You haven't changed by a hair. As if it's only been a few months — which I guess it has, in your terms ..."

"It hasn't seemed so!" Ils whispered. "We thought you were *dead* ... you imbecile, idiot, you ... you *human!*"

"You note, of course," remarked Kermorvan in an elaborate aside to Roc, "that no such compliments came to us ..."

Roc, equally straight-faced, spread his hands helplessly. "Nor *that* sort of greeting my way, my lord. Seems we're just hangers-on ..."

"Bystanders," amplified Kermorvan. "Forgotten men ..."

Ils tore loose and whirled round on Roc with her clenched fist darting at his middle. "I'll give you greeting, you tub of lard!" she snapped, then flung her arms around his neck and kissed him with a force that lifted his bulky frame from the ground, leaving him scarlet-faced and staggering. Kermorvan's reserve shattered; he gave one of his rare shouts of laughter, and spread his arms wide to embrace them all. "Peace, you madmen all! By the sign of the sun, it's good beyond measure to have you both back!"

Then he pulled free, gesturing up at the town. "I must countermand the alert!" he said. "Before too much panic spreads!"

Trygkar, who had scrambled up onto the wall, coughed. "And the warship, my lord? May we bring our prize in before the waves break her?"

"And without some fool unleashing a volley!" nodded Kermorvan. "Yes, you may!" He turned to one of the horsemen. "See they are signalled at once, Athayn, and the guards stood down!" The young aide saluted and cantered away. Trygkar bowed, and was about to return to the ship when Kermorvan laid a hand on his arm. "You are of Kerys? A shipmaster, by the cut of you, who has helped my friends voyage back across this vast ocean?"

Trygkar bowed again. "My lads and I; Trygkar at your service, shipmaster as you guessed. My privilege, my lord. And some amends for the hard welcome my land gave them."

Kermorvan shook his head, stern-faced. "That should not fall to such as you, sir! Our debt to you remains."

Elof grinned. "They might be interested in settling here."

"If you've a need of more seamen, my lord. Though I've never seen the like of these great ships of yours ..."

Kermorvan pursed his lips judiciously. "And there was I wondering how I might persuade you! I always need more ship-wise men, and those who have crossed an ocean ... But for now, go bring in your ship to the quayside there, and then toil no more; you and yours will be our honoured guests. There is much to be told, I see."

"And much to be done!" answered Elof. "Kerys is in peril, and its peril may be ours also, and that of all the world! For if what I suspect is true, Louhi is on the verge of victory, of tipping the balance decisively in favour of the Ice. I think I know how she means to achieve it. We must take counsel at once!"

Kermorvan nodded. "So be it! My lady, you have your mount? We'll ride up to the palace. A more fitting place for your welcome than out here, at any rate. Dismount, you two, and let us have your horses! Then arrange carriage for the crew when they reach the quay –"

As Kermorvan turned aside to give his orders Trygkar plucked Elof by the sleeve. "So that's your king!

Younger than I'd bargained for, but a fine man regardless! There's one to follow, if any! And this land of yours looks worthy of him, aye, and yourselves as well! You've kept your pledge, Mastersmith!"

They invited the old shipmaster to join their council, but he declined, much amused, saying it was late in life for him to start meddling in princely matters. So they left him with their thanks to bring in the black ship, and mounted up to return to the palace. "Help the Mastersmith up, there!" Kermorvan commanded. "You can ride pillion with me, or Roc if you prefer –"

"Neither, by your leave!" growled Elof, hating the indignity of bumping through town at someone's saddleback. "Just get me into the saddle – and bind my feet loosely into the stirrups, so ..."

He swayed in the saddle; he had not ridden for too many years, and his legs had grown weak. It gave him some sense of freedom, but nothing compared to flying. He looked up at the tower atop the promontory, and hungered for his wings, longing to soar about it as he had with Kara long ago, to take in all this new city from above, laid out like a living traject. Roc cocked an eye at him. "Sure you won't come a cropper?"

"I'm all right! I may have to sit like a sack of meal, but I can still clasp with my knees, so; I'll manage. But Trygkar, will you see my wings safely unloaded and sent after me? Many thanks!"

"Wings?" inquired Kermorvan with innocent interest, then held up a hand. "No, not a word! I can see I will have to hear all this from the beginning to make sense of it. So to the palace, without delay!" The little cavalcade trotted off down the sea wall towards the city; Elof winced as he saw crowds flocking along the wider end of the wall. It might have been the alarum that brought them out, but they were evidently staying to cheer. Many came rushing out to hurl flowers or clasp hands with the returning seafarers, and Elof was surprised to hear the accents of Kerbryhaine thoroughly blended with those of the east, and see so many brown-skinned folk of Nordeney in harmony with both; to them he was an especial hero, and he spoke to them in their own dialect. Strangest of all, though, was to see duergar among the ranks of men. "They make us welcome here!" said Ils, slipping her plump hand into Elof's. "Even the folk of Kerbryhaine are learning that we are not vermin, working with us to rebuild."

"The towers?"

Ils nodded. "When the west was abandoned at last, the syndics did not wish to leave the Ekwesh such a strong place; they were going to throw down wall and tower, but we offered to bring the towers east and rebuild them. It was the long lad's idea, and a good one; that more than anything made us friends. It took two years with the fleet, and they're not yet finished, but it was time well spent. We took charge of much of the other construction, also, and taught their masons a thing or two; their smiths, also. But we have never found any to match you, Elof! To have you back —" She squeezed his hand, hard....

He looked down into her dark eyes. "To be back, my lady! It seems more than I deserve. But my heart tells me I must not stay, not now."

She sat silent for a moment. "Is it only your quest that draws you?" she asked at last. "Or is there other reason?"

"There is; and you shall all hear it. You, especially, Ils; for it concerns matters in which the duergar are wise."

"I will hear," she said. "And yet I could find it in me to deny all, if it would persuade you to stay."

Then, as they neared the end of the wall, Roc let out a startled oath and pointed. Ahead lay Plen Perthau, the Landfall Square, where the tall statues of the Watchers stood; but it had changed. On its farther side, where a block of rather dilapidated storehouses had stood, there was now a park of many young trees; but it was not that alone which startled them. For out of the trees, tall and grim, rose what was unmistakably the Tower of Vayde, that had stood in Kerbryhaine for well-nigh a thousand years. And at its foot, along the seaward edge of the park, stood two more statues, in line with the Watchers and of no less stature, upon a common plinth;

the faces were living likenesses of Roc and Elof. Across the base were carved the words *Mhar Dasunyans*. *"In the hope of return!"* said Elof, deeply moved, in the northern tongue, and then he saw that there was a third place on the dais, standing empty.

"That one is not yet finished," said Ils tonelessly. "Not even my folk can easily capture so fair a likeness in stone." Elof did not reply; nor would he look at her as they rode on towards the palace.

"I scarcely know what to make of it!" said Kermorvan, when after some hours all was told to his satisfaction. He stretched out a long hand, and poured more wine for them all. "Save that I grieve for the sorrows of that ancient land; and for yours no less, Elof. But I would fear you, if you were not my friend."

Elof made no answer. They sat in Kermorvan's own apartments, at the summit of the palace, overlooking the harbour far below. The king held up his own goblet to the falling sun, watching the dark wine turn the faceted glass to a fire-ruby. "Now, I have heard what you have heard, seen with your eyes, yet I still do not perceive this plan of Louhi's. I find only dark suspicions. Why so?"

Elof sought to rise, and sank back angrily; he had a great need to pace the room. He felt pent with energy, like one of his crystals, with no way to release it. "I still have doubts myself. They made me slow to voice my thoughts, and yet –" He wrung his fingers tightly. "Yet I am sure. The swelling of the earthfires ..."

"I noted that!" said Kermorvan. "What caused it, think you?"

"The Ice!" Elof answered curtly.

Kermorvan shrugged. "Very likely! But how? Louhi's power is the reverse of heat, as you yourself ..."

The table quivered as the flat of Elof's hand cracked down, and the glasses rang. "Not Louhi! The Ice! That vast bulk of frozen water spread across the land! Have you ever thought what it must be doing to it?"

"Grinding it down ..." began Roc, but Elof overtook him.

"And then? Lying on its new base, still carrying all the weight it's ground away, and all its own great weight of frozen water as well – what must it be doing to the land beneath? Crushing it down, that's what –"

Kermorvan snapped his fingers. "And forcing the earthfires up ..."

"Squeezing them out like juice from a fruit!" Roc chipped in. "Yes, that'd be it! They'd come boiling up, as the furnace-fires did!"

"And the Vale of Kerys is rich in the fires, as Roc found out; they run in a great line right across it, almost straight in places – a seam in the earth itself. And now every single breach on that seam is cracking, every fire-mountain erupting skyward!"

"Aye, but what's the Ice to do with such fires? Surely they'd hinder more than help?"

"No! Remember what we guessed – and what Louhi herself boasted to me! The Ice seeks to chill the world, by mirroring back a great part of the sunlight that falls upon it; but it cannot chill it enough to allow the Ice to spread without check – not yet. In free lands, warmed by the sun, the seasons hold the balance; the winters at their worst are neither cold enough nor long enough to advance the Ice further than the summers can melt back. And the sun is a sign of hope, warming the hearts and minds of men, that Louhi fears almost as much! But if she could find a way to block off that sunlight –"

"The clouds of ash!" said Kermorvan. "But – surely they only rise briefly, and then fall?"

"Not the finest ash! It was all around me in the upper airs, and higher still, as high as I could see; at that height it might hang there for days –"

"Years!" said Ils unexpectedly. "My people know of this; the airs owe their colour to the dust they bear, and the sunsets are known to grow more colourful after truly great eruptions. The effect may last years –" She sat up suddenly. "And many have thought this may affect the climes, as well! By filtering the sunlight, blocking its richness a little. But no more than a little, a few wet summers, a trifling time! That could not aid the Ice very much!"

Elof shook his head grimly. "One eruption, no. But

along the length of Kerys I passed by something like twenty! Not counting," he grimaced, "one more I unleashed myself. And these eruptions are continuous, not dying, but growing, spreading, laying waste the land about. All that in one small region – small, compared with the rest of the world, anyway. The last few winters have been terrible, long and cold; pure chance, perhaps. But every year the ice-islands have been coming further south – till now they are lodging in the very inflow of the Great River ..."

Kermorvan stared into his wine a moment, then downed it in one swift draught. "I understand now," he said softly. "I believe you are right. Though it is hard to think on such a scale – but not so for the Ice, no doubt ... But if it is so gradual, what makes you think the balance will be tipped so soon?"

"For several reasons! First, because Louhi told me the Ice need only advance a little further; second, because the upsurge of the earthfires has been so sudden and violent only in this last year; and thirdly – though I am less sure of this – because Louhi was relaxing her war against Kerys. Because she was ready to conclude a show of peace – with me as the price!"

Kermorvan tapped his fingers on the table. "Let me see if I follow that. It cannot have been only out of revenge; she must have feared you could thwart her, somehow ... But how, by the High Gate?" Then he slammed down his fist. "That's how! Thanks to you this man Nithaid had driven back her armies, defied the worst she could do. Another season, and he might have assailed her in the Gate itself – and that she could not risk! Because she must have that place to be sure of freezing the Great River!"

Elof sat back with a sigh. "The Gate! That was the missing piece of the pattern! That was what I did not understand! And it comforts me; for as you say, she must have had the next season in mind, just as Tapiau warned! I feared she might strike sooner!"

Ils shook her head. "Unlikely! She will need time to build up a great enough cloud; there will be no mistaking it then! It will hang like a pall over the land. Nor would she waste its power striking in summer, when its effect is least; most likely she will wait till the end of winter, and then build it up gradually to prevent a thaw."

"So we've got some time?" Roc demanded. "Fine; but how can we use it, that's the question! How thwart a power that turns earth and air against us? Elof, you said you'd some idea ..."

"A weapon – it might help. Though mere men cannot assail the whole mass of the Ice ..."

"But the Gate?" demanded Kermorvan. "The Gate is her weak point here! What men built, men may assail!" He rose abruptly, and strode to the window, surveying the city that was his life's achievement. "Less than Kerys or Morvan we may be; but where they are sundered, we are united! Where they have faltered or fallen, we stand free! We have a fleet, great enough to bear the strongest force we can raise across the Seas of the Sunrise. And we have you, Mastersmith of the Skilled Hand, and your weapons; they may give our spear-shaft its striking head. That spear we shall cast into the balance of the world. Then let us see which way it turns!"

CHAPTER TEN

The Shieldwall Breaks

THE *WIND BLOWS FAIR*
Across the wide sea –
My blackhaired girl
It takes from me!
Sorrow, you winds above,
Sigh for me and my love!
You Western girl,
Ah, you blackhaired girl,
You wild lover of mine ...

The voice came echoing eerily down through the gloom from the masthead above, chanting in time to the slow splash of the sweeps. Whichever young sailor it was had a fine voice, but it ground upon Elof's nerves like the wail of a pent-up dog. He shifted uncomfortably where he sat, hunched up against the high stern-post, but only made himself more uncomfortable. His life had left his body a mass of scars, and in this damp weather it seemed that every single separate one of them grew taut and ached. The scars around the silver rings had even begun to bleed a little. But Kermorvan was not the kind of man to countenance silencing the singer for so petty a reason – nor, he had to face it, was he himself. Besides, it helped keep the ships together. He pulled his cowl over his head and rested his head upon his knees; but because he had to support them with his arms, it was hardly restful. Just as he gave up and resolved to enjoy the song, it broke off abruptly and became a shout.

"Dawn ho!"

The order was given to dim the lanthorns, and looking where he knew the east must be Elof became aware of a trace of light, pallid and sourceless, spreading like thin milk. "Not before time!" said Kermorvan, watching his officers scurrying about, seeking the sun with their navigation devices. "Between playing ducks and drakes with ice-islands and striving to keep the fleet together, we're losing track of where we are!"

"Somewhere close!" said Elof. "I feel it! In my bones, in my blood I feel it!"

"A shame we cannot ask them for our heading!" remarked the king wryly, shifting his fur cloak more firmly around him. "All mine can sense is this numbing clammy chill! The very flesh will not shut it out. When I awoke this morning my cabin was full of it, my mail-shirt a mass of rime where it hung. And this is spring!"

"No!" said Ils grimly, from somewhere beside him. "This is still winter, a long winter, a Winter of the World. Its cold fingers reach out even across the oceans now; how fares the land, I wonder?"

"*Dawn ho!*" sang the lookout once again. "*And the mists are clearing! Wind arising, mists lifting!*"

"What wind?" called Kermorvan through his cupped hands. There was no reply for a moment. Elof bit his lip; most probably it would be from the north, as usual, and bring down more ice among the fleet. It was a miracle they had lost no more than two ships so far, and no lives; a miracle, and Kermorvan's keen planning and brilliant seamanship.

"*South wind! South and fair!*" The mastheader's whoop of joy, echoed from the deck, flowed naturally into song once more.

My sweetheart, pray the southern winds
To speed me to you once more –
Ah, smiling wind, blow stronger still,
My girl lies lone ashore . . .

But then all voices died away, for around them the fog seemed to heave and shrug like some vast indolent beast, before rolling the deck. Behind it trailed a mass of serpentine streamers like ghostly banners, shredded and pale, through which they saw faint shapes gradually appear to left and right of them, their fellow ships like rime-encrusted skeletons under their bare masts. But ahead of them, at the margins of sight, it was as if the mists grew solid, drew aside only to settle and condense on the rim of the world, becoming, as it seemed, a great jagged reef of whiteness rising straight out of the waters. High against a sky of sullen lead it towered, and glittered bright and cold.

"*Land ho!*" sang the watcher. "*Land* ..." But then his voice faltered; in face of that eerie mass he could not be sure.

"What is this?" exclaimed Kermorvan in amazement. "Whole mountains of ice rising from the very sea itself? The glaciers cannot have come this far south already!"

"No!" said Elof, rising awkwardly and shading his eyes with a hand. "Nearest us, yes, those are ice-islands, fused almost into a ridge. But for all the snow that shrouds them, those are true hills behind! You look upon the eastern shores of the ocean, my lord; and if I mistake not, the coastlands of Kerys itself. The end of our voyage is within sight!"

"And the beginning of something more terrible, I doubt not!" muttered Kermorvan. "Battle, war, slaughter, while the foes of life look on and laugh!" But then his grim features softened with wonder, and he seized Elof's arm. "Kerys!" he repeated. "The shores of Kerys ..." His blue-grey eyes glittered like the sea beneath. "It is much to have come so far, to have looked upon them ..." He sighed, and then his mouth tightened again. "However, we must reach them. And we cannot pass that ice-wall. See how it curves away there, to either side! Elof, could this be the Bay of the Gate ahead? And that be the wall you passed through in your escape, the grounded ice-islands?"

"Yes!" breathed Elof. "Yes, it could! So if we follow it north or south, we will come to land!"

"South, if you please!" smiled Kermorvan grimly. "Better we do not sail straight into the arms of the Ice at once, but try to reach whatever endures of Kerys first. Always assuming," he added, "that we're allowed to reach the shore unmolested ..."

The cry from the masthead cut like an arrow through his words, all yearning and all joy drained from the young voice, yielding place to urgency and alarm. "*A sail! Sail to landward! Two – six – no, many sails! Black sails! A host of them! Running cross-wind towards us – a bloody host!*"

"As I expected," said Kermorvan calmly, amid all the frantic flurry on the deck around him. "After the barriers, the picket forces; after the mist, the guard-ships. The lady Tauounehtar sets her sieges entirely in accordance with the old texts! She has not forgotten to provide against relief; the strange theft of a ship may have made her more alert. In which case she may also have some swift-moving reserves ready to reinforce the guards; for that too is laid down in the best authorities."

Elof grinned, though he felt a sudden taut empti-ness behind his belt. "And what do they recommend to the relievers?"

"Swiftness, and little else. Save to avoid battle, where possible, for delay can only bring down greater forces upon you. But it is too late for that now, I guess. You there, Oste! My armour! And rouse that slugabed Roc while you're about it!"

Roc was on deck and clad in his mail before the guard-ships came clearly into sight, though he grumbled about being roused. "And all for a mere thirty reiver ships! I thought this fleet could pick its teeth with such numbers! There's not one of them the size of our dromunds or the *Korentyn*, is there?"

Kermorvan frowned. "No; but they are all fair-sized ships, and heavily manned, by the look of them. They can afford to be, not carrying supplies. They'll fight the bloodiest delaying action they can, to win their kinsmen time either to bar us from landing, or fall on us while we are in the midst of it. I have ordered the dromunds forward; our best hope is to ram as many as possible, and clear a passage through."

Elof watched the black specks swell gradually against the forbidding walls of ice, finding it strange to think that only a year past he had sailed these waters beneath such a sail himself. They were moving out now into lines of battle, in staggered rows and spaced well

apart to make them hard to ram, a shield of ships across
the hidden land beyond. In just the same way Kermorvan's heaviest ships, the great man-carriers, were gliding
up between the sleek warships in the van of the fleet,
every inch of sail hoisted, every oar straining, to form a
swift-moving spearhead shape. Spear would strike
against shield – he shuddered at the thought; the collision would be bloody, costly, and he had had enough of
such cost. The rams he himself had shaped hissed
through the water as if it were still their quenching-
trough, soaking in hides and offal to harden the steel;
would they grow any harder in the blood of men? He
peered at the ships ahead, stark and clear in the pale
light, striving to find some detail that would stop him
thinking of them as faceless menaces. His hatred of the
Ekwesh, conceived in his first harsh captivity, had never
left him; but as he peered at the ships ahead, stark and
clear in the pale light, he could not forget that they
were still crewed by men. It would be their blood too.

Suddenly he stiffened, shaded his eyes and strained
to see. "What is it?" demanded Kermorvan, who even
among the pressures of command missed nothing.
"D'you see something, man?"

Elof rounded on him. "My lord, will you have the
braziers made ready at once? And give the order for my
wings –"

It was no answer, but Kermorvan passed on the
curt orders before he questioned Elof again, and that
only with a sardonic eyebrow. Elof swallowed. "I can see
– but I do not know if you can ..."

The tall man stared a moment, his lips moving, and
then gave vent to a very unkingly whistle. "Is that what
you told me of? Louhi's swift reserves?"

"It may well be! And if it is – then, as we agreed, it
falls to me to meet it ..."

"Alone?" cried Ils. "That was never the plan! Use
the new weapon!"

Roc echoed her, but Elof shook his head. "You
know better than that, whatever you say! Once seen, it
can be countered. We keep it for the last! Now help me
arm!"

The braziers had been lit for the fog, and in the excitement not yet extinguished; they were ready before Elof was. The steel lids clanged back, sending up a shower of little sparks. Kermorvan and his officers jumped and looked blackly, for no mariner likes the least spark in the little world of timber and tar and tow around him; a ship is a world too easily ended. But the dark wings folded about them, and that embrace no spark escaped. The least cinder that touched the deck was already dull and dead. One of the officers touched a spent brazier and gave a cry of surprise. "The very metal is cold!"

Elof smiled. "A man is no light weight to lift! Even with all that fire I cannot stay aloft long; I must await the last moment!"

"It will not be long delayed!" said Kermorvan grimly, and with a gesture sent his archers swarming up the shrouds to the masthead. "And we are almost within shot of the guard-ships now. *See!*" For the others it came too fast; but he had never quite taken his eyes off the enemy. A giant's hand seemed to slap the hull, then something passed between sail and deck, making all in its path duck, and hissed over into the sea. The *Korentyn's* bow catapults sang, but on the dromund next to them an invisible scythe slashed along the crowded deck, and cries arose. Kermorvan, tight-lipped, was about to order the rowers to a last burst of speed, when Elof caught his arm.

"Wait!" he said. "If I fail –"

"If I wait I risk more lives!" grated the king. "Be swift, my friend, or do not venture it at all!" There was a cry over their heads; a figure folded and dropped from the masthead, bounced off the the mainyard and dropped all asprawl to the deck. Elof swallowed, hoping it was not the singer, and flung his arms high above his head. With a rush and sweep his wings unfolded across the sterncastle, his maimed legs buckled and he fell forward on their great beat. Over the deck he swooped, and up, half wild with relief and exhilaration, like a man who has lain months abed able to walk again, to run free and unfettered.

He climbed high to gain speed, and saw beneath him the massed masts of the fleet of Morvanhal, swaying like a floating forest out of the dispersing mists. It seemed to cover the sea, more than three hundred ships strong, bearing well-nigh ten thousand men. Yet against the fifty thousand or more that Kerys might field after centuries of war, or the unknown throngs of the Ekwesh and the unhuman servants of the Ice, that number would be all too few. It might dwarf that dark phalanx ahead, a mere thirty ships, yet against the threat that approached it seemed nothing. Seeking an updraft, he swooped over the Ekwesh ships, and caught his breath as the white emblems on bow and flank became clear to him. They were all the same, following the patterns that iron custom had laid down – an upraised head, arrogant and crested, tongue erect to scream with laughter or contempt, its long beak gaping to grasp at the sun-disc behind it. That changed everything. There was little time to waste, but he must risk it; he plunged straight towards the leading ship. He glimpsed an Ekwesh cata-pult dart shoot wide and targetless, skimming the harm-less waves; they had seen him, all right. Now let them hear!

The leader was a dark hull longer than the rest, and it was careful to keep squarely in the path of the *Prince Korentyn's* looming bow; they valued bravery, this folk, if little else. Above the leader's maindeck he pulled up sharply and came riding down the southwind, wings thrashing like a great black crow as the ploughman passes. A hissing fountain of bolts and arrows rose up at him, but he hardly minded; he was hard to hit, and each was one less at the fleet. Swiftly he cupped hands to mouth and cried out, in what he knew of the Ekwesh speech.

"Clan of the Raven! Warriors of the Kokuen! Why bow you to shamans, why grovel to the Ice and she who rules it? Why do you counter the will of him you most revere?"

No arrow was loosed. But among the uplifted faces, well-nigh as dark as their leathern armour, there was a flurry of movement; out onto the shaman's platform sprang a burly warrior, his white hair streaming in the downdraft. His cloak of marten furs billowed out amid a jangle of ornaments as he flung up an arm. Instinctively Elof flinched, but only words were hurled.

"*Again you, steel-shaman! Twice a handcount of years, and to the serpent's tongue you stole you add the Raven's wing! But are you truly his voice, then let him shield you now! Or look to yourself, shaman! For behold – Her hunter comes!*"

It might have been thunder that came shivering down the airs, but Elof knew that it was not. Gorthawer leaned into his hand, he flexed his shoulders and saw the black sail beaten aback against the mast by the gust that hurled him upward. Like a startled horse the black ship reared and plunged, then it shrank away beneath him. With a chill in his heart he rose to meet the winged spear that came plunging down through the clouds.

Immediately he had seen that speeding speck he had guessed the moment he and Kermorvan had long debated was here. He had hoped it would be later, over land, with the bright sun at his back, the force of an army beneath him, and, hopefully, his latest and most powerful weapon; now he was armed only with what he bore, and not for the first time he mourned the loss of helm and hammer. But late or soon, come it would, he had known that; as well, perhaps that he face it now.

To reach the Ekwesh he had sacrificed height and speed; it was nearly the end of him. Those vast yellow eyes must have seen him even as he rose, so much greater than any seabird, and known him for an enemy and a challenge; that swoop was aimed not at the fleet but at himself. Barely in time he raised his left hand, open in defiance; then the sky vanished around him, and suddenly he was back in his furnace, blinded and choking amid roaring flame. It was only agonised reflex that clenched his fists and dropped him just as suddenly into clear air once again, or as clear as it could be with a cloud of stinking oily vapour about him. He knew then what had happened, and twisting about he saw the brute circling, coming about to make another pass. But for a moment he had the height, and as the broad back swept below him he swooped in his turn, and flung out his fist. Ahead of him, the mistcloud exploded about the muzzle of the great dragon as the heat the gauntlet had drained from it lanced back. Caught in the fireball, the long head was flung back and the vast body, as long as any dromund, curled and ducked away, wings folded, dropping towards the dark waters beneath.

Elof cursed, and circled for height once more; he had hoped to kindle the beast's fire within its own throat, as he had served another once before. But this was an older, vaster creature, and undoubtedly wilier; it had shielded eye and muzzle and let the flame wash harmlessly over its scales, then sought to tempt him down by shamming defeat. Its wings unfolded suddenly, and the fall became a wide, sweeping glide well clear of the sea, away towards the advancing fleet. Elof cursed again and ducked after it, as it knew he would have to. It was man-cunning, this creature, if not more; he had fallen into the snare of thinking it a beast, and now it was leading the fight. Abruptly that serpentine body bent back on itself and came lancing back at him as fast as it had fled a heartbeat since. The jaws opened, and in near panic he thrust out his gauntlet to turn the flame –

There was no flame. The gigantic jaws, long as a small boat and lined with teeth longer than his hands, twisted and snapped at him with a vicious speed he could not avoid. Barely in time he swung his left arm clear and in the same movement hewed hard with Gorthawer. Dark blood leapt into the air, the jaws clashed shut and twisted away. A bellow of pain and rage shivered the air around Elof, and the light was blotted out. In horror he saw vast leathery wing, dwarfing his own puny span, come sweeping down upon him like a toppling wall; in desperation he struck again, a slashing blow taking all his strength from head to foot, a blow so hard that it spun him around in the air. A glancing impact stunned him, nearly tearing the blade from his hand, a spray of hot blood scorched his skin, a waft of foulness choked him and another cry rang through his skull, no bellow but a tearing shriek of pain and fury whose sheer force struck him as hard as any blow and numbed his mind anew. "They'll hear that leagues hence!" was his only clear thought as he tumbled down the airs. "Louhi'll know her pet's been stung –"

Then, once more at the margins of disaster, he half unconsciously spread his arms, and felt the wings bite the air above him and halt his fall. As the dragon had, he glided, letting the wind-rush clear the pain in his head, and sought frantically about him for his antagonist; he had been helpless for minutes now, why had the brute not finished him? Then, looking up, he saw the dragon plunge overhead, and realised what he had done. That giant wing was not, like his own, modelled after a bird's; it was a membrane of leathery skin stretched over bone, without feathers to part around an obstacle. His desperate slash had cut a way right through the membrane near the root, out to the trailing edge, so that only a loose shred had slapped at him; and with every wing-beat that tear was spreading. He could guess at the pain of it, and the horror of losing control out over the dark ocean; perhaps now the thing would turn back for the land ...

He had reckoned without the power of its wrath. The malign yellow eye fixed on him, and madness glazed it. Unable to fly freely, its mind clouded by anguish and fear, the great dragon opened its jaws and vomited a stream of flame upon its tormentor. Elof had just time to thrust up the gauntlet; but he might as well have sought to dam a river with it. The fire-blast streamed about him and could not be extinguished, for that which the gauntlet cooled was lit anew. It was shielding his face and body a little, no more, and it was not enough. Desperate once more, Elof flung his wings wide, his head back, and clenched his fist tight. At once the flame rushed in upon him. But it caught him full on his chest, as he had intended, and fell upon the gems of his corselet. These, too, could not stop such a rush of fire; but they did not need to. They drank deep of it before it touched Elof's flesh, and gave his wings such a surge of strength as they had never before received save from the furnace that saw their birth. The force of their stroke hurled Elof free of the flame; but it did more. It lashed the fire-stream back upon the dragon, and from below, beneath the edges of its shield-strong scales.

Startled, the dragon plunged aside, or the wash of flame might have taken it full in the jaws; but its torn wing hampered it, and the fire struck it full on its right side, and spattered across its unprotected wing. The dragon shrieked, a high thin agonized note so loud it whipped the ears like a white-hot wire, as if to transmit the pain. Elof's head rang, his eyes stung, but as he climbed free he saw the dragon drop away across the sky, trailing a great plume of smoke. The wind stank of scorched flesh. Its left wing shredded, its right perforated in many places and still ablaze, the creature was making a desperate lunge to reach the safety of the land and the cool snow-clad hills. What became of it Elof never saw; but that it came to land is recorded, for its fall was seen and the place of it noted, where a great fire sprang up among the snow. No doubt it was worse injured then, yet not slain; for a crawling trail led from that spot far off into the hills of the Wild Lands, and no man cared to follow further. What became of the dragon after that time is less certain, but that it lived on, maimed yet formidable, is beyond doubt; for even when its kind had withered in the changes of the world, it remained a legend of terror among the mountains of the ancient north long after the passing of these events, and the closing of their chronicles.

But Elof, riding a great surge of joy and relief, wheeled back on wings that throbbed with strength and hurled himself down upon the masts of the black flotilla beneath. And where the shadow of those wings passed, many a strong warrior flung himself face down upon the deck. He rejoiced at that, though there was no vainglory in him; he knew how close he had pressed his luck. But now at least he could seek to save lives, rather than spill them, and for that the Ekwesh had to be impressed. He glanced quickly behind him, and saw to his relief that Morvanhal's stained sails had slackened their onrush, although they still advanced; he had the few minutes he needed. Again he held the air above the bows of the chieftain's ship, and again he cried out to them.

"*Is it well, then, Sons of the Raven? Look to your-self, you bade me; and that I have done! Now I bid you do as much! Ask this of yourselves! Will you follow her still who would have you feast upon the flesh of men? Who sets you apart on the land, to walk the wastes and win no honour in war? Who sets you apart at sea, where you will strike the hardest against fellow follow-ers of the Raven? Where your deeds will be drowned in the sea's cold silence and forgotten? Who has bidden you throw your lives away, not for your own good reasons but for hers?*" Furiously he gestured at the oncoming fleet, at the inexorable glitter of the rams. "*Then go! Go follow home her hunter, whom you bade me fear! Begone, ere she whips you in! Like curs to your kennels! Leave the Raven banner to those who work his will!*"

From the black ships came no word or sign; but neither was any weapon loosed or hand raised against Elof, though the very air felt taut as a bowstring. He could see the chieftain, standing by the helm, glancing slowly from Elof back to the white-clad hills behind, and the hidden presence of the Gate. Among these impassive folk that probably betrayed a panic of indecision, but it was scarcely enough. It was one thing to claim the will of Raven, another to convince them. He had hoped to overawe them utterly; but at their best they were a fell folk, grim and dour, and the long service of the Ice had hardened them to sights awesome and terrible. What else was left him, if even defeating the dragon had not served? He looked up despairingly to where the smoke of the battle still hung in the middle airs, and thought for one awful moment that others had been sent out after him. But he saw at once that it was not so, and he laughed aloud for wonder. From out of the plume of smoke, as it spread and straggled upon the south wind, dropped the two specks that he had seen, circling, spiralling downward to settle in a flurry of wings as dark as his own upon either end of the black ship's mainyard. They snapped their high curved bills and cocked bright eyes down at the staring faces below; but then they peered back, cackling like malign old men over hunched shoulders, and stared straight at him.

"*Thinking!*" croaked the first.

"*Remembering!*" cackled the other, exactly as they had so many years since. He shivered with apprehension, and the effort to understand.

"*Live!*"

"*Thrive!*"

"*Blood!*"

"*Brood!*"

Then "*Stay! Pass! Weigh!*" over and over, very fast, batting the words between each other like a game, till one suddenly added "*Choose!*"

"*Speak!*" spat the other, and rattled its black blade of a beak.

Elof caught his breath; then he threw back his head and laughed again as all his exaltation flowed back to him, and shouted down to the silent ship below.

"*Behold, I ride upon black wings, over land and sea he has sped me to speak words of fire to you, words of sun's fire that shall shine through the pale Ice and melt it to a mist! I am his emissary!*" He heard his words come rolling back like thunder from against the distant barriers of the Ice. "*Well? Will you hear what he wills?*" Not a boy stirred on the decks below; even the sea seemed hushed.

"*You shall not fight! For the lives Louhi commanded you to cast away are not hers to rule – nor his – but yours alone! You need not surrender, nor bow the knee, nor in any way lessen your honour and your pride! But in the name of your mighty forefathers of old and their allegiance, older than the Ice itself, he asks you to stand aside, to let pass the fleet before you! For they also are a part of the Raven's brood, sprung like you from the common blood of the fathers of men, that first he sheltered beneath his wing! Weigh well; choose freely! That is the Raven's word!*"

Even as he finished, the black birds squawked and shrilled, and rising on their cruel talons they shook their wide wings. The chieftain looked up at them, and beyond to meet Elof's own intense gaze. For a moment they stared at one another, and at the black birds between them; then the chief made a single curt gesture, spoke a short word, and the sharp-edged sweeps splashed into the water, the steersman bore down on his oar. In a swift flurry of wings the two huge ravens flung themselves aloft, almost colliding with Elof and whirling him aside; when he collected himself, he saw that the dark ships were moving forward no longer, but turning away, aside. Numb with excitement, Elof came swooping down past the masthead of the *Prince Korentyn* as it passed beneath him, and all but collapsed upon the deck.

The shield split before the spearhead. If signals were exchanged, no man saw any, nor heard any hail; but the line of black ships parted, and peeled back on either side to give the great warship passage. In two long lines they formed up like sullen guards, and rode there, sails furled, silently watching the fleet pass. But as the last ship went by they hoisted sail once more, and the two ranks silently closed in behind it and followed the fleet to land.

On board the *Korentyn* confusion had reigned. Elof was bombarded with loud praise of his valour and wild enquiry as to what the savages meant, often in the same voices at the same time, till Kermorvan's dry voice cut through the hubbub and extracted an account of what had passed. "So Raven takes an interest!" mused Kermorvan, tapping the gold-damasked Raven and sun emblem on his breastplate. "He seems to think you did the right thing. And I agree. But I crave to know just what those ships intend now!"

Later that day he found out. As the day declined they sighted the southern hills, still green and free of snow, and at their feet many small bays without any ice, that might make good anchorages. Kermorvan had the best of them swiftly sounded, then ordered the fleet in. He would waste no time, for, as he told Elof, Louhi's minions were probably herding a huge army of Ekwesh southward across the snow that very minute, or preparing to land one from the sea. But the scouts he sent out, among them Elof aloft, reported both sea and land empty within their sight, and he gave the orders to disembark.

It was a disciplined force that landed, but confusion and problems were inevitable. The land was cool and windswept under that grim and sunless sky, a country of barren cliffs and grassland only a little less harsh than the north had been; by the sea tough grass and thorny gorse were all that grew, save for the odd stunted tree. Here and there in sheltered vales and hollows some plants of warmer climes struggled on, but to no great effect. There was little to replenish their supplies, and no sign of men; but there was fresh water in plenty, and that they needed most. Their greatest concerns, as Kermorvan detailed them to the council of war he held on the *Korentyn's* deck, were first, to establish and fortify their place of landing, and second, to seek afield for folk of Kerys and establish a link with them before Louhi's forces could cut across the land between.

The matter of defences Kermorvan set to Ils and the small group of young duergar she had brought, and even before the main body of the force was ashore they were busy throwing up ditch and earthwork, complaining bitterly of the poor sandstone of the cliffs. Faring afield posed a worse problem. On so long a voyage they had not been able to bring many horses, and of those they had, some had died, and most were weakened by seasickness; even Kermorvan's hardy white warhorses, well used to sea voyages, were looking leaner in the ribs. Seasickness had taken its toll of men also, though they had guarded scrupulously against other disease, and many of the force were still not fit for long riding or heavy labour. Kermorvan's plan, therefore, was this: that while the main body of the force guarded fleet and shore, a swift band of such as were fittest should at once ride inland and seek the southland cities of Kerys; this, he informed them, meeting all protest with a chilly gleam in his eye, he would himself lead. Elof would go with them, as scout and courier. "But none of this we may safely begin," he added grimly, "till our third and most urgent problem is solved; what we do about our obliging escort out there?" He gestured over his shoulder to the gaggle of black ships.

"Chances are that'll be resolving itself any time now!" remarked Roc cheerfully. "One of the buggers is rowing this way!" There was a general rush to the side, but it was clear the newcomer meant no attack. There was something hesitant in the manner in which it hove to a discreet length from the *Korentyn*, and hailed for a parley. Elof was there when its boat drew under the warship's lee, and the chieftain of the Ravens climbed on board. He was grim of face, and there was fresh blood among the many stains on his mantle, but he saluted Kermorvan with respect, and Elof with awe.

"No man fares best alone," he began, without preamble. "To gladden the eye of Raven we set a spear between us and the other clans of the Aikiya'wahsa, and defied the Woman of the Ice. Now we think we will gladden Raven's eye further if we join those others who follow him."

Kermorvan's angry gesture silenced the outbursts of disbelief that arose all around, but the chieftain folded his arms and said no more. Kermorvan pushed his long hair back from his forehead, and regarded him steadily awhile before he answered. "You did what was honourable," he answered at last, very calmly, "and we take notice of it; we should have had hard fighting, for all our numbers. What it has cost you, we can guess. But your kin has never shown any love for ours, and there is an ocean of blood between us. When one shieldwall joins with another, each man must trust his neighbour, or the wall is weaker than it was before. I cannot forget that you might be cunning traitors, preferring a sudden strike from within our ranks to an open clash of shield-walls that must in the end cost all your lives. I do not say you are traitors, but I would be a fool not to think of it." The chieftain gave a contemptuous grunt, but said nothing. Kermorvan leaned back in his heavy chair. "We must know more. We also are honourable; aid for aid we will return as generously as we may – but to have you join us is a longer step, and one we should both test first. How truly do you wish it? Is it not rather fear of Louhi's wrath that urges you on?"

Kermorvan had taken care, Elof noticed, to speak in simple terms the Ekwesh would understand instantly, and to avoid offending him; and yet he had accused him of fear. The chieftain bristled visibly, but controlled his temper, and allowed himself a frigid nod. "Not to turn face from the Unending is foolishness; and the Ravens of the Aikiya'wahsa are not fools, King-over-sea. Else should we chafe under her rule so long? We thought then, Raven sleeps, or, Raven is weak, because he has no moving mountains, no warriors, no beasts, no sights or sendings, save, some say, himself. So we think, to serve well, we can do no better. Now we see this may not be so, there are other ways, that you serve him and yet are not his slaves, that you have power to wield as he shows you and yet is your own." The black eyes glittered as cold as Kermorvan's own, and the stolid face grinned with sudden savage vitality. "To fight the Hunter as you did, steel-shaman ... *ayeh!* Would I had done that deed! She was wise not to send the Ravens to fight in your land, but keep us to this, whose folk are rotten in their heart and strive among themselves. We saw you, we knew the time had come. So, King-over-sea, our wish to join your force is true, not a turning of the face. If he follows you, we shall also. In all you command!"

Elof felt intensely uncomfortable. "You make too much of me!" he said. "The King-over-sea is a man to follow indeed, a terrible warrior but wise also in the ways of peace. Look rather to him!"

Kermorvan smiled wryly. "Whatever the truth of this, I begin to understand your wish, and to believe you. But it is not something that can be decided in a moment. For one, are all your clan of the same mind?"

"There are many yet in our own land. Here, there are many still ashore, some forty ships or more; them also we put in peril. But of those here at sea, all who remain are of the same mind."

"All who remain?"

"A few were foolish, or face-turners. But have no concern! No ship is weaker save by a handcount, and

the clan is stronger without them." He touched the
bloodstain on his mantle. "They served us for luck-
offerings."

"Then hear me!" said Kermorvan into the ensuing
silence, as they pictured in their minds what bloody
moments had passed upon those still ships. "For now
you find it well to join us, and I should be glad to
welcome such powerful fighters under the Raven and
Sun; but much of what we command might chafe upon
you. We do not offer lives, for one thing; and you may
not be so glad when the day comes that you must strike
against your own kin." He paused, and the chieftain
nodded curtly again. "Very well then! Against all this,
and treason, we must guard. Our welcome is hard, but
the times admit no better. You and yours must live and
act only as we direct, till such time as we hold you
proven!"

The chieftain said nothing, made no move; but a
strong pulse beat visibly at his jaw, and a stony pride
was in his eyes. Abruptly Kermorvan surged to his feet,
towering over him and all others on deck, and whipped
from his belt his grey-gold sword. "This the Mastersmith
Elof Valantor made me in the forges of the mountain
folk! Say, will you swear fealty and obedience on it? For
else upon its edge you dwell; and it has never yet been
blunted! Speak now, or begone; I will have everything,
or nothing!"

For a long moment the old man gazed at him, then
with a sigh he seemed to collapse like a punctured bladder. He bowed his head, and fell to his knees and beat
his forehead upon the planking. "As you wish it, King-
over-the-sea! We are your hounds, and at heel we
follow!"

In truth, as he explained readily enough afterwards,
he had expected no less. It was agreed, among lesser
precautions, that his ships should moor well apart, his
men camp ashore in small groups under guard, in return
for which they would both receive and help to gather
supplies, chiefly fish; and that in battle by land or sea
they would be set in a place where they might prove
themselves at once. To this the chieftain assented,

adding with a cold twinkle in his eye "But hurry the battle, lord! For we are not mild folk, to sit idle at the doors of our tents! We breathe honour as the air!"

"Battle and honour you shall have soon enough!" said Kermorvan. "For now nothing hinders the searching party! See that it is made ready, for it departs within this very hour!"

In his place he left Ils, as was his wont at home; but to aid her he commanded Roc as marshal of the fleet, much to his astonishment and disgust. "For you know the land, and are a man of hard counsel, well suited to such a rank; and," he added in a lower voice, with a wry smile, "that is a thing you have achieved yourself. It is no accident of birth, like smithcraft, or, for that matter, kingship; and that Marja will not forget!" Roc snorted. To his vast chagrin, or so he gave out, Marja, instead of finding someone else, had waited out his nine year's absence quite faithfully, leaving him no honourable alternative but to cleave to her. In truth she obviously suited him much better than he pretended, for the years had settled him; only the matter of standing had rankled between them. Now Kermorvan had more than made that up, and chosen so vital a time that none would claim he favoured Roc from friendship only.

Certainly Elof was glad that two such solid natures were left in charge, as he and Kermorvan led their few squadrons of horsemen up the steep defiles above the landing site. It would not do to allow the Ekwesh to stage a surprise attack from the sea, and destroy the ships; the landing could be penned in then, and left to starve with no way of escape. As they passed below the crest of the hills, Kermorvan called to Elof, and together they left the column and rode up to the summit. Clinging to his saddle, Elof was too exhausted to speak when they reached the top, but he was able to seize Kermorvan's arm and point; there, barely distinguishable from the hill-crests against that grey horizon, was the distant shape of the Gate-tower. No dragon-coils crowned it now, no great head lifted towards the louring overcast; yet its aura of menace seemed undiminished. "I feel it too!" muttered Kermorvan. "Once so great, yet what has it become?"

"What has all this land become?" countered Elof harshly. "We linger from finding out, and night comes early; would there were more sun ..." The two friends looked at one another, struck by the same thought; then they looked upward at the lowering clouds, already tinged with red by the low sunbeams. "It can't be!" exclaimed Elof. "Not already!"

But as the sun sank in a riot of hues, scarlet and peach and glaring dark gold, mantled overall in black, Elof took wing once more; when he returned his hair seemed strangely faded, his wings greyed, till he clapped them together and blew a rich dust of pumice about the company. "On every hand the fire-mountains belch smoke and ash!" he reported. "They look like pillars upholding this canopy! As in a sense they are. The Wild Lands are still thick with snow; the Yskianas is well-nigh frozen in its upper reaches, the rest awash with ice. In early summer! The attack has begun!"

"What of the Ekwesh?" rasped Kermorvan. "Or any force of Louhi's? Did you see anything of them?"

"I saw something – here on the southern bank, no more than three or four leagues hence. I could not get close enough before the light failed, but it looked to me like a great encampment around a town."

"A siege? Or a muster?"

Elof shrugged. "Either. I said I could not see. And there were a few small flickers along the northern shore, fires of picket camps perhaps; Ekwesh, if so. Those lands have been long deserted. Nothing more – and Powers, but it was cold up there! The Ice rides the upper airs now!"

Kermorvan looked grave, but he helped Elof unbuckle his harness. "Come warm yourself by the ovens, then; we dare not build open fires in this bare place. We must get away from it soon, even if that means pressing on through the night."

To nobody's surprise, it did. The cold grew fierce enough to discourage even the weariest from thoughts of sleep; the danger of never waking was too great. The earth rang flinty beneath the hooves of their mounts, their breath burned in their nostrils and steamed out in

great clouds. Only a few stars glinted through the suffocating cloak of the upper airs, like the spear-points of a
night assault; the moon when it rose shone a few pale
beams through the ragged cloud, but the frost-bound
land glinted enough to give them light to ride by. They
cantered on like a column of dark-cloaked ghosts, and
made good speed; near dawn they were already on the
southern slopes of the hills, encamped beneath a
stand of dead corkbark oaks, winter's victims, and were
grateful to snatch a few hours sleep beneath the rising
sun. Then fire was kindled, and Elof lifted once more into
the air, climbing so high that to any casual eye he must
be mistaken for a bird. But he knew well that among his
foes there were eyes less casual, eyes of freezing blue,
eyes of blazing green, and he held Gorthawer ready at
his belt, the gauntlet on his arm. Only his heart felt
unready to face either.

The land swept by beneath him as if his wing-beats
brushed it away; there was little warmth in the light,
but enough to keep him aloft for many leagues yet, and
the warm south wind that had brought them ashore
contended with the cold flow down from the north;
their conflict sped him swiftly eastward towards the
town he had glimpsed. He could remember the name of
only one fortified town in this region, Torvallen, a holding whose lords had been a particular thorn in Nithaid's
side. It did not augur well; like many of their northern
cousins they might have sought to compact with the
Ekwesh. Again and again he wondered what he had
done in slaying Nithaid; the ruthlessness that had
dogged him all through his life, that Korentyn in naming
him had hung around his neck, had it betrayed him as
before, and perhaps the whole world with it? All the
bitter self-disgust of old came welling up in his throat,
all the old ghosts flew mockingly beside him. What was
he, who was he, that he should do such things, bear
such burdens? He had never really known. But long
before he reached his goal he saw a change that drove
the phantoms of the past from his waking mind; that
dark smudge in the lands around had changed shape,
grown longer to the west, like some amorphous crea-

ture stretching out an arm of its substance. And there was something moving among the river-ice … Puzzled, he went gliding down towards it.

They had agreed that while he was scouting, Kermorvan should not wait, but continue his drive eastward. Time was too short to waste; Elof could find them on the move easily enough, and it would shorten his journey back. So it was that he came upon the column as it was making its way across the southward slopes, and seeing for the first time the Vale of Kerys laid out before it. So intent were they all, even Kermorvan, on the sight of this, their ancestral homeland and the focus of all their legends and tales, that there was near panic as Elof came down among them, with men shouting and horses milling and rearing, ready to bolt. "I might have been another dragon!" grinned Elof breathlessly, as the alarm settled. "Could've settled on your wrist like a falcon!"

"You could hardly have caused more of a row!" said Kermorvan, irritably; then he grinned ruefully. "Oh, very well, I admit it; I was too struck by the sight to see a proper watch kept. What news, then, with such haste? Do you bring a band of reivers down on us?"

"Far from it! There'd better be none this side of the Great River, if they value their hides; there's a host of Kerys on the march!"

Kermorvan seized him by the arm. "You're sure?"

"Of course! All straggling out along the high roads, with cogs plying back and forth on the River; they're breaking channels in the Ice as they go. I saw banners and standards I've seen before; on my second pass I stooped low enough to see the very shade of their faces, and nearly caused a riot –"

"Evidently a habit of yours; but small wonder, when the tale of Nithaid's death must now be well known. As well they did not singe your plumes with this smith's fire of yours!"

Elof frowned. "They hardly looked able. That's no orderly force, from the glimpse I got, save for a few under the banners of lords; and even the banners are ragged. The rest – straggling off in any order, a rabble army. No colours, armour smirched and gear fouled, as if they've fought through mires and slept in them too!"

"*After fierce winter, flooding thaw!*" mused Kermorvan, quoting an old piece of weather-lore. "Even a miserable failed thaw such as this. Very likely they have. But they cannot hope to meet the Ekwesh thus, not in their full array of battle, with Louhi to general them. Still, their coming would explain why she has not been free to strike at us across the land. I guess that the sooner we join them, the better!"

Three days later, when Kermorvan's force came trotting out of the hills above the march, it became clear that Elof's surmise had been right. The army was at its noonday rest, straggling out across the land like a ragged scar, stretching far into the distance; only here and there was there any trace of order. Yet when the first sounds of hooves reached the flanking columns, they saw sentinels enough spring to their feet, and if the weapons in their hands glinted dully, still they were held steady, and no man turned. Horns sounded, and the whole long line erupted; the country seethed like an ant's nest. Kermorvan exclaimed in astonishment as he saw it. "There must be tens of thousands here!"

"Such is the might of Kerys," said Elof quietly. "Each campaign Nithaid could raise a force thrice the size of ours, and still leave his lords some garrison. Did I not tell you?"

"You did, and I believed you; but it is another matter to see it before us. As well we make ourselves known ere it rolls over us!" He gestured to the riders to form up, and led them off downhill at a brisk canter, their mail and weapons jingling merrily across the breeze. "Now sound your horns!" he ordered. "And, standard-bearer, unfurl that banner!"

The hubbub had begun to die down, as the sentries realised this was only a small party, and saw their pale skins, and Kermorvan's long bronze hair blowing in the breeze. But when the silver cavalry horns split the air, and the long black pennon broke out and floated over the tossing crests of the helms, the mêlée broke out anew, men shading their eyes and pointing, gesturing furiously at the design of the Raven and the sun on the banner. For this was the emblem of the Ysmerien kings, that had not flown in this land for three generations, and had scarcely been seen above the heads of warriors for centuries before that.

At the very margins of the army Kermorvan wheeled his horsemen and brought them, still in their tight formation, cantering cheerfully along the ranks. He kept a careful eye on Elof, who was having some difficulty staying in his saddle, let alone holding the line; but it did not stop either of them from noting how men who seemed sunk in weariness and filth, who looked up with disheartened desperation on their faces, sprang up with astonishment at the sight of this trim band of horsemen, and the banner they bore. Kermorvan at their head was a sight in himself, clad in the grim black mail coat of his fathers, but with a cloak of rich furs streaming out behind, and the Raven crest damascened on his breastplate glittering even in that sullen light. He wore no helm; his blowing hair served him for crest and crown, and above that stern and ageless face it made him look every inch a king.

He reined in when he came to the first of the banners in the van, and bade his horns sound once more. Men came thronging around him, but though he held up a hand to them he was obviously looking for some man such as the one who came riding up through the crowd on a tall chestnut warhorse, a burly, balding man in a stained black tunic set at the breast with the same red shield as upon the banner, patterned with gold mascles; a heavy broadsword with an intricate cage hilt swung at his side, and his hand was never far from it as he cursed the common kerns out of his way. "And who in the name of Verya d'you think you are, riding in under that banner?" he demanded in a sibilant southern drawl.

Kermorvan smiled, and shaping his words as Elof had taught him, he replied "I had best answer to the commander of this army, whom I seek. Are you he, or will you take me to him?"

"Commander?" glared the burly nobleman, his

short beard bristling. "Where've you sprung from? Fallen with yesterday's rain? You don't think this mob can boast a commander, do you? We're long past such things; we're bound to fight, man, and that's about the best we can manage. If you've a mind to die beside us, why then muck in and welcome to you! No politenesses needed, I do assure you. Needn't even answer your bloody name."

"But I will, nonetheless." Kermorvan's cold eyes sparkled. "I will join you gladly; but I have no mind to die quite yet. I am the Lord Keryn Kermorvan of Morvan, King of Morvanhal, heir of the line of the Ysmerien, lord of all the children of Kerys in the land of High Brasayhal, far across the oceans. We have heard of your need, and brought such force as we can to your aid; even now our fleet disembarks upon the coast. And though we have but half your number, we are fresh and hardened, and our hearts are in the trim! For we also have faced the Ice and the Ekwesh in our lands, and though it has cost us dearly we have beaten them back!"

The big man looked at him blankly. "You're kin of ours from oversea? Of Ysmerien blood? And you've landed ..." He sounded about to choke. "Some ... ten thousand men to help us? Ten thousand fighting men?"

Kermorvan nodded. "And well armed. Though a few are also smiths, such as my court mastersmith here."

The baron glanced at Elof, then his eyes bulged, and he clapped hand to sword with such violence his horse almost reared under him. "You! You're the sorcerer who slew Nithaid!"

Elof nodded calmly. "As I had promised him, for good cause. And ere he died I promised him I would bring his folk a worthier figure of a king ..."

"So it was true, what you said!" muttered the baron. "I was at court when you came – aye, you had cause ... But an Ysmerien!" He gazed at Kermorvan from keen dark eyes, then anxiously around at the throng of men who were pressing in, hanging on every word. "He has the look of it ... Gentles, you had better come with me. The lords must hear of this!" He swung the heavy horse about, beckoning them to follow him, and curdled the air as he sought to clear a way through the press.

But others have heard of it first, thought Elof, looking down on faces dulled and haggard catching new life from a spark of hope. Then, as the column wheeled to follow the baron, he caught his friend's eye and was startled by the twinkle in it, wintry but unmistakable. It was too easy to forget that Kermorvan, though almost painfully honest and honourable in himself, had a king's upbringing, and kingship in his blood; it made him, among other things, extremely adept at getting his own way. He had deliberately attracted the attention of large numbers of common soldiers before announcing himself and his purpose; he had seized the chance to do so in their hearing, and drive home the message that Ice and Ekwesh could be beaten – or had he very gently manoeuvered the baron into giving him it? Elof had warned him of the squabbles and jealousies he must expect among the lords of Kerys, and he had passed them by before they even knew it.

So it was that while the loose alliance of nobles who had strung together this last, desperate army of Kerys were welcoming Kermorvan effusively, and at the same time striving either to put him in his place, or, as they got the measure of him, to win some personal alliance with him, the word was spreading through the army outside, like sparks spreading before a forest fire. And for confirmation they had Kermorvan's horsemen, men of Morvanhal and of Kerbryhaine together in amity, common men like themselves but equipped and armed better than most of the lords. They were only too ready to tell tales of Kermorvan's defeat of the Mastersmith in the Westlands, of his journey east and liberation of Morvannec from its oppressors, of how he had rescued the besieged folk of Nordeney and Kerbryhaine and united them into a strong and peaceful eastern kingdom, all in the short space of seventeen years; and all, they were careful to add, when he was no more than forty-four years old himself, and could, if he lasted the long span of his line, look to another forty or fifty active years. Before the lords had spent more than an hour or

two in talk, they were astonished to hear a growing murmur outside their great tent, lively but restive, and sent out to see what it was about. When answer was returned that the soldiers wished to see the King, they looked at one another in dawning dismay, and some in sharp displeasure. Elof, who had been observing their manoeuvering with amusement tempered with disgust, grew tense, and made sure Gorthawer was to hand; but Kermorvan looked blandly astonished, and sat at ease where he was. "*King?*" barked one of the more piratical lords from the northern shore. "The only king here's from a far land, and doesn't mean to go poking his nose into the matters of Kerys! Tell that to the swine!" He had forgotten that he was not within the thick walls of his tower, now reduced by the Ekwesh, nor surrounded by his own unquestioning peasantry as of old. The ragged and desperate soldiers outside those walls of oiled cloth and leather were of a very different mood, and they heard him clearly. A loud rumble and hiss of anger, like a wave breaking on gravel, answered him at once, and his florid face grew pale; the others rounded on him in anger and panic. They were not evil men, thought Elof; they had at least had the wisdom to swallow their differences, the will and courage to muster this last force, to give a morsel of leadership where it was needed. Nor were they battening on their followers, as some lords might have; their gear was as grimy, their armour as rusty, their board as bare, their faces as gaunt and desperate as any of their men's. But it was obviously their power they were most concerned about, and the independence they had looked forward to since Nithaid's death; even before his forefathers usurped the kingship the lords of this land had lost any respect for it, or any idea that they might benefit under a central rule. Or the common folk, either; it was not impossible that they cared for them, in their way. Now, though, they were in for a shock. Outside the murmur of the crowd was rising, growing louder and more rythmical, becoming a chant there was no mistaking. *The King! The King!*
Show us the King!

We'll see the King! We want the King! Bring out our King!

"Outrageous!" blared the young lord of Keruelen, the great city in the south. "Get out there and silence them!"

"Who're you talking to?" growled an older and poorer lord. "Go silence 'em yourself, puppy! They'll rend you limb from limb! They've had a scent of something they want, and woe betide any of us dares tell 'em they can't have it!"

There was a long silence while the lords assembled digested this unpleasant truth, and then, for the first time, many pairs of hostile eyes lit upon Kermorvan. "You must tell them, then!" said Irouac, who had been Nithaid's steward. "Say to them that you have come to help and have no other ambitions, that being a stranger you must naturally submit to our command ..." He faltered. Kermorvan's lean features had hardly changed, but there was a faint and alarming smile on his lips.

"Must I?" He spread his hands, as the faces grew downright menacing. "Speak to them so, I mean." They relaxed a little, and so did Elof; he had Gorthawer's hilt in his right hand, the weight of the long trestle table in his left, ready to hurl it in their faces if they sprang. But Kermorvan's smile hardened, and became a wry and angry grimace. "My lords, consider! What you ask me to say would be justified if there were some strong, some solid captaincy here! Some leader or leaders fit to direct such a force as this in so crucial a campaign. But what do I find? What do you find, if you look honestly at yourselves? You are so strained with suppressing your rivalries that you can barely agree which direction to march in! And though you are all capable warriors, not one among you has ever held such a command as this. I know that because I have listened to your talk, and because Nithaid would never have risked giving an underling such power. Speak to my lords, when you meet them, and you may hear a different tale; but that is not now at issue. What is, is captaincy!" He rose from his seat. "Look upon me, my lords! You know little of me save what I have told you; but I think that simply not being one of you, not being caught up in your ancient strife, would be a great asset in a leader. However, I can offer you more. I was born to war. I have fought by land and sea, as penniless wanderer, as common sailor, as leader of half-armed mobs and marshal of great armies. I have fought men and monsters, I have raised my sword against the very Walls of Winter themselves; and I have not been defeated." In the gloomy light of the tent his pale face seemed grey and stony, implacable, resolute. "I ask you, am I not better suited to command than any one of you – let alone your ramshackle confederacy? Ask yourselves, where lies your greatest chance to save your land, your estates, your power that you cherish so much? I do not say there is much hope. This land has been let slip far, and perhaps it must fall further yet ere it can be cleansed. But I urge you, do not let it slip away altogether, to gratify your own resentments! Do not bury your good sense beneath stale rivalries of rank and lineage! But if you must, what of mine? I am the last of the Ysmerien, and descended from a line which, had it not balked at kin-strife, could have held the kingship of Kerys more rightfully than the one that did. I could step out of this tent and assert my ancient right – *and dare you think it would not be upheld?*"

The cold eyes blazed, the calm voice thundered. The assembled lords gave back, astonished; they had seen Nithaid in his wrath, but never this mood of stone and centuries that descended upon Kermorvan in his righteous anger. "My lords," he said, amid a sudden hush outside, "I will make no such claim unless you force me. Unless there is no other way to stop you casting away the lives of your followers and mine; to stop you ruining the last hope of this desperate land, and perhaps of the whole living world, with your selfish follies and distrusts. I will lead you now, if you will it, as war-leader only; as to kingship, let that rest until there is a land to be king of once more. Then we shall see!"

"Indeed, and by then you'll have your claws well fixed in the throne anyway!" grunted a sour-faced southern lord.

Kermorvan's look was bleak but unoffended. "You seem very certain that I would want it ..." That left them silent with confusion and suspicion blended. To them Kerys was the world. They knew well enough that Kermorvan had his own land, his own realm, but could hardly bring themselves to credit that he might prefer it.

"Anyway, what's in the name?" added the baron of the red shield. "Whatever we called any leader we chose – Warlord, Overlord, Marshal of the Field – *they'll* call him king! They trust kings; they don't trust us. And I don't blame them one blind bit!"

The lords were drawing breath to turn on him next when Kermorvan's voice, pitched to carry to the outside, curled around them like the fine tip of a lash. "I came this great distance to strike at the Ice, my lords; that is all. And with you or without you, fight I shall! If I cannot wring some sense from you, shall I ask your men? I do not think they will refuse me; others have not. We are not without other allies ..."

Elof watched warily as Kermorvan told just who they were, and how they had come to serve beneath the Raven banner, expecting a great outburst. But when he had done there was only silence, broken at last by the burly baron. "Ekwesh ..." he drawled thoughtfully. "Thirty shiploads, which is to say some four thousand of 'em ... And the dragon. Well, gentles? To whom shall fall the honour of proclaiming our new warlord?"

"It won't last, you know," warned Elof, as he and Kermorvan rode out in the van of the ragged army, towards the northern flanks of the hills they had passed through. "This sudden meekness of theirs. You've daunted them well for now, yes. But if things go ill, even briefly – or the moment the fighting's done ..."

Kermorvan smiled. "I know. But that moment is a fair step into the future; and I am preparing for it. Now do you don your wings, for you must take word to Roc and Ils at once, while there is light. Our two forces must move swiftly to unite, march night and day if need be; if Louhi realises we have met, let alone made alliance, she will hurl everything she can between us! So go

now, guide them to the tryst; we shall be hurrying on
your heels!"

It was four days later that the two armies met; it
could scarcely have been sooner. The place appointed
was a shallow cleft in the hills above the southern cliffs
of the Vale, just beyond the angle where the Yskianas
narrowed sharply, more or less opposite where Elof and
Roc had first looked out over the great valley. Its
surrounding hills, though they were no protection from
the icy north wind, screened it well from the sight of
the distant Gate. The mood in both armies was one of
rejoicing at the finding of kin long lost, and it made
mingling them an easier task. When the lords and
captains of both armies came together, united by the
common demands of commanding so great a body of
men, and of establishing a new battle order, the soldiers
soon followed their example; and by morning Kermorvan commanded a reasonably unified army. But it was
not without its problems. If Kermorvan's force had
found their rations meagre before, when they saw the
plight of their fellows they portioned them gladly; that
created great good will, but something of a problem.
"It'll leave us little enough to fall back on," was Roc's
verdict. "But then, if this goes ill, there'll be nowhere to
fall back *to*, will there?" So it came about that the men
of Kerys went on to their war somewhat strengthened,
and in many cases armed anew with spare weapons
from the store Elof and his mastersmiths had built up;
shields alone were denied them, though the fleet had
brought a great store of light metal shields, tall curved
rectangles large enough to shelter the whole body. But
it appeared that these were of some special kind, which
only trained men could use properly, and Kermorvan
had forbidden their being given away. This did create
some resentment, but it was a small enough point,
passed over easily in the glad meeting of the armies.
More troublesome was the strong presence in the fleet
of Nordeney men with the same copper skin as the
Ekwesh; many Kerysmen met them with lively and vocal
distrust and scorn, and as the northerners were not given
to suffering insult mildly it took all of Kermorvan's

authority to quell the resulting dissension. The wiser Kerysmen accepted them then, at least when they found they talked and behaved much like their own northerners; the rest soon found it politic to keep their resentment silent.

Only the Ravens stood apart from the gathering, eating the mass of fish they had caught and smoked while Kermorvan was away, and loath to share; most men were glad of that, for they remained a fell and uncanny folk, and there was hardly a man there of either camp who had not suffered some loss at the hands of their fellows, whether of home or kinsfolk or his own blood. Among the Kerysmen in particular there was great ill-feeling against them, but it was mitigated by the belief that their desertion was a potent omen; also, Kermorvan had put Elof, who spoke their tongue best, in charge of them, to see that they neither offered nor suffered any treachery, and every man was too much in awe of him to risk anything.

Kermorvan lingered only long enough at that camp to send out scouts, Elof among them, and plot what they found onto the maps the nobles brought him. Then, shortly before dawn on a day of mist and rain, a whisper ran through the camp that was more thrilling than any trumpet or drum. The new king had commanded silence; and all his subjects, old and new, were already given to heed him. In a pale half-light, with no fanfare save the muted thunder of their own bustle and tread, the last army of men formed up and marched away to do battle with the ancient Powers of the world.

CHAPTER ELEVEN
The Hammer of the Sun

THERE WAS NO WAY now their presence could be concealed from the Gate; it grew before them as they trudged along the snow-bound hills above the Great River's southern shore, from a notch of grey between hummocks of white to the great crowned ridge that Elof knew only too well. Roc, riding as ever at his side, spat and cursed. But as they drew closer, coming out of the hills onto open plains, frosty and snow-sprinkled, they agreed that its aspect seemed to have changed again, though clearly there was no dragon coiled around its crown now. The grey walls seemed to glisten blue in the sun, as if filmed with ice; and above them there was snow, thick crests of white crowning every roof, outlining every rail, every balustrade, every plinth, picking them out clearly so that each man of the army could see, even at this distance, the towering strength of the stronghold they must face. Ils whistled, and turned to the chief of her duergar. "Not so bad for man's work – eh, Gurri?"

His dark eyes scanned the ridge, and he rubbed his flat-chinned jaw. "Man's work, and ours, I guess, in days when such things were. Long in the breaching, long in the under-mining. Months, perhaps."

"Time is Louhi's servant," remarked Kermorvan. "But I doubt if she will leave us free to try either. If we are to besiege that burg, we must first get by ..." He stopped, and reined in his warhorse. From somewhere ahead of them, the High Gate or near it, a weird sound arose, a deep pulsing rattle, rhythmical as a heartbeat, and beneath it a soft roaring note, hollow and thunderous, that rose and fell upon the bitter wind but never quite faded. Elof could not for the life of him identify it, and to judge from the excited comments he heard among Kermorvan's guard, neither could anyone else.

"Like a heartbeat, hey? But *dry*…"

"More like hammering…"

"Like breath!" said a nervous voice. "Another bloody monster, panting for air…"

"Or flapping its wings…"

Ils snorted. "Might be some kind of an engine, maybe!"

"Aye!" said Roc fiercely. "A huge waterwheel, bigger than the Mastersmith's even! What deviltry's she about, up there?"

But Kermorvan made no answer; he was gazing around him with furrowed brow, considering the scene, looking across the open space to where it dropped away, no longer to cliffs but onto the steep slopes leading down to the chain of deep lakes that flowed from the Gate falls. A cold gleam came into his eyes then, and a wry smile; he frowned once more, and called to one of his captains. "Have the Raven chieftain come to me!" He turned back to the others. "I was going to say, we must get by her defenders; and if I mistake not, this heralds their coming. The Ravens cannot or will not say how many there are, save that there are more than us; which is not hard to believe…" Even as he spoke, the sound faded away altogether; the sudden silence quivered like a tautened wire. He thought for a moment, then gestured to another captain. "Sound the halt! Then the battle order, and see them formed up! Send out the rest of the scouts! We go no further in marching order, it's too vulnerable; we'll give battle while we're still in the open, not among Louhi's hills!"

The horns sang in strident discord through the ranks, and the long serpentine columns halted, broke and began to cluster together on the plain, gathering slowly into a series of concentric rings, so wide they covered more than half the plain. For a time all was chaos, horns signalling, men shouting, horses neighing; for although the twenty thousand of Kerys had all seen some campaigning, they had less experience of the tight and flexible formations that Kermorvan demanded. Foreseeing this, he had had to divide his own well-trained men, weaken their dependable lines to leaven the mix and pass on as much of their knowledge as they could on the march. He took his stand with his captains and friends upon a rocky eminence atop a low rise of ground.

With the many banners of the two armies floating above his head he was easily visible as a pillar of calm above the milling masses, one moment conferring urgently with captains and nobles, the next calling cool orders that disposed one group or another about the lines, or set another to scraping shallow breast-works out of the hardened ground; but those close to him saw how his mouth worked, and how closely he scanned the hillsides for any signal from the scouts.

"What ails you, my long lad?" demanded Ils. "You've seen bad battles enough in your day!"

"Aye, and never loved a single one of them!" retorted Kermorvan grimly. "But least of all one in which I am doomed to hang back, to command thousands to spill their blood before I so much as risk any drop of my own."

He turned sharply as the Raven chieftain struggled through the mêlée and hailed him with grim respect, raising spear and shield. "*Ayeha!* Where will you have the Ravens perch?"

Kermorvan lifted a hand. "Gather them below the hillock here, where you can hear me!"

The old man eyed him a moment. "I thought, he will place us in the front line, that his foes may seem to strike against themselves." He paused doubtfully. "Clan has fought clan often enough. It is a place of some honour ..."

Kermorvan shook his head. "I have a better for you. Hold yourselves ready to my command – and keep down your banners till then!" Abruptly the air was shuddering about them with the same rattling thunder and roar as before, but nearer, much nearer. The Ekwesh tensed, spun about and sniffed at the wind like a hunting hound, this way and that. Then he lifted his spear and pointed at the rounded crest of the high hill before them. All eyes followed him, but upon its unstained whiteness there seemed to be nothing to see. Suddenly it was as if the sharp skyline of the hill grew blurred; another breath and it had grown a fine fringe, that swelled and wavered and rose higher. All along the rim of the hills that spear swung, and as it passed, as if somehow calling it up, the line arose, shimmering like wind-blown grass. In the utter silence Elof heard Roc, standing beside him, swallow convulsively, and realised then how dry his own throat had become. The line stretched out in a great half-moon around them, from the hills inland to where the land fell away down steep slopes into the valley; at that end small specks were still bounding to complete the line, and rank upon rank behind it. For this was the shieldwall of the armies of the Ekwesh, and every seeming grass-blade was one of their long oval shields, man-high. The army below, that a moment before had seemed so vast in its numbers, dwindled and shrank in Elof's eyes before that shimmering mass. He saw men's faces grow pale all round him, their knuckles whiten upon rein and weapon. Kermorvan, apparently impassive, was quietly and unnecessarily losening his grey-gold sword in its scabbard.

"Look at them!" breathed one of his captains, appalled. "Look at the numbers of them! There must be fifty thousand if there's a man!"

"And more in yon tower!" growled Ils. "But we'll deal with them later. For now, it's only slay two to one; and in the old days it was a poor duergh couldn't manage that now and again!"

Still in the eerie silence, save for the crunch of feet among the snow-clad stones, a long section of the northernmost line detached themselves and padded downward, hunched down and slipping swiftly behind hillocks and along gullies, till they were just beyond bowshot of Kermorvan's lines. They stopped there as if waiting, for one long breathless moment, and then, at an order howled from the hill, they swung up their short spears in a glittering mass, whirled about, away from both armies and towards the tower of the Gate itself. It seemed to Elof, straining his eyes that he saw high on the balcony below the round tower a soft gleam of gold that shifted, as it might be fair hair; but dark hair he was too distant to make out. Then the Ekwesh cried out a single word, unmistakably a salute, and lifting their shields of stiffened hide over wood they sang out a hooting, carrying call and rattled the blades of their spears flat against them.

Aotu-u-eh!

Across the ridges the whole vast army echoed them, and the drumming of the shields swelled and rang off the cold rock walls of the valley, a savage, terrifying music of war.

"That's what the row was!" barked Ils, her large eyes creased into deep wrinkles as she squinted across the snow.

"Not quite!" said Elof. "There was more ..." Below the rise the old Raven chieftain, growing impatient, seized his shield and slammed it hard, and all of his men would have echoed him had not Kermorvan barked for quiet; they subsided at once, but looked sullen and resentful. Even as he spoke, the foremost of the enemy whirled back suddenly; among them a chant began, a sung line and a massed response, almost like a sea-shanty.

Awey-yeh!
Heugh!
Awey-yey-yeh!
Heugh!
Aotu-u-ueh!

On that last word all joined in, brandished their spears and rattled them against their shields once more. "You speak their tongue better than I, Elof!" Kermorvan murmured. "Can you catch any of that?"

"Only the salute, the last word. *Aotu.* It means *Slay!*" They were leaping in time to it, dancing even, a strange bounding step, on the spot at first, then carrying them forward a step, one, two –

With frightening suddenness, and a great howling shout of *Aotu!* the dance became a charging run, and the first wave of Ekwesh swept forward towards the lines of Kerys and Morvanhal. A shoal of arrows hissed out to meet them, and many fell beneath the feet of their fellows; another shout from the hill, and the rush halted, but did not retreat, remaining there, the copper-skinned men dancing and chanting in mockery while the deadly shafts sang into their uneven lines and sent one after another sprawling in agony on the frozen soil, impaled and contorted, grotesquely propped up by the embedded shafts. It was an evil spectacle, so much bravery so ill-used, and for one long moment it held all eyes in horror; all eyes save those of the Ravens, who had looked upon worse and laughed. It was their shout that brought Kermorvan whirling around. "A decoy, by the Powers!" yelled the king. Like a grey tide creeping, the southernmost quarter of the shieldwall had detached itself and advanced, was even now padding stealthily down the lower slopes and onto the plain. "*Sound, horns! Stand to your posts!*"

As they saw their ruse discovered the black-clad chieftains upon the hill stretched out their spears and called in baying voices; the advancing troops abandoned their stealthy, crouching gait, and with a great shout and rattling of spear upon shield they sprang up and broke into a fast trot that rapidly became a headlong downhill plunge. The crisp snow flew up beneath their feet and hid them, so that the shields seemed to glide forward across an icy cloud, and the crunch of each man's footfall, magnified many a thousandfold, became at last the mounting, unearthly roar that they had heard across the hills.

Kermorvan measured the distance with a keen eye, then waved his hand. A horn sounded, and from within the ranks the catapults he had taken from the ships sang and slammed. It was a well-timed stroke. Rocks and darts went whistling down upon the advancing lines; black-armoured warriors were transfixed, dashed down like skittles or crushed outright, but they left hardly a gap in that immense line, nor slowed the onrush. Some rocks overshot, but came tumbling back down the slope to take the Ekwesh from behind; here and there the snow-cover broke and slid away in little avalanches, sweeping warriors away helpless as insects struggling in sand. The catapults were frantically, reloaded, and some even had time to fire. But the main lines were already under the arc of their flight, and it was only the few stragglers they caught. Now arrows began to sing down from the hilltops, a long shot, but in the tight-packed formation Kermorvan had ordered they seldom wanted a mark. Men fell groaning and screaming, but their cries sounded thin and ridiculous against the rising thunder of oncoming feet. For the first time Elof actually felt a thing he had only read of, the earth shuddering beneath him at an army's tread. Amid their snow-cloud the Ekwesh came on like the stormy surf of a vast ocean. And like surf that first massive onrush struck Kermorvan's shieldwall, and burst over it with a roar.

Or so it seemed. An endless moment of flurry and confusion, roaring and screaming and the rattle of arms, took hold. Hide shield boomed against metal, pike and sword clinked against the Ekwesh spears, short-shafted, broad-bladed, that could be wielded as either, while from the second rank long spears stabbed out over the shoulders of the defenders. Elof itched to take wing, to see and fight from above; but in this barren land they had little fuel to burn, and he must save it for great need. It was too much to take in, too complex and terrible a sight, this mutual slaughter of many thousands of men; even to Elof's sharp eyes only fragmentary images registered among the confusion, small scenes that seemed to be repeated, played out over and over again wherever one looked along that long line of battle, like recurring patterns on some potent work of smithcraft, some immense and frenzied frieze, patterns brief, bloody, all too vivid. Here a pike sheared away a hide shield and the arm that held it, raking open the black-armoured ribs behind; there a sword wedged in the wooden frame of another such shield, grey and serpent-crested, then fell from its wielder's hand as like the serpent's tongue the deadly spear flicked out. Here a tall warrior sprang up on bodies sprawled across the breast-works, only to rise straight up into the air, thrashing like a fish upon the spear that impaled him; there a man of Morvanhal was knocked back across the breastworks by a hide shield, and had time to scream in terror at the spear that plunged towards his heart. But a metal shield felled his slayer to his knees in the snow as a man of the second rank stepped into his place, and a long spear drove under the Ekwesh armour. He fell thrashing, dragging the spear with him, and his assailant drew blade to confront the man behind. Over and over again such scenes took place, made all the more uniform when distance or the clouds of powder snow, pink-tinged now, hid the adversaries' faces; to Elof then it took on a dream-like quality, as if two armies of ghosts were condemned to eternal battle, where each man who fell rose at once to fight again.

Then, quite suddenly, like glass that cools or ice that melts, the scene cleared. The confusion resolved to reveal most of the Ekwesh milling and thrashing against the ring of shields, still sparring viciously with its defenders but to little effect. Kermorvan's tight formation had played the strong sea-wall to that human surf; most it had held, and what passed it had scattered like flecks of foam. Alone, intruders burst like foam indeed against the second rank, thrust through even as they yelled their triumph; and for larger groups also Kermorvan had made ready. His few squadrons of horses and picked bands of pikemen ranged freely between the ranks, blocking any breach and falling upon any who passed through; no intruders lived more than seconds. Only at the apex of the charge was the shieldwall truly breached, brave men borne down with broad spears biting at their vitals, and there at once the horns sounded and men of the second lines moved up around the gap, enclosing the influx of Ekwesh in a shallow arrowhead hedged with shields and thorned with spear and pike. Those at the fore, isolated in the narrow channel and beset from three sides, were driven onto their points by the sheer weight of the press from behind, and their bodies piled up to serve their slayers as a grisly breast-work of their own. The chieftains on the hill, seeing how ill even this breach was faring, bayed new commands. All along the line, the black-armoured warriors broke off their skirmishing and dropped back; but those caught within the arrowhead could not move so quickly, to their undoing. With a hungry roar the two ends of the reinforced line rolled over the uncertain press in their path, stabbing and slashing, trampling what fell, narrowing and closing the arrowhead till the line stood whole once more.

The ranks of the Ekwesh drew back, many still dancing and chanting mockingly as they trotted back up the slopes once more; but they left the ground before the shieldwall a stinking trampled slush, brown with blood, strewn with bodies like rain-felled grass. A wild cheer went up from within the Kerys lines, and some, foolish or blood-drunk, broke ranks to follow. Their captains roared them back, and they came all the faster when a couple of the foremost dropped with Ekwesh darts in their bellies. The archers on the hills began to fire further and faster, now there was less danger of hitting their own ranks.

"Well, we've held 'em!" said Roc tensely, and without any note of rejoicing. "But that was just their first wave. What next, Kermorvan? More of the same?"

'I think not!" said Kermorvan. "They have failed to

whelm our lines; now they will strive to break them. The chiefest question is, where? On which flank will they strike?"

"Why not on all?" growled Ils. "There's enough of 'em, by Ilmarinen!"

"No. In such a mêlée they could not keep control of their forces, and that would serve us better than anything ..." He danced hurriedly aside as a heavy catapult arrow came hissing down and skipped across the stone near his feet. "Nor could they fire down into it so freely, lest they hit their own. They will sooner try the lance, I think, now the club has failed; and they will tip that lance with hardened warriors. But where? Where?"

"I think I know," said Elof quietly. "Look there!" High on the hillside there was activity behind that motionless front wall. Grey shields were streaming over the hill-brow and down into the centre of the shieldwall, to the west of them.

"It may be ..." began Kermorvan, then he broke off. Even as the last few grey shields bounced into the line a wailing call rang out from the hill, the outer shieldwall parted and melted back, and the greys took their place. Their shields bore the same serpent pattern as the banners that lifted and fluttered overhead. There were no chants now, no dance; one more wail from above, one jabbing spear lifted in answer, and with a single shout of *Hoh!* the grey shields swept down the hill. As they ran their line bent back from the middle into a wedge shape, and all the rest of the vast phalanx on the central slope, some nine or ten thousand men, fell in behind it. Well-nigh as many warriors as Morvanhal's whole army raced in a great spearhead towards the western edge of Kermorvan's lines, with the grey serpents tossing at its point.

"If we'd had but a few hours more for earthworks −" hissed Ils between her large teeth as she watched that inexorable rush, then she winced in sympathy as the two lines collided with a terrible juddering crash of shield on shield. So might two mountains sound that made war upon the plains, hurling down their slopes of stone. Elof held his breath, for it seemed no mere wall of human thews could sustain that impact. Even as he thought that, he heard the horns bray alarum around him, saw the outer lines seem to shudder and dissolve, falling back, aside, inwards, any way, as the great column of Ekwesh came charging through and the writhing banners came driving with breathless speed straight towards the heart of the ring, the king's rock. He cursed and snatched at his sword, but even as Gorthawer sang out of its scabbard he realised that the fragmented lines had not dissolved, only shifted once again. For a moment they had curled in on themselves, spirals of shuffling men, then suddenly they were sharp-edged squares, islands shored with shields and forested with blades, solid and impregnable among the churning Ekwesh, their charge thrown into confusion by the sudden dissipation of its target. The smaller surface the squares presented meant that only a few at a time could come against each face, and they met the same double or triple ranks as before, and an impenetrable press of men behind; the rest, angry and impatient, could only mill around and shout. The veterans of the Serpent clan alone kept their heads, it seemed; for they held together and drove hard against the inner rings that had not been pierced, but had drawn closer about the king's rock. Many fell, but the press began to tell, and Elof saw that they would burst through any moment. Kermorvan paid them no apparent heed, but strode over to the edge and called down. "*Ravens all! Now is your hour! Pluck me down that Serpent!*"

He gestured, horns sounded; the hard-pressed lines gave back and with a hoarse yell of triumph the Serpents came streaming through. But the old chieftain had sprung up with a cry of his own, and hammered spear-shaft against shield; his followers echoed him, and took up the cry – *Kokju'awatle! The Raven is upon you!* With no more ado they fell upon their fellow-tribe.

Around the rock chaos flowed, and from the throng, of a sudden, the Serpent banner burst, around it a tight knot of hard-faced men. Up the slope they charged, and throwing aside the cares of the greater battle the captains drew blade and turned to fight for themselves. Roc cast down his bow and unhooked his mace from his belt; Ils plucked up her axe. Kermorvan, drawing on his helm and fastening down the fearsome jewelled eye-mask that was its visor, turned to

Elof. "Stay here; you cannot walk on this rough stone, and there is no time for your wings! None shall reach you while we are on our feet!" Then sweeping the grey-gold blade from its scabbard he bounded down the steep crag with Roc and Ils on his heels, and hurled himself into the onrush. To left and right of him he hewed with all the fierce art of his youth, harnessing the impact of each savage blow to launch himself into the next; he became the centre of a grotesque death-dance, black-armoured figures springing in then rebounding back, flung bodily from his path, or capering a moment and collapsing like clumsy dolls. From the moment of his coming the onrush was stemmed.

Elof, perched on his crutches, cursed his infirmity and all who had caused it; for though he was not naturally a war-like man, it galled him to be left helpless, watching his friends at risk. Gorthawer seemed to shiver and sing in his grasp, and he began to hobble and clamber painfully down towards the fighting, striving to see more clearly. Neither Roc nor Ils could he make out, their short figures lost in the crush; but Kermorvan, taller even than the Ekwesh, stood out clearly. He seemed at no peril; indeed the fight was swirling away from him as the Ekwesh saw him hew down their strongest by twos and threes. Elof saw him bend down then over somebody fallen, and hurried to look closer; it was Ils, with blood streaming from her leg. But then two tall Ekwesh made a sudden rush; Ils cried out, Kermorvan whirled, but a shield clubbed him on the side of the neck and sent him staggering back. One Ekwesh raised his spear to stab; Elof, still beyond sword's reach, leaned on one crutch and lashed out with the other. The stabbing arm was stopped in midair; then Gorthawer thrust deep into the bared armpit, and the man fell with a retching gasp. The other rounded on Elof, but the crutch struck him in the face and the black sword took him below his breastplate, up behind his ribs. Another ran up, shield raised; Elof slammed the crutch against it, knocking him sprawling, and thrust him through the back with Gorthawer, then wrenched it free, slashed another across the breast and with a growl of effort toppled him from the rock. Now the attackers were themselves attacked; beneath the banner a huge man, head crowned with bobbing white plumes, face and arms ringed with the swirling bluish cicatrices of high rank, roared out an order, gathered such of his men as he still could about him. As swiftly as they had come they gave back, turned and vanished into the fray.

Elof turned to his friends; Ils, forgetting her own injury, had removed Kermorvan's helm, and he was already staggering up, grimacing with disgust as he fingered his bruised neck. "Let no man call you cripple evermore. Mastersmith!" he gasped. "Afoot or awing, my friend, you are the great man-slayer I once named you!"

Elof grimaced. "Mastersmith I prefer! Are you all right?"

Kermorvan's clear laugh rang with triumph. "I am, by your good grace! And all the better for seeing how the field stands now!"

Elof knew that the old Raven had spoken truly; until first the Mastersmith, and then Louhi, had managed to tame their rivalries, the great tribes of the Ekwesh had made constant war over the scanty resources of their barren homeland. Anywhere else the Serpents might have been wary of their kin; but here they had fought their way, as they thought, into the very heart of their enemies, only to find there a strong force of their own kind. For a moment, evidently, they had assumed that these were their fellows coming to their aid; and that moment was fatal. The Ravens' attack struck them as a stunning shock, an awesome stroke of magecraft that thus stood the battle on its head; and the Ravens, with the weapons of Kerys many had adopted, were terrifying opponents. The Serpents' charge stopped dead; they lifted their shields in a feeble attempt to defend themselves, but panic blazed through their ranks, and those behind turned at once to flee. Out into the milling mass around the squares they charged, and in that disordered hubbub their fright was contagious. Heads turned, warriors already balked and frustrated by the disorder saw them flee and began to draw back themselves; the press eased and the squares, still holding doggedly together, began little by little to move. Two came together and joined, and bore down upon another that was hardest pressed; there too the Ekwesh gave back at sight of this creeping dragon-thing of shields that slowly but surely trampled over any in its path;

they began to stream away. In moments the chieftains were again yelling from the hill-tops, and the men of the great onrush turned and went pounding away. But there was no dancing nor mockery now; for of that great wedge of men over half lay dead among slime and mud, the heat of their spilled blood thawing even this frosty ground. And behind that mighty heap of corpses Kermorvan's sundered lines were already forming anew.

Elof heaved a deep sigh of relief, but Kermorvan's countenance was grim. "Why so, my long lad?" demanded Ils, leaning on his arm. "Your plan worked well. Our losses are light compared to theirs."

"Losses they remain, and there is worse to come. Nevertheless, I am thankful ... But what's this?"

Through the press shouldered the leaders of the Ravens, bearing something towards the rock. Before Kermorvan's feet they unrolled it, with a bellow of laughter; the chiefest banner of the Serpents, and within, impaled upon the staff, a naked corpse, obscenely mutilated but with those chains of cicatrices still recognisable. Ils whistled, and chuckled softly in Elof's ear. "As well we didn't recruit the *real* savages, I guess!"

But Kermorvan remained imperturbable. Stepping down from the rock, he gave the grisly trophy grave attention, commended the talons of the Ravens who had seized the Serpent, then ordered the chieftain wrapped in his banner again and laid honourably aside with the other slain. This surprised the Ravens, accustomed to displaying the bodies of their more notable foes, but appeared to impress them deeply, the more so when Kermorvan ordered their banners to be flown above the hill with all the rest. "They have earned it!" he said, returning to his vantage, "And it will confirm the tale of those who fled. That may be of use to us; to cover their shame they will magnify the numbers they met. Among the common warriors rumour will spread that Ekwesh can be our friends and fight beside us; it may even unnerve the true fanatics a little."

"Are you so sure?" demanded Elof. "It may weaken the hold on their minds a little – but enough? And how soon?"

"Not enough to win us this battle, of course. But if we win it ... Ah yes, then it may make a great difference. If. But that remains to be seen. No, my old friend, there is only one thing I am sure of, and that is that there is hard hewing ahead before the night comes."

In this Kermorvan proved himself a true prophet. There are many accounts in the Chronicles of that last and greatest of battles in the defence of Kerys, and they differ over many points; for so vast a conflict can seldom look alike to any one pair of eyes, and to each man his own standpoint must often have seemed the most hard-pressed and perilous. Yet all agree that between midday and evening four more such great onslaughts were unleashed against the combined ranks of Kerys and Morvanhal, and smaller assaults unnumbered, and that many broke through even to the king's rock. But though they differ as to how, they agree that the ranks, though sadly diminished and frequently broken, never panicked nor sought to run, and that all these assaults were turned, though at great cost; all, save the very last.

For there came a point towards evening, when Kermorvan, squinting out across his re-grouping lines, turned a weary head to his friends and said, quite calmly, "They have done bravely, very bravely. But I do not believe they can withstand the next assault."

A grim silence fell. Elof, looking out at the sinking sun glaring from a grey sky, realised that he had long ago accepted that this would be so; it had scarcely seemed to matter. Ils, refastening the bandage around her slashed leg, lifted an eyebrow, but said nothing; evidently she felt much the same. Kermorvan looked from one to another of his captains, then at the grey-gold blade he held, the blood of many men intermingled upon it; a catapult arrow whined overhead, and he nodded, as if coming to some further conclusion. Then he turned to Elof. "There is one stroke we might essay, still; but those archers on the southward hills with their long view may ruin it. I have not asked this of you before, because it was too perilous to justify; but they must be dealt with, or at the least distracted, even as the onslaught comes. At all events their attention must be held, if only for a few minutes. That you can do, and no other."

Elof grinned, felt his mouth tense and turn wolfish. He hefted Gorthawer and raised himself on the one crutch left him. "Build me a good fire, then!" was all he said.

Out on the slopes the ranks of shields were moving
again, and another chant beginning, along the lines of the
first but louder, more mocking; they too scented victory,
fearfully depleted as their numbers were. *Dey-oh-
towayhiau!* sang a single voice, and deep voices a guttural
response *Iho-te-cheugh!* Then the line was repeated, but to
a different response, a singing bass line *Kawei-oh-hoh!
Kawei-oh!* to which spears were brandished, sawing the air.
Then they were struck against shields – no longer merely
rattled, but hammered butt-first, three savage blows that
made the hide boom like a metallic drum. The ring and
crash of it burst like thunderclaps among the hills and
echoed shivering from the cliffs; snow dropped from ledges,
rocks split and tumbled away with a roar. Though his head
reeled with the noise, Elof caught the meaning of the song
all too clearly.

> *Sheep of the valley*
> *Come to the slaughter!*
> *Sheep of the valley*
> *Come and be slain! Come die!*
> *Calves of the bison*
> *Stand for the arrow!*
> *Calves of the bison,*
> *Come to the bloodtrough! Come bleed!*

All eyes were on him, and he felt appallingly alone. He
realised suddenly that he had no idea what Kermorvan
intended; his hands full with the Ravens, he had taken little
part in the actual planning of the battle. But then the fire
blazed and crackled, and he had no time left to ask; he swept
down his wings, held them a moment as fierce heat beat on
his numbed cheeks, then swept them back with a rush that
caused the draggled banners overhead to thrash and stiffen.
The heat vanished with painful suddenness; he dared not
linger, but raised an arm in salute to Kermorvan and his
friends, and letting fall his crutches he swept up into the icy
airs. A great shout went up from the ranks below as he rose,
as if he was some living banner, and he knew the fleet men
must be remembering how once before he had plucked

victory from defeat for them, and hoping. They were a burden, those hopes; they weighed down his spirit, so that he found no release in his flight, only grim necessity. A wailing command drifted up to him, and a deep shout in answer; he looked down across the hills, and saw the great lines of shields, sweeping forward like the incoming tide. The orange sun glinted dully off his plumage; he was high enough, he would have to be. He hovered a moment, wings thrashing, gauging his time, and drew Gorthawer from his belt. Then as the Ekwesh shieldwalls reached the plain and broke into their last run,, he tilted in the air and dropped, the black blade out-thrust before him, falling as fast, he felt, as the lightning that had forged it. He did not, could not see that moment when among a shivering crash of shields the two great armies collided for the last time; but in his very bones he felt it.

There were the archers, a rough line of catapults and a few hundred men scattered widely across the hill top, taking advantage of whatever small eminence they could find. He saw one perched in the blackened carcass of a tree, and swooped towards him. The man had time to see, to whirl around, loose one wild shot and shriek; for so Elof had intended. All eyes turned to him as the black blade struck, and the fountaining body fell headlong through the branches: then the air was alive with shafts. They fell far behind him, some among the catapults. Another archer, perched on a rock, fell right in his path and was cut down; two more dived for cover, a third was less swift and paid the penalty. Elof whirled around, wings thrashing, and headed for the catapults. Only the lightest had a chance to fire before he was among them, hewing out at their cords and the arms that drew them; windlasses spun and sang, men shrieked and fell, many under the panicky shafts of their fellows, as he passed. Compared to the slaughter on the plains below it was nothing, but it ensured what Kermorvan desired, that every eye on that southern ridge should be fastened on him as he glided up and away. His, though, turned towards the plain, seeking some assurance that his flight had worked.

He found only dismay. The ranks of Kerys and Morvanhal, so sorely tried, had broken even as Kermorvan predicted. No longer was there any calculated regrouping, no squares, no order at all; it seemed that no man had any sense of it left in him, had any thought left at all save to flee and save his own skin as best he could. Elof was appalled to see the king's rock empty, abandoned, and the many banners bobbing this way and that near the head of the throng, fleeing desperately over the valley's edge and down onto the steep slopes beyond; they must have fled almost at once, before the collision even. The Ekwesh, abandoning their own shieldwall in triumphant contempt, were streaming this way and that after the stragglers. Where was Kermorvan, then? He would never have allowed this, if he were still in command. With leaden heart Elof soared up, fighting an urge to fall like a thunderbolt upon the Ekwesh chieftains; that would help nobody, neither his friends nor Kara – but what could, now?

Then from his greater height he saw over the valley's rim, and laughed aloud in glory and amazement. A wilder gamble he had never witnessed, nor a more marvellous feat of order. Perhaps the Ekwesh thought so also, as in their bloodthirsty pursuit they poured over the rim of the slopes, ready to butcher all they overtook. For what they found there was no terrified trail of fugitives, but the same fearsome shieldwalls they had faced all that day long, regrouped now in three solid ranks all along the slope, with more forming behind as the seeming fugitives poured in. The rear ranks must have pulled back first, pretending to flee while the outer ranks held, and used the time to order their array; the archers could have seen that happening, and passed a warning to the main force. But because Kermorvan had unleashed Elof onto them, they had not, and the greater part of that last onslaught poured over the slope at speed like maddened beasts stampeded into a spike-lined pit.

And like beasts they perished. Many, unable to stop themselves, plunged headlong onto the spear-points; others sought to turn but slipped and fell on the trodden snow; some managed to turn, only to be knocked back down by their own eager fellows rushing along behind, or struck down by the stragglers they had thought to harry. In the blinking of an eye the slope had turned to a scarlet fall of blood, so many died in those first chaotic seconds; chaotic for the Ekwesh, for among the ranks of their foes there reigned an implacable calm, as if Kermorvan's cool mind lay like a mantle across them.

The onrush of the Ekwesh slackened, as from the cries below some realization dawned that all was not as they thought it. But even as they stumbled gradually to a halt horns sounded, and with a single hoarse shout the shield-wall rose and paced forward, up to the edge of the slope and over. Even to Elof it seemed a fearsome sight, those solid walls of shields, rank after rank, arising suddenly over the valley's rim, blood-reddened, flashing with red fire as they caught the last long rays of the sunset. To the Ekwesh, seized by sudden uncertainty after the intoxication of victory, it must have seemed appalling. Many must have thought it a whole new army, come in the nick of time to the relief of the one they had broken; but even to those who did not it must have seemed no less marvellous that ranks once scattered should cohere once more. Grim fighters as the Ekwesh were, they had never been held together by the same strong bonds of discipline as the men of Morvanhal, or followed a leader out of regard and love, rather than fear. Thus all the awe and terror that Louhi and her shadowy kindred of the Ice relied upon in dealing with their thralls turned at that crucial point against her. For all their subservience to their chieftains, for all the hold the shamans of the Hidden Clan had on the hearts of the Ekwesh, they had always been prone to panic. For those who are dominated through fear are in the end ruled by it, and their hearts may fail them sooner than those whose obedience is freely given, and truly earned.

So it had been before with the Ekwesh, when the Mastersmith fell. So it had proved in the Eastlands, when Kara's influence was taken from them; and here, for all the fire that she, Morghannen, Warrior of the Powers, Chooser of the Slain, could pour into their hearts, it was so again. They saw what they could not understand, a menace arising where none should have been; and being accustomed to fear such things, they could not confront it. They looked back to their chieftains, only to see, high in the airs above them, the vision of an armed man aloft on immense wings. The greater part of them took fright, and turned on their heels to run. Many did not; but they were out of their shield-wall now, each man for himself against an army of men they had moulded in their own likeness, as fell and grim as any, and better armed. They stood, and perished; and the rest, seeing this, fled all the faster. In vain the chieftains cried out from the hill-tops, in vain they came down onto the plain and harangued the fugitives, sought to seize them, and in the end menaced them with weapons; their own men cut them down. Into the passes of the hills a broken rabble streamed, leaderless, heedless; above them the sun set and to their minds the sudden darkness and bitter cold seemed only another device of their foes. They sank down and sought shelter, or ran on mindless till they fell, without thought of food or fire or the means to make either; and the frost settled upon them like the wrath of the Ice they had betrayed, and tightened its grip. They were hardy men, but they had fought a long day, and that last run sapped their endurance. Of those who ran from the battle more than two third parts are thought to have perished that night among the hills; and it is said that some fell not to the cold, but to the many kinds of nightwalkers and trolls the Ice had sent to haunt those lands, who cared not whose blood they took. To the High Gate and the wrath of Louhi only a fragment returned of the vast force that had been sent out; yet in her pride, and the nearness of her victory, she gave no thought to flight, but made ready for the siege she guessed must follow.

On the field they had fled few thought ahead to that. There was no rejoicing, for so utterly drained and exhausted were they in body and mind that they could scarce take in the fact of victory, let alone its scale and consequence. When the horns sounded their release the weary soldiers of the shieldwalls could only sink down among the bloody mud, grateful for even a brief respite, a moment of life where neither man nor weapon menaced them. Gradually, as they grew used to the vast wind-scoured silence that had replaced frenzied tumult, they began to realise what they had done; but the awful cost of it was clear to all. Of the armies of Kerys and Morvanhal together, that had numbered some thirty thousand men, there remained only seventeen thousand alive, and well-nigh two thousand of those grievously enough wounded to be unable to fight. How many Ekwesh had fallen was never tallied; but it is generally agreed that out of a full force of some fifty thousand not twelve thousand had joined that mad flight into the darkness, and four thousand at most survived it. All around them, then, as far as the distant foothills, as near as the trampled paste at their feet, the stench in their nostrils utterly inescapable, that darkling plain was carpeted with the broken limbs and the spilled blood of at least fifty thousand men. No other description of the scene than that is given in any chronicle; and none is needed.

There could be scant celebration in the midst of that horrendous carnage. The salute with which the armies greeted Elof as he came gliding clumsily in on the back of night rose hoarse and grim from their throats; but a salute it was. Exhausted, the force of his wings long spent, he missed his precarious footing and landed hard in that noisome mud; but he lost no time in reporting to the king all that he had seen. Kermorvan nodded, as if he had conjured up the rout already in his mind's eye. "I hoped as much. Victory is ours; and yet it only flutters before us, to be blown hence if we do not stretch out a hand to seize it, however weary. We must march out at once to lay siege to the High Gate itself!"

"Must we indeed?" interrupted one of the nobles of Kerys. "My lord, you have worked great wonders, but at great cost; do not wastefully make it greater!" Elof bit his lip; it had swiftly become clear that the vast majority of their fallen, as many as eleven thousand, were Kerysmen. This might easily have been because they were so much wearier and worse fed for months before, less well fed and skilled in war; but malicious tongues would not be found lacking to suggest that Kermorvan had spilled those lives to shield his own folk. His horsemen, in particular, he had been most sparing with.

"Aye, my lord!" put in another noble. "Your will swayed the battle well enough, but can it whip up limbs whose strength is spent, hasten hearts at the brink of cracking? For your own folk I cannot speak, but the men of Kerys are foredone; they must rest, or perish!"

"If they try resting on this freezing butcher's slab they'll perish anyway!" growled Roc. "Of cold in the night or pestilence tomorrow! Better die on the march than that!"

But Kermorvan raised a commanding hand. "You are both of you right, my friends. But no dispute need arise, because our forces must be divided in any case. The High Gate has two approaches, and we must lay siege to them both. What I command, therefore, is this; hot on the heels of the Ekwesh shall go the forces of Morvanhal, and any others who wish it. But the men of Kerys, who have suffered more in the march here, may descend into the valley and there find shelter and fuel for fires among the trees. But having rested for a few hours, they will cross the frozen river, climb the northern slopes and lay siege to the Gate from that flank, blocking all approaches, and watchful for new forces coming from the north. You will travel faster than we then, because you know the land, and will not have to deal with stragglers. But all this must be accomplished by dawn, and no later; that is your charge, my lords."

So it was that three long columns filed away from that terrible field, and left it empty beneath the gathering darkness. Three, for not even the wounded could be suffered to linger, lest the carnage breed disease; Kermorvan was sending them, with such comforts as could be spared, southward towards the landings. But his own forces he led with little or no respite up into the hills, walking like the least of his footmen to spare the strength of his horses for when it might be needed. In this, and in much else, he was proven wise; for many times that night, as the column wound like a long snake through a mass of little hills and vales, it was set upon by bands of Ekwesh diehards, willing to make desperate and damaging strikes in search of food, or simply revenge. Cavalry proved the most effective answer to such depredations, charging swiftly and frightenly up and down the long lines; it was for such a chance, in victory or retreat, that Kermorvan had reserved them.

But there were other enemies abroad against whom cavalry was of little use. The breeze was freshening as they neared the sea, but the clouds stayed obstinately solid; they marched without light of moon or star, and as few torches as they dared. In the shifting of darkness shapes seemed to move, shadows to skulk at the edge of vision. They were not all illusions. Among the deepest shadows of the dales dark things snarled and slunk away from Ekwesh corpses, or flitted up like great bats. Men who straggled or strayed from the main column, even a short way all too often vanished without trace; in one deep dell, overgrown with thorns, three men vanished. When Roc took a party of Ravens to search for them, they found only bloodstains and strange foot prints; and at the sight of those the Ravens all but dragged him away. The mounted scouts seemed to rove safely enough, until Elof, serving as one since he had perforce to ride, found two of them dismembered in the shadow of a giant boulder; even as he summoned help he himself was snared by the huge arms that reached over the top, and almost met the same fate before lancers and mounted bowmen arrived to slay the brutes. Kermorvan, inspecting the scene as the column plodded past, grimaced at the rivulets of dark blood upon the rock, the tangles of greyish fur hanging over its edge, and the yellow tusks grinning moistly between tautening lips. "Our old friends the snow-trolls," he remarked, his face drawn and pale, as he watched the columns come plodding up the slope. "Three of them, come back to finish what their cousins of our land failed in long ago. I almost thought they had succeeded."

Cold shivered on Elof's neck. "Thanks to your foresight, they did not."

"Thanks to my horsemen; they heard you before we did. Those brutes! They were not even killing out of hunger; the remains of some twenty men lie behind that rock, set neatly to keep in the snow." He shuddered. "I could curse this land, but it is accursed already; what will cleanse it? What will sweep away this dreadful night?"

"The wind, maybe," remarked Ils, limping up to them. "Feel it; it blows stronger, and we have marched a good five hours now. We must be nearing the sea." The chill breath touched Elof's neck again, and he realised it was real; it blew away the reek of slaughter, and touched his lips with the keen tang of drift. Together they hurried up to the hill-top, and even as they climbed they saw that the heavy clouds had begun to shift, solid no longer but stirring, rending, tearing; here and there pale gleams shone through the gaps, and the snow-clad hills around them stood out silver-clear against the deep blue skies.

"The banners of the Ice break and grow ragged!" said Elof. "Let it be a signal to her!" But even as he spoke they reached the summit, and Ils cried out and pointed. They had reached the sea indeed; at the base of that long slope it lay, its surf all but deadened by the ice that choked its shores. But they hardly spared it a second glance, for there, only a little way to the north of them, the High Gate also had awoken to life, shining and shimmering like some monstrous jewel beneath the sinking moon.

From the battle plains they had seen the gleam of ice enshrouding it; but now they stared in wonder and horror, and many rubbed their eyes, as if some glamour of magecraft were laid upon their sight. Even in the few short hours since last they saw it, it had changed and grown, its battlements glittering beneath crowns of dazzling snow, its galleries hung about with icicles of incalculable size and beauty, its stern walls lost beneath rippling depths of translucent blue and green, rich as sapphire, deep as the sunlit sea. They seemed a greater architecture in themselves, a palace of ice that encased, enveloped the ancient stronghold of stone almost mockingly, a shell of vast columns that dwarfed the original structure, immense blue-lit pillars that tapered down even into the frozen cascade of the waterfall below Its stern lines softened into curves as sweeping as an ice-bound wave, its straight unworn walls swirled and orna-mented with fantastic shapes, the High Gate in all its grandeur was reduced only to the barren core upon which something vastly more majestic was founded. It was a towering vision of the might and nobility of the ancient Powers, a creation of unhuman beauty and strength so great that it awoke a yearning ache in the hearts of all who gazed upon it, as if they were children looking from their own scrawled slates to the supreme jewel of some great master's mind and hand, and seeing the vast gulf that separated them, their own joys shrivelling the petty things they had been so proud of. It was beauty that struck men like a blow, and cowed them.

And just as it mocked their ideals, so equally it seemed to laugh at their warlike ambitions; for what could any assault launched by men mean to such walls as those? How could they be assailed, being ice deeply overlaid upon stone, doubling the strengths of both? Who could scale that wall of slippery glass, or hurl stone or dart against it? The largest throwing weapons of men would be as helpless against it as slingshots in the hands of their children. In every sense it seemed to tower above them, this awesome thing, as indifferent to their hatred as it would be to their worship; they might do either, and it would scarcely matter. A great silence fell over that whole army; men fell upon their knees, or shrank down behind their shields, or simply stood and stared at that eerie fortress of the cold as the moon sank slowly down behind it, crowning it with light and leaving them once more in darkness. By its mere existence it cast down their hearts and held their minds in thrall.

Elof felt no such urge to bow down, though he shared in their awe; the undertow of horror and revulsion it awoke in his mind was too great for that. In the fate of that noble fortress, encased within that sternly glittering shell, he seemed to see a vision of the impending fate of the whole rich and varied world that he loved, and of Kara most of all; and it came to him now that it might be too late to prevent it. Was the chilly triumph of that vision, the sudden burgeoning of it, an earnest that the crucial point had already passed, the balance already tilted? Had the cold hands of the Ice closed at last upon the world?

So he was held, as was each of them in their own way. In the end it was Ils' voice, loud and sardonic, that broke the silence upon the hill. "A pretty toy, if it's to your mind! But don't mistake it for more solid craft! What's this beside the high mountains, eh? That Ilmarinen forged from the very earthfires; and gave to us as a refuge and a home, when last these chilly Powers sought to plaster the world thus in their tuppenny trumpery!" She gave a snort of scornful laughter, echoed by Gurri and the other duergar, and thumped Elof and Kermorvan hard upon the back. "Look with the eyes of the Elder Folk, you fools of men, and don't be deceived by mere melting charms!"

Kermorvan shook himself, massaging his neck and blinking like a man awaking from a long and haunted sleep. "I wondered why the clouds broke so conveniently," he muttered. "When she might have held them. She was readying her defences; she meant us to see the place clearly."

"And now it'll work against her!" whooped Ils triumphantly. "Look alive, man, and don't just stand there blinking! It'll be dawn soon – a clear dawn! And what have we laboured so long on our weapon for, if not for this?"

Kermorvan gazed down at her a moment, then flinging aside his customary dignity he caught her up and kissed her with startling vehemence. Then, setting her down gently he seized a horn from one of his captains, and blew a piercing blast. It coursed like a shock of lightning through those still ranks; men jumped and shuddered where they stood shaking off the subtle thrall the vision had laid upon them. "*Morvan morlanhal!*" he shouted, the ancient and bitter battlecry of his line. "*Movan shall arise!* Up, all of you, and into your ranks once more! Stand firm upon the living earth, feel your blood flow and heed no sendings of the barren Ice! Form up, and await the dawn!"

His clear voice rang against those glittering battlements, challenging and defiant; and it seemed to awaken a response in the world around them, from the depths to the heights of the very skies. For even as the army took up his battlecry and sent it roaring like a tide against the castellations of the Ice, so in the east behind them came the first faint gleam of light, grey at first but turning swiftly to the palest gold. And as the men came streaming past, summoned by horn calls to form their shieldwalls across the hill-top, answering calls came echoing out of the still-dark chasms below the falls. Kermorvan nodded in satisfaction, and pointed; up the far flank of the vale wound what looked like a serpent of golden lights. It was the army of Kerys, hurrying up from its warm fires to take its appointed place among the northern hills, and close the siege of the Gate. "I commanded them to keep well back from the fortress, in the shelter of the hills, until any actual assault," he remarked.

"That was wise," Elof answered, though inwardly he writhed at the thought of what must follow. "It gives us a freer hand. And I think we will need it."

Kermorvan nodded. "I fear you are right. She will scorn to answer us if we seek to talk with her now; each moment may be a gain to her, any one might be critical. I will not deny Louhi a chance of terms – if only for Kara's sake; but first we must make her feel the power you have given us.

Make ready, then, and I will sound the call."

Elof stood rooted as the tall man strode away, feeling helpless, feeling as if the Ice flowed through him, veins and vitals frozen to crystal. Ils, oddly hesitant, touched his arm, and when he made no response she looped her own through it. He smiled at her thinly, "You're slipping, my lady. When he kissed you you didn't hack him on the shins."

Ils shrugged. "He learns, that long lad. Decidedly he learns."

"Would you kick me?"

For answer Ils twisted around and pulled his face down to her a moment, then as swiftly released him. Kermorvan's horns, marching out before the host, were sounding a single braying challenge, and the first full rays of the sun were blazing up over the eastern rim of the world. "Now go! Go, and may our work blister the pale hide off her!"

That first call had set the soldiers swiftly to work. They laid down those great shields, upon which Elof and every smith of Kermorvan's and Ils's realms, from apprentice to master, had laboured through many long months; the remorseless heat and sweat of that time came back to him as he watched, but also a growing thrill of excitement. Those who had lost or damaged their shields in the battle had gathered more from the slain, and from the store of spare ones they had brought. Now they were unscrewing the heavy bosses of the shields; behind these were the bolts which held on their wooden grips, and their covers of sturdy fabric. Off came the grips, and were laid aside; then off came the covers, and a swift golden shimmer seemed to play among the ranks. Quickly then the shields were laid down, and the grips refastened; then the horns sounded another call, and because this was a set and practised drill the whole army picked up its reversed shields almost as one man. Cursing sergeants ran to berate the inevitable few who had failed, but also to assist; speed was the all-important thing here.

Behind Elof stood some of the few Kerys folk who had chosen to follow Kermorvan rather than rest; they were mostly young and hardy, and two of them, to his surprise, were among the few women who had come out to fight. They had stayed close to Roc because he could talk to them easily in their own dialect, and they were plying him with puzzled questions. But all he would say was "Do you watch!" And it was not such a bad answer, Elof thought, for even as the next call sounded and the ranks reformed, some earnest of their purpose could not help but appear. The ice-wall nearest them came suddenly alive, shot with fleeting shimmers and sparkles of golden radiance, beautiful but so bright one hardly dared look at it, for it left blazing streaks of purple in one's sight.

One of the Kerysmen gasped and swore in astonishment, then fell silent, as Elof turned to him with what must have been a death's-head grin. "Well?" Elof demanded.

"A – a mirror!" stammered the Kerysman, in horrified fascination. "A mirror of the sun! A ... b-burning-glass!"

"Aye, lad," said Roc with grim satisfaction. "That's just exactly what it is! The most mirrors there's ever been, or the biggest, however you care to look at it. But not just any mirror turns the sun better, gathering rather than scatter-turning a blow better than a flat one. And an inward-curving mirror turns the sun betrer, gathering rather than scatter-ing the light. It was Hella's own job trying to find a shape good for both, let me tell you! But Master Elof did it!" For long moments the Kerysmen and women watched that great burst of light pulse and shiver upon the fortress wall, awed and fascinated; but evidently one of the women was also deeply disturbed by something.

"Well?" demanded Elof again. "Speak up, woman, I won't bite!"

"It's just that – even though the mirrors gather the light – can it really be enough – against ice such as that? True, there are many – but they would still all need to cast the light close together, into one single narrow place! How may they aim all for that one small target, for the time they will need?"

Elof nodded gravely. "There might be the makings of smiths in you folk still. As you say, men's arms weaken, their aim wavers; we could not depend on it for a moment. So within that metal we mastersmiths set virtues, potencies and attributes fitting to both its tasks; for what fits a shield better than to hold firm with its fellows in the shieldwall? Did you wonder at how tight ours held? If they had been made of lodestone they would not have held faster, nor moved more as one; yet when needed they could be plucked apart again without effort. And so it is with them now; or it will be, when all is prepared, and the command is given. Roc – by your leave …"

Roc nodded curtly, and turning to Elof's mount he handed him down the great shield slung from its saddlebow; the grips had already been reversed. Elof tore the cover from it, revealing a surface still mirror-bright after its long voyage; that was a work of virtues also, and of subtle alloys. "This is one of the master-shields," he said quietly. "There are others, here and there among the host; but they will command only if this and others of greater precedence are turned from the sun. We tested this weapon when we had only a few shields; where the master-shield's light falls, all follow. One or two, even ten, do little. But thirty under a clear noon sun could fire a tree, given time – or a hundred, a man. And though some, and their wielders, are lost to us, we have – what would you say? – some eight thousand still." He held the shield to his lips, and they heard him murmur a few words in a tongue of old; only his friends knew their origins.

> *Eynhere elof hallns styrmer*
> *Stallans imars olnere elof …*

It was the phrase the Mastersmith had first shown him, the words of power that had governed the shaping of Tarnhelm and sword, and even of himself; for in one word of ambiguity, signifying both *one alone* and *smith*, they had given him his name.

> *A lone thing gains power surpassing*
> *When joined among many by a smith …*

So it had been with him; for without his friends, what would he have been? And so it was with this. He cried out suddenly, and brandished the shield aloft. From along the slope above Kermorvan answered him, and other commanders about the hill. Then slowly, carefully, Elof angled his shield to catch the sun as it lifted above the horizon, and cast it into the heart of that amorphous glow. And as he did so, he caught his breath; for with a sudden brilliant flicker, like coals shifting in a fire, all eight thousand shields, each the height and breadth of a man, tilted to follow him.

For a moment it was as if the sun had stretched forth, not the long and lazy beams of dawning, but a limb of its own blazing substance, a great arm of flame that struck against that glittering wall. An image of fire like a living thing danced mockingly upon it. For long seconds nothing seemed to happen; then, as Elof's arm settled and grew steadier, and the other shields followed it ever more closely, the dancing image grew finer, more concentrated, impossible to look at. Even the reflected radiance of it was dazzling, and the air about them, that had been so frosty a moment since, grew slowly warm as spring. It settled and steadied until it seemed that the mirrors had captured the sun itself, and sent it out to fight; for upon that bright surface there formed a perfect image of the blazing disk high above.

In that very moment there came a deafening, explosive report, and across the face of the Ice a great white line sprang out, a crack that coursed and spread across the shining surface in a mad fusillade of sound, thrusting out others like living roots, crazing and opaquing all its transparency. From the heart of the blazing light there came a sudden frenzied shriek, the cry of the steam that boiled out through the cracks. But not fast enough, for with a sudden dull roar a great chunk of the ice was blasted out by its pressure, and went crashing down in a mad shattering music onto the frozen falls below. A wild wolfish cheer went up from the host, and Elof, his face taut with concentration, began very delicately to swing the beam of sunfire around towards the centre of the tower. He had played such games as this in childhood, in his few precious moments of idleness, turning the sun with a bright flake of mica or metal; it was strange to turn the light in such deadly earnest now. If he brought down one of those great ice-pillars ...

But a warning shout from above showed him the activity upon the upper reaches of the castle; men were moving, files of black-clad warriors pouring out of the gates onto the paths along the ridge that led around the slopes of the Pillars of the Gate and up towards the army above. He winced, hating Louhi more than ever for what she was making him do. Slowly, very carefully, he began to shift his shield once more, as Kermorvan, breathless, came bounding down to his side. "Easy now!" breathed the king. "There's time enough; and with luck we need only give them a slight lesson!"

"I hope so!" grated Elof, fighting down his nausea. But it was too late for regrets; the first mass of warriors had reached the hill's edge. So had the light. Flame and fire flashed up as it touched; for there was no chill in the bodies of men to match that of the Ice. Like heedless insects they rushed into that burst of sunfire, and like insects they blazed up, withered and dwindled to a charred nothingness. Those at the light's edge were not instantly consumed, but leaped and capered as it touched them, and burst into little pillars of flame; those behind fell back, blinded, and found their hair and clothes catch about them. This way and that they rushed, fell on the steep slope and rolled crazily downhill through the melting snow till they fell like blazing star-stones out into the abyss. The disk of light played searingly back and forth across the hillsides, splitting stones, steaming snow and blasting the black earth beneath to white powder; there was no shelter from it, for even those who sought it sprang up shrieking as air like the breath of some immense furnace wrapped itself around them, flaying their skin and blistering their lungs. The light began to tremble then, till Kermorvan put a steadying hand on the edge of the master-shield, countering Elof's unsteadiness.

But it was more also than his foes could stand. From shameful defeat they had fled to the fastness of the Gate, that to them embodied the Ice's conquering invulnerability, only to find it menaced also, and themselves driven forth to perish against a force they could not understand, let alone fight. That point of sunfire seemed to them more fearsome and awful than any of the terrors and wonders by which the Ice had fastened its thrall upon them, a greater, more devouring horror than all the dark rituals it demanded. It broke more than their onrush; it broke them. They obeyed that ancient enthrall, and died instantly; or they cast it off, and fled. Still they streamed from the doors of the Gate; but no longer in any order, and not towards the shieldwalls on the distant slopes. This way and that they ran, scuttling like pale things from beneath an overturned stone, no longer thralls of anything save their own terror. In pride and despair some flung themselves down from the heights, or ran headlong into the flame; but most fled incontinently into the vale or the hills once more, and there perished in the hardships of the days that followed. A few who kept some shred of sanity ran southward, around and behind the slopes where Kermorvan's army stood, for there neither Ice nor Sun could reach them. But there the Ravens were waiting, for Kermorvan had stationed them against such a chance. A few offered fight, and were cut down; the remainder were gathered in, and by Kermorvan's command well treated. They were no longer a threat to anyone. In one blazing day of wrath the cold grip on their people had been tried in an ordeal of fire; and in that fire it melted away. So also melted the ice upon the walls of the Gate; for Elof, glad to be free of such slaughter, had already swung back his shield. and after it he drew the sun, as if like Raven in the old tale he had stolen it for the succour of mankind.

Against the tallest of all the glassy pillars he flung it like a coin of whitehot gold, and ice and image shattered together, cracking, splintering, exploding outwards in a cloud of flying spicules; downward he played it, and cracks ran ahead of it, all the long length of the pillar. Great showers of shattered whiteness came plummeting after, fell through the beam and blasted back up as steam; then, with a tormented moaning crunch, the whole top-heavy column blew free of the main sheet and tilted out into emptiness. With the same momentous deliberation as the glacier-face falling into the sea it toppled away, away and down into the valley below. It struck the frozen falls with a ringing crash of glassy thunder, rebounded off with sickening slowness, and rolled down the flank of the vale, crushing a great swathe through the pines and plummeting at last onto the frozen surface of one of the lakes, splitting it to fragments and raising a huge fountain of dark water. Heads turned to watch, for that was an awesome fall; but their shields seemed to stir in their hands, for Elof, with a savage grimace of triumph, was already swinging the beam back against the patch of bared stone. Back and forth it coursed, and as the cold stone grew swiftly warm the ice began to melt outwards. A growing stream of meltwater poured down, and the searing air boiled into the gap; cracks exploded along the wall, and suddenly, with great tearing crashes, pillar after pillar began to tear free under its own weight and drop down into the chasm.

All the army of Morvanhal cheered wildly as they felt the power in their own hands blast those daunting walls to nothing; even Kermorvan was yelling in delight, crying out ancestral vows of vengeance for the razing of Morvan. Only Elof's face was grim, a mask as set as any Ekwesh shaman's, feeling the might of the sun tearing at the heart of his foe. He caught Kermorvan's eye, and called "Is that enough of a taste for her, think you?" Kermorvan nodded, and signalled to his men, and through the rumble of falling ice the bright-voiced horns rang clear. For long moments it seemed as if there would be no response from within the Gate; it stood there, silent and unmoving, while its shattered ice continued to sizzle and melt and fall away from the heated stone. Angrily Kermorvan signalled that the call should be repeated more loudly, and his heralds blew till they were scarlet-faced. As the sound died they all heard, quite clearly, the thin cold music of icicles vibrating in sympathy; but still there was no response. Elof frowned. He tilted his shield with unhurried care, and the sun-disc began to creep slowly up towards the still untouched crown of the Gate. As it settled on the rim of the first balcony a great cloud of steam arose, and meltwater poured down in a sudden stream. Then at last from within the battlements a single horn rang out in answer. Elof stared, cursed, and the light juddered violently. Within the very heart of that blazing orb, full in its glare, a door had opened, and onto the central dais of the balcony, raised high upon stairs, stepped a majestic figure. About her blonde hair the fire danced in a corona of light, against the sleek whiteness of her robe that sunblast shimmered and glowed; yet neither she nor the shadowy shapes behind her shrivelled or vanished, or seemed in any way affected.

She leaned out, resting her hands lightly upon the balustrade before her, and a swift whiteness seemed to course along it, spreading as milk whitens water, glittering as it grew thicker, radiating cold flashes of rainbow hues from the true sun overhead. As it ran out along the outer battlements men filed out behind it, tall warriors of the Ekwesh, but with their black shields painted only with plain bars of white; Elof knew them at once for men of the Hidden Clan, deepest and most fanatical votaries of the Ice. And behind them other shapes came lumbering, nightmarish, inhuman, trolls and worse beasts of shadow. Elof had no eyes for them; for he had glimpsed another, slighter shape. Bare-limbed and slender in a corselet of bright mail, helmless so that her short dark hair showed, she came to Louhi's side as she beckoned, suffered an arm to be laid about her slim shoulders, and inclined her head to rest it against the white-clad breast.

"Well, brave men of Morvanhal?" called a smoothly mocking voice. "What of all your brave deeds now?"

"What indeed?" Kermorvan shouted back. "We have defeated your army, driven away your rear-guard and shattered your walls of ice. If you do not surrender and submit yourself to us, we will melt the very stone beneath you!"

The laugh that drifted down was sweet and silvery. "Will you indeed? And can you now? See, I bathe in this brightness of yours; for the heat is not in it that can burn me! I drink such petty fires, and make them my own; ask the clever smithling who made you your toy! So what then, my brave man-child? You must move swiftly, remember; for your power dies with the day's end; and the night is mine! What then, man-child? What then?"

Looks of dismay flickered across men's faces, much as the heat across their shields; but Kermorvan smiled calmly. "What then? Another dawn, my lady Louhi! And by that dawn you will be alone, and your life at risk. Can all the Ice stand thus against men, with such power as this in their hands? Whatever a winter achieves, the first suns of spring will undo more swiftly. Your power is slow, my lady, so slow that but for its strength it would be laughable. And now we have found a greater. You are defeated."

The bright peal of laughter that drifted down to them sounded disturbingly true; there was almost an affectionate ring to it, delighting as an adult might in the absurd follies of a child. "*I?* defeated? Believe me, my fair lordling, those of my kind are not so easily defeated, nor lightly slain. The

Great Ice has come and gone many a thousand times since this world of ours was gathered out of dust and given to us to direct; do you really think your toy can change that at a few strokes? But, let us suppose it might – have you thought what must follow?" She shook her blond hair till it foamed about her shoulders and fell across her breasts. "Of course you have not. But, man-child, the Ice you would melt, what will become of it? It will not simply vanish, will it? It must turn to water, of course. As much water; and what then?" Her voice hardened suddenly, and became queenly, regal, stern as cold steel mirroring the light that played still about her. "Fool, shall I tell you what must happen? Into the seas that vastness of water shall flow as all waters must, and swell them mightily, and they shall rise and overwhelm the land! And with it shall sink all the petty realms of men, and the last pitiful hopes of your ill-starred race! Destroy the Ice, and you destroy yourselves!"

A shudder of dismay fell across the army at her words, and the disregard she still showed for the consuming sunfire; rumour rumbled among the ranks. But it was Kermorvan's turn to laugh, a broad, confident chuckle not at all like his rare outbursts of mirth; he meant it to be heard. "Lady, lady," he laughed, "you have learned to threaten well; but you threaten too cleverly for simple folk like us! If the Ice cannot overwhelm all the land as Ice, then why should it do any better as water?" Answering guffaws broke out among the ranks, and the mood of the army was turned again in an instant. But Elof did not laugh; he could not take his eyes from that slender figure by Louhi's side, all but eclipsed by her brilliant light.

"No, lady," said Kermorvan then, growing more grimly serious with every word, "I fear nobody believes you. But I tell you this – even if I did, still all your threats would not divert me the breadth of one of your fair golden hairs from my purpose."

His words echoed against the bared stone, and the tall woman swayed suddenly, as if struck in the body. Kermorvan caught Elof by the shoulder, and said sharply "Above her head!" Elof hissed his agreement, and tilted back his shield with minute precision. The sun settled on the upper galleries as if it was caught between the high towers of Kerys, and their icy sheathing exploded. Steam boiled out around the people on the battlements, and Louhi had to throw herself aside to avoid a rain of jagged fragments.

"Stop it!" they heard her scream, stumbling up, "*Stop it!*" She was raging now, all pretence of suavity gone. "Mind-less vermin, can you not even see? All that you have, all that you are you owe to us! Our chance creation – a by-blow, an accident of our power ..." With savage precision Elof shone the sunlight closer. Then he stopped abruptly as he saw her hurl a figure forward against the balustrade; it was Kara, looking out with wide alarmed eyes among the boiling steam, but making no effort to struggle. The sun's image shook and danced wildly in his quivering grasp. "*You!*" yelled Louhi, and he had no doubt whom she meant. "*Mas-tersmith!* It was your mind dreamed up this pretty toy; who else of your verminkind would have the wit? And it's your hand that sways it now, I'll be bound! Well, do you turn that meddling hand away from me, away from the Ice! Or you'll see its power at work indeed! This creature you claim to care for, though little she thinks of you now – what of her, when your beam is upon us? I need only lift my hand from her and she'll burn to ashes as swift as any common mortal! And what then? We may not die, we higher-born, if we are unbodied against our will; but we do change, and change in the changing. She is weak, and change hangs over her, a change neither you nor I can guess. Bring it upon her, little mastersmith, and how will you ever find her again within the puny lifespan of a man? And would she know you, if you did?"

Elof shot a horrified glance at Kermorvan; but even as he did so, and before the king could answer, the whole great army of shields parted as one, as if they moved of their own accord, dispersing the light in many directions. Elof bowed his head. "Your will is in them," said Kermorvan sombrely. "When it is so strong they heed it even as it forms. You must turn it again, my friend, or we are lost!"

"But there must be something we can do!" cried Elof in dire anguish.

"What then?" Kermorvan demanded bleakly. "Rescue her? But does she want to be rescued? Look at her; she might strike you down as soon as Louhi would, if you tried!"

Elof ground his teeth. "She would want it! She will, can I but win her away again! You should know there are shackles upon her, though you cannot see them!"

"I know!" said the king bitterly. "But can I set that, set her against all the lives at risk, all we have spent already – and all the future of this world? If you cannot nerve yourself to it, I could not blame you; but I also hold a master-shield, and if I must ..."

"Kermorvan!" cried Elof, desperate with anger and alarm. "The ruin of all that is yours would not deter you, you say; *but who are you to command the ruin of mine?*" Roc and Ils sprang up; for they had seen his hand drop to the silver hilt.

Kermorvan did not answer. Instead he said "We have a minute, while Louhi is still gathering her wits. A swift strike at her might free Kara; it is a better chance than none, at all events."

"I could crawl close," offered Roc hoarsely. "With our best archers. Fetch down the bitch with an arrow ..."

Kermorvan shook his head. "They are watching for that, those guards ... Elof, what could reach that balcony in time? A catapult –"

"No; too inaccurate. If only I still had my hammer! But hurling that into such great heat might awaken a worse danger ... My wings, now – but we've no fire ..."

A thin faint smile hovered about Kermorvan's lips. "Do we need it?" Elof slapped hand to palm, and swore.

Within minutes he was strapping his wings about him, and Ils, with infinite care, was directing a growing number of shields around and onto his corselet. For long moments he felt the flaring radiance envelop him, his sight flamed scarlet and his skin prickled agonizingly; then it faded, and his broad pinions drove the searing air from about him, beating with a promise of strength they had never before known. His whole being seemed to tingle with energy, and he grew impatient for his sight to clear. When it did, Kermorvan stood before him, in full armour and helm.

"Can you bear a heavy burden thus?"

"Kara, you mean? Twice over, with ease!"

Kermorvan nodded, lacing his helmet tight for battle.

"Then you can bear me also. You may need me to occupy that guard."

"But – but you're the king ..."

"Of where, save for my friends? You more than any, perhaps; and Kara was my friend also." The grey-gold blade slid from its scabbard. "And in truth, do you know any other warrior who would serve?"

Elof, half smiling, shook his head quickly, once, and his wings spread high above his shoulders; Kermorvan hooked an arm about his neck, Elof caught him by his broad belt, and they lifted. Ils swung back the beam to distract his foes, Elof's wings thrashed like a stormwind and they soared up towards the looming heights of the High Gate. Lean though he looked, Kermorvan was a heavy man, but the smith's strength and the power of the wings bore them both up easily and fast. The wind burned in their faces with the speed of their rush, and the arrows loosed by the guards above flew harmless in their wake. In a few fast breaths, they were crossing the balustrade just below the dais steps, out of sight of those above; a mêlée of startled guards rushed in on them, and Kermorvan, loosing his grip, dropped lightly onto the balcony. His feet skidded upon the rimed tiles, but in the very act of recovering his balance he hewed the first-comer's head from his shoulders; Elof angled his wings, and bowled down three more, one right over the balustrade. The others dropped back, shields raised, and Kermorvan sprang at them. Elof, drawing Gorthawer, was turning to speed up the steps when he heard a scream of wrath from above, and from below a warning blare of horn-calls; a speeding shadow fell across him, and he twisted around in alarm, squinting up at the dark shape that dived out of the sun's glare towards him.

In that blaze of light he judged his distance ill. His first thought was only to warn; his second, that he was responsible for the king's safety, at whatever cost. With that thought the shadow was on him, and the collision sent him spinning around in the air, his ears ringing with a terrible cry of pain. Gorthawer was wrenched from his fingers; he saw something plummet past him and crash upon the balcony tiles, and heard from above him an echoing scream, and a peal of sobbing laughter. Then as he rolled upward and regained control, he himself screamed at what he saw there. It had the ghastly clarity of a dream; the slender form of a woman arched high against the sun, the wings that were her arms flung back from her out-thrust breast, and standing in it among a flood of scarlet the shining hilt of a black-bladed sword.

It seemed an endless age of agony and horror that she hung there before him. Then it was as if she crumpled up around the blade that transfixed her; she toppled sideways, her wings folding about her like a shroud, and even as he leaped out to her, crying her name, she fell away in a cloud of black feathers into the deep vale below. After her he sped, so fast the wind whipped the very tears from his eyes, but it was hopeless. For all that long fall Elof's eyes never left her; but of what thoughts passed behind them, no chronicle can tell. Light but swift she fell, the merest speck plummeting into the distance, lost to him in an instant against the dark waters of a new-opened lake, still churning with the ice-fall. A frozen moment passed, and a speck of white leaped up upon its surface; a rage of whiteness swirled there a moment, and Kara was gone.

In a void he whirled, and a void opened within him, a raging turmoil of agonizing emptiness and loss. The shouts he heard he heeded without understanding, less will in him than in the least thing of his devising. Back against the balustrade he crashed, and would have fallen had hard hands not hauled him in. There was Kermorvan, his mail spattered with blood, Louhi's guards scattered writhing or still about his feet; but in his eyes a greater horror dwelt. "You were right …" whispered Elof. "She attacked …" But Kermorvan, his lips set hard and grey as cold granite, was lifting something from among a mass of splintered tiles. He hefted it a moment, his head bowed, and then stretched out his hand to Elof. In it was Elof's hammer.

Light and dark seemed to spin around in Elof's head, forming a cruel mask of a face, stern, grey-bearded, cruelly lined, laughing a bitter laugh that echoed into infinite emptinesses, mocking the twisted web of destiny that twined there. It was the face of the Watcher, the image of Vayde, it was not his own; and yet, somehow he knew that it laughed for him, because it had never learned to weep.

But he himself, it is said, rose shakily on his knees, staring at the hammer that Kara, in one last defiant act of love, had risked her existence to bring him. Risked – but she had never dreamed the risk was from him.

A sudden slash of pain cut through his legs. All thoughts save one died and shrivelled in his mind, all fires save one in his heart. He looked up, and saw there another, fair, deadly fair as the shining summits of the Ice itself; and she too was laughing, no less terribly, leaning far out over the whitened balustrade and brandishing her fist at him. Within him a cold knot of compassion twisted; for she too had loved, in her way. Had he not had Kermorvan to protect – With a howl of sheer animal pain he seized the tall man by belt and arm, and sprang up and out with him over the balustrade as if he meant to dash them both to their deaths below. But his wings flung out, and back towards the blazing shieldwall he swooped. At the slope's foot, he glided low and dropped his burden crying out in a great voice *"Down, all of you! Behind the shields! And cover your eyes! Do not look!"*

Then high into the middle airs he arrowed, and even as he rose the shields of his craft seemed to come alive in the hands of their wielders, twisting like serpents till the sunfire they ensnared found focus upon him. To the few who dared look a moment longer he seemed to vanish for a moment, as if he had met the fate of so many that day. Yet Kermorvan, as he sped back among his ranks, saw him still hanging there at the heart of the glare, shining like a shape new-cast in white-hot gold. On the balcony of the Gate the Ekwesh too stared at that terrible sight, and many cast themselves headlong, hiding their eyes. But she whom they cried to, tall and pale, made no move to look away. The white gems of the corselet drank in the whole force of that fire, and from them the gem of his gauntlet, till his whole arm blazed with the terrible radiance of contained power. A moment more, and it would have consumed him; but in that moment he acted. Louhi shrank back; she screamed aloud, and her arms flew up as if to ward off a blow. It availed her nothing. Out from that glowing shape, as the fingers flashed apart, burst all that pent-up force, in a single incandescent shape; and in its path, straight and fast as if to shatter mountains, flew the devastating hammer.

Kermorvan, forewarned, reached the shieldwall and threw himself down among his followers, crouched down with covered eyes. Yet the flash of light they saw even through tight-shut lids, so white it seemed to burn deep into the depths of their minds. Thunder crashed about them, the very air seized them and shook them and threw them half scorched upon the steaming earth, as it twitched and shivered beneath them like the hide of a branded beast. The drum-beats of avalanches resounded through earth and sky as the faces of cliff and slope crumbled and slid away beneath that single overwhelming blow, that violent impact upon the face of the world. Yet through it, above it, louder than any voice they had ever heard, it seemed to all who were there that they heard that last desperate cry echoing still, a shriek of anguish and defeat and ultimate, infinite loss. Like lightning it leaped from sky to earth and back again, and rove the air asunder; but whether they heard it with their ears or in their hearts few cared to say.

Elof heard it. A searing blast hurled him skyward so high, so fast, the breath was crushed from him; and when at last he could breath again, the air lanced thin and cold through his straining lungs. It stung his scorched skin unbearably, and the sunlight, brighter sharper, fell on him like a sleeting shower of needles, as if to flay him for his presumption in having channeled its power. Something was happening to him, something frightening, as if the shrieking winds were shredding the flesh from his bones like leaves from dead branches, as if he was being torn apart and reformed. He groped for understanding, but that convulsion of nature, and ringing through it that last terrible scream, had shivered his thoughts like thin ice. His wings had shielded him, and they were ragged now, they hardly bore him, and yet he felt unable to fall. It was as if only fragments of him were left to float upon the wind, a ragged shred through which a clear light could shine. But it was a strange light, at once limpid and fiery, and it seemed to

well up, out of the infinite abyss below. Visions it bore
with it, visions and truths, clear sights of things that had
been, that were taking shape even now, or that might
yet be, all weaving together in one vast coil. In wonder
he perceived that coil, and gazing upon it knew that
slowly but surely, as he once had crafted a sword, the
many strands were being twisted into greater strands,
and those strands hammered together into one bright
infinite shaping, one awesome work of craft. No vision
lingered, though he grasped at them as might a child at
butterflies; he glimpsed them only, as one might
through the gaps in a tattered tapestry draped across a
wide casement. But he saw enough to grasp one truth.
He himself was that tapestry. Seconds passed, perhaps,
before he knew he was falling once more; but they
might as well have been hours.

As he turned over in the air, the clearest vision of
all came to him. His tortured eyes, and more than his
eyes, looked down upon the churning sea, scattered
with jagged shards of ice, fragmented, melting, and at its
margins a great scorched scar upon the land. There the
fortress of the High Gate had stood; but it was gone, and
the very ridge it was built upon. The mountains that
flanked it still stood, but their faces had collapsed in
rubble into the yawning gap. And through that gap,
bounding like a horse newly freed from harness and
stall, the sea came rushing in. Down it crashed from
heights to depths in falls and rapids of awesome height,
tumbling the shattered mountain-ribs like fine gravel,
spitting brilliant spray skyward as if to mock the force
that had lately held it in icy bonds. Into the upper
reaches of the Yskianas, still frozen, it spilled, and
further and further downstream the ice bulged up from
beneath and exploded into floating shards as the dark
waters swelled.

He looked after them, and to his sight time and
space merged and became one. Down the river of days
he followed their surging progress, and watched the
ending of a land. Wider they spread, smoothly, slowly,
and up bank and barrier the darkly gleaming line rose;
there was no wave, no wash of devastation, only a

smooth slow devouring. Water-side and island seemed to shrink and sink down into the sparkling maw of the waters with scarcely a wash of foam, grasses waved their heads to the flow as they had to the wind, till they were swallowed up. Trees at the river-side stood straight even as the waters climbed their trunks; only at the last, like men awakening in a sinking ship, did they flail their dark heads frantically. Their fear availed them nothing; they too sank. But down to the haunts of men that fear was swiftly borne, by the waves that lapped at wharf and wall, boomed at water-gates and shook bridges. Bells rang from tower to tower, bronze voices that sang their warning peal all along the shores of that once mighty country, till it seemed that the whole land quivered; back and forth they swung, as if the waves themselves were ringing them. Even in the Horns of the Bull they swung, in the towers that crowned the Strength of Kerys, telling of a subtle foe that neither outermost wall nor highest bastion could bar, of the cool darkness that even now was filling the docks, swinging ships at anchor, swelling channel and canals like riven veins. With many voices they sang, but one word only was their message to all men, from furthest farmstead to the streets of Kerys the City itself; and that was *flee!*

It was heeded. Those fled, who could; and most fled in time. Men who had boats took to them, but large numbers were sunk by the frantic fugitives who sought to struggle aboard. Others fled mounted or on foot, in carts and carriages, or with what conveyance they might; but it was little enough they managed to take with them. Many farmers drove their beasts inland, but some not far enough; for at the first the Yskianas rose as fast as a weary man might run. It met the tributaries, and drove back their flows. Into the crevices of the fire-mountains it spilled, recoiled in steam and patiently, insistently, washed once more. The defences that Elof had created with such care it touched, tried and found wanting; into their depths it sent a probing tendril, and even as the tiny garrison escaped it was lapping the dark blood from its rough-hewn stone. Down it came to a green island whose crown still smoked and smouldered, and the little mammuts among the rushes squealed and trampled their way to the high ground; nobody dared set foot there now, and they were safe. Wider and wider it spread, that Great River no longer a river; men fled to north and to south, as the sundering waters rose between them. They saved their lives; but the land and realm of which once they had been a part was engulfed at their heels, and lost beyond recall. The peril of the Ice was lifted from the world; but upon the land it had corrupted, and upon the city at its heart, the mightiest that then was in all the world, a still greater cleansing was come. But already Elof's eyes were gazing far beyond it; for the hunger of the waters was not yet sated, and the cleansing not yet at an end.

CHAPTER TWELVE
The Coming of the Spring

SO MUCH CAME TO Elof in his vision, and many things else both near and far; perhaps among them he saw also what passed beneath him, as he drifted among the uppermost reaches of the airs. But for an account of that, whatever its origin, the chronicles must answer. Awesome as were the forces he had unleashed, the armies gathered among the hills had escaped them. The Kerysmen, almost a league away to the north and westward, were well sheltered by the intervening hills; but it seems that the light in the sky and the terrible blast that followed were too much for them. They were brave men, but they had fought too long and hard against forces they scarcely understood; almost to a man they took to their heels, and those few captains who sought to restrain them were borne along in the rush. And in the end that was as well; for they were not cut off from their homes and kin by the rising waters.

The men of Morvanhal might have been less fortunate, had they not heeded Elof's warning and been crouched down behind the shieldwall. Those among the duergar wise in such arcane matters believed that the shields had mirrored more than light that day; for it was certain that such strange metals as were bound within that hammer could unleash a hundred unseen deaths if ill-handled. But none who were there, save perhaps Ils and her folk, guessed anything of this. It is told in the chronicles that even as the roar and thunder of the riven land abated, and the earth grew still again, the first gusts blew of a mighty gale that scoured the smoke and dust from the air, and for a few minutes left the skies clear. Then the bravest among them ventured to peer shakily over their shield-rims, marvelling at the catastrophe that had occurred and even more at their own preservation. And as they gathered courage and stood up upon shaky limbs, humbled and fragile in the face of so vast an event, they saw that outside the shelter of the shields the snow and frost had been scorched from the hillside, and withered grasses were steaming in the sun. Their wonder grew when they perceived that all around them, upon every hill as far as the eye could reach, even beyond the possible reach of that blast, it was the same. The cloud that had maintained that wintry landscape was gone, blown apart and dispersed; and so no less was the will that had created it. Only then, with a shaky lift in their hearts, did they begin to understand.

One of the first afoot was Kermorvan, and though he was as awed as any by the spectacle of such utter devastation he turned at once to see that his people were safe. He helped Ils up, her wounded leg stiff beneath her, and kept her hand clasped tight in his own as he gazed around that shattered scene; and he it was who first voiced the hesitant hope that was slowly swelling to a certainty in all their minds. "A great change is come upon the world!" he cried, his clear voice carried upon the wind. "The balance is turned back! The power of the Ice is swept away!"

And down that wind as though in answer, as if he had heard those words or perceived them in his vision, came Elof. Spiralling from the sky he fell like a moth from a candleflame, whirling and tumbling like one of his own plumes upon ruined and smouldering wings. They saw him at once by the trail of smoke he left. Down over their heads he glided, black against the red of the sinking sun, and crashed onto the hillside above in a sprawl of limbs. Up the hill they streamed after him, his friends to the fore, though they dreaded what they were sure they would find. But some long strides away Roc, who was first, stopped, hesitated, whispered "Is that him?"

For the man who lay upon the scorched grass, arms and legs outflung, had skin darkened to the hue of old bronze, and hair of purest white. "Ah!" breathed Ils, her voice choked and hoarse. "He might almost be that Watcher ... Fool! Of course it's him! But ... living?" As if hearing her somehow, the man stirred, moving his legs slowly, and Ils cried out; beneath them silver gleamed against the black ground, and a slow trickle of blood ran from the rags of his clothes. Forgetting her own pains, she hastened to tend him; and found, when she did so, that the anklets set in his legs had shattered, violently as it seemed, and the fragments were gradually working loose from his wounds.

"He lives, then; but what more?" demanded Kermorvan, returning with men bearing a shield lined with blankets, and bending over the anxious knot of figures. The gale was blowing ever more strongly from the south, a warm wind rich with the promise of rain, and heavy clouds were rising over the southward hills. "Will he waken?" Ils looked up at him, her huge dark eyes troubled.

"The wounds to his legs are healing already; his burns not so, but we have salved them ... But as to wakening, well ..." The first shadows of the night touched the hillside, and she sighed. Above the noise of the torrents a distant rumble sounded in the sky. "His eyes are open, as they were from the first. I think he has heard all we said to him – but he does not seem to understand. It is as if he looks elsewhere, at things we cannot see; and we are not real to him."

"He has flown too close to the sun," said a deep voice quietly from behind them. "That man may not do, and yet live."

Kermorvan jerked upright. An awful chill had lanced through him at the very sound of that voice, and he knew at once whose it was. The huge figure that stooped beside him had not been there only a moment since; and though from the huge rough-shafted spear the man leaned upon he had the look of a warrior, no one in all the army wore such a long and dusty mantle of midnight blue, nor such a wide-brimmed hat. But even had Kermorvan been a man of less swift thought, that chill would have warned him.

"*You!*" he said, his words forming thick as blood upon his tongue with the wrath that welled up within him. "*You! Raven!* And well you are named, coming to settle upon a battlefield, and batten upon the fallen! May you fall in your turn, you callous crow of carrion, and drag down all your kind with you! Your kind, that in their eternal squabbling trample unheeding upon the brief lives of men!" He waved a furious hand at the devastation in the vale below. "Why could you not have prevented *that*, friend of men that you claim to be? Why could you not save *him*, at least, rather than come prate above him? What better have you wrought, with all your endless wars? Your kind or the Ice-kind, one Power is as bad for mankind as another! Why will you twist and turn the world this way and that between you? A lasting curse upon the whole pack of you! Why will you not leave men be, to live their own lives?"

The figure turned its head, and he found himself staring into a single eye that gleamed bright as black waters beneath the shadows of the brim. The face in the shadows was lean, hook-nosed, seamed as an ancient oak with lines that were a cryptic chart of long years of wisdom, and perhaps also a vast and joyous laughter; the rest was hidden beneath shaggy white hair and beard. But the eye was young and clear, that of a man in his vigorous prime, as he was himself; it surveyed him gravely, without anger, and with only the faintest tinge of mockery, before it spoke. "That will come; and this day has hastened it. That is worth a higher price than is paid. Be content."

Kermovan glared at him. "I may not be Elof, to cross blades with the Powers; but since he lies at death's door I will at least have my say nonetheless, you despoiler of our ..."

"*No!*"

The commanding strength of the voice astonished him; but though it was deep and fair, it was not Raven's tone. Kermorvan turned again, and though a man of courage he found himself shaking uncontrollably. Elof stood before him, upright and straight upon his own strong legs; and though it obviously hurt his deep-burned face, he smiled. "I heard you. But folk such as I don't die so easily, old friend."

Kermorvan, limp with astonishment, looked back at the Raven. "You ... did come to help? You saved him?"

The white beard tossed. "I? I did nothing. All that was done, he did. But if it is help you wish, I may spare you some, my lord Keryn, under my ancient bond with your folk and line, and because I am indebted to you for your work today. I give you advice, and it is this: Begone from here at once! Back to your ships with all your folk, and begone! At once!"

"But Kerys!" said Kermorvan angrily. "The unleashed waters threaten it and all its folk! We must stay to succour them, at least; not only because they are our kindred, but all the more so!"

Raven growled impatiently. "You cannot aid them! Nor should you try! Do you not see why? But you knew that a great Change was impending, that once again the world hung in the balance! Surely you realised that such things cannot be avoided, that the balance cannot be stayed, only tipped one way, or another? This way, or that? Very well; the balance has been tipped the better way, away from the changeless Ice towards the side of life. You have had a hand in that; why rail against it now? Did you not know that Life means change, constant change?"

"No," said Kermorvan dully. "I did not guess."

"But why not?" The deep voice was rich, almost rejoicing. "Nothing endures forever unchanged, not the stone beneath your feet nor the stars above your head! Not men, and not Powers! Everything changes, everything shifts." His eye gleamed brightly, as if at some secret only he knew. Overhead the stars were coming out, and the pale ribbon of the River stretched across the heavens. "And why should it not? Would you have the River frozen and dead, as that one was below, or the River flowing? For if it did not, how would anything ever reach the Sea?"

Silence lay across the shattered land; even the thunder of the new forces below them seemed stilled for that time. The clouds were gathering fast, hiding the stars. The tall figure raised his spear. "In the end there are only two choices – call them what you will, growth or decay, life or death, a clear river or a stagnant pool. The fate of Kerys is hard; none know that better than I, who have watched over it since its birth, and joined my blood to its royal line. But it was old as the lands and races of men are reckoned, long overdue to alter, one way or another; yet so entrenched was it in its ways that only some such disaster might bring that about . . . Its folk must forget what was theirs, and struggle to find something new in a new land, as their ancestors did, and yours also. Harsh, yes; but consider how much harder the other way would have been!"

Kermorvan lowered his eyes. "You are right; and I should not have spoken as I did."

The grey head nodded, and the voice became softer. "All things go their way appointed, and in their own time! But I should not blame you for not grasping that truth. Even

I did not, not wholly, till Ilmarinen taught it me, greatest of the Elder Powers. Most of his fellows never learned it, least of all Taoune, and Taounehtar after him. Well, she knows it now. And she has paid a grievous price for her knowledge. For like all her rebel kind she has resisted change longest of all; yet now it has been forced upon her, and her loss is all the more grievous. She was trapped in her body with no chance to leave it; and so she is severed from her power, reduced as Taoune was to a shadow of her former self. It will fade now, that power; and with it, the Ice. That will be a change for the better, will it not? But since all things are linked in the world, each acting upon another, you must accept one change as part of many others; you cannot pick and choose."

Kermorvan raised his head suddenly, and stared in horror; he made as if to speak, reached out to seize the old man's mantle. Elof called out a warning, but faster even than his thought the spear swung about in the gnarled hand, and the tip of the blade dug in beneath the point of Kermorvan's jaw. "No more! You . . . your duty is to your land. Linger here and you will not live to fulfil it. The forces that were wielded today have flooded land and sky with poisons; my storm-winds bear the worst of them northward to the Ice, to speed the cleansing of what lurks there; but enough is left to put you all in peril!"

Kermorvan's mouth hardened with anger, and he pulled free of the insistent spear-point; but without wasting time he whirled about and shouted to the silent throng below the hill "*Captains, to me! Heralds, sound! Form up for the march! We're going home!*"

No other words could have aroused so thunderous a cheer from those weary throats, drowning even the thunderclap that burst overhead. But Kermorvan did not stay to acknowledge it; he turned back at once, with a question hovering on his lips – and then stood staring. The figure of the Raven had vanished. "Did you see him go?" he demanded of Ils, and of Roc; but neither of them had. "And you?"

Elof shrugged. "That's a dark mantle he wears. He seemed simply to . . . merge with the dark."

Kermorvan looked at him strangely. "You had nothing

much to say to each other, he and you; yet it was to you he always came."

Elof returned the look. "Everything he said was as true for me."

Understanding widened Kermorvan's eyes. "Of course ... You have lost more to change; far more. I grieved with you, my friend; I grieve now. Words will not serve me better ..."

Roc grunted his agreement; he could not meet Elof's look. Ils took his hand, very gently, perhaps because of the burns. "You deserved better," she said softly. "After so long a struggle ..." From the shadows below the horns were sounding, summoning the army to the march. "Do you feel able to ... walk, now? To ride?"

Elof nodded. "I do. In body, at least, I am healing. For the rest ..." His eyes seemed to lose their focus once more, to gaze into distances undreamt of. "That is harder to tell. But I will come with you, for now." A slow rain began to fall about them as they set off down the hill.

The march to the sea was a silent one at first, but by the second day it became more triumphal in mood, as the true measure of their victory at last began to dawn upon the weary soldiers, and the promise of going home. Even the prospect of short commons and a long voyage could not dampen their joy; but they kept it muted out of respect for their king, and for the mastersmith who had wielded such awesome power, at such cost to himself. For the most part both men rode in silence, and Kermorvan most of all, to Ils' deep concern. "Something troubles him, something more than I can understand," she told Elof as they rode. "Do you know what it might be?"

Elof looked at her, and took her hand in his. "I cannot help, Ils," was all he said.

With the column marched the Ravens, and their many captives, whom Kermorvan pardoned, and proclaimed free. When they came to the coast and their landing he offered them all their freedom and their ships to seek out their homeland, but to a man they declined; they were his followers and his people, and preferred to follow his fortunes if he would permit it. To this he agreed, since there was land enough and to spare in his eastern realm. "And through them I may one day come to some peace with the Ekwesh settlers in the West," he added, to his friends. "With the grip of the Ice loosening upon them, they may become more reasonable. In time," he added, looking hard at Elof.

"A wise hope, I think," was all Elof replied; it did not seem to satisfy the king. It was an exchange neither Ils nor Roc understood, and it grieved them that there seemed to be some cause of tension between two such fast friends. But neither would give any clue as to what it might be, until the dawn when the fleet at last set sail. Last of all to weigh anchor was the *Prince Korentyn*, and at its stern stood the King and his friends, looking back. As the great ship turned its head out into the bay, catching the freshening wind, Elof leaned back intently, as if listening to some remote sound.

"I don't hear ..." began Roc, but Kermorvan held up his hand, and together they listened.

A moment later Ils looked around sharply. "It sounds like ... bells," she said, and bit her full lip.

"Aye!" said Roc uneasily. "Couldn't make it out, but ... bells, it must be. From Kerys ..."

Kermorvan nodded. "So it is, but they are swinging with the waves now. Soon the waters will ring the bells even in that great city, in those high towers I have never seen, save in my dreams. And where else, Mastersmith? *Where else?*"

Such was the anger in his voice that Ils caught him by the arm. "He knows," said Kermorvan softly. "What I was about to ask the Raven. He knows the question; he may even know the answer. But he will not tell me!" He controlled himself with difficulty, and stood up, very straight. "As your friend I might have a claim on your truthful answer, Mastersmith. But as a king you owe it to me!"

Elof ran his fingers through his whitened mane. He had never felt older or wearier than then. "You shall have it," he said. "But not now."

"When, then?" demanded Kermorvan tautly.

"When I choose. But it will not be long delayed; that I promise you."

The voyage back was by all accounts swift and sure; but to Kermorvan, it must not have seemed so. Nevertheless, it was clear to Elof that he was doing his best to be content with that promise, and be the friend he had always been; and that was what Elof most desired. He surrounded himself with his friends as much as he could, and this did not go unnoticed. "Almost as if you're ... savouring us." said Roc bluntly. "Storing us up, so you won't forget. Not thinking of setting out on one more lunatic search, are you? Because lunatic it will be, I promise you! At your age? In your condition?"

Ils put an arm around his shoulders. "If she remembers you still, she will do the searching; there is nobody now who can hold her back. Louhi will have problems of her own!"

Elof smiled, but it became a grimace of pain. "What I did to her ... that may hold her back. Even at the last I betrayed her, Ils ..."

"No!" said Kermorvan, pouring him a stoup of wine, made doubly precious by their short supplies. "Drink this, man, and take heart! I was there; I saw! And I will judge you, as is my right; as once before I declined to. You did what was inevitable, with no time for thought; and you were shielding me. If the old Kara is there, she will not forget that."

"Maybe," said Elof quietly. "What you say may be true. But meanwhile ... I am waiting for a sign. And though I am happy among you all, I grow weary."

At long last there came a sunset when the mastheads hailed land on the horizon. That brought Kermorvan and the others on deck, but to their surprise they found Elof already there; he was huddled up by the steersman's bench against the cold night wind, and coughing. He looked up as the king approached. "I said I would answer your question one day, Kermorvan. And this is the day."

Kermorvan's face went grey, and he sat down heavily on the bench. "I feared it might be." Visibly he gathered his strength. "Tell me, then, and have done with it. What Louhi threatened me with, and I laughed away for the army's sake – it has haunted me all these days and nights since. I see it in my dreams, even. *Was it true?*"

"Yes," said Elof quietly. "It was. It is." Ils and Roc stared down at him aghast, but he shook his head sadly. "Think of it! Where did the waters come from, that make up the great glaciers of the Ice? From the seas, in the end; and their level fell. New coastlines were laid bare; new land emerged, as other land was covered. And men took that land, because it was farthest from the Ice; and because no other Power held it as their dominion, as Tapiau does the forests. The old kingdoms of men were crushed, and it was in coastal lands that their new realms sprang up, even those of the Ekwesh. Why was the Vale of Kerys so deep, think you? Because once before it was a sea, and waves broke over that smooth ridge where the Gate was built; the Yskianas was all that remained of that sea. It only reclaims what was taken from it." He laughed, till it turned to a coughing fit. "Ironic, is it not? Kerys, Morvannec, Morvan, Kerbryhaine, men settled those great realms to escape the Ice; men held them against it. Yet all the time they were the Ice's own creation, as unnatural in the world as it was. And now Taounehtar is weakened, the others of her kind will not be able to sustain it. It has ceased its advance. Slowly it will melt and withdraw, and the oceans will reclaim their own."

"How soon?" demanded Roc in horror. "*How soon?* Are you telling us we've no home left awaiting us over the horizon there? Was that why you waited?"

Elof smiled, and lifted a hand. From overhead came a joyous cry. "*Morvanhal in sight! Morvanhal to starboard, palace and tower! Home, we're home!*"

"That at least I can spare you," he said. "It comforts me somewhat. And you did not notice the glaciers shrinking before we sailed, did you? They almost made themselves the ruling forces in the climes of the world, and such a presence will be slow to disperse. It will take time; many lifetimes of men, I think. But not so many; three, four, five perhaps, before the waters begin to swallow the coasts. But after that it will become swift."

"New lands will be laid bare, when the glaciers melt!" said Ils encouragingly. "As they were before! That's something, isn't it?"

Kermorvan did not lift his head when he spoke. "As I feared. That cannot be enough time to find and clear enough new land, even if the Powers that linger will let us. And the lands that were under the Ice will take longer still to recover. Oh, we will manage something, somehow, with your folk to help us. Men will endure; but not their realms. We will dwindle, as did your folk, or revert to simple, rustic folk; even savages and barbarians. It happens even now to

Kerys; but soon we also shall be devoured!" He stood suddenly, and his face was bitter and bleak, his fists clenched white at his breast. "So ends my fool's dream! My dream of founding a realm and a dynasty, a land of prosperity and wisdom, of strength and justice. Not one that would last forever; I needed no Raven to tell me that. But that would last as long as Kerys, and leave as great a name; or at the least, some tangible mark and memory in the hearts of men. But whatever I achieve still, it will melt and vanish, and be dissolved in the eternal changes of the seas. I should have known better, this world being what it is. It was all in vain."

Elof also rose, though with difficulty. "No," he said quietly, and put a hard hand on Kermorvan's shoulder. "it was not. And it will not be."

The tall man turned, his bronze hair streaming in the breeze with the look in his face of one who hears a distant horn-call.

"It will not be!" repeated Elof. "I did you an injustice, my old friend. You spoke still of the future, of what you might still achieve, hopeless or not; had I been sure you would, I would have answered you sooner, and not delayed till I had to. Hear then, and hope on! Without your kingship, without *you*, there would have been no victory, no chance of any men at all surviving, civilised or not. But they will, now. Civilisation will come again, where without you, without all of you, it could not have. It will come again, because from the fires you light in the years to come, small sparks will be kept alight, little enclaves of wisdom in a world newborn, and ignorant as all things newborn are. Some of their knowledge, some of their wisdom, that will survive to pass down the years, even if men forget whence it came, and keep only a dim memory of legend, of an age of vanished glory. All save that memory may be lost, yet still it will inspire them to glories of their own. Your name, all our names they may forget, but the image of your kingdom, your line, shall burn bright in their hearts. They will cross seas in quest of it once more, and perhaps the name of Kerys, of the glorious City of Ys, will not be wholly forgotten. Men may hear its bells ringing still, there beneath the waves. You shall have your dynasty, Keryn Kermorvan; and no king ever founded one greater. It shall be all mankind."

When Kermorvan spoke at last, it was with difficulty. "It is greater than I deserve, then. I am comforted. And I am humbled; I can hope, still. May our children and theirs be worthier – eh, my lady Ils?"

She smiled then; but she also could not speak. It was Roc who spoke first. "That goes for me also – but Elof . . . I don't know if I should ask, but . . . how can you be so bloody *sure?*"

"And you said you *had* to tell now!" whispered Ils. "Why, Elof, why?"

Kermorvan nodded. "I wonder also. Yet I do not doubt you. What sight is given you, Elof Valantor?"

Elof smiled again, though a cough racked him painfully. "The sight of the bird that breaks its shell. As a bird indeed I saw it first, blown this way and that on the heights. A light shone all about me, it seemed; and only my own poor self was in the way of it. As Louhi said, we do not die so easily, our kind; but Kara was right to sense a change coming. It was for us both."

"*Who are you?*" Kermorvan whispered. "I have asked you that before, but . . . Who are you?"

"A man, like yourself," answered Elof, with only a tinge of amusement. "Exceptional in some ways, perhaps; but then all men are, if only they can discover how. I live by eating and drinking; I grow ill, I feel pain, I bleed, age comes upon me – what more would you have? I have smithcraft in me; but then so do all men in whom the blood of the Powers is still mingled richly enough – yourself included, Kermorvan. But . . ." He hesitated. "Once, I was something more. No, more than once."

"What in Hella's curlies are you talking about?" demanded Roc.

Elof grinned. "In no place so arcane. Bear with me; it is hard to explain. There is still so much that I can't remember, or only have a brief glimpse of; more than my mind will hold . . . Say, if you like, that I have lived many lives – *stay!*" So commanding was the word, so absolute the gesture that instead of springing up in astonishment or fear they swayed towards him, and were silent. "Or that someone has. Each one different, none of them resulting in the man who speaks to you now. How could they, when so many different memories must make up a man? Yet each began from a common core; each was a different path to an end. And that core endured. Most were failures; but I am not." He grimaced. "Not entirely, not at the last. For if I learned one thing in all those lifetimes, learned it with pain and suffering and damnable follies, it was this –" He coughed, so that his whole body shook. "That only a man free of the Powers could free men from them."

He smiled again. "As free they must become in the end, Kermorvan. However great the cost ... So I forswore all that was mine, knowledge and power beyond your comprehension – and now beyond mine. Forswore it wholly, as I had never before dared to do. On that path there was no going back. I forgot entirely who I had been. When I became the infant fondling they named Alv, I set myself forever within the limits of men."

"And you chose Asenby ..." murmured Kermorvan, as if in a dream. "Where a sceptre was being used as a cattle-goad ..."

"A sceptre that would draw me through my great smithcraft to its rightful lord, in the end," said Elof, and became aware of a vast laughter bubbling up within him. "And where an agent of Louhi would come – drawn in his turn, though neither of us ever guessed it! Only I had reckoned without the Raven. He knew of me, none better; no other did, not Tapiau, not even Louhi, though she saw something in me she did not understand. Raven chose to shorten my ways somewhat, in his own twisted fashion. But never freely; I had always to earn his help, however paltry. Of my own I had nothing, save one legacy left myself against great need; and that was the sword Talathar, which I renamed Gorthawer, and the knowledge that lay bound up in it. And both of those I had to find anew for myself."

"Vayde's sword ..." said Roc quietly. "As they knew, in Kerys . And you were drawn to Vayde's forge. So it was Vayde you were, right enough ..."

"Vayde was himself, and for what he was he perished in the Great Marshes, though nobly enough at the last. Poor creature! He knew too much of what he was, and not enough of men, and both were torment to him; he failed, though not completely. Him you might have feared, for he was more than a man; but I ..." He laid his hands in his lap. "I am a man. All my life that is what I have thought myself; and now that I know my history, I feel only the more sure of it. I'm afraid that you might think otherwise; that you, my oldest friends, might not accept me as you always have." He smiled wryly. "Whatever my human failings."

No one answered at first, and the sound of the waves grew very loud in their ears; but then, impulsively, Ils caught his hand and held it tight. "Ass! Of course you're a man! Does it take a duergar girl to tell you that?"

"Well," said Roc thoughtfully. "You *look* like the same lad I've chased around and about half this world with. And I reckon nobody but a man could get in some of the scrapes I've hauled you out of ..." He chuckled. "Or haul me out of mine. So we'll give you the benefit of the doubt – eh, Kermorvan?"

"I think that might be arranged," said Kermorvan dryly, though a great wonder was still in his eyes. "Indeed, I have known you too well, too long to think otherwise. And I always thought it an honour, even then. Yet ..." But there he caught himself, and said no more.

Ils snorted. "There he goes again, too damned court-eous! Elof, you are who you are, and you're a fool to think we'd have you otherwise ... after the first surprise, that is! But once you were someone else, you've told us. Someone, apart from those other lives. Have you ... have you remembered who?"

Elof laughed suddenly, and fell to coughing so hard his hand clenched tight upon hers. "I'm sorry ... My chest seems afire. I was only remembering you and I, Kermorvan, in the earliest days arguing about what your Kerbryhaine philosophers thought, about whether the Powers could take human shape, and why – whether it was to understand men better! I wish they could have met Louhi! It is not the shape that gives understanding, but the life. I as I was, I never understood the hearts of men, and I longed to. So at last I plucked up the courage, and made what I thought a great sacrifice, frighteningly great. Freely I forgot all of myself, leaving only the essence, the inner fire. And fire it was, indeed! For the light and fire that gave life to the world, they were my element once, as the waters are Niarad's and

Saithana's, and the forests Tapiau's; as the airs were Taou-nehtar's and Taoune's once, till they armoured themselves in the dead Ice. We were the minds that roved in those forces, set within them to the long labours of shaping a world, destined in the end to change, and become a part of it. To join with men ... We take human shape more easily than any other, because that is the shape we must all take in the end, and the destiny we must share. Louhi may, soon, and I wish her joy of it, ill-prepared as she is; though she will still have something of her beauty to help her. I embraced that change, because I knew it must come; and oddly enough I feel more myself than ever before. For I was Ilmar-inen, Forger of Mountains, Smith of the Powers; an I am all of him that remains."

"*Ilmarinen!*" gasped Ils, and would have sunk down at his feet, had he not caught her and raised her, though she shivered at his touch. "Small wonder that I ... I ..."

Elof smiled. "Saw something in me? It is so; and it is not out of place. For in his way Ilmarinen always loved your race as much as they, him. But I would rather be your friend still, than what he has been to you, for I share your world, and not his. Save only in this; we who have dwelt upon the heights, we cannot enjoy the surcease of a single life, a single death. It may be that men cannot, either; of that knowledge only a glimmering remains. But this I know; we at least may rest between our human lives, may find long surcease from our labours. I have earned it, and perhaps more. For when I took courage at last and embraced that change I found something new rewarded me, something I had never managed to find before; and if it is lost to me as a man, then by pursuing that change I may find it yet. You asked me, Ils, why I had to tell you now. It is this; I was waiting for a sign. And that sign has come."

He stood, and they stood with him. "It is time to say farewell, my friends. But not forever; I will never be far from you, in this life or any other. For harsh as the world may seem, yet against all hope we may make things of worth endure. Even that most fragile thing of all, that we call love. *For see there!*"

The voice was a man's; but such a weight even of remembered power resounded within it that, as the tale is told, no man on board could look anywhere but where his lifted arm pointed. High above the coasts of Morvanhal, where red stone and white tower gleamed in distant harmony, a dark speck appeared, flying swift against the wind that bore them home. And it seemed to those who had been the friends of Elof Valantor, greatest of all master-smiths among men, that for a moment that wind blew strong and fierce and warm about them, as if great wings beat within; and when they turned to Elof the deck was empty where he had stood.

Only a few fragments of silver lay there, and an arm-ring of pale gold, abandoned as things childish are when their need and use is past. No man heeded them, for their eyes were held skyward, higher and ever higher to where two great swans flew up, circling ever closer in a graceful spiral until they seemed to vanish among the clouds, into the last rich light of the sun. And though to them it set, the watchers knew in their hearts that elsewhere it arose again in spreading, undying fire.

Coda

It came to pass even as Elof had foretold. Under the wise rule of Keryn Kermorvan and his queen the last kingdom of men flourished and spread far along that eastern shore, ever joining and mingling more with the duergar as the years passed. King Keryn lived to an astonishing age, far beyond the span of his eldest subjects save only his great chancellor, the Lord Roc, and till their end they both kept strength and vigour. In that, perhaps, the lady Ils had a hand, and the healing arts of the duergar; but it may have been another's gift. After the King's death Ils returned to her own folk, and with her aged father long ruled that remnant who would not mingle with men, but chose to live out their lives under stone; and though they stayed long in friendship with the kingdom of her children, she herself never came there again.

But it is said that on the morning King Keryn died, two black swans came to perch a brief while upon the heights of the palace, and then flew off to the southwest, filling the dawn air with cries that seemed not of sorrow, but of gladness. And the Chronicles affirm that two like them returned ever and again in later years, at the death of Roc and of all they had known, and of all the kings of Kermorvan's line, till at last the city was abandoned to the rising waters, and a lasting end was come of the days both dark and heroic of the long Winter of the World.

Appendix

Of the Land of Kerys, its form, nature and climate, and of its peoples and their several histories, such as are set forth in that volume of the Winter Chronicles called the Book of the Armring.

In reducing to a single tale the long span of years covered in the Book of the Armring, the many strands of lives and events that weave and intertwine throughout, the many details of people and places, much has had to be omitted, or told only from afar. For it was the Mastersmith Elof Valantor who proved, unknown even to himself, to be the prime mover in that troubled time, and his tale is the one that matters most. Also, as before, the authors of the Chronicles could scarcely help writing for their own times and their own folk; so, inevitably, they leave much unexplained that we no longer know, or explain at length matters we would today take for granted. This account cannot replace all that is missing, or has had to be curtailed; but it may at least paint in more detail the backdrop, like a remote and misty landscape, against which these events took place.

THE LAND

The land of Kerys, with which the Book of the Armring is principally concerned, was like no other in the world at that time, uniquely suited to provide a refuge for men against the ravages of the Long Winter, and a fit cradle for the birth of a great civilization. In form it was as Elof and Roc saw it, a river valley of immense size; in extent it must have been greater even than they realised, stretching at its widest some six or seven hundred leagues from the western oceans to its eastern margins, and from north to south over two hundred leagues at its widest. In former days, when it also included great regions of the hinterlands above its northern and southern walls, its area can only be guessed at; but these were gradually lost to the Ice, and to the desert that crept relentlessly northward, like its malign shadow. By the time of Elof's arrival the last of them had become the Wild Lands, home to none save the scattered remnants of the duergar.

The account given by Elof of the origin of Kerys is substantially correct; however, it had gone through many such changes before. Originally it appears to have been a low-lying landlocked basin, probably a barren desert, founded upon rock chiefly of granite and limestone types. It was held back from the oceans by a land barrier at its eastern end; gradually this was eroded away, until at last the seas came flooding in and over, in a waterfall of astonishing size and height. This probably created the ridge upon which the Gate was built; the shape depicted on surviving marginal sketches, though obviously much narrowed and steepened on its seaward side by men to make a defence, still suggests the shallow crescent typical of wide falls such as Niagara, or the awesome rockface, long dry, at Malham Cove in Yorkshire, England. The waters that poured over that fall turned the basin into an inland sea; but in the succession of Long Winters launched against the living world, enchaining more and more of the world's waters, its level sank and it became land once more, only to rise again as each Winter came to its end. This the duergar seem to have known, but among men, more recent arrivals, it was either never realised, or wholly forgotten.

These successive floodings were not without their effect on the once infertile land. The waters had eroded much hard rock to sand, and into this inflowing rivers, as well as diluting the salt content, poured rich loads of upland silt; fertile volcanic debris, distributed by the waters into which it fell, may also have played a part. As the level of the seas outside gradually declined, the waters drew back and left these deposits open to the air. Land plants came to grow on this new soil, bound it and enriched it with their remains, and after them trees and animals, establishing a whole fertile cycle. Certainly the result, by the time men first came there, was a black alluvial soil of remarkable richness, and on the higher ground "brown earths" of the podzol type, developed under the vast tracts of deciduous forest which then covered the land; in the more southerly areas the less fertile *terra rossa* soils formed on limestone. By later days, however, the richest soils had been exhausted by over-farming, and the forests cleared altogether from much of the land; the unity of the soil was destroyed, and much of it was simply blown or washed away. Even before its drowning Kerys, rich as it seemed, was a dying land.

The Great River

So it was that Kerys was in a very real sense created by the River. And the River continued to dominate it, as the name the Penruthya, or sothran, peoples gave it, *Yskianas*, acknowledged. *Kian* was a rather poetic name for a vein, and so this meant *Vein of the Heartland*, or as it was understood, *River at the Heart of the World*. The Svarhath, inhabiting the north of the land, took a less central view and called it simply *Myklstavathan*, the Great River. As sea levels had declined, so the falls over the ancient barrier had ceased to flow, save for a small central cranny or channel that the river cut itself, probably by following some crack or flaw in the eroded rock, or some softer intrusion.

This admitted a relatively restricted flow of seawater, but it was soon swelled, and its salt diluted, by inflows from various tributaries to north and south. Some of these were created, or swelled, by meltwater directly from the Ice, and this brought with it the same terrors as did the upper reaches of the Gorlafros to the Marshlands in Nordeney. But the Great River dispersed these in its vastness as it rode peaceably through the centre of the land; and if some trace of darker influence remained, a slow poison for the minds and spirits of the people, it cannot now be said.

Past the warm lands where men founded Kerys the River flowed, until at last it broadened to become a great lake, more properly an inland sea,. Those waters were little navigated or frequented. The lands around their shores were hot and unwelcoming when men first arrived there, with many regions of marsh along the coasts, and tempted nobody to settle save the most desperate of outlaws. By Nithaid's time, thousands of years later, the marshes had spread and the rest degenerated into barrens in the north and near desert in the south. Through those marshes, along many small streams and channels, the waters of the Yskianas drained southward, and though much was lost by sheer evaporation at least one river was thought to reach the mysterious oceans to the south. But it was not navigable, and its course, if it ever was known, had long been lost. Adventurers in those lands had brought back little of worth, but many plagues and spreading maladies, until the reputation of the area for disease was such that landing there was forbidden on pain of death. If any ventured it, therefore, they left no records, and no certain maps have survived.

The High Gate

Such was the course of the Great River, and a vein it was indeed to the land of Kerys, bearing its heart's blood, the water that fed its rich fields and the ships that carried their produce to feed the great city at its heart, and at need their soldiers to enforce its defence and royal authority. That so many of their towns were built along its shores and at its confluences is ample witness of this. Its importance was obvious to the people of the land even from the earliest years. Very soon they began building, over that narrow crevice in the ancient barrier and the falls that came through it, the first stages of what was to become the High Gate. They had many reasons for siting such a fortress there, but high among them was the desire to protect the source of the river that was their land's life. At that time they had not yet grown complacent, and lost their awareness of what the Ice or some other enemy might do. Generation after generation built the Gate higher and grander, and as the sea-level fell outside they cut down and narrowed the ancient barrier into a well too steep for any enemy to scale. In the end the Gate towered high over the ancient ridge, an imposing palace atop walls smooth and utterly unscaleable, guarding the River that thundered through its depths; and it became a sign in the minds of men, a symbol of the fountainhead of the land they loved. A fire was set on its roof, guiding mariners by day with its smoke, and by night with its flame, and to them in particular it became an almost sacred sight, their last upon setting sail and their first upon their return. Since it was the greatest and most adventurous mariners who discovered the new lands across the ocean, it became especially important to them; and for those who fled into exile to found a new realm there, it was a poignant memory, the last they were ever to see of Kerys. So it was that even when with the decline of Kerys the Gate had ceased to mean so much to its people, their kin beyond the seas were still invoking its name.

Climes

The compression of climes that the Long Winter created throughout the world was particularly acute in Kerys at the time of Elof's coming. This was because the Ice had been able to distribute itself very differently than in Brasayhal. To onlookers such as Elof and Roc the great icesheets appeared at first to have extended far further south; but in fact the borders of the main sheets followed much the same parallel as across the oceans. What they had been able to do, however, was create an advance guard of secondary icesheets by the means Ansker described in the Book of the Sword, "colonizing" the heights of more southerly mountan ranges by extending glaciations from mountain snowcaps.

The land immediately beyond the main ice-sheets had no such peaks, but was hilly and uneven enough to impede their advance; it became the *tundra* landscape of Taoune'la, snowy, bleak and haunted, an evil place in whose northern reaches nothing save the hardiest lichens could live. Over this, however, cold airs and subtler influences spread to the mountain-peaks beyond; gradually their icecaps swelled and gathered strength and gave birth to glaciers that flowed down below the snowlines, joined and became vast enveloping icesheets that no longer changed with the seasons, but were as permanent as the main body of the Ice. In fact, it was the Iceglow from these, and not from the main body, that Ilof and Roc saw from Elan Ghorhenyan.

There were now two of them, each the size of a substantial country, and steadily growing by the same process. Each winter the cold fingers of the glaciers would spread further along the more southerly peaks, and leave them that fraction colder; and though with the thaw they would retreat again, it would not be all the way. Each year they had gained a little more ground, until now in winter they thrust deep into what had been the north of Kerys, and spun their webs of frost and snow over valleys that had once been high green pastures, home to hardy farmers of the Svarhath folk. Now they were miserable barrens, and even when the snow had drawn back many evils stalked them under the shadow of those peaks.

South of these troubled lands the land was still fertile and rich, though it suffered from severe winters that killed off a great part of its game. Once it had been the main home of the Svarhath, who were for the most part free landholders and cultivators save when they lived by the sea. Then it had held their pastures and grainfields, for they raised both, and many other crops besides; there had even been orchards for the more robust fruits, and a few vineyards on the most southerly slopes. But most of that people had fled the advance of the Ice thousands of years since, and now these were the Wild Lands, overgrown and tangled, home only to the duergar and human outlaws, and much feared on that account. From time to time, under some more vigorous king, attempts had been made to clear and resettle parts of them, but in winter these little colonies were isolated for long periods, and sooner or later they came to a bad and mysterious end. Many blamed the duergar rather than the Ice; and it is not impossible that they were right.

But to the people of the Vale its steep sides, in many places impass-able cliffs, remained an effective barrier against the worsening conditions above; and for centuries this seemed to be so. In their shelter the land north of the Great River enjoyed a warm temperate climate, growing gradually warmer as the river angled away to the southeast. The lands of the southern shore were much the same in the regions about the Gate; but as they sloped away sharply southward they grew increasingly warm and humid, basking in a warmth semi-tropical and even fully tropical, with high humidity. A great belt of dense rainforest covered the southernmost slopes of the vale and extended out to envelop the southern mountains. Beyond these, however, the land grew equally swiftly hot and dry, and the forest gave way to parched scrubland, sunbaked barrens and at last sheer desert; and though it was hardly noticeable at first, this too was advancing, as the Ice drained more and more of the free water from the cycle of life, and bound it in chill and sterile chains. Thus the extremes of clime that had first brought Kerys into being were all the millennia of its existence closing upon it like the jaws of a nutcracker; and all the while the shell was growing rotten from within.

The Last Winter

This was the closing of the jaws, the disordering of climes in whose fell grip the fleets of Morvannec found Kerys. It began soon after Nithaid's death and Elof's flight, as if either or both of them had been holding it somehow at bay; and this may be the case. It started as an early, fierce autumn, with stormy rains that ruined the harvest, and frosty nights that froze the sodden ground hard. Bitter blasts whipped the southern forests, blowing ever more of their tenuous topsoil from the great areas that man had cleared for his own husbandry, or simply laid waste. The first snows for thousands of years fell there, and the plants shrivelled. In the North the snows fell heavier, and the River began to slow and freeze; then at last men saw their folly in neglecting the Gate, and cursed the Lonuen line that had let it slip from the grasp. Somehow men managed to survive the winter, though food was scarce and many dark perils stalked the land, eagerly awaiting the spring, and some kind of a thaw. But the time came, and there was no thaw the snows did not slacken, nor did the glaciers relinquish their hold upon the mountains high above the walls. Ice stopped the inflow of the Great River at last, and its level began to fall.

What was happening to the northward can only be guessed at; but it is likely that the main body of the Ice was beginning its long-delayed advance at last, and setting in motion the final stages of Louhi's plan. Certainly the hilly *tundra* was more densely covered in snow than ever before. With the weather so propitious, in a very short time, weeks or days even, it might be about to form a solid sheet, and allow the main body to reach and merge with its two offshoots, and they in turn to stretch forward and join up with the enclave of ice around the Gate, where Louhi was exerting her own power. From there the path of the Ice would have been easy and obvious; down the Great River, and into the heart of Kerys. Formerly its sheer size must have made it almost impossible to freeze, keeping a constant temperature in its depths, and also its salinity. Ever since its flow had been reduced at the Gate falls, however, only its tributaries were feeding it, and it had been growing fresher; this may explain the dearth of fish Elof found around the island. Now, with many of the northern tributaries themselves frozen, it was also dwindling in size; already half-frozen, with the Ice itself behind her she could undoubtedly transform it almost at a stroke from river to glacier, from a bearer of life to a harbinger of death, overwhelming a vast area of land. Whether this in itself would have been enough to overturn the climatic balance of the world, and make the Ice permanent, we cannot now tell; but from the urgency all the Powers seem to have sensed, it almost certainly was the crucial point.

As to what brought this about, the chronicles offer no better explanations than Elof's and they seem to be right. Recent research suggests that the forces he saw at work would indeed have produced the results he feared; and ironically, it is from the icesheets that the evidence comes. The Antarctic icecap preserves a remarkable record of many atmospheric events and changes, and among these any particularly great volcanic eruptions. These hurl vast amounts of dust and gases, in particular sulphur dioxide, high into the atmosphere, and it is this gas, converted to fine droplets of sulphuric acid, that the ice preserves. Comparing concentrations of this in ice of known age with records of climactic changes over the same period have produced remarkable correlations between, for example, the enormous eruption of Tambora in Indonesia and the extraordinarily severe weather in the Northern Hemisphere in the first years of the nineteenth century – known, significantly, as the "Little Ice Age". Studies of later eruptions when more accurate records exist, such as Krakatoa in 1883 or more recently Mount St. Helen's, establish that the temperature not only of the particular region, but of the Earth as a whole, falls by several tenths of a degree in the years following a major eruption, chiefly because of the filtration effect of the dust in the upper atmosphere upon received solar radiation; most of that dust falls to earth in only a few days, but enough remains to make a significant difference. The effect of a number of such active volcanoes over a period of many years, capped at the climax by a period of extra-violent eruptions, and in a restricted area where the Ice could at least strongly influence wind patterns to gather and sustain more dust than usual, is difficult wholly to imagine; it would certainly be savage, turning the sky to a permanent lowering grey, chilling the air and stifling photosynthesis in plants. The sudden glaciation of the River might well increase the vulcanism still further, but even without that it would have been quite conclusive enough for Louhi's needs.

THE PEOPLES

THE PEOPLE OF KERYS

It is accurate to say "people", for the division between Svarhath and Penruthya, northerner and sothran, that so bedevilled the Westlands had always mattered less in Kerys, and by the time of Elof's coming was almost extinct. Nevertheless, it had its roots there, and they help to understand its history. Originally it may have reflected the merging of two distinct peoples, relics perhaps of the forgotten racial strands in the little kingdoms of the North before the Ice came, and that now were less than legendary. "Kingdom", indeed, may have been too grand a word; more probably most were mere tribal leagues as loose as the Ekwesh, and at best small and fluid monarchies of various kinds like Northumberland or Mercia in Dark Age England, or the Burgundian and Frankish realms that grew up around the Roman Empire. Almost certainly the dominant kingdom among the Penruthya was a city-state, because it was a cultural mould they never escaped, but simply expanded to fit the land; even in so vast a realm as Kerys, which had perforce to have several great cities, one immense community dominated all the rest. The Svarhath never showed quite the same tendency; their preference was always for towns of moderate size among a loose federation of villages. Probably it was the threat of the Ice that first drove these related but disparate peoples to unite; but nothing certain is known of that. It is well established, however, that in even the earliest records of Kerys they thought of themselves as one nation, owing allegiance to one lord, intermarrying freely and speaking one another's tongues. It was chiefly a preference for different climes and manners of life that kept them separate at all, and perhaps also kept them friendly; for they seldom if ever competed for the same land.

The character of both peoples was much the same as in the realms of Brasayhal. The Penruthya of Kerys were always the more numerous race, probably because their way of life allowed it. They were a lowland folk, fond of warm climes and the rich flat farmland of riverine plains; they grew much grain and many orchards and vineyards, but raised little meat or dairy produce, and almost no fish. Their lands tended to be divided into large estates whose farms were held in tenancy from the great lords; but this tenancy was not a burdensome thing, and until the last years the land was worked at all levels by free men. Some of the estates on the southern shore, settled later, were of astonishing size, their labourers numbered by the thousand, and their lords, men of great consequence. Their cities showed the same tendency towards size, but in a well-ordered form; they were masters of buildings as of all the other arts, and had a surprising command of the basic requirements in water supply and sanitation that alone make such large communities practicable. Their laws regarding public health were strict and carried severe penalties, and they were supported by all levels of the community, even the lowest; almost certainly this was a result of the state's provision of basic instruction for all its citizens. What was provided varied widely, but in Kerys the City at its height there was almost no citizen of sound mind who could not read and write, and recite the basic table of laws. The Penruthya had a strong tradition of hierarchy and the rule of law from above, but set against this an equally strong tradition of freedom, if not of equality, for all men; this often took the form of opposition to their kings, commonly by powerful lords in pursuit of their own independence.

The Svarhath, on the other hand, had no particular tradition of order, and few if any great lords; they reserved their respect for wise elders and rich men, and regarded the king much as a clan might its chieftain – their ruler, but by right of kinship more than law. They chose to dwell chiefly among the cooler uplands above the northern walls of Kerys Vale, a land that seemed far too coarse and wild to the Penruthya, but could in fact yield a rich living to men who knew how to cultivate it. They grew some grain, wine grapes and other fruit in the sheltered valleys, but meat and dairying were their main products; upon hill and mountain pastures they raised their huge cattle, and upon higher slopes of coarser vegetation sheep or goats. Wise in all matters relating to ships and seafaring, they fished not only the rivers but also the rich seas around the coast. They also thrived upon forestry and hunting, for they took better care of their wooden lands than did the sothrans. Landholdings were mostly no larger than an individual could manage; even the richest men might own no more than a single manorial farm, albeit a very large one, and some woods and hunting preserves. Tenancy was almost unknown, and treated with deep suspicion. Some villages, however, owned and worked large holdings in common, and so also some families, for a particular reason. Land was inherited not by the eldest male heir, as with the Penruthya, but by all sons jointly; only if it could not support them all would some have to seek their support elsewhere. Since large families were rare among the Svarhath, this usually worked well enough. There were plenty of opportunities for such sons; shipping and the crafts were honourable and prosperous occupations that supportd many, and also matters financial and scholarly. The Penruthya appeared to dominate trade, but never to the exclusion of an energetic northerner; indeed, since it was Svarhath-owned ships that handled the cream of the swift river traffic, they had considerable influence in it, and many a Southern lord owed his fortune to the acumen and industry of his Svarhath stewards. And in scholarship and statecraft – which they tended to associate – both strains mingled readily, the Penruthya excelling only by their numbers.

In general this union of peoples was a strong one, each fulfilling somewhat different roles, each benefitting from what the other lacked and respecting the other for it; it was a strong foundation upon which to build such a realm. Such friction as there was appears to have been mild, easily contained by the Ysmerien kings who mingled the blood of both races; and it is noticeable that when serious factional problems did break out in Kerys the division was more social than racial. The plebeian and patrician factions that appeared among the Penruthya were reflected among the Northerners, though less aggressively; but then the distinctions between lord and commoner were never so important there. The factions plagued the land, but never seriously divided it. The real difficulties began when the might and wealth of Kerys were at their peak, and the land seemed a strength unassailable. It was then the menace of the Ice first began to make itself felt among the Svarhath lands, and the remotest northerners had to flee southwards, even into the Vale. Then, a generation later, a serious conflict of kinship and succession broke out for the first time among the Ysmerien.

The Sundering of the Peoples

The details are simple enough; a king, Gherannen, died leaving a son and a daughter by different wives. The laws of succession were strict. Daughters could inherit at need, but the son, Barech, was the elder, and there was never any doubt that he would be the rightful successor; but he died suddenly within days of his father. And though he was of mature years and his wife had recently borne him a son, there was grave doubt as to whether the child, though named for him, was in fact his; and what followed fed that doubt. His widow Amer immediately installed as regent not Barech's younger sister, Authe, as was customary, but their cousin Dormaidh, one of the most able and powerful southern lords. By a coincidence of ancestry he was a pure-blooded Ysmerien, a well-made man of great charm and vigour; and he was also a former suitor of Amer. The resultant furore threatened to split the country, for, if the child was not Barech's, then Authe was the rightful heir, and after her her son Keryn; but Dormaidh enjoyed great support among powerful men of both Penruthya and Svarhath, and of both ancestral factions. Fewer supported Authe, young widow of an Ysmerien landholder, and of no great distinction; but she showed great firmness in claiming the throne on behalf of her son. For many years the whole land simmered, without ever quite bursting into the flame of civil war. Even the ancestral factions were split down the middle, although the older aristocracy tended to support Authe and the newer Dormaidh. Dormaidh was the effective ruler, but his power was never absolute enough to put down his enemies; and to do him justice, he had no particular wish to, restraining the most hot-headed of his followers. It was charged he had murdered Barech, but his later behaviour made this less likely. Authe was less retrained, but could never whip up enough sure support; however, her supporters' minor insurrections seriously disrupted the trade of the land, and deepened divisions. When the garrison of the High Gate declared for her she occupied it and set up her own court there, and over a period of yeas intrigued to little effect against Dormaidh.

Meanwhile the two children were growing up, the younger Barech as a powerless shadow under Dormaidh's overwhelming personality, and Keryn as an independent and intelligent young prince; as he grew up it became obvious that he was the most attractive character in the whole tangle. When he reached his first manhood, in his sixteenth year as the custom then was, his mother was persuaded to hand over her claim to him, and swiftly he gained greater support than she ever had. Dormaidh himself, eager to end the disruption, offered him joint succession with Barech; but Barech, for the first time in his life, objected violently. He threatened Keryn's life, and swore bloody retribution against the least man who supported him. Civil war now began to seem inevitable when Dormaidh died, if not sooner, and men on either side began to arm and prepare, and break off what slight contact they had kept with their opponents; towns on one side or the other hounded out minorities lest they launch a surprise attack, and murders and brawls began to multiply. This prospect, on top of the years of squabbling he had known, saddened and disgusted Keryn; and the news of the advancing Ice brought by northern refugees, remote as it seemed to most, filled this far-sighted prince with alarm for the future. He was in the mood to find some new alternative, when one presented itself.

Mariners had long suspected the existence of another land across the oceans; wide-ranging fishermen claimed to have fished off its shores, though none had dared to land. Now some bold Svarhath shipowners, desperate for new profits after some fourteen years of decaying trade, set out to find it in earnest. One party succeeded, after great privations, and returned to tell of a vast new land of forests and high mountains, wild and uninhabited as far they could tell, but fertile and full of promise. Most significantly of all, it was relatively untroubled by the Ice. For Keryn that was enough, and he resolved to seek out a new home in this land. To Dormaidh and Barech he sent a defiant challenge, saying that though he asserted his birthright still, he preferred to extend his realm rather than lay it waste with war; since the folk must be divided, let those who favoured his cause come with him to settle this new land. If Dormaidh would not hinder any who wished to go, but would assist them with ships and resources, then, rightfully or not, he might rule those who remained. Dormaidh accepted this with relief, for he too hated the prospect of war; he ignored the wrath of Barech, who foresaw, rightly, that many would desert the land rather than face his rule, shrinking his inheritance and injuring his pride. In fact, many even among his own supporters were piqued by the idea, and the taste of adventure; and the number who responded surprised even Keryn. Men and women of every quality, of every allegiance and faction joined with him, until the size of the expedition began to alarm Dormaidh; but by then events had gathered momentum, and there was little he could do. Barech's attempt to deter recruits by threatening the kin they were leaving behind simply swelled their numbers further, as he might have expected, and led to open conflict between Dormaidh and himself. In the end, some five years later, it is said that more than a fifth of the entire Penruthya population of Kerys chose to follow Keryn, and close to half the Svarhath; and the majority of these were able-bodied folk in their prime years, so that the loss to the land was far greater. Many more would have come, if they could have hoped to survive the voyage. More ships were needed than the land could possibly dispose of; and it may well be that the great clearing of forests began at this time, and that the timber taken was never fully replanted. There is no reason to doubt the chronicles' picture of the fleet at last assembled on the shores below the Gate, darkening the ocean and stilling its waves by the very number of its hulls; the number of people who sailed in them is harder to be sure of. But since at that time Kerys was mightier and better peopled than when Elof and Roc came there, it is possible that a hundred thousand at least set sail with Keryn that day, and like him looked their last upon the beacon of the Gate until even its last wisp of smoke had vanished utterly beneath the remorseless horizon.

It was a blow from which, perhaps, Kerys never quite recovered. Soon after the sailing Barech, supported by many who were suffering its consequences, raised a rebellion against Dormaidh and toppled him. He became king, and his heirs after him, and save for one act of cruelty he was not as bad a ruler as his beginning had promised; his worst fault was a certain weakness and indecision, which had perhaps been seen in Dormaidh also, and inability to restrain the warring factions. Yet it is not unlikely that he did indeed represent some altered strain in the Ysmerien. For though after him, as before, there were kings strong and weak, good and less good, that indecisive nature appeared more and more often, till in the end the kings were reduced to puppets of their powerful warlords and marshals, and were at the last overthrown by one such of the Lonuen line, who took their place; and his great-grandson was Nithaid.

That act of cruelty was significant. It is said that Barech took Dormaidh to the shore and mockingly sent the defeated regent and a few close companions to sea in an ill-equipped hulk, bidding them also seek new kingdoms to conquer. Cruel as this was to a man very likely his own father, it is possible to understand the grievance he bore. The land was cruelly impoverished by losing so many, and the nature of its people changed. The Svarhath in particular dwindled from that time, becoming a far smaller adjunct to the Penruthya than they were anywhere in the new lands save only Kerbryhaine; and without them, as Elof suspected, Kerys began to follow the same downward slope. Together, both strains added up to a great people; but with their mutual influence removed, each followed their own particular downward paths, into harsh and demoralized decadence or sullen rusticity respectively. Clearly some more radical blending was needed in them both; and it may be that it was this, harsh as it seemed, that the downfall of all their lands in the ending of the Long Winter provided.

Of the fortunes of the folk of Kerys in its immediate aftermath a little is known, for one or two fortunate ships still managed to escape across the oceans to Morvanhal in the years that followed. Relatively few lives were lost, for in the wake of that unnatural winter a sudden and balmy summer followed, and a sudden explosion of growth. The Wild Lands, to which most in the north had escaped, took flower and fruited, and rough patches could be cleared and sown here and there, and shelters built against the coming winter; in the south the jungle also provided some food. So few if any starved; but the life they clung to was hard, with hardly a trace of its former luxury, or even of civilization. The duergar might have helped, fallen as they too were; but the gulf between them and men was grown too wide. Objects of fear they were and remained to the sundered folk. Of the north the last that was heard, a generation later, spoke of a reversion to the levels of the stone age; and of the south, nothing. In so short a time was the glory of that land brought at last to the dust; yet against the span of time, even all the millennia of its rise and fall seem little longer, and are swallowed up in that greater river so thoroughly that they might as well never have been.

Languages

The tongues of Kerys were, like its peoples, very close to those of their kin in Brasayhal, and more has been said of these in earlier appendices. However, they were less close than would appear from the text of the chronicles, and it is likely that Roc and Elof had a great deal more trouble making themselves understood than the account suggests. The grammar of both versions of Penruthya appears to have remained substantially intact over the long period of their separation; but such matters as word termination had altered drastically, and even the meanings of many common words. The accents also had changed; Roc had the advantage here, for Elof's clear Northern accents sounded alien to the Penruthya, though not unpleasant, and startlingly august to northerners such as Trygvar. It was as if an Englishman of today were addressed by a fine speaker of Shakespeare's English. The Northern tongue had changed less, for its speakers had become an extreme minority, and as minorities do they guarded their tongue jealously, hugging it close to them and teaching and using it with meticulous care.

Arcane Beliefs and Arts

Of these also much else has been said earlier; but some points arise only in the Book of the Armring. In Kerys, for example, the probable origin of the River as a concept of time and the cycles of the world, and as a border and barrier to the land of the dead, are best seen, for to the first men who looked upon it that awesome flow must have seemed like the bounds of the world indeed. At some later date, though, the Milky Way seems to have become identified with the metaphysical River, and been given the same name. But by Kermorvan's day it was no longer seriously thought of in that sense, save by the least educated of folk, and the River had become a wholly philosophical concept. Yet nevertheless, that misty streak across the night skies persisted as a symbol of potent meaning, at least as significant as the Iceglow which seemed to be forever and futilely seeking to blot it out.

By that time the rather vague concept of reincarnation the peoples of Kerys favoured had coalesced, and for that also the River became a symbol. As something set afloat upon the Yskianas' waters would eventually find shore elsewhere, so might the returning spirit; unless it were weighted or dragged down. It is interesting that Elof is not made by the chroniclers to endorse that, as one might expect; but to declare his ignorance of it. Evidently they wished to stress that within this world even the Powers have bounds, for better or for worse.

Smithcraft

In the chronicles the nature of Elof's smithcraft is discussed and debated at every turn, as to whether it was an attribute of a human or a power; but this these present accounts could hardly reflect, without revealing more than Elof himself knew at the time. The conclusion come to is the one that Elof suggests in passing; that all smithcraft in humanity was a gift of the Powers, a counterbalance to what they knew its foes would one day hurl against it. Whether or not that gift was reclaimed or exhausted, or simply lies dormant for want of knowledge to awaken it, cannot be said. But Elof's case is clearer. Those who came before him had been more than human, and that was their glory and all too often their downfall; so Elof had, by the very nature of his mission, to be no more than human if he was to succeed. So though the power he had was great, it must have been no more than the most a human might have had, albeit an exceptional one; or, more probably, it was as great as any human might have found within himself, had he only the will to awaken it.

It was a great endowment; yet without the dedication to learn its uses and the skills to exploit them, it would have been meaningless. It was in these that Elof's true achievement lay, and in these that his mastery truly surpassed any other of that time. Certainly the materials and processes he used, though mysterious, are not wholly beyond our own comprehension.

The mirror-shields seem to have been no more than some light and hard alloy, perhaps upon a bracing frame of wood or metal tube. Their chiefest subtlety lay in their shape which caught and concentrated the sun so well, and in the truly mysterious influence that held them in such unison both as shieldwall and as solar mirror. Such tight coordination and focussing is the problem which bedevils modern solar furnaces; they are capable of astonishing temperatures, such is the power the sun sheds upon us, but are very clumsy at concentrating it. Nevertheless there is evidence that some part of this problem was solved in ancient times. The Greek philosopher Archimedes, among the defences he created for his home city of Syracuse, is said to have fired enemy ships by just such a burning-glass, a feat historians have long sneered at because of the problems such mirrors involve. But recently a more practical archaeologist realised that he might have used the long Greek shields, highly polished, and tried an experiment with some twenty modern replicas of these, representing quite a good-sized area of reflector. Under the noon sun their combined beams were well able to set afire the timbers of a boat moored in the harbour. Elof's shields represented a surface thousands of times greater, and much more carefully and uniformly shaped. In such greater numbers and more skilfully shaped, and with their beams concentrated by the mastershields into near-perfect intensity, they must have achieved astonishing temperatures. It is ironic that the Ice's ultimate plan was to raise the world's albedo and so reflect away the life-giving solar energy; for Elof simply reflected it back at them.

That fine fibre of which both Gorthawer and his wings were shaped is rather more mysterious to our eyes. Yet essentially it was almost certainly more refinement of carbon or graphite fibres, many varieties of which we can produce under a very great and sustained heat; and of such a heat, in his day, some kinds of lava-flow would have been an adequate source. Such fibres depend for their remarkable properties upon their crystalline structure, and the ability the duergar taught him to study this under heat must have given him wide control over them. This, incidentally, the chronicles speak of as if it was a natural ability; but more probably he made use of some device, and his own subtlety lay in the true interpreting of it. For in this, as in all else, he was as he wished his friends to think him, a man only.

Such signposts as he left himself, all those generations past, would have been meaningless as his power without the will and daring to exploit them, and the sheer disregard of himself. Had he not shed his old life willingly, it is likely his labours, and most of all those in the furnace would have curtailed it, or at any rate brought on him a miserable and suffering old age; but the greater flame that burned within him spared him that.

THE DUERGAR

In the Book of the Sword some brief glimpses remain of the Duergar people at what, in these latter years, was very probably their peak. In the Book of the Helm their decline and disappearance is hinted at; and in the Book of the Armring its progress is seen. They were undoubtedly a very ancient folk, and equally a very strange one by the standards of ordinary men. To grasp something of how alien they were, one needed only consider a race who were aware of many of the possibilities of science and technology, up to and including some grasp of the structure of matter and the potential energies it could unleash; yet who chose not to pursue or exploit that knowledge. Neither their dwelling underground, nor their characteristic physical shape, can set them further apart from men than that; for they were enough like us to interbreed, and they had not always dwelt beneath the earth. Some of them could understand men, and even become friends with them and more, as has been seen; in the end, as the world changed about them, many united with men, and brought with them their many virtues. But these were always a small minority. Ildryan, as he is shown to us, is much more characteristic of the majority of duergar, a cold and remote personality, with his concept of ethics governed by payment and return, even in a forced bargain. Elof's assessment of him shows how well he understood these people, for reasons that he could not have realised at the time. It is ironic that, when he first sought their help, he was himself, without knowing it, demanding a *quid pro quo*; for it was to the Power he had once been that the whole race owed its very survival.

The Beginnings of the Duergar

Some words of Ils', which are not included in the tale, throw a grim light upon this; they were spoken in royal council, to support Kermorvan's plan to aid Kerys, and promise the duergar's aid. "We should act! And act in time! For once before we have stood here, and failed to; and it was almost the end of us. Not for nothing do you call us the Elder Folk; for all that you are we once were, all and more. Once we too had spread out across the world, had explored the secrets of nature to their depths, only to find what gulfs lay beyond them. We too dreamed ourselves rulers of the world, not brief tenants of another's halls. Then the Ice came. Then that earlier Long Winter rolled over us, and scoured away all that we had built. Had Ilmarinen not helped us, shaped us our refuges beneath the hollow hills, and taught us new ways to live and to survive, then we should have been altogether destroyed. We were neither as numerous nor as aggressive as you humans; we were not so ready to rip the whole wide world apart and tack it back together again to suit us. We might have been driven back to savagery; and if both your race and mine do not act for themselves now, we may yet be. One alone came to help us, when it seemed that all other doors were shut, and many hope he will again; but I fear even his face is turned from us now."

This was not so; for Elof himself sat by her as she spoke these words, as she afterwards recalled. But she was right, in that he had no intention of maintaining the duergar in the state he had left them, even had he the power to do. As he himself had suggested in his plea to the old king Andvar, Ilmarinen had saved them for a purpose, that the riches of their culture might not wholly vanish from the world, that they might serve as a bridge and an inspiration to struggling future generations, just as he promised Kermorvan he should. To that end he had sought almost to "store" them underground, in an environment and a way of life that was relatively fixed, hoping that when the Winter was spent and the Ice withdrew, they would emerge and join the new men coming into their lands, and teach them their ancient wisdom.

To some extent his plan worked. As Ils suggested, many of the greatest works of men of the elder days were created with advice, at least, from the duergar; the High Gate, for example, would not have been possible without their skill with stone. Even in less happy days men might, from time to time, awake their interest or their compassion, which was greater than might have been expected, and learn from them again. So it was with the Mastersmith, and so also Elof himself; though it may have counted for much with the more obdurate of them that he had saved many of their people's lives, and had only his own and one other in return, for on such petty balances their ethics might rest. They could be generous with their gifts, if they took to a human, and undoubtedly he learned much from them, more even than smithcraft, either directly or from what the Mastersmith had gleaned. His skill in navigation came from them, and more arcane knowledge, often of a quite startling extent. The account of the reasoning by which he grasped Louhi's intention to use the volcanos of Kerys (and perhaps of the Westlands, before that) is notable because it suggests that he had some knowledge of the existence of continental platforms, the so-called "plates"; but equally he seems not to have understood anything of their movement and interaction, or any of the processes with which modern plate tectonics is concerned. Most probably, therefore, his knowledge was second-hand, and not a result of his own deductions; there is nowhere else he could have come by it save from the duergar, and it is more likely his fault than theirs that he did not grasp the full concept. And indeed such drift would be a hard thing to grasp, in a world half shelled in ice; but the duergar remembered it differently.

But a certain amount of teaching and advice was as much as the duergar would ever give, in the years before his coming, and these were exceptions. Even in their best relations with men they would rarely do more than dwell among them for a brief while, then return with relief to their own. Ultimately Ilmarinen's plan proved a failure – because, no doubt, much as he loved the race he had made the duergar, he understood them little better than their human cousins. The Elder Folk, buffeted by climate and destiny, had come to despise the outside world, and grown contemplative and inward-looking, suspicious even of their own kin from elsewhere. They forgot their purpose, or scorned it, and for the most part an enmity grew up between them and men that they made little effort to avoid. Instead they fled, shunning the animals, as they deemed them, and joined their kin in scattered halls elsewhere. In the end, as Andvar told, they fled halfway round the world to escape mankind; but they could not flee forever. Man was their destiny, and with him they were doomed to mingle, or perish in their own isolation; yet that bleak end was what many at last preferred, and it is doubtful whether any of that race yet walk the world. Yet some did join with men, and their influence was a good one. For it is known that members of that race which was born of their mingling sank to the simplest savagery ere they rose again; but what little we have of them speaks well. Even their crude stone tools were fairly made; and they buried their dead with care, and filled the graves with flowers.

The Duergar Languages

In earlier books of the chronicles mention is made of the sound of the duergar tongue – or tongues, for there were several – but few attempts are made to reproduce any of them; the Book of the Armring has more than the others that concern Elof, and that only a few scattered words and phrases, clumsily transliterated. Even these survive from a single text, probably the oldest surviving; in later copies they are omitted altogether. This probably indicates the reason; the tongues in which the chronicles were written were preserved long after they fell from use, first as a "classical" tongue of refined expression, and later as a "mystery" language guarding secrets only for the initiate. But the duergar languages no man of later ages knew. Even those duergar who, in the general changing of the world, chose to throw in their lot with men, never taught them any duergar tongue, lest it compromise the safety of their kin who remained apart. For this reason little can be made of what is left. The original author had no alternative but to transcribe it phonetically, using whatever ideographic characters sounded approximately right; and it must be remembered that each character in itself also stood for a word. The effect of this may be gauged by comparing the pseudonym a Japanese writer borrowed from his favourite Western author, Edogawa Rampo, to the original. He was referring to Edgar Allan Poe. What an immense span of time could do to this, in which characters and soundforms changed and mistakes and "improvements" were introduced into the copying, is best left to the imagination. So, to the later copyists, whatever duergar words were included must have seemed like meaningless gibberish. Sooner or later they were bound to be edited out. From what little remains, as has been said before, some deductions have been made. One or two words suggest some ancestral affinity with the rather unusual Finno-Ugric family of languages; but this cannot be proven. It seems to have sounded much more like a Slavic tongue, however, and for that reason it has been rendered into a Slavic form. Attempts have been made to make the meaning of what is spoken clear from the accompanying dialogue; though it should be noted that Ildryan's final comment appears to be moderately obscene. The duergar were never known for primness; and there are signs that some of Ils' more pungent comments have been censored by later generations – if so, most unfairly, as she was renowned even among her own folk for the imaginative nature of her insults.

In most cases where a human being was present, of course, duergar would speak the northern tongue. This was partly for reasons of secrecy, but also because they found it a very convenient *lingua franca* between themselves. Which of their languages took precedence could often have some social or political significance, and was hard to settle; the human tongue, which they found easy to master, avoided the question neatly. Why it was Svarhath they spoke is uncertain; Ils, who spoke both Svarhath ande Penruthya, claimed it was because the "furry" northern speech sat more easily in their mouths than the southern, which she thought sounded "slimy". This may well have been so, but it may have been adopted simply because duergar tended to prefer the same slightly cooler climates as the Svarhath, and so came into contact with them more often. By Elof's time almost all duergar spoke some Svarhath; even their names, though they originated in their own tongues, they habitually rendered into Northern form. And only in that form are they preserved.

THE EKWESH PEOPLES

The various books of the Winter Chronicles contain much incidental lore concerning these savage folks, but the Book of the Armring most of all, probably because it tells of the first encounter with the Ravens; for that reason it is best gathered here. As with the duergar, examples of their speech are preserved in the oldest texts only; and no doubt for the same reasons.

The Ekwesh Tongues

It is known that there were many of these, three at least; they were naurally closely related, but not always mutually understandable because they had so many dialects. The majority tongue, like Mandarin Chinese, became almost universally spoken, but jealousies between tribes and clans ensured that it did not oust their own tongues; it became almost a point of honour to speak it or any foreign speech as badly and curtly as possible. The result was that most Ekwesh sounded crude and monosyllabic to outsiders. The Ravens, however, spoke the majority tongue as their own, in a particularly old-fashioned form much like the one Elof had learned a little of from the Mastersmith. It may have flattered the Raven chieftain to hear him speak it.

None, however, had any written form. A few Ekwesh could read and write the Kerys-born languages, but this was not an achievement highly regarded, even when it proved useful; it was, after all, something thralls regarded, even when it proved useful; it was, after all, something thralls could do. Even the shamans and chieftains preserved their lore orally, reinforced only by a mnemonic system, patterns of odd characters that operated as a more sophisticated equivalent of the Inca *quipu* or medieval tally sticks, totally unintelligible when its sphere of reference was unknown. It is thought that this was forced upon them by the Ice, to keep them dependent on it for dribs and drabs of knowledge which could be handed out over and over again as some new gift; and also, very probably, to prevent any true culture developing. For this reason even in the oldest texts of the chronicles only a few words of Ekwesh are preserved, spelt much as they sounded to Svarhath or Penruthya speakers; and since we cannot tell from an ideographic system exactly how those tongues sounded, the Ekwesh speech is well and truly lost. It appears to have been an agglutinative type, highly expressive but cumbersome and fiendishly complicated to those who had not grown up with it. The whole phrase "vault out of a boat" became a single verb "out-of-a-boat-with-one hand-to-leap", as it might in many "primitive" languages today, for example certain Inuit and Northwest Coast tongues. Such words as can be salvaged have been included in the text, but they amount at best to an informed guess.

The Ekwesh realm and its origins

Much information about the land and history of the Ekwesh peoples is put by the chroniclers into the mouth of their chieftain, speaking with Elof – more, certainly, than he would ever have told a prisoner, even one he had come to respect. But this is a common enough device in such histories, and it was undoubtedly from the Ravens that most such lore came; of their homeland, in particular, no outsider left any account. It is not hard to guess why.

It is known to have lain in the lands far east of Kerys, separated from it by a land so trackless and wild that the Ice actually became the safest means for the Ekwesh to cross, and to have reached the further shores of the oceans that lapped upon the Westlands of Bryhaine, where Elof and Kermorvan grew up. Its exact extent is unknown, but undoubtedly it covered more actual land than any other realm among men at that time – perhaps more than all the rest put together. But so miserable and barren was most of this land, barely able to sustain life, that population densities were very low. The Ekwesh people arose as hardy hunter-gatherers with only the simplest of cultures, living a nomadic, seasonal existence and making the best of the savage and hostile environment which was all they knew. At this stage they seem to have lived not unlike the natives of Tierra del Fuego, who astonished European explorers by their ability to live more or less naked, with only crude shelters of branches and grass; within five degrees of the South Polar icepack. The Ekwesh lands also lay in the proximity of the Ice, and it dominated their climate, adding to the long and terrible winters it sent the brief fierce summer that was natural to the region. Each season brought extremes, from heavy snow to floods to drought to torrential rains and snow again, in a ruthless cycle. So bleak was their land that it is a marvel these ancestors of the Ekwesh survived; with only a little more effort the Ice might well have exterminated them entirely, as it sought to do to all other races of men. Why, then, did it fail to?

There is some suggestion that the Ekwesh lands were a reservation created by the Ice – or, more properly, an arena. By pushing the lands to the limits of habitability, therefore, they sought to create a breed of men apt to their ways. Whether this is so, or whether some among the Powers of the Ice simply seized upon what they found, the fact remains they soon began to take an active part in the shaping of the Ekwesh folk. Formerly they had relied for warriors upon the lesser powers among their own numbers, forcing them into strange and fearsome forms, and upon lesser creatures they had bred and deformed into monsters, and only secondarily upon men; they had recruited such renegades as can always be found, individuals or tribes, but these proved rare and highly undependable, and often at a crucial moment chose the kinship of their true kind. For even in the worst among men some small spark may not be wholly extinguished. So, after a series of formidable defeats – not least those inflicted by Kerys in the days of its first grandeur – they seem to have concluded that only men could defeat men, and sought to reshape these troublesome creatures to their own ideas. And, perhaps, their own preconceptions.

The Cult of the Ice

Undoubtedly these rebel Powers saw men as substantially base, brutish and vicious; and this judgement may have been reinforced by the urges which came to bedevil them whenever they assumed human form, and which they had never learned to control. So they began to force these strong but unformed folk, whose society already had all the savagery and ruthlessness necessary to hunters who must kill to live, into a society that, so they thought, would best express this human baseness, and channel it in ways useful to them. In subtle ways they began to take hold of the ancestors of the Ekwesh, and to lead them along the paths they chose.

These were often very dark, for it was among the depths of the human mind that the Ice sought its hold, and among the blacker desires and pleasures of men. Perhaps it amused those cold minds to dominate those they despised by what harmed them most, by unleashing their own worst urges, by cruelty and torture and the bonds that bind those who have done a thing unthinkable to others. The Ekwesh under the tutelage of the Ice became a folk bloody and fell, to whom the causing of pain and the shedding of blood were not an evil, not even a means to an end, but an end in themselves, a propitiation to be offered and a pleasure to be shared. From Elof's intimacy with the Mastersmith we know that it enforced austerities upon its highest initiates, no doubt, as the chronicler suggests, to direct their energy and avoid distractions, and fearsome journeys into the heart of the Ice to commune there with its rulers, which must have involved the initiate forcing himself to survive in an environment that made little or no concession to the human body. The lives of the Hidden Clan lost in its march eastward over the Ice to Morvannec were simply what is expected of dedicated men. From Bryhon's revelations we know that self-torment or even mutilation was demanded of them, and from accounts of Ekwesh captives, and grisly discoveries aboard their ships and in their camps, we know that it demanded human torture and sacrifice from its followers. But of the actual rites of its worship, we know only the most general details, mostly from thralls who were fortunate enough to see them and survive to be freed. As was mentioned in earlier appendices, the shamans relied on ecstatic and visionary rites, dancing themselves into a frenzy to drumbeats to release their inner powers; this appears to have been a cruder analogue of the concentration and labour of smithcraft, and its effects, naturally, were more transient. This their followers appeared to have imitated, but to what end, and in what ways, is unknown.

Unless, perhaps, we may see some distant reflection of them in the many strange rites of veneration and fear still associated with glaciers, such as those practised, in a thinly Christian guise, by native South Americans across a wide range of the Andes in the *Cholleriti* festival. In this the participants, the so-called *Ucucu* dancers, wear bear masks; carrying a great cross, they climb up to the glaciers that loom over their mountain homes and there spend a night above the snowline in a vigil, initiated by a symbolic whipping. This is intended to propitiate the *condenados*, ghoul-spirits (now said to be those of the damned) who are supposed to inhabit the glacier, and protect the festival pilgrims from them. In the morning they use their whips as saws to cut out huge lumps of the glacier, and these they carry as a penance down to the festival sanctuary, in a procession accompanied by the pilgrims with wild hooting cries. This ritual destruction of the glacier is thought to enact the penance of the *condenados* and release both them and their intended victims. In this and many other examples some relic of the dominion and terror of the Ice may yet remain.

The Ekwesh Empire

In fact, of course, human beings are neither so simple nor so easily coerced, whatever the Ice may have believed. Even under that yoke at its worst the Ekwesh kept many natural human virtues the Ice could not suppress; these it had to contain by channelling them inwards. Love was limited to the closest of kindred only, and became a fierce and jealous thing, that many times led to a slaying when it was in any way baulked or betrayed; man and wife, father and children, were linked by a bond whose very strength and rigidity made it perilous. Loyalty and respect extended only to the tribe, and no further; intermarriage was possible, but the wife was seldom well regarded – nor, sometimes, the children. Those outside the family could command no affection; those outside the tribe might be foes or allies, but never friends. Those who were not Ekwesh were only potential victims or thralls; and thralls were scarcely human. An Ekwesh might father children upon a thrall woman; but those children would be marked thralls, and so also their children's children to the end of their line, even if all the fathers were Ekwesh, and the blood be almost pure. An Ekwesh woman conceiving by a thrall, if something so unthinkable were to happen, would be slaughtered out of hand, and her child with her, by her closest kin, as being unfit even for sacrifice. Yet even in this harsh society, individual Ekwesh still retained surprising depths. Some families, especially among the Ravens, had a tradition of treating their thralls humanely; and though this earned them the contempt of others, it often gained them greater labour, and so greater riches. For slaves have little to gain by working harder; but these wished their master to prosper, if only for their own protection. So, such masters often became rich and powerful, and some slight force for better ways.

However, there were stronger voices set against them. For the Ice had chosen its chief spokesmen with cunning; these were the shamans, the wise men of the tribes. From the earliest days it had recruited them and trained them in its cult, arming them with arcane knowledge and teaching them to enhance and develop the innate power that men of Kerys called smithcraft, but which the Ice claimed was its gift. From their association with the Ice they derived great prestige and authority, and from presiding over the atrocious rites it prescribed. Often they became the true rulers behind the tribal chiefs, who became mainly warleaders; but sometimes they became chieftains themselves. The one whom Elof first encountered in Asenby seems to have been of this breed, as also their younger captor in Morvannec.

It was under the influence of the earliest and most charismatic of these leaders, men trained by the Ice powers or even the powers themselves in human form, that the most savage tribes in the north of the land first began to link up. Sometimes by alliance, most often by conquest, they gathered into a few very large tribes under the name-totem of whichever group had made itself dominant. The strength of unity gave them greater mastery of their land, and their numbers began to increase rapidly. Soon they were outstripping the land's ability to support them; and under the pressure of the Ice and the goading of necessity they began to raid their most southerly neighbours to live, and at last press down into their land. So the pattern of the Ekwesh expansion – grow, raid and then settle to grow again – was set in motion, and for a thousand years it did not change; the same process drove them over the seas to the West-lands and overland to Kerys.

Some of these southern tribes had abandoned a nomadic existence and developed the beginnings of agriculture, and the Ekwesh were not slow to see that this was a surer way of gaining food. But it posed a problem. To them hunting and warfare were proper occupations for men, and the practise of crafts; gathering was woman's work, at best, and the drudgery of cultivation inconceivably demeaning, not to say impossible for a nomad. So, perhaps with guidance from the Ice, their attitude began to change; instead of butchering their adversaries outright, they made thralls of them, and set them to produce food. They themselves remained semi-nomadic, and developed that mode of life to great heights; they moved as overlords between these communities of thrall sessors, still nomadic and free. They would oversee a planting and return to oversee the harvest, leaving the thralls to cultivate the land meanwhile, knowing that if they slacked or failed their masters would consume their own food, and perhaps them also. Though unusual, this society was a recognisable, if more extreme version of the periodic "taxing" rounds levied by the Rus of Kiev or the Norwegian Vikings upon the Slav towns of the interior, as described by the warrior Ohtere (Ottar) who visited the court of Alfred the Great. The Ekwesh, however, carried it further, extending the same principle to mines and shipyards, and even small manufactories and market towns; the thralls became almost a mercantile subclass, but always at the mercy of their fundamentally less civilised overlords. Any development more advanced, however, was always held back by the Ekwesh's understandable fear of giving thralls too much power, as the Spartans feared the Helots; and this goes some way to explain the Ekwesh's instant hatred of more civilised lands such as Kerys or Morvannec, or even rural Nordeney. To them they represented what might happen when thralls got out of hand, and were to be subjugated as soon as possible lest they set their own thralls a bad example. Any awe or impression civilization might have made upon them, that fear, encouraged no doubt by the Ice, swallowed up.

Up to that point, however, the Ekwesh prospered. The surpluses created increased their population still further, and redoubled their need to expand. By now many of their remaining neighbours, who were mostly along the eastern seaboard, saw what was coming, and fled over-sea, or even, in desperation, over the Ice. These were the hapless fugitives who poured ito Nordeney only a brief time after the Svarhath refugees from Morvan, and made common cause with them. Those who did not flee were swiftly overwhelmed. But as the Ekwesh ran out of land and neighbours to conquer, they ran into their first serious check; and it was one of the Ice's own making. It had bred the Ekwesh to be its conquerors, spreading savagery over the other realms of men; but for them to expand into those realms they had to achieve some degree of unity, some semblance of empire, or organise their armies. And it was precisely those aspects of human nature which make unity possible that the Ice had suppressed. The tribes had always fought one another, making and breaking alliances as the moment's advantage dictated; but for centuries it had been chiefly their thralls who suffered, and that too drove the Ekwesh outwards. A defeated tribe would lose some possessions, then seek to conquer some more. But now, with none left to conquer, save far off over unknown lands and seas, they were beginning to turn on each other in savage earnest. The ties of common kinship had been made too slack to restrain them. The Ice had to tighten its grip somehow, and force unity upon them; and to do so it sought to rely upon the influence it had long wielded over men, the sheer superstitious awe it could evoke.

The Hidden Clan

The Hidden Clan, therefore, which came into being around this time, seems to have been wholly a development of the Ice, a secret blood-brotherhood of chosen shamans and shaman-chieftains from all the tribes, in which the bonds established through elaborate ordeal and ceremonial, and reinforced by shared purpose, overrode the limited interests of individual tribes. In this it somewhat resembled the intertribal "freemasonry" practised among the Australian aborigines, being signified by elaborate patterns of cicatrice scars, but in a much more organized form, and wholly sinister in its practises and aspirations. At first, as its name suggests, it had to remain secret, so strong was the intertribal distrust; many members were lynched outright by their own followers. But as time passed and the benefits of some degree, at least, of coordination between tribes became clearer to the ordinary clansmen, membership commanded first tolerance and then respect and fear. Many initiates came to display and even to vaunt their status as a point of pride, by negative means such as bearing an abstract pattern (perhaps with an arcane meaning) instead of their totem. Lesser men began to copy them, and such secret societies grew up at a lower level between the tribes, but without seriously affecting the barriers between them; when there was conflict, tribe still told over society almost every time.

It was the Hidden Clan that organised the armies that crossed the Ice to begin the centuries of campaign against Kerys, and a century or two later developed the arts of shipbuilding and sailing that sent the black ships raiding oversea on the trail blazed by the fugitives, to assail the Westlands of Kerbryhaine and Nordeney. These were achievements; but they were slow in coming, many times hindered by intertribal jealousy and strife, even within the Clan itself. Some lesser clans, of which the Ravens were the most significant, distrusted its domination by the larger tribes, and held aloof. The Hidden Clan and its imitators were an imperfect means to an end, and the Ice was forever in search of something better. But none came, until the Mastersmith Mylio appeared on the scene.

The Mastersmith's Design

Over the centuries the Ice had seduced a number of men to its side, including smiths of greater power than he; but never before such a scholar. His fanatical energy drove him to acquire the greatest library of any man living at his time, to seek ancient knowledge among the duergar, and among the Ekwesh themselves, at his continual peril. This he found, as the Book of the Sword recounts, chiefly from observation and study of the subtle ways in which the shamans had refined the magecraft taught them by the Ice to help them control their folk. He synthesized this knowledge with others, as the shamans could not do; and he applied it to human minds with a finesse the Ice could never match. So he conceived the mindsword; and so, equally, his inability to forge such a thing. He sought one who could do the work for him, leaving only the last and simplest for him to complete; but when he tricked Elof into doing so, he was startled by the boy's ability to complete it, and even more so by the power of the result. With such a force in his hands he set out to second-guess his masters, and rather than turning the sword over to Louhi, leaving him no more than a useful appendage, to unite the Ekwesh under his own leadership, making him indispensable. Almost certainly he hoped to gain status among the powers, even to be made one of them; for such promises they often made to their useful dupes, producing images of the dead as proof. If so, it was a deluding hope, for they were only the mindless shades of Taoune, constructs of memories with no controlling intelligence at their heart save the rebel powers. But those who wished to believe were easy to delude, and the Mastersmith undoubtedly won great status by uniting the Ekwesh; Louhi may have meant to keep him alive, at least, or to bring him more securely under her domination. The changes in him, that eerie "bleaching" may have been caused by some spiritual exhaustion of his powers in Louhi's service, but equally they may have been intended to change his body, to fit him for life in a cold environment as Tapiau altered men for the forests. For there are living things even today that may survive in such conditions, icefish for example that live in freezing water, by having no haemoglobin in the blood; and they have just that white and pallid look.

He had undoubtedly earned some reward, if reward this was; for it was he who, as the old chieftain told Elof and Kermorvan, first united the tribes into a single solid fighting force. And, ironically, it was an achievement that his death only reinforced. When Elof destroyed him and the mindsword together the sudden slackening of the sword's hold on their minds, added to the sheer shock of seeing one they had thought a demigod slain and cast down, caused the Ekwesh to flee in panic. But such was the humiliation of this that for the first time it gave the tribes a common cause strong enough to outweigh their mutual mistrust, the more so as

Louhi played upon it. When less than two years later the elite troops of the Hidden Clan, to a man chieftain's and shaman's sons from many tribes, were wiped out in Morvannec, she had no trouble in bringing them together at last. Even the Ravens, who still scorned the Hidden Clan, and had never shared in the assaults on the Westlands or the madness of the mindsword, joined in the oaths to avenge that defeat; and without the witness of Raven himself even Elof probably could not have swayed them. With Kara to set their hearts ablaze with battle-fury the Ekwesh were in Louhi's grip as much as they had ever been in the Mastersmith's; and when that grip broke many a mind and heart among them shattered with it, and the old hierarchy of the tribes was broken for ever.

The Aftermath

In the time that followed, the fate of the Ekwesh became joined once again to that of other men. The Ravens became more humane as the influence of the Ice over them dwindled; but they kept much of their stern pride, and gathered the other Ekwesh who joined them under their sway. They posed Kermorvan something of a problem in settling them among his own folk, but to him and his line they remained fiercely loyal, and never forgot that allegiance. As the generations passed they mingled increasingly with their ancient foes, and in particular with the Northerners who resembled them; but their blood was always the hardiest and best suited to life in the increasingly harsh conditions of the declining land. They came to dominate it, until it was in the end wrested from them, with cruelties as great as any the Ekwesh practised; but that, alas, is the way of men, in which the Ice was not wholly mistaken. In the areas of that land they settled longest, some echoes of that terrible time may still linger; for there it is said of some tribes that they once earned a dark name among their neighbours, peaceful, hunter-gatherers and fishers for the most part, for dark practises, grim pride, fell magic, the taking of thralls and the eating of man's flesh. Today there is so little evidence of this that it has been disputed; and it may be that such tales are simply an ancestral memory, harking back to times more remote than any can now imagine.

In their own homeland, so far as can be told, their empire fragmented and fell apart far more swiftly, for most of those who had held it together perished in the Battle of the Gate, or subsequently. Every major clan was shorn of at least half its leaders, generally the more energetic and fanatical ones, and its most accomplished and dedicated warriors; and from those who remained the grip of the Ice was lifted. At first, perhaps, there was little outward change in their way of life; but as the years passed and new generations arose, and it became clear that the Ice was retreating, the old concerns soon lost their force, and the fierce energy waned. The remaining shamans lost much of their power and dominance; hierarchies of tribe and clan withered, and the barriers between master and thrall softened. Little by little the realm fragmented as the rising sea swallowed its coasts, and the Ekwesh as a people fragmented with it. Many still sailed over sea to Nordeney, but as settlers rather than reivers; and it is from them, through the tenuous links to the East, that the last was heard of the once-feared Ekwesh realm. All else was silence; but those lands have since been the cradle of many a formidable and conquering people, whose names have become as great a byword for savagery in their time as the Ekwesh were in theirs. Yet they rarely deserved it quite so thoroughly as did the Ekwesh, and it may be that there also some faint memory of their forgotten ancestors has ridden before them like a ghostly banner. Which, perhaps, is the memorial they would have wished.

But a better one may remain elsewhere. Those few stragglers who remained in Kerys, and were not slaughtered out of hand in the confusion and madness of the early days, also came to mingle with their lighter-skinned neighbours. Unmanned and humbled by what they had experienced, they responded much as the Ravens had, and sought new allegiance. There also they won it with their great skill at surviving in the wild, and more swiftly; mild as was the winter that followed the fall of the Gate, many Kerys folk would have perished were it not for their aid. One or two became men of great account in the crude tribal life to which the survivors were reduced, but there were never enough of them for their physical type to dominate, as it did in Brasayhal, and the race of the Akiya'wahsa was lost, becoming no more than a name. But when, many long thousands of years later, such another tribe of fierce searovers arose in those lands, that name was remembered, and either bestowed upon or taken by them in defiant assumption of a heritage. To their earliest enemies these Sea Peoples were called *Akiyawa* or *Ekwesh* as their hieroglyphics rendered it, and that is the form we have used. But they are better known to us as the Achaeans, the warlike Greeks of Homer.

FLORA AND FAUNA

The Book of the Armring has much to tell of the living things of Kerys, for Elof and Roc, having travelled from another continent, often found them very strange. Something is said of the different varieties of tree they saw from the cog on their long river journey, and elsewhere. But since Elof was forced to remain on the island for so long, animals are mostly mentioned in connection with Roc's travels, which are not germane to the tale. For the most part it can be said that the animal life is recognisably similar to that in similar latitudes of Elof's own land at this time. Many, however, are made to sound strange, because they are described only in their modern winter colouration; it may well be that they were wearing it all year round, an anomaly that may reflect the worsening state of the climate, and perhaps also the more direct effects of the Ice on living things. These were markedly more severe than in Brasayhal, because there the mountain ranges were ranged predominantly on north to south axes, and large areas of flat land and forest remained open to migration. In Kerys, however, most of the mountains extended from east to west, and as the Ice advanced they left few easy avenues southward; the creation of the secondary icesheets must have worsened matters even further. Adaptation must have been forced upon animals and plants much more swiftly.

Small and Domestic Animals

Among the commonest small beasts were squirrels, hares, rabbits, lemmings, mustelid predators such as martens and wolverines, and foxes; hedgehogs and water-shrews flourished on the island, and were totally new to Elof. Mercifully it was free of rats and mice, though the city of Kerys was not; dogs and wild kites were the main agents for controlling such vermin, the more efficient cat still rare as a domestic animal outside the houses of wealthy noblemen. These were probably unlike modern cats; from their descriptions they sound more like domesticated breeds derived from some wilder breed such as *Felis lunensis*, ancestor of *Felis silvestris*, the modern wildcat.

Other domesticated beasts included the huge and temperamental cattle of Kerys, the same breed Elof had herded as a child, and some much smaller beast which yielded a wooly fleece, but from its description sounds otherwise more like a goat than a sheep; certainly no very sharp distinction was then drawn between the two caprine types. It may well have looked a little like the primitive Soay sheep, lean and long-limbed with substantial horns, but must have been much larger. Less common were domesticated pigs, savage creatures barely distinguishable from the wild hogs they were bred from; these, and their cousins the wild boars, were still common enough to make hunting worthwhile. It was hardly less dangerous than keeping them. Horses were not only ridden, but were the main draft animals of the land, oxen being stronger but more dangerous; it seemed strange to Elof that there were none of the hardy little pony-like species native to his own land, with their vestigial extra hooves.

Wild Animals

Among larger wild animals the various breeds of *mammut* were rare, probably through hunting, but still to be found in the north eastern plains of the Wild Lands; the same was true of some breed of wooly rhinoceros. Deer and wisent were still quite common, some breeds of very great size; one deer Roc shot was larger, he claimed, even than the huge deer of Tapiau's forests, and had a wider spread of antlers. If so, this must almost certainly have been the so-called Irish elk, *Megaceros*. In the warmer areas wild cattle of similar enormous bulk still roamed, probably ancestors of the recently extinct *aurochs*; and there were both wild boar and wild hogs in the forests. In the higher areas chamois were common, and some breed of mountain goat. Large predators seem to have been rare, probably because the land had been so long settled by men. It is known that the early settlers of Kerys faced some big cat of appalling size, probably the so-called "cave lion" *Felis leo spelaea*, a third again as large as modern lions, but this had been quite deliberately hunted down and all but exterminated throughout the land; some had reappeared in the Wild Lands, but Elof and Roc ran little risk of encountering them where game was so scarce. Another somewhat smaller cat, probably a descendant of the giant cheetah *Acinonyx pardinensis*, was still an occasional threat to livestock in the southlands. In the northern woodlands lynxes were still to be found, and on the grasslands a cat of similar size, probably the steppe cat, *Felis manul*; wildcats very like today. The bears, as in Elof's land, were very large, but chiefly vegetarian and rarely aggressive if not provoked. Wolves, once again, were large, but rare, although they had begun to move into the western lands once more as men deserted them, and found fat pickings after the battles that raged there.

These creatures are mentioned only incidentally among the many strands of the chronicles; but one or two creatures feature so prominently that they deserve some further remarks.

Amicac This astonishing creature, the Sea-Devourer, is so unlike any known seabeast, either in living or fossil form, that it might be thought some strange anomalous form natural to a minor power, as were dragons, or yet another of the creations or distortions of the Ice. The strong impression of intelligence it left with Elof and Roc is echoed by other surviving witnesses, and suggests this. Yet manifestly the creature was no servant of the Ice, for it destroyed its thralls with appalling ferocity and cunning, yet spared their quarry with an almost regal grace. It has been suggested that it might have been a shape assumed by Niarad or some other sea-dwelling power, but this is unlikely; there is no record of them ever containing themselves within a single beast, preferring shoals and throngs much as Tapiau preferred his trees. What then can it have been? It bore the shape of the plesiosaurs, long-necked prehistoric sea-reptiles, but they were long extinct, much smaller and lived differently;

nor could two such keen observers ever mistake such creatures for any kind of seal or other pinniped. It seems best to accept their identification, therefore, and look for some other evidence; and this exists. In studying the many sightings of so-called "Sea Serpents" around the world, the Dutch scientist Dr. H.C. Oudemans produced a composite picture of a very large marine carnivore resembling a type of seal or otter, but by the same evolutionary convergence that made icthyosaurs appear almost identical to dolphins, shaped like a gigantic plesiosaur; he christened it, somewhat misleadingly, *Megophias*, or Great Serpent. Though the evidence has been interpreted differently by later researchers, most notably by Dr. Bernard Heuvelmans of Belgium as two distinct species of different size, the distinctive shape and dimensions remain; and they fit the Sea Devourer all too well. More, it is generally agreed to inhabit colder northern waters, where it was much feared by seamen of previous generations in their small sailing vessels. This might be thought of as a superstition, but in one or two Norwegian fishing museums giant iron traps can still be found, that were set in fjords to ensnare long and questing necks; in a pre-industrial society the labour of shaping such a trap is not usually devoted to hunting phantoms. It may be worth noting the quite startling intelligence often displayed by sea mammals, not only dolphins and whales but also seals such as H.G. Hurrell's Atlanta, able to distinguish command words spoken in complex context in a normally-toned voice – a feat unusual in any creature. And it is not impossible that with an increased brain size this might also be enhanced; which is not to say that such intelligence would produce anything like a human mind. What use would a human outlook be in so different a body and lifestyle? But even a very different mind might well be able to share the same repugnance for the common enemy of all things living, and recognise a call for help – not least from so powerful a mind as Elof's.

Small Mammut The miniature proboscideans with whom Elof and Roc shared Elan Ghorhenyan might sound even more problematic than the Sea Devourer, but in fact the existence of such creatures during the Long Winter is well established. Like similarly dwarfed deer, hippopotami and ground sloths at various times, they seem to have evolved in island environments where food and living space were limited. Various very different breeds existed in different parts of the world, but the most likely candidate would be *Loxodonta falconeri*, or a close relative. This was in fact a true elephant rather than a mammoth or mastodon, with long straight tusks, and it stood no more than three feet tall. If it was as curious as its living relatives it might well have strayed into the smithy in search of food.

Swans The guise of a great black swan, though undoubtedly it reflected something in Kara's nature, may not have been so strange and eerie as it appears. It may have been a shape well adapted to passing unnoticed through the skies of Kerys, and perhaps of other lands also. The only living black swan is confined to a small space of the southern hemisphere, is smaller than some northern breeds, and has a slightly comical squeaky cry. But during the Long Winter a swan of immense size undoubtedly lived in the Northlands. Fossil evidence suggests that it was among the largest of flying birds; but can tell us little more. Of the hue of its feathers no trace remains.

Trees and Plants

The impression gained from Elof's journey, and from the map of Kerys, may be somewhat deceptive. The text of the chronicle tells a truer story. There were still large areas of wooded land in the Vale of Kerys, both north and south; but they were sadly reduced from what they had once been, and accounted for a relatively small land area. Much of what remained was mere secondary growth where the old-established forests had been cut down, sometimes even a stunted aftergrowth of little use to men and fit only for the smaller beasts. Tapiau's accusation was quite justified; Kerys had played the spendthrift with its woodlands, as with every other resource it tapped. This was less true in those that were predominantly Svarhath, both because they were better foresters, and because they had a much smaller population and agriculture. Along the snowline near the gates of the duergar birch forests still persisted, with dwarf juniper and alpine alders in the barrens, and scrubland of heather and gorse. In the Wild Lands species related to all the common evergreen trees of Elof's homeland could be found, save for the redwoods he loved so much; the same was true of deciduous trees; though, as he noticed, they tended to be smaller. Pines – from the descriptions Scots pine, spruce and firs – beech, and oaks were the commonest trees there, and in the south sweet chestnut, which was new to him; the Svarhath had been fond of these, and planted them throughout the forests. Most of these were also found within the warmer climes of the Vale itself, along with less familiar species such as planes, cypresses, cork oaks, tamarisks and even some fig-cactus and date-palms spread from the southern shore, though in the north they were non-fruiting. Beyond Kerys itself, in the warmer east, cypress and olive trees were commonest, and along the coasts maritime and Aleppo pines; there were some of these on Elan Ghorhenyan, among a characteristically fragrant scrubland that seems to have been chiefly the evergreen shrub known today as the rock-rose, *Cistus*, mingled with broom and gorse, and perhaps also laurel.

SHIPS

Less can be said of the types of ship with which this book deals, the huge ships that Kermorvan built with the aid of the Duergar, and the cogs which were the main model in use on the rivers of Kerys, than of earlier ones, because no reliable marginalia survive. Evidently such large ships fell quite swiftly from use as the land declined, and later copyists had never seen them; their attempts to draw them are fanciful in the extreme. Large warships such as the *Prince Korentyn* seem to have had hulls of a very modern profile, and a system of multiple sails such as the larger rivercraft of the duergar used. The dromunds have been given that name to distinguish them, because they seem to have been simply larger versions of the standard "double-ended" Kerbryhaine model, though with a variety of more complex rigs. As the extent to which he kept his smiths and shipwrights busy suggests, Kermorvan was constantly experimenting to improve the performance of his ships. What heights he may eventually have reached are suggested by the cutter that bore Roc and Elof across the ocean. If he was able to develop fore-and-aft rigs sufficiently to apply them to his larger and leaner hulls, he could have achieved craft almost as fast and efficient as the great China clippers.

The cog could hardly be more of a contrast. It is given that name because it somewhat resembled the breed of craft that was common on the seas of medieval Europe, a round-bellied tun of a ship well suited to carrying heavy loads or companies of troops with equal seaworthiness and ill grace under a simple squaresail, with at most a smaller topsail. In versions made or adapted for fighting, as was Trygvar's, towers of planking were added at bow and stern to give archers height to fire down onto an opposing deck. In his boat, and probably in most others of his land, these were kept to a sensible height, but in an early breed of arms race the European types were raised higher and higher till they often made the ship dangerously unstable, more a threat to its crew than its enemies. "*Where now are the bones of Wayland the wise?*" Boethius. *Consolation of Philosophy*, in the rendering of Alfred the Great.